Alexander M. Sullivan

The story of Ireland

A narrative if Irish history from the earliest ages to the insurrection of 1867

I0592302

Alexander M. Sullivan

The story of Ireland
A narrative if Irish history from the earliest ages to the insurrection of 1867

ISBN/EAN: 9783741195075

Manufactured in Europe, USA, Canada, Australia, Japa

Cover: Foto ©Andreas Hilbeck / pixelio.de

Manufactured and distributed by brebook publishing software
(www.brebook.com)

Alexander M. Sullivan

The story of Ireland

THE

STORY OF IRELAND;

A NARRATIVE OF IRISH HISTORY,

From the Earliest Ages to the Insurrection of 1867.

WRITTEN FOR THE YOUTH OF IRELAND

BY

ALEXANDER M. SULLIVAN, M. P.

CONTINUED TO THE PRESENT TIME

BY JAMES LUBY, OF NEW YORK.

Illustrated with Numerous Engravings.

"She's not a dull or cold land;
No! she's a warm and bold land!
Oh! she's a true and old land,—
This native land of mine."
DAVIS.

.NEW YORK:.
P. J. KENEDY,
Excelsior Catholic Publishing House,
5 BARCLAY STREET.

TO

MY YOUNG FELLOW-COUNTRYMEN

AT HOME AND IN EXILE,

IN THE COTTAGE AND THE MANSION,

AMIDST THE GREEN FIELDS AND IN THE CROWDED CITIES,

SOON TO BE

THE MEN OF IRELAND,

I DEDICATE

THIS LITTLE BOOK, WHICH CONTAINS

THE STORY OF OUR COUNTRY,

AND SUBSCRIBE MYSELF

THEIR FRIEND,

THE AUTHOR

ILLUSTRATIONS.

—SKETCH—

LIFE OF ALEXANDER M. SULLIVAN, M. P.

———

MR. A. M. SULLIVAN was born in 1830, in one of the most picturesque spots in the south of Ireland, at the head of Bantry Bay, where is situated the village of Bantry. In one of his books he tells us how, roaming among the mountains and sea-girt crags of his native place, his soul drank in a love of its magnificent scenery which nourished his artistic instinct and perhaps impelled him in the choice of his future profession. His parents were in an humble walk of life, but, like many an Irish family who have fallen upon evil days, they cherished traditions of a time when their people were among the great of the land. The shadow of the famine fell over Mr. Sullivan's youth ; and this, perhaps, imparted to his character a certain sad cast which is to be noticed among most of the Irish people who passed through that terrible experience, and which is missing from the brighter enthusiasm of the present generation. " My native district," he writes in *New Ireland*, " figures largely in the gloomy record of that dreadful time. I saw the horrible phantasmagoria— would to God it were but that!—pass before my eyes. Blank, stolid dismay—a sort of stupor—fell upon the people, contrasting remarkably with the fierce energy put forth a year before. It was no uncommon sight to see the cottier and his little family seated on the garden fence, gazing all day long in gloomy silence at the blighted plot that had been their last hope. Nothing could arouse them. If you spoke they answered not. If you tried to cheer them they shook their heads. I never saw so sudden and so terrible a trans-

Mr. Sullivan had determined to adopt the career of an ar-
tist, and in 1853 he left Bantry for Dublin to take up a position on the staff of an illustrated paper. During this period
he contributed sometimes to the *Nation*—the *Nation* revived
by Charles Gavan Duffy after his release from prison. In
1855 the treachery of Keogh and Sadlier and their " Brass
Band " had left Irish politics in such a hopeless condition
that Mr. Duffy threw up his post and went to Australia.
Two years later his successor, John Cashel Hoey, retired
from the paper. It was to such a heritage of despair A. M.
Sullivan succeeded. He took the *Nation* on his shoulders as
its sole proprietor, and began a heroic struggle to revivify a
national public opinion in Ireland. To a man who was not a
very incarnation of hopefulness the task would have been
impossible. It is not overstating the case to say that but for
A. M. Sullivan the work of O'Connell and Young Ireland
would have been in vain and the Irish movements of to-day
would never have been possible, or at least would have been
indefinitely postponed. The appeal to conspiracy, to secret
plannings for armed revolution, was the only appeal that the
people, disgusted with the Parliamentary traitors, would
listen to. But A. M. Sullivan condemned conspiracy and
every resort to physical force with a religious ardor. What,
then, did he hope to do ? To restore confidence in, to restore
interest in, constitutional agitation ! Wild as the hope appeared, it was, nevertheless, this that he succeeded in accomplishing. Aided by a band of fellow-workers, chief of
whom was his brother, Mr. T. D. Sullivan, the poet (at
present proprietor of the *Nation* and member of Parliament
for Westmeath), he worked at this task like a giant, advo-
cating every movement or enterprise that tended to honor the
Irish name or foster the spirit of genuine Irish patriotism.
He even started a daily paper, the *Morning News*, with the
aid of his friend, Mr. Donegan, the patriotic Dublin jeweller,
and for a time made this organ the most dreaded foe of the
Whigs and the " Anglo-Irish Irishmen." Mr. Sullivan in
due time shared the inevitable lot of the Irish patriot. He
was arrested and imprisoned. In February, 1868, he, with

John Martin, James J. Lalor, and Thomas Bracken, was indicted by the government on a charge of seditious assembling for participation in the erection of the monument to the " Manchester Martyrs "—Allen, Larkin, and O'Brien. The jury disagreed ; but Mr. Sullivan was indicted on a separate charge in the same court, and found guilty of publishing seditious matter in the *Weekly News*. This paper was a sort of tender to the *Nation*, and had denounced the packing of juries. Mr. Sullivan was sentenced to six months' imprisonment and to give security in £1,000 for his good behavior for two years after his release. He was at this time a member of the Dublin Corporation, and that body, on his being sentenced, offered to elect him Lord Mayor, but he declined the honor. While he was in jail a committee had been formed to present him with a national testimonial, but he declined to receive it, as it took a pecuniary shape ; and a sum of £300 which had been collected in the meantime he caused to be made the nucleus of a fund for the erection of the statue of Grattan, by Foley, which now stands in front of the old Parliament House on College Green.

In May, 1870, Mr. Sullivan was one of the most active promoters of the Home Rule Association. He was returned to Parliament for the County Louth in 1874, defeating a cabinet minister, the Right Hon. Chichester Fortescue, now Lord Carlingford. Mr. Sullivan revealed the possession of extraordinary power as a Parliamentary orator, and soon acquired a reputation as one of the most eloquent speakers and ablest statesmen in the House. In 1880, on the election of Mr. Parnell for Cork, Mr. Sullivan was unanimously chosen to succeed him in the representation of Meath. He held this position until, to the regret of all parties, failing health compelled him to resign it and cease taking an active share in Irish politics.

Mr. Sullivan's literary works are widely popular. His STORY OF IRELAND is the best introduction to Irish history that can he put into the hands of a young student.

Mr. Sullivan was a member of the English bar. This was because an anti-national clique denied him admission to the

bar of his native country. He was steadily conquering the
prejudices which met him in England on account of his share
in Irish politics, and his great abilities were securing him
an increasing practice, when his career was suddenly cut
off during a visit to Ireland. He died on Irish soil, in
Dublin, on the 17th of October, 1884. The Irish benchers
had, a few years previously, repented of their churlishness
and made him a member of the Irish bar. Two of the most
eloquent orations heard in the Dublin law-courts since the
days of Curren were delivered by him in this capacity—one
at the state trials of the Land-Leaguers, the other in defence
of Mr. William O'Brien, M. P., of *United Ireland*, who was
indicted for a similar offence as he himself had been in the
same court fourteen years before.

In addition to Irish politics Mr. Sullivan took an active interest in all questions of social reform, and was the most
powerful ally Cardinal Manning had on the temperance
question in England. He was a most fervent Catholic, and
his well-known religious zeal lent additional weight to his
opinion when he gave it—as he did not hesitate to do on
more than one occasion—against the position taken by certain prominent ecclesiastics in Irish politics. On the reception of the Simeoni circular condemning the Parnell fund,
Cardinal Manning and Mr. Sullivan forwarded to Rome a
joint letter, putting the case justly before the Holy See, and
this document is mainly accountable for the more favorable
attitude of the Holy see on the Irish question since.

In 1882 Mr. Sullivan visited America, by order of his physicians; but so thoroughly devoted and unselfish was this
patriot that, at the request of the Irish leaders, he consented
to convert this health-trip into a lecturing tour for the information of the American people as to the true merits of the
Irish question. An idea of the sacrifice he thus made may
be gathered from the fact that three times during this
tour his health broke down in a seriously alarming manner.
But he stuck to his task with characteristic pluck and ten-
acity. It was a brilliant tour in every sense of the word.
Wherever he appeared he was paid the highest marks of re-

spect in the power of the American people to bestow. Governors of states, mayors of cities, Catholic bishops, and clergymen of every denomination crowded his platforms to do him honor.

He married in 1861 an American lady of rare gifts and accomplishments, a daughter of the late Mr. John Donovan, of New Orleans. Mrs. Sullivan and a large family survive him. The generous Irish nation has made itself the guardian of Mr. Sullivan's family. The very week of his death a national testimonial was started which reached noble proportions before it was closed. The subscription-list of this testimonial gives an indication of the respect in which Mr. Sullivan was held. Men of every shade of politics in England, Ireland, America, and Australia are represented on it—Mr. Gladstone, the Liberal Prime Minister ; Sir Stafford Northcote, the leader of the Tory opposition ; the Protestant archbishop, the Catholic cardinal, Mr. Parnell, and Earl Spencer—and men of every social grade, from the Lord-Lieutenant to the poorest peasant.

T. P. G.

PUBLISHER'S NOTICE.

In placing this work at the disposal of the Irish American public, the publisher is glad to be able to announce that he has the authority and good will of Mr. A. M. Sullivan, M.P., the author, and also of Mr. T. D. Sullivan, M.P., the present holder of the author's rights. When he first determined upon the publication, the publisher opened correspondence with the former of these gentlemen. The reply came from Mr. T. D. Sullivan, and from it the following passage is quoted :

My brother, Mr. A. M. Sullivan, M P., has sent me a note which he recently received from you relative to the reprinting of "The Story of Ireland," by you in America. He has done so because the copyright of that work passed from him to me on my purchase of this concern from him three years ago. * * * * In writing to me, he said he regarded your offer as an honorable one, and felt confident that you would act up to it, and he advised me, as the owner of the copyright, to accord you the permission you desired. I have much pleasure in doing so, on the conditions mentioned by you, and I hope your publication of the work will be in every way successful.

Subsequent correspondence regarding the exact financial arrangements resulted in an agreement satisfactory to both parties.

In one of his letters, Mr. Sullivan remarks, "The sale in this country, (Ireland,) has been and continues to be very great." This is not surprising. The book has all the qualities necessary to meet the wants of the general public. It is so simply and clearly written as to form the best introduction to a knowledge of Irish history that the young, or those hitherto uninstructed in the subject, can find ; at the same time it is so spirited in style, so accurate in detail, and so patriotic in tone, that even the well-informed may read it with pleasure and advantage.

In the American edition, all the original illustrations are re-produced, and, besides, many portraits have been added, which, it is believed, will give the volume an additional in-terest. In this edition too, the author's plan of spelling the old Irish names, for the most part, as they are pronounced has been followed, as it is considered that the principal aim, in a popular work such as this, should be to contribute, in all possible respects, to the convenience of the reader.

To the kind courtesy of Mr. Lawrence Kehoe, Manager of the Catholic Publication Society Co., 9 Barclay St., New York, I am indebted for the sketch of Mr. A. M. Sullivan's life, printed in this volume.

PREFACE TO THE AMERICAN EDITION.

In the chapters which I have written at the close of this volume I have aimed not so much to continue as to supplement Mr. Sullivan's narrative. The work of that gentleman remains as it came from his pen, unaltered and unabridged. It is, so far as it goes, distinct and complete in itself. Similarly what I have written, I desire to be held separate and distinct from all that precedes it.

Mr. Sullivan, throughout his book, expresses his honest opinions of men and things. I must be in no sense held responsible for these; for, though in general I coincide with him in his views, there are expressions, notably as regards the Fenian movement, which I could in no degree endorse. On the other hand, Mr. Sullivan is equally little responsible for my opinions. He has never seen my work, and I have permitted my own best judgment alone to dictate my utterances.

I am well pleased to aid in bringing before the Irish American public so useful and patriotic a work as the "Story of Ireland." I trust my efforts may contribute to a true understanding of the nation's history, during an era pregnant with future result. I have made such endeavor as was possible, to present the facts of the last sixteen years, clearly and truthfully. My first reliance has been on my own recollections of scenes and events which I have myself witnessed; I have besides collected information orally from those whom I believed to be at once well informed and honest. I have consulted few books, but have been materially aided by Mr. Sullivan's "New Ireland," and other works of his; and Mr. John

Devoy's sketch of the Land League, recently published. Finally, I have referred occasionally to the files of the "New York Herald," the Dublin "Irishman," the New York 'Irish World," and John Devoy's "Irish Nation," the only newspapers to which I had reasonably easy access.

I have only one word more to say. I desire to heartily join with Mr. Sullivan in his dedication of the book to the youth of Irish race in Ireland and America.

J. L.

AUTHOR'S PREFACE.

THIS little book is written for young people. It does not pretend to the serious character of a History of Ireland. It does not claim to be more than a compilation from the many admirable works which have been published by painstaking and faithful historians. It is an effort to interest the young in the subject of Irish history, and attract them to its study.

I say so much in deprecation of the stern judgment of learned critics. I say it furthermore and chiefly by way of owning my obligations to those authors the fruits of whose researches have been availed of so freely by me. To two of these in particular, Mr. M'Gee and Mr. Haverty, I am deeply indebted. In several instances, even where I have not expressly referred to my authority, I have followed almost literally the text supplied by them. If I succeed in my design of interesting my young fellow-countrymen in the subject of Irish history, I recommend them strongly to follow it up by reading the works of the two historians whom I have mentioned. They possess this immeasurable advantage over every other previously published history of Ireland, that in them the authors were able to avail themselves of the rich stores of material brought to light by the lamented O'Curry and O'Donovan, by Todd, Greaves, Wilde, Mehan, Gilbert, and others. These revelations of authentic history, inaccessible or unknown to previous history-writers, not only throw a flood of light upon many periods of our history heretofore darkened and obscured, but may be said to have given to

many of the most important events in our annals an aspect
totally new, and in some instances the reverse of that commonly assigned to them. Mr. Haverty's book is Irish history
clearly and faithfully traced, and carefully corrected by recent
invaluable archæological discoveries ; Mr. M'Gee's is the
only work of the kind accessible to our people which is yet
more than a painstaking and reliable record of events. It
rises above mere chronicling, and presents to the reader
the philosophy of history, assisting him to view great movements and changes in their comprehensive totality, and to
understand the principles which underlay, promoted, guided,
or controlled them.

In all these, however, the learned and gifted authors have
aimed high. They have written for adult readers. Mine is
an humble, but I trust it may prove to be a no less useful aim.
I desire to get hold of the young people, and not to offer them
a learned and serious " history," which might perhaps be associated in their minds with school tasks and painful efforts
to remember when this king reigned or whom that one slew ;
but to have a pleasant talk with them about Ireland ; to tell
them its story, after the manner of simple story-tellers ; not
confusing their minds with a mournful series of feuds, raids,
and slaughters, merely for the sake of noting them ; or with
essays upon the state of agriculture or commerce, religion
or science, at particular periods—all of which they will find
instructive when they grow to an age to comprehend and
be interested in more advanced works. I desire to do for our
young people that which has been well done for the youth
of England by numerous writers. I desire to interest them
in their country ; to convince them that its history is no wild,
dreary, and uninviting monotony of internecine slaughter,
but an entertaining and instructive narrative of stirring
events, abounding with episodes, thrilling, glorious and
beautiful.

I do not take upon myself the credit of being the first to
remember that " the Child is father of the Man." The Rev.
Iohn O'Hanlon's admirable " Catechism of Irish History "

follow many besides myself to cater for the amusement and instruction of the young people. They deserve more attention than has hitherto been paid them by our Irish book-writers. In childhood or boy-hood to-day, there rapidly approaches for them a to-morrow, bringing manhood, with its cares, duties, responsibilities. When we who have preceded them shall have passed away for ever, they will be the men on whom Ireland must depend. They will make her future. They will guide her destinies. They will guard her honor. They will defend her life. To the service of this "Irish Nation of the Future" I devote the following pages, confident that my young friends will not fail to read aright the lesson which is taught by "The Story of Ireland."

INTRODUCTORY.

HOW WE LEARN THE FACTS OF EARLY HISTORY.

*I*T may occur to my young friends, that, before I begin my narration, I ought to explain how far or by what means any one now living can correctly ascertain and narrate the facts of very remote history. The reply is, that what we know of history anterior to the keeping of written records, is derived from the traditions handed down "by word of mouth" from generation to generation. We may safely assume that the commemoration of important events by this means, was, at first, unguarded or unregulated by any public authority, and accordingly led to much confusion, exaggeration, and corruption; but we have positive and certain information that at length steps were taken to regulate these oral communications, and guard them as far as possible from corruption. The method most generally adopted for perpetuating them was to compose them into historical chants or verse-histories, which were easily committed to memory, and were recited on all public or festive occasions. When written records began to be used, the events thus commemorated were set down in the regular chronicles. Several of these latter, in one shape or another, are still in existence. From these we chiefly derive our knowledge, such as it is, of the ancient history of Erinn.

It is, however, necessary to remember that all history of very early or remote times, unless what is derived from the

degree, with doubt and obscurity, and is, to a greater or
lesser degree, a hazy mixture of probable fact and manifest
fable. When writing was unknown, and before measures
were taken to keep the oral traditions with exactitude and
for a public purpose, and while yet events were loosely handed down by unregulated "hearsay" which no one was
charged to guard from exaggeration and corruption, some of
the facts thus commemorated became gradually distorted,
until after great lapse of time, whatever was described as mar-
vellously *wonderful* in the past, was set down as at least
partly *supernatural*, and the long dead heroes whose prowess
had become fabulously exaggerated, came to be regarded as
demi-gods.

It is thus as regards the early history of ancient Rome and
Greece. It is thus with the early history of Ireland, and indeed of all other European countries.

It would, however, be a great blunder for any one to conclude that because some of those old mists of early tradition
contain such gross absurdities, they contain no truths at all.
Investigation is every day more and more clearly establishing
the fact that, shrouded in some of the most absurd of those
fables of antiquity, there are indisputable and valuable truths
of history.

THE STORY OF IRELAND.

I.—HOW THE MILESIANS SOUGHT AND FOUND " THE PROMISED ISLE"—AND CONQUERED IT.

THE earliest settlement or colonization of Ireland of which there is tolerably precise and satisfactory information, was that by the sons of Miledh or Milesius, from whom the Irish are occasionally styled Milesians. There are abundant evidences that at least two or three "waves" of colonization had long previously reached the island; but it is not very clear whence they came. Those first settlers are severally known in history as the Partholanians, the Nemedians, the Firbolgs, and the Tuatha de Danaans. These latter, the Tuatha de Danaans, who immediately preceded the Melesians, possessed a civilization and a knowledge of " arts and sciences" which,

limited as we may be sure it was, greatly amazed the earlier
settlers (whom they had subjected) by the results it produced.
To the Firbolgs (the more early settlers) the wonderful things
done by the conquering new-comers, and the wonderful knowledge they displayed, could only be the results of supernatural
power. Accordingly they set down the Tuatha de Danaans
as " magicians," an idea which the Milesians, as we shall presently see, also adopted.

The Firbolgs seem to have been a pastoral race; the Tuatha
de Danaans were more of a manufacturing and commercial
people. The soldier Milesian came, and he ruled over all.

The Milesian colony reached Ireland from Spain,* but they
were not Spaniards. They were an eastern people who had
tarried in that country on their way westward, seeking, they
said, an island promised to the posterity of their ancestor,
Gadelius. Moved by this mysterious purpose to fulfil their
destiny, they had passed from land to land, from the shores
of Asia across the wide expanse of Southern Europe, bearing
aloft through all their wanderings the Sacred Banner, which
symbolized to them at once their origin and their mission, the
blessing and the promise given to their race. This celebrated
standard, the "Sacred Banner of the Milesians," was a flag
on which was represented a dead serpent and the rod of
Moses; a device to commemorate for ever amongst the posterity of Gadelius the miracle by which his life had been
saved. The story of this event, treasured with singular per-
tinacity by the Milesians, is told as follows in their traditions,
which so far I have been following:—

While Gadelius, being yet a child, was sleeping one day,
he was bitten by a poisonous serpent. His father—Niul, a
younger son of the king of Scythia—carried the child to the
camp of the Israelites, then close by, where the distracted
parent with tears and prayers implored the aid of Moses.
The inspired leader was profoundly touched by the anguish
of Niul. He laid the child down, and prayed over him; then

---

* The settled Irish account; but this is also disputed by theorists, who contend that
all the waves of colonization reached Ireland from the continent across Britain.

he touched with his rod the wound, and the boy arose healed. Then, say the Milesians, the man of God promised or prophesied for the posterity of the young prince, that they should inhabit a country in which no venomous reptile could live, an island which they should seek and find in the track of the setting sun.

It was not, however, until the third generation subsequently that the descendants and people of Gadelius are found setting forth on their prophesied wanderings; and of this migration itself—of the adventures and fortunes of the Gadelian colony in its journeyings—the history would make a volume. At length we find them tarrying in Spain, where they built a city, Brigantia, and occupied and ruled a certain extent of territory. It is said that Ith (pronounced " Eeh"), uncle of Milesius, an adventurous explorer, had, in his cruising northward of the Brigantian coast, sighted the Promised Isle, and landing to explore it, was attacked by the inhabitants (Tuatha de Danaans), and mortally wounded ere he could regain his ship. He died at sea on the way homeward. His body was reverentially preserved and brought back to Spain by his son, Lui (spelled Lugaid),* who had accompanied him, and who now summoned the entire Milesian host to the last stage of their destined wanderings—to avenge the death of Ith, and occupy the promised isle. The old patriarch himself, Miledh, had died before Lui arrived : but his sons all responded quickly to the summons; and the widowed queen, their mother, Scota, placed herself at the head of the expedition, which soon sailed in thirty galleys for " the isle they had seen in dreams." The names of the sons of Milesius who thus sailed for Ireland were,

---

* Here let me at the outset state, once for all, that I have decided after mature consideration, to spell most of the Irish names occurring in our annals according to their correct pronunciation or sound, and not according to their strictly correct orthography in the Irish language and typography. I am aware of all that may fairly be said against this course; yet consider the weight of advantage to be on its side. *Some* of our Irish names are *irretrievably* Anglicized in the worst form—uncouth and absurd. Choosing, therefore, between difficulties and objections, I have decided to rescue the correct *pronunciation* in this manner; giving, besides, with sufficient frequency, the correct orthography.

Heber the Fair, Amergin, Heber the Brown, Colpa, Ir, and
Heremon; and the date of this event is generally supposed
to have been about fourteen hundred years before the birth
of our Lord.

At that time Ireland, known as Innis Ealga (the Noble Isle),
was ruled over by three brothers, Tuatha de Danaan princes,
after whose wives (who were three sisters) the island was alternately called, Eire, Banba (or Banva), and Fiola (spelled
Fodhla), by which names Ireland is still frequently styled in
national poems. Whatever difficulties or obstacles beset the
Milesians in landing they at once attributed to the " necromancy" of the Tuatha de Danaans, and the old traditions narrate
amusing stories of the contest between the resources of magic
and the power of valor. When the Milesians could not discover land where they thought to sight it, they simply agreed
that the Tuatha de Danaans had by their black arts rendered
it invisible. At length they descried the island, its tall blue
hills touched by the last beams of the setting sun, and from
the galleys there arose a shout of joy ; Innisfail, the Isle of
Destiny, was found ! * But lo, next morning the land was
submerged, until only a low ridge appeared above the ocean.
A device of the magicians, say the Milesians. Nevertheless
they reached the shore and made good their landing. The
" magician" inhabitants, however, stated that this was not a
fair conquest by the rules of war; that they had no standing
army to oppose the Milesians; but if the new-comers would
again take to their galleys, they should *if able once more to
effect a landing*, be recognized as masters of the isle by the
laws of war.

---

* In Moore's *Melodies* the event here related is made the subject of the following
verses :

> " They came from a land beyond the sea,
> And now o'er the western main
> Set sail, in their good ships, gallantly,
> From the sunny land of Spain.
> " Oh, where's the Isle we've seen in dreams,
> Our destin'd home or grave ? "
> Thus sung they as, by the morning's beams,
> They swept the Atlantic wave.

The Milesians did not quite like the proposition. They feared much the " necromancy" of the Tuatha de Danaans. It had cost them trouble enough already to get their feet upon the soil, and they did not greatly relish the idea of having to begin it all over again. They debated the point, and it was resolved to submit the case to the decision of Amergin, who was the Ollave (the Learned Man, Lawgiver, or Seer) of the expedition. Amergin, strange to say, decided on the merits against his own brothers and kinsmen, and in favor of the Tuatha de Danaans. Accordingly, with scrupulous obedience of his decision, the Milesians relinquished all they had so far won. They reëmbarked in their galleys, and, as demanded, withdrew "nine waves off from the shore." Immediately a hurricane, raised, say their versions, by the spells of the magicians on shore, burst over the fleet, dispersing it in all directions. Several of the princes and chiefs and their wives and retainers were drowned. The Milesians paid dearly for their chivalrous acquiescence in the rather singular proposition of the inhabitants endorsed by the decision of Amergin. When they did land next time, it was not in one combined force, but in detachments widely separated ; some at the mouth of the Boyne ; others on the Kerry coast. A short but fiercely contested campaign decided the fate of the kingdom. In the first great pitched battle, which was fought in a glen a few miles

---

" And, lo, where afar o'er ocean shines
A sparkle of radiant green,
As though in that deep lay emerald mines,
Whose light through the wave was seen.
'Tis Innisfail—'tis Innisfail !
Rings o'er the echoing sea !
While, bending to heav'n, the warriors hail
That home of the brave and free.

" Then turned they unto the Eastern wave,
Where now their Day-God's eye
A look of such sunny omen gave
As lighted up sea and sky.
Nor frown was seen through sky or sea,
Nor tear o'er leaf or sod,
When first on their Isle of Destiny
Our great forefathers trod."

south of Tralee,* the Milesians were victorious. But they
lost the aged Queen-Mother, Scota, who fell amidst the slain,
and was buried beneath a royal cairn in Glen Scohene, close
by. Indeed the Queens of ancient Ireland figure very prominently in our history, as we shall learn as we proceed. In
the final engagement, which was fought at Tailtan in Meath,
between the sons of Milesius and the three Tuatha de Danaan
kings, the latter were utterly and finally defeated, and were
themselves slain. And with their husbands, the three brothers,
there fell upon that dreadful day, when crown and country,
home and husband, all were lost to them, the three sisters,
Queens Eire, Banva, and Fiola!

---

* All that I have been here relating is a condensation of traditions, very old, and
until recently little valued or credited by historical theorists. Yet singular corrobor-
ations have been turning up daily, establishing the truth of *the main facts* thus handed down. Accidental excavations a few years since in the glen which tradition has
handed down as the scene of this battle more than *three thousand years ago*, brought
to light full corroboration of this fact, at least, that a battle of great slaughter was
fought upon the exact spot some thousands of years ago.

QUEEN SCOTA UNFURLS THE SACRED BANNER.

See page 13.

II.—HOW IRELAND FARED UNDER THE MILESIAN DYNASTY.

T is unnecessary to follow through their details the proceedings of the Milesian princes in the period immediately subsequent to the landing. It will suffice to state that in a comparatively brief time they subdued the country, entering, however, into regular pacts, treaties, or alliances with the conquered but not powerless Firbolgs and Tuatha de Danaans. According to the constitution under which Ireland was governed for more than a thousand years, the population of the island were distinguished in two classes —the Free Clans, and the Unfree Clans ; the former being the descendants of the Milesian legions, the latter the descendants of the subjected Tuatha de Danaans and Firbolgs. The latter were allowed certain rights and privileges, and to a great extent regulated their own internal affairs ; but they could not vote in the selection of a sovereign, nor exercise any other of the attributes of full citizenship without special leave. Indeed, those subject populations occasioned the conquerors serious trouble by their hostility from time to time for centuries afterwards.

The sovereignty of the island was jointly vested in, or assumed by, Heremon and Heber, the Romulus and Remus of ancient Ireland. Like these twin brothers, who, seven hundred years later on, founded Rome, Heber and Heremon quarrelled in the sovereignty. In a pitched battle fought between them Heber was slain, and Heremon remained sole ruler of the island. For more than a thousand years the dynasty thus established reigned in Ireland, the sceptre never passing out of the family of Milesius in the direct line of descent, unless upon one occasion (to which I shall more fully advert at the proper time) for the brief period of less than twenty years. The Milesian sovereigns appear to have exhibited considerable energy in organizing the country and establishing what we may call "institutions," some of which have been adopted or copied, with improvements and adaptations, by the most civilized governments of the present day ;

and the island advanced in renown for valor, for wealth, for manufactures, and for commerce.

By this, however, my young readers are not to suppose that anything like the civilization of our times, or even faintly approaching that to which ancient Greece and Rome afterwards attained, prevailed at this period in Ireland. Not so. But, compared with the civilization of its own period in Northern and Western Europe, and recollecting how isolated and how far removed Ireland was from the great centre and source of colonization and civilization in the East, the civilization of pagan Ireland must be admitted to have been proudly eminent. In the works remaining to us of the earliest writers of ancient Rome, we find references to Ireland that attest the high position it then held in the estimation of the most civilized and learned nations of antiquity. From our own historians we know that more than fifteen hundred years before the birth of our Lord, gold mining and smelting, and artistic working in the precious metals, were carried on to a great extent in Ireland. Numerous facts might be adduced to prove that a high order of political, social, industrial, and intellectual intelligence prevailed in the country. Even in an age which was rudely barbaric elsewhere all over the world, the superiority of intellect over force, of the scholar over the soldier, was not only recognized but *decreed by legislation* in Ireland ! We find in the Irish chronicles that in the reign of Eochy the First (more than a thousand years before Christ) society was classified into seven grades, each marked by the number of colors in its dress, and that in this classification *men of learning, i. e.* eminent scholars, or *savants* as they would now be called, were by law ranked *next to royalty.*

But the most signal proof of all, attesting the existence in Ireland at that period of a civilization marvellous for its time, was the celebrated institution of the Feis Tara, or Triennial Parliament of Tara, one of the first formal parliaments or legislative assemblies of which we have record.* This great

---

* The Amphictyonic Council did not by any means partake to a like extent of the

national legislative assembly was instituted by an Irish monarch, whose name survives as a synonym of wisdom and justice, Ollav Fiola (Ollaiu poola,), who reigned as Ard Ri of
Erinn about one thousand years before the birth of Christ.
To this assembly were regularly summoned :—

Firstly—All the subordinate royal princes or chieftains;

Secondly—Ollaves and bards, judges, scholars, and historians; and

Thirdly—Military commanders.

We have in the old records the most precise accounts of
the formalities observed at the opening and during the sitting
of the assembly, from which we learn that its proceedings
were regulated with admirable order and conducted with the
greatest solemnity.

Nor was the institution of "triennial parliaments" the only
instance in which this illustrious Irish monarch, two thousand
eight hundred years ago, anticipated to a certain extent the
forms of constitutional government of which the nineteenth
century is so proud.   In the civil administration of the kingdom the same enlightened wisdom was displayed. He organized the country into regular prefectures. "Over every can-
tred," says the historian, "he appointed a chieftain, and over
every townland a kind of prefect or secondary chief, all being
the officials of the king of Ireland." After a reign of more than
forty years, this "true Irish king" died at an advanced age,
having lived to witness long the prosperity, happiness, and
peace which his noble efforts had diffused all over the realm.
His real name was Eochy the Fourth, but he is more familiarly
known in history by the title or soubriquet of "Ollav Fiola,"
that is, *the* "Ollav", or law giver, preëminently of Ireland or
" Fiola."

Though the comparative civilization of Ireland at this remote time was so high, the annals of the period disclose the
usual recurrence of wars for the throne between rival members
of the same dynasty, which early and mediæval European history in general exhibits. Reading over the history of ancient
Ireland, as of ancient Greece, Rome, Assyria, Gaul, Britain,
or Spain, one is struck by the number of sovereigns who fell

by violent deaths, and the fewness of those who ended their reigns otherwise.   But those were the days when between kings and princes, chiefs and warriors, the sword was the ready arbiter that decided all causes, executed all judgments, avenged all wrongs, and accomplished all ambitions.   Moreover, it is essential to bear in mind that the kings of those times commanded and led their own armies, not merely in theory or by "legal fiction," but in reality and fact ; and that personal participation in the battle and prowess in the field was expected and was requisite on the part of the royal commander. Under such circumstances one can easily perceive how it came to pass, naturally and inevitably, that the battle-field became ordinarily the deathbed of the king.   In those early times the kings who did not fall by the sword, in fair battle or unfair assault, were the exceptions everywhere.   Yet it is a remarkable fact, that we find the average duration of the reigns of Irish monarchs, for fifteen hundred or two thousand years after the Milesian dynasty ascended the throne, was as long as that of most European reigns in the seventeenth, eighteenth, and nineteenth centuries.   Several of the Milesian sovereigns enjoyed reigns extending to over thirty years; some to fifty years.   Many of them were highly accomplished and learned men, liberal patrons of arts, science, and commerce ; and as one of them, fourteen hundred years before the Christian era, instituted regularly convened parliaments, so we find others of them instituting orders of knighthood and Companionships of Chivalry long before we hear of their establishment elsewhere.

The Irish kings of this period, as well as during the first ten centuries of the Christian age, in frequent instances intermarried with the royal families of other countries—Spain, Gaul, Britain, and Alba ; and the commerce and manufactures of Ireland were, as the early Latin writers acquaint us, famed in all the marts and ports of Europe.

III.—HOW THE UNFREE CLANS TRIED A REVOLUTION; AND WHAT CAME OF IT. HOW THE ROMANS THOUGHT IT VAIN TO ATTEMPT A CONQUEST OF IRELAND.

DURING those fifteen hundred years preceding the Christian era, the other great nations of Europe, the Romans and the Greeks, were passing, by violent changes and bloody convulsions, through nearly every conceivable form of government—republics, confederations, empires, kingdoms, limited monarchies, despotisms, consulates, etc. During the like period (fifteen centuries) the *one* form of government, a limited monarchy, and the *one* dynasty, the Milesian, ruled in Ireland. The monarchy was *elective*, but elective out of the eligible members of the established or legitimate dynasty.

Indeed the principle of "legitimacy," as it is sometimes called in our times—the hereditary right of a ruling family or dynasty—seems from the earliest ages to have been devotedly, I might almost say superstitiously, held by the Irish. Wars for the crown, and violent changes of rulers, were always frequent enough; but the wars and the changes were always between members of the ruling family or "blood royal;" and the two or three instances to the contrary that occur, are so singularly strong in their illustration of the fact to which I have adverted, that I will cite one of them here.

The Milesians and the earlier settlers never completely fused. Fifteen hundred years after the Milesian landing, the Firbolgs, the Tuatha de Danaans, and the Milesians were still substantially distinct races or classes, the first being agriculturists or tillers of the soil, the second manufacturers and merchants, the third soldiers and rulers. The exactions and oppressions of the ruling classes at one time became so grievous that in the reign succeeding that of Creivan the Second, who was the ninety-ninth Milesian monarch of Ireland, a wide-spread con-

Milesian princes and aristocracy. After three years of secret
preparation, everything being ready, the royal and noble Milesian families, one and all, were invited to a "monster meeting"
for games, exhibitions, feastings, etc., on the plain of Knock
Ma, in the county Galway. The great spectacle had lasted
nine days, when suddenly the Milesians were set upon by the
Attacotti (as the Latin chroniclers called the conspirators), and
massacred to a man. Of the royal line there escaped, however,
three princes, *children yet unborn.* Their mothers, wives of
Irish princes, were the daughters respectively of the kings of
Scotland, Saxony, and Brittany. They succeeded in escaping
into Albion, where the three young princes were born and
educated. The successful conspirators raised to the throne
Carbry the First, who reigned five years, during which time
say the chronicles, the country was a prey to every misfortune ; the earth refused to yield, the cattle gave no milk, the
trees bore no fruit, the waters had no fish, and " the oak had but
one acorn." * Carbry was succeeded by his son, Moran, whose
name deservedly lives in Irish history as " Moran the Just."
He refused to wear the crown, which belonged, he said, to
the royal line that had been so miraculously preserved ; and he
urged that the rightful princes, who by this time had grown to
man's estate, should be recalled. Moran's powerful pleading
commended itself readily to the popular conscience, already
disquieted by the misfortunes and evil omens which, as the
people read them, had fallen upon the land since the legitimate
line had been so dreadfully cut down. The young princes were
recalled from exile, and one of them, Faradah the Righteous,
was, amidst great rejoicing, elected king of Ireland. Moran
was appointed chief judge of Erinn, and under his administra-

---

* Such was the deep faith the Irish had in the principle of legitimacy in a dynasty !
This charactertistic of nearly all the Celtic nations survives in all its force in the Jacobite
Relics of Ireland, the outburst of Irish national feeling *seventeen hundred years subsequently.* Ex. gr. Compare the above, taken from an old chronicle of the period
with the well-known Jacobite song translated from the Irish by Callanan : —

> " No more the cuckoo hails the spring ;
> No more the woods with staunch-hounds ring ;
> *The sun scarce lights the sorrowing day,*
> *Since the rightful prince is far away."*

tion of justice the land long presented a scene of peace, happiness, and contentment. To the gold chain of office which Moran wore on the judgment seat, the Irish for centuries subsequently attached supernatural powers. It was said that it would tighten around the neck of the judge if he was unjustly judging a cause!

The dawn of Christianity found the Romans masters of nearly the whole of the known world. Britain, after a short struggle, succumbed, and eventually learned to love the yoke. Gaul, after a gallant effort, was also overpowered and held as a conquered province. But upon Irish soil the Roman eagles were never planted. Of Ireland, or Ierne, as they called it, of its great wealth and amazing beauty of scenery and richness of soil, the all-conquering Romans heard much. But they had heard also that the fruitful and beautiful island was peopled by a soldier race, and, judging them by the few who occasionally crossed to Alba to help their British neighbors, and whose prowess and skill the imperial legions had betimes to prove, the conquest of Ierne was wisely judged by the Romans to be a work better not attempted.

The early centuries of the Christian era may be considered the period preëminently of pagan bardic or legendary fame in Ireland. In this, which we may call the " Ossianic" period, lived Cuhal or Cumhal, father of the celebrated Fin Mac Cumhal, and commander of the great Irish legion called Fiana Erion, or Irish militia. The Ossianic poems* recount the most marvellous stories of Fin and the Fiana Erion, which stories are compounds of undoubted facts and manifest fictions, the prowess of the heroes being in the course of time magnified into the supernatural, and the figures and poetic allegories of the earlier bards gradually coming to be read as realities. Some of these poems are gross, extravagant, and absurd. Others of them are of rare beauty, and are, moreover, valuable for the insight they give, though obliquely, into the manners and customs, thoughts, feelings, guiding principles, and moving passions of the ancient Irish.

---

* So called from their author, Oisin, or Ossian, the warrior poet, son of Fin, and

IV.—BARDIC TALES OF ANCIENT ERINN. "THE SORROWFUL
FATE OF THE CHILDREN OF USNA."

NE of the oldest, and **perhaps the
most** famous, of all **the great
national** history-poems **or bardic** tales of the ancient **Irish, is**
called " The Fate of the **Children** of
Usna," the incidents of **which belong**
to the period preceding by **half a century** the Christian era, or **anno mundi**
3,960. Indeed it was always classified
by the bards as one of "The Three
Sorrowful Tales of Erinn." Singularly enough, the story
contains much less poetic fiction, and keeps much closer to
the simple facts of history, than do several of the poems of
Ossian's time written much later on. From the highly
dramatic and tragic nature of the events related, one can well
conceive that, clad in the beautiful idiom of the Irish tongue
and told in the fanciful language of poetry, "The story of the
children of Usnach" was calculated to win a prominent place
amongst the bardic recitals of the pagan Irish. A semi-fan-
ciful version of it has been given in English at great length
by Dr. Ferguson in the *Hibernian Nights' Entertainment ;* but

perhaps, be interesting to my young readers, I summarize the various versions here, as the only specimen I mean to give of the semi-imaginative literature of the pagan Irish:

When Conor Mac Nessa was reigning king of Ulidia and Eochy the Tenth was Ard Ri of Erinn, it happened one day that Conor had deigned to be present at a feast which was given at the house of Felemi, son of the laureate of Ulster. While the festivities were going on, it came to pass that the wife of the host gave birth to a daughter; and the infant being brought into the presence of the king and the other assembled guests, all saw that a beauty more than natural had been given to the child. In the midst of remark and marvel on all hands at the circumstance, Kavaiee, the chief druid of the Ulidians, cried out with a loud voice and prophesied that through the infant before them there would come dark woe and misfortune to Ulster, such as the land had not known for years. When the warriors heard this they all demanded that the child should instantly be put to death. But Conor interposed and forbade the deed. "I," said the king, "will myself take charge of this beautiful child of destiny. I shall have her reared where no evil can befall through her or to her, and in time she may become a wife for me." Then the chief druid, Kavaiee, named the child Deirdri, which means alarm or danger. Conor placed the infant under the charge of a nurse or attendant, and subsequently a female tutor, in a residence situated in a district which no foot of man was allowed to tread; so that Deirdri had grown to the age of woman before she saw a human form other than those of her female attendants. And the maiden was beautiful beyond aught that the eye of man had ever beheld.

Meanwhile, at the court of the Ulidian king was a young noble named Naeisi, son of Usna, whose manly beauty, vigor, activity, and bravery were the theme of every tongue. One day, accompanied only by a faithful deerhound, Naeisi had hunted the deer from the rising of the sun, until towards evening, he found the chase had led him into a district quite strange to his

homeward, when suddenly the terrible idea flashed across his
mind, that he was within the forbidden ground which it was
death to enter—the watchfully-guarded retreat of the king's
mysterious *protégé* Deirdri. While pondering on his fatal position, he came suddenly upon Deirdri and her nurse, who were
strolling in the sunset by a running stream. Deirdri cried out
with joy to her attendant, and asked what sort of a being it
was who stood beyond ; for she had never seen any such before. The consternation and embarrassment of the aged attendant was extreme, and she in vain sought to baffle Deirdri's
queries, and to induce her to hasten homeward. Naeisi too,
riveted by the beauy of Deirdri, even though he knew the
awful consequences of his unexpected presence there, stirred
not from the scene. He felt that even on the penalty of death
he would not lose the enchanting vision. He and Deirdri spoke
to each other and eventually the nurse, perplexed at first,
seems to have become a confident to the attachment which
on the spot sprung up between the young people.

It was vain for them, however, to hide from themselves the
fate awaiting them on the king's discovery of their affection,
and accordingly Naeisi and Deirdri arranged that they would
fly into Alba, where they might find a home. Now Naeisi
was greatly loved by all the nobles of Ulster ; but most of
all was he loved by his two brothers, Anli and Ardan, and his
affection for them caused him to feel poignantly the idea of leaving them forever. So he confided to them the dread secret of
his love for Deirdri, and of the flight he and she had planned.
Then Anli and Ardan said that wherever Naeisi would fly, thither also would they go, and with their good swords guard their
brother and the wife for whom he was sacrificing home and
heritage. So, privately selecting a trusty band of one hundred and fifty warriors, Naeisi, Anli, and Ardan, taking Deirdri with them, succeeding in making their escape out of
Ireland and into Alba, where the king of that country, aware
of their noble lineage and high valor, assigned them ample
"maintenance and quarterage," as the bards express it.
There they lived peacefully and happily for a time, until the

restless and envious, reflecting that he might, as sovereign, himself claim her as wife, which demand at length he made. Naeisi and his brothers were filled with indignation at this; but their difficulty was extreme, for whither now could they fly? Ireland was closed against them forever; and now they were no longer safe in Alba! The full distress of their position was soon realized; for the king of Alba came with force of arms to take Deirdri. After many desperate encounters and adventures, however, any one of which would supply ample materials for a poem-story, the exiled brothers and their retainers made good their retreat into a small island off the Scottish coast.

When it was heard in Ulidia that the sons of Usna were in such sore strait, great murmurs went round amongst the nobles of Ulster, for Naeisi and his brothers were greatly beloved of them all. So the nobles of the province eventually spoke up to the king, and said it was hard and a sad thing that these three young nobles, the foremost warriors of Ulster, should be lost to their native land and should suffer such difficulty "on account of one woman." Conor saw what discontent and disaffection would prevail throughout the province if the popular favorites were not at once pardoned and recalled. He consented to the entreaties of the nobles, and a royal courier was despatched with the glad tidings to the sons of Usna.

When the news came, joy beamed on every face but on that of Deirdri. She felt an unaccountable sense of fear and sorrow, "as if of coming ill." Yet, with all Naeisi's unbounded love for her, she feared to put it to the strain of calling on him to choose between exile with her or a return to Ireland without her. For it was clear that both he and Anli and Ardan longed in their hearts for one glimpse of the hills of Erinn. However, she could not conceal the terrible dread that oppressed her, and Naeisi, though his soul yearned for home, was so moved by Deirdri's forebodings, that he replied to the royal messenger by expressing doubts of the safety promised to him if he returned.

content against the king, and the nobles agreed that it was but right that the most solemn guarantees and ample sureties should be given to the sons of Usna on the part of the king. To this also Conor assented ; and he gave Fergus Mac Roi, Dutha del Ulad, and Cormac Colingas as guarantees or hostages that he would himself act toward the sons of Usna in good faith.

The royal messenger set out once more, accompanied by Fiachy, a young noble of Ulster, son of Fergus Mac Roi, one of the three hostages, and now there remained no excuse for Naeisi delaying to return. Deirdri still felt oppressed by the mysterious sense of dread and hidden danger ; but (so she reflected) as Naeisi and his devoted brothers had hitherto uncomplainingly sacrificed everything for her, she would now sacrifice her feelings for their sakes. · She assented, therefore (though with secret sorrow and foreboding), to their homeward voyage.

Soon the galleys laden with the returning exiles reached the Irish shore. On landing, they found a Dalaraidian legion waiting to escort them to Emania, the palace of the king ; and of this legion the young Fiachy was the commander. Before completing the first day's march some misgivings seem occasionally to have flitted across the minds of the brothers, but they were allayed by the frank and fearless, brave and honourable Fiachy, who told them to have no fear, and be of good heart. But every spear's length they drew near to Emania, Deirdri's feelings became more and more insupportable, and so overpowered was she with the forebodings of evil, that again the cavalcade halted, and again the brothers would have turned back but for the persuasions of their escort. Next day, towards evening, they sighted Emania. "O·Naeisi," cried Deirdri, "view the cloud that I here see in the sky ! I see over Eman Green a chilling cloud of blood-tinged red." But Naeisi tried to cheer her with assurances of safety and pictures of the happy days that were yet before them.

Next day came Durthact, chieftain of Fermac(now Farney), saying that he came from the king, by whose orders the charge

haps at this stage began to have misgivings as to what was in
meditation, answered, that to no one would he surrender the
honorable trust confided to him on the stake of his father's
life and honor, which with his own life and honor he would
defend.

And here, interrupting the summarized text of the story, I
may state, that it is a matter of doubt whether the king was
really a party to the treachery which ensued, or whether
Durthacht and others themselves moved in the bloody business without his orders, using his name and calculating that
what they proposed to do would secretly please him, would
be readily forgiven or approved, and would recommend them
to Conor's favor. Conor's character as it stands on the page
of authentic history, would forbid the idea of such murderous
perfidy on his part ; but all the versions of the tale allege the
king's guilt to be deep and plain.

Fiachy escorted his charge to a palace which had been assigned for them in the neighborhood ; and much to the discon-
certing of Durthacht of Fermae, quartered his legion of Dalar-
aidians as guards upon the building. That night neither the
chivalrous Fiachy nor the children of Usna disguised the
now irresistible and mournful conviction, that foul play was to
be apprehended ; but Naeisi and his brothers had seen enough
of their brave young custodian to convince them that, even
though his own father should come at the palace gate to bid
him connive at the surrender of his charge, Fiachy would
defend them while life remained.

Next morning the effort was renewed to induce Fiachy to
hand over the charge of the returned exiles. He was immovable. " What interest is it of yours to obstruct the king's
orders?" said Durthacht of Fermea ; " can you not turn over
your responsibility to us, and in peace and safety go your
way ? " " It is of the lasti nterest to me," replied Fiachy,
"to see that the sons of Usna have not trusted in vain on the
word of the king, on the hostage of my father, or on the honor of
my father's son." Then all chance of prevailing on Fiachy
being over, Durthacht gave the signal for assault and the pal-

Then spoke Naeisi, touched to the heart by the devotion and fidelity of Fiachy : " Why should you perish defending us? We have seen all. *Your* honor is safe, noblest of youths. We will not have you sacrificed vainly resisting the fate that for us now is clearly inevitable. We will meet death calmly, we will surrender ourselves, and spare needless slaughter." But Fiachy would not have it so, and all the entreaties of the sons of Usna could not prevail upon him to assent. " I am here," said he, " the representative of my father's hostage of the honor of Ulster, and the word of the king. To these and on me you trusted. While you were safe you would have turned back, but for me. Now, they who would harm you must pass over the lifeless corpse of Fiachy."

Then they asked that they might at least go forth on the ramparts and take part in the defence of the palace ; but Fiachy pointed out that by the etiquette of knightly honor in Ulidia, this would be infringing on his sacred charge. He was the pledge for their safety, and he alone should look to it. They must, under no circumstances, run even the slightest peril of a spear-wound, unless he should first fall, when by the laws of honor, his trust would have been acquitted, but not otherwise. So ran the code of chivalry amongst the warriors of Dalariada.

Then Naeisi and his brothers and Deirdri withdrew into the palace, and no more, even by a glance, gave sign of any inter- est or thought whatsoever about their fate ; whether it was near or far, brightening or darkening ; " but Naeisi and Dier- dri sat down at a chess-board and played at the game."

Meanwhile, not all the thunders of the heavens could equal the resounding din of the clanging of shields, the clash of swords and spears, the cries of the wounded, and the shouts of the combatants outside. The assailants were twenty to one ; but the faithful Fiachy and his Dalariadians performed prod- igies of valor, and at noon they still held the outer ramparts of all. By the assailants nothing had yet been won.

An attendant rushed with word to Naeisi. He raised not his eyes from the board, but continued the game.

returned to the charge with increased desperation. For an hour there was no pause in the frightful fury of the struggle. At length the first rampart was won.

A wounded guard rushed in with the dark news to Naeisi, who "moved a piece on the board, but never raised his eyes." The story in this way goes on to describe how, as each fosse surrounding the palace was lost and won, and as the din and carnage of the strife drew nearer and nearer to the doomed guests inside, each report from the scene of slaughter, whether of good or evil report, failed alike to elicit the slightest motion of concern or interest one way or another from the brothers or from Deirdri. In all the relics we possess of the old poems or bardic stories of those pagan times, there is nothing finer than the climax of the tragedy which the semi-imaginative story I have been epitomizing here proceeds to reach. The deafening clangor and bloody strife outside, drawing nearer and nearer, the supreme equanimity of the noble victims inside, too proud to evince the slightest emotion, is most powerfully and dramatically antithesized; the story culminating in the final act of the tragedy, when the faithful Fiachy and the last of his guards having been slain, "the Sons of Usna" met their fate with a dignity that befitted three such noble champions of Ulster."

When Fergus and Duthah heard of the foul murder of the Sons of Usna, in violation of the pledge for which they themselves were sureties, they marched upon Emania, and, in a desperate encounter with Conor's forces, in which the king's son was slain and his palace burned to the ground, they inaugurated a desolating war that lasted in Ulster for many a year, and amply fulfilled the dark prophecy of Kavaiee the druid in the hour of Deirdri's birth.

Deirdri, we are told, "never smiled" from the day of the slaughter of her husband on Eman Green. In vain the king lavished kindness and favors upon her. In vain he exhausted every resource in the endeavor to cheer, amuse, or interest her. One day, after more than a year had been passed by Deirdri in this settled but placid despair and melancholy,

He attempted to jest her sarcastically about her continued grieving for Naeisi, when suddenly she sprang out of the chariot, then flying at the full speed of the steeds, and falling head foremost against a sharp rock on the road side, was killed upon the spot.

Well known to most Irish readers, young and old, is Moore's beautiful and passionate " Lament for the Children of Usna :"—

> Avenging and bright falls the swift sword of Erin
>   On him who the brave sons of Usna betrayed !—
> For every fond eye he hath waken'd a tear in,
>   A drop from his heart-wounds shall weep o'er her blade !
>
> By the red cloud that hung over Conor's dark dwelling,
>   When Ulad's three champions lay sleeping in gore—
> By the billows of war, which so often, high swelling,
>   Have wafted those heroes to victory's shore—
>
> We swear to revenge them !—No joy shall be tasted,
>   The harp shall be silent, the maiden unwed,
> Our halls shall be mute, and our fields shall lie wasted,
>   Till vengeance is wreak'd on the murderer's head !
>
> Yes, monarch, tho' sweet are our home recollections ;
>   Though sweet are the tears that from tenderness fall ;
> Though sweet are our friendships, our hopes, our affections,
>   Revenge on a tyrant is sweetest of all !

V.— THE DEATH OF KING CONOR MAC NESSA.

HAVE alluded to doubts suggested in my mind by the facts of authentic history, as to whether King Conor Mac Nessa was likely to have played the foul part attributed to him in this celebrated bardic story, and for which, certainly, the "sureties" Fergus, Duthach, and Cormac, held him to a terrible account. All that can be said is, that no other incident recorded of him would warrant such an estimate of his character; and it is certain he was a man of many brave and noble parts. He met his death under truly singular circumstances. The ancient bardic version of the event is almost literally given in the following poem, by Mr. T. D. Sullivan :—

DEATH OF KING CONOR MAC NESSA.

'Twas a day full of sorrow for Ulster when Conor Mac Nessa went forth
To punish the clansman of Connaught who dared to take spoil from the North ;
For his men brought him back from the battle scarce better than one that was dead,
With the brain-ball of Mesgedra* buried two-thirds of its depth in his head.
His royal physician bent o'er him, great Fingin who often before
Staunched the war-battered bodies of heroes and built them for battle once more,
And he looked on the wound of the monarch, and heark'd to his low-breathed sighs,
And he said, " In the day when that missile is loosed from his forehead, he dies.

II.

" Yet long midst the people who love him King Conor Mac Nessa may reign,
If always the high pulse of passion be kept from his heart and his brain;
And for this I lay down his restrictions :—no more from this day shall his place
He with armies, in battles, or hostings, or leading the van of the chase ;
At night, when the banquet is flashing, his measure of wine must be small,
And take heed that the bright eyes of woman be kept from his sight above all ;
For if heart-thrilling joyance or anger awhile o'er his being have power,
The ball will start forth from his forehead, and surely he dies in that hour."

---

* The pagan Irish warriors sometimes took the brains out of champions whom they had slain in single combat, mixed them up with lime, and rolled them into balls, which hardened with time, and which they preserved as trophies. It was with one of these balls, which had been abstracted from his armory, that Conor Mac Nessa

III.

Oh ! woe for the valiant King Conor, struck down from the summit of life,
While glory unclouded shone round him, and regal enjoyment was rife—
Shut out from his toils and his duties, condemned to ignoble repose,
No longer to friends a true helper, no longer a scourge to his foes !
He, the strong-handed smiter of champions, the piercer of armor and shields,
The foremost in earth shaking onsets, the last out of blood-sodden fields—
The mildest, the kindest the gayest, when revels ran high in his hall—
Oh, well might his true-hearted people feel gloomy and sad for his fall !

IV.

The princes, the chieftains, the nobles, who met to consult at his board,
Whispered low when their talk was of combats, and wielding the spear and the
    sword :
The bards from their harps feared to waken the full-pealing sweetness of song,
To give homage to valor or beauty, or praise to the wise and the strong ;
The flash of no joy-giving story made cheers or gay laughter resound,
Amidst silence constrained and unwonted the seldom-filled wine-cup went round :
And, sadder to all who remembered the glories and joys that had been,
The heart-swaying presence of woman not once shed its light on the scene.

V.

He knew it, he felt it, and sorrow sunk daily more deep in his heart ;
He wearied of doleful inaction, from all his loved labors apart.
He sat at his door in the sunlight, sore grieving and weeping to see
The life and the motion around him, and nothing so stricken as he.
Above him the eagle went wheeling, before him the deer galloped by,
And the quick-legged rabbits went skipping from green glades and burrows a-nigh.
The-song-birds sang out from the copses, the bees passed on musical wing,
And all things were happy and busy, save Conor Mac Nessa the king !

VI.

So years had passed over, when, sitting midst silence like that of the tomb,
A terror crept through him as sudden the noonlight was blackened with gloom.
One red flare of lightning blazed brightly, illuming the landscape around,
One thunder-peal roared through the mountains, and rumbled and crashed un-
    derground ;
He heard the rocks bursting asunder, the trees tearing up by the roots,
And loud through the horrid confusion the howling of terrified brutes.
From the halls of his tottering palace came screamings of terror and pain,
And he saw crowding thickly around him the ghosts of the foes he had slain i

VII.

And as soon as the sudden commotion that shuddered through nature had ceased.
The king sent for Barach, his druid, and said : " Tell me truly, O priest,
What magical arts have created this scene of wild horror and dread ?
What has blotted the blue sky above us, and shaken the earth that we tread ?

Are the gods that we worship offended? what crime or what wrong has been done?
Has the fault been committed in Erin, and how may their favor be won?
What rites may avail to appease them? what gifts on their altars should smoke?
Only say, and the offering demanded we lay by your consecrate oak."

VIII.

"O king," said the white-bearded druid, " the truth unto me has been shown,
There lives but *one* God, the Eternal; far up in high Heaven is His throne.
He looked upon men with compassion, and sent from His kingdom of light
His Son, in the shape of a mortal, to teach them and guide them aright.
Near the time of your birth, O King Conor, the Saviour of mankind was born,
And since then in the kingdoms far eastward He taught, toiled, and prayed, till this morn,
When wicked men seized Him, fast bound Him with nails to a cross, lanced his side,
And that moment of gloom and confusion was earth's cry of dread when He died.

IX.

"O King, He was gracious and gentle, His heart was all pity and love,
And for men he was ever beseeching the grace of his Father above ;
He helped them, He healed them, He blessed them, He labored that all might attain
To the true God's high kingdom of glory, where never comes sorrow or pain ;
But they rose in their pride and their folly, their hearts filled with merciless rage,
That only the sight of his life-blood fast poured from His heart could assuage :
Yet while on the cross-beams uplifted, His body racked, tortured, and riven,
He prayed—not for justice or vengeance, but asked that His foes be forgiven."

X.

With a bound from his seat rose King Conor, the red flush of rage on his face,
Fast he ran through the hall for his weapons, and snatching his sword from its place,
He rushed to the woods, striking wildly at boughs that dropped down with each blow,
And he cried : "Were I midst the vile rabble, I'd cleave them to earth even so !
With the strokes of a high king of Erinn, the whirls of my keen-tempered sword,
I would save from their horrible fury that mild and that merciful Lord."
His frame shook and heaved with emotion ; the brain ball leaped forth from his head,
And commending his soul to that Saviour, King Conor Mac Nessa fell dead.

VI.—THE "GOLDEN AGE" OF PRE-CHRISTIAN ERINN.

AS early as the reign of Ard-ri Cormac the First—the first years of the third century—the Christian faith had penetrated into Ireland. Probably in the commercial intercourse between the Irish and continental ports, some Christian converts had been made amongst the Irish navigators or merchants. Some historians think the monarch himself, Cormac, towards the close of life adored the true God, and attempted to put down druidism. "His reign," says Mr. Haverty, the historian, "is generally looked upon as the brightest epoch in the entire history of pagan Ireland. He established three colleges; one for War, one for History, and the third for Jurisprudence. He collected and remodelled the laws, and published the code which remained in force until the English invasion (a period extending beyond *nine hundred years*), and outside the English Pale for many centuries after! He assembled the bards and chroniclers at Tara, and directed them to collect the annals of Ireland, and to write out the records of the country from year to year, making them synchronize with the history of other countries, by collating events with the reigns of contemporary foreign potentates, Cormac himself having been the inventor of this kind of chronology. These annals formed what is called the 'Psalter of Tara,' which also contained full details of the bounderies of provinces, districts, and small divisions of land throughout Ireland; but unfortunately this great record has been lost, no vestige of it being now, it is believed, in existence. The magnificence of Cormac's palace at Tara was commensurate with the greatness of his power and the brilliancy of his actions; and he fitted out a fleet which he sent to harass the shores of

acknowledge him as sovereign. He wrote a book or tract called *Teaguscna-Ri*, or the ' Institutions of a Prince,' which is still in existence, and which contains admirable maxims on manners, morals, and government." This illustrious sovereign died A. D. 266, at Cleitach, on the Boyne, a salmon bone. it is said, having fastened in his throat while dining, and defied all efforts of extrication. He was buried at Ross-na-ri, the first of the pagan monarchs for many generations who was not interred at Brugh, the famous burial place of the pre-Christian kings. A vivid tradition relating the circumstances of his burial has been very beautifully versified by Dr. Ferguson in his poem, " The Burial of King Cormac":

"Crom Cruach and his sub-gods twelve,"
Said Cormac "are but craven treene;
The axe that made them, haft or helve,
Had worthier of our worship been :

But He who made the tree to grow,
And hid in earth the iron-stone,
And made the man with mind to know
The axe's use, is God alone."

The druids hear of this fearful speech and are horrified:

Anon to priests of Crom was brought
(Where girded in their service dread
They ministered on red Moy Slaught)—
Word of the words King Cormac said.

They loosed their curse against the king,
They cursed him in his flesh and bones,
And daily in their mystic ring
They turned the maledictive stones.

At length one day comes the news to them that the king is dead, "choked upon the food he ate," and they exultantly sound "the praise of their avenging God." Cormac, before he dies, however, leaves as his last behest a direction that he shall not be interred in the old pagan cemetery of the kings at Brugh, but at Ross-na-ri :

But ere the voice was wholly spent
That priest and prince should still obey,
To awed attendants o'er him bent
Great Cormac gathered breath to say :

" Spread not the beds of Brugh for me,
    When restless death-bed's use is done ;
But bury me at Ross-na-ree,
    And face me to the rising sun.

For all the kings who lie in Brugh
    Put trust in gods of wood and stone ;
And 'twas at Ross that first I knew   ,
    One Unseen, who is God alone.

His glory lightens from the east,
    His message soon shall reach our shore,
And idol-god and cursing priest
    Shall plague us from Moy Slaught no more."

King Cormac dies, and his people one and all are shocked ·
at the idea of burying him anywhere save in the ancient pagan
cemetery where all his great forefathers repose.   They agree
that he must have been raving when he desired otherwise ;
and they decide to bury him in Brugh, where his grandsire,
Conn of the Hundred Battles, lies armor-clad, upright, hound
at foot and spear in hand :

Dead Cormac on his bier they laid :
    " He reigned a king for forty years ;
And shame it were," his captains said,
    " He lay not with his royal peers :

His grandsire, Hundred Battles, sleeps
    Serene in Brugh, and all around
Dead kings, in stone sepulchral keeps,
    Protect he sacred burial ground.

What though a dying man should rave
    Of changes o'er the eastern sea,
In Brugh of Boyne shall be his grave,
    And not in noteless Ross-na-ree. "

Then northward forth they bore the bier,
    And down from Sleithac's side they drew
With horseman and with charioteer,
    To cross the fords of Boyne to Brugh.

Suddenly "a breath of finer air" touches the river "with
rustling wings."

And as the burial train came down
    With dirge, and savage dolorous shows,
Across their pathway broad and brown,
    The deep full-hearted river rose.

From bank to bank through all his fords,
   'Neath blackening squalls he swelled and boiled
And thrice the wond'ring gentile lords
   Essay'd to cross and thrice recoil'd.

Then forth stepped gray-haired warriors four ;
   They said : "Through angrier floods than these,
On link'd shield once our king we bore
   From Dread-spear and the hosts of Deece;

And 'ong as loyal will holds good,
   And limbs respond with helpful thews,
Nor flood nor fiend within the flood
   Shall bar him of his burial dues."

So they lift the bier, and step into the boiling surge

And now they slide and now they swim,
   And now amid the blackening squall,
Gray locks afloat with clutchings grim,
   They plunge around the floating pall.

While as a youth with practised spear
   Through justling crowds bears off the ring—
Boyne from their shoulders caught the bier,
   And proudly bare away the King !

The foaming torrent sweeps the coffin away ; next day it is found far down the river, stranded on the bank under Ross-na-ri ; the last behest of Cormac is fulfilled after all !

At morning on the grassy marge
   Of Ross-na-ree the corpse was found,
And shepherds at their early charge,
   Entombed it in the peaceful ground.
      *   *   *   *
And life and time rejoicing run ;
   From age to age their wonted way ;
But still he waits the risen Sun,
   For still 'tis only dawning Day.

In the two centuries succeeding, there flourished among other sovereigns of Ireland less known to fame, the celebrated Niall of the Nine Hostages, and King Dahi.* During these two hundred years the flag of Ireland waved through continental Europe

over victorious egions and fleets ; the Irish monarchs leading
powerful armies across the plains of Gaul, and up to the very
confines of "the Cæsars' domains" in Italy.   It was the day
of Ireland's military power in Europe; a day which subsequently waned so disastrously, and, later on, set in utter gloom.
Neighboring Britain, whose yoke a thousand years subsequently Ireland was to wear, then lay helpless and abject at the
mercy of the Irish hosts ; the Britons, as history relates, absolutely weeping and wailing at the departure of the enslaving
Roman-legions, because now there would be naught to stay
the visits of the Scoti, or Irish, and the Picts ! The courts of
the Irish princes and homes of the Irish nobility were filled
with slave attendants, brought from abroad, some from
Gaul, but the most from Anglia.   It was in this way the
youthful Patricus, or Patrick, was brought a slave into Ireland
from Gaul.   As the power of imperial Rome began to pale,
and the outlying legions were being every year drawn in nearer
and nearer to the great city itself, the Irish sunburst blazed
over the scene, and the retreating Romans found the cohorts
of Erinn pushing dauntlessly and vengefully on their track.
Although the Irish chronicles of the period themselves say
little of the deeds of the armies abroad, the continental records
of the time give us pretty full insight into the part they played on the European stage in that day.*   Niall of the Nine
Hostages met his death in Gaul, on the banks of the Loire,
while leading his armies in one of those campaigns. The
death of King Dahi, who was killed by lightning at the foot
of the Alps, while marching at the head of his legions, one
of our national poets, Davis, has immortalized in a poem, from
which I quote here :—

---

* Haverty the historian says : " It is in the verses of the Latin poet Claudian that we
read of the sending of troops by Stilichio, the general of Theodosius the Great to
repel the Scottish hosts led by the brave and abventurous Niall One of the passages
of Claudian thus referred to is that in which the poet says:

' Totam cum Scotus Iernem
Movit, et infesto spumavit remige Tethys.'

That is, as translated in Gibson's *Candem*:

" 'When Scots came thundering from the Irish shores

Darkly their glibs o'erhang,
Sharp is their wolf-dog's fang,
Bronze spear and falchion clang—
    Brave men might shun them
Heavy the spoil they bear—
Jewels and gold are there—
Hostage and maiden fair—
    How have they won them?

From the soft sons of Gaul,
Roman, and Frank, and thrall,
Borough, and hut, and hall,—
    These have been torn.
Over Britannia wide,
Over fair Gaul they hied,
Often in battle tried,—
    Enemies mourn!

          *   *   *

Up on the glacier's snow,
Down on the vales below,
Monarch and clansmen go—
    Bright is the morning.
Never their march they slack,
Jura is at their back,
When falls the evening black,
    Hideous, and warning.

Eagles scream loud on high;
Far off the chamois fly;
Hoarse comes the torrent's cry,
    On the rocks whitening.
Strong are the storm's wings;
Down the tall pine it flings;
Hail-stone and sleet it brings
    Thunder and lightning.

Little these veterans mind
Thundering hail, or wind;
Closer their ranks thay bind—
    Matching the storm.
While, a spear-cast or more,
On, the first ranks before,
Dathi the sunburst bore—
    Haughty his form.

Forth from the thunder-cloud
Leaps out a foe as proud—
Sudden the monarch bowed—

Wildly the king they raise—
Struck by the lightning's blaze—
Ghastly his dying gaze,
    Clutching his standard !
  *   *   *   *   *
Mild is the morning beam,
Gently the rivers stream,
Happy the valleys seem ;
    But the lone islanders—
Mark how they guard their king !
Hark, to the wail they sing !
Dark is their counselling—
    Helvetia's highlanders.

Gather like ravens, near—
Shall Dathi's soldiers fear?
Soon their home-path they clear—
    Rapid and daring ;
On through the pass and plain,
Until the shore they gain,
And, with their spoil, again
    Landed in Eirinn.

Little does Eire care
For gold or maiden fair—
" Where is king Dathi ?—where,
    Where is my bravest ? "
On the rich deck he lies.
O'er him his sunburst flies;
Solemn the obsequies,
    Eire ! thou gavest.

See ye that countless train
Crossing Ros-Comain's plain,
Crying, like hurricane,
    Uile liú ai ?
Broad is his *cairn's* base—
Nigh the '' King's burial place'',
Last of the Pagan race,
    Lieth King Dathi !

VII.—HOW IRELAND RECEIVED THE CHRISTIAN FAITH.

O these foreign expeditions Ireland was destined to be indebted for her own conquest by the spirit of Christianity. As I have already mentioned, in one of the military excursions of King Niall the First into Gaul, he captured and brought to Ireland amongst other white slaves, Patricius, a Romano-Gallic youth of good quality, and his sisters Darerca and Lupita. The story of St. Patrick's bondage in Ireland, of his miraculous escape, his entry into holy orders, his vision of Ireland—in which he thought he heard cries of a multitude of people, entreating him to come to them in Erinn—his long studies under St. Germain, and eventually his determination to undertake in an especial manner the conversion of the Irish, will all be found in any Irish Church History or Life of St. Patrick.* Having received the sanction and benediction of the holy pontiff Pope Celestine, and having been consecrated bishop, St. Patrick, accompanied by a few chosen priests, reached Ireland in 432. Christianity had been preached in Ireland long before St. Patrick's time. In 431 St. Palladius, Archdeacon of Rome, was sent by Pope Celestine as a bishop to the Christians in Ireland. These, however, were evidently but few in number, and worshipped only in fear or secrecy. The attempt to preach the faith openly to the people was violently suppressed, and St. Palladius sailed from Ireland. St. Patrick and his missioners landed on the spot where now stands the fashionable watering

---

* My young readers will find this glorious chapter in our religious annals, related with great simplicity, beauty, and truth, in a little publication called, "St. Patrick's: how it was restored," by the Rev James Gaffney, of the diocese of Dublin, whose admirable volume on "The Ancient Irish Church", as well as the Rev. S. Malone's

place called Bray, near Dublin. The hostility of the Lagenian
prince and people compelled him to reëmbark. He sailed
northwards, touching at Innis-Patrick near Skerries, county
Dublin, and eventually landed at Magh Innis, in Strangford
Lough.

Druidism would appear to have been the form of paganism
then prevailing in Ireland, though even then some traces remained of a still more ancient idol-worship, probably dating
from the time of the Tuatha de Danaans, two thousand years
before. St. Patrick, however, found the Irish mind much
better prepared, by its comparative civilization and refinement,
to receive the truths of Christianity, than that of any other
nation in Europe outside imperial Rome. The Irish were
always—then as they are now—preëminently a reverential
people, and thus were peculiarly susceptible of religious
truth. St. Patrick's progress through the island was marked
by success from the outset. Tradition states that, expound-
ing the doctrine of the Holy Trinity, he used a little sprig of
trefoil, or three-leaved grass, whence the Shamrock comes
to be the National Emblem, as St. Patrick is the National
Saint or Patron of Ireland.

Ard-Ri Laori* was holding a druidical festival in Tara, at
which the kindling of a great fire formed a chief feature of the
proceedings, and it was a crime punishable with death for
any one to light a fire in the surrounding country on the
evening of that great festival, until the sacred flame on Tara
Hill blazed forth. To his amazement, however, the monarch
beheld on the Hill of Slane, visible from Tara, a bright fire
kindled early in the evening. This was the Paschal fire which
St. Patrick and his missionaries had lighted, for it was Holy
Saturday. The king sent for the chief druid, and pointed
out to him on the distant horizon the flickering beam that so
audaciously violated the sacred laws. The archpriest gazed
long and wistfully at the spot, and eventually answered : " O
king, there is indeed a flame lighted on yonder hill, which, *if*

it be not put out to-night will never be quenched in Erinn." Much disquieted by this oracular answer, Laori directed that the offenders, whoever they might be, should be instantly brought before him for punishment. St. Patrick, on being arrested, arrayed himself in his vestments, and, crozier in hand, marched boldly at the head of his captors, reciting aloud as he went along, a litany which is still extant, in which he invoked, " on , that momentous day for Erinn," the Holy Trinity, the Father, the Son, and the Holy Spirit, ever Blessed Mary the Mother of God, and the saints around the throne of heaven. Having arrived before the king and his assembled courtiers and druidical high priests, St. Patrick, undismayed, proclaimed to them that he had come to quench the fires of pagan sacrifice in Ireland, and light the flame of Christian faith. The king listened amazed and angered, yet no penalty fell on Patrick. On the contrary, he made several converts on the spot, and the sermon and controversy in the king's presence proved an auspicious beginning for the glorious mission upon which he had just entered.

It would fill a large volume to chronicle the progress of the saint through the island. Before his death, though only a few of the reigning princes had embraced the faith (for many years subsequently pagan kings ruled the country) the good seeds had been sown far and wide, and were thriving apace, and the cross had been raised throughout Ireland, "from the centre to the sea." Ours was the only country in Europe, it is said, bloodlessly converted to the faith. Strictly speaking, only one martyr suffered death for the evangelization of Ireland, and death in this instance had been devised for the saint himself. While St. Patrick was returning from Munster a pagan chieftain formed a design to murder him. The plan came to the knowledge of Odran, the faithful charioteer of Patrick, who, saying nought of it to him, managed to change seats with the Saint, and thus received himself the fatal blow intended for his master.

Another authentic anecdote may be mentioned here. At the baptism of Aengus, King of Mononia or Munster, St. Pat-

the king with his pastoral staff,* which terminated in an iron spike, and which it was the Saint's custom to strike into the ground by his side, supporting himself more or less thereby, while preaching or baptising. The king bore the wound without wincing, until the ceremony was over, when St. Patrick with surprise and pain beheld the ground covered with blood, and observed the cause. Being questioned by the Saint as to why he did not cry out, Aengus replied, that *he thought it was part of the ceremony*, to represent, though faintly, the wounds our Lord had borne for man's redemption.

In the year of our Lord 493, on the 17th of March—which day is celebrated as his feast by the Catholic Church and by the Irish nation at home and in exile—St. Patrick departed this life in his favorite retreat of Saul, in the county of Down, where his body was interred. " His obsequies," say the old annalists, "continued for twelve days, during which the light of innumerable tapers seemed to turn night into day ; and the bishops and priests of Ireland congregated on the occasion."

Several of the saint's compositions, chiefly prayers and litanies, are extant. They are full of the most powerful invocations of the saints, and in all other particulars are exactly such prayers and express such doctrines as are taught in our own day in the unchanged and unchangeable Catholic Church.

---

* " The staff of Jesus" is the name by which the crozier of St. Patrick is always mentioned in the earliest of our annals ; a well preserved tradition asserting it to have been a rood or staff which our Lord carried. It was brought by St. Patrick from Rome when setting forth by the authority of Pope Celestine to evangelize Ireland. This staff was treasured as one of the most precious relics on Irish soil for *more than one thousand years*, and was an object of special veneration. It was sacrilegiously destroyed in the reign of Henry the Eighth by one of Henry's "reforming" bishops, who writes to the king boasting of the deed !

DEATH OF KING DAHI.

See pages 42, 43.

VIII.—A RETROSPECTIVE GLANCE AT PAGAN IRELAND.

E have now, my dear young friends, arrived at a memorable point in Irish history; we are about to pass from pagan Ireland to Christian Ireland. Before doing so, it may be well that I should tell you something about matters which require a few words apart from the brief narrative of events which I have been relating for you. Let us pause, and take a glance at the country and the people, at the manners and customs, laws and institutions of our pagan ancestors.

The geographical subdivisions of the country varied in successive centuries. The chief subdivision, the designations of which are most frequently used by the ancient chroniclers, was effected by a line drawn from the hill or ridge on the south bank of the Liffey, on the eastern end of which the castle of Dublin is built, running due west to the peninsula of Marey, at the head of Galway Bay. The portion of Ireland south of this line was called Leah Moha ("Moh Nua's half"), the portion to the north of it Leah Cuinn ("Conn's half "); As these names suggest, this division of the island was first made between two princes, Conn of the Hundred battles, and Moh Nua, or Eoghan Mor, otherwise Eugene the Great, the former being the head or chief representative of the Milesian families descended from Ir, the latter the head of those descended from Heber. Though the primary object of this partition was achieved but for a short time, the names thus given to the two territories are found in use, to designate the northern and southern halves of Ireland, for a thousand years subsequently.

Within these there were smaller subdivisions. The ancient names of the four provinces into which Ireland is still divided were, Mononia (Munster), Dalaradia, or Ulidia (Ulster),

Again, Mononia was subdivided into Thomond and Desmond,
i.e., north and south Munster. Besides these names, the
territory or district possessed by every sept or clan had a
designation of its own.

The chief palaces of the Irish kings, whose splendois are
celebrated in Irish history, were : the palace of Emania, in
Ulster, founded or built by Macha, queen of Cinbaeth the
First (pronounced Kimbahe), about the year B.C. 700; Tara
in Meath ; Cruachan, in Conact, built by Queen Maeve, the
beautiful, albeit Amazonian, Queen of the West, about the
year B.C. 100 ; Aileach, in Donegal, built on the site of an
ancient Sun-temple, or Tuatha de Danaan fort-palace.

Kincora had not at this period an existence, nor had it for
some centuries subsequently. It was never more than the
local residence, a palatial castle, of Brian Boruma. It stood
on the spot where now stands the town of Killaloe.

Emania, next to Tara the most celebrated of all the royal
palaces of Ancient Erinn, stood on the spot now marked by a
largerath called the Navan Fort, two miles to the west of
Armagh. It was the residence of the Ulster kings for a
period of 855 years.

The mound or Grianan of Aileach, upon which, even for
hundreds of years after the destruction of the palace, the
O Donnells were elected, installed, or " inaugurated," is still
an object of wonder and curiosity. It stands on the crown
of a low hill by the shores of Lough Swilly, about five miles
from Londonderry.

Royal Tara has been crowned with an imperishable fame
in song and story. The entire crest and slopes of Tara Hill
were covered with buildings at one time ; for it was not alone
a royal palace, the residence of the Ard-Ri (or High king) of
Erinn, but, moreover, the legislative chambers, the military
buildings, the law courts, and royal universities that stood
thereupon. Of all these, naught now remains but the moated
mounds or raths that mark where stood the halls within which
bard and warrior, ruler and lawgiver, once assembled in a
glorious pageant.

and chivalry, mentioned in pagan Irish history, the two principal were : the Knights of the (Craev Rua, or) Red Branch of Emania, and the Clanna Morna, or Damnonian Knights of Iorras. The former were a Dalaradian, the latter a Conacian body ; and, test the records how we may, it is incontrovertible that no chivalric institutions of modern times eclipsed in knightly valor and romantic daring those warrior companionships of ancient Erinn.

Besides these orders of knighthood, several military legions figure familiarly and prominently in Irish history ; but the most celebrated of them all, the Dalcassians—one of the most brave and "glory-crowned" bodies of which there is record in ancient or modern times—did not figure in Irish history until long after the commencement of the Christian era.

The Fianna Eirion, or National Militia of Erinn, I have already mentioned. This celebrated enrolment had the advantage of claiming within its own ranks a warrior-poet, Ossian (son of the commander Fin), whose poems, taking for their theme invariably the achievements and adventures of the Fenian host, or of its chiefs, have given to it a lasting fame. According to Ossian, there never existed upon the earth another such force of heroes as the Fianna Eirion ; and the feats he attributes to them were of course unparalleled. He would have us believe there were no taller, straighter, stronger, braver, bolder men in all Erinn, than his Fenian comrades ; and with the recital of their deeds he mixes up the wildest romance and fable. What is strictly true of them is, that at one period undoubtedly they were a splendid national force ; but ultimately they became a danger rather than a protection to the kingdom, and had to be put down by the regular army in the reign of king Carbri the Second, who encountered and destroyed them finally on the bloody battle field of Gavra, about the year A.D. 280.

Ben Eder, now called the Hill of Howth, near Dublin, was the camp or exercise ground of the Fianna Eirion when called out annually for training.

The laws of pagan Ireland, which were collected and

throughout the kingdom as long subsequently as a vestige of native Irish regal authority remained—a space of nearly fifteen hundred years—are, even in this present age, exciting considerable attention amongst legislators and savans. A royal commission—the " Brehon Laws Commission"—appointed by the British government in the year 1856 (chiefly owing to the energetic exertions of Rev. Dr. Graves and Rev. Dr. Todd, of Trinity College, Dublin), has been laboring at their translation, parliament voting an annual sum to defray the expenses. Of course only portions of the original manuscripts are now in existence, but even these portions attest the marvellous wisdom and the profound justness of the ancient Milesian Code, and give us a high opinion of Irish jurisprudence two thousand years ago!

The Brehon Laws Commission published their first volume, the " Seanchus Mor," in 1865, and a most interesting publication it is. Immediately on the establishment of Christianity in Ireland a royal commission of *that* day was appointed to revise the statute laws of Erinn, so that they might be purged of everything applicable only to a pagan nation and inconsistent with the pure doctrines of Christianity. On this commission, we are told, there were appointed by the Irish monarch three chief Brehons or judges, three Christian bishops, and three territorial chiefs or viceroys. The result of their labors was presented to the Irish parliament of Tara, and being duly confirmed, the code thenceforth became known as the Seanchus Mor.

From the earliest age the Irish appear to have been extremely fond of games, athletic sports, and displays of prowess or agility. Amongst the royal and noble families chess was the chief domestic game. There are indubitable proofs that it was played amongst the princes of Erinn two thousands years ago ; and the oldest bardic chants and verse-histories mention the gold and jewel inlaid chessboards of the kings.

Of the passionate attachment of the Irish to music, little need be said, as this is one of the national characteristics which

as a national emblem of Ireland. Even in the pre-Christian period we are here reviewing, music was an " institution" and a power in Erinn.

———◆—◆—◆———

IX.—CHRISTIAN IRELAND. THE STORY OF COLUMBA, THE " DOVE OF THE CELL."

THE five hundred years, one-half of which preceded the birth of our Lord, may be considered the period of Ireland's greatest power and military glory as a nation. The five hundred years which succeeded St. Patrick's mission may be regarded as the period of Ireland's Christian and Scholastic fame. In the former she sent her warriors, in the latter her missionaries, all over Europe. Where her fierce hero-kings carried the sword, her saints now bore the cross of faith. It was in this latter period, between the sixth and the eighth centuries particularly, that Ireland became known all over Europe as the *Insula Sanctorum et Doctorum*—" the Island of Saints and Scholars."

covered the island. From even the most distant parts of
Europe, kings and their subjects came to study in the Irish
schools. King Alfred of Northumberland was educated in
one of the Irish universities. A glorious roll of Irish saints
and scholars belong to this period : St. Columba or Colum-
cille, St. Columbanus, St. Gall, who evangelized Helvetia, St.
Frigidian, who was bishop of Lucca in Italy, St. Livinus, who
was martyred in Flanders, St. Argobast, who became bishop
of Strasburg, St. Killian, the apostle of Franconia, and quite
a host of illustrious Irish missionaries, who carried the blessings of faith and education all over Europe. The record of
their myriad adventurous enterprises, their glorious labors,
their evangelizing conquests, cannot be traced within the
scope of this book. There is one, however, the foremost of
that sainted band, with whom exception must be made—the
first and the greatest of Irish missionary saints, the abbot of
Iona's isle, whose name and fame filled the world, and the
story of whose life is a Christian romance—Columba, the
" Dove of the Cell."*

The personal character of Columba and the romantic incidents of his life, as well as his preëminence amongst the missionary conquerors of the British Isles, seem to have had a
powerful attraction for the illustrious Montalembert, who, in
his great work, " The Monks of the West," traces the eventful
career of the saint in language of equisite beauty, eloquence,
and feeling. Moreover, their is this to be said further of that
Christian romance, as I have called it, the life of St. Columba,
that happily the accounts thereof which we possess are complete, authentic, and documentary ; most of the incidents related we have on the authority of well-known writers, who
lived in Columba's time and held personal communication
with him or with his companions.

The picture presented to us in these life-portraitures of
Iona's saint is assuredly one to move the hearts of Irishmen
young and old. In Columba two great features stand out in
bold prominence ; and never perhaps were those two charac-

teristics more powerfully developed in one man—devotion to
God and passionate love of country.   He was a great saint,
but he was as great a "politician," entering deeply and
warmly into everything affecting the weal of Clan Nial, or
the honor of Erinn.   His love for Ireland was something beyond description.   As he often declared in his after-life exile,
the very breezes that blew on the fair hills of holy Ireland
were to him like the zephyrs of paradise.   Our story were
incomplete indeed, without a sketch, however brief, of " the
Dove of the Cell."

Columba* was a prince of the royal race of Nial, his father
being the third in descent from the founder of that illustrious
house, Nial of the Nine Hostages.   He was born at Gartan,
in Donegal, on the 7th December, 521.   " The Irish legends,"
says Montalembert, "which are always distinguished, even
amidst the wildest vagaries of fancy, by a high and pure morality, linger lovingly upon the childhood and youth of the
predestined saint."   Before his birth (according to one of
these traditions) the mother of Columba had a dream, " which
posterity has accepted as a graceful and poetical symbol of
her son's career.   An angel appeared to her, bringing her a
veil covered with flowers of wonderful beauty, and the sweet-
est variety of colors ; immediately after she saw the veil carried away by the wind, and rolling out as it fled over the
plains, woods, and mountains.   Then the angel said to her,
' Thou art about to become the mother of a son, who shall
blossom for Heaven, who shall be reckoned among the pro-
phets of God, and who shall lead numberless souls to the
heavenly country.' "

But indeed, according to the legends of the Hy Nial, the
coming of their great saint was foretold still more remotely.
St. Patrick, they tell us, having come northward to bless the
territory and people, was stopped at the Daol—the modern
Deel or Burndale river—by the breaking of his chariot wheels.
The chariot was repaired, but again broke down ; a third time
it was refitted, and a third time it failed at the ford.   Then

Patrick, addressing those around him, said: "Wonder no more: behold, the land from this stream northwards needs no blessing from me; for a son shall be born there who shall be called the Dove of the Churches; and he shall bless that land, in honor of whom God has this day prevented my doing so." The name Ath-an-Charpaid (lord of the chariot) marks to this day the spot memorized by this tradition. Count Montalembert cites many of these stories of the "childhood and youth of the predestined saint." He was, while yet a child, confided to the care of the priest who had baptized him, and from him he received the first rudiments of education. " His guarding angel often appeared to him; and the child asked if all the angels in Heaven were so young and shining as he. A little later, Columba was invited by the same angel to choose among all the virtues that which he would like best to possess. 'I choose,' said the youth, 'chastity and wisdom;' and immediately three young girls of wonderful beauty but foreign air, appeared to him, and threw themselves on his neck to embrace him. The pious youth frowned, and repulsed them with indignation. 'What,' they said, 'then thou dost not know us?' 'No, not the least in the world.' 'We are three sisters, whom our Father gives to thee to be thy brides.' 'Who then is your Father?' 'Our Father is God, He is Jesus Christ, the Lord and Saviour of the world.' 'Ah, you have indeed an illustrious Father. But what are your names?' 'Our names are Virginity, Wisdom, and Prophecy; and we come to leave thee no more, to love thee with an incorruptible love.' "

From the house of this early tutor Columba "passed into the great monastic schools which were not only a nursery for the clergy of the Irish Church, but where also young laymen of all conditions were educated."

" While Columba studied at Clonard, being still only a deacon," says his biographer, " an incident took place which has been proved by authentic testimony, and which fixed general attention upon him by giving a first evidence of his supernatural and prophetic intuition. An old Christian bard (the

live near the Abbot Finnian, asking from him, in exchange for his poetry, the secret of fertilizing the soil. Columba, who continued all his life a passionate admirer of the tradition-ary poetry of his nation, determined to join the school of the bard, and to share his labors and studies. The two were reading together out of doors, at a little distance from each other, when a young girl appeared in the distance pursued by a rob-ber. At the sight of the old man the fugitive made for him with all her remaining strength, hoping, no doubt, to find safety in the authority exercised throughout Ireland by the national poets. Germain, in great trouble, called his pupil to his aid to defend the unfortunate child, who was trying to hide herself un-der their long robes, when her pursuer reached the spot. With-out taking any notice of her defenders, he struck her in the neck with his lance, and was making off, leaving her dead at their feet. The horrified old man turned to Columba. 'How long,' he said 'will God leave unpunished this crime which dishonors us?' 'For this moment only,' said Columba, 'not longer; at this very hour, when the soul of this innocent creature ascends to heaven, the soul of the murderer shall go down to hell.' At the instant, like Ananias at the words of Peter, the assassin fell dead. The news of this sudden punishment, the story goes, went over Ireland, and spread the fame of the young Columba far and wide."

At the comparatively early age of twenty-five, Columba had attained to a prominent position in the ecclesiastical world, and had presided over the creation of a crowd of monasteries. As many as thirty-seven in Ireland alone recognized him as their founder. "It is easy," says Montalembert, "to per-ceive, by the importance of the monastic establishments which he had brought into being, even before he had attained to man-hood, that his influence must have been as precocious as it was considerable. Apart from the virtues of which his after life afforded so many examples, it may be supposed that his roy-al birth gave him an irresistible ascendancy in a country where, since the introduction of Christianity, all the early saints, like the principal abbots, belonged to reigning families.

still continue, even to this day, to a degree unknown in other
lands. Springing, as has been said, from the same race as the
monarch of all Ireland, and consequently himself eligible for
the same high office, which was more frequently obtained by
election or usurpation than inheritance—nephew or near
cousin of the seven monarchs who successively wielded the
supreme authority during his life—he was also related by ties
of blood to almost all the provincial kings. Thus we see him
during his whole career treated on a footing of perfect intimacy and equality by all the princes of Ireland and of Caledonia,
and exercising a sort of spiritual sway equal or superior to
the authority of secular sovereigns."

His attachment to poetry and literature has been already
glanced at. He was, in fact, an enthusiast on the subject ; he
was himself a poet and writer of a high order of genius, and
to an advanced period of his life remained an ardent devotee
of the muse, ever powerfully moved by whatever affected the
weal of the minstrel fraternity. His passion for books (all
manuscript, of course, in those days, and of great rarity and
value) was destined to lead him into that great offence of his life,
which he was afterwards to expiate by a penance so grievous.
"He went everywhere in search of volumes which he could
borrow or copy ; often experiencing refusals which he resent-
ed bitterly." In this way occurred what Montalembert calls
" the decisive event which changed the destiny of Columba,
and transformed him from a wandering poet and ardent book-
worm, into a missionary and apostle." While visiting one of his
former tutors, Finian, he found means to copy clandestinely the
abbot's Psalter by shutting himself up at nights in the church
where the book was deposited. " Indignant at what he considered as almost a theft, Finian claimed the copy when it was

" King Diarmid, or Dermott, supreme monarch of Ireland, was, like Columba, descended from the great king Niall, but by another son than he whose great-grandson Columba was. He lived, like all the princes of his country, in a close union with the Church, which was represented in Ireland, more completely than anywhere else, by the monastic order. Exiled and persecuted in his youth, he had found refuge in an island situated in one of those lakes which interrupt the course of the Shannon, the chief river of Ireland, and had there formed a friendship with a holy monk called Kieran, a zealous comrade of Columba at the monastic school of Clonard, and since that time his generous rival in knowledge and in austerity. Upon the still solitary bank of the river the two friends had planned the foundation of a monastery, which, owing to the marshy nature of the soil, had to be built upon piles. ' Plant with me the first stake,' the monk said to the exiled prince, putting your hand under mine, and soon that hand shall be over all the men of Erinn ; ' and it happened that Diarmid was very shortly after called to the throne. He immediately used his new power to endow richly the monastery which was rendered doubly dear to him by the recollection of his exile and of his friend. This sanctuary became, under the name of Clonmacnoise, one of the greatest monasteries and most frequented schools of Ireland, and even of Western Europe.

" This king might accordingly be regarded as a competent judge in a contest at once monastic and literary ; he might even have been suspected of partiality for Columba, his kinsman,—and yet he pronounced judgment against him. His judgment was given in a rustic phrase which has passed into a proverb in Ireland—To every cow her calf, and, consequently, to every book its copy. Columba protested loudly. ' It is an unjust sentence,' he said, 'and I will revenge myself." After this incident a young prince, son of the provincial king of Connaught, who was pursued for having committed an involuntary murder, took refuge with Columba, but was seized and put to death by the king. The irritation of the poet-monk knew no bounds. The ecclesiastical im-

of several monasteries, ought to have, in his opinion, created
a sort of sanctuary around his person, and this immunity had
been scandalously violated by the execution of a youth whom he
protected. He threatened the king with prompt vengeance.
' I will denounce, ' he said, ' to my brethren and my kindred
thy wicked judgment, and the violation in my person of the
immunity of the Church ; they will listen to my complaint,
and punish thee sword in hand. Bad king, thou shall no more
see my face in thy province, until God, the just judge, has subdued thy pride. As thou has humbled me to-day before thy
lords and thy friends, God will humble thee on the battle-day
before thine enemies.' Diarmid attempted to retain him by
force in the neighborhood ; but, evading the vigilance of his
guards, he escaped by night from the court of Tara, and directed his steps to his native province of Tyrconnell.

 " Columba arrived safely in his province, and immediately
set to work to excite against king Diarmid the numerous and
powerful clans of his relatives and friends, who belonged to a
branch of the house of Niall, distinct from and hostile to that
of the reigning monarch. His efforts were crowned with
success. The Hy-Nialls of the north armed eagerly against
the Hy-Nialls of the south, of whom Diarmid was the special
chief.

 " Diarmid marched to meet them, and they met in battle
at Cool Drewny, or Cul-Dreimhne, upon the borders of Ul-
tonia and Connacia. He was completely beaten, and was
obliged to take refuge at Tara. The victory was due, according to the annalist Tighernach, to the prayers and songs of
Columba, who had fasted and prayed with all his might to obtain from Heaven the punishment of the royal insolence, and
who, besides, was present at the battle, *and took upon himself
before all men the responsibility of the bloodshed.*

 " As for the manuscript which had been the object of this
strange conflict of copyright elevated into a civil war, it was
afterwards venerated as a kind of national, military and religious palladium. Under the name of Cathach or Fightu, the
Latin Psalter transcribed by Columba, enshrined in a sort of
portable altar, became the national relic of the O'Donnell

clan. For more than a thousand years it was carried with them to battle as a pledge of victory, on the condition of being supported on the breast of a clerk free from all mortal sin. It has escaped as by miracle from the ravages of which Ireland has been the victim, and exists still, to the great joy of all learned Irish patriots." *

But soon a terrible punishment was to fall upon Columba for this dread violence. He, an anointed priest of the Most High, a minister of the Prince of Peace, had made himself the cause and the inciter of a civil war, which had bathed the land in blood—the blood of Christian men—the blood of kindred! Clearly enough, the violence of political passions, of which this war was the most lamentable fruit, had, in many other ways, attracted upon the youthful monk the severe opinions of the ecclesiastical authorities. "His excitable and vindictive character," we are told, "and above all his passionate attachment to his relatives, and the violent part which he took in their domestic disputes and their continually recurring rivalries, had engaged him in other struggles, the date of which is perhaps later than that of his first departure from Ireland, but the responsibility of which is formally imputed to him by various authorities, and which also ended in bloody battles." At all events, immediately after the battle of Cool Drewney, " he was accused by a synod, convoked in the centre of the royal domain at Tailte, of having occasioned the shedding of Christian blood." The synod seems to have acted with very uncanonical precipitancy ; for it judged the cause without waiting for the defence—though, in sooth, the facts,

---

* The Annals of the Four Masters report that in a battle waged in 1497, between the O'Donnells and M'Dermotts, the sacred book fell into the hands of the latter, who, however, restored it in 1499. It was preserved for thirteen hundred years in the O'Donnell family, and at present belongs to a baronet of that name, who has permitted it to be exhibited in the museum of the Royal Irish Academy, where it can be seen by all. It is composed of fifty-eight leaves of parchment, bound in silver. The learned O'Curry (p. 322) has given a fac-simile of a fragment of this MS., which he does not hesitate to believe is in the handwriting of our saint, as well as that of the fine copy of the Gospels called the Book of Kells, of which he has also given a facsimile. See Reeves' note upon Adamnan, p. 250, and the pamphlet upon Marianus Scotus, p. 12."—*Count Montalembert's note.*

beyond the power of any defence to remove, were ample and
notorious. However, the decision was announced—sentence
of excommunication was pronounced against him!

"Columba was not a man to draw back before his accusers
and judges. He presented himself before the synod which
had struck without hearing him. He found a defender in the
famous Abbot Brendan, the founder of the monastery of Birr.
When Columba made his appearance, this abbot rose, went
up to him, and embraced him. 'How can you give the kiss
of peace to an excommunicated man?' said some of the other
members of the synod. 'You would do as I have done,' he
answered, 'and you never would have excommunicated him,
had you seen what I see—a pillar of fire which goes before
him, and the angels that accompany him. I dare not disdain
a man predestined by God to be the guide of an entire people
to eternal life.' Thanks to the intervention of Brendan, or to
some other motive not mentioned, the sentence of excommunication was withdrawn, but Columba was charged to
win to Christ, by his preaching, as many pagan souls as the
number of Christians who had fallen in the battle of Cool-
Drewny."

Troubled in soul, but still struggling with a stubborn self-
will, Columba found his life miserable, unhappy, and full of
unrest; yet remorse had even now "planted in his soul the
germs at once of a startling conversion and of his future apostolic mission." "Various legends reveal him to us at this
crisis of his life, wandering long from solitude to solitude, and
from monastery to monastery, seeking out holy monks, masters of penitence and Christian virtue, and asking them
anxiously what he should do to obtain the pardon of God for
the murder of so many victims."

At length, after many wanderings in contrition and mortification, "he found the light which he sought from a holy
monk, St. Molaise, famed for his studies of Holy Scripture,
and who had already been his confessor."

" This severe hermit confirmed the decision of the synod;
but to the obligation of converting to the Christian faith an
equal number of pagans as there were of Christians killed in

the civil war, he added a new condition, which bore cruelly upon a soul so passionately attached to country and kindred. The confessor condemned his penitent to *perpetual exile from Ireland !* "

Exile from Ireland! Did Columba hear the words aright? *Exile from Ireland !* What! See no more that land which he loved with such a wild and passionate love! Part from the brothers and kinsmen all, for whom he felt perhaps too strong and too deep an affection! Quit for aye the stirring scenes in which so great a part of his sympathies were engaged! Leave Ireland!

Oh ! it was more hard than to bare his breast to the piercing sword ; less welcome than to walk in constant punishment of suffering, so that his feet pressed the soil of his worshipped Erinn !

But it was even so. Thus ran the sentence of Molaise : "*perpetual exile from Ireland !* "

Staggered, stunned, struck to the heart, Columba could not speak for a moment. But God gave him in that great crisis of his life the supreme grace of bearing the blow and embracing the cross presented to him. At last he spoke, and in a voice agitated with emotion he answered : "*Be it so ; what you have commanded shall be done.*"

From that instant forth his life was one prolonged act of penitential sacrifice. For thirty years—his heart bursting within his breast the while—yearning for one sight of Ireland —he lived and labored in distant Iona. The fame of his sanctity filled the world ; religious houses subject to his rule arose in many a glen and isle of rugged Caledonia ; the gifts of prophecy and miracle momentously attested him as one of God's most favored apostles : yet all the while his heart was breaking ; all the while in his silent cell Columba's tears flowed freely for the one grief that never left him—the wound that only deepened with lengthening time—*he was away from Ireland !* Into all his thoughts this sorrow entered. In all his songs—and several of his compositions still remain to us— this one sad strain is introduced. Witness the following,

retains much of the poetic beauty and exquisite tenderness of
the original by Columba in the Gaelic tongue:

What joy to fly upon the white-crested sea; and watch the waves break upon the
Irish shore!

 *   *   *   *   *

My foot is in my little boat; but my sad heart ever bleeds!
*There is a gray eye which ever turns to Erinn; but never in this life shall it see
Erinn, nor her sons, nor her daughters!*
From the high prow I look over the sea; and great tears are in my eyes when I turn
to Erinn —
To Erinn, where the songs of the birds are so sweet, and where the clerks sing like
the birds:
Where the young are so gentle, and the old are so wise; where the great men are
so noble to look at, and the women so fair to wed!
Young traveller! carry my sorrows with you; carry them to Comgall of eternal life!
Noble youth, take my prayer with thee, and my blessing: one part for Ireland—
seven times may she be blest—and the other for Albyn.
Carry my blessing across the sea; carry it to the West. My heart is broken in my
breast!
If death comes suddenly to me, it will be because of the great love I bear to the Gael! *

It was to the rugged and desolate Hebrides that Columba
turned his face when he accepted the terrible penance of Molaise.   He bade farewell to his relatives, and, with a few monks
who insisted on accompanying him whithersoever he might go,
launched his frail currochs from the northern shore.   They
landed first, or rather were carried by wind and steam, upon
the little isle of Oronsay, close by Islay; and here for a moment
they thought their future abode was to be.   But when Columba, with the early morning, ascending the highest ground on
the island, to take what he thought would be a harmless look
towards the island of his heart, lo! on the dim horizon a faint
blue ridge—the distant hills of Antrim!   He averts his head
and flies downwards to the strand!   Here they cannot stay,
if his vow is to be kept.   They betake them once more to the
currochs, and steering further northward, eventually land upon Iona, thenceforth, till time shall be no more, to be famed
as the sacred isle of Columba!   Here landing, he ascended
the loftiest of the hills upon the isle, and "gazing into the

---

* This poem appears to have been presented as a farewell gift by St. Columba to
some of the Irish visitors at Iona, when returning home to Ireland.   It is deservedly

distance, found no longer any trace of Ireland upon the horizon." In Iona accordingly he resolved to make his home. The spot from whence St. Columba made this sorrowful survey is still called by the isles-men in the Gaelic tongue, *Carn-cul-ri-Erinn*, or the Cairn of Farewell—literally, *The back turned on Ireland.*

Writers without number have traced the glories of Iona.*

Here rose, as if by miracle, a city of churches; the isle became one vast monastery, and soon much too small for the crowds that still pressed thither. Then from the parent isle there went forth to the surrounding shores, and all over the mainland, off-shoot establishments and missionary colonies (all under the authority of Columba), until in time the Gospel light was ablaze on the hills of Albyn ; and the names of St. Columba and Iona were on every tongue from Rome to the utmost limits of Europe !

" This man, whom we have seen so passionate, so irritable, so warlike and vindictive, became little by little the most gentle, the humblest, the most tender of friends and fathers. It was he, the great head of the Caledonian Church, who, kneeling before the strangers who came to Iona, or before the monks returning from their work, took off their shoes, washed their feet, and after having washed them, respectfully kissed them. But charity was still stronger than humility in that transfigured soul. No necessity, spiritual or temporal, found him indifferent. He devoted himself to the solace of all infirmities, all misery, and pain, weeping often over those who did not weep for themselves.

" The work of transcription remained until his last day the occupation of his old age, as it had been the passion of his

---

* " We are now," said Dr. Johnson, " treading that illustrious island which was once the luminary of the Caledonian regions ; whence savage clans and roving barbarians derived the benefits of knowledge and the blessings of religion . . . Far from me and from my friends be such frigid philosophy as may conduct us indifferent and unmoved over any ground which has been dignified by wisdom, bravery, or virtue. That man is little to be envied whose patriotism would not gain force upon the plain of Marathon, or whose piety would not grow warmer among the ruins of Iona. "—Bos.

youth; it had such an attraction for him, and seemed to him
so essential to a knowledge of the truth, that, as we have already said, three hundred copies of the Holy Gospels, copied
by his own hand, have been attributed to him."

But still Columba carried with him in his heart the great
grief that made life for him a lengthened penance. "Far from
having any prevision of the glory of Iona, his soul," says Montalembert, "was still swayed by a sentiment which never
abandoned him—regret for his lost country. All his life he
retained for Ireland the passionate tenderness of an exile, a
love which displayed itself in the songs which have been preserved to us, and which date perhaps from the first moment
of his exile. . . . . . 'Death in faultless Ireland is better
than life without end in Albyn.' After this cry of despair
follow strains more plaintive and submissive.

" 'But it was not only in these elegies, repeated and perhaps
retouched by Irish bards and monks, but at each instant of
his life, in season and out of season, that this love and passionate longing for his native country burst forth in words
and musings; the narratives of his most trustworthy bio-
graphers are full of it. The most severe penance which he
could have imagined for the guiltiest sinners who came to confess to him, was to impose upon them the same fate which he
had voluntarily inflicted on himself—never to set foot again
upon Irish soil! But when, instead of forbidding to sinners
all access to that beloved isle, he had to smother his envy of
those who had the right and happiness to go there at their
pleasure, he dared scarcely trust himself to name its name;
and when speaking to his guests, or to the monks who were
to return to Ireland, he would only say to them, 'you will
return to the country that you love.' "

At length there arrived an event for Columba full of excruciating trial—*it became necessary for him to revisit Ireland!*
His presence was found to be imperatively required at the
general assembly or convocation of the princes and prelates
of the Irish nation, convented A. D. 573, by Hugh the Second. *

At this memorable assembly, known in history as the great Convention of Drumceat, the first meeting of the States of Ireland held since the abandonment of Tara, there were to be discussed, amongst other important subjects, two which were of deep and powerful interest to Columba: firstly, the relations between Ireland and the Argyle or Caledonian colony ; and secondly, the proposed decree for the abolition of the Bards.

The country now known as Scotland was, about the time of the Christian era, inhabited by a barbarous and warlike race called Picts. About the middle of the second century, when Ireland was known to the Romans as Scotia, an Irish chieftain, Carbri Riada (from whom were descended the Dalraids of Antrim), crossed over to the western shores of Alba or Albyn, and founded there a Dalaraidan or Milesian colony. The colonists had a hard time of it with their savage Pictish neighbors ; yet they managed to hold their ground, though receiving very little aid or attention from the parent country, to which nevertheless they regularly paid tribute. At length, in the year 503, the neglected colony was utterly overwhelmed by the Picts, whereupon a powerful force of the Irish Dalraids, under the leadership of Leorn, Aengus, and Fergus, crossed over, invaded Albany, and gradually subjugating the Picts, reëstablished the colony on a basis which was the foundation eventually of the Scottish monarchy of all subsequent history. To the reëstablished colony was given the name by which it was known long after, Scotia Minor ; Ireland being called Scotia Major.

In the time of St. Columba, the colony, which so far had continuously been assessed by, and had duly paid its tribute to, the mother country, began to feel its competency to claim independence. Already it had selected and installed a king (whom St. Columba had formally consecrated), and now it sent to Ireland a demand to be exempted from further tribute. The Irish monarch resisted the demand, which, however, it was decided first to submit to a national assembly, at which the Scottish colony should be represented, and where it might plead its case as best it could. Many and obvious considera-

cause of the young nationality on this momentous occasion.
He was peculiarly qualified to act as umpire in this threatening quarrel between the old country, to which he felt bound
by such sacred ties, and the new one, which by adoption was
now his home. He consented to attend at the assembly. He
did so the more readily, perhaps, because of his strong feelings
in reference to the other proposition named, viz., the proscription of the bards.

It may seem strange that in Ireland, where, from an early
date, music and song held so high a place in national estimation, such a proposition should be made. But by this time
the numerous and absurd immunities claimed by the bardic
profession had become intolerable ; and by gross abuses of
the bardic privileges, the bards themselves had indubitably
become a pest to society. King Hugh had, therefore, a strong
public opinion at his back in his design of utterly abolishing
the bardic corporation.

St. Columba, however, not only was allied to them by a
fraternity of feeling, but he discerned clearly that by purify-
ing and conserving, rather than by destroying, the national
minstrelsy, it would become a potential influence for good,
and would entwine itself gratefully around the shrine within
which at such a crisis it found shelter. In fine, he felt, and
felt deeply, as an Irishman and as an ecclesiastic, that the proposition of King Hugh would annihilate one of the most treasured institutions of the nation—one of the most powerful aids
to patriotism, and religion.

So, to plead the cause of liberty for a young nationality,
and the cause of patriotism, religion, literature, music and
poetry, in defending the minstrel race, St. Columba to Ireland
would go !

To Ireland ! But then his vow ! His penance sentence,
that he should never more see Ireland ! How his heart surged !
O great allurement ! O stern resolve ! O triumph of sacrifice !

Yes ; he would keep his vow, yet attend the convocation
amidst those hills of Ireland which he was never more to see !
With a vast array of attendant monks and lay princes, he em

d for the unforgotten land ; but when the galleys came within some leagues of the Irish coast and before it could yet be sighted, St. Columba *caused his eyes to be bandaged with a white scarf*, and thus blindfolded was he led on shore! It is said that when he stepped upon the beach, and for the first time duning so many years felt that he trod the soil of Ireland, he trembled from head to foot with emotion.

When the great saint was led blindfold into the Convention, the whole assemblage—kings, princes, prelates, and chieftains —rose and uncovered as reverentially as if Patrick himself had once more appeared amongst them.* It was, we may well believe, an impressive scene; and we can well understand the stillness of anxious attention with which all waited to hear once more the tones of that voice which many traditions class amongst the miraculous gifts of Columba. More than one contemporary writer has described his personal appearance at this time; and Montalembert says : " All testimonies agree in celebrating his manly beauty, his remarkable height, his sweet and sonorous voice, the cordiality of his manner, the gracious dignity of his deportment and person."

Not in vain did he plead the causes he had come to advo-cate. Long and ably was the question of the Scottish colony debated. Some versions allege that it was amicably left to the decision of Columba, and that his award of several inde-pendence, but fraternal alliance, was cheerfully acquiesced in. Other accounts state that king Hugh, finding argument pre-vailing against his views, angrily drawing his sword, declared he would *compel* the colony to submission by force of arms ; whereupon Columba, rising from his seat, in a voice full of solemnity and authority, exclaimed : " In the presence of this threat of tyrannic force, I declare the cause ended, and proclaim the Scottish colony free forever from the yoke!" By which-ever way, however, the result was arrived at, the indepen-dence of the young Caledonian nation was recognized and voted by the convention through the exertions of St. Columba.

---

* Some versions allege that, although the saint himself was received with reverence, almost with awe, a hostile demonstration was designed, if not attempted, by the king's

His views in behalf of the bards likewise prevailed. He admitted the disorders, irregularities, and abuses alleged against the body ; but he pleaded, and pleaded successfully, for reform instead of abolition. Time has vindicated the far-sighted policy of the statesman saint. The national music and poetry of Ireland, thus purified and consecrated to the service of religion and country, have ever since, through ages of persecution, been true to the holy mission assigned them on that day by Columba.

The Dove of the Cell made a comparatively long stay in Ireland, visiting with scarf-bound brow the numerous monastic establishments subject to his rule. At length he returned to Iona, where far into the evening of life he waited for his summons to the beatific vision. The miracles he wrought, attested by evidence of weight to move the most callous sceptic, the myriad wondrous signs of God's favor that marked his daily acts, filled all the nations with awe. The hour and the manner of his death had long been revealed to him. The precise time he concealed from those about him until close upon the last day of his life ; but the manner of his death he long foretold to his attendants. " I shall die," said he, " without sickness or hurt ; suddenly, but happily, and without accident." At length one day, while in his usual health, he disclosed to Diarmid, his "minister" or regular attendant monk, that the hour of summons was nigh. A week before he had gone around the island, taking leave of the monks and laborers ; and when all wept, he strove anxiously to console them. Then he blessed the island and the inhabitants. " And now," said he to Diarmid, " here is a secret ; but you must keep it till I am gone. This is Saturday, the day called Sabbath, or day of rest : and that it will be to me, for it shall be the last of my laborious life." In the evening he retired to hi cell, and began to work for the last time, being then occupied in transcribing the Psalter. When he had come to the thirty-third Psalm, and the verse, "*Inquirentes autem Dominum non deficient omni bono*," he stopped short. "*I* cease here," said he : " Baithin must do the rest."

" As soon as the midnight bell had rung for the matins of the Sunday festival, he rose and hastened before the other monks to the church, where he knelt down before the altar. Diarmid followed him ; but, as the church was not yet lighted, he could only find him by groping and crying in a plaintive voice 'Where art thou, my father ?' He found Columba lying before the altar, and, placing himself at his side, raised the old abbot's venerable head upon his knees. The whole community soon arrived with lights, and wept as one man at the sight of their dying father. Columba opened his eyes once more, and turned them to his children on either side with a look full of serene and radiant joy. Then, with the aid of Diarmid, he raised as best he might his right hand to bless them all. His hand dropped, the last sigh came from his lips, and his face remained calm and sweet, like that of a man who in his sleep had seen a vision of heaven."

Like the illustrious French publicist whom I have so largely followed in this sketch, I may say that I have " lingered perhaps too long on the grand form of this monk rising up before us from the midst of Hebridean sea." But I have, from the missionary saint-army of Ireland, selected this one—this typical apostle—to illustrate the characters that illumine one of the most glorious pages of our history. Many, indeed, were the " Columbs " that went forth from Ireland, as from an ark of faith, bearing blessed olive branches to the mountain tops of Europe, then slowly emerging from the flood of paganism. Well might we dwell upon this period of Irish history ! It was a bright and glorious chapter. It was soon, alas ! to be followed by one of gloom. Five hundred years of military fame and five hundred years of Christian glory were to be followed by five hundred years of disorganizing dissensions, leading to centuries of painful bondage.

X.—THE DANES IN IRELAND.

THE first dark cloud came from Scandinavia. Towards the close of the eighth century the Danes made their appearance in Ireland. They came at first as transitory coast marauders, landing and sacking a neighboring town, church, or monastery. For this species of warfare the Irish seem to have been as little prepared as any of the other European countries subjected to the like scourge, that is to say, none of them but the Danes possessed at this period of history a powerful fleet. So when the pirates had wreaked their will upon the city or monastery, in order to plunder which they had landed, they simply reëmbarked and sailed away comparatively safe from molestation.

At length it seems to have occurred to the professional pirates, that in place of making periodical dashes on the Irish coast, they might secure a permanent footing thereupon, and so prepare the way for eventually subjugating the entire kingdom. Accordingly, they came in force and possessed themselves of several spots favorably placed for such purposes as theirs— sites for fortified maritime cities on estuaries affording good shelter for their fleets, viz.: Dublin, Drogheda, Waterford, Limerick, Wexford, etc.

In the fourth year of Nial the Third (about the year A. D. 840), there arrived a monster fleet of these fierce and ruthless savages, under the command of Turgesius. They poured into the country and carried all before them. For nearly seven years, Turgesius exercised over a considerable district kingly authority, and the Irish groaned under the horrors of oppression the most heartless and brutal. Turgesius converted the cathedral at Clonmacnoise into a palace for his own use, and from the high alter, used as a throne, the fierce idolator gave forth his tyrannical commands. Meantime the

plundered, the gold and jewels were kept by the spoilers, but the holy relics were sacrilegiously given to destruction. The schools were dispersed, the books and chronicles burned, and finally the " successor of Patrick, "the Archbishop of Armagh, was seized, the cathedral sacked, and the holy prelate brought a captive into the Danish stronghold.

But the day of retribution was at hand. The divided and disorganized tribes were being bitterly taught the necessity of union. These latest outrages were too much for Christian Irish flesh and blood to bear. Concerting their measures, the people simultaneously rose on their oppressors. Turgesius was seized and put to death by Malachy, prince of Westmeath, while the Irish Ard-Ri, Nial the Third, at length able to rally a powerful army against the invaders, swooped down upon them from the north and drove them panic-stricken to their maritime fortressses, their track marked with slaughter. Nial seems to have been a really noble character, and the circumstances under which he met his death, sudden and calamitous, in the very midst of his victorious career, afford ample illustration of the fact. His army had halted on the banks of the Callen river, at the moment swollen by heavy rains. One of the royal domestics or attendants, a common *Giolla*, in endeavoring to ford the river for some purpose was swept from his feet and carried off by the flood. The monarch, who happened to be looking on, cried aloud to his guards to succor the drowning man, but quicker than any other he himself plunged into the torrent. He never rose again. The brave Nial, who had a hundred times faced death in the midst of reddened spears, perished in his effort to save the life of one of the humblest of his followers.

The power of the Danes was broken, but they still clung to the seaports, where either they were able to defy efforts at expulsion, or else obtained permission to remain by paying heavy tribute to the Irish sovereign. It is clear enough that the presence of the Danes, came, in course of time, to be regarded as useful and profitable by the Irish, so long as they did not refuse tribute to the native power. The history of

Danish struggle—exhibits a singular spectacle. The Danes mades themselves fully at home in the great maritime cities, which they may be said to have founded, and which their commerce certainly raised to importance. The Irish princes made alliances betimes with them, and Danes frequently fought on opposite sides in the internecine conflicts of the Irish princes. Occasionally seizing a favorable opportunity—(when the Irish were particularly weakened by internal feud, and when a powerful reinforcement for themselves arrived from Scandinavia)—they would make a firce endeavor to extend their dominion on Irish soil. These efforts were mostly successful for a time, owing to the absence of a strong centralized authority amongst the Irish ; but eventually the Irish, by putting forth their native valor, and even partially combining for the time, were always able to crush them.

Yet it is evident that during the three hundred years over which this Danish struggle spreads, the Irish nation was undergoing disintegration and demoralization. Towards the middle of the period, the Danes became converted to Christianity; but their coarse and fierce barbarism remained long after, and it is evident that contact with such elements, and increasing political disruption amongst themselves, had a fatal effects on the Irish. They absolutely *retrogadcd* in learning and civilization during this time and contracted some of the worst vices that could pave the way for the fate that a few centuries more were to bring upon them.

National pride may vainly seek to ignore or hide the great truth here displayed. During the three hundred years that preceded the Anglo-Norman invasion, the Irish princes appeared to be given over to a madness marking them for destruction ! At a time when consolidation of national authority was becoming the rule all over Europe, and was becoming so necessary for them, they were going into the other extreme. As the general rule, each one sought only his personal or family ambition or aggrandisement, and strove for it lawlessly and violently. Frequently when the Ard-Ri of Erinn was nobly grappling with the Danish foe, and was on

prince would seize what seemed to him the golden opportunity for throwing off the authority of the chief king, or for treacherously endeavoring to grasp it himself! During the whole time—three centuries—there was scarcely a single reign in which the Ard-Ri did not find occupation for his arms as constantly in compelling the submission of the subordinate native princes, as in combating the Scandinavian foe.

Religion itself suffered in this national declension. In these centuries we find professedly Christian Irish kings themselves as ruthless destroyers of churches and schools as the pagan Danes of a few years previous. The *titles* of the Irish episcopacy were sometimes seized by lay princes for the sake of the revenues attached to them ; the spiritual functions of the offices, however, being performed by ecclesiastics meanwhile. In fine, the Irish national character in those centuries is to be censured, not admired. It would seem as if by adding sacrilege and war upon religion and on learning to political suicide and a fatal frenzy of factiousness, the Irish princes of that period were doing their best and their worst to shame the glories of their nation in the preceding thousand years, and to draw down upon their country the terrible chastisement that eventually befel it, a chastisement which never could have befallen it, but for the state of things I am here pointing out.

Yet was this gloomy period lit up by some brilliant flashes of glory, the brightest, if not the last, being that which surrounds the name of Clontarf, where the power of the Danes in Ireland was crushed totally and for ever.

XI.—HOW "BRIAN OF THE TRIBUTE" BECAME A HIGH KING OF ERINN.

EW historical names are more widely known amongst Irishmen than that of **Brian the** First—" Brian Boru, or Borumha ;"* and the story of his life is a necessary and an interesting introduction to an account of the battle of Clontarf.

About the middle of the tenth century the crown of Munster was worn by Mahon, son of Ceineidi (pr. Kennedy), a prince of the Dalcassian family. Mahon had a young brother, Brian, and by all testimony the affection which existed between the brothers was something touching. Mahon, who was a noble character—" as a prince and captain in every way worthy of his inheritance"—was accompanied in all his expeditions, and from an early age, by Brian, to whom he acted not only as a brother and prince, but as military preceptor. After a brilliant career, Mahon fell by a deed of deadly treachery. A rival prince of south Munster—"Molloy, son of Bran, Lord of Desmond"—whom he had vanquished, proposed to meet him in friendly conference at the house of Donovan, an Eugenian chief. The safety of each person was guaranteed by the Bishop of Cork, who acted as mediator between them. Mahon, chivalrous and unsuspecting, went unattended and unarmed to the conference. He was seized by an armed band of Donovan's men, who handed him over to a party of Molloy's retainers, by whom he was put to death. He had with him, as the sacred and (as it ought to have been) inviolable "safe-conduct" on the faith of which he had trusted himself into the power of his foes, a copy of the Gospels written by the hand of St. Barre. As the assassins drew their swords upon him, Mahon snatched up the sacred scroll, and held it on his breast, as if he could not credit that a murderous hand would dare to wound him through such a shield ! But the murderers plunged their swords into his heart, piercing right through the vellum, which became all stained and matted with his blood. Two priests had, horror-stricken, witnessed the outrage. They caught up the bloodstained Gospels and fled to the bishop, spreading through the country as they went the dreadful news which they bore. The venerable successor of St. Fin Bar, we are told, wept bitterly and uttered a prophecy concerning the fate of the murderers, which was soon and remarkably fulfilled.

"When the news of his noble-hearted brother's death was brought to Brian at Kincora, he was seized with the most violent grief. His favorite harp was taken down, and he sang the death-song of Mahon, recounting all the glorious actions of his life. His anger flashed out through his tears as he wildly chaunted—

'My heart shall burst within my breast,
Unless I avenge this great king.
They shall forfeit life for this foul deed,
Or I must perish by a violent death.'

" But the climax of his grief was, that Mahon ' had not fallen
behind the shelter of his shield, rather than trust the treacherous word of Donovan.' " *

A " Bard of Thomond " in our own day—one not unworthy
of his proud pseudonym—Mr. M. Hogan of Limerick, has
supplied the following very beautiful version of " Brian's
Lament for King Mahon : "—

> Lament, O Dalcassians ! the Eagle of Cashel is dead !
> The grandeur, the glory, the joy of her palace is fled ;
> Your strength in the battle —your bulwark of valor is low,
> But the fire of your vengeance will fall on the murderous foe !
>
> His country was mighty—his people were blest in his reign,
> But the ray of his glory shall never shine on them again ;
> Like beauty of summer his presence gave joy to our souls,
> When bards sung his deeds at the banquet of bright golden bowls.
>
> Ye maids of Temora, whose rich garments sweep the green plain !
> Ye chiefs of the sunburst, the terror and scourge of the Dane!
> Ye gray-haired *Ard-Fileas!* whose songs fire the blood of the brave !
> Oh! weep, for your Sun-star is quenched in the night of the grave.
>
> He clad you with honors—he filled your high hearts with delight,
> In the midst of your councils he beamed in his wisdom and might ;
> Gold, silver, and jewels were only as dust in his hand,
> But his sword like a lightning-flash blasted the foes of his land.
>
> Oh ! Mahon, my brother ! we've conquer'd and marched side by side,
> And thou wert to the love of my soul as a beautiful bride ;
> In the battle, the banquet, the council, the chase and the throne,
> Our beings were blended—our spirits were filled with one tone.
>
> Oh ! Mahon, my brother ! thou'st died like the hind of the wood,
> The hands of assassins were red with thy pure noble blood ;
> And I was not near, my beloved, when thou wast overpower'd,
> To steep in their hearts' blood the steel of my blue-beaming sword.
>
> I stood by the dark misty river at eve dim and gray,
> And I heard the death-cry of the spirit of gloomy Craghlea ;
> She repeated thy name in her *caoine* of desolate woe,
> Then I knew that the Beauty and Joy of Clan Tail was laid low.
>
> All day and all night one dark vigil of sorrow I keep,
> My pirit is bleeding with wounds that are many and deep,
> My banquet is anguish, tears, groaning, and wringing of hands,
> In madness lamenting my prince of the gold-hilted brands.

---

* M'Gee.

O God! give me patience to bear the affliction I feel,
But for every hot tear a red blood-drop shall blush on my steel ;
For every deep pang which my grief-stricken spirit has known,
A thousand death-wounds in the day of revenge shall atone.

And he smote the murderers of his brother with a swift and
terrible vengeance. Mustering his Dalcassian legions, which
so often with Mahon he had led to victory, he set forth upon
the task of retribution. His first effort, the old records tell us,
was directed against the Danes of Limerick, who were Donovan's allies, and he slew Ivor, their king, and his two sons.
Foreseeing their fate, they had fled before him, and had taken
refuge in "Scattery's Holy Isle." But Brian slew them even
"between the horns of the altar." Next came the turn of
Donovan, who had meantime hastily gathered to his aid the
Danes of South Munster. But " Brian," say the Annals of
Innisfallen, " gave them battle, and Auliffe and his Danes, and
Donovan and his allies, were all cut off." Of all guilty in the
murder of the brother whom he so loved, there now remained but one—the principal, Molloy the son of Bran. After
the fashion in those times, Brian sent Molloy a formal summons or citation to meet him in battle until the terrible issue
between them should be settled. To this Molloy responded
by confederating all the Irish and Danes of South Munster
whom he could rally, for yet another encounter with the avenging Dalcassian. But the curse of the Comharba of St. Barre was
upon the murderers of Mahon, and the might of a passionate
vengeance was in Brian's arm. Again he was victorious. The
confederated Danes and Irish were overthown with great
slaughter ; Brian's son, Morrogh, then a mere lad, "killing the
murderer of his uncle Mahon with his own hand." " Molloy
was buried on the north side of the mountain where Mahon
had been murdered and interred : on Mahon the sun shone
full and fair ; but on the grave of his assassin the black shadow
of the northern sky rested always. Such was the tradition
which all Munster piously believed. After this victory Brian
was universally acknowledged king of Munster, and until
Ard-Ri Malachy won the battle of Tara, was justly considered the first Irish captain of his age." *

This was the opening chapter of Brian's career. Thenceforth his military reputation and his political influence are found extending far beyond the confines of Munster.

The supreme crown of Ireland at this time was worn by a brave and enlightened sovereign, Malachy the Second, or Malachy Mor. He exhibited rare qualities of statesmanship, patriotism, and valor, in his vigorous efforts against the Danes. On the occasion of one of his most signal victories over them, he himself engaged in combat two Danish princes, overcame and slew both of them, taking from off the neck of one a massive collar of gold, and from the grasp of the other a jewel-hilted sword, which he himself thenceforward wore as trophies. To this monarch, and to the incident here mentioned, Moore alludes in his well-known lines : —

> Let Erin remember the days of old,
> Ere her faithless sons betrayed her,
> *When Malachy wore the collar of gold*
> *That he won from the proud invader.*

Whether it was that Ard-Ri Malachy began to fear the increasing and almost over-shadowing power and influence of his southern tributary, or that Brian had in his pride of strength refused to own his tributary position, it seems impossible to tell; but unfortunately for Ireland the brave and wise Ard-Ri Malachy, and the not less brave and wise tributary Brian, became embroiled in a bitter war, the remote but indubitable consequences of which most powerfully and calamitously affected the future destinies of Ireland. For nearly twenty years the struggle between them continued. Any adversary less able than Malachy would have been quickly compelled to succumb to ability such as Brian's; and it may on the other hand be said that it was only a man of Brian's marvellous powers whom Malachy could not effectively crush in as many months. Two such men united could accomplish anything with Ireland ; and when they eventually did unite, they absolutely swept the Danes into their walled and fortified cities, from whence they had begun once more to overrun the country during the distractions of the struggle be-

tween Malachy and Brian. During the short peace or truce between himself and the Ard-Ri, Brian—who was a sagacious
diplomatist as well as a great general—seems to have attached
to his interest nearly all the tributary kings, and subsequently
even the Danish princes; so that it was easy to see that already
his eye began to glance at the supreme crown. Malachy saw
it all, and when the decisive moment at last arrived, and
Brian, playing Cæsar, "crossed the Rubicon," the now only
titular Ard-Ri made a gallant but brief defence against the ambitious usurper—for such Brian was on the occasion. After this
short effort Malachy yielded with dignity and calmness to the
inevitable, and gave up the monarchy of Erinn to Brien. The
abdicated sovereign thenceforward served under his victorious rival as a subordinate, with a readiness and fidelity which
showed him to be Brian's superior at least in unselfish patriotism and in readiness to sacrifice personal pride and personal rights to the public interests of his country.

Brian, now no longer king of Munster, but Ard-Ri of Erinn,
found his ambition fully crowned. The power and authority
to which he had thus attained, he wielded with a wisdom, a
sagacity, a firmness, and a success that made his reign as
Ard-Ri, while it lasted, one of almost unsurpassed glory,
prosperity, and happiness for Ireland. Yet the student of
Irish history finds no fact more indelibly marked on his mind
by the thoughtful study of the great page before him, than
this, namely, that, glorious as was Brian's reign—brave, generous, noble, pious, learned, accomplished, politic, and wise,
as he is confessed on all hands to have been—his seizure of the
supreme national crown was a calamity for Ireland. Or
rather, perhaps, it would be more correct and more just to
say, that having reference not singly to his ambitious seizure
of the national crown, but also to the loss in one day of his
own life and the lives of his next heirs (both son and grandson), the event resulted calamitously for Ireland. For, " it
threw open the sovereignty to every great family as a prize
to be won by policy or force, and no longer an inheritance to
be determined by law and usage. The consequences were
what might have been expected. After his death the O'Con-

nors of the West competed with both O'Neills and O'Briens
for supremacy, and *a chronic civil war prepared the way for
Strongbow and the Normans.* The term 'kings with opposition'
is applied to nearly all who reigned between king Brian's
time and that of Roderic O'Connor" (the Norman invasion),
"meaning thereby kings who were unable to secure general
obedience to their administration of affairs."*

Brian, however, in all probability, as the historian I have
quoted pleads on his behalf, might have been moved by the
great and statesmanlike scheme of consolidating and fusing
Ireland into one kingdom ; gradually repressing individuality
in the subordinate principalities, and laying the firm foundation of an enduring and compact monarchical state, of which
his own posterity would be the sovereigns. "For Morrogh,
his first-born, and for Morrogh's descendants he hoped to
found an hereditary kingship after the type universally copied throughout Christendom. He was not ignorant of what
Alfred had done for England, Harold for Norway, Charle-
magne for France, and Otho for Germany." If any such design really inspired Brian's course, it was a grandly useful
one, comprehensive, and truly national. Its realization was
just what Ireland wanted at that period of her history. But
its existence in Brian's mind is a most fanciful theory. He
was himself, while a tributary king, no wondrous friend or
helper of centralized authority. He pushed from the throne
a wise and worthy monarch. He grasped at the sceptre, not
in a reign of anarchy, but in a period of comparative order,
authority, and tranquillity.

Be that as it may, certain it is that Brian was "every inch
a king." Neither on the Irish throne, nor on that of any
other kingdom, did sovereign ever sit more splendidly qualified to rule ; and Ireland had not for some centuries known
such a glorious and prosperous, peaceful, and happy time as
the five years preceding Brian's death. He caused his authority to be not only unquestioned, but obeyed and respected in
every corner of the land. So justly were the laws adminis-

---

* M'Gee.

tered in his name, and so loyally obeyed throughout the kingdom, that the bards relate a rather fanciful story of a young and exquisitely beautiful lady, making, without the slightest apprehension of violence or insult, and in perfect safety, a tour of the island on foot, alone and unprotected, though bearing about her the most costly jewels and ornaments of gold! A national minstrel of our own times has celebrated this illustration of the tranquillity of Brian's reign in the well-known poem, " Rich and rare were the gems she wore."

————o————

XII.—HOW A DARK THUNDER-CLOUD GATHERED OVER IRELAND.

ABOUT this time the Danish power all over Europe had made considerable advances. In France it had fastened itself upon Normandy, and in England it had once more become victorious, the Danish prince, Sweyne, having been proclaimed king of England in 1013, though it was not until the time of his successor, Canute, that the Danish line were undisputed monarchs of England. All these triumphs made them turn their attention the more earnestly to Ireland, which they so often and so desperately, yet so vainly, sought to win. At length the Danes of this country— holding several of the large sea port cities, but yielding tribute to the Irish monarch—seem to have been roused to the design of rallying all the might of the Scanian race for one gigantic and supreme effort to conquer the kingdom : for it was a reflection hard for northmen to endure, that they who had conquered England almost as often as they tried, who had now placed a Danish sovereign on the English throne, and had established a Danish dukedom of Normandy in France, had never yet been able to bring this dearly coveted western isle into subjection and had never once given a monarch to its line of kings. Coincidently with the victories of Sweyne in England, several Danish expeditions appeared

Foyle in the north ; but these were promptly met and repelled by the vigor of the Ard-Ri, or of the local princes. These
forays, however, though serious and dangerous enough, were
but the prelude of the forthcoming grand assault, or as it has
been aptly styled, "the last field-day of Christianity and
Paganism on Irish soil."

 "A taunt thrown out over a game of chess at Kincora is
said to have hastened this memorable day. Maelmurra, prince
of Leinster, playing or advising on the game, made or recommended a false move, upon which Morrogh, son of Brian, observed it was no wonder his friends the Danes (to whom he
owed his elevation) were beaten at Glenmana, if he gave them
advice like that. Maelmurra, highly incensed by the allusion—
all the more severe for its bitter truth—arose, ordered his horse,
and rode away in haste. Brian, when he heard it, despatched
a messenger after the indignant guest, begging him to return ; but Maelmurra was not to be pacified, and refused.
We next hear of him as concerting with certain Danish agents,
always open to such negotiations, those measures which led
to the great invasion of the year 1014, in which the whole
Scanian race, from Anglesea and Man, north to Norway, bore
an active share.

 " These agents passing over to England and Man, among
the Scottish isles, and even to the Baltic, followed up the design of an invasion on a gigantic scale. Suibne, earl of Man,
entered warmly into this conspiracy, and sent 'the war-arrow'
through all those 'out-islands' which obeyed him as lord. A yet
more formidable potentate, Sigurd, of the Orkneys, next joined
the league. He was the fourteenth earl of Orkney, of Norse
origin, and his power was at this period a balance to that of
his nearest neighbor, the king of Scots. He had ruled since
the year 996, not only over the Orkneys, Shetland, and the
Northern Hebrides, but the coasts of Caithness and Sutherland,
and even Ross and Moray rendered him homage and tribute.
Eight years before the battle of Clontarf, Malcolm the Second
of Scotland had been fain to purchase his alliance by giving
him his daughter in marriage, and the kings of Denmark and
Norway treated with him on equal terms. The hundred in-

habited isles which lie between Yell and Man,—isles which after their conversion contained 'three hundred churches and chapels'—sent in their contingents, to swell the following of the renowned earl Sigurd. As his fleet bore southward from Kirkwall, it swept the subject coast of Scotland, and gathered from every lough its galleys and its fighting-men. The rendez-vous was the Isle of Man, where Suibne had placed his own forces, under the command of Brodar, or Broderick, a famous leader against the Britons of Wales and Cornwall. In conjunction with Sigurd, the Manxmen sailed over to Ireland, where they were joined, in the Liffey, by earl Canuteson, prince of Denmark, at the head of fourteen hundred champions clad in armor. Sitric of Dublin stood, or effected to stand, neutral in these preparations, but Maelmurra of Leinster had mustered all the forces he could command for such an expedition."*

Here was a mighty thunder-storm gathering over and around Ireland! Never before was an effort of such magnitude made for the conquest of the island. Never before had the Danish power so palpably put forth its utmost strength, and never hitherto had it put forth such strength in vain. This was the supreme moment for Ireland to show what she could do when united in self-defence against a foreign invader. Here were the unconquered Northmen, the scourge and terror of Europe, the conquerors of Britain, Normandy, Anglesea, Orkney, and Man, now concentrating the might of their whole race, from fiord and haven, from the Orkneys to the Scilly Isles, to burst in an overwhelming billow upon Ireland! If before a far less formidable assault England went down, dare Ireland hope now to meet and withstand this tremendous shock? In truth it seemed a hard chance. It was a trial-hour for the men of Erinn. And gloriously did they meet it! Never for an instant were they daunted by the tidings of the extensive and mighty preparations going forward; for the news filled Europe, and a hundred harbors in Norway, Denmark, France, England, and the Channel Isles resounded day

---

* M'Gee.

and night with the bustle preparatory for the coming war.
Brian was fully equal to the emergency. He resolved to meet
force by force, combination by combination, preparation by
preparation ; to defy the foe, and let them see " what Irishmen
could do." His efforts were nobly seconded by the zeal of all
the tributary princes (with barely a few exceptions), but most
nobly of all by the deposed Malachy, whose conduct upon
this occasion alone would entitle him to a proud place in the
annals of Ireland. In one,of the preliminary expeditions of
the Danes a few years previously, he detected more quickly
than Brian the seriousness of the work going forward ; he
sent word hurriedly to Kincora, that the Danes, who had landed near Dublin, were marching inward, and entreated of Brian
to hasten to check them promptly. The Ard-Ri, however,
was at that time absolutely incredulous that anything more
serious than a paltry foray was designed ; and he refused, it
is said, to lend any assistance to the local prince. But Malachy had a truer conception of the gravity of the case. He
himself marched to meet the invaders, and in a battle which ensued, routed them, losing, however, in the hour of victory, his
son Flann. This engagement awakened Brian to a sense of
the danger at hand. He quickly despatched an auxiliary force,
under his son Morrogh, to Malachy's aid ; but the Danes, driv-
en into their walled city of Dublin by Malachy, did not
venture out ; and so the Dalcassian force returned southwards,
devastating the territory of the traitor, Maelmorha, of Leinster, whose perfidy was now openly proclaimed.

XIII.—THE GLORIOUS DAY OF CLONTARF.

RIAN soon became fully aware of the scheme at which the Danes all over Europe were laboring, and of the terrible trial approaching for Ireland. Through all the autumn of that year, 1013, and the spring months of the year following, the two powers, Danish and Irish, were working hard at preparations for the great event, each straining every energy and summoning every resource for the crisis. Towards the close of March, Brian's arrangements being completed, he gave the order for a simultaneous march to Kilmainham,* usually the camping ground and now the appointed rendezvous of the national forces. By the second week in April there had rallied to the national standard a force which, if numerically unequal to that assembled by the invaders, was, as the result showed, able to compensate by superior valor for whatever it lacked in numbers. The lords of all the southern half of the kingdom—the lords of Decies, Inchiquin, Fermoy, Corca-Baiskin, Kinalmeaky, and Kerry—and the lords of Hy-Manie and Hi-Fiachra in Connacht, we are told, hastened to Brian's standard. O'More and O'Nolan of Leinster, and Donald, Steward of Marr, in Scotland, continues the historian, "were the other chieftains who joined him before Clontarf, besides those of his own kindred," or the forces proper of Thomond.† Just one faint shadow catches the eye as we sur-

---

* The district north and south of the Liffey at this point—the Phoenix Park, Kilmainham, Inchicore, and Chapel-Izod—was the rendezvous.

† " Under the standard of Brian Borumha also fought that day the Maermors, or Great Stewards of Lennox and Mar, with a contingent of the brave Gaels of Alba. It would even appear, from a Danish account, that some of the Northmen who had always been friendly to Brian, fought on his side at Clontarf. A large body of hardy men came from the distant maritime districts of Connemara ; many warriors flocked from other territories, and, on the whole, the rallying of the men of Ireland in the cause of their country upon that occasion, as much as the victory which their gal-

vey the picture presented by Ireland in the hour of this great
national rally. The northern chieftains, the lords of Ulster,
alone held back. Sullen and silent, they stirred not. "They
had submitted to Brian; but they never cordially supported
him. "

The great Danish flotilla, under Brodar, the admiral-in-chief,
entered Dublin Bay on Palm Sunday, the 18th of April, 1014.
The galleys anchored, some of them at Sutton, near Howth,
others were moored in the mouth of the river Liffey, and the
rest were beached or anchored in a vast line stretching along
the Clontarf shore, which sweeps between the two points indicated. Brian immediately swung his army round upon
Glasnevin, crossed the Tolka at the point where the Botanical
Gardens now stand, and faced his line of battle southward
towards where the enemy were encamped upon the shore.
Meantime, becoming aware that Maelmorra, prince of Leinster, was so eager to help the invader, that he had entered
the Danish camp with every man of his following, Brian
secretly despatched a body of Dalcassians, under his son Don-
agh, to dash into the traitor's territory and waste it with fire
and sword. The secret march southward of the Dalcassians
was communicated to Maelmorra by a spy in Brian's camp,
and, inasmuch as the Dalcassians were famed as the "invincible legion " of the Irish army, the traitor urged vehemently upon his English allies that this was the moment to give battle—
while Brian's best troops were away. Accordingly, on Holy
Thursday, the Danes announced their resolution to give battle next day. Brian had the utmost reluctance to fight upon
that day, which would be Good Friday, thinking it almost a
profanation to engage in combat upon the day on which our
Lord died for man's redemption. He begged that the engagement might be postponed even one day ; but the Danes were
all the more resolute to engage on the next morning, for, says
an old legend of the battle, Brodar, having consulted one of
the Danish pagan oracles, was told that if he gave battle upon the Friday *Brian would fall.*

With early dawn next day, Good Friday, 23d of April,

1014, all was bustle in both camps.* The Danish army, facing inland, northwards or north-east, stretched along the shore of Dublin Bay; its left flank touching and protected by the city of Dublin, its centre being about the spot where Clontarf castle now stands, and its right wing resting on Dollymount. The Irish army, facing southwards, had its right on Drumcondra, its centre on Fairview, and its extreme left on Clontarf. The Danish forces were disposed of in three divisions, of which the first, or left, was composed of the Danes of Dublin, under their king, Sitric, and the princes Dolat and Conmael, with the thousand Norwegians, already mentioned as clothed in suits of ringed mail, under the youthful warriors Carlus and Anrud; the second, or central division, was composed chiefly of the Lagenians, commanded by Mealmorha himself, and the princes of Offaly and of the Liffey territory; and the third division, or right wing, was made up of the auxiliaries from the Baltic and the Islands, under Brodar, admiral of the fleet, and the Earl of Orkneys, together with some British auxiliaries from Wales and Cornwall. To oppose these the Irish monarch also marshalled his forces in three corps or divisions. The first, or right wing, composed chiefly of the diminished legions of the brave Dalcassians, was under the command of his son Morrogh, who had also with him his four brothers, Tiege, Donald, Conor, and Flann, and his own son (grandson of Brian), the youthful Torlogh, who was but fifteen years of age. In this division also fought Malachy

---

* Haverty says: "The exact site of the battle seems to be tolerably well defined. In some copies of the Annals it is called 'the Battle of the Fishing-weir of Clontarf;' and the weir in question must have been at the mouth of the Tolka, about the place where Ballybough Bridge now stands. It also appears that the principle destruction of the Danes took place when in their flight they endeavored to cross the Tolka, probably at the moment of high water, when great numbers of them were drowned; and it is expressly stated that they were pursued with great slaughter 'from the Tolka to Dublin.'" I, however, venture, though with proper diffidence, to suggest that the 'Fishing weir' stood a short distance higher up the river, to wit, at Clonliffe, directly below where the College of the Holy Cross now stands. For there is, in my opinion, ample evidence to show that at that time the sea flowed over the flats on the city side, by which Ballybough Bridge is now approached, making a goodly bay, or wide estuary, there; and that only about the point I indicate was a fishing-weir

with the Meath contingent. The Irish centre division comprised the troops of Desmond, or South Munster, under the
command of Kian, son of Molloy, and Donel, son of Duv
Davoren (ancestor of The O'Donoghue), both of the Eugenian
line. The Irish left wing was composed mainly of the forces
of Connaught, under O'Kelly, prince of Hy-Manie (the great
central territory of Connact) O'Heyne, prince of Hy-Fiachra
Ahna ; and Echtigern, king of Dalaradia. It is supposed that
·Brian's army numbered about 20,000 men.*

All being ready for the signal of battle, Brian himself,
mounted on a richly-caparisoned charger, rode through the
Irish lines, as all the records are careful to tell us, " with his
sword in one hand, and a crucifix in the other," exhorting the
troops to remember the momentous issues that depended upon the fortunes of that day—Religion and Country against
Paganism and Bondage. It is said, that on this occasion he
delivered an address which moved his soldiers, now to tears
and anon to the utmost pitch of enthusiasm and resolution.
And we can well imagine the effect, upon an army drawn up
as they were for the onset of battle in defence of " Faith and
Fatherland," of such a sight and of such an appeal—their aged
and venerable monarch, "his white hair floating in the wind
riding through their lines, with sacred symbol of Redemption borne aloft, and adjuring them, as the chronicles tell us,
to " *remember that on this day Christ died for us, on the Mount
of Calvary.*" Moreover, Brian himself had given them an
earnest, such perhaps as monarch had never given before, of
his resolve, that with the fortunes of his country he and his
sons and kinsmen all would stand or fall. He had brought
" his sons and nephews there," says the historian, who might
have added, *and even his grand-children,* " and showed that he
was prepared to let the existence of his race depend upon the
issue of the day." We may be sure a circumstance so effecting as this was not lost upon Brian's soldiers. It gave force
to every word of his address. He recounted, we are told, all
the barbarities and the sacrileges perpetrated by the invaders

* Abridged from Haverty.

in their lawless ravages on Irish soil, the shrines they had plundered, the holy relics they had profaned, the brutal cruelties they had inflicted on unarmed non-combatants—nay, on " the servants of the Altar." Then, raising the crucifix aloft, he invoked the Omnipotent God to look down upon them that day, and to strengthen their arms in a cause so just and holy.

Mr. William Kenealy (now of Kilkenny) is the author of a truly noble poem which gives, with all the native vigor and force of the original, this thrilling " Address of Brian to his army."

Stand ye now for Erin's glory!   Stand ye now for Erin's cause!
Long ye've groaned beneath the rigor of the Northmen's savage laws.
What though brothers league against us ?   What, though myriads be the foe ?
Victory will be more honored in the myriads' overthrow.

Proud Connacians !   oft we've wrangled in our petty feuds of yore ;
Now we fight against the robber Dane upon our native shore ;
May our hearts unite in friendship, as our blood in one red tide,
While we crush their mail-clad legions, and annihilate their pride !

Brave Eugenians !   Erin triumphs in the sight she sees to-day—
Desmond's homesteads all deserted for the muster and the fray !
Cluan's vale and Galtees' summit send their bravest and their best—
May such hearts be theirs for ever, for the Freedom of the West !

Chiefs and Kernes of Dalcassia !   Brothers of my past career,
Oft we've trodden on the pirate-flag that flaunts before us here;
You remember Inniscattery, how we bounded on the foe,
As the torrent of the mountain bursts upon the plain below !

They have razed our proudest castles—spoiled the Temples of the Lord—
Burnt to dust the sacred relics—put the Peaceful to the sword—
Desecrated all things holy—as they soon may do again,
If their power to-day we smite not—if to-day we be not men !
    *   *   *   *   *   *
On this day the God-man suffered—look upon the sacred sign—
May we conquer 'neath its shadow, as of old did Constantine !
May the heathen tribe of Odin fade before it like a dream,
And the triumph of this glorious day in our future annals gleam !

God of heaven bless our banner—nerve our sinews for the strife !
Fight we now for all that's holy—for our altars, land, and life—
For red vengeance on the spoiler, whom the blazing temples trace—

Should I fall before the foemen, 'tis the death I seek to-day ;
Should ten thousand daggers pierce me, bear my body not away,
Till this day of days be over—till the field is fought and won—
Then the holy Mass be chaunted, and the funeral rites be done.

    *   *   *   *   *   *   *

Men of Erin ! men of Erin ! grasp the battle-axe and spear !
Chase these Northern wolves before you like a herd of frightened deer!
Burst their ranks, like bolts from heaven !   Down on the heathen crew,
For the glory of the Crucified, and Erin's glory too !

Who can be astonished that, as he ceased, a shout wild,
furious, and deafening, burst from the Irish lines ? A cry arose
from the soldiers, we are told, demanding instantly to be led
against the enemy. The aged monarch now placed himself
at the head of his guards, to lead the van of battle ; but at this
point his sons and all the attendant princes and commanders
protested against his attempting, at his advanced age, to take
part personally in the conflict ; and eventually, after much
effort, they succeeded in prevailing upon him to retire to his
tent and to let the chief command devolve upon his eldest son
Morrogh.

"The battle," says a historian, " then commenced ; 'a spirited, fierce, violent, vengeful and furious battle ; the likeness
of which was not to be found at that time,' as the old annalists
quaintly describe it.   It was a conflict of heroes.   The chieftains engaged at every point in single combat ; and the
greater part of them on both sides fell.   The impetuosity of
the Irish was irresistible, and their battle-axes did fearful
execution, every man of the ten hundred mailed warriors of
Norway having been made to bite the dust, and it was against
them, we are told, that the Dalcassians had been obliged to
contend single-handed.   The heroic Morrogh performed pro-
digies of valor throughout the day.   Ranks of men fell before
him ; and, hewing his way to the Danish standard, he cut
down two successive bearers of it with his battle-axe.   Two
Danish leaders, Carolus and Conmael, enraged at this success,
rushed on him together, but both fell in rapid succession by
his sword. Twice, Morrogh and some of his chiefs retired to
slake their thirst and cool their hands, swollen from the
violent use of the sword ; and the Danes observing the vigor

BRIAN ON THE MORNING OF CLONTARF.

See pages 93, 94.

with which they returned to the conflict, succeeded, by a desperate effort, in cutting off the brook which had refreshed them. Thus the battle raged from an early hour in the morning—innumerable deeds of valor being performed on both sides, and victory appearing still doubtful, until the third or fourth hour in the afternoon, when a fresh and desperate effort was made by the Irish, and the Danes, now almost destitute of leaders, began to waver and give way at every point. Just at this moment the Norwegian prince, Anrud, encountered Morrogh, who was unable to raise his arms from fatigue, but with the left hand seized Anrud and hurled him to the earth, and with the other placed the point of the sword on the breast of the prostrate Northman, and leaning on it plunged it through his body. While stooping, however, for this purpose, Anrud contrived to inflict on him a mortal wound with a dagger, and Morrogh fell in the arms of victory. According to other accounts, Morrogh was in the act of stooping to relieve an enemy when he received from him his death wound. This disaster had not the effect of turning the fortune of the day, for the Danes and their allies were in a state of utter disorder, and along their whole line had commenced to fly towards the city or to their ships. They plunged into the Tolka at a time, we may conclude, when the river was swollen with the tide, so that great numbers were drowned. The body of young Turlogh was found after the battle 'at the weir of Clontarf,' with his hands entangled in the hair of a Dane whom he had grappled with in the pursuit.

"But the chief tragedy of the day remains to be related. Brodar, the pirate admiral, who commanded in the point of the Danish lines remotest from the city, seeing the route general, was making his way through some thickets with only a few attendants, when he came upon the tent of Brian Borumha, left at that moment without his guards. The fierce Norseman rushed in and found the aged Monarch at prayer before the Crucifix, which he had that morning held up to the view of his troops, and attended only by his page. Yet, Brian had time to seize his arms, and died sword in hand.

only overcome by numbers; but the Danish version in the
Niala Saga is more probable, and in this Brodar is represented
as holding up his reeking sword, and crying : ' Let it be proclaimed from man to man that Brian has been slain by Brodar.'
It is added, on the same authority, that the ferocious pirate
was then hemmed in by Brian's returned guards and captured
alive, and that he was hung from a tree, and continued to rage
like a beast of prey until all his entrails were torn out—the
Irish soldiers thus taking savage vengeance for the death of their
king, who but for their own neglect would have been safe."*

Such was the victory of Clontarf—one of the most glorious
events in the annals of Ireland! It was the final effort of the
Danish power to effect the conquest of this country. Never
again was that effort renewed. For a century subsequently
the Danes continued to hold some maritime cities in Ireland ;
but never more did they dream of conquest. That design was
overthrown forever on the bloody plain of Clontarf.

It was, as the historian called it truly, "a conflict of heroes."
There was no flinching on either side, and on each side fell nearly every commander of note who had entered battle! The
list of the dead is a roll of nobility, Danish and Irish; amongst
the dead being the brave Caledonian chiefs, the great Stewards
of Mar and Lennox, who had come from distant Alba to
fight on the Irish side that day.

But direst disaster of all—most woful in its ulterior results
affecting the fate and fortunes of Ireland—was the slaughter
of the reigning family : Brian himself, Morrogh, his eldest
son and destined successor, and his grandson, "the youthful
Torlagh," eldest child of Morrogh—three generations cut
down in the one day upon the same field of battle !

"The fame of the event went out through all nations. The
chronicles of Wales, of Scotland, and of Man ; the annals of
Ademar and Marianus ;† the sagas of Denmark and the Isles,
all record the event. The Norse settlers in Caithness saw

---

* Haverty.

† "Brian, king of Hibernia, slain on Good Friday, the 9th of the calends of May
(23rd April), with his mind and his hands turned towards God."—*Chronicles of Mar-*

terrific visions of Valhalla ' the day after the battle.' " * " The annals state that Brian and Morrogh both lived to receive the last sacraments of the Church, and that their remains were conveyed by the monks to Swords (near Dublin), and thence to Armagh by the Archbishop ; and that their obsequies were celebrated for twelve days and nights with great splendor by the clergy of Armagh ; after which the body of Brian was deposited in a stone coffin on the north side of the high altar in the cathedral, the body of his son being interred on the south side of the same church. The remains of Torlogh and of several of the other chieftains were buried in the old church-yard of Kilmainham, where the shaft of an Irish cross still marks the spot. "†

XIV.—"AFTER THE BATTLE." THE SCENE " UPON OSSORY'S PLAIN." THE LAST DAYS OF NATIONAL FREEDOM.

HREE days after the battle the decimated but victory-crowned Irish legions broke up camp and marched homewards to their respective provinces, chanting songs of triumph. The Dalcassians (who had suf-fered terribly in the battle) found their way barred by a hostile prince, Fitzpatrick, lord of Ossory, whose opposing numbers vastly exceeded their effective force which indeed was barely enough to convey or convoy their wounded homeward to Kincora. In this extremity the wounded soldiers entreated that they might be allowed to fight with the rest. "Let stake ," they said, " be driven into the ground, and suffer each of us, *tied to and supported by one of these stakes*, to be placed in his rank by the side of a sound man." " Between seven and eight hundred wounded men," adds the historian, " pale, ema-ciated, and supported in this manner, appeared mixed with the foremost of the troops! Never was such another sight exhibited !"‡ Keating's quaint narrative of the event is well

worthy of quotation. He says : " Donogh then again gave orders that one-third of his host should be placed on guard as a
protection for the wounded, and that the other two-thirds should
meet the expected battle. But when the wounded men heard
of these orders, they sprung up in such haste that their wounds
and sores burst open ; but they bound them up in moss, and
grasping their lances and their swords, they came thus equipped into the midst of their comrades. Here they requested of
Donncadh, son of Brian, to send some men to the forest with instructions to bring them a number of strong stakes, which they
proposed to have thrust into the ground, and to these
stakes,' said they, 'let us be bound with our arms in our hands,
and let our sons and our kinsmen be stationed by our sides ;
and let two warriors, who are unwounded, be placed near
each one of us wounded, for it is thus that we will help one
another with truer zeal, because shame will not allow the
sound man to leave his position until his wounded and bound
comrade can leave it likewise.' This request was complied
with, and the wounded men were stationed after the manner
which they had pointed out. And, indeed, that array in
which the Dalg-Cais were then drawn, was a thing for the
mind to dwell upon in admiration, for it was a great and amazing wonder."

Our national minstrel, Moore, has alluded to this episode
of the return of the Dalcassians in one of the melodies:

> Remember our wounded companions, who stood
>   In the day of distress by our side :
> When the moss of the valley grew red with their blood,
>   They stirred not, but conquered and died.
> The sun that now blesses our arms with its light
>   Saw them fall upon Ossory's plain:
> O ! let him not blush, when he leaves us to-night,
>   To find that they fell there in vain !

With the victory of Clontarf the day of Ireland's unity and
power as a nation may be said to have ended. The sun of
her national greatness, that had been waning previously, set
suddenly in a brilliant flash of glory. If we except the eight

knew the blessing of national unity—never more was a kingdom, in the full sense of the word. Malachy Mor—well worthy of his title "the great"—the good, the magnanimous, the patriot, and brave king, whom Brian had deposed, was unanimously recalled to the throne after Brian's death. The eight years during which Malachy ruled in this the second term of his sovereignty, were marked by every evidence of kingly ability and virtue on his part. At length, finding death approaching, he retired for greater solitude to an island in Lough Ennel (now called Cormorant Island), whither repaired sorrowfully to his spiritual succor "Amalgaid, Archbishop of Armagh, the Abbots of Clonmacnoise and of Durrow, and a good train of clergy;" and where, as the old chronicles relate it, "after intense penance, on the fourth of the nones of September, died Malachy, the pillar of the dignity and nobility of the western world."

He was the last "unquestioned" monarch of Ireland. The interval between his death and the landing of Henry the Second (over one hundred and fifty years) was a period of bloody and ruinous contention, that invited—and I had almost said merited—the yoke of a foreign rule. After Malachy's death Brian's younger son, Donogh, claimed the throne; but his claim was scorned and repudiated by a moiety of the princes, who had, indeed, always regarded Brian himself as little better than an usurper, though a brave and a heroic sovereign. Never afterwards was an Ard-Ri fully and lawfully elected or acknowledged. There were frequently two or more claimants assuming the title at the same time, and desolating the country in their contests for sovereignty. Brian had broken the charmed line of regulated succession, that had, as I have already detailed, lasted through nearly two thousand years. His act was the final blow at the already loosened and tottering edifice of centralized national authority. While he himself lived, with his own strong hand and powerful mind to keep all things in order, it was well; no evil was likely to come of the act that supplied a new ground for wasting discords and bloody civil strife. But when the powerful hand and the strong mind had passed away; when the

splendid talents that had made even the deposed monarch,
Malachy, bow to their supremacy, no longer availed to
bind the kingdom into unity and strength, the miseries that
ensued were hopeless. The political disintegration of Ireland was aggravated a thousand-fold. The idea of national
unity seemed as completely dead, buried, and forgotten, when
the Normans came in, as if it never had existence amongst
the faction-split people of Erinn.

> 'Twas self-abasement paved the way
> For villain bonds and despot's sway.

Donogh O'Brien, never acknowledged as Ard-Ri, was driv-
en from even his titular sovereignty by his own nephew,
Torlogh. Aged, broken, and weary, he sailed for Rome,
where he entered a monastery and ended his life "in penance,"
as the old chronicles say. It is stated that this Donogh took
with him to Rome the crown and the harp of his father, the
illustrious Brian, and presented them to the Pope.* This
donation of his father's diadem to the Pope by Donogh has
sometimes been referred to as if it implied a bestowal of the
Irish sovereignty; a placing of it, as it were, at the disposal
of the Father of Christendom, for the best interests of faction-
ruined Ireland herself, and for the benefit of the Christian religion. Perhaps the Pope was led so to regard it. But the
Supreme Pontiff did not know that such a gift was not Donogh's to give! Donogh never owned or possessed the Irish
sovereignty; and even if he had been unanimously elected
and acknowledged Ard-Ri (and he never was), the Irish sovereignty was a trust to which the Ard-Ri was elected for life,
and which he could not donate even his own son, except by
the consent of the Royal Electors and Free Clans of Erinn.

---

* The harp is still in existence. It is in the Museum of Trinity College, Dublin.

XV.—HOW ENGLAND BECAME A COMPACT KINGDOM, WHILE IRELAND WAS BREAKING INTO FRAGMENTS.

E now approach the period at which, for the first time, the history of Ireland needs to be read with that of England.

A quarter of a century after the rout of the Danes by the Irish at Clontarf, the Anglo-Saxons drove them from the English throne, the Anglo-Saxon line being restored in the person of Edward the Confessor. A quarter of a century subsequently, however, the Anglo-Saxons were again dethroned, and England was again conquered by new invaders—or the old ones with a new name—the Normans. In this last struggle, the Anglo-Saxons were aided by troops from Ireland; for the Normans were kith and kin of the Norse foes whom Ireland had such reason to hate. An Irish contingent fought side by side with the Saxons in their struggle against William; and when the brave but unfortunate Harold fell at Hastings, it was to Ireland his children were sent for friendly asylum.

The Normans treasured a bitter remembrance of this against Ireland; and there is evidence that from the first they meant to essay the subjugation of *that* island also, as soon as they should have consolidated their British conquest. These same Normans were a brave race. They possessed every quality requisite for military conquerors. To the rough fierce vigor of the Norse ancestors they had added the military discipline and scientific skill which the Gauls had learned from their Roman masters. They conquered united England in one year. Yet they were *five hundred* years unsuccessfully laboring to conquer *dis*-united Ireland!

During the one hundred and fifty years following Brian's death (devoted by the Irish princes to every factious folly and their country), the Normans in England were solidifying and strengthening their power. England was becoming a compact nation, governed by concentrated national authority, and possessed of a military organization formidable in numbers and in arms, but most of all in scientific mode of warfare and perfection of military discipline ; while Ireland, like a noble vessel amid the breakers, was absolutely going to pieces—breaking up into fragments, or " clans," north, south, east, and west. As a natural result of this anarchy or wasting strife of factions, social and religious disorders supervened ; and as a historian aptly remarks, " the Island of Saints" became an "Island of Sinners." The state of religion was deplorable. The rules of ecclesiastical discipline were in many places overthrown, as was nearly every other necessary moral and social safeguard ; and, inevitably, the most lamentable disorders and scandals resulted. The bishops vainly sought to calm this fearful war of factions that was thus ruining the power of a great nation, and destroying or disgracing its Christian faith. They threatened to appeal to the Supreme Pontiff, and to invoke his interposition in behalf of religion thus outraged, and civil society thus desolate. St. Malachy, the primate of Armagh, the fame of whose sanctity, piety and learning had reached all Europe, labored heroically amidst these terrible afflictions. He proceeded to Rome, and was received with every mark of consideration by the reigning Pope, Innocent the Second, who, "descending from his throne, placed his own mitre on the head of the Irish saint, presented him with his own vestments and other religous gifts, and appointed him apostolic legate in the place of Gilbert, bishop of Limerick, then a very old man." St. Malachy petitioned the Pope for the necessary recognition of the Irish archiepiscopal sees, by the sending of the palliums to the archbishops; but the Pope pointed out that so grave a request should proceed from a synod of the Irish Church. The primate returned to Ireland ; and after some time devoted to still more energetic measures to cope with the difficulties created by perpetual civil war, he eventually convened a national synod, which was held at Innis-Patrick, near Skerries, county Dublin. St. Malachy was authorized again to proceed to the Holy Father, and in the name of the Irish Church beseech him to grant the palliums. The aged primate set out on his journey. But while on his way, having reached Clairvaux, he was seized with his death-sickness, and expired there (2d November, 1148), attended by the great St. Bernard, between whom and the Irish primate a personal friendship existed, and a correspondence passed, portion of which is still extant. Three years afterwards the palliums, sent by Pope Eugene the Third, were brought to Ireland by Cardinal Paparo, and were solemnly conferred on the archbishops the year following, at a national synod held at Kells.

But all the efforts of the ministers of religion could not compensate for the want of a stable civil government in the land. Nothing could permanently restrain the fierce violence of the chiefs; and it is clear that at Rome, and throughout Europe, the opinion at this time began to gain ground that Ireland was a hopeless case. And, indeed, so it must have seemed. It is true that the innate virtue and morality of the Irish national character began to assert itself the moment society was allowed to enjoy the least respite; it is beyond question that, during and after the time of the sainted primate, Malachy, vigorous and comprehensive efforts were afoot, and great strides made towards reforming the abuses with which chronic civil war had covered the land. But, like many another reformation, it *came to late*. Before the ruined nation could be reconstituted, the Nemesis of invasion arrived, to teach all peoples, by the story of Ireland's fate, that when national cohesiveness is gone, national power has departed and national suffering is at hand.

XVI.—HOW HENRY THE SECOND FEIGNED WONDROUS ANXIETY TO HEAL THE DISORDERS OF IRELAND.

HE grandson of William of Normandy, Conqueror of England, Henry the Second, was not an inattentive observer of the progressing wreck of the Irish Church and Nation. He inherited the Norman design of one day conquering Ireland also, and adding that kingdom to his English crown. He was not ignorant that at Rome Ireland was regarded as derelict. An Englishman, Pope Adrian, now sat in the Chair of Peter; and the English ecclesiastical authorities, who were in constant communication with the Holy See, were transmitting the most alarming accounts of the fearful state of Ireland. It is now known that these accounts were, in many cases, monstrously exaggerated; but it is true that, at best, the state of affairs was very bad.

The cunning and politic Henry saw his opportunity. Though his was the heart of a mere conqueror, sordid and callous, he clothed himself in the garb of the most saintly piety, and wrote to the Holy Father, calling attention to the state of Ireland, which for over a hundred years has been a scandal to Europe. But oh! it was the state of religion there that most afflicted his pious and holy Norman heart! It was all in the interests of social order, morality, religion, and civilization,* that he now approached the Holy Father with a proposition. In those times (when Christendom was an unbroken family, of which the Pope was the head), the Supreme Pontiff was, by the voices of the nations themselves, invested with a certain kind of arbitrative civil authority for the general good. And, indeed, even infidel and non-Catholic historians declare to us that, on the whole, and with scarcely a possible exception

---

* Even in *that* day—seven hundred years ago—English subjugators had learned the use of these amiable pretexts for invasion and annexation !

the Popes exerted the authority thus vested in them with a pure, unselfish, and exalted anxiety for the general public good and the ends of justice, for the advancement of religion, learning, civilization, and civil freedom. But this authority rested merely on the principle by which the Arcadian farmers in Longfellow's poem constituted their venerable pastor supreme lawgiver, arbitrator, and regulator in their little community ; a practice which, even in our own day, prevails within the realms of fact here in Ireland and in other countries.

Henry's proposition to the Pope was that he, the English king, should, with the sanction of the Holy Father, and (of course) purely in the interests of religion, morality, and social order, enter Ireland and restore order in that region of anarchy. He pleaded that the Pope was *bound* to cause some such step to be taken, and altogether urged numerous grounds for persuading the Pontiff to credit his professions as to his motives and designs. Pope Adrian is said to have complied by issuing a bull approving of Henry's scheme *as presented to him*, and with the purposes and on the conditions therein set forth. Their is no such bull now to be found in the Papal archives, yet it is credited that some such bull was issued; but its contents, terms, and permissions have been absurdly misrepresented and exaggerated in some versions coined by English writers.

The Papal bull or letter once issued, Henry had gained his point. He stored away the document until his other plans should be ripe ; and, meanwhile, having no longer any need of feigning great piety and love for religion, he flung off the mask and entered upon that course of conduct which, culminating in the murder of St. Thomas A'Becket, Archbishop of Canterbury, drew down upon him the excommunication of Rome.

Meantime events were transpiring in Ireland destined to afford him a splendid opportunity for practically availing of his fraudulently obtained Papal letter, and making a commencement in his scheme of Irish conquest.

XVII.—THE TREASON OF DIARMID M'MURROGH.

BOUT the year 1152, in the course of the interminable civil war desolating Ireland, a feud of peculiar bitterness arose between Tiernan O'Ruarc, prince of Brefni, and Diarmid M'Murrogh, prince of Leinster. While one of the Ard-Righana favorable to the latter was for the moment uppermost, O'Ruarc had been dispossessed of his territory, its lordship being handed over to M'Murrogh. To this was added a wrong still more dire. Devorgilla, the wife of O'Ruarc, eloped with M'Murrogh, already her husband's most bitter rival and foe! Her father and her husband both appealed to Torlogh O'Connor for justice upon the guilty prince of Leinster. O'Connor, although M'Murrough had been one of his supporters, at once acceded to this request. M'Murrogh soon found his territory surrounded, and Devorgilla was restored to her husband. She did not, however, return to domestic life. Recent researches amongst the ancient "Manuscript Materials for Irish History," by O'Curry and O'Donovan, throw much light upon this episode, and considerably alter the long prevailing popular impressions in reference thereto. Whatever the measure of Devorgilla's fault in eloping with M'Murrogh—and the researches illuded to bring to light many circumstances invoking for her more of commiseration than of angry scorn—her whole life subsequently to this sad event, and she lived for forty years afterwards, was one prolonged act of contrition and of penitential reparation for the scandal she had given. As I have already said, she did not return to the home she had abandoned. She entered a religious retreat; and thenceforth, while living a life of practical piety, penance, and mortification, devoted the immense dower which she possessed in her own right, to works of charity, relieving the poor, building hospitals, asylums, convents, and churches.

Thirteen years after this event, Roderick O'Connor, son and successor of the king who had forced M'Murrogh to yield up the unhappy Devorgilla, claimed the throne of the kingdom. Roderick was a devoted friend of O'Ruarc, and entertained no very warm feelings towards M'Murrogh. The king claimant marched on his "circuit," claiming "hostages" from the local princes as recognition of sovereignty. M'Murrogh, who hated Roderick with intense violence, burned his city of Ferns, and retired to his Wicklow fastnesses, rather than yield allegiance to him. Roderick could not just then delay on his circuit to follow him up, but passed on southward, took up his hostages there, and then returned to settle accounts with M'Murrogh. But by this time O'Ruarc, apparently only too glad to have such a pretext and opportunity for a stroke at his mortal foe, had assembled a powerful army and marched upon M'Murrogh from the north, while Roderick approached him from the south. Diarmid, thus surrounded, and deserted by most of his own people, outwitted and overmatched on all sides, saw that he was a ruined man. He abandoned the few followers yet remaining to him, fled to the nearest seaport, and, with a heart bursting with the most deadly passions, sailed for England (A.D. 1168), vowing vengeance, black, bitter, and terrible, on all that he left behind!

"A solemn sentence of banishment was publicly pronounced against him by the assembled princes, and Morrogh, his cousin—commonly called 'Morrogh *na Gael*,' (or 'of the Irish,') to distinguish him from 'Morrogh *na Gall*' (or 'of the Foreigners')—was inaugurated in his stead."*

Straightway he sought out the English king, who was just then in Aquitaine quelling a revolt of the nobles in that portion of his possessions. M'Murrogh laid before Henry a most piteous recital of his wrongs and grievances, appealed to him for justice and for aid, inviting him to enter Ireland, which he was sure most easily to reduce to his sway, and finally offering to become his most submissive vassal if his majesty would but aid him in recovering the possessions from which he had

been expelled. " Henry," as one of our historians justly remarks, " must have been forcibly struck by such an invitation
to carry out a project which he had long entertained, and for
which he had been making grave preparations long before."
He was too busy himself, however, just then to enter upon
the project; but he gave M'Murrogh a royal letter or proclamation authorizing such of his subjects as might so desire
to aid the views of the Irish fugitive. Diarmid hurried back
to England, and had all publicity given to this proclamation
in his favor; but though he made the most alluring offers of
reward and booty, he was a long time before he found any
one to espouse his cause. At length Robert Fitzstephen, a
Norman relative of the prince of North Wales, just then held
in prison by his Cambrian kinsman, was released or brought
out of prison by M'Murrogh, on condition of undertaking his
service. Through Fitzstephen there came into the enterprise
several other knights, Maurice Fitzgerald, Meyler Fitzhenry
and others—all of them men of supreme daring, but of needy
circumstances. Eventually there joined one who was destined
to take command of them all. Richard de Clare, earl of Pen-
broke, commonly called "Strongbow;" a man of ruined fortune, needy, greedy, unscrupulous, and ready for any desperate adventure; possessing unquestionable military skill and
reckless daring, and having a tolerably strong following of like
adventurous spirits amongst the knights of the Welsh marches
—in fine, just the man for Diarmid's purpose. The terms
were soon settled. Strongbow and his companions undertook
to raise a force of adventurers, proceed to Ireland with
M'Murrogh, and reinstate him in his principality. M'Murrogh was to bestow on Strongbow (then a widower between
fifty and sixty years of age) his daughter Eva in marriage,
with succession to the throne of Leinster. Large grants of
land also were to be distributed amongst the adventurers.

Now, Diarmid knew that "succession to the throne" was
not a matter which any king in Ireland, whether provincial
or national, at any time could bestow; the monarchy being
elective out of the members of the reigning family. Even if
he was himself at the time in full legal possession of " the

throne of Leinster," he could not promise, secure, or bequeath it, as if *right*, even to his own son.

In the next place, Diarmid knew that his offers of "grants of land "struck directly and utterly at the existing land system, the basis of all society in Ireland, For, according to the Irish constitution and laws for a thousand years, the fee-simple or *ownership* of the soil was vested in the sept, tribe, or clan ; its *use or occupancy* (by the individual members of the sept or others) being only regulated on behalf of and in the interest of the whole sept, by the elected king for the time being. "Tribe land" could not be alienated unless by the king, with the sanction of the sept. The users and occupiers were, so to speak, a coöperative society of agriculturists, who *as a body* or a community, owned the soil they tilled, while individually renting it from that body or community under its administrative official—the king.

While Strongbow and his confederates were, completing their arrangements in Chester, M'Murrogh crossed over to his native Wexford privately to prepare the way there for their reception. It would seem that no whisper had reached Ireland of his movements, designs, proclamations, and preparations on the other side of the channel. The wolf assumed the sheep's clothing. M'Murrogh feigned great humility and contrition, and pretended to aspire only to the recovery, by grace and favor, of his immediate patrimony of Hy-Kinsella. Amongst his own immediate clansmen, no doubt, he found a friendly meeting and a ready following, and, more generally, a feeling somewhat of commiseration for one deemed to be now so fallen, so helpless, so humiliated. This secured him from very close observation, and greatly favored the preparations he was stealthily making to meet the Norman expedition with stout help on the shore.

XVIII.—HOW THE NORMAN ADVENTURERS GOT A FOOTHOLD ON IRISH SOIL.

HE fatal hour was now at hand. Early in the month of May a small flotilla of strange vessels ran into a little creek on the Wexford coast, near Bannow, and disembarked an armed force upon the shore. This was the advanced guard of the Norman invasion ; a party of thirty knights, sixty men in armor, and three hundred footmen, under Robert Fitzstephen. Next day at the same point of disembarkation arrived Maurice de Prendergast, a Welsh gentleman who had joined the enterprise, bringing with him an additional force. Camping on the coast, they quickly despatched a courier to M·Murrogh to say that they had come. Diarmid hastened to the spot with all the men he could rally. The joint force at once marched upon and laid siege to Wexford, which town, after a

tant victory, and strengthened in numbers, Diarmid now marched into Ossory. Here he was confronted by Fitz-patrick, prince of Ossory, commanding, however, a force quite inferior to M'Murrogh's. A sanguinary engagement ensued. The Ossorians bravely held their own throughout the day, until decoyed from their chosen position into an open ground where the Norman cavalry had full play, the "poise of the beam" was turned against them ; they were thrown into confusion, pressed by the enemy, and at length overthrown with great slaughter.

Roderick the Second, titular Ard-Ri, now awakened to the necessity of interposing with the national forces ; *not* as against an *invasion ;* for at this period, and indeed for some time afterwards, none of the Irish princes attached such a character or meaning to the circumstance that M'Murrogh had enlisted into his service some men of England. It was to check M'Murrogh, the deposed king of Leinster, in his hostile proceedings, that the Ard-Ri summoned the national forces to meet him at the Hill of Tara. The provincial princes, with their respective forces, assembled at his call ; but had scarcely done so, when, owing to some contention, the northern contingent, under Mac Dunlevy, prince of Ulidia, withdrew. With the remainder, however, Roderick marched upon Ferns, the Lagenian capital, where M'Murrogh had entrenched himself. Roderick appears to have exhibited weakness and vacillation in the crisis, when boldness, promptitude, and vigor were so vitally requisite. He began to parley and diplomatise with M'Murrogh, who cunningly feigned willingness to agree to any terms ; for all he secretly desired was to gain time till Strongbow and the full force

wisely saw the danger of importing a foreign force into the country. He and the other princes really believed that the only object M'Murrogh had was to regain the sovereignty of Leinster.

The crafty and perfidious Diarmid in this treaty gained the object he sought—time. Scarcely had Roderick and the national forces retired, than the Leinster king, hearing that a further Norman contingent, under Maurice Fitzgerald, had landed at Wexford, marched upon Dublin—then held by the Danes under their prince Hasculf Mac Turkill, tributary to the Irish Ard-Ri—and set up a claim to the monarchy of Ireland. The struggle was now fully inaugurated. Soon after a third Norman force, under Raymond le Gros (or " the Fat"), landed in Waterford estuary, on the Wexford side, and hastily fortified themselves on the rock of Dundonolf, awaiting the main force under Strongbow.

And now we encounter the evil and terrible results of the riven and disorganized state of Ireland, to which I have already sufficiently adverted. The hour at last had come, when the curse was to work, when the punishment was to fall!

It was at such a moment as this—just as Roderick was again preparing to take the field to crush the more fully developed designs of Diarmid—that Donogh O'Brien, Prince of Thomond, chose to throw off allegiance to the Ard-Ri, and precipitate a civil war in the very face of a foreign invasion! Meanwhile, Strongbow was on the point of embarking at Milford Haven with a most formidable force, when king Henry, much mistrusting the adventurous and powerful knight—and having, secretly, his own designs about Ireland, which he feared the ambition of Strongbow, if successful, might thwart—imperatively forbade his sailing. Strongbow disregarded the royal mandate, and set sail with his fleet. He landed at Waterford (23rd August, 1171), and joined by the force of Raymond, which had been cooped up in their fort on the rock of Dundonolf, laid siege to the city. Waterford, like Dublin, was a Dano-Irish city, and was governed and commanded by Reginald, a prince of Danish race. The neighbor-

hurried to the assistance of the Danish citizens; and the city was defended with a heroism equal to that of the three hundred at Thermopylae. Again and again the assailants were hurled from the walls; but at length the Norman sieging skill prevailed; a breach was effected; the enemy poured into the town, and a scene of butchery shocking to contemplate ensued. Diarmid arrived just in time to congratulate Strongbow on this important victory. He had brought his daughter Eva with him, and amidst the smoking and bloodstained ruins of the city the nuptials of the Norman knight and the Irish princess were celebrated.

Strongbow and M'Murrogh now marched for Dublin. The Ard-Ri, who had meantime taken the field, made an effort to intercept them, but he was out-manœuvred, and they reached and commenced to siege the city. The citizens sought a parley. The fate of Waterford had struck terror into them. They dispatched to the besiegers' camp as negotiator or mediator their archbishop, Laurence, or Lorcan O'Tuahal, the first prelate of Dublin of Irish origin.

"This illustrious man, canonized both by sanctity and patriotism, was then in the thirty-ninth year of his age, and the ninth of his episcopate. His father was Lord of Imayle and chief of his clan; his sister had been wife of Dermid and mother of Eva, the prize bride of Earl Richard. He himself had been a hostage with Dermid in his youth, and afterwards abbot of Glendalough, the most celebrated monastic city of Leinster. He stood, therefore, to the besieged, being their chief pastor, in the relation of a father; to Dermid, and strangely enough to Strongbow also, as brother-in-law and uncle by marriage. A fitter ambassador could not be found.

"Maurice Regan, the 'Latiner,' or secretary of Dermid, had advanced to the walls and summoned the city to surrender, and deliver up 'thirty pledges' to his master their lawful prince. Asculph, son of Torcall, was in favor of the surrender, but the citizens could not agree among themselves as to hostages. No one was willing to trust himself to the notoriously untrustworthy Dermid. The archbishop was then

detail. He was received with all reverence in the camp, but
while he was deliberating with the commanders without, and
the townsmen were anxiously awaiting his return, Milo de
Cogan and Raymond the Fat, seizing the opportunity, broke
into the city at the head of their companies, and began to put
the inhabitants ruthlessly to the sword. They were soon followed by the whole force eager for massacre and pillage.
The Archbishop hastened back to endeavor to stay the havoc
which was being made of his people. He threw himself before the infuriated Irish and Normans, he threatened, he denounced, he bared his own breast to the swords of the assassins. All to little purpose: the blood fury exhausted itself
before peace settled over the city. Its Danish chief Asculph,
with many of his followers, escaped to their ships, and fled to
the Isle of Man and the Hebrides in search of succor and revenge. Roderick, unprepared to besiege the enemy who had
outmarched and outwitted him, at that season of the year—it
could not be earlier than October—broke up his encampment
at Clondalkin and retired to Connaught. Earl Richard having appointed De Cogan his governor of Dublin, followed on
the rear of the retreating Ard-Righ, at the instigation of
M'Murrogh, burning and plundering the churches of Kells,
Clonard, and Slane, and carrying off the hostages of East-
Meath."*

Roderick, having first vainly noticed M'Murrogh to return
to his allegiance on forfeit of the life of his hostage, beheaded
the son of Diarmid, who had been given as surety for his
father's good faith at the treaty of Ferns. Soon after
M'Murrogh himself died, and his end, as recorded in the
chronicles, was truly horrible. "His death, which took place
in less than a year after his sacrilegious church burnings in
Meath, is described as being accompanied by fearful evidence
of divine displeasure. He died intestate and without the
sacraments of the church. His disease was of some unknown
and loathsome kind, and was attended with insufferable pain,
which, acting on the naturally savage violence of his temper,

renaerea him so furious, that his ordinary attendants must have
been afraid to approach him, and his body become at once a
putrid mass, so that its presence above ground could not be
endured. Some historians suggest that this account of his
death may have been the invention of enemies, yet it is so
consistent with what we know of M'Murrogh's character
and career from other sources, as to be noways incredible.
He was at his death eighty-one years of age, and is known
in Irish history as Diarmaid-na-Gall, or Dermot of the
Foreigners."

An incident well calculated to win our admiration presents
itself, in the midst of the dismal chapter I have just sketched
in outline; an instance of chivalrous honor and good faith on
the part of a Norman lord in behalf of an Irish chieftain!
Maurice de Prendergast was deputed by Earl "Strongbow"
as envoy to Mac Gilla Patrick, prince of Ossory, charged to
invite him to a conference in the Norman camp. Prendergast
undertook to prevail upon the Ossorian prince to comply, on
receiving from Strongbow a solemn pledge that good faith
would be observed towards the Irish chief, and that he should
be free and safe coming and returning. Relying on this
pledge, Prendergast bore the invitation to Mac Gilla Patrick,
and prevailed upon him to accompany him to the earl. "Understanding, however, during the conference," says the historian, "treachery was about to be used towards Mac Gilla
Patrick, he rushed into Earl Strongbow's presence and, 'swore
by the cross of his sword that no man there that day should dare
lay hands on the king of Ossory.'" And well kept he his word.
Out of the camp, when the conference ended, rode the Irish
chief, and by his side, good sword in hand, that glorious type
of honor and chivalry, Prendergast, ever since named in Irish
tradition and history as "the Faithful Norman"—"faithful
among the faithless" we might truly say! Scrupulously did
he redeem his word to the Irish prince. He not only conducted him safely back to his own camp, but encountering on
the way a force belonging to Strongbow's ally, O'Brien, returning from a foray into Ossory, he attacked and defeated

118   THE STORY OF IRELAND.

old chronicler has it, "in the woods," the guest of the Irish chief, and next day returned to the English lines. This truly pleasing episode—this little oasis of chivalrous honor in the midst of a trackless expanse of treacherous and ruthless warfare has been made the subject of a short poem by Mr. Aubrey De Vere, in his *Lyrical Chronicle of Ireland:*

THE FAITHFUL NORMAN.

Praise to the valiant and faithful foe !
Give us noble foes, not the friend who lies !
We dread the drugged cup, not the open blow :
We dread the old hate in the new disguise.

To Ossory's king they had pledged their word :
He stood in their camp, and their pledge they broke;
Then Maurice the Norman upraised his sword :
The cross on its hilt he kiss'd, and spoke :

"So long as this sword or this arm hath might,
I swear by the cross which is lord of all
By the faith and honor of noble and knight,
Who touches you, prince, by this hand shall fall ! "

So side by side through the throng they pass'd ;
And Eire gave praise to the just and true,
Brave foe ! the past truth heals at last :
There is room in the great heart of Eire for you !

It is nigh seven hundred years since ' the faithful Norman " linked the name of Prendergast to honor and chivalry on Irish soil. Those who have read that truly remarkable work, Prendergast's *Cromwellian Settlement of Ireland*, will conclude that the spirit of Maurice is still to be found amongst some of those who bear his name.

"BARTERED AWAY!" THE NUPTIALS OF EVA AND STRONGBOW.

See page 115.

XIX.—HOW HENRY RECALLED THE ADVENTURERS. HOW HE CAME OVER HIMSELF TO PUNISH THEM AND BEFRIEND THE IRISH.

STRONGBOW having now assumed the sovereignty of Leinster, king Henry's jealousy burst into a flame. He issued a proclamation ordering Strongbow and every other Englishman in Ireland to return forthwith to England on pain of outlawry! Strongbow hurriedly despatched ambassador after ambassador to soothe Henry's anger; but all was vain. At length he hastened to England himself, and found the English sovereign assembling an enormous fleet and army with the intent of himself invading Ireland! The crafty knight humiliated himself to the utmost; yet it was with great difficulty the king was induced even to grant him audience. When he did, Strongbow, partly by his own most abject protestations of submission, and partly by the aid of mediators, received the royal pardon for his contumacy, and was confirmed in his grants of land in Wexford.

Early in October, 1171, Henry sailed with his armada of over four hundred ships, with a powerful army; and on the 18th of that month landed at Crooch, in Waterford harbor. In his train came the flower of the Norman knights, captains, and commanders; and even in the day of Ireland's greatest unity and strength she would have found it difficult to cope with the force which the English king now led into the land.

Coming in such kingly power, and with all the pomp and pageantry with which he was particularly careful to surround himself—studiously polished, politic, plausible, dignified, and courtier like towards such of the Irish princes as came within his presence—proclaiming himself by word and act angry with the lawless and ruthless proceedings of Strongbow, Raymond,

to the Irish of the neighborhood something like an illustrious deliverer! They had full and public knowledge of his strong proclamation against Strongbow and his companions, calling upon all the Norman auxiliaries of Dermot to *return forthwith to England on pain of outlawry.* On every occasion subsequent to his landing Henry manifested a like feeling and purpose ; so much so that the Irish of Wexford, who had taken Fitz-stephen prisoner, sent a deputation to deliver him up to be dealt with by Henry, and the king imprisoned him forthwith in Reginald's tower to await further sentence ! In fine, Henry pretended to come as an angry king to chastise his own contumacious subjects—the Norman auxiliaries of the Leinster prince—and to adjudicate upon the complicated issues which had arisen out of the treaties of that prince with them. This most smooth and plausible hypocrisy, kept up with admirable skill, threw the Irish utterly off their guard, and made them regard his visit as the reverse of hostile or undesirable. As I have already pointed out, the idea of national unity was practically defunct among the Irish at the time. For more than a hundred years it had been very much a game of " everyone for himself " (varied with "every man against every body else ") with them There was no stable or enduring national government or central authority in the land, since Brian's time. The nakedly hostile and sanguinary invasion of Strongbow, they were all ready enough, in their disintegrated and ill-organized way, to confront and bravely resist to the death ; and had Henry on this occasion really appeared to them to come as an invader, they would have instantly encountered him sword in hand ; a truth most amply proven by the fact that when subsequently (but *too late*) they found out the real nature of the English designs, not all the power of united, compact, and mighty England was able, for hundreds and hundreds of years, to subdue the broken and weakened, deceived and betrayed, but still heroic Irish nation.

Attracted by the fame of Henry's magnanimity, the splendor of his power, the (supposed) justice and friendliness of his intentions, the local princes one by one arrived at his tempor-

by the courtier affabilities, of the great English king. To several of them it seems very quickly to have occurred, that, considering the ruinously distracted and demoralized state of the country and the absence of any strong central governmental authority able to protect any one of them against the capricious lawlessness of his neighbors, the very best thing they could do—*possibly* for the interests of the whole country, *certainly* for their own particular personal or local interests— would be to constitute Henry a friendly arbitrator, regulator, and protector, on a much wider scale than (as *they* imagined) he intended. The wily Englishman only wanted the whisper of such a desirable pretext. It was just what he had been angling for. Yes; he, the mighty and magnanimous, the just and friendly, English sovereign would accept the position. They should all, to this end, recognize him as a nominal liege lord; and then he, on the other hand, would undertake to regulate all their differences, tranquillize the island, and guarantee to each individual secure possession of his own territory.

Thus, by a smooth and plausible diplomacy, Henry found himself, with the consent or at the request of the southern Irish princes, in a position which he never could have attained, except through seas of blood, if he had allowed them to suspect that he came as a hostile invader, not as a neighbor and powerful friend.

From Waterford he marched to Cashel, and from Cashel to Dublin, receiving on the way visits from the several local princes; and now that the news spread that the magnanimous English king had consented to be their arbitrator, protector, and liege lord, every one of them that once visited Henry went away wheedled into adhesion to the scheme. Amongst the rest was Donald O'Brien, prince of Thomond, who the more readily gave in his adhesion to the new idea, for that he, as I have already mentioned of him, had thrown off allegiance to Roderick, the titular Ard-Ri, and felt the necessity of protection by some one against the probable consequences of his conduct. Arrived at Dublin, Henry played the king on a still grander scale. A vast palace of wicker-work was erected* for his especial residence; and here, during the winter, he kept up a continued round of feasting, hospitality, pomp, and pageantry. Every effort was used to attract the Irish princes to the royal court, and once attracted thither, Henry made them the object of the most flattering attentions. They were made to feel painfully the contrast between the marked superiority in elegance, wealth, civilization—especially in new species of armor and weapons, and in new methods of war and military tactics—presented by the Norman-English, and the backwardness of their own country in each particular ; a change wrought, as they well knew, altogether or mainly within the last hundred and fifty years!

Where was the titular Ard-Ri all this time? Away in his western home, sullen and perplexed, scarcely knowing what to think of this singular and unprecedented turn of affairs. Henry tried hard to persuade Roderick to visit him ; but neither Roderick nor any of the northern princes could be persuaded to an interview with the English king. On the contrary, the Ard-Ri, when he heard that Henry was likely to come westward and visit him, instantly mustered an army and boldly took his stand at Athlone, resolved to defend the integrity and independence of at least his own territory. Henry, however, disclaimed the idea of conflict ; and, once again trusting more to smooth diplomacy than to the sword, despatched two ambassadors to the Irish titular monarch. The result was, according to some English versions of very doubtful and suspicious authority, that Roderick so far came in to the scheme of constituting Henry general suzeraine, as to agree to offer it no opposition on condition (readily acceded to by the ambassadors) that his own sovereignty, as, at least, next in supremacy to Henry, should be recognized. But there is no reliable proof that Roderick made any such concession, conditional or unconditional ; and most Irish historians reject the story.

Having spent the Christmas in Dublin, and devoted the

---

* On the spot where now stands the Protestant church of St. Andrew, St. Andrew Street, Dublin.

winter season to feasting and entertainment on a right royal scale, Henry now set about exercising his authority as general pacificator and regulator; and his first exercise of it was marked by that profound policy and sagacity which seem to have guided all his acts since he landed. He began, not by openly aggrandising himself or his followers—that might have excited suspicion—but by evidencing a deep and earnest solicitude for the state of religion in the country. This strengthened the opinion that estimated him as a noble, magnanimous, unselfish, and friendly protector, and it won for him the favor of the country. As his first exercise of general authority in the land, he convened a synod at Cashel; and at this synod, the decrees of which are known, measures were devised for the repression and correction of such abuses and irregularities in connection with religion as were known to exist in the country. Yet, strange to say, we find by the statutes and decrees of this synod nothing of a doctrinal nature requiring correction; nothing more serious calling for regulation than what is referred to in the following enactments then made :—

1. That the prohibition of marriage within the canonical degrees of consanguinity be enforced.

2. That children should be regularly catechized before the church door in each parish.

3. That children should be baptized in the public fonts of the parish churches.

4. That regular tithes should be paid to the clergy rather than irregular donations from time to time.

5. That church lands should be exempt from the exaction of "livery," etc.

6. That the clergy should not be liable to any share of the eric or blood-fine, levied off the kindred of a man guilty of homicide.

7. A decree regulating wills.

Such and no more were the reforms found to be necessary in the Irish Church under Henry's own eye, notwithstanding all the dreadful stories he had been hearing, and which he (not without addition by exaggeration) had been so carefully

however, require the confession, that the reason why there
was so little, comparatively, needing to be set right just then
was because there had been during, and ever since, St. Malachy's time vigorous efforts on the part of the Irish prelates,
priests, princes, and people themselves, to restore and repair
the ruins caused by long years of bloody convulsion.

The synod over, Henry next turned his attention to civil
affairs. He held a royal court at Lismore, whereat he made
numerous civil appointments and regulations for the government of the territories and cities possessed by the Norman
allies of the late prince of Leinster, or those surrendered by
Irish princes to himself.

While Henry was thus engaged in adroitly causing his
authority to be gradually recognized, respected, and obeyed
in the execution of peaceful, wise, and politic measures for the
general tranquillity and welfare of the country—for, from the
hour of his landing, he had not spilled one drop of Irish blood,
nor harshly treated a native of Ireland—he suddenly found
himself summoned to England by gathering troubles there.
Papal commissioners had arrived in his realm of Normandy
to investigate the murder of St. Thomas A'Becket, and threatening to lay England under an interdict, if Henry could not
clear or purge himself of guilty part in that foul deed.   There
was nothing for it, but to hasten thither with all speed, abandoning for the time his Irish plans and schemes, but taking the
best means he could to provide meantime for the retention of
his power and authority in the realm of Ireland.

I do not hesitate to express my opinion that, as the Normans had fastened at all upon Ireland, it was unfortunate that
Henry was called away at this juncture.   No one can for an
instant rank side by side the naked and heartless rapacity and
bloody ferocity of the Normans who proceded and who succeeded him in Ireland, with the moderation, the statesmanship,
and the tolerance exhibited by Henry while remaining here.
Much of this, doubtless, was policy on his part: but such a
policy, though it might result in bringing the kingdom of Ire-
and under the same crown with England many centuries

would have spared our country centuries of slaughter, persecution, and suffering unexampled in the annals of the world. There are abundant grounds for presuming that Henry's views and designs originally were wise and comprehensive, and certainly the reverse of sanguinary. *He* meant simply to win the sovereignty of another kingdom; but the spirit in which tne Normans who remained and who came after him in Ireland acted was that of mere freebooters—rapacious and merciless plunderers—whose sole redeeming trait was their indomitable pluck and undaunted bravery.

XX.—HOW HENRY MADE A TREATY WITH THE IRISH KING— AND DID NOT KEEP IT.

SOON the Irish began to learn the difference between king Henry's friendly courtesies and mild adjudications, and the rough iron-shod rule of his needy, covetous, and lawless lieutenants. On all sides the Normans commenced to encroach upon, outrage, and despoil the Irish, until, before three years had elapsed, Henry found all he had won in Ireland lost, and the English power there apparently at the last extremity. A signal defeat which Strongbow encountered in one of his insolent forays, at the hands of O'Brien, prince of Thomond, was the signal for a general assault upon the Normans. They were routed on all sides; Strongbow himself being chased into and cooped up with a few men in a fortified tower in Waterford. But this simultaneous outbreak lacked the unity of direction, the reach of purpose, and the perseverance which would cause it to accomplish permanent rather than transitory results. The Irish gave no thought to the necessity of following up their victories; and the Norman power, on the very point of extinction, was allowed slowly to recruit and extend itself again.

Henry was sorely displeased to find affairs in Ireland in this condition; but, of course, the versions which reached him

laid all the blame on the Irish, and represented the Norman settlers as meek and peaceful colonists driven to defend themselves
against treacherous savages. The English monarch, unable
to repair to Ireland himself, bethought him of the Papal letters, and resolved to try their influence on the Irish. He
accordingly commissioned William Fitzadelm De Burgo and
Nicholas, the prior of Wallingford, to proceed with these
documents to Ireland, and report to him on the true state of
affairs there. These royal commissioners duly reached that
country, and we are told that, having assembled the Irish prelates, the Papal letters were read. But no chronicle, English
or Irish, tells us what was said by the Irish bishops on hearing
them read. Very likely there were not wanting prelates to
point out that the Pope had been utterly misinformed and
kept in the dark as to the truth about Ireland; and that so
far the bulls were of no valid force as such; that as to the authority necessary to king Henry to effect the excellent designs
he professed, it had already been pretty generally yielded to
him for such purpose by the Irish princes themselves without
these letters at all: that, *for the purposes* and *on the conditions*
specified in the Papal letters, he was likely to receive every
coöperation from the Irish princes; but that it was quite another thing if he expected them to yield themselves up to be
plundered and enslaved—*that* they would resist for ever and
ever; and if there was to be peace, morality, or religion in the
land, it was his own Norman lords and governors he should
recall or curb.

Very much to this effect was the report of the royal commissioners when they returned, and as if to confirm the conclusion that these were the views of the Irish prelates and
princes at the time, we find the Irish monarch, Roderick, sending special ambassadors to king Henry to negotiate a formal
treaty, recording and regulating the relations which were to
exist between them. "In September, 1175," we are told, "the
Irish monarch sent over to England as his plenipotentiaries,
Catholicus O'Duffy, the archbishop of Tuam; Concors, abbot
of St. Brendan's of Clonfert; and a third, who is called Master Laurence, his chancellor, but who was no other than the

holy Archbishop of Dublin, as we know that that illustrious man was one of those who signed the treaty on this occasion. A great council was held at Windsor, within the octave of Michaelmas, and a treaty was agreed on, the articles of which were to the effect, that Roderick was to be king under Henry, rendering him service as his vassal ; that he was to hold his hereditary territory of Connaught in the same way as before the coming of Henry into Ireland ; that he was to have jurisdiction and dominion over the rest of the island, including its kings and princes, whom he should oblige to pay tribute, through his hands, to the king of England ; that these kings and princes were also to hold possession of their respective territories as long as they remained faithful to the king of England and paid their tribute to him ; that if they departed from their fealty to the king of England, Roderick was to judge and depose them, either by his own power, or, if that was not sufficient, by the aid of the Anglo-Norman authorities ; but that his jurisdiction should not extend to the territories occupied by the English settlers, which at a later period was called the English Pale, and comprised Meath and Leinster, Dublin with its dependent district, Waterford, and the country thence to Dungarvan.

The treaty between the two sovereigns, Roderick and Henry, clearly shows that the mere recognition of the English king as suzeraine was all that appeared to be claimed on the one side or yielded on the other. With this single exception or qualification, the native Irish power, authority, rights, and liberties, were fully and formally guaranteed. What Henry himself thought of the relations in which he stood by this treaty towards Ireland, and the sense in which he read its stipulations, is very intelligibly evidenced in the fact that he never styled, signed, or described himself as either king or lord of Ireland, in the documents reciting and referring to his relations with and towards that country.

But neither Henry nor his Norman barons kept the treaty. Like that made with Ireland by another English king, five hundred years later on, at Limerick, it was

I am inclined to credit Henry with having at one time intended to keep it. I think there are indications that he was in a certain sense coerced by his Norman lords into the abandonment, or at least the alteration, of his original policy, plans, and intentions as to Ireland, which were quite too peaceful and afforded too little scope for plunder to please those adventurers. In fact the barons revolted against the idea of not being allowed full scope for robbing the Irish; and one of them, De Courcy, resolved to fling the king's restrictions overboard, and set off on a conquering or freebooting expedition on his own account! A historian tells us that the royal commissioner Fitzadelm was quite unpopular with the colony. " His tastes were not military ; *he did not afford sufficient scope for spoliation;* and he was openly accused of *being too friendly to the Irish.* De Courcy, one of his aides in the government, became so disgusted with his inactivity, that he set out, in open defiance of the viceroy's prohibition, on an expedition to the north. Having selected a small army of twenty-two knights and three hundred soldiers, all picked men, to accompany him, by rapid marches he arrived the fourth day at Downpatrick, the chief city of Ulidia, and the clangor of his bugles ringing through the streets at the break of day, was the first intimation which the inhabitants received of this wholly unexpected incursion. In the alarm and confusion which ensued, the people became easy victims, and the English, after indulging their rage and rapacity, entrenched themselves in a corner of the city. Cardinal Vivian, who had come as legate from Pope Alexander the Third to the nations of Scotland and Ireland, and who had only recently arrived from the Isle of Man, happened to be then in Down, and was horrified at this act of aggression. He attempted to negotiate terms of peace, and proposed that De Courcy should withdraw his army on the condition of the Ulidians paying tribute to the English king; but any such terms being sternly rejected by De Courcy, the Cardinal encouraged and exhorted Mac Dunlevy, the king of Ulidia and Dalarania, to defend his territories manfully against the invaders. Coming as this advice did from

Ireland to king Henry the Second was regarded by the Pope himself."

It became clear that whatever policy or principles Henry might originally have thought of acting on in Ireland, he should abandon them and come into the scheme of the barons, which was, that he should give them free and full license for the plunder of the Irish, and they in return, would extend his realm. So we find the whole aim and spirit of the royal policy forthwith altered to meet the piratical views of the barons.

One of Roderick's sons, Murrogh, rebelled against and endeavored to depose his father (as the sons of Henry endeavored to dethrone *him* a few years subsequently), and Milo de Cogan, by the lord deputy's orders, led a Norman force into Connaught to aid the parricidal revolt! The Connacians, however, stood by their aged king, shrank from the rebellious son, and under the command of Roderick in person gave battle to the Normans at the Shannon. De Cogan and his Norman treaty-breakers and plunder-seekers were utterly and disastrously defeated; and Murrogh, the unnatural son, being captured, was tried for his offence by the assembled clans, and suffered the eric decreed by law for his crime.

This was the first deliberate rent in the treaty by the English. The next was by Henry himself, who, in violation of his kingly troth, undertook to dub his son John, yet a mere child, either lord or king of Ireland, and by those plausible deceits and diplomatic arts in which he proved himself a master, he obtained the approbation of the Pope for his proceeding. Quickly following upon these violations of the treaty of Windsor, and suddenly and completely changing the whole nature of the relations between the Irish and the Normans as previously laid down, Henry began to grant and assign away after the most wholesale fashion, the lands of the Irish, apportioning amongst his hungry followers whole territories yet unseen by an English eye! Naturalists tell how the paw of a tiger can touch with the softness of velvet or clutch with the force of a vice, according as the deadly

treated with the velvet smoothness ; they were now to be torn
by the lacerating fangs of that tiger grip to which they had
yielded themselves up so easily.

XXI.—DEATH-BED SCENES.

IT is a singular fact — one
which no historian can
avoid particularly noticing
—that every one of the
principal actors on the English
side in this eventful episode of the
first Anglo-Norman invasion, ended life violently, or under most
painful circumstances.

Murrogh the traitor died, as we have already seen, of a
mysterious disease, by which his body became putrid while
yet he lingered between life and death.   Strongbow died under somewhat similar circumstances ; an ulcer in his foot
spread upwards, and so eat away his body that it almost fell
to pieces.   Strongbow's son was slain by the father's hand.

horror. He died cursing with the most fearful maledictions his own sons! In vain the bishops and ecclesiastics surrounding his couch, horror-stricken, sought to prevail upon him to revoke these awful imprecations on his own offspring! *"Accursed be the day on which I was born; and accursed of God be the sons that I leave after me,"* were his last words.* Far different is the spectacle presented to us in the death-scene of the hapless Irish monarch Roderick! Misfortunes in every shape had indeed overwhelmed him, and in his last hours sorrows were multiplied to him. " Near the junction of Lough Corrib with Lough Mask, on the boundary line between Mayo and Galway, stand the ruins of the once populous monastery and village of Cong. The first Christian kings of Connaught had founded the monastery, or enabled St. Fechin to do so by their generous donations. The father of Roderick had enriched its shrine by the gift of a particle of the true cross, reverently enshrined in a reliquary, the workmanship of which still excites the admiration of antiquaries. Here Roderick retired in the seventieth year of his age, and for twelve years thereafter—until the 29th day of November, 1198—here he wept and prayed and withered away. Dead to the world, as the world to him, the opening of a new grave in the royal corner at Clonmacnoise was the last incident connected with his name which reminded Connaught that it had lost its once prosperous prince, and Ireland, that she had seen her last Ard-Righ, according to the ancient Milesian constitution. Powerful princes of his own and other houses the land was destined to know for many generations, before its sovereignty was merged in that of England, but none fully entitled to claim the high sounding but often fallacious title of Monarch of all Ireland."

One other death-bed scene, described to us by the same historian, one more picture from the Irish side, and we shall take our leave of this eventful chapter of Irish history, and the actors who moved in it. The last hours of Roderick's ambassador, the illustrious archbishop of Dublin, are thus

described: "From Rome he returned with legatine powers
which he used with great energy during the year 1180. In
the autumn of that year, he was intrusted with the delivery
to Henry the Second of the son of Roderick O'Conor, as a
pledge for the fulfilment of the treaty of Windsor, and with
other diplomatic functions. On reaching England he found
the king had gone to France, and following him thither, he
was seized with illness as he approached the monastery of Eu,
and with a prophetic foretaste of death, he exclaimed, as he
came in sight of the towers of the convert, 'Here shall I make
my resting place.' The Abbot Osbert and the monks of the
order of St. Victor received him tenderly and watched his
couch for the few days he yet lingered. Anxious to fulfil his
mission, he despatched David, tutor of the son of Roderick,
with messages to Henry, and awaited his return with
anxiety. David brought him a satisfactory response from the
English king, and the last anxiety only remained. In death,
as in life, his thoughts were with his country. 'Ah, foolish
and insensible people,' he exclaimed in his latest hours, 'what
will become of you? Who will relieve your miseries? Who
will heal you?' When recommended to make his last will he
answered with apostolic simplicity: 'God knows out of all
my revenues I have not a single coin to bequeath.' And thus
on the 11th of November, 1180, in the forty-eighth year of his
age, under the shelter of a Norman roof, surrounded by
Norman mourners, the Gaelic statesman-saint departed out
of this life bequeathing one more canonized memory to
Ireland and to Rome."

XXII.—HOW THE ANGLO-NORMAN COLONY FARED.

HAVE, in the foregoing pages, endeavored to narrate fully and minutely all the circumstances leading to, and attendant upon, the Anglo-Norman landing and settlement in this country, A.D. 1169-1172. It transcends in importance all other events in our history, having regard to ulterior and enduring consequences; and a clear and correct understanding of that event will furnish a key to the confused history of the troubled period which immediately succeeded it.

It is not my design to follow the formal histories of Ireland in relating at full length, and in consecutive detail, the events of the four centuries that succeeded the date of king Henry's landing. It was a period of such wild, confused, and chaotic struggle, that youthful readers would be hopelessly bewildered in the effort to keep its incidents minutely and consecutively remembered. Moreover, the history of those four centuries fully written out, would make a goodly volume in itself; a volume abounding with stirring incidents and effecting tragedies, and with episodes of valor and heroism, adventurous daring, and chivalrous patriotic devotion, not to be surpassed in the pages of romance. But the scope of my story forbids my dwelling at any great length upon the events of this period. Such of my readers as may desire to trace them in detail will find them succinctly related in the formal histories of Ireland. What I propose to do here, is to make my youthful readers acquainted with the general character, course, and progress of the struggle; the phases, changes, or mutations through which it passed; the aspects it presented, and the issues it contested, as each century rolled on, dwelling only upon events of comparative importance, and incidents illustrating the actions and the actors of the period.

king Henry's visit to Ireland—that event which Englishmen who write Irish history affect to regard as an "easy conquest" of our country. Let us see what the Normans have achieved by the end of one hundred years in Ireland. They required but *one year* to conquer England; and, accordingly, judging by all ordinary calculations and probabilities, we ought surely, in one hundred times that duration, to find Ireland as throughly subdued and as completely pacified as England had been in the twelvemonth that sufficed for its utter subjugation.

The nature of the struggle waged by the Anglo-Normans against Ireland during this period was rather peculiar. At no time was it an open and avowed effort to conquer Ireland as England had been conquered, though, as a matter of fact the military force engaged against the Irish throughout the period exceded that which had sufficed the Normans to conquer England. King Henry, as we have already seen, presented himself and his designs in no such hostile guise to the Irish. He seems to have concluded that broken and faction-spilt, disorganized and demoralized, as the Irish princes were, they would probably be rallied into union by the appearance of a nakedly hostile invasion, and he knew well that it would be easier to conquer a dozen Englands than to overcome this soldier race if only united against a common foe. So the crown of England did not, until long after this time, openly profess to pursue a *conquest* of Ireland, any more than it professed to pursue a conquest in India in the time of Clive. An Anglo-Norman colony was planted on the south-eastern corner of the island. This colony, which was well sustained from England, was to push its own fortunes, as it were, in Ireland, and to extend itself as rapidly as it could. To it, as ample excitement, sustainment, and recompense, was given, prospectively, the land to be taken from the Irish. The planting of such a colony—composed, as it was, of able, skilful, and desperate military adventurers—and the endowing of it, so to speak, with such rich prospect of plunder, was the establishment of a perpetual and self-acting mechanism for the gradual reduction of Ireland.

Against this colony the Irish warred in their own desultory

way, very much as they warred against each other, neither better nor worse ; and in the fierce warring of the Irish princes with each other, the Anglo-Norman colonists sided now with one, now with another ; nay, very frequently in such conflicts Anglo-Normans fought on *each* side !   The colony, however, had precisely that which the Irish needed—a supreme authority ever guiding it in the one purpose ; and it always felt strong in the consciousness that, at the worst, England was at its back, and that in its front lay, not the Irish nation, but the broken fragments of that once great and glorious power.

The Irish princes, meantime, each one for himself, fought away as usual, either against the Norman colonists or against some neighboring Irish chief.   Indeed, they may be described as fighting each other with one hand, and fighting England with the other !   Quite as curious is the fact, that in all their struggles with the latter, they seem to have been ready enough to admit the honorary lordship or suzerainty of the English king, but resolved to resist to the death the Norman encroachments beyond the cities and lands to the possession of which they had attained by reason of their treaties with, or successes under Dermott M'Murrogh.   The fight was all for the soil. Then, as in our own times, the battle cry was " Land or Life !"

But the English power had two modes of action ; and when one failed the other was tried.   As long as the rapacious freebooting of the barons was working profitably, not only for themselves but for the king, it was all very well.   But when that policy resulted in arousing the Irish to successful resistance, and the freebooters were being routed everywhere, or when they had learned to think too much to their own profit and too little of the king's, then his English majesty could take to the *role* of magnanimous friend, protector, or suzeraine of the Irish princes, and angry punisher of the rapacious Norman barons.

We have already seen that when Henry the Second visited Ireland it was (pretendedly at least) in the character of a justminded king, who came to chastise his own subjects, the Norman settlers.   When next an English king visited these shores,

and during his entire stay in this country he was occupied,
not in wars or conflicts with the Irish ; quite the contrary—
in chastising the most powerful and presumptuous of the great
Norman lords ! What wonder that the Irish princes were
confirmed in the old idea, impressed upon them by king Henry's words and actions, that though in the Norman barons,
they had to deal with savage and merciless spoliators, in the
English king they had a friendly suzeraine ? As a matter of
fact, the Irish princes who had fought most stoutly and victoriously against the Normans up to the date of John's arrival, at once joined their armies to his, and at the head of this
combined force the English king proceeded to overthrow
the most piratical and powerful of the barons! Says M‘Gee :
"The visit of king John, which lasted from the 20th of June
to the 25th of August, was mainly directed to the reduction
of those intractable Anglo-Irish princes whom Fitz-Henry
and Gray had proved themselves unable to cope with. Of
these the De Lacys of Meath were the most obnoxious. They
not only assumed an independent state, but had sheltered de
Braos, lord of Brecknock, one of the recusant barons of Wales,
and refused to surrender him on the royal summons. To assert his authority and to strike terror into the nobles of other
possessions, John crossed the channel with a prodigious fleet
—in the Irish annals said to consist of seven hundred sail.
He landed at Crook, reached Dublin, and prepared at once
to subdue the Lacys. With his own army, and the coöperation of Cathal O'Conor, he drove out Walter de Lacy, Lord
of Meath, who fled to his brother, Hugh de Lacy since de
Courcy's disgrace, Earl of Ulster. From Meath into Louth
John pursued the brothers, crossing the lough at Carlingford
with his ships, which must have coasted in his company.
From Carlingford they retreated, and he pursued to Carrickfergus, and that fortress, being unable to resist a royal fleet
and navy, they fled into Man or Scotland, and thence escaped
in disguise into France. With their guest de Braos, they
wrought as gardeners in the grounds of the Abbey of Saint
Taurin Evreux, until the abbot, having discovered by their

John for their restoration to their estates. Walter agreed to pay a fine of 2,500 marks for his lordship in Meath, and Hugh 4,000 for his possessions in Ulster. Of de Braos we have no particulars ; his high-spirited wife and children were thought to have been starved to death by order of the unforgiving tyrant in one of his castles.

In the next succeeding reign (that of Henry the Third), we find a like impression existing and encouraged amongst the Irish princes; the king of Connacht proceeding to England and complaining to the king of the unjust, oppressive, and rapacious conduct of the barons. And we find king Henry ordering him substantial redress, writing to his lord justice in Ireland, Maurice Fitzgerald, to "pluck up by the root" the powerful De Burgo, who lorded it over all the west. There is still in existence a letter written by the Connacian king to Henry the Third, thanking him for the many favors he had conferred upon him, but particularly for this one.

XXIII.—" THE MER THAT CONQUERED." THE STORY OF GOD-
FREY OF TYRCONNELL.

HAVE remarked that the Irish chiefs may be said to
have fought each other with one hand, while they
fought the English with the other. Illustrating this
state of things, I may refer to the story of Godfrey,
prince of Tyrconnell—as glorious a character as ever
adorned the page of history. For years the Normans had
striven in vain to gain a foot-hold in Tyrconnell. Elsewhere—
in Connacht, in Munster, throughout all Leinster, and in
southern Ulster—they could betimes assert their sway, either
by dint of arms or insidious diplomatic strategy! But never
could they over-reach the wary and martial Cinel-Connal,
from whom more than once the Norman armies had suffered
overthrow. At length the lord justice, Maurice Fitzgerald,
felt that this hitherto invulnerable fortress of native Irish
power in the north-west had become a formidable standing
peril to the entire English colony ; and it was accordingly resolved that the whole strength of the Anglo-Norman force
in Ireland should be put forth in one grand expedition against
it! and this expedition the lord justice decided that he himself would lead and command in person! At this time Tyrconnell was ruled by a prince who was the soul of chivalric
bravery, wise in council, and daring in the field—Godfrey
O'Donnell. The lord justice, while assembling his forces,
employed the time, moreover, in skilfully diplomatizing, playing the insidious game which, in every century, most largely
helped the Anglo-Norman interest in Ireland—setting up
rivalries and inciting hostilities amongst the Irish princes!
Having, as he thought, not only cut off Godfrey from all
chance of alliance or support from his fellow-princes of the

Fitzgerald marched on Tyrconnell. His army moved with all the pomp and panoply of Norman pride. Lords, earls, knights, and squires, from every Norman castle or settlement in the land, had rallied at the summons of the king's representative. Godfrey, isolated though he found himself, was nothing daunted by the tremendous odds which he knew were against him. He was conscious of his own military superiority to any of the Norman lords yet sent against him— he was in fact one of the most skilful captains of the age—and he relied implicitly on the unconquerable bravery of his clansmen. Both armies met at Credan-kille in the north of Sligo. A battle which the Normans describe as fiercely and vehemently contested, ensued and raged for hours without palpable advantage to either side. In vain the mail-clad battalions of England rushed upon the saffron-kilted Irish clansmen; each time they reeled from the shock and fled in bloody rout! In vain the cavalry squadrons—long the boasted pride of the Normans—headed by earls and knights whose names were rallying cries in Norman England, swept upon the Irish lines! Riderless horses alone returned,

"Their nostrils all red with the sign of despair."

The lord justice in wild dismay saw the proudest army ever rallied by Norman power on Irish soil, being routed and hewn piecemeal before his eyes! Godfrey, on the other hand, the very impersonation of valor, was everywhere cheering his men, directing the battle and dealing destruction to the Normans. The gleam of his battle-axe or the flash of his sword, was the sure precursor of death to the haughtiest earl or knight that dared to confront him. The lord justice—than whom no abler general or braver soldier served the king— saw that the day was lost if he could not save it by some desperate effort, and at the worst he had no wish to survive the overthrow of the splendid army he had led into the field. The flower of the Norman nobles had fallen under the sword of Godfrey, and him the Lord Maurice now sought out, dash-

single combat. Fitzgerald dealt the Tyrconnell chief a deadly wound; but Godfrey, still keeping his seat, with one blow of his battle-axe, clove the lord justice to the earth and the proud baron was carried senseless off the field by his followers. The English fled in hopeless confusion and of them the chroniclers tell us there was made a slaughter that night's darkness alone arrested. The Lord Maurice was done with pomp and power after the ruin of that day. He survived his dreadful wound for some time; he retired into a Franciscan monastery which he himself had built and endowed at Youghal, and there taking the habit of a monk, he departed this life tranquilly in the bosom of religion. Godfrey, meanwhile, mortally wounded, was unable to follow up quickly the great victory of Credan-kille; but stricken as he was, and with life ebbing fast, he did not disband his army till he had demolished the only castle the English had dared to raise on the soil of Tyrconnell. This being done, and the last soldier of England chased beyond the frontier line, he gave the order for dispersion, and himself was borne homewards to die.

This, however, sad to tell, was the moment seized upon by O'Neill, prince of Tyrone, to wrest from the Cinel-Connall submission to his power! Hearing that the lion-hearted Godfrey lay dying, and while yet the Tyrconnellian clans, disbanded and on their homeward roads, were suffering from their recent engagement with the Normans, O'Neill sent envoys to the dying prince demanding hostages in token of submission? The envoys, say all the historians, no sooner delivered this message than they fled for their lives! Dying though Godfrey was, and broken and wounded as were his clansmen by their recent glorious struggle the messengers of Tirowen felt but too forcibly the peril of delivering this insolent demand! And characteristically was it answered by Godfrey! His only reply was to order an instantaneous muster of all the fighting men of Tyrconnell. The army of Tyrowen meanwhile pressed forward rapidly to strike the Cinel-Connal, if possible, before their available strength, such as it was, could be rallied. Nevertheless, they found the quickly re-assembled victors of Credan-kille awaiting them.

But alas, sorrowful story! On the morning of the battle,
death had but too plainly set his seal upon the brow of the
heroic Godfrey! As the troops were being drawn up in line,
ready to march into the field, the physicians announced that
his last moments were at hand; he had but a few hours to
live! Godfrey himself received the information with sublime
composure. Having first received the last sacraments of the
Church, and given minute instructions as to the order of battle,
*he directed that he should be laid upon the bier which was to have
borne him to the grave; and that thus he should be carried at the
head of his army on their march!* His orders were obeyed,
and then was witnessed a scene for which history has not a
parallel! The dying king, laid on his bier, was borne at the
head of his troops into the field! After the bier came the
standard of Godfrey—on which was emblazoned a cross with
the words, *In hoc signo vinces**—and next came the charger of

---

* On the banner and shield of Tyrconnel were emblazoned a Cross surrounded by
the words *In hoc signo vinces.* One readily inclines to the conjecture that this was
borrowed from the Roman emperor Constantine. The words may have been ; but
amongst the treasured traditions of the Cinel-Connal was one which there is reason
for regarding as historically reliable, assigning to an interesting circumstance the adoption by them of the Cross as the armorial bearings of the sept. One of the earliest
of St. Patrick's converts was Conall Crievan, brother of Ard-Ri-Laori, and ancestor
of the Cinel-Connall. Conall was a prince famed for his courage and bravery, and
much attached to military pursuits ; but on his conversion he desired to become a
priest ; preferring his request to this effect to St. Patrick, when either baptizing or
confirming him. The saint, however, commanded him to remain a soldier ; but to
fight henceforth as became a Christian warrior ; "and under this sign serve and conquer," said the saint, raising the iron-pointed end of the "Staff of Jesus," and marking
on the shield of Conall a cross. The shield thus marked by St. Patrick's crozier was
ever called "Sciath Bachlach," or the "Shield of the Crozier." Mr. Aubrey de Vere
very truly calls this the "inauguration of Irish (Christian) chivalry," and has made
the incident the subject of the following poem:—

ST. PATRICK AND THE KNIGHT.

"Thou shalt not be a priest," he said ;
 "Christ hath for thee a lowlier task :
Be thou his *soldier !* Wear with dread
 His cross upon thy shield and casque !
Put on God's armor, faithful knight !
 Mercy with justice, love with law ;
Nor e'er, except for truth and right,
 This sword, cross hilted, dare to draw."

He spake, and with his crozier pointed
Graved on the broad shield's brazen boss

the dying king, caparisoned as if for battle! But Godfrey's last fight was fought! Never more was that charger to bear him where the sword-blows fell thickest. Never more would his battle-axe gleam in the front of the combat. But as if his presence, living, dead, or dying, was still a potential assurance of triumph to his people, the Cinel-Connal bore down all opposition. Long and fiercely, but vainly, the army of Tyrowen contested the field. Around the bier of Godfrey his faithful clansmen made an adamantine rampart which no foe could penetrate. Wherever it was borne, the Tyrconnel phalanx, of which it was the heart and centre, swept all before them. At length when the foe was flying on all sides, they laid the bier upon the ground to tell the king that the day was won. But the face of Godfrey was marble pale, and cold and motionless! All was over! His heroic spirit had departed amidst his people's shouts of victory!

Several poems have been written on this tragic yet glorious episode. That from which I take the following passages, is generally accounted the best : *—

> All worn and wan, and sore with wounds from Credan's bloody fray
> In Donegal for weary months the proud O'Donnell lay ;
> Around his couch in bitter grief his trusty clansmen wait,
> And silent watch, with aching hearts, his faint and feeble state.

The chief asks one evening to be brought into the open air, that he may gaze once more on the landscape's familiar scenes :—

> " And see the stag upon the hills, the white clouds drifting by :
> And feel upon my wasted cheek God's sunshine ere I die."

Suddenly he starts on his pallet, and exclaims:

> " A war-steed's tramp is on the heath, and onward cometh fast,
> And by the rood ! a trumpet sounds ! hark ! 'tis the Red Hand's blast !"
> And soon a kern all breathless ran, and told a stranger train
> Across the heath was spurring fast, and then in sight it came.

> (That hour baptized, confirmed, anointed,
> S'ood Erin's chivalry) the Cross :
> And there was heard a whisper low—
> (St. Michael, was that whisper thine ?)—
> Thou sword, keep pure thy virgin vow,
> And trenchant thou shalt be as mine.

* The name of the author is unknown.

GODFREY OF TYRCONNELL BORNE INTO BATTLE.

See page 143.

"Go, bring me, quick, my father's sword," the noble chieftain said ;
" My mantle o'er my shoulders fling, place helmet on my head ;
And raise me to my feet, for ne'er shall clansmen of my foe
Go boasting tell in far Tyrone he saw O'Donnell low."

The envoys of O'Neill arrive in Godfrey's presence, and
deliver their message, demanding tribute :

" A hundred hawks from out your woods, all trained their prey to get ;
A hundred steeds from off your hills, uncrossed by rider yet ;
A hundred kine from off your hills, the best your land doth know ;
A hundred hounds from out your halls, to hunt the stag and roe."

Godfrey, however, is resolved to let his foes, be they Norman or native, know that, though dying, he is not dead yet.
He orders a levy of all the fighting men of Tyrconnel :—

"Go call around Tyrconnell's chief my warriors tried and true,
Send forth a friend to Donal More, a scout to Lisnahue ;
Light baal-fires quick on Esker's towers, that all the land may know
O'Donnell needeth help and haste to meet his haughty foe.

"Oh, could I but my people head, or wield once more a spear,
Saint Angus ! but we'd hunt their hosts like herds of fallow deer.
But vain the wish, since I am now a faint and failing man ;
Yet, ye shall bear me to the field, in the centre of my clan.

"Right in the midst, and lest, perchance upon the march I die,
In my coffin ye shall place me, uncovered let me lie ;
And swear ye now, my body cold shall never rest in clay,
Until you drive from Donegal O'Niall's host away."

Then sad and stern, with hand on skian, that solemn oath they swore,
And in a coffin placed their chief and on a litter bore.
Tho' ebbing fast his life-throbs came, yet dauntless in his mood,
He marshalled well Tyrconnell's chiefs, like leader wise and good

*   *   *   *   *   *   *

Lough Swilly's sides are thick with spears, O'Niall's host is there,
And proud and gay their battle sheen, their banners float the air ;
And haughtily a challenge bold their trumpets bloweth free,
When winding down the heath-clad hills, O'Donnell's band they see !

No answer back those warriors gave, but sternly on they stept,
And in their centre, curtained black, a litter close is kept ;
And all their host it guideth fair, as did in Galilee
Proud Judah's tribes the Ark of God, when crossing Egypt's sea.

Then rose the roar of battle loud, as clan met clan in fight ;
The axe and skian grew red with blood, a sad and woful sight ;
Yet in the midst o'er all, unmoved, that litter black is seen,

Yet once, when blenching back fierce Bryan's charge before,
Tyrconnell wavered in its ranks, and all was nearly o'er,
Aside those curtains wide were flung, and plainly to the view
Each host beheld O'Donnell there, all pale and wan in hue.

And to his tribes he stretch'd his hands—then pointed to the foe,
When with a shout they rally round, and on Clan Hugh they go ;
And back they beat their horsemen fierce and in a column deep,
With O'Donnell in their foremost rank, in one fierce charge they sweep.
　　*　　　*　　　*　　　*　　　*　　　*
Lough Swilly's banks are thick with spears !—O'Niall's host is there,
But rent and tost like tempest clouds —Clan O'Donnell in the rear !
Lough Swilly's waves are red with blood, as madly in its tide
O'Niall's horsemen wildly plunge, to reach the other side.

And broken is Tyrowen's pride, and vanquished Clannaboy,
And there is wailing thro' the land, from Bann to Aughnacloy.
The red hand's crest is bent in grief, upon its shield a stain,
For its stoutest clans are broken, its stoutest chiefs are slain.

And proud and high Tyrconnell shouts ; but blending on the gale,
Upon the ear ascendeth a sad and sullen wail,
For on that field, as back they bore, from chasing of the foe,
The spirit of O'Donnell fled !—oh, woe for Ulster, woe !

Yet died he there all gloriously—a victor in the fight ;
A chieftain at his people's head, a warrior in his might ;
They dug him there a fitting grave upon that field of pride,
And a lofty cairn raised above, by fair Lough Swilly's side.

In this story of Godfrey of Tyrconnell we have a perfect
illustration of the state of affairs in Ireland at the time.
Studying it, no one can marvel that the English power eventually prevailed ; but many may wonder that the struggle
lasted so many centuries. What Irishman can contemplate
without sorrow the spectacle of those brave soldiers of Tyrconnell and their heroic prince, after contending with, and
defeating, the concentrated power of the Anglo-Norman settlement, called upon to hurriedly re-unite their broken and
wounded ranks that they might fight yet another battle against
fresh foes—those foes their own countrymen ! Only amongst
a people given over to the madness that precedes destruction
could conduct like that of O'Neill be exhibited. At a moment
when Godfrey and his battle-wounded clansmen had routed

weakened after such a desperate combat—at a moment when they should have been hailed with acclaim, and greeted with aid and succor by every chief and clan in Ireland—they are foully taken at disadvantage, and called upon to fight anew, by their own fellow-countrymen and neighbors of Tyrowen!

The conduct of O'Neill on this occasion was a fair sample of the prevailing practice amongst the Irish princes. Faction-split to the last degree, each one sought merely his own personal advantage or ambition. Nationality and patriotism were sentiments no longer understood. Bravely in battle, dauntless courage, heroic endurance, marvellous skill, we find them displaying to the last ; but the higher political virtues, so essential to the existence of a nation—unity of purpose and of action against a common foe—recognition of and obedience to a central national authority—were utterly absent. Let us own in sorrow that a people amongst whom such conduct as that of O'Neill towards Godfrey of Tyconnell was not only possible but of frequent occurrence, deserved subjection—invited it—rendered it inevitable. Nations, like individuals, must expect the penalty of disregarding the first essentials to existence. " Eternal vigilance is the price of liberty." Factionism like that of the Irish princes found its sure punishment in subjugation.

XXIV.—HOW THE IRISH NATION AWOKE FROM ITS TRANCE, AND FLUNG OFF ITS CHAINS. THE CAREER OF KING EDWARD BRUCE.

ARLY in the second century of the Norman settlement we find the Irish for the first time apparently realizing their true position in relation to England. They begin to appreciate the fact that it is England and not the Anglo-Norman colony they have to combat, and that recognition of the English power means loss of liberty, loss of honor, loss of property, alienation of the soil! Had the Irish awakened sooner to these facts, it is just possible they might have exerted themselves and combined in a national struggle against the fate thus presaged. But they awoke to them too late—

> The fatal chain was o'er them cast,
> And they were men no more !

As if to quicken within them the stings of self-reproach, they saw their Gaelic kinsmen of Caledonia bravely battling in compact national array against this same English power that had for a time conquered them also. When king Edward marched northward to measure swords with the Scottish "rebel," Robert Bruce, he summoned his Norman lieges and all other true and loyal subjects in Ireland to send him aid. The Anglo-Norman lords of Ireland did accordingly equip considerable bodies, and with them joined the king in Scotland. The native Irish, on the other hand, sent aid to Bruce ; and on the field of Bannockburn old foes on Irish soil met once more in deadly combat on new ground—the Norman lords and the Irish chieftains. "Twenty-one clans, Highlanders and Islesmen, and many Ulstermen fought on the side of Bruce on the field of Bannockburn. The grant of ' Kincar-line-O'Neill,' made by the victor-king to his Irish followers, remains a striking evidence of their fidelity to his person and their sacrifices in his cause. The result of that glorious day was, by the testimony of all historians, English as well as Scottish, received with enthusiasm on the Irish side of the channel." *

Fired by the glorious example of their Scottish kinsmen, the native Irish princes for the first time took up the design of a really national and united effort to expel the English invaders root and branch. Utterly unused to union or combination as they had been for hundreds of years, it is really wonderful how readily and successfully they carried out their design. The northern Irish princes with few exceptions entered into it; and it was agreed that as well to secure the prestige of Bruce's name and the alliance of Scotland, as also to avoid native Irish jealousies in submitting to a national leader or king, Edward Bruce, the brother of king Robert, should be invited to land in Ireland with an auxiliary liberating army, and should be recognized as king. The Ulster princes, with Donald O'Neill at their head, sent off a memorial to the Pope (John the Twelfth), a document which is still extant, and is, as may be supposed, of singular interest and importance. In this memorable letter the Irish princes acquaint his Holiness with their national design; and having reference to the bulls or letters of popes Adrian and Alexander, they proceed to justify their resolution of destroying the hated English power in their country, and point out the fraud and false pretence upon which those documents were obtained by king Henry from the pontiffs named. The sovereign pontiff appears to have been profoundly moved by the recital of facts in this remonstrance or memorial. Not long after he addressed to the English king (Edward the Third) a letter forcibly reproaching the English sovereigns who had obtained those bulls from popes Adrian and Alexander, with the crimes of deceit and violation of their specific conditions and covenants. To the objects of those bulls, his Holiness says, "neither king Henry nor his successors paid any regard; but, passing the bounds that had been prescribed for them, they had heaped upon the

Irish the most unheard-of miseries and persecutions, and had during a long period, imposed on them *a yoke of slavery which could not be borne.*

The Irish themselves were now, however, about to make a brave effort to break that unbearable yoke, to terminate those miseries and persecutions, and to establish a national throne once more in the land. On the 25th May, 1315, Edward Bruce, the invited deliverer, landed near Glenarm in Antrim, with a force of six thousand men. He was instantly joined by Donald O'Neill, prince of Ulster, and throughout all the northern half of the island the most intense excitement spread. The native Irish flocked to Bruce's standard ; the Anglo-Normans, in dismay, hurried from all parts to encounter this truly formidable danger, and suceeded in compelling, or inducing the Connacian prince, O'Conor, to join them. Meanwhile the Scoto-Irish army marched southward, defeating every attempt of the local English garrisons to obstruct its victorious progress. The lord justice, coming from Dublin with all the forces he could bring from the south, and Richard de Burgo, Anglo-Norman titular earl of Ulster, hurrying from Athlone with a powerful contingent raised in the west, came up with the national army at Ardee, too late, however, to save that town, which the Irish had just captured and destroyed. This Earl Richard is known in Anglo-Irish history as "the Red Earl." He was the most prominent character, and in every sense the greatest—the ablest and most powerful and influential—man of that century amongst the Anglo-Norman rulers or nobles. As a matter of fact, his influence and power overtopped and over-shadowed that of the lord justice ; and, singular to relate, the king's letters and writes, coming to Ireland, were invariably, as a matter of form, addressed to him in the first instance, that is, his name came first, and that of the lord justice for the time being next. He was, in truth, king of the Anglo-Normans in Ireland. He raised armies, levied war, made treaties, conferred titles, and bestowed lands, without the least reference to the formal royal deputy—the lord justice in Dublin—whom he looked down upon with disdain. Accordingly, when these two magnates met on this occasion,

him back to his castle of Dublin as quickly as he pleased, for
that he himself, Earl Richard, as befitted his title rank of earl
of Ulster, would take in hands the work of clearing the province of the Scottish-Irish army, and would guarantee to deliver Edward Bruce, living or dead, into the justice's hands
ere many days. Notwithstanding this haughty speech, the lord
justice and his forces remained, and the combined army now
confronted Bruce, outnumbering him hopelessly; whereupon
he commenced to retreat slowly, his object being to effect,
either by military strategy or diplomacy, a separation of the
enemy's forces. This object was soon accomplished. When
the Connacian king, Felim O'Connor, joined the Red Earl, and
marched against Bruce, in his own principality his act was
revolted against as parricidal treason. Ruari, son of Cathal
Roe O'Conor, head of the Clanna-Murtough, unfurled the
national flag, declared for the national cause, and soon struck
for it boldly and decisively. Hurriedly despatching envoys
to Bruce tendering adhesion, and requesting to be commissioned or recognized as prince of Connact in place of Felim,
who had forfeited by fighting against his country at such a
crisis, he meanwhile swept through all the west, tearing down
the Norman rule and erecting in its stead the national authority,
declaring the penalty of high treason against all who favored
or sided with the Norman enemy or refused to aid the national
cause. Felim heard of these proceedings before Ruari's envoys reached Bruce, and quickly saw that his only chance of
safety—and in truth the course most in consonance with his
secret feelings—was, himself, to make overtures to Bruce,
which he did ; so that about the time Ruari's envoys arrived,
Felim's offers were also before the Scoto-Irish commander.
Valuable as were Ruari's services in the west, the greater and
more urgent consideration was to detach Felim from the
Norman army, which thus might be fought, but which otherwise could not be withstood. Accordingly, Bruce came to
terms with Felim, and answered to Ruari that he was in no
way to molest the possessions of Felim, who was now on the
right side, but to take all he could from the common enemy

ward, whereupon Bruce and O'Neill, no longer afraid to encounter the enemy, though still superior to them in numbers,
gave battle to the lord justice. A desperate engagement
ensued at Connoyr, on the banks of the river Bann, near
Ballymena. The great Norman army was defeated; the
haughty Earl Richard was obliged to seek personal safety in
flight; his brother, William, with quite a number of other
Norman knights and nobles, being taken prisoners by that
same soldier-chief whom he had arrogantly undertaken to
capture and present, dead or alive, within a few days, at
Dublin Castle gate! The shattered forces of the lord justice
retreated southward as best they could. The Red Earl fled
into Connact, where, for a year, he was fain to seek safety
in comparative obscurity, shorn of all power, pomp, and possessions. Of these, what he had not lost on the battle field at
Connoyre, he found wrested from him by the Prince of
Tyrconnel, who, by way of giving the Red Earl something
to do near home, had burst down upon the Anglo-Norman
possessions in the west, and levelled every castle that flew
the red flag of England! The Irish army now marched
southward once more, capturing all the great towns and
Norman castles on the way. At Loughsweedy, in Westmeath,
Bruce and O'Neill went into winter quarters, and spent their
Christmas " in the midst of the most considerable chiefs of
Ulster, Meath, and Connact."

Thus closed the first campaign in this, the first really national war undertaken against the English power in Ireland. "The
termination of his first campaign on Irish soil," says a historian,
" might be considered highly favorable to Bruce. More than
·   half the clans had risen, and others were certain to follow
their example; the clergy were almost wholly with him, and
his heroic brother had promised to lead an army to his aid
in the ensuing spring."

In the early spring of the succeeding year (1316) he opened
the next campaign by a march southwards. The Anglo-
Norman armies made several ineffectual efforts to bar his
progress. At Kells, in King's County of the present day,

utterly routing this the last army of any proportions now op-posed to them. Soon after this decisive victory, Bruce and O' Neill returned northwards in proud exultation. Already it seemed that the liberation of Ireland was complete. Hav-ing arrived at Dundalk, the national army halted, and prepar-ations were commenced for the great ceremonial that was to consummate and commemorate the national deliverance. At a solemn council of the native princes and chiefs, Edward Bruce was elected king of Ireland ; Donald O'Neill, the heart 'and head of the entire movement, formally resigning by letters patent in favor of Bruce such rights as belonged to him as son of the last acknowledged native sovereign. After the election, the ceremonial of inauguration was carried out in the native Irish forms, with a pomp and splendor such as had not been wit-nessed since the reign of Brian the First. This imposing ceremony took place on the hill of Knocknemelan, within a mile of Dundalk ; and the formal election and inauguration being over, the king and the assembled princes and chiefs marched in procession into the town, where the solemn consecration took place in one of the churches. King Edward now established his court in the castle of Northburg, possessing and exercising all the prerogatives, powers, and privileges of royalty, holding courts of justice, and enforcing such regulations as were necessary for the welfare and good order of the country.

XXV.—HOW THIS BRIGHT DAY OF INDEPENDENCE WAS TURNED
    TO GLOOM. HOW THE SEASONS FOUGHT AGAINST IRELAND,
    AND FAMINE FOR ENGLAND.

THE Anglo-Irish power was almost extinct. It would
    probably never more have been heard of, and the
    newly-revived nationality would have lasted long,
    and prospered, had there not been behind that bro-
ken and ruined colony all the resources of a great and powerful nation. The English monarch summoned to a conference
with himself in London several of the Anglo-Irish barons,
and it was agreed by all that nothing but a compact union
amongst themselves, strong reinforcements from England,
and the equipment of an army of great magnitude for a new
campaign in Ireland, could avert the complete and final extinction of the English power in that country. Preparations
were accordingly made for placing in the field such an army
as had never before been assembled by the Anglo-Irish colony.
King Edward of Ireland, on the other hand, was fully conscious
that the next campaign would be the supreme trial, and both
parties, English and Irish, prepared to put forth their utmost
strength. True to his promise, king Robert of Scotland arrived to the aid of his brother, bringing with him a small
contingent. The royal brothers soon opened the campaign.
Marching southwards at the head of thirty-six thousand men,
they crossed the Boyne at Slane, and soon were beneath the
walls of Castleknock, a powerful Anglo-Norman fortress,
barely three miles from the gate of Dublin. Castleknock was
assaulted and taken, the governor Hugh Tyrell being made
prisoner. The Irish and Scotch kings took up their quarters
in the castle, and the Anglo-Normans of Dublin, gazing from
the city walls, could see between them and the setting sun
the royal standards of Ireland and Scotland floating proudly

ited a spirit of indomitable courage and determination. To their action in this emergency—designated by some as the desperation of wild panic, but by others, in my opinion more justly, intrepidity and heroic public spirit—they saved the chief seat of Anglo-Norman authority and power, the loss of which at that moment would have altered the whole fate and fortunes of the ensuing campaign. Led on by the mayor, they exhibited a frantic spirit of resistance, burning down the suburbs of their city, and freely devoting to demolition even their churches and priories outside the walls, lest these should afford shelter or advantage to a besieging army. The Irish army had no sieging materials, and could not just then pause for the tedious operations of reducing a walled and fortified city like Dublin, especially when such a spirit of vehement determination was evinced not merely by the garrison but by the citizens themselves. In fact, the city could not be infested without the coöperation of a powerful fleet to cut off supplies by sea from England. The Irish army, therefore, was compelled to turn away from Dublin, and leave that formidable position intact in their rear. They marched southward as in the previous campaigns, this time reaching as far as Limerick. Again, as before, victory followed their banners. Their course was literally a succession of splendid achievements. The Normans never offered battle that they were not utterly defeated.

The full strength of the English, however, had not yet been available, and a foe more deadly and more formidable than all the power of England was about to fall upon the Irish army.

By one of those calamitous concurrences which are often to be noted in history, there fell upon Ireland in this year (1317) a famine of dreadful severity. The crops had entirely failed the previous autumn, and now throughout the land the dread consequences were spreading desolation. The brothers Bruce each day found it more and more difficult to provision the army, and soon it became apparent that hunger and privation were destroying and demoralizing the national force. This evil in itself was bad enough, but a worse followed upon it.

food, and soon there sprung up between the Scottish contingent and the Irish troops and inhabitants bitter ill feeling
and contention. The Scots—who from the very outset appear to have discriminated nought in plundering castles and
churches when the opportunity came fairly in their way—now,
throwing off all restraint, broke into churches and broke open
and rifled shrines and tombs. The Irish, whose reverence for
religion was always so intense and solemn, were horrified at
these acts of sacrilege and desecration, and there gradually
spread through the country a vague but all-powerful popular belief that the dreadful scourge of famine was a " visita-·
tion of heaven" called down upon the country by the presence
of the irreverent Scots!

Meanwhile the English were mustering a tremendous force
in the rear of the wasted Irish army. The Bruces, on learning the fact, quickly ordered a night retreat, and pushed
northwards by forced marches. An Anglo-Irish army of
thirty thousand men, well appointed and provisioned, lay
across their path ; yet such was the terror inspired by vivid
recollection of the recent victories of the Irish and the prestige of Bruce's name, that this vast force, as the historian tells
us, hung around the camp of the half-starved and diminished
Scoto-Irish army, without ever once daring to attack them
in a pitched battle ! On the 1st of May, after a march full of
unexampled suffering, the remnant of the Irish army safely
reached Ulster.

The famine now raged with such intensity all over Ireland,
that it brought about a suspension of hostilites. Neither
party could provision an army in the field. King Robert of
Scotland, utterly disheartened, sailed homeward. His own
country was not free from suffering, and in any event, the
terrible privations of the past few months had filled the Scottish contingent with discontent. King Edward, however,
nothing daunted, resolved to stand by the Irish kingdom to
the last, and it was arranged that whenever a resumption of
hostilities became feasible, Robert should send him another
Scottish contingent.

both parties sprang to arms. The English commander-in-chief John de Birmingham, was quickly across the Boyne at the head of twelve thousand men, intent on striking king Edward before his hourly expected Scottish contingent could arrive. The Irish levies were but slowly coming in, and Edward at this time had barely two or three thousand men at hand. Nevertheless he resolved to meet the English and give them battle. Donald O'Neill and the other native princes saw the madness of this course, and vainly endeavored to dissuade the king from it. They pointed out that the true strategy to be adopted under the circumstances was to gain time, to retire slowly on their northern base, disputing each inch of ground, but risking no pitched battle, until the national levies would have come in, and the Scottish contingent arrived, by which time, moreover, they would have drawn Birmingham away from his base, and would have him in a hostile country. There can be no second opinion about the merits of this scheme. It was the only one for Edward to pursue just then. It was identical with that which had enabled him to overthrow the Red Earl three years before and had won the battle of Connoyre. But the king was immovable. At all times headstrong, self-willed, and impetuous, he now seemed to have been rendered extravagantly over-confident by the singular fact (for fact it was), that never yet had he met the English in battle on Irish soil that he did not defeat them. It is said that some of the Irish princes, fully persuaded of the madness of the course resolved upon, and incensed by the despotic obstinacy of the king, withdrew from the camp. "There remained with the iron-headed king," says the historian, "the lords Mowbray de Soulis and Stewart, with three brothers of the latter, Mac Roy, Lord of the Isles, and Mac Donald, chief of his clan. The neighborhood of Dundalk, the scene of his triumphs and coronation, was to be the scene of the last act of Bruce's chivalrous and stormy career." From the same authority (M'Gee) I quote the following accounts of that scene :

"On the 14th of October, 1318, at the Hill of Faughard,

hostile armies came into the presence of each other, and made ready for battle. Roland de Jorse, the foreign Archbishop of Armagh, who had not been able to take possession of his see, though appointed to it seven years before, accompanied the Anglo-Irish, and moving through their ranks, gave his benediction to their banners. But the impetuosity of Bruce gave little time for preparation. At the head of the vanguard, without waiting for the whole of his company to come up, he charged the enemy with impetuosity. The action became general, and the skill of De Bermingham as a leader was again demonstrated. An incident common to the warfare of that age was, however, the immediate cause of the victory. Master John de Maupas, a burgher of Dundalk, believing that the death of the Scottish leader would be the signal for the retreat of his followers, disguised as a jester or a fool, sought him throughout the field. One of the royal esquires named Gilbert Harper, wearing the surcoat of his master, was mistaken for him and slain; but the true leader was at length found by De Maupas, and struck down with the blow of a leaden plummet or slung-shot. After the battle, when the field was searched for his body, it was found under that of De Maupas, who had bravely yielded up life for life. The Hiberno-Scottish forces dispersed in dismay, and when King Robert of Scotland landed, a day or two afterwards, he was met by the fugitive men of Carrick, under their leader Thompson, who informed him of his brother's fate. He returned at once into his own country, carrying off the few Scottish survivors. The head of the impetuous Edward was sent to London, but the body was interred in the Churchyard of Faughard, where, within living memory, a tall pillar of stone was pointed out by every peasant in the neighborhood as marking the grave of King Bruce."

Thus ended the first grand effort of Ireland as an independent nation to expel the Anglo-Norman power. Never was so great an effort so brilliantly successful, yet eventually defeated by means outside and beyond human skill to avert, or human bravery to withstand. The seasons fought against

EDWARD BRUCE CROWNED KING OF IRELAND.

See page 182.

struck down the country in the very moment of national triumph.   The arm that was victorious in battle fell lifeless at the breath of this dread destroyer.   To the singular and calamitous coincidence of a famine so terrible at such a critical moment for Ireland, and to this alone, was the ruin of the national cause attributable.   The Irish under the king of their choice had, in three heavy campaigns, shown themselves able to meet and overcome the utmost force that could be brought against them.   England had put forth her best energies and had been defeated.   Prestige was rapidly multiplying the forces and increasing the moral and material resources of the Irish ; and but for the circumstances which compelled the retreat northwards from Limerick, reducing and disorganizing the national army, and leading in a long train of still greater evils, as far as human ken could see, the independent nationality of Ireland was triumphantly consolidated and her freedom securely established.

The battle of Faughard—or rather the fall of Edward under such circumstances—was a decisive termination of the whole struggle.   The expected Scottish contingent arrived soon after ; but all was over, and it returned home.   The English king, some years subsequently, took measures to guard against the recurrence of such a formidable danger as that which had so nearly wrested Ireland from his grasp—a Scoto-Irish alliance.   On the 17th March, 1328, a treaty between England and Scotland was signed at Edinburg by which it was stipulated that, in the event of a rebellion against Scotland in Skye, Man, or the Islands, *or against England in Ireland*, the respecttive kings would not assist each other's "rebel subjects."   Ireland had played for a great stake, and lost the game.   The nation that had reappeared for a moment, again disappeared and once more the struggle against the English power was waged merely by isolated chiefs and princes, each one acting for himself alone.

XXVI.—HOW THE ANGLO-IRISH LORDS LEARNED TO PREFER IRISH MANNERS, LAWS, AND LANGUAGE, AND WERE BECOMING " MORE IRISH THAN THE IRISH THEMSELVES." HOW THE KING IN LONDON TOOK MEASURES TO ARREST THAT DREADED EVIL.

BUT a new danger arose to the English power. It was not alone fresh armies and a constant stream of subsidies that England found it necessary to be pouring into Ireland, to insure the retention of the Anglo-Norman Colony. Something more became requisite now. It was found that a constant stream of fresh colonization from England, a frequent change of governors, nay further, the most severe repressive laws, could alone keep the colony English in spirit, in interest, in language, laws, manners, and customs. The descendants of the early Anglo-Norman settlers—gentle and simple, lord and burgher—were becoming thoroughly Hibernicized. Norwithstanding the ceaseless warfare waged between the Norman lords and the Irish chiefs, it was found that the former were becoming absorbed in to or fused with the native element. The middle of the fourteenth century found the Irish language and Brehon law, native Irish manners, habits and customs, almost universally prevalent amongst the Anglo-Normans in Ireland ; while marriage and " fosterage "—that most sacred domestic tie in Gaelic estimation— were becoming quite frequent between the noble families of each race. In fact, the great lords and nobles of the Colony became Chieftains and their families and following, Septs. Like the Irish chiefs, whom they imitated in most things, they fought against each other or against some native chief or sided with either of them if choice so determined. Each earl or baron amongst them kept his bard and his brehon, like any native prince ; and, in several instances, they began to drop their Anglo-Norman names and take Irish ones instead.

council in London, to discern in this state of things a peril far
and away more formidable than any the English power had
yet encountered in Ireland. True the Anglo-Irish lords had
always as yet professed allegiance to the English sovereign,
and had, on the whole, so far helped forward the English designs. But it was easy to foresee that it would require but a
few more years of this process of fusion with the native Irish
race to make the Anglo-Irish element Irish in every sense.
To avert this dreaded and now imminent evil the London Government resolved to adopt the most stringent measures.
Amongst the first of these was a royal ordinance issued in 1341,
declaring that whereas it had appeared to the King (Edward the
Third) and his council that they would be better and more
usefully served in Ireland by Englishmen whose revenues
were derived from England than by Irish or English who
possessed estates only in Ireland, or were married there, the
king's judiciary should therefore, after diligent inquiries, remove all such officers as were married or held estates in Ireland, and replace them by fit Englishmen, having no personal
interest whatever in Ireland. This ordinance set the Anglo-
Irish colony in a flame. Edward's lord deputy, Sir John Mor-
ris, alarmed at its effect on the proud and powerful barons,
summoned them to a parliament to meet in Dublin to reason
over the matter. But they would have no reasoning with
him. They contemptuously derided his summons, and called
a parliament of their own, which, accordingly, met at Kilkenny in November, 1342, whereat they adopted a strong remonstrance, and forwarded it to the king, complaining of the
royal ordinance, and recriminating by alleging, that to the
ignorance and incapacity of the English officials, sent over
from time to time to conduct the government of the colony,
was owing to the fact that the native Irish had repossessed
themselves of nearly all the land that had ever hitherto been
wrested from them by "the gallant services of themselves
(the remonstrancers) of their ancestors." Edward was obliged to temporize. He answered this remonstrance graciously,
and "played" the dangerous barons.

was to be pushed on as opportunity offered. Eight years subsequent to the above proceedings—in 1360—Lionel, son of king
Edward, was sent over as lord lieutenant. He brought with
him a considerable army, and was to inaugurate the new system with great *eclat*. He had personal claims to assert as well
as a state policy to carry out. By his wife, Elizabeth de
Burgh, he succeeded to the empty titles of earl of Ulster and
lord of Connaught, and the possessions supposed to follow
them ; but these were just then held by their rightful Irish
owners, and one of Lionel's objects was to obtain them by force
of arms for himself. Soon after landing he marched against
" the Irish enemy," and confident in the strength of newly-
landed legions, he issued a proclamation "forbidding any of
Irish birth to come near his army." This arrogance was soon
humbled. His vaunted English army was a failure. The
Irish cut it to pieces ; and prince Lionel was obliged to abandon
the campaign, and retreated to Dublin a prey to mortification
and humiliation. His courtiers plied him with flatteries in
order to cheer him. By a process not very intelligible, they
augered that he conquered Clare, though O'Brien had utterly
defeated him there, and compelled him to fly to Dublin ; and
they manufactured for him out of this piece of adulatory invention the title of " *Clarence*." But he only half-accepted these
pleasant fictions, the falseness of which he knew too well. He recalled his arrogant and offensive proclamation, and besought the
aid of the Anglo-Irish. To gain their favor he conferred additional titles and privileges on some of them and knighted several
of the most powerful commoners. After an administration of
seven years it was deemed high time for Lionel to bring the
new policy into greater prominence. In 1367 he convened
a parliament at Kilkenny whereat he succeeded in having
passed that memorable statute known ever since in history as
" The Statute of Kilkenny"—the first formal enactment in
that " penal code of race " which was so elaborately developed
by all subsequent English legislation for hundreds of years.
The act sets out by reciting that, " Whereas, at the conquest
of the land of Ireland, and for a long time after, the English

apparel, and were governed and ruled, both they and their subjects, called Betaghese (villeins) according to English law, etc.; but now many English of the said land, forsaking the English language, manners, mode of riding, laws, and usages, live and govern themselves according to the manners, fashion, and language of the Irish enemies, and also have made divers marriages and alliances between themselves and the Irish enemies aforesaid ; it is therefore enacted (amongst other provisions,) that all intermarriages, fosterings, gossipred, and buying or selling with the enemy shall be accounted treason ; that English names, fashions, and manners shall be resumed under penalty of the confiscation of the delinquent's lands ; that March laws and Brehon laws are illegal, and that there shall be no law but English laws ; that the Irish shall not pasture their cattle on English lands ; that the English shall not entertain Irish rhymers, minstrels, or newsmen ; and moreover, that no 'mere Irishman' shall be admitted to any ecclesiastical benefice or religious house situated within the English district."

The Anglo-Irish barons must have been strangely over-awed or over-reached when they were brought to pass this statute ; several of themselves being at that moment answerable to all its penalties! Its immediate result, however, well nigh completed the ruin of the power it was meant to restore and strengthen. It roused the native Irish to a full conception of the English policy, and simultaneously, though without the least concert, they fell upon the colony on all sides, drove in the outposts, destroyed the castles, hunted the barons, and reoccupied the country very nearly up to the walls of Dublin. " O'Connor of Connact and O'Brien of Thomond," says Hardiman, " laid aside for the moment their private feuds, and united against the common foe. The earl of Desmond, lord justice, marched against them with a considerable army, but was defeated and slain (captured) in a sanguinary engagement, fought A.D. 1369, in the county of Limerick. O'Farrel, the chieftain of Annaly, committed great slaughter in Meath. The O'Mores, Cavanaghs, O'Byrnes, and O'Tooles, pressed upon Leinster, and the O'Neills raised the red arm in the North.

dismay, and terror and confusion reigned in their councils. while the natives continued to gain ground upon them in every direction.   At this crisis an opportunity offered such as had never before occurred, of terminating the dominion of the English in Ireland ; but if the natives had ever conceived such a project, they were never sufficiently united to achieve it. The opportunity passed away, and the disunion of the Irish saved the colony."

As for the obnoxious statute, it was found impossible to enforce it further.   Cunning policy did not risk permanent defeat by pressing it at such a moment.   It was allowed to remain "a dead letter " for a while ; not dead, however, but only slumbering.

XXVII.—HOW THE VAIN-GLORIOUS RICHARD OF ENGLAND AND HIS OVERWHELMING ARMY FAILED TO " DAZZLE" OR CONQUER THE PRINCE OF LEINSTER. CAREER OF THE HEROIC ART M'MURROGH.

THE close of the century which witnessed the events I have been mentioning, brought about another " royal visit " to Ireland. The weak, vain, and pomp-loving Richard the Second visited this country twice in the course of his ill-fated career—for the first time 1394. I would not deem either worth more than a passing word (for both of them were barren of results), were it not that they interweave with the story of the chivalrous Art M'Murrogh" Kavanagh," prince of Leinster, whose heroic figure stands out in glorious prominence on this page of Irish history.

If the M'Murroghs of Leinster in 1170 contributed to our

to give, two centuries later on, another, illustrious in all that ennobles or adorns the patriot, the soldier, or the statesman. Eva M'Murrogh, daughter of Diarmid the Traitor, who married Strongbow the Freebooter, claimed to be the only child of her father born in lawful wedlock. That there were sons of her father then living, was not questioned ; but she, or her husband on her behalf, setting up a claim of inheritance to Diarmid's possessions, impugned their legitimacy. However this may have been, the sept proceeded according to law and usage under the Irish constitution, to elect from the reigning family a successor to Diarmid, and they raised to the chieftaincy his son Donal. Thenceforth the name of M'Murrogh is heard of in Irish history only in connection with the bravest and boldest efforts of patriotism. Whenever a blow was to be struck for Ireland, the M'Murroghs were the readiest in the field—the " first in front and last in rear." They became a formidable barrier to the English encroachments, and in importance were not second to any native power in Ireland. In 1350 the sept was ruled by Art, or Arthur the First, father of our hero. "To carry on a war against him," we are told,"the whole English interest was assessed with a special tax. Louth contributed twenty pounds, Meath and Waterford, two shillings on every carucate (140 acres) of tilled land ; Kilkenny the same sum, with the addition of 6d. in the pound on chattels. This Art captured the strong castles of Kilbelle, Galbarstown, Rathville ; and although his career was not one of invariable success, he bequeathed to his son, also called Art, in 1375, an inheritance extending over a large portion—perhaps one-half—of the territory ruled by his ancestors before the invasion."

From the same historian* I take the subjoined sketch of the early career of that son, Art the Second. "Art M'Murrogh, or Art Kavanagh, as he is commonly called, was born in the year 1357, and from the age of sixteen and upwards was distinguished by his hospitality, knowledge, and feats of arms. Like the great Brian, he was a younger son, but the fortune of war removed one by one those who would otherwise have preceded him in the captaincy of his clan and connections. About the year 1375—while he was still under age—he was elected successor to his father, according to the annalists, who record his death in 1417, 'after being forty-two years in the government of Leinster.' Fortunately he attained command at a period favorable to his genius and enterprise. His own and the adjoining tribes were aroused by tidings of success from other provinces, and the partial victories of their immediate predecessors, to entertain bolder schemes, and they only waited for a chief of distinguished ability to concentrate their efforts. This chief they found, where they naturally looked for him, among the old ruling family of the province. Nor were the English settlers ignorant of his promise. In the parliament held at Castle Dermot in 1377, they granted to him the customary annual tribute paid to his house. . . . Art M'Murrogh the younger not only extended the bounds of his inheritance and imposed tribute on the English settlers in adjoining districts during the first years of his rule, but having married a noble lady of the 'Pale,' Elizabeth, heiress to the barony of Norragh, in Kildare, which included Naas and its neighborhood, he claimed her inheritance in full, though forfeited under 'the statute of Kilkenny,' according to English notions. So necessary did it seem to the deputy and council of the day to conciliate their formidable neighbor, that they addressed a special representation to king Richard, setting forth the facts of the case, and adding that M'Murrogh threatened, until this lady's estates were restored and the arrears of tribute due to him fully discharged, he should never cease from war, 'but would join with the Earl of Desmond against the Earl of Ormond, and afterwards return with a great force out of Munster to ravage the country'. . . . By this time the banner of Art M'Murrogh floated over all the castles and raths on the slope of the Ridge of Leinster, or the steps of the Blackstair hills; while the forests along the Barrow and the Upper Slaney, as well as in the plain of Carlow and in the south-western angle of Wicklow (now the barony of Shillelagh), served still better his purposes of defensive warfare. So en-

native sway, that John Griffin, the English bishop of Leighlin and chancellor of the exchequer, obtained a grant in 1389 of the town of Gulroestown, in the county of Dublin, 'near the marches of O'Toole, seeing he could not live within his own see for the rebels.' In 1390, Peter Creagh, bishop of Limerick, on his way to attend an Anglo-Irish parliament, was taken prisoner in that region, and in consequence the usual fine was remitted in his favor. In 1392, James, the third earl of Ormond, gave M'Murrogh a severe check at Tiscoffin, near Shankil, where six hundred of his clansmen were left dead among the hills.

" This defeat, however, was thrown into the shade by the capture of New Ross, on the very eve of Richard's arrival at Waterford. In a previous chapter we have described the fortifications erected around this important seaport towards the end of the thirteenth century. Since that period its progress had been steadily onward. In the reign of Edward the Third the controversy which had long subsisted between the merchants of New Ross and those of Waterford, concerning the trade monopolies claimed by the latter, had been decided in favor of Ross. At this period it could muster in its own defence 363 cross-bowmen, 1,200 long bowmen, 1,200 pikemen, and 104 horsemen—a force which would seem to place it second to Dublin in point of military strength. The capture of so important a place by M'Murrogh was a cheering omen to his followers. He razed the walls and towers, and carried off gold, silver, and hostages."

From the first sentence in the concluding passage of the foregoing extract it will be gathered, that it was at this juncture the vain-glorious Richard made his first visit to Ireland. He had just recently been a candidate for the imperial throne of the Germanic empire, and had been rejected in a manner most wounding to his pride. So he formed the project of visiting Ireland with a display of pomp, power, and royal splendor, such as had not been seen in Europe for a long time, and would, he was firmly persuaded, enable him to accomplish the complete subjugation of the Irish kingdom after the manner of that Roman general who came and saw and conquered. Early in October he landed at Waterford with a force of 30,000 bowmen and 4,000 men-at-arms ; a force in those days deemed ample to over-run and conquer the strongest kingdom, and far exceeding many that sufficed to change the fate of empires previously and subsequently in Europe. This vast army was transported across the channel in a fleet in some three hundred ships or galleys. Great pains were taken to provide the expedition with all the appliances and features of impressive pageantry ; and in the king's train, as usual, came the chief nobles of England—his uncle, the duke of Glo'ster, the young earl of March (heir apparent), and of earls and lords a goodly attendance, besides several prelates, abbots, and other ecclesiastical dignitaries. But with this vast expedition king Richard accomplished in Ireland just as much as that king in the ballad, who "marched up the hill, and then marched down again." He rehearsed king Henry and king John on Irish soil. The Irish princes were invited to visit their "friend" the mighty and puissant king of England. They did visit him, and were subjected, as of old, to the "dazzling" process. They were patronizingly fondled ; made to understand that their magnanimous suzerain was a most powerful, and most grand, and most gorgeous potentate, own brother of the Sun and Moon. They accepted his flattering attentions ; but they did not altogether so clearly understand or accept a proposition he made them as to surrendering their lands and chieftaincies to him, and receiving, instead, royal pensions and English titles from his most gracious hand. Many of the Irish princes yielded, from one motive or another, to this insidious proposition. But foremost amongst those who could not be persuaded to see the excellence of this arrangement was the young prince of Leinster, whose fame had already filled the land, and whose victories had made the English king feel ill at ease. Art would not come to "court" to reason over the matter with the bland and puissant king. He was obdurate. He resisted all "dazzling." He mocked at the royal pageants, and snapped his fingers at the brother of the Sun and Moon. All this was keenly mortifying to the

a royal commissioner to treat with Art. He accordingly
despatched the earl marshall (Mowbray) to meet and treat
with the prince of Leinster. On the plain of Balligory, near
Carlow, the conference took place, Art being accompanied by
his uncle Malachi. The earl marshall soon found that he had
in Art a statesman as well as a soldier to treat with. Art
proudly refused to treat with an *inferior :* If he was to treat
at all, it should be with the king himself! Mowbray had to
bend to this humiliating rebuff and try to palaver the stern
M'Murrogh. In vain! Art's final answer was, that "so far
from yielding his own lands, his wife's patrimony in Kildare
should instantly be restored to him ; or——." Of course
this broke up the conference. The earl marshall returned
with the unwelcome news to the king, who flew into a rage !
What ! He, the great, the courtly, the puissant, and gorgeous
king Richard of England, thus haughtily treated by a mere
Irish prince ! By the toe-nails of William the Conqueror,
this astounding conduct should meet a dreadful chastisement !
He would wipe out this haughty prince ! The defiant
M'Murrogh should be made to feel the might of England's
royal arm ! So, putting himself at the head of his grand army,
king Richard set out wrathfully to annihilate Art.

But the Lagenian chief soon taught him a bitter lesson.
Art's superior military genius, the valor of his troops, and the
patriotism of the population, soon caused the vastness of the
invading English host to be a weakness, not a strength.
Richard found his march tedious and tardy. It was impossible to make in that strange and hostile country commissariat
arrangements for such an enormous army. Impenetrable forests and impassable bogs were varied only by mountain defiles
defended with true Spartan heroism by the fearless M'Murrogh clansmen. Then the weather broke into severity awful
to endure. Fodder for the horses, food for the men, now became the sole objects of each day's labor on the part of king
Richard's grand army ; "but," says the historian, "M'Murrogh swept off everything of the nature of food—took advantage of his knowledge of the country to burst upon the enemy

cavalry from the foot, and by many other stratagems to thin their ranks and harass the stragglers." In fine, king Richard's splendid army, stuck fast in the Wicklow mountains, was a wreck ; while the vengeful and victorious Lagenians hovered around, daily growing more daring in their disastrous assaults. Richard found there was nothing for it but to supplicate Art, and obtain peace at any price. A deputation of "the English and Irish of Leinster" was despatched to him by the king, making humble apologies and inviting him to a conference with his majesty in Dublin, where, if he would thus honor the king, he should be the royal guest, and learn how highly his valor and wisdom were esteemed by the English sovereign. Art acceded, and permitted Richard to make his way in peace northward to Dublin, crestfallen and defeated, with the relics of his grand army and the tattered rags of the gilt silk banners, the crimson canopies and other regal " properties" that were to have " dazzled" the sept of M'Murrogh.

Art, a few months afterwards, followed, according to invitation ; but he had not been long in Dublin—where Richard had by great exertions once more established a royal court with all its splendors—when he found himself in the hands of treacherous and faithless foes. He was seized and imprisoned on a charge of "conspiring" against the king. Nevertheless, Richard found that he dared not carry out the base plot of which this was meant to be the beginning. He had already got a taste of what he might expect if he relied on *fighting* to conquer Ireland ; and, on reflection, he seems to have decided that the overreaching arts of diplomacy, and the seductions of court life were pleasanter modes of extending his nominal sway, than conducting campaigns like that in which he had already lost a splendid army and tarnished the tinsel of his vain prestige. So Art was eventually set at liberty, but three of his neighboring fellow-chieftains were retained as " hostages" for him ; and it is even said, that before he was released, some form or promise of submission was extorted from him by the treacherous "hosts" who had so basely violated the sanctity of hospitality to which he had frankly trusted. Not long after, an attempt was made to entrap and murder him in one of

the Norman border castles, the owner of which had invited
him to a friendly feast. As M'Murrogh was sitting down to
the banquet, it happened that the quick eye of his bard detected
in the court-yard outside certain movements of troops that
told him at once what was afoot. He knew that if he or his
master openly and suddenly manifested their discovery of the
danger, they were lost; their perfidious hosts would slay
them at the board. Striking his harp to an old Irish
air the minstrel commenced to sing to the music; but the
words in the Gaelic tongue soon caught the ear of M'Murrogh.
They warned him to be calm, circumspect, yet ready and resolute, for that he was in the toils of the foe. The prince
divined all in an instant. He maintained a calm demeanor
until, seizing a favorable pretext for reaching the yard, he
sprang to horse, dashed through his foes, and, sword in hand,
hewed his way to freedom. This second instance of perfidy
completely persuaded M'Murrogh that he was dealing with
faithless foes, whom no bond of honor could bind, and with
whom no truce was safe; so, unfurling once more the Lagenian standard, he declared war *à la mort* against the English
settlement.

It was no light struggle he thus inaugurated. Alone, unaided, he challenged and fought for twenty years the full
power of England; in many a dearly bought victory prov-
ing himself truly worthy of his reputation as a master of military science. The ablest generals of England were one by
one sent to cope with him; but Art outmatched them in strategy
and outstripped them in valor. In the second year's campaign the strongly fortified frontier town and castle of Carlow
fell before him; and in the next year (20th July, 1398) was
fought the memorable battle of Kenlis. "Here," says a historian, "fell the heir presumptive to the English crown, whose
premature removal was one of the causes which contributed
to the revolution in England a year or two later."* We can
well credit the next succeeding observation of the historian
just quoted, that "the tidings of this event filled the Pale
with consternation, and thoroughly aroused the vindictive

---

* M'Gee.

temper of Richard. He at once dispatched to Dublin his half-brother, the earl of Kent, to whom he made a gift of Carlow castle and town, to be held (if taken) by knight's service. He then, as much perhaps to give occupation to the minds of his people as to prosecute his old project of subduing Ireland, began to make preparations for his second expedition thither."

XXVIII.—HOW THE VAIN-GLORIOUS ENGLISH KING TRIED ANOTHER CAMPAIGN AGAINST THE INVINCIBLE IRISH PRINCE, AND WAS UTTERLY DEFEATED AS BEFORE.

F this second expedition of King Richard there is extant an account written by a Frenchman who was in his train. In all its main features expedition number two was a singular repetition of expedition number one ; vast preparations and levies of men and materials, ships and armaments, as if for the invasion and subjugation of one of the most powerful empires of the world ; gorgeous trappings, courtly attendants, and all the necessaries for renewed experiments with the royal " dazzling " policy. Landing at Waterford, Richard, at the head of his panoplied host, marched against M'Murrogh, who to a lofty and magniloquent invitation to seek the king's gracious clemency, had rudely replied, "that he would neither submit nor obey him in any way ; and that he would never cease from war and the defence of his country until his death." To the overawing force of the English king, Art had, as the French narrator informs us, just " three thousand hardy men, who did not appear to be much afraid of the English. " M'Murrogh's tactics were those which had stood him in such good stead on the previous occasion. He removed all the cattle and corn, food and fodder of every kind, as well as the women, children, aged and helpless, of his people, into the interior, while he himself at the head of his Spartan band, " few, but undismayed," took up a position at Idrone awaiting the invaders. Once more Richard

med in by bogs, morass, and mountain—M'Murrogh fighting
and retiring with deadly craft to draw him deeper and deeper into difficulty, "harassing him dreadfully, carrying off everything fit for food for man or beast, surprising and slaying his
foragers, and filling his camp nightly with alarm and blood."
A crumb of consolation greatly regarded by the mortified
and humiliated English king was the appearance one day in
his camp of Art's uncle giving in submission, supplicating for
himself "pardon and favor." This Richard only too joyfully
granted ; and, allowing the incident to persuade him that Art
himself might also be wavering, a royal message was sent to
the Leinster prince assuring him of free pardon, and "castles
and lands in abundance elsewhere," if only he would submit.
The Frenchman records M'Murrogh's reply : " MacMor told
the king's people that for all the gold in the world he would
not submit himself, but would continue to war and endamage
the king in all that he could." This ruined Richard's last hope
of anything like a fair pretext for abandoning his enterprise.
He now relinquished all idea of assailing M'Murrogh, and
marched as best he could towards Dublin, his army meanwhile suffering fearfully from famine. After some days of
dreadful privation they reached the sea-shore at Arklow,
where ships with provisions from Dublin awaited them. The
soldiers rushed into the sea to reach at the food, fought for it
ravenously, and drank all the wine they could seize. Soon
after this timely relief, a still more welcome gleam of fortune
fell upon the English host. A messenger arrived from Art expressing his willingness to meet some accredited ambassador
from the king and discuss the matters at issue between them.
Whereupon, says the chronicler, there was great joy in the
English camp. The earl of Glo'ster was at once despatched
to treat with Art. The French knight was among the earl's
escort, and witnessed the meeting, of which he has left a
quaint description. He describes Art as a " fine large man,
wondrously active. To look at him he seemed very stern and
savage and a very able man." The horse which Art rode
especially transfixed the Frenchman's gaze. He declares, that

had never beheld. "In coming down it galloped so hard, that in my opinion, I never saw hare, deer, sheep, or any other animal, I declare to you for a certainty, run with such speed as it did." This horse Art rode " without housing or saddle," yet sat like a king, and guided with utmost ease in the most astounding feats of horsemanship. " He and the earl," the Frenchman tells, " exchanged much discourse, but did not come to agreement. They took short leave and hastily parted. Each took his way apart, and the earl returned to king Richard." The announcement brought by his ambassador was a sore disappointment to the king. Art would only agree to " peace without reserve ; " " otherwise he will never come to agreement." "This speech," continues the Frenchman, " was not agreeable to the king. It appeared to me that his face grew pale with anger. He swore in great wrath by St. Bernard that no, never would he depart from Ireland till, alive or dead, he had him in his power."

Rash oath—soon broken. Little thought Richard when he so hotly swore against Art in such impotent anger, that he would have to quit Ireland, leaving Art free, unconquered, and defiant, while he returned to England only to find himself a crownless monarch, deposed and friendless, in a few brief days subsequently to meet a treacherous and cruel death in Pontefract castle !

All this, however, though near at hand, was as yet in the unforeseen future ; and Richard, on reaching Dublin, devoted himself once more to "dazzling" revels there. But while he feasted he forgot not his hatred of the indomitable M'Murrogh. " A hundred marks in pure gold" were publicly proclaimed by the king to any one who should bring to him in Dublin, *alive or dead*, the defiant prince of Leinster ; against whom, moreover, the army, divided into three divisions, were despatched upon a new campaign. Soon the revels and marchings were abruptly interrupted by sinister news from England. A formidable rebellion had broken out there, headed by the banished Lancaster. Richard marched southward with all speed to take shipping at Waterford, collecting on the way the several divisions of his army. He embarked for

M'Murrogh had cost him his crown, eventually his life; had changed the dynasty in England, and seated the house of Lancaster upon the throne.

For eighteen years subsequently the invincible Art reigned over his inviolate territory; his career to the last being a record of brilliant victories over every expedition sent against it. As we wade through the crowded annals of those years, his name is ever found in connection with some gallant achievement. Wherever else the fight is found going against Ireland, whatever hand falters or falls in the unbroken struggle, in the mountains of Wicklow there is one stout arm, one bold heart, one glorious intellect, ever nobly daring and bravely conquering in the cause of native land. Art, " whose activity defied the chilling effects of age, poured his cohorts through Sculloge Gap on the garrisons of Wexford, taking in rapid succession in one campaign (1406) the castles of Camolins, Ferns, and Enniscorthy. A few years subsequently his last great battle, probably the most serious engagement of his life, was fought by him against the whole force of the Pale under the walls of Dublin. The Duke of Lancaster, son of the king and lord lieutenant of Ireland, issued orders for the concentration of a powerful army for an expedition southwards against M'Murrogh's allies. But M'Murrogh and the mountaineers of Wicklow now felt themselves strong enough to take the initiative. They crossed the plain which lies to the north of Dublin, and encamped at Kilmainham, where Roderic, when he besieged the city, and Brian before the battle of Clontarf, had pitched their tents of old. The English and Anglo-Irish forces, under the eye of their prince, marched out to dislodge them, in four divisions. The first was led by the duke in person; the second by the veteran knight, Jenicho d'Artois; the third by Sir Edward Perrers, an English knight; and the fourth by Sir Thomas Butler, prior of the order of St. John, afterwards created by Henry the Fifth, for his distinguished service, earl of Kilmain. With M'Murrogh were O'Byrne, O'Nolan, and other chiefs, besides his sons, nephews, and relatives. The numbers on each side could hardly fall short of ten thousand

decisive of those times. The duke was carried back wounded into Dublin ; the slopes of Inchicore and the valley of the Liffey were strewn with the dying and the dead ; the river at that point obtained from the Leinster Irish the name of *Athcroc*, or the ford of slaughter ; the widowed city was filled with lamentation and dismay."

This was the last endeavor of the English power against Art. " While he lived no further attacks were made upon his kindred or country." He was not, alas! destined to enjoy long the peace he had thus conquered from his powerful foes by a forty-four years' war! On the 12th of January, 1417, he died at Ross in the sixtieth year of age, many of the chroniclers attributing his death to poison administered in a drink. Whether the enemies whom he had so often vanquished in the battle-field resorted to such foul means of accomplishing his removal, is, however, only a matter of suspicion, resting mainly on the fact, that his chief brehon, O'Doran, who with him had partaken of a drink given them by a woman on the wayside as they passed, also died on the same day, and was attacked with like symptoms. Leeches' skill was vain to save the heroic chief. His grief-stricken people followed him to the grave, well knowing and keenly feeling that in him they had lost their invincible tower of defence. He had been called to the chieftaincy of Leinster at the early age of sixteen years ; and on the very threshold of his career had to draw the sword to defend the integrity of his principality. From that hour to the last of his battles, more than forty years subsequently, he proved himself one of the most consummate military tacticians of his time. Again and again he met and defeated the proudest armies of England, led by the ablest generals of the age. " He was," say the four Masters, ' a man distinguished for his hospitality, knowledge, and feats of arms ; a man full of prosperity and royalty ; a founder of churches and monasteries by his bounties and contributions." In fine, our history enumerates no braver soldier, no nobler character, than Art M'Murrogh "Kavanagh," prince of Leinster.

XXIX.—HOW THE CIVIL WARS IN ENGLAND LEFT THE ANGLO-
IRISH COLONY TO RUIN. HOW THE IRISH DID NOT GRASP
THE OPPORTUNITY OF EASY LIBERATION.

ITHIN the hundred years next succeeding the events
we have just traced—the period embraced between
1420 and 1520—England was convulsed by the great
civil war of the White and Red Roses, the houses
of York and Lancaster. Irish history during the same
period being chiefly a record of the contest for mastery
between the two principal families of the Pale—the Butlers
and the Geraldines. During this protracted civil struggle,
which bathed England in blood, the colony in Ireland had,
of course, to be left very much to its own resources; and,
as a natural consequence, its dimensions gradually contracted, or rather it ceased to have any defined boundary
at all, and the merest exertion on the part of the Irish must
have sufficed to sweep it away completely. Here was, in
fine, the opportunity of opportunities for the native population, had they but been in a position to avail of it, or
had they been capable of profiting by *any* opportunity, to
accomplish with scarcely an effort the complete deliverance
of their country. England was powerless for aggression,
torn, distracted, wasted, paralyzed, by a protracted civil war.
The lords of the Pale were equally disunited and comparatively helpless. One-hundredth part of the exertion put forth so
bravely, yet so vainly, by the native princes in the time of
Donald O'Neil and Robert Bruce would have more than
sufficed them now to sweep from the land every vestige of
foreign rule. The chain hung so loosely that they had but
to arise and shake it from their limbs. They literally needed
but to will it, and they were free !

Yet not an effort, not a movement, not a motion, during

away forever—was made by the native Irish to grasp the prize thus almost thrust into their hand—the prize of national freedom! They had boldly and bravely striven for it *before* when no such opportunity invited them; they were subsequently to strive for it yet again with valor and daring as great, when every advantage would be arrayed against them. But now, at the moment when they had but to reach out their hand and grasp the object of all their endeavors, they seemed dead to all conceptions of duty or policy. The individual chiefs, north, south, east, and west, lived on in the usual way. They fought each other or the neighboring Anglo-Norman lord just as usual, or else they enjoyed as a pleasant diversification a spell of tranquillity, peace, and friendship. In the relations between Pale and the Irish ground there was, for the time, no regular government "policy" of any kind on either hand. Each Anglo-Norman lord, and each Irish chieftain, did very much as he himself pleased; made peace or war with his neighbors, or took any side he listed in the current conflicts of the period. Some of the Irish princes do certainly appear to have turned this time of respite to a good account, if not for national interests, for other not less sacred interests. Many of them employed their lives during this century in rehabilitating religion and learning in all their pristine power and grandeur. Science and literature once more began to flourish; and the shrines of Rome and Compostello were thronged with pilgrim chiefs and princes, paying their vows of faith, from the Western Isle. Within this period lived Margaret of Offaly, the beautiful and accomplished queen of O'Carroll, king of Ely. She and her husband were munificent patrons of literature, art, and science. On queen Margaret's special invitation the literati of Ireland and Scotland, to the number of nearly three thousand, held a "session" for the furtherance of literary and scientific interests, at her palace, near Killeagh, in Offaly, the entire assemblage being the guests of the king and queen during their stay. "The nave of the great church of Da Sinchell was converted, for the occasion, into a banqueting hall,

placing two massive chalice of gold, as offerings, on the high altar, and committing two orphan children to the charge of nurses to be fostered at her charge. Robed in cloth of gold, this illustrious lady, who was as distinguished for her beauty as for her generosity, sat in queenly state in one of the galleries of the church, surrounded by the clergy, the brehons, and her private friends, shedding a lustre on the scene which was passing below, while her husband, who had often encountered England's greatest generals in battle, remained mounted on a charge outside the church to bid the guests welcome, and see that order was preserved. The invitations were issued, and the guests arranged, according to a list prepared by O'Connor's chief brehon ; and the second entertainment, which took place as Rathangan, was a supplemental one, to embrace such men of learning as had not been brought together at the former feast."

————:∞:————

XXX.—HOW A NEW ELEMENT OF ANTAGONISM CAME INTO THE STRUGGLE. HOW THE ENGLISH KING AND NATION ADOPTED A NEW RELIGION, AND HOW THE IRISH HELD FAST BY THE OLD.

HE time was now at hand when, to the existing elements of strive and hatred between the Irish and the English nations, there was to be added one more fierce than all the rest ; one bitterly intensifying the issues of battle already knit with such deadly vehemence between the Celt and Saxon. Christendom was being rent in twain by a terrible convulsion. A new religion had flung aloft the standard of revolt and revolution against the successors of St. Peter; and the Christian world was being divided into two hostile camps—of the old faith and the new. This was not the mere agitation of new theories of subverting tendencies, pushed and preached with vehemence to the overturning of the old ; but the crash of a volcano, and as suddenly spreading confusion and change far and wide. The political policy and the personal aims and interests of kings and princes gave to the new doctrines at their very birth a range of dominion greater than original Christianity itself had been able to attain in a century. Almost instantaneously, princes and magnates grasped at the new theories, according as personal or state policy dictated. To each and all of them those theories offered one most tempting and invaluable advantage—*supremacy*, spiritual and temporal, unshadowed, unrestrained, unaccountable, and irresponsible on earth. No more of vexing conflicts with the obstinate Roman Pontiffs. No more of supplications to the Holy See " with whispering breath and bated humbleness," if a divorce was needed or a new wife sighted while yet the old one was alive. No more of humiliating submissions to the penances or conditions imposed by that antique tribunal in the Eternal City ; but each one a king, spiritual as well as temporal, in his own dominions. Who would not hail such a system? There was perhaps not one amongst the kings of Europe who had not, at one time or another, been made to feel unpleasantly the restraint put on him by the Pope, acting either as spiritual pontiff or in his capacity of chief arbiter in the disputes of the Christian family. Sometimes, though rarely, this latter function—entirely of human origin and authority —seemed to sink into mere state policy, and like all human schemes had its varying characteristics of good and ill. But that which most frequently brought the Popes into conflict with the civil rulers of the world was the striving of the Holy See to mitigate the evils of villeinage or serfdom appertaining to the feudal system ; to restrain by the spiritual authority the lawless violence and passion of feudal lords and kings ; and, above all, to maintain the sanctity and inviolability of the marriage tie, whether in the cottage of the bondman or the palace of the king. To many of the Europeans sovereigns, therefore, the newly propounded system—(which I am viewing solely as it affected the public policy of individual princes, prescinding entirely from its doctrinal aspect)— held forth

So far, identity of faith had prevailed between England and
Ireland ; albeit English churchmen—archbishops, bishops,
priests and monks—waged the national war in their own way
against the Irish hierarchy, clergy, and people, as hotly as the
most implacable of the military chiefs. With the cessation of the
civil war in England, and the restoration of English national
power during the reign of the seventh Henry, the state policy
of strengthening and extending the English colony in Ireland was vigorously resumed; and the period which witnessed
the outbreak of the religious revolution in Germany found
the sensual and brutal Henry the Eighth engaged in a savage
war upon the Irish nation. Henry early entered the lists
against the new doctrines. He wrote a controversial pamphlet in refutation of Luther's dogmas, and was rewarded therefore by an encomiastic letter from the Pope conferring on
him the title of " Defender of the Faith." Indeed, ever since
the time of Adrian, the Popes had always been wondrously friendly towards the English kings ; much too ready to
give them "aid and comfort" in their schemes of Irish subjugation, and much too little regardful of the heroic people
that were battling so persistently in defence of their nationality. A terrible lesson was now to awaken Rome to remorse
and sorrow. The power she had aided and sanctioned in
those schemes was to turn from her with unblushing apostacy,
and become the most deadly and malignant of her foes ; while
that crushed and broken nation whom she had uninquiringly
given up to be the prey of merciless invaders, was to shame
this ingratitude and perfidy by a fidelity and devotedness not
to be surpassed in the history of the world.

Henry—a creature of mere animal passions—tired of his
lawful wife, and desired another. He applied to Rome for a
divorce. He was, of course, refused. He pressed his application again in terms that but too plainly foreshadowed to
the Supreme Pontiff what the result of a refusal might be.
It was, no doubt, a serious contingency for the Holy See to
contemplate—the defection to the new religion of a king and
a nation so powerful as the English. In fact, it would give to
the new creed a status and a power it otherwise would not

required to wrong one woman; merely to permit a lustful king to have his way, and sacrifice to his brute passions his helpless wife. With full consciousness, however, of all that the refusal implied, the Holy See refused to permit to a king that which could not be permitted to the humblest of his subjects—refused to allow a wife's rights to be sacrificed, even to save to the side of Catholicity for three centuries the great and powerful English nation.

Henry had an easy way out of the difficulty. According to the new system, he would have no need to incur such mortifying refusals from this intractable, antiquated, and unprogressive tribunal of Rome, but could grant to himself divorces and dispensations *ad libitum*. So he threw off the Pope's authority, embraced the new religion, and helped himself to a new wife as often as he pleased; merely cutting off the head of the discarded one after he had granted himself a divorce from her.

In a country where feudal institutions and ideas prevailed, a king who could appease the lords carried the nation. In England, at this period, the masses of the people, though for some time past by the letter of the law freed from villeinage, were still, practically, the creatures of the lords and barons, and depended upon, looked up to, and followed them with the olden stolid docility. Henry, of course, though he might himself have changed as he listed, could never have carried the nation over with him into the creed, had he not devised a means for giving the lords and barons also a material interest in the change. This he effected by sharing with them the rich plunder of the Church. Few amongst the English nobility were proof against the great temptations of kingly favor and princely estates, and the great perils of kingly anger and confiscations. For, in good truth, even at a very early stage of the business, to hesitate was to lose life as well as possessions, inasmuch as Henry unceremoniously chopped off the heads of those who wavered or refused to join him in the new movement. The feudal system carried England bodily over with the king. Once he was able to get

abbey lands) a sufficient number of the nobles, the game was all in his hands. The people counted for nothing in such a system. They went with their lords, like the cattle stock on the estates. The English bishops, mostly scions of the noble houses, were not greatly behind in the corrupt and cowardly acceptance of the king's scheme ; but there were in the episcopacy noble and glorious exceptions to this spectacle of baseness. The body of the clergy, too, made a brave struggle for a time ; but the king and the nobles made light of what *they* could do. A brisk application of the axe and the block—a rattling code of penalties for premunire and so forth—and soon the troublesome priests were all either killed off or banished.

But now, thought Henry, what of Ireland ! How is the revolution likely to be received by the English colony there ? In truth, it was quite a ticklish consideration ; and Henry appears to have apprehended very nearly that which actually resulted—namely, that in proportion as the Anglo-Irish lords had become Hibernicized, they would resist that revolution, and stand by the old faith ; while those of them least imbued with Irish sentiment would proportionately be on his side. Amongst the former, and of all others most coveted now and feared for their vast influence and power, were the Geraldines. Scions of that great house had been amongst the earliest to drop their distinctive character as Anglo-Norman lords, and become Anglo-Irish chiefs—adopting the institutions, laws, language, manners, and customs of the native Irish. For years the head of the family had been kept on the side of the English power, simply by confiding to him its supreme control in Ireland; but of the Irish sympathies of Clan Gerald, Henry had misgivings sore, and ruefully suspected now that it would lead the van in a powerful struggle in Ireland against his politico-religious revolution. In fact, at the very moment in which he was plunging into his revolt against the Pope, a rebellion, led by a Geraldine chief, was shaking to its foundations the English power in Ireland—the rebellion of " Silken Thomas."

XXXI.—" THOSE GERALDINES ! THOSE GERALDINES ! "

HE history of the Geraldine family is a perfect romance, and in many respects outrivals the creations of fiction. From the earliest period of their settlement in Ireland. they attained to a position of almost kingly power, and for full five hundred years were the foremost figures in Anglo-Irish history. Yet with what changing fortunes! Now vice-kings reigning in Dublin, their vast estates stretching from Maynooth to Lixnaw, their strong castles sentinelling the land from sea to sea! Anon captive victims of attainder, stripped of every earthly honor and possession; to-day in the dungeon, to-morrow led to the scaffold! Now a numerous and powerful family—a fruitful, strong, and wide-spreading tree. Anon hewn down to earth, or plucked up seemingly root and branch, beyond the possibility of further existence; yet mysteriously preserved and budding forth from some single seedling to new and greater power! Often the Geraldine stock seemed extinct; frequently its jealous enemies—the English king or his favorites—made safe and sure (as they thought) that the dangerous line was extirpated. Yet as frequently did they find it miraculously resurgent, grasping all its ancient power and renewing all its ancient glory.

At a very early period the Geraldine line was very nearly cut off for ever, but was preserved in the person of one infant child, under circumstances worthy of narration. In the year 1261 a pitched battle was fought between the justiciary, Lord Thomas Fitzgerald, and the MacCarthy More, at a glen a few miles east of Kenmare in Kerry. It was a formidable engagement, in which each side put forth all its resources of military generalship and strength of levies. The Irish commander completely out-generalled the Normans. At the close of a protracted and sanguinary battle they were routed with fearful slaughter, Lord Thomas being mortally wounded, and his

field. "Alas!" continues the narrative of O'Daly (who wrote in the year 1655), "the whole family of the Geraldines had well nigh perished; at one blow they were cut off—father and son; and now there remained but an infant one year old, to wit, the son of John Fitz-Thomas, recently slain. The nurse, who had heard the dismal tidings at Tralee, ran about here and there distraught with grief, and left the cradle of the young Geraldine without a watcher; thereupon an ape (which was kept for amusement sake) came and raised the infant out of the cradle and carried him to the top of the castle. There, to the astonishment of those who passed by, the ape took off the babe's swaddling clothes, licked him all over, clothed him again, and brought him back to his cradle safe and sound. Then coming to the nurse, as it were in reproof for her neglect, he dealt her a blow. Ever after was that babe called Thomas *a n' Appa;* that is, 'of the Ape;' and when he grew to man's estate he was ennobled by many virtues. Bravely did he avenge his father's and grandfather's murder, and reërect the fortunes of his house.* He left a son, Maurice Fitz-Thomas, who was the first earl of Desmond."

Of Lord Thomas, the sixth earl, is related a romantic, yet authentic story, known to many Irish readers. While on a hunting expedition in some of the lonely and picturesque glens in North Kerry, he was benighted on his homeward way. Weary and thirsting, he urged his steed forward through the tangled wood. At length, through the gloom he discerned close by an humble cottage, which proved to be the dwelling of one of his own retainers or clansmen, named MacCormick. Lord Thomas rode to the door, halted, and asked for a drink. His summons was attended to and his request supplied by Catherine, the daughter of the cottage, a young girl whose simple grace and exquisite beauty struck the young earl with astonishment—and with warmer feelings too. He dismounted and rested awhile in the cottage, and became quite charmed with the daughter of its humble host. He bade her farewell, resolving to seek that cottage soon again. Often subsequently

---

* To this incident is attributed the circumstance that the armorial ensigns of the

his horse bore him thither; for Lord Thomas loved Catherine MacCormick, and loved her purely and honorably. Not perhaps without certain misgivings as to the result did he resolve to make her his wife; yet never did he waver in that resolve. In due time he led the beautiful cottage girl to the altar, and brought her home his wife.

His worst fears were quickly realized. His kindred and clansmen all rose against him for this *mésalliance*, which, according to their code, forfeited for him lands and title! In vain he pleaded. An ambitious uncle, James, eventually seventh earl, led the movement against him, and, claiming for himself the title and estates thus "forfeited," was clamorous and uncompassionate. Lord Thomas at the last nobly declared that even on the penalty thus inexorably decreed against him, he in no wise repented him of his marriage, and that he would give up lands and titles rather than part his peasant wife. Relinquishing everything, he bade an eternal adieu to Ireland, and sailed with his young wife for France, where he died at Rouen in 1420. This romantic episode of authentic history furnished our national melodist with the subject of the following verses:

By the Feal's wave benighted
 No star in the skies,
To thy door by love lighted,
 I first saw those eyes.
Some voice whispered o'er me,
 As the threshold I cross'd,
There was ruin before me;
 If I lov'd, I was lost.

Love came, and brought sorrow
 Too soon in his train;
Yet so sweet, that to-morrow
 'Twere welcome again!
Though misery's full measure
 My portion should be,
I would drain it with pleasure
 If poured out by thee!

You, who call it dishonor
 To bow to love's flame,
If you've eyes, look but on her,

Hath the pearl less whiteness
Because of its birth?
Hath the violet less brightness
For growing near earth?

No : man for his glory
To ancestry flies :
But woman's bright story
Is told in her eyes.
While the monarch but traces
Through mortals his line,
Beauty, born of the graces,
Ranks next to divine!

In the reign of the eighth Henry, as well as for a long time
previous thereto, the Geraldine family comprised two great
branches, of which the earl of Desmond and the earl of Kildare were respectively the heads ; the latter being paramount.
Early in Henry's reign Gerald earl of Kildare, or "The Great
Earl," as he is called in the Irish annals, died after a long life,
illustrious as a soldier, statesman, and ruler.   He was succeeded by his son, Garret Oge, or Gerald the younger, who was
soon appointed by the crown to the high office and authority
of lord deputy as vested in his father.   Gerald Oge found
his enemies at court active and restless in plotting his overthrow.   He had more than once to proceed to England to
make his defence against fatal charges, but invariably succeeded in vindicating himself with the king.   With Henry,
indeed, he was apparently rather a favorite ; while, on the
other hand, Cardinal Wolsey viewed him with marked suspicion.   Kildare, though at the head of the English power in
Ireland, was, like many of the Geraldines, nearly as much of
an Irish chief as an English noble.   Not only was he, to the
sore uneasiness of the court at London, in friendly alliance
with many of the native princes, but he was allied by the
closest ties of kindred and alliance with the royal houses of
Ulster.   So proud was he of this relationship, that, upon one
occasion, when he was being reinstated as lord deputy, to the
expulsion of Ormond, his accusing enemy, we are told, that
at Kildare's request "*his kinsman, Con O'Neill*, carried the

entertained the king's commissioners and others at a sumptuous banquet."

But soon Gerald's enemies were destined to witness the accomplishment of all their designs against his house. James, earl of Desmond, "a man of lofty and ambitious views," entered into a correspondence with Charles the Fifth, king of Spain, and Francis the First of France, for the purpose, some hold, of inducing one or other of those sovereigns to invade Ireland. What follows I quote textually from O'Daly's quaint narrative, as translated by the Rev. C. P. Meehan :—

"Many messages passed between them, of all which Henry the Eighth was a long time ignorant. It is commonly thought that Charles the Fifth at this time meditated an invasion of Ireland ; and when at length the intelligence of these facts reached the king of England, Cardinal Wolsey (a man of immoderate ambition, most inimical to the Geraldines, and then ruling England as it were by his nod) caused the earl to be summoned to London ; but Desmond did not choose to place himself in the hands of the cardinal, and declined the invitation. Thereupon the king despatched a messenger to the earl of Kildare, then viceroy in Ireland, ordering him to arrest Desmond and send him to England forthwith. On receipt of the order, Kildare collected troops and marched into Munster to seize Desmond ; but, after some time, whether through inability or reluctance to injure his kinsman, the business failed and Kildare returned. Then did the cardinal poison the mind of the king against Kildare, asseverating that by his connivance Desmond had escaped—(this, indeed, was not the fact, for Kildare, however so anxious, could not have arrested Desmond). Kildare was then arraigned before the privy council, as Henry gave willing ear to the cardinal's assertions ; but before the viceroy sailed for England, he committed the state and administration of Ireland to Thomas, his son and heir, and then presented himself before the council. The cardinal accused him of high treason to his liege sovereign, and endeavored to brand him and all his family with the ignominious mark of disloyalty. Kildare, who was a man of

polished, yet vehement language; and though the cardinal
and court were hostile to him, nevertheless he so well managed the matter, that he was only committed to the tower of
London. But the cardinal, determined to carry out his designs of vengance, without knowledge of the king, sent private instructions to the constable of the tower ordering him
to behead the earl without delay. When the constable received his orders, although he knew how dangerous it was to
contravene the cardinal's mandate, commiserating the earl,
he made him aware of his instructions. Calmly, yet firmly,
did Kildare listen to the person who read his death-warrant ;
and then launching into a violent invective against the cardinal, he caused the constable to proceed to the king, to learn
if such order had emanated from him, for he suspected that it
was the act of the cardinal unauthorized. The constable, re-
gardless of the risk he ran, hastened to the king, and, about
ten o'clock at night, reported to his majesty the order of the
cardinal for destroying Kildare. Thereon the king was bitterly incensed against Wolsey, whom he cursed, and forbade
the constable to execute any order not sanctioned by his own
sign-manual; stating, at the same time, that he would cause
the cardinal to repent of his usurped authority and unjust
dislike to Kildare. The constable returned, and informed the
earl of his message; but Kildare was nevertheless detained a
prisoner in the tower to the end of his days."

" There is," says O'Daly's translator, " a chapter in Galt's
Life of Wolsey full of errors and gross misrepresentations of
Ireland and the Irish. It is only fair, however, to give him
credit for the spirited sketch he has given of the dialogue between Wolsey and Kildare. 'My lord,' said Wolsey, 'you
will remember how the earl of Desmond, your kinsman, sent
letters to Francis, the French king, what messages have been
sent to you to arrest him (Desmond), and it is not yet done. . .
but, in performing your duty in this affair, merciful God ! how
dilatory have you been !....what ! the earl of Kildare dare
not venture ! nay, the king of Kildare ; for you reign more
than you govern the land.' 'My lord chancellor,' replied the

I have no school tricks nor art of recollection; unless you hear me while I remember, your second charge will hammer the first out of my head. As to my kingdom, I know not what you mean . . . . I would you and I, my lord, exchanged kingdoms for one month; I would in that time undertake to gather more crumbs than twice the revenues of my poor earldom. While you sleep in your bed of down, I lie in a poor hovel; while you are served under a canopy, I serve under the cope of heaven; while you drink wine from golden cups, I must be content with water from a shell; my charger is trained for the field, your jennet is taught to amble.' O'Daly's assertion that Wolsey issued the earl's death-warrant does not appear to rest on any solid foundation; and the contrary appears likely, when such usurpation of royalty was not objected in the impeachment of the cardinal."

XXXII.—THE REBELLION OF SILKEN THOMAS.

HEN Kildare was summoned to London—as it proved
to be for the last time—he was called upon to nominate
some one who should act for him in his absence, and
for whom he himself would be responsible. Unfortunately he nominated his own son Thomas,* a hot, impetuous, brave, daring, and chivalrous youth, scarce one-and-
twenty years of age. For some time the earl lay in London
tower, his fate as yet uncertain ; the enemies of his house meanwhile striving steadily to insure his ruin.

It was at this juncture that the events detailed in bygone
pages—Henry's quarrel with the Pope, and the consequent
politico-religious revolution in England—flung all the English
realm into consternation and dismay. Amidst the tidings of
startling changes and bloody executions in London brought
by each mail to Ireland, came many disquieting rumors of the
fate of the Geraldine earl. The effect of these stories on the
young Lord Thomas seems to have suggested to the anti-Geral-
dine faction a foul plot to accomplish his ruin. Forged letters
were circulated giving out with much circumstantiality how
the earl his father had been beheaded in the tower of London,
notwithstanding the king's promise to the contrary. The
effect of this news on the Geraldine party, but most of all on
the young Lord Thomas, may be imagined. Stunned for an
instant by this cruel blow, his resolution was taken in a burst
of passionate grief and anger. Vengeance ! vengeance on the
trebly perjured and blood-guilty king, whose crimes of lust,
murder, and sacrilege called aloud for punishment, and forfeited for him allegiance, throne, and life ! The youthful dep-

---

* Known in history as "Silken Thomas." He was so called, we are told, from the
silken banners carried by his standard-bearers—other say, because of the richness of

uty hastily assembling his guards and retainers, and surrounded by a crowd of his grief-stricken and vengeful kinsmen,
marched to Mary's Abbey, where the privy council was already sitting, waiting for him to preside over its deliberations.
The scene at the council-chamber is picturesquely sketched by
Mr. Ferguson, in his *Hibernian Nights' Entertainment.**

"Presently the crowd collected round the gates began to
break up and line the causeways at either side, and a gallant
cavalcade was seen through the open arch advancing from
Thomas' Court towards the drawbridge. 'Way for the lord
deputy,' cried two truncheon bearers, dashing through the
gate, and a shout arose on all sides that Lord Thomas was
coming. Trumpeters and pursuivants at arms rode first, then
came the mace-bearer with his symbol of office, and after him
the sword of state, in a rich scabbard of velvet, carried by its
proper officer. Lord Thomas himself, in his robes of state,
and surrounded by a dazzling array of nobles and gentlemen,
spurred after. The arched gateway was choked for a moment
with tossing plumes and banners, flashing arms and gleaming
faces, as the magnificent troop burst in like a flood of fire
upon the dark and narrow precincts of the city. But behind
the splendid cortege which headed their march, came a dense
column of mailed men-at-arms, that continued to defile through
the close pass long after the gay mantles and waving pennants
of their leaders were indistinct in the distance.

"The gate of Mary's Abbey soon received the leaders of
the revolt ; and ere the last of their followers had ceased to
pour into the echoing court-yard, Lord Thomas and his friends
were at the door of the council-chamber. The assembled
lords rose at his entrance, and way was made for him to the
chair of state

"'Keep your seats, my lords,' said he, stopping midway
between the entrance and council table, while his friends
gathered in a body at his back. 'I have not come to preside

---

* The book here alluded to, it may be right to remind young readers, does not
purport to be more than a fanciful story founded on facts ; but the author so closely

over this council, my lords; I come to tell you of a blood
tragedy that has been enacted in London, and to give
you to know what steps I have thought fit to take in consequence.'

"'What tragedy, my lord?' said Alan, the archbishop of
Dublin; 'your lordship's looks and words alarm me: what
means this multitude of men now in the house of God? My
lord, my lord, I fear this step is rashly taken; this looks like
something, my lord, that I would be loth to name in the presence of loyal men.'

"'My lord archbishop,' replied Thomas, 'when you pretend an ignorance of my noble father's murder'——

"'Murder!' cried the lord chancellor, Cromer, starting
from his seat, and all at the council table uttered exclamations
of astonishment in horror, save only Alan and the lord high
treasurer.

"'Yes, my lord,' the young Geraldine continued with
a stern voice, still addressing the archbishop,"when you pretend ignorance of that foul and cruel murder, which was done
by the instigation and traitorous procuring of yourself and
others, your accomplices, and yet taunt me with the step which
I have taken, rashly, as it may be, but not, I trust unworthily
of my noble father's son, in consequence, you betray at once
your teachery and your hypocrisy.' By this time the tumult
among the soldiery without who had not till now heard of the
death of the earl, was as if a thousand men had been storming the Abbey. They were all native Irish, and to a man
devoted to Kildare. Curses, lamentations, and cries of rage
and vengeance sounded from every quarter of the court-yard;
and some who rushed into the council-hall with drawn swords,
to be revenged on the authors of their calamity, were with difficulty restrained by the knights and gentlemen around the
door from rushing on the archbishop, and slaying him as they
heard him denounced by their chief, on the spot. When the
clamor was somewhat abated, Alan, who had stood up to
speak at its commencement, addressed the chancellor.

"'My lord, this unhappy young man says he knows not
what. If his noble father, which God forbid, should have

have suffered—although I know not that he hath—the penalty of his numerous treasons'——

" ' Bold priest, thou liest !' cried Sir Oliver Fitzgerald ; my murdered brother was a truer servant of the crown than ever stood in thy satin shoes !'

" Alan and the lord chancellor Cromer, also an archbishop and primate of Armagh, rose together ; the one complaining loudly of the wrong and insult done his order ; the other beseeching that all present would remember they were Christians and subjects of the crown of England ; but, in the midst of this confusion, Lord Thomas, taking the sword of state out of the hands of its bearer, advanced up the hall to the council-table with a lofty determination in his bearing that at once arrested all eyes. It was plain he was about to announce his final purpose, and all within the hall awaited what he would say in sullen silence. His friends and followers now formed a dense semicircle at the foot of the hall ; the lords of the council had involuntarily drawn round the throne and lord chancellor's chair ; Thomas stood alone on the floor opposite the table, with the sword in his hands. Anxiety and pity were marked on the venerable features of Cromer as he bent forward to hear what he would say ; but Alan and the treasurer Lord James Butler, exchanged looks of malignant satisfaction.

" ' My lord,' said Thomas, ' I come to tell you that my father has been basely put to death, for I know not what alleged treason, and that we have taken up arms to avenge his murder. Yet, although we be thus driven by the tyranny and cruelty of the king into open hostility, we would not have it said hereafter that we have conspired like villains and churls, but boldly declared our purpose as becomes warriors and gentlemen. This sword of state, my lord, is yours, not mine. I received it with an oath, that I would use it for your benefit ; I should stain my honor if I turned it to your hurt. My lords, I have now need of my own weapon, which I can trust ; but as for the common sword, it has flattered me not— a painted scabbard, while its edge was yet red in the best blood of my house—aye and is even now whetted anew for further destruction of the Geraldines. Therefore, my lords, save yourselves from us as from open enemies. I am no longer Henry Tudor's deputy—I am his foe. I have more mind to conquer than to govern—to meet him in the field than to serve him in office. And now, my lords, if all the hearts in England and Ireland, that have cause thereto, do but join in this quarrel, as I look that they will, then shall the world shortly be made sensible of the tyranny, cruelty, falsehood, and heresy, for which the age to come may well count this base king among the ancient traitors of most abominable and hateful memory.

"'Croom aboo!' cried Neale Roe O'Kennedy, Lord Thomas's bard, who had pressed into the body of the hall at the head of the Irish soldiery. He was conspicuous over all by his height and the splendor of his native costume. His legs and arms were bare; the sleeves of his yellow cothone, parting above the elbow, fell in voluminous folds almost to the ground, whilst its skirts, girded at the loins, covered him to the knee. Over this he wore a short jacket of crimson, the sleeves just covering the shoulders, richly wrought and embroidered, and drawn round the waist by a broad belt, set with precious stones and fastened with a massive golden buckle. His laced and fringed mantle was thrown back, but kept from falling by a silver brooch, as broad as a man's palm, which glittered on his breast. He stretched out his hand, the gold bracelets rattling as they slid back on the thickness of his arm, and exclaimed in Irish :—

"'Who is the young lion of the plains of Liffey, that affrights the men of council, and the ruler of the Saxon, with his noble voice?

"'Who is the quickened ember of Kildare, that would consume the enemies of his people, and the false churls of the cruel race of clan-London?

"'It is the son of Gerald—the top branch of the oak of Offaly!

"'It is Thomas of the silken mantle—Ard-Righ Eireann!'

"'Righ Tomas go bragh!' shouted the soldiery; and many of the young lord's Anglo-Irish friends responded—'Long live King Thomas!' but the chancellor, archbishop Cromer, who had listened to his insane avowal with undisguised distress

SILKEN THOMAS FLINGS UP THE SWORD OF STATE.

See page 203.

and who had already been seen to wring his hand, and even to shed tears as the misguided nobleman and his friends thus madly invoked their own destruction, came down from his seat, and earnestly grasping the young lord by the hand, addressed him :

" ' Good my lord,' he cried, while his venerable figure and known attachment to the house of Kildare, attested as it was by such visible evidences of concern, commanded for a time the attention of all present. ' Good my lord, suffer me to use the privilege of an old man's speech with you, before you finally give up this ensign of your authority and pledge of your allegiance.' "

The archbishop reasoned and pleaded at much length and with deep emotion ; but he urged and prayed in vain.

" ' My Lord Chancellor,' replied Thomas, ' I came not here to take advice, but to give you to understand what I purpose to do. As loyalty would have me know my prince, so duty compels me to reverence my father. I thank you heartily for your counsel ; but it is now too late. As to my fortune, I will take it as God sends it, and rather choose to die with valor and liberty, than live under King Henry in bondage and villainy. Therefore, my lord, I thank you again for the concern you take in my welfare, and since you will not receive this sword out of my hand, I can but *cast it from me, even as here I cast off and renounce all duty and allegiance to your master.*'

" So saying, he flung the sword of state upon the council table. The blade started a hand's breadth out of its sheath, from the violence with which it was dashed out of his hands. He then, in the midst of a tumult of acclamation from his followers and cries of horror and pity from the lords and prelates around, tore off his robes of office and cast them at his feet. Stripped thus of his ensigns of dignity, Lord Thomas Fitzgerald stood up, amid the wreck of his fair fortune, an armed and avowed rebel, equipped in complete mail, before the representatives of England and Ireland. The cheering from his adherents was loud and enthusiastic, and those without replied with cries of fierce exultation.

The gallant but hapless Geraldine was now fully launched

on his wild and desperate enterprise. There is no doubt that, had it partaken less of a hasty burst of passionate impetuosity, had it been more deliberately planned and organized, the revolt of Silken Thomas might have wrested the Anglo-Irish colony from Henry's authority. As it was, it shook the Anglo-Irish power to its base, and at one time seemed irresistible in its progress to success. But, however the ties of blood, kindred, and clanship might draw men to the side of Lord Thomas; most persons outside the Geraldine party soon saw the fate that surely awaited such a desperate venture, and saw too that it had all been the result of a subtle plot of the Ormond faction to ruin their powerful rivals. Moreover, in due time the truth leaked out that the old earl had not been beheaded at all, but was alive a prisoner in London. Lord Thomas now saw the gulf of ruin into which he had been precipitated, and knew now that his acts would only seal the doom or else break the heart of that father, the news of whose murder had driven him into this desperate course. But it was all too late to turn back. He would see the hopeless struggle through to the bitter end.

One of his first acts was to besiege Dublin city while another wing of his army devastated the possessions and reduced the castles of Ormond. Alan, the Archbishop of Dublin, a prominent enemy of the Geraldines, fled from the city by ship. The vessel, however, was driven ashore on Clontarf, and the archbishop sought refuge in the village of Artane. News of this fact was quickly carried into the Geraldine camp at Dublin; and before day's-dawn Lord Thomas and his uncles, John and Oliver, with an armed party, reached Artane, and dragged the archbishop from his bed. The unhappy prelate pleaded hard for his life; but the elder Geraldines, who were men of savage passion, barbarously murdered him as he knelt at their feet. This foul deed ruined any prospect of success which their cause might have had. It excited universal horror, and drew down upon its perpetrators, and all who should aid or shelter them, the terrible sentence of excommunication. This sentence was exhibited to the hapless earl of Kildare in his dungeon in London tower, and it is said, so affected him that he never rallied more. He sank under the great load of his afflictions, and died of a broken heart.

Meanwhile, Lord Thomas was pushing the rebellion with all his energies, and for a time with wondrous success. He despatched ambassadors to the emperor Charles the Fifth, and to the Pope, demanding aid in this war against Henry as the foe of God and man. But it is clear that neither the Pope nor the emperor augured well of Silken Thomas's ill-devised endeavors. No succors reached him. His fortunes eventually began to pale. Powerful levies were brought against him; and, finally, he sought a parley with the English commander-in-chief, Lord Leonard Gray, who granted him terms of life for himself and uncles. Henry was wroth that any terms should have been promised to such daring foes: but as terms had been pledged, there was nothing for it, according to Henry's code of morality, but to break the promise. Accordingly, the five uncles of Silken Thomas, and the unfortunate young nobleman himself, were treacherously seized—the uncles at a banquet to which they were invited, and which was, indeed, given in their honor, by the lord deputy Gray —and brought to London, where, in violation of plighted troth, they were all six beheaded at Tyburn, 3d January, 1537.

This terrible blow was designed to cut off the Geraldine family forever; and to all appearance it seemed, and Henry fondly believed, that this wholesale execution had accomplished that design, and left neither root nor seed behind. Yet once again that mysterious protection, which had so often preserved the Geraldine line in like terrible times, saved it from the decreed destruction. "The imprisoned earl (Lord Thomas's father) having died in the tower on the 12th December, 1534, the sole survivor of this historic house was now a child of twelve years of age, whose life was sought with an avidity equal to Herod's, but who was protected with a fidelity which defeated every attempt to capture him. Alternately the guest of his aunts, married to the chiefs of Offaly and Donegal, the

the northern and southern chiefs, which had long been wanting. A loose league was formed, including the O'Neils of
both branches, O'Donnell, O'Brien, the earl of Desmond, and
the chiefs of Moylurg and Breffni. The lad, the object of so
much natural and chivalrous affection, was harbored for a
time in Munster, thence transported through Connaught into
Donegal, and finally, after four years, in which he engaged
more of the minds of statesmen than any other individual
under the rank of royalty, was safely landed in France."

The Geraldine line was preserved once more! From this
child Gerald it was to branch out as of yore, in stately
strength and princely power.

XXXIII.—HOW THE "REFORMATION," WAS ACCOMPLISHED IN ENGLAND, AND HOW IT WAS RESISTED IN IRELAND.

I HAVE so far called the event, usually termed the Reformation, a politico-religious revolution, and treated of it only as such. With phases of religious belief or the propagandism of new religious doctrines, unless in so far as they affected political events or effected marked national changes, I do not purpose dealing in this Story. As a matter of fact, however, the Reformation was during the reign of Henry much less of a religious than a political revolution. The only points Henry was particular about were the matters of *supremacy* and *church property*. For a long period the idea of adopting the new form of faith in all its doctrinal sequence seemed quite foreign to his mind. The doctrine, firstly, that he, Henry, was supreme king, spiritual as well as temporal, within his own realms: the doctrine, secondly, that he could, in virtue of such spiritual supremacy, give full rein to his beastly lusts, and call concubinage marriage; and lastly, that whatever property the Church possessed, bequeathed for pious uses, he might rob and keep for himself, or divide as bribes between his abetting nobles, legislators, and statesmen—these were the "reforms," so-called, upon which the king set most value. Other matters he allowed for a time to have their way; at least it was so wherever difficulty was anticipated in pulling down the old and setting up new forms of worship. Thus we find the king at the same time sending a "reforming" archbishop to Dublin while sanctioning prelates of the old faith in other dioceses, barely on condition of taking the oath of allegiance to him. Doctrine or theology had scarcely any concern for him or his statesmen, and it is clear and plain to any student of history, that if the Catholic Church would only sanction to him his polygamy, and to them the rich plunder they had clutched, they would never have gone further, and would still be wondrous zealous "defenders of the faith." But the Catholic Church, which could have avoided the whole disaster at the outset by merely suffering one lawful wife to be unlawfully put away, was not going to compromise with him or with them, an iota of sacred truth or public morality, much less to sacrifice both wholesale after this fashion. So, in time, the king and his party saw that having gone so far, they must needs go the whole way. Like the panther that has tasted blood, their thirst for plunder was but whetted by their taste of Church spoil. They should go farther or they might lose all. They knew right well that of these spoils they never could rest sure as long as the owner, the Catholic Church, was allowed to live; so to kill the Church outright became to them as much of a necessity as the sure "dispatching" of a half-murdered victim is to a burglar or an assassin. Had it not been for this question of Church property—had there been no plunder to divide—in all human probability there would have been no "reformation" consummated in these countries. But by the spoils of the sanctuary Henry was able to bribe the nobles to his side, and to give them

perpetuation of the new system, that no king or queen coming after him would be able permanently to restore the old
order of things.

Here the reflection at once confronts us—what a mean,
sordid, worldly-minded kennel these same "nobles" must have
been! Aye, mean and soulless indeed! If there was any pretence of religious convictions having anything to say in the
business, no such reflection would arise; no such language
would be seemly. But few or none of the parties cared to
get up even a semblance of interest in the doctrinal aspect of
the passing revolution. One object, and one alone, seemed
fixed before their gaze—to get as much as possible of " what
was going;" to secure some of the loot, and to keep it. Given
this one consideration, all things else might remain or be
changed a thousand times over for all they cared. If any one
question the correctness of this estimate of the conduct of the
English and Anglo-Irish lords of the period before us, I need
only point to the page of authentic history. They were a
debased and cowardly pack. As long as Henry fed them
with bribes from the abbey lands, they made and unmade
laws "to order" for him. He asked them to declare his marriage with Catherine of Arragon invalid—they did it; his
marriage with Anna Boleyn lawful—they did it; this same
marriage *un*-lawful and its fruits illegitimate—they did it;
his marriage with Jane Seymour lawful—they did it. In fine,
they said and unsaid, legitimatized and illegitimatized, just as
he desired. Nor was this all. In the reign of his child Edward, they enacted every law deemed necessary for the more
complete overthrow of the ancient faith and the setting up of
the new. But no sooner had Mary come to the throne, than
these same lords, legislators, and statesmen instantaneously
wheeled around, beat their breasts, became wondrously pious
Catholics, whined out repentantly that they had been frightful
criminals; and, like the facile creatures that they were, at the
request of Mary, or to please her, undid in a rush all they
had been doing during the two preceding reigns—but all on one
condition, most significant and most necessary to mark, viz.:

beth comes to undo all that Mary had restored, and lo ! the
venal lords and legislators in a instant wheel around once
more; they decree false and illegitimate all they had just declared true and lawful; they swallow their own words, they
say and unsay, they repeal and reënact, do and undo, as the
whim of the queen, or the necessity of conserving their sacrilegious robberies dictates !

Yes; the history of the world has nothing to parallel the
disgusting baseness, the mean, sordid cowardice of the English
and Anglo-Irish lords and legislators. Theirs was not a
change of religious conviction, right or wrong, but a greedy
venality, a facile readiness to change *any* way or *every* way
for worldly advantage. Their model of policy was Judas
Iscariot, who sold our Lord for thirty pieces of silver.

That Ireland also was not carried over into the new system
was owing to the circumstance that the English authority
had, so far, been able to secure for itself but a partial hold on
the Irish nation. It must have been a curious reflection with
the supreme pontiffs, that Ireland might in a certain sense
be said to have been saved to the Catholic Church by its
obstinate disregard of exhortations addressed to it repeatedly,
if not by the popes, under cover or ostensible sanction of
papal authority, in support of the English crown; for had
the Irish yielded all that the English king demanded, with
Papal bull in hand, and become part and parcel of the English
realm,Ireland, too, was lost to the old faith. At this point
one is tempted to indulge in bitter reflections on the course
of the Roman pontiffs towards Ireland. " Hitherto"—(so one
might put it)—"that hapless nation in its fearful struggle
against ruthless invaders found Rome on the side of its foes.
It was surely a hard and a cruel thing for the Irish, so devotedly attached to the Holy See, to behold the rapacious and
blood-thirsty Normans, Plantagenets and Tudors, able to
flourish against them Papal bulls and rescripts, until now
when Henry quarrelled with Rome. Now—henceforth—*too
late*—all that is to be altered ; henceforth the bulls and the
rescripts are all to exhort the broken and ruined Irish nation to
fight valiantly against that power to which, for four hundred

it to submit. Surely Ireland has been the sport of Roman policy, if not its victim !"

These bitter reflections would be not only natural but just, if the facts of the case really supported them. But the facts do not quite support this view, which, it is singular to note, the Irish themselves never entertained. At all times they seem to have most justly and accurately appreciated the real attitude of the Holy See towards them, and fixed the value and force of the bulls and rescripts obtained by the English sovereign at their true figure. The conduct of the popes was not free from reproach in a particular subsequently to be noted ; but the one thing they had really urged, rightly or wrongly, on the Irish from the first was the acceptance of the sovereignty of the English king, by no means implying an incorporation with the English nation, or an abandonment of their nationality. In this sense the popes' exhortations were always read by the native Irish ; and it will be noted that in this sense from the very beginning the Irish princes very generally were ready to acquiesce in them. The idea, rightly or wrongly, appears to have been that this strong sovereignty would be capable of reducing the chaotic elements in Ireland (given up to such hopeless disorder previously) to compactness and order—a good to Ireland and to Christendom. This was the guise in which the Irish question had always been presented by plausible English envoys, civil or ecclesiastical, at Rome. The Irish themselves did not greatly quarrel with it so far ; but there was all the difference in the world between this the theory and the bloody and barbarous fact and practice as revealed in Ireland.

What may be said with truth is, that the popes inquired too little about the fact and practice, and were always too ready to write and exhort upon such a question at the instance of the English. The Irish chiefs were sensible of this wrong done them ; but in their every act and word they evidenced a perfect consciousness that the rectitude of the motives animating the popes was not to be questioned. Even when the authority of the Holy See was most painfully misused against them,

at length arrived, however, when Rome was to mourn over whatever of error or wrong had marked its past policy towards Ireland, and for ever after nobly and unchangeably to stand by her side.   But alas! too late—all too late now for succeeding! All the harm had been done, and was now beyond repairing.   The grasp of England had been too firmly tightened in the past.   At the very moment when the Pope desired, hoped, urged, and expected Ireland to arise triumphant and glorious, a free Catholic nation, a recompense for lost England, she sank broken, helpless, and despairing under the feet of the sacrilegious Tudor.

————:∞:————

XXXIV.—HOW THE IRISH CHIEFS GAVE UP ALL HOPE AND YIELDED TO HENRY; AND HOW THE IRISH CLANS SERVED THE CHIEFS FOR SUCH TREASON.

HENRY THE EIGHTH was the first English sovereign styled King of Ireland, and it must be confessed he had more to show for assuming such a title than his predecessors had for the lesser dignities of the kind which they claimed; inasmuch as the title was "voted" to him in the first formal parliament in which Irish chieftains and Anglo-Norman lords sat side by side.   To be sure the Irish chieftains had no authority from the septs (from whom alone they derived any authority or power) to give such a vote; and, as we shall learn presently, some of those septs instantly on becoming aware of it and the consequences it implied, deposed the chiefs thus acting, and promptly elected (in each case from the same family, however) others in their stead.   But never previously had so many of the native princes in a manner so formal given in their acknowledgment of the English dynasty, and their renunciation of the ancient institutions of their nation.   Utterly broken down in spirit, reft of hope, weary of struggle, they seem to have yielded themselves up to inevitable fate.   "The arguments," says one of our historians, "by which many of the chiefs might have

the inevitable laws of necessity, in rendering homage to Henry the Eighth, were neither few nor weak. Abroad there was no hope of an alliance sufficient to counterbalance the immense resources of England; at home, life-wasting private wars, the conflict of laws, of languages, and of titles to property had become unbearable. That fatal family pride which would not permit an O'Brien to obey an O'Neill, nor an O'Connor to follow either, rendered the establishment of a native monarchy (even if there had been no other obstacle) wholly impracticable." Another says: "The chief lords of both English and Irish descent were reduced to a state of deplorable misery and exhaustion. . . . . It was high time, therefore, on the one side to think of submission, and prudent on the other to propose concession ; and Henry was just then fortunate in selecting a governor for Ireland who knew how to take advantage of the favorable circumstances." This was Saint-leger, whose politic course of action resulted in the assembling at Dublin, 12th June, 1541, of a parliament at which, besides all the principal Anglo-Norman lords, there attended, Donogh O'Brien, tanist of Thomond, the O'Reilly, O'More, M'William, Fitzpatrick, and Kavanagh.* The speeches in the English language were translated in the Gaelic tongue to the Irish chiefs by the Earl of Ormond. The main business was to consider a bill voting the crown of Ireland to Henry, which was unanimously passed—registered rather ; for, as far as the native " legislators" were concerned, the assemblage was that of conquered and subdued chieftains, ready to acknowledge their subjection in *any* way. O'Neill and O'Donnell refused to attend. They held out sullenly yet awhile in the North. But in the next year they "came in," much to the delight of Henry, who loaded them with flatteries and attentions. The several chiefs yielded up their ancient Irish titles, and consented to receive English instead. O'Brien was created Earl of Thomond ; Ulick M William was created Earl of Clanrickard and Baron Dunkellin ; Hugh O'Donnell was made Earl

---

*Son of M'Murrogh who had just previously " submitted, " renouncing the title of M'Murrogh, adopting the name of Kavanagh, and undertaking on the part of his

of Tyrconnel ; O'Neill was made Earl of Tyrone ; Kavanagh was made Baron of Ballyann ; and Fitzpatrick, Baron of Ossory.   Most of these titles were conferred by Henry in person at Greenwich palace, with extravagant pomp and formality, the Irish chiefs having been specially invited thither for that purpose, and sums of money given them for their equipment and expenses.   In many instances, if not in all, they consented to receive from Henry royal patents or title deeds for "their" lands, as the English from their feudal stand-point would regard them ; not *their* lands, however, in point of fact and law, but the "tribe-lands" of their septs. The acceptance of these "patents" of land proprietorship, still more than the acceptance of English titles, was " a complete abrogation of the Gaelic relation of clansman and chief." Some of the new earls were moreover apportioned a share of the plundered Church lands.   This was yet a further outrage on their people.   Little need we wonder, therefore, that while the newly created earls and barons were airing their modern dignities at the English court, feted and flattered by Henry, the clans at home, learning by dark rumor of these treasons, were already stripping the backsliding chiefs of all authority and power, and were taking measures to arrest and consign them to punishment on their return !   O'Donnell found most of his clan, headed by his son, up in arms against him ; O'Brien, on his return, was confronted by like circumstances ; the new " Earl of Clanrickard" was incontinently attainted by his people, and a Gaelic " M'William" was duly installed in his stead.   O'Neill, " the first of his race who had accepted an English title," found that his clansmen had formally deposed him, and elected as the O'Neill, his son John, surnamed " John the Proud "—the celebrated "Shane " O'Neill so called in the jargon of the English writers.   On all sides the septs repudiated and took formal and practical measures to disavow and reverse the acts of their representatives. The hopelessness that had broken the spirit of the chief found no place in the heart of the clan.

This was the beginning of new complications in the already tangled skein of Irish affairs.   A new source of division and disorganization was now planted in the country. Hitherto the clans at least were intact, though the nation was shattered. Henceforth the clans themselves were split into fragments. From this period forward we hear of a king's or a queen's O'Reilly and an Irish O'Reilly; a king's O'Neill and an Irish O'Neill; a king's O'Donnell and an Irish O'Donnell. The English government presented a very artful compromise to the septs—offering them a chief of the native family stock, but requiring that he should hold from the crown, not from the clan. The nominee of the government, backed by all the English power and interest, was generally able to make head for a time at least against the legitimate chief duly and legally chosen and elected by the sept. In many instances the English nominee was able to rally to his side a considerable section of the clan, and even without external aid to hold the chosen chief in check. By the internal feuds thus incited, the clans were utterly riven, and were given over to a self-acting process of extinction. Occasionally, indeed, the crown nominee, once he was firmly seated in the chieftaincy, threw off all allegiance to his foreign masters, declared himself an *Irish* chief, cast away scornfully his English earlship, and assumed proudly the ancient title that named him head of his clan. In this event the government simply declared him "deposed," proceeded to nominate another chief in his place, and sent an army to install the new nominee on the necks of the stubborn clan. This was the artful system—copied in all its craft and cruelty by the British in India centuries afterwards—pursued towards the native princes and chiefs of Ireland from the reign of Henry the Eighth to the middle of the seventeenth century.

XXXV.—HENRY'S SUCCESSORS: EDWARD, MARY, AND ELIZABETH. THE CAREER OF "JOHN THE PROUD."

THE changes of English sovereigns little affected English policy in Ireland. Whatever meaning the change from Henry to Edward, from Edward to Mary, and from Mary to Elizabeth, may have had in England, in Ireland it mattered little who filled the throne: the policy of subjugation, plunder, and extirpation went on. In Mary's reign, indeed, incidents more than one occurred to show that, though of course bent on completing the conquest and annexation of Ireland, she was a stranger to the savage and cruel passions that had ruled her father, and that were so fearfully inherited by his other daughter, Elizabeth. The aged chief of Offaly, O'Conor, had long lain in the dungeons of London Tower, all efforts to obtain his release having failed. At length his daughter Margaret, hearing that now a queen—a *woman*—sat on the throne, bethought her of an appeal in person to Mary for her father's life and freedom. She proceeded to London and succeeded in obtaining an audience of the queen. She pleaded with all a woman's eloquence, and with all the fervor of a daughter petitioning for a father's life. Mary was touched to the heart by this instance of devotedness. She treated young Margaret of Offaly with the greatest tenderness, spoke to her cheeringly, and promised her that what she had so bravely sought should be freely granted. And it was so. O'Conor Faly returned with his daughter to Ireland a free man.

Nor was this the only instance in which Mary exhibited a womanly sympathy for misfortune. The fate of the Geraldines moved her to compassion. The young Gerald—long time a fugitive among the glens of Muskery and Donegal, now an exile sheltered in Rome—was recalled and restored to all

the young Geraldine there were allowed to return to their homes, we are told, the heirs of the houses of Ormond and Upper Ossory, "to the great delight of the southern half of the kingdom."

To Mary there succeeded on the English throne her Amazonian sister, Elizabeth. The nobles and commoners of England, had, as in Mary's case, at her father's request, declared and decreed as the immortal and unchangeable truth that she was illegitimate; but, according to their code of morality, that was no earthly reason against their now declaring and decreeing as the immortal and unchangeable truth that she was legitimate. For these very noble nobles and most uncommon commoners eat dirt with a hearty zest, and were ready to decree and declare, to swear and unswear, the most contradictory and irreconcilable assertions, according as their venality and servility suggested.

Elizabeth was a woman of marvellous ability. She possessed abundantly the talents that qualify a statesman. She was greatly gifted indeed: but nature, while richly endowing her with so much else besides, forgot or withheld from her one of the commonest gifts of human kind—Elizabeth had no heart. A woman devoid of heart is, after all, a terrible freak of nature. She may be gifted with marvellous powers of intellect, and endowed with great personal beauty, but she is still a monster. Such was Elizabeth; a true Tudor and veritable daughter of King Henry the Eighth; one of the most remarkable women of her age, and in one sense one of the greatest of English sovereigns.

Her reign was memorable in Irish history. It witnessed at its opening the revolt of John the Proud in Ulster; later on the Desmond rebellion: and towards the close the great struggle that to all time will immortalize the name of Hugh O'Neill.

John the Proud, as I have already mentioned, was elected to the chieftaincy of the O'Neills on the deposition of his father by the clan. He scornfully defied all the efforts of the English to dispute his claim, and soon they were fain to re-

man little more can be said in praise than that he was an indomitable and, up to the great reverse which suddenly closed
his career, a successful soldier, who was able to defy and defeat the best armies of England on Irish soil, and more than
once to bring the English government very submissively to
terms of his dictation. But he lacked the personal virtues
that adorned the lives and inspired the efforts of the great
and brave men whose struggles we love to trace in the annals
of Ireland. His was, indeed, a splendid military career, and
his administration of the government of his territory was undoubtedly exemplary in many respects, but he was in private
life no better than a mere English noble of the time ; his conduct towards the unfortunate Calvach O'Donnell·leaving a
lasting stain on his name.* The state papers of England
reveal an incident in his life, which presents us with an
authenticated illustration of the means deemed lawful by the
English Government often enough in those centuries for the
removing of an Irish foe. John had reduced all the north to his
sway, and cleared out every vestige of English dominion in
Ulster. He had encountered the English commander-in-chief
and defeated him. He had marched to the very confines of
Dublin, spreading terror through the Pale. In this strait
Sussex, the lord lieutenant, bethought him of a good plan for
the effectual removal of this dangerous enemy to the crown
and government. With the full cognizance and sanction of
the queen, he hired an assassin to murder O'Neill. The plot,
however, miscarried, and we should probably have never
heard of it, but that, very awkwardly for the memory of Elizabeth and of her worthy viceroy, some portions of their cor-

* He invaded the O'Donnell's territory, and acting, it is said, on information secretly supplied by the unfaithful wife of the Tyrconnell chief, succeeded in surprising
and capturing him. He kept O'Donnell, who was his father-in-law, for years a close
prisoner, and lived in open adultery with the perfidious wife of the imprisoned chief,
the step-mother of his own lawful wife! 'What deepens the horror of this odious
domestic tragedy," says M'Gee, " is the fact that the wife of O'Neill, the daughter
of O'Donnell, thus supplanted by her shameless step-mother under her own roof,
died soon afterwards of ' horror loathing grief and deep anguish' at the spectacle
afforded by the private life of O'Neill, and the severities inflicted on her wretched

respondence on the subject remained undestroyed amongst the state papers, and are now to be seen in the State Paper Office! The career of John the Proud closed suddenly and miserably. He was utterly defeated (A.D. 1567) in a great pitched battle by the O'Donnells; an overthrow which it is said affected his reason. Flying from the field with his guilty mistress, his secretary, and a bodyguard of fifty horsemen he was induced to become the guest of some Scottish adventurers in Antrim, upon whom he had inflicted a severe defeat not long previously. After dinner, when most of those present were under the influence of wine—John it is said, having been purposely plied with drink—an Englishman who was present, designedly got up a brawl, or pretence of a brawl, about O'Neill's recent defeat of his then guests. Daggers were drawn in an instant, and the unfortunate John the Proud while sitting helplessly at the banqueting board, was surrounded and butchered!

XXXVI.—HOW THE GERALDINES ONCE MORE LEAGUED AGAINST ENGLAND UNDER THE BANNER OF THE CROSS. HOW "THE ROYAL POPE" WAS THE EARLIEST AND THE MOST ACTIVE ALLY OF THE IRISH CAUSE.

HE death of John the Proud gave the English Power respite in the north; but, respited for a moment in the north, that power was doomed to encounter danger still as menacing in the south. Once more the Geraldines were to put it severely to the proof.

Elizabeth had not witnessed and studied in vain the events of her father's reign: She very sagaciously concluded, that if she would safely push her war against the Catholic faith in Ireland, she must first get the dreaded Geraldines out of the way. And she knew, too, from all previous events, how necessary it was to guard that not even a solitary seedling of that dangerous race was allowed to escape. She wrote to Sydney, her lord lieutenant, to lay a right cunning snare for the catching of the Geraldines in one haul. That faithful viceroy of a gracious queen forthwith " issued an invitation for the nobility of Ireland to meet him on a given day in the city of Dublin, to confer with him on some matters of great weight, particularly regarding religion." The bait took. "The dynasts of Ireland, little suspecting the design, hasten to the city, and along with them the Earl of Desmond and his brother John." They had a safe conduct from Sydney, but had scarcely arrived when they were seized and committed to the castile dungeons, whence they were soon shipped off to the tower of London. This was the plan Elizabeth had laid, but it had only partially succeeded. All the Geraldines had not come into the snare, and she took five years to decide whether it would be worth while murdering these (according to law), while so many other members of the family were yet outside her grasp. The earl and his

to residence under surveillance in London. According to the version of the family chronicler, they found means of transmitting a document or message to their kinsmen and retainers, appointing their cousin James, son of Maurice—known as James Fitzmaurice—to be the head and leader of the family in their absence, " for he was well-known for his attachment to the ancient faith, no less than for his valor and chivalry." " Gladly," says the old chronicler, " did the people of Earl Desmond receive these commands, and inviolable was their attachmento him who was now their appointed chieftain."

This was that James Fitzmaurice of Desmond—" James Geraldine of happy memory," as Pope Gregory calls him—who originated, planned, and organized the memorable Geraldine League of 1579, upon the fortunes of which for years the attention of Christendom was fixed. With loftier, nobler, holier arms than the righting of mere family wrongs he conceived the idea of a great league in defence of religion ; a holy war, in which he might demand the sustainment and intervention of the Catholic powers. Elizabeth's own conduct at this juncture in stirring up and subsidizing the Huguenots in France supplied Fitzmaurice with another argument in favor of his scheme. First of all he sent an envoy to the Pope—Gregory the Thirteenth—demanding the blessing and assistance of the Supreme Pontiff in this struggle of a Catholic nation against a monarch nakedly violating all title to allegiance. The act of an apostate sovereign of a Catholic country drawing the sword to compel his subjects into apostacy on pain of death, was not only a forfeiture of his title to rule, it placed him outside the pale of law, civil and ecclesiastical. This was Henry's position when he died ; to this position, as the envoy pointed out, Elizabeth succeeded " with a vengeance ;" and so he prayed of Pope Gregory, " his blessing on the undertaking and the concession of indulgences which the Church bestows on those who die in defence of the faith." The Holy Father flung himself earnestly and actively into the cause. " Then," says the old Geraldine chaplain, " forth flashed the sword of the Geraldine ; like chaff did he scatter the host of reformers ; fire and devastation did

won many a glorious victory, and carried off innumerable
trophies."

This burst of rhapsody, excusable enough on the part of the
old Geraldine chronicler, gives, however, no faithful idea of
what ensued; many brilliant victories, it is true, James Geraldine achieved in his protracted struggle. But after five years
of valiant effort and of varied fortunes, the hour of reverses
came. One by one Fitzmaurice's allies were struck down or
fell away from him, until at length he himself with a small
force stood to bay in the historic Glen of Aherlow, which " had
now become to the patriots of the south what the valley of
Glenmalure had been for those of Leinster—a fortress dedicated by nature to the defence of freedom." Here he held out
for a year, but, eventually, he despatched envoys to the lord
president at Kilmallock to make terms of submission, which
were duly granted. Whether from motives of policy, or in
compliance with these stipulations, the imprisoned earl and
his brother were forthwith released in London; the queen
making them an exceedingly smooth and bland speech against
the sin of rebellion. The gallant Fitzmaurice betook himself
into exile there to plot and organize with redoubled energy
in the cause of Faith and Country; while the earl of Desmond, utterly disheartened no doubt by the result of James's
revolt, and "only too happy to be tolerated in the possession
of his 570,000 acres, was eager enough to testify his allegiance
by any sort of service."

Fitzmaurice did not labor in vain. He went from court to
court pleading the cause he had so deeply at heart. He was
received with honor and respect everywhere; but it was only
at Rome that he obtained that which he valued beyond personal honors for himself—aid in men, money, and arms for
the struggle in Ireland. A powerful expedition was fitted out
at Civita Vecchia by the sovereign pontiff; and from various
princes of Europe secret promises of further aid were showered upon the brave Geraldine. He little knew, all this time,
while he in exile was toiling night and day—was pleading,
urging, beseeching—planning, organizing, and directing—full
of ardor and of faithful courageous resolve, that his coun-

trymen at home—even his own kinsmen—were temporizing and
compromising with the lord president! He little knew that,
instead of finding Ireland ready to welcome him as a deliverer,
he was to land in the midst of a prostrate, dispirited, and
apathetic population, and was to find some of his own relatives,
not only fearing to countenance, but cravenly arrayed against
him! It was even so. As the youthful Emmett exclaimed of
his own project against the British crown more than two hundred years subsequently, we may say of Fitzmaurice's—" There
was failure in every part." By some wild fatality everything
miscarried. There was concert nowhere: there was no one
engaged in the cause of ability to second James's efforts; and
what misfortune marred, incompetency ruined. The Pope's
expedition, upon which so much depended, was diverted from
its destination by its incompetent commander, an English ad-
venturer named Stukely, knave or fool, to whom, in an evil
hour, James had unfortunately confided such a trust. Stukely,
having arrived at Lisbon on his way to Ireland, and having
there learned that the king of Portugal was setting out on an
expedition against the Moors, absolutely joined his forces to
those of Dom Sebastian, and accompanied him,* leaving James
of Desmond to learn as best he might of his inexplicable imbecility, if not cold-blooded treason!

Meanwhile, in Ireland, the air was thick with rumors, vague
and furtive, that James was " on the sea," and soon to land
with a liberating expedition. The government was of course,
on the alert, fastening its gaze with lynx-eyed vigilance on all
men likely to join the " foreign emissaries," as the returning
Irish and their friends were styled; and around the south-
western coast of Ireland was instantly drawn a line of British
cruisers. The government fain would have seized upon the
earl of Desmond and his brothers, but, it was not certain
whether this would aid or retard the apprehended revolt; for,
so far, these Geraldines protested their opposition to it, and
to them—to the earl in particular—the population of the south

---

* Stukely, and most of his force, perished on the bloody field of Alcazarquebir,
where Dom Sebastian and two Moorish kings likewise fell.

looked for leadership. Yet, in sooth, the English might have believed the earl, who, hoping nothing of the revolt, yet sympathizing secretly with his kinsmen, was in a sad plight what to do, anxious to be "neutral," and trying to convince the lord president that he was well affected. The government party, on the other hand, trusting him nought, seemed anxious to goad him into some "overt act" that would put him utterly in their power. While all was excitement about the expected expedition, lo! three suspicious strangers were landed at Dingle from a Spanish ship! They were seized as "foreign emissaries," and were brought first before the earl of Desmond. Glad of an opportunity for showing the government his zeal, he forthwith sent them prisoners to the lord president at Kilmallock. In vain they protested that they were not conspirators or invaders. And indeed they were not, though they were what was just as bad in the eyes of the law, namely, Catholic ecclesiastics, one of them being Dr. O'Haly, bishop of Mayo, and another, Father Cornelius O'Rorke. To reveal what they really were would serve them little; inasmuch as hanging and beheading as "rebels" was in no way different from hanging and beheading as "Popish ecclesiastics." Yet would the authorities insist that they were vile foreign emissaries. They spoke with a Spanish accent; they wore their beards in the Spanish fashion, and their boots were of Spanish cut. So to force a confession of what was not truth out of them, no effort was spared. They were "put to every conceivable torture," says the historian, "in order to extract intelligence of Fitzmaurice's movements." After their thighs had been broken with hammers they were hanged on a tree, and their bodies used as targets by the soldiery.

By this time James, all unconscious of Stukely's defection, had embarked from Spain for Ireland, with a few score Spanish soldiers in three small ship. He brought with him Dr. Saunders, Papal legate, the bishop of Killaloe, and Dr. Allen. The little fleet, after surviving shipwreck on the coast of Gallicia, sailed into Dingle Harbor 17th July, 1579. Here James first tasted disheartening disillusion. His great kinsman the earl, so far from marching to welcome him and summoning the country to rise, "sent him neither sign of friendship nor promise of coöperation." This was discouragement indeed ; yet Fitzmaurice was not without hope that when in a few days the main expedition under Stukely would arrive, the earl might think more hopefully of the enterprise, and rally to it that power which he alone could assemble in Munster. So, weighing anchor, James steered for a spot which no doubt he had long previously noted and marked as preëminently suited by nature for such a purpose as this of his just now— Illan-an-Oir, or Golden Island, in Smerwick harbor, on the north-west Kerry coast, destined to be famed in story as fort del Ore. This was a singular rock, a diminutive Gibraltar jutting into the harbor or bay of Smerwick. Even previously its natural strength as a site for a fort had been noticed, and a rude fortification of some sort crowned the rock. Here James landed his small force, threw up an earthwork across the narrow neck of land connecting " the Isle of Gold" with the mainland, and waited for news of Stukely.

But Stukely never came ! There did come, however, unfortunately for James, an English man of war, which had little difficulty in capturing his transports within sight of the helpless fort. All hope of the expected expedition soon fled, or mayhap its fate became known, and matters grew desperate on Illan-an-Oir. Still the earl made no sign. His brothers John and James, however, less timid or more true to kinship, had chivalrously hastened to join Fitzmaurice. But it was clear the enterprise was lost. The government forces were mustering throughout Munster, and nowhere was help being organized. In this strait it was decided to quit the fort and endeavor to reach the old fastnesses amidst the Galtees. The little band in their eastward march were actually pursued by the earl of Desmond, not very much in earnest indeed—in downright sham, the English said, yet in truth severely enough to compel them to divide into three fugitive groups, the papal legate and the other dignitaries remaining with Fitzmaurice. Making a desperate push to reach the Shannon, his horses utterly exhausted, the brave Geraldine was obliged to impress into his

whose lands he was then passing.   Burke, indeed, was a relative of his, and Fitzmaurice thought that revealing his
name would silence all objection.   On the contrary, however,
this miserable Burke assembled a force, pursued the fugitives
and fell upon them, as " few and faint," jaded and outworn,
they had halted at the little river Mulkern in Limerick county.
Fitzmaurice was wounded mortally early in the fray, yet his
ancient prowess flashed out with all its native brilliancy at the
last.   Dashing into the midst of his dastard foes, at one blow
he clove to earth Theobald Burke, and in another instant laid
the brother of Theobald mortally wounded at his feet.   The
assailants, though ten to one, at once turned and fled.   But alas !
vain was the victory—James Geraldine had received his death
wound !   Calmly receiving the last rites of the Church at
the hands of Dr. Allen, and having in his last breath dictated
a message to his kinsmen enjoining them to take up the banner
fallen in his hand, and to fight to the last in the holy war—
naming his cousin John of Desmond as leader to succeed him—
the chivalrous Fitzmaurice breathed his last sigh.   " Such,"
says the historian, " was the fate of the glorious hopes of Sir
James Fitzmaurice !   So ended in a squabble with churls
about cattle, on the banks of an insignificant stream, a career
which has drawn the attention of Europe, and had inspired
with apprehension the lion-hearted English queen ! "

Faithful to the dying message of Fitzmaurice, John of Desmond now avowed his resolution to continue the struggle ;
which he did bravely, and not without brilliant results.   But
the earl still "stood on the fence." Still would he fain persuade
the government that he was quite averse to the mad designs
of his unfortunate kinsmen ; and still the government, fully
believing him a sympathizer with the movement, lost no opportunity of scornfully taunting him with insinuations.
Eventually htey commenced to treat his lands as the possessions of an enemy, wasting and harrying them; and at length the
earl, finding *too late* that in such a struggle there was for him
no neutrality, took the field. But this step on his part, which if
it had been taken earlier, might have had a powerful effect,

upon the lost cause. Yet he showed by a few brilliant victories at the very outset that he was, in a military sense, not all unworthy of his position as First Geraldine. The Spanish king, too, had by this time been moved to the aid of the struggle. The Fort del Ore once more received an expedition from Spain, where this time there landed a force of 700 Spaniards and Italians, under the command of Sebastian San Josef Hercules Pisano, and the Duke of Biscay. They brought moreover arms for 5,000 men, a large supply of money, and cheering promises of still further aid from over the sea. Lord Grey, the deputy, quickly saw that probably the future existence of British power in Ireland depended upon the swift and sudden crushing of this formidable expedition; accordingly with all vehemence did he strain every energy to concentrate with rapidity around Fort del Ore, by land and sea, an overwhelming force before any aid or coöperation could reach it from the Geraldines. "Among the officers of the besieging force were three especially notable men—Sir Walter Raleigh, the poet Spenser, and Hugh O'Neill—afterwards Earl of Tyrone, but at this time commanding a squadron of cavalry for her majesty, queen Elizabeth. San Josef surrendered the place on conditions; that savage outrage ensued, which is known in Irish history as ' the massacre of Smerwick.' Raleigh and Wingfield appear to have directed the operations by which 800 prisoners of war were cruelly butchered and flung over the rocks. The sea upon that coast is deep, and the tide swift ; but it has not proved deep enough to hide that horrid crime, or to wash the stains of such wanton bloodshed from the memory of it authors ! "*

It may be said that the Geraldine cause never rallied after this disaster. " For four years longer," says the historian whom I have just quoted, "the Geraldine League flickered in the South. Proclamations offering pardon to all concerned, except earl Gerald and a few of his most devoted adherents, had their effect. Deserted at home, and cut off from foreign assistance, the condition of Desmond grew more and more intolerable. On one occasion he narrowly escaped capture by rushing with his countess into a river, and remaining concealed

---

*M'Gee.

up to the chin in water. His dangers can hardly be paralleled
by those of Bruce after the battle of Falkirk, or by the more
familiar adventures of Charles Edward. At length, on the
night of the 11th November, 1584, he was surprised with only
two followers in a lonesome valley, about five miles distant from
Tralee, among the mountains of Kerry. The spot is still remembered, and the name of ' the Earl's Road' transports the
fancy of the traveller to that tragical scene. Cowering over the
embers of a half-extinct fire in a miserable hovel, the lord of a
country which in time of peace had yielded an annual rental of
'40,000 golden pieces,' was despatched by the hands of common soldiers, without pity, or time, or hesitation. A few followers watching their creaghts or herds, farther up the valley,
found his bleeding trunk flung out upon the highway; the
head was transported over seas to rot upon the spikes of
London Tower."

Such was the end of the great Geraldine League of 1579.
Even the youngest of my readers must have noticed in its
plan and constitution, one singular omission which proved a
fatal defect. It did not raise the issue of national independence at all. It made no appeal to the national aspirations
for liberty. It was simply a war to compel Elizabeth to desist from her bloody persecutions of the Catholic faith. Furthermore it left out of calculation altogether the purely Irish
elements. It left all the northern half of the kingdom out of
sight. It was only a southern movement. The Irish princes
and chiefs—those of them most opposed to the English power
—never viewed the enterprise with confidence or sympathy.
Fitzmaurice devoted much more attention to foreign aid than
to native combination. In truth, his movement was simply
an Anglo-Irish war to obtain freedom of conscience, and never
raised issues calculated to call forth the united efforts of the
Irish nation in a war against England.

Before passing to the next great event of this era, I may
pause to note here a few occurrences worthy of record, but for
which I did not deem it advisable to break in upon the consecutive narration of the Geraldine war. My endeavor throughout
is to present to my young readers in clear and distinct outline,

a sketch of the *chief* event of each period more or less complete
by itself, so that it may be easily comprehended and remembered. To this end I omit many minor incidents and occurrences, which, if engrafted or brought in upon the main narrative, might have a tendency to confuse and bewilder the facts
in one's recollection.

————:∞:————

XXXVII.—HOW COMMANDER COSBY HELD A "FEAST" AT MUL-
LAGHMAST; AND HOW "RUARI OGE" RECOMPENSED THAT
"HOSPITALITY." A VICEROY'S VISIT TO GLENMALURE, AND
HIS RECEPTION THERE.

IT was within the period which we have just passed over,
that the ever-memorable massacre of Mullaghmast
occurred. It is not, unhappily, the only tragedy of the
kind to be met with in our blood-stained annals; yet it
is of all the most vividly perpetuated in popular traditions. In 1577, Sir Francis Cosby, commanding the queen's
troops in Leix and Offaly, formed a diabolical plot for the
permanent conquest of that district. Peace at the moment
prevailed between the government and the inhabitants; but
Cosby seemed to think that in *extirpation* lay the only effectual security for the crown. Feigning, however, great friendship, albeit suspicious of some few "evil disposed" persons,
said not to be well-affected, he invited to a grand feast all the
chief families of the territory; attendance thereat being a sort
of test of amity. To this summons responded the flower of
the Irish nobility in Leix and Offaly, with their kinsmen and
friends—the O'Mores, O'Kellys, Lalors, O'Nolans, etc. The
"banquet"—alas!—was prepared by Cosby in the great Rath
or Fort of Mullach-Maisten, or Mullaghmast, in Kildare
county. Into the great rath rode many a pleasant cavalcade
that day; but none ever came forth that entered in. A gentleman named Lalor who had halted a little way off, had his

while many went into the rath, none were seen to reappear
outside.   Accordingly he desired his friends to remain behind
while he advanced and reconnoitred.   He entered cautiously.
Inside, what a horrid spectacle met his sight!   At the very
entrance the dead bodies of some of his slaughtered kinsmen!
In an instant he himself was set upon; but drawing his sword,
he hewed his way out of the fort and back to his friends, and
they barely escaped with their lives to Dysart!   He was the
only Irishman, out of more than four hundred who entered
the fort that day, that escaped with life!   The invited guests
were butchered to a man; one hundred and eighty of the
O'Mores alone having thus perished.

The peasantry long earnestly believed and asserted that on
the encircled rath of slaughter rain nor dew never fell, and
that the ghosts of the slain might be seen, and their groans
distinctly heard "on the solemn midnight blast"!-

O'er the Rath of Mullaghmast,
On the solemn midnight blast,
What bleeding spectres pass'd
                With their gashed breasts bare !

Hast thou heard the fitful wail
That o'erloads the sullen gale
When the waning moon shines pale
                O'er the cursed ground there !

Hark ! hollow moans arise
Through the black tempestuous skies,
And curses, strife, and cries,
                From the lone rath swell ;

For bloody Sydney there
Nightly fills the lurid air
With the unholy pompous glare
                Of the foul, deep hell.

     *   *   *   *   *
False Sydney ! knighthood's stain !
The trusting brave—in vain
Thy guests—ride o'er the plain
                To thy dark cow'rd snare;

Flow'r of Offaly and Leix,
They have come thy hoard to grace—
Fools !.to meet a faithless race,

While cup and song abound,
The triple lines surround
The closed and guarded mound,
      In the night's dark noon.

Alas! too brave O'Moore,
Ere the revelry was o'er,
They have spill'd thy young heart's gore,
      Snatch'd from love too soon!

At the feast, unarmed all,
Priest, bard, and chieftain fall
In the treacherous Saxon's hall,
      O'er the bright wine bowl;

And now hightly round the board,
With unsheath'd and reeking sword,
Strides the cruel felon lord
      Of the blood stain'd souL

Since that hour the clouds that pass'd
O'er the Rath of Mullaghmast,
One tear have never cast
      On the gore dyed sod;

For the shower of crimson rain
That o'erflowed that fatal plain,
Cries aloud, and not in vain,
      To the most high God!

A sword of vengeance tracked Cosby from that day. In Leix or Offaly after this terrible blow there was no raising a regular force; yet of the family thus murderously cut down, there remained one man who thenceforth lived but to avenge his slaughtered kindred. This was Ruari Oge O'Moore, the guerilla chief of Leix and Offaly, long the terror and the scourge of the Pale. While he lived, none of Cosby's "undertakers" slept securely in the homes of the plundered race. Swooping down upon their castles and mansions, towns and settlements, Ruari became to them an Angel of Destruction. When they deemed him farthest away, his sword of vengeance was at hand. In the lurid glare of burning roof and blazing granary, they saw like a spectre from the rath, the face of an O'Moore; and, above the roar of the flames, the shrieks of victims, or the crash of falling battlements, they heard in the hoarse voice of an implacable avenger—

And the sword of Ireland still was swift and strong to pursue the author of that bloody deed, and to strike him and his
race through two generations.   One by one they met their
doom—

> In the lost battle
> Borne down by the flying :
> Where mingle war's rattle
> With the groans of the dying.

On the bloody day of Glenmalure, when the red flag of
England went down in the battle's hurricane, and Elizabeth's
proud viceroy, Lord Gray de Wilton, and all the chivalry of
the Pale were scattered and strewn like autumn leaves in the
gale, Cosby of Mullaghmast fell in the rout, sent swiftly to
eternal judgment with the brand of Cain upon his brow.   A
like doom, a fatality, tracked his children from generation to
generation ! They too perished by the sword or the battle-axe
—the last of them, son and grandson, on one day by the stroke
of an avenging O'More*—until it may be questioned if there
now exists a human being in whose veins runs the blood of
the greatly infamous knight commander, Sir Francis Cosby.
The battle of Glenmalure was fought 25th of August, 1580.
That magnificent defile, as I have already remarked, in the
words of one of our historians, had long been for the patriots
of Leinster "a fortress dedicated by nature to the defence of freedom : " and never had fortress of freedom a nobler soul to
command its defence than he who now held Glenmalure for
God and Ireland—Feach M'Hugh O'Byrne, of Ballinacor,
called by the English " The Firebrand of the Mountains."
In his time no sword was drawn for liberty in any corner of
the island, near or far, that his own good blade did not leap
responsively from its scabbard to aid " the good old cause."
Whether the tocsin was sounded in the north or in the south,
it ever woke pealing echoes amidst the hills of Glenmalure. As
in later years, Feach of Ballinacor was the more trusted and
faithful of Hugh O'Neill's friends and allies, so was he now

---

* "Ouney, son of Ruari Oge O'More, slew Alexander and Francis Cosby, son and
grandson of Cosby of Mullaghmast, and routed their troops with great slaughter, at

in arms stoutly battling for the Geraldine league. His son-in-law, Sir Francis Fitzgerald, and James Eustace, Viscount Baltinglass, had rallied what survived of the clansmen of Idrone, Offaly, and Leix, and had effected a junction with him, taking up strong positions in the passes of Slieveroe and Glenmalure. Lord Grey of Wilton arrived as lord lieutenant from England on the 12th August. Eager to signalize his advent to office by some brilliant achievement, he rejoiced greatly that so near at hand—within a day's march of Dublin Castle—an opportunity presented itself. Yes! He would measure swords with this wild chief of Glenmalure who had so often defied the power of England. He would extinguish the "Firebrand of the Mountain," and plant the cross of St. George on the ruins of Ballinacor! So, assembling a right royal host, the haughty viceroy marched upon Glenmalure. The only accounts which we possess of the battle are those contained in letters written to England by Sir William Stanley and others of the lord lieutenant's officials and subordinates; so that we may be sure the truth is very scantily revealed. Lord Grey having arrived at the entrance to the glen, seems to have had no greater anxiety than to "hem in" the Irish. So he constructed a strong earthwork or entrenched camp at the mouth of the valley the more effectually to stop "escape!" It never once occurred to the vain-glorious English viceroy that it was he himself and his royal army that were to play the part of fugitives in the approaching scene! All being in readiness, Lord Grey gave the order of the advance; he and a group of courtier friends taking their place on a high ground commanding a full view up the valley, so that they might lose nothing of the gratifying spectacle anticipated. An ominous silence prevailed as the English regiments pushed their way into the glen. The courtiers waxed witty; they wondered whether the game had not "stolen away;" they sadly thought there would be "no sport;" or they halloed right merrily to the troops to follow on and "unearth" the "old fox." After a while the way became more and more tedious. "We were," says Sir William Stanley, "forced to our feet;" the way being "full of stones, rocks, logs, and wood; in the bottom thereof a river full of loose stones which we were driven to cross divers times." At length it seemed good to Feach M'Hugh O'Byrne to declare that the time had come for action. Then from the forest-clad mountain sides there burst forth a wild shout whereat many of the jesting courtiers turned pale ; and a storm of bullets assailed the entangled English legions. As yet the foe was unseen ; but his execution was disastrous. The English troops broke into disorder. Lord Grey, furious and distracted, ordered up the reserves ; but now Feach passed the word along the Irish lines to charge the foe. Like the torrents of winter pouring down those hills, down swept the Irish force from every side upon the struggling mass below. Vain was all effort to wrestle against such a furious charge. From the very first it became a pursuit. How to escape was now each castle courtier's wild endeavor. Discipline was utterly cast aside in the panic rout! Lord Grey and a few attendants fled early, and by fleet horses saved themselves; but of all the brilliant hosts the viceroy had led out of Dublin a few days before, there returned but a few shattered companies to tell the tale of disaster, and to surround with new terrors the name of Feach M'Hugh, the " Firebrand of the Mountains."

XXXVIII.—" HUGH OF DUNGANNON," HOW QUEEN ELIZA-
BETH BROUGHT UP THE YOUNG IRISH CHIEF AT COURT
WITH CERTAIN CRAFTY DESIGNS OF HER OWN.

THERE now appears upon the scene of Irish history
that remarkable man whose name will live in song
and story as long as the Irish race survives; leader of
one of the greatest struggles ever waged against the
Anglo-Norman subjugation;   (pronounced Aeh), Angli-
cised Hugh O'Neill; called in English "patents" Earl of
Tyrone.

Ever since the closing years of the eighth Henry's reign—
the period at which, as I have already explained, the policy
of splitting up the clans by rival chiefs began to be adopted by
the English power—the government took care to provide itself,
by fair means or by foul, with a supply of material from which
crown chiefs might be taken. That is to say, the government
took care to have in its hands, and trained to its own purposes,
some member or members of each of the ruling families—the
O'Neills, O'Reillys, O'Donnells, M'Guires, O'Connors, etc.,
ready to be set up as the king's or queen's O'Neill, O'Reilly, or
O'Donnell, as the case might be, according as policy dictated
and opportunity offered. One of these government *protégés* was
Hugh O'Neill, who, when yet a boy, was taken to London
and brought up in the court of Elizabeth. As he was a
scion of the royal house of O'Neill, and, in English planning
destined one day to play the most important part as yet
assigned to a queen's chief in Ireland, viz., the reducing to
subserviency of that Ulster which formed the standing menace
of English power, the unconquerable citadel of nationality,
the boy Hugh—the young Baron of Dungannon as he was
called—was the object of unusual attention. He was an
especial favorite with the queen, and as may be supposed

able obeisance. No pains were spared with his education.
He had the best tutors to attend upon him, and above all he
was assiduously trained into court finesse, how to dissemble,
and with smooth and smiling face to veil the true workings
of mind and heart, In this way it was hoped to mould the
young Irish chief into English shape for English purposes ;
it never once occurring to his royal trainers that nature
some day might burst forth and prove stronger than courtly
artificiality, or that the arts they were so assiduously teaching the boy chief for the ruin of his country's independence,
might be turned against themselves. In due time he was
sent into the army to perfect his military studies, and eventually (fully trained, polished, educated, and prepared for the
role designed for him by his English masters) he took up his
residence at his family seat in Dungannon.

Fortunately for the fame of Hugh O'Neill, and for the Irish
nation in whose history he played so memorable a part, the
life of that illustrious man has been written in our generation
by a biographer worthy of the theme. Amongst the masses
of Irishmen, comparatively little would be known of that
wondrous career had its history not been popularized by
John Mitchel's *Life of Hugh O'Neill.* The dust of centuries
had been allowed to cover the noble picture drawn from life
by the master hand of Don Philip O'Sullivan Beare—a writer
but for whom we should now be without any contemporaneous record of the most eventful period of Anglo-Irish history save the unjust and distorted versions of bitterly partizan
English officials.* Don Philip's history, however, was practically inaccessible to the masses of Irishmen ; and to Mr.
Mitchel is almost entirely owing the place O'Neill now
holds— his rightful prominence—in popular estimation.

---

* To Don Philip's great work the *Historiæ Catholicæ Iberniæ*, we are indebted for
nearly all that we know of this memorable struggle. "He is," says Mr. Mitchel,
"the only writer, Irish or foreign, who gives an intelligible account of O Neill's
battles ; but he was a soldier as well as a chronicler." Another writer says, "The
loss of this history could not be supplied by any work extant." Don Philip was
nephew to Donal, last lord of Beare, of whom we shall hear more anon. The
Historiæ Iberniæ was written in Latin and published about the year 1621, in Lisbon,

Mr. Mitchel pictures the great Ulster chieftain to us a patriot from the beginning; adroitly and dissemblingly biding his time; learning all that was to be learned in the camp of the enemy; looking far ahead into the future, and shaping his course from the start with fixed purpose towards the goal of national independence. This, however, cannot well be considered more than a " view," a "theory," a "reading." O'Neill was, during his earlier career, in purpose and in plan, in mind, manner, and action, quite a different man from the O'Neill of his later years. It is very doubtful that he had any patriotic aspirations after national independence—much less any fixed policy or design tending thereto—until long after he first found himself, by the force of circumstances, in collision with the English power. In him we see the conflicting influences of nature and nature-repressing art. His Irishism was ineradicable, though long dormant. His court tutors strove hard to eliminate it, and to give him instead a " polished" Englishism ; but they never more than partially succeeded. They put a court lacquer on the Celtic material, and the superficial wash remained for a few years, not more. The voice of nature was ever crying out to Hugh O'Neill. For some years after leaving court, he lived very much like any other Anglicized or English baron, in his house at Dungannon. But the touch of his native soil, intercourse with neighboring Irish chieftains, and the force of sympathy with his own people, now surrounding him, were gradually telling upon him. His life then became a curious spectacle of inconsistencies, as he found himself pulled and strained in opposite directions by opposite sympathies, claims, commands, or impulses ; sometimes, in proud disregard of his English masters, behaving like a true Irish O'Neill ; at other times swayed by his foreign allegiance into acts of very obedient suit and service to the queen's cause. But the day was gradually nearing when these struggles between two allegiances were to cease, and when Hugh, with all the fervor of a great and noble heart, was to dedicate his life to one unalterable purpose, the overthrow of English rule and the liberation of his native land !

XXXIX.—HOW LORD DEPUTY PERROT PLANNED A RIGHT CUN-
NING EXPEDITION, AND STOLE AWAY THE YOUTHFUL PRINCE
OF TYRCONNELL. HOW, IN THE DUNGEONS OF DUBLIN CAS-
TLE, THE BOY CHIEF LEARNED HIS DUTY TOWARDS ENGLAND;
AND HOW HE AT LENGTH ESCAPED AND COMMENCED DIS-
CHARGING THAT DUTY.

MEANWHILE, years passed
by, and another **Hugh had
begun** to rise **above the**
northern horizon, **amidst**
signs and perturbations **boding**
no good to the crown **and gov-**
ernment of the Pale. **This was**
Hugh O'Donnell—"**Hugh Roe**"
or "Red Hugh"—son of **the reign-**
ing chief of Tyrconnell. **Young**
O'Donnell, who was at this time "a fiery stripling of fifteen,
was already know throughout the five provinces of Ireland,
not only ' by the report of his beauty, his agility, and his noble deeds,' but as a sworn foe to the Saxons of the Pale:" and

of Tyrone and Hugh of Tyrconnell—ever forming a combination, sufficed to fill Dublin Castle with dismay. For already indeed, Hugh O'Neill's "loyalty" was beginning to be considered rather unsteady. To be sure, as yet no man durst whisper a word against ·him in the queen's hearing ; and he was still ready at call to do the queen's fighting against southern Geraldine, O'Brien, or Mac Caura. But the astute in these matters noted that he was unpleasantly neighborly and friendly with the northern chiefs and tanists ; that, so far from maintaining suitable ill-will towards the reigning O'Neill (whom the queen meant him some day to overthrow), Hugh had actually treated him with respect and obedience. Moreover " the English knew," says the chronicler of Hugh Roe, "that it was Judith, the daughter of O'Donnell, and sister of the before-mentioned Hugh Roe, that was the spouse and best beloved of the Earl O'Neill." "Those six companies of troops also," says Mr. Mitchel, " that he kept on foot (in the queen's name, but for his own behoof) began to be suspicious in the eyes of the state ; for it is much feared that he changes the men so soon as they thoroughly learn the use of arms, replacing them by others, all of his own clansmen, whom he diligently drills and reviews for some unknown service. And the lead he imports—surely the roofing of that house of Dungannon will not need all these ship-loads of lead ; —lead enough to sheet Glenshane, or clothe the sides of Cairnocher. And, indeed, a rumor does reach the deputy in Dublin, that there goes on at Dungannon an incredible casting of *bullets*. No wonder that the eyes of the English government began to turn anxiously to the north."

"And if this princely Red Hugh should live to take the leading of his sept—and if the two potent chieftains of the north should forget their ancient feud, and unite for the cause of Ireland," proceeds Mr. Mitchel, " then, indeed, not only this settlement of the Ulster ' counties ' must be adjourned, one knows not how long ; but the Pale itself or the Castle of Dublin might hardly protect her majesty's officers. These were contingencies which any prudent agent of the queen

" Near Rathmullan, on the western shore of Lough Swilly, looking towards the mountains of Innishowen, stood a monastery of Carmelites and a church dedicated to the Blessed Virgin, the most famous place of devotion in Tyronnell, whither all the clan-Connell, both chiefs and people, made resort at certain seasons to pay their devotions. Here the young Red Hugh, with Mac Swyne of the battle-axes, O'Gallagher of Ballyshannon, and some other chiefs were in the summer of 1587 sojourning a short time in that part to pay their vows of religion ; but not without stag-hounds and implements of chase, having views upon the red-deer of Fanad and Innishowen. One day, while the prince was here, a swift-sailing merchant ship doubled the promontory of Dunaff, stood up the lough, and cast anchor opposite Rathmullan ; a ' bark, blackhatched, deceptive,' bearing the flag of England, and offering for sale, as a peaceful trader, her cargo of Spanish wine. And surely no more courteous merchant than the master of that ship had visited the north for many a year. He invited the people most hospitably on board, solicited them, whether purchasers or not, to partake of his good cheer, entertained them with music and wine, and so gained very speedily the good will of all Fanad. Red Hugh and his companions soon heard of the obliging merchant and his rare wines. They visited the ship, where they were received with all respect, and, indeed, with unfeigned joy ; descended into the cabin, and with connoisseur discrimination tried and tasted, and finally drank too deeply ; and at last when they would come on deck and return to the shore, they found themselves secured under hatches ; their weapons had been removed ; night had fallen ; they were *prisoners* to those traitor Saxons. Morning dawned, and they looked anxiously towards the shore ; but, ah! where is Rathmullan and the Carmelite church? and what wild coast is this? Past Malin and the cliffs of Innishowen ; past Benmore, and southward to the shores of Antrim and the mountains of Mourne flew that ill-omened bark, and never dropped anchor till she lay under the towers of Dublin. The treacherous Perrot joyully received his prize, and 'exult-

he had procured hostages for the peaceable submission of O'Donnell.' And the prince of Tyrconnell was thrown into 'a strong stone castle,' and kept in heavy irons three years and three months, 'meditating,' says the chronicle, 'on the feeble and impotent condition of his friends and relations, of his princes and supreme chiefs, of his nobles and clergy, his poets and professors.' "*

Three long and weary years—oh! but they seemed three ages—the young Hugh pined in the grated dungeons of that "Birmingham Tower," which still stands in Dublin Castle yard. How the fierce hot spirit of the impetuous northern youth chafed in this cruel captivity! He, accustomed daily to breathe the free air of his native hills in the pastimes of the chase, now gasped for breath in the close and fetid atmosphere of a squalid cell! He, the joy and pride of an aged father—the strong hope of a thousand faithful clansmen—was now the helpless object of jailers' insolence, neglect, and persecution! "Three years and three months," the old chroniclers tell us, —when hark! there is whispering furtively betimes as young Hugh and Art Kavanagh, and other of the captives meet on the stone stairs, or the narrow landing, by the warders' gracious courtesy. Yes; Art had a plan of escape. Escape! Oh! the thought sends the blood rushing hotly through the veins of Red Hugh. Escape! Home! Freedom on the Tyrconnell hills once more! O blessed, thrice blessed words!

It is even so. And now all is arranged, and the daring attempt waits but a night favorably dark and wild—which comes at last; and while the sentries shelter themselves from the pitiless sleet, the young fugitives, at peril of life or limb, are stealthily scaling or descending bastion and battlement, fosse and barbican. With beating hearts they pass the last sentry, and now through the city streets they grope their way southwards; for the nearest hand of succor is amidst the valleys of Wicklow. Theirs is a slow and toilsome progress; they know not the paths, and they must hide by day and fly as best they can in the night-time through wooded country.

At length they cross the Three Rock Mountain, and look down upon Glencree. But alas! Young Hugh sinks down exhausted! Three years in a dungeon have cramped his limbs, and he is no longer the Hugh that bounded like a deer on the slopes of Glenvigh! His feet are torn and bleeding from sharp rock and piercing bramble; his strength is gone; he can no further fly. He exhorts his companions to speed onwards and save themselves, while he secretes himself in the copse and awaits succor if they can send it. Reluctantly, and only yielding to his urgent entreaties, they departed. A faithful servant, we are told, who had been in the secret of Hugh's escape, still remained with him, and repaired for succor to the house of Felim O'Tuhal, the beautiful site of whose residence is now called Powerscourt. Felim was known to be a friend, though he dared not openly disclose the fact. He was too close to the seat of the English power, and was obliged to keep on terms with the Pale authorities. But now "the flight of the prisoners had created great excitement in Dublin, and numerous bands were despatched in pursuit of them." It was next to impossible—certainly full of danger —for the friendly O'Tuhal, with the English scouring-parties spread all over hill and vale, to bring in the exhausted and helpless fugitive from his hiding place, where nevertheless he must perish if not quickly reached. Sorrowfully and reluctantly Felim was forced to conclude that all hope of escape for young Hugh this time must be abandoned, and that the best course was to pretend to discover him in the copse, and to make a merit of giving him up to his pursuers. So, with a heart bursting with mingled rage, grief, and despair, Hugh found himself once more in the gripe of his savage foes. He was brought back to Dublin "loaded with heavy iron fetters," and flung into a narrower and stronger dungeon, to spend another year cursing the day that Norman foot had touched the Irish shore.

There he lay until Christmas Day, 25th December, 1592, "when," says the old chronicle, "it seemed to the Son of the Virgin time for him to escape." Henry and Art O'Neill,

flight. In fact the lord deputy, Fitzwilliam, a needy and corrupt creature, had taken a bribe from Hugh O'Neill to afford opportunity for the escape. Hugh of Dungannon had designs of his own in desiring the freedom of all three ; for events to be noted further on had been occurring, and already he was, like a skilful statesman, preparing for future contingencies. He knew that the liberation of Red Hugh would give him an ally worth half Ireland, and he knew that rescuing the two O'Neills would leave the government without a "queen's O'Neill" to set up against him at a future day. Of this escape Haverty gives us the following account :—

"They descended by a rope through a sewer which opened into the Castle ditch ; and leaving there the soiled outer garments, they were conducted by a young man, named Turlough Roe O'Hagan, *the confidential servant or emissary of the Earl of Tyrone,* who was sent to act as their guide. Passing through the gates of the city, which were still open, three of the party reached the same Slieve Rua which Hugh had visited on the former occasion. The fourth, Henry O Neill, strayed from his companions in some way—probably before they left the city—but eventually he reached Tyrone, where the earl seized and imprisoned him. Hugh Roe and Art O'Neill, with their faithful guide, proceeded on their way over the Wicklow mountains towards Glenmalure, to Feagh Mac Hugh O'Byrne, a chief famous for his heroism, and who was then in arms against the government. Art O'Neill had grown corpulent in prison, and had besides been hurt in descending from the Castle, so that he became quite worn out from fatigue. The party were also exhausted with hunger, and as the snow fell thickly, and their clothing was very scanty, they

youths lay. 'Their bodies,' says the Four masters, 'were
covered with white-bordered shrouds of hailstones freezing
around them, and their light clothes adhered to their skin,
so that, covered as they were with the snow, it did not appear to
the men who had arrived that they were human beings at all,
for they found no life in their members, but just as if they
were dead.' On being raised up, Art O'Neill fell back and
expired, and was buried on the spot ; but Red Hugh was revived with some difficulty, and carried to Glenmalure, where
he was secreted in a sequestered cabin and attended by a
physician."

Mr. Mitchel describes for us the sequel. "O'Byrne brought
them to his house and revived and warmed and clothed them,
and instantly sent a message to Hugh O'Neill (with whom
he was then in close alliance) with the joyful tidings of
O'Donnell's escape. O'Neill heard it with delight, and sent
a faithful retainer, Tirlough Buidhe O'Hagan, who was well
acquainted with the country, to guide the young chief into
Ulster. After a few days of rest and refreshment, O'Donnell
and his guide set forth, and the Irish chronicler minutely
details that perilous journey ;—how they crossed the Liffey
far to the westward of Fitzwilliam's hated towers, and rode
cautiously through Fingal and Meath, avoiding the garrisons
of the Pale, until they arrived at the Boyne, a short distance
west of Inver Colpa (Drogheda), 'where the Danes had built
a noble city' ; how they sent round their horses through the
town, and themselves passed over in a fisherman's boat ; how
they passed by Mellifont, a great monastery, 'which belonged
to a noted young Englishman attached to Hugh O'Neill,' and
therefore met with no interruption there ; rode right through
Dundalk, and entered the friendly Irish country, where they
had nothing more to fear. One night they rested at Feadth
Mor (the Fews), where O'Neill's brother had a house, and
the next day crossed the Blackwater at Moy, and so to
Dungannon, where O'Neill received them right joyfully.
And here ' the two Hughs ' entered into a strict and cordial
friendship, and told each other of their wrongs and of their

imagine to the story of the youth's base kidnapping and cruel imprisonment in darkness and chains; and the impetuous Hugh Roe heard with scornful rage of the English deputy's atrocity towards Mac Mahon, and attempts to bring his accursed sheriffs and juries amongst the ancient Irish of Ulster. And they deeply swore to bury forever the unhappy feuds of their families, and to stand by each other with all the powers of the North against their treacherous and relentless foe. The chiefs parted, and O'Donnell, with an escort of the Tyrowen cavalry, passed into Mac Guire's country. The chief of Fermanagh received him with honor, eagerly joined in the confederacy, and gave him a black polished boat,' in which the prince and his attendants rowed through Lough Erne, and glided down that 'pleasant salmon-breeding river' which leads to Ballyshannon and the ancient seats of the Clan-Conal.

" We may conceive with what stormy joy the tribes of Tryconnell welcomed their prince; with what mingled pity and wrath, thanksgivings and curses, they heard of his chains, and wanderings, and sufferings, and beheld the feet that used to bound so lightly on the hills, swollen and crippled by that cruel frost, by the crueller fetters of the Saxon. But little time was now for festal rejoicing or the unprofitable luxury of cursing; for just then, Sir Richard Bingham, the English leader in Connaught, relying on the irresolute nature of old O'Donnell, and not aware of Red Hugh's return, had sent two hundred men by sea to Donegal, where they took by surprise the Franciscan monastery, drove away the monks (making small account of their historic studies and learned annals), and garrisoned the buildings for the queen. The fiery Hugh could ill endure to hear of these outrages, or brook an English garrison upon the soil of Tyrconnell. He collected the people in hot haste, led them instantly into Donegal, and commanded the English by a certain day and hour to betake themselves with all speed back to Connaught, and leave behind them the rich spoils they had taken; all which they thought it prudent without further parley to do. And so the monks of St. Francis returned to their home and

XL.—HOW HUGH OF DUNGANNON WAS MEANTIME DRAWING
OFF FROM ENGLAND AND DRAWING NEAR TO IRELAND.

URING the four years over which the imprisonment
of Red Hugh extended, important events had been
transpiring in the outer world ; and amidst them
the character of Hugh of Dungannon was under.
going a rapid transmutation.   We had already seen him
cultivating friendly relations with the neighboring chiefs,
though most of them were in a state of open hostility to
the queen.   He, by degrees, went much farther than this.
He busied himself in the disloyal work of healing the
feuds of the rival clans, and extending throughout the north
feelings of amity—nay, a net-work of alliances between
them.   To some of the native princes he lends one or two
of his fully trained companies of foot ; to others, some troops
of his cavalry.   He secretly encourages some of them (say
his enemies at court) to stouter resistance to the English.
It is even said that he harbors Popish priests.   " North of
Slieve Gullion the venerable brehons still arbitrate undisturb-
ed the causes of the people ; the ancient laws, civilization, and
religion stand untouched.   Nay, it is credibly rumored to
the Dublin deputy that this noble earl, forgetful apparently
of his coronet and golden chain, and of his high favor with so
potent a princess, does about this time get recognized and
solemnly inaugurated as chieftain of his sept, by the proscribed name of ' The O' Neill , ' and at the rath of Tulloghoge,
on the Stone of Royalty, amidst the circling warriors, amidst
the bards and ollamhs of Tyr-eoghain, ' receives an oath to
preserve all the ancient former customs of the country inviolable, and to deliver up the succession peaceably to his
tanist ; and then hath a wand delivered to him by one whose
proper office that is, after which, descending from the stone,

even as the O'Neills had done for a thousand years; altogether in the most un-English manner, and with the strangest ceremonies which no garter king-at-arms could endure."

While matters were happening thus in Ulster, England was undergoing the excitement of apprehended invasion. The Armada of Philip the Second was on the sea, and the English nation—queen and people—Protestant and Catholic—persecutor and persecuted—with a burst of genuine patriotism, prepared to meet the invaders. The elements, however, averted the threatened doom. A hurricane of unexampled fury scattered Philip's flotilla, so vauntingly styled "invincible;" the ships were strewn, shattered wrecks, all over the coasts of England and Ireland. In the latter country the crews were treated very differently, according as they happened to be cast upon the shores of districts amenable to English authority or influences, or the reverse. In the former instances they were treated barbarously—slain as queen's enemies, or given up to the queen's forces. In the latter, they were sheltered and succored, treated as friends, and afforded means of safe return to their native Spain. Some of these ships were cast upon the coast of O'Neill's conntry, and by no one were the Spanish crews more kindly treated, more warmly befriended, than by Hugh, erstwhiles the queen's most favored *protégé*, and still professedly her most true and obedient servant. This hospitality to the shipwrecked Spaniards, however, is too much for English flesh and blood to bear. Hugh is openly murmured against in Dublin and in London. And soon formal proof of his "treason" is preferred. An envious cousin of his, known as John of the Fetters—a natural son of John the Proud, by the false wife of O'Donnell—animated by a mortal hatred of Hugh, gave information to the lord deputy that he had not only regaled the Spanish officers right royally at Dungannon, but had then and there planned with them an alliance between himself and king Philip, to whom Hugh —so said his accuser—had forwarded letters and presents by the said officers. All of which the said accuser undertook to prove, either upon the body of Hugh in mortal combat, or before a jury well and truly packed or empanelled, as the case might be. Whereupon there was dreadful commotion in Dublin Castle. Hugh's reply was—to arrest the base informer on a charge of treason against the sacred person and prerogatives of his lawful chief. Which charge being proved, John of the Fetters was at once executed. Indeed some accounts say that Hugh himself had to act as executioner; since in all Tyrone no man could be prevailed upon to put to death one of the royal race of Niall—albeit an attained and condemned traitor. Then Hugh, full of a fine glowing indignation against these accusing murmurers in Dublin, sped straightway to London, to complain of them to the queen, and to convince her anew, with that politic hypocrisy taught him (for quite a different use, though) in that same court, that her majesty had no more devoted admirer than himself. And he succeeded. He professed and promised the most ample loyalty. He would undertake to harbor no more popish priests; he would admit sheriffs into Tyrone; he would no more molest chiefs friendly to England, or befriend chiefs hostile to the queen; and as for the title of "The O'Neill," which, it was charged, he gloried in, while feeling quite ashamed of the mean English title, "Earl of Tyrone," he protested by her majesty's most angelic countenance (ah, Hugh!) that he merely adopted it lest some one else might possess himself thereof; but if it in the least offended a queen so beautiful and so exalted, why he would disown it for ever!* Elizabeth was charmed by that dear sweet-spoken young noble—and so handsome too. (Hugh, who was brought up at court, knew Elizabeth's weak points.) The Lord of Dungannon returned to Ireland higher than ever in the queen's favor; and his enimies in Dublin Castle were overturned for that time.

The most inveterate of these was Sir Henry Bagnal, commander of the Newry garrison. "The marshal and his English garrison in the castle and abbey of Newry," says Mr.

---

* Thus, according to the tenor of English chroniclers; but as a matter of fact Hugh had not at this time been elected as The O'Neill. This event occurred subsequently; the existing O'Neill having been persuaded or compelled by Hugh Roe of Tyrconnell to abdicate, that the clans might, as they desired to do, elect Hugh of Dungannon in his place.

RED HUGH O'DONNELL'S WELCOME HOME.

Mitchel, "were a secret thorn in the side of O'Neill. They lay upon one of the main passes to the north, and he had deeply vowed that one day the ancient monastery, *de viridi ligno,* should be swept clear of this foreign soldiery. But in that castle of Newry the Saxon marshal had a fair sister, a woman of rarest beauty, whom O'Neill thought it a sin to leave for a spouse to some churl of an English undertaker. And indeed we next hear of him as a love-suitor at the feet of the English beauty." Haverty tells the story of this romantic love-suit as follows :—

"This man—the marshal, Sir Henry Bagnal—hated the Irish with a rancor which bad men are known to feel towards those whom they have mortally injured. He had shed a great deal of their blood, obtained a great deal of their lands, and was the sworn enemy of the whole race. Sir Henry had a sister who was young and exceedingly beautiful. The wife of the Earl of Tyrone, the daughter of Sir Hugh Mac Manus O'Donnell, had died, and the heart of the Irish chieftain was captivated by the beautiful English girl. His love was reciprocated, and he became in due form a suitor for her hand; but all efforts to gain her brother's consent to this marriage were in vain. The story, indeed, is one which might seem to be borrowed from some old romance, if we did not find it circumstantially detailed in the matter-of-fact documents of the State Paper Office. The Irish prince and the English maiden mutually plighted their vows, and O'Neill presented to the lady a gold chain worth one hundred pounds; but the inexorable Sir Henry removed his sister from Newry to the house of Sir Patrick Barnwell, who was married to another of his sisters, and who lived about seven miles from Dublin. Hither the earl followed her. He was courteously received by Sir Patrick, and seems to have had many friends among the English. One of these, a gentleman named William Warren, acted as his confidant, and at a party at Barnwell's house, the earl engaged the rest of the company in conversation while Warren rode off with the lady behind him, accompanied by two servants and carried her safely to the residence of a friend at Drum-

Protestant Bishop of Meath, Thomas Jones, a Lancashire man, was easily induced to come and unite them in marriage the same evening. This elopement and marriage, which took place on the 3d of August, 1591, were made the subject of violent accusations againt O'Neill. Sir Henry Bagnal was furious. He charged the earl with having another wife living; but this point was explained, as O'Neill showed that this lady, who was his first wife, the daughter of Sir Brian Mac Felim O'Neill, had been divorced previous to his marriage with the daughter of O'Donnell. Altogether the government would appear to have viewed the conduct of O'Neill in this matter rather leniently; but Bagnal was henceforth his most implacable foe, and the circumstance was not without its influence on succeeding events."

——:☙:——

XLI.—HOW RED HUGH WENT CIRCUIT AGAINST THE ENGLISH IN THE NORTH. HOW THE CRISIS CAME UPON O'NEILL.

BY this time young Hugh Roe O'Donnell had, as we have already learned, escaped from his cruel captivity in Dublin, mainly by the help of that astute and skilful organizer, Hugh of Dungannon. In the spring of the year following, "on the 3d of May, 1593, there was a solemn meeting of the warriors, clergy, and bards of Tyrconnell, at the Rock of Doune, Kilmacrenan, ' the nursing place of Columbcille.' And here the father of Red Hugh renounced the chieftaincy of the sept, and his impetuous son at nineteen years of age was duly inaugurated by Erenach O'Firghil, and made the O'Donnell with the ancient ceremonies of his race."

The young chief did not wear his honors idly. In the Dublin dungeons he had sworn vows, and he was not the man to break them : vows that while his good right hand could draw a sword, the English should have no peace in Ireland. Close by the O'Donnell's territory, in Strabane, old Torlogh Lynagh O'Neill had admitted an English force as "auxiliaries" forsooth.

" And it was a heart break," says the old chronicler, " to Hugh O'Donnell, that the English of Dublin should thus obtain a knowledge of the country." He fiercely attacked Strabane, and chased the obnoxious English " auxiliaries " away, " pardoning old Torlogh only on solemn promise not to repeat his offence. From this forth Red Hugh engaged himself in what we may call a circuit of the north, rooting out English garrisons, sheriffs, seneschals, or functionaries of what sort soever, as zealously and scrupulously as if they were plague-pests. Woe to the English chief that admitted a queen's sheriff within his territories! Hugh was down upon him like a whirlwind! O'Donnell's cordial ally in this crusade was Maguire, lord of Fermanagh, a man truly worthy of such a colleague. Hugh of Dungannon saw with dire concern this premature conflict precipitated by Red Hugh's impetuosity. Very probably he was not unwilling that O'Donnell should find the English some occupation yet awhile in the north ; but the time had not at all arrived (in his opinion) for the serious and comprehensive undertaking of a stand up fight for the great stake of national freedom. But it was vain for him to try remonstrance with Hugh Roe, whose nature could ill brook restraint, and who, indeed, could not relish or comprehend at all the subtle and politic slowness of O'Neill. Hugh of Dungannon, however, would not allow himself at any hazard to be pushed or drawn into open action a day or an hour sooner than his own judgment approved. He could hardly keep out of the conflict so close beside him, and so, rather than be precipitated prematurely into the struggle which, no doubt, he now deemed inevitable, and for which, accordingly, he was preparing, he made show of joining the queen's side and led some troops against Maguire. It was noted, however, that the species of assistance which he gave the English generally consisted in " moderating " Hugh Roe's punishment of them, and pleading with him merely to sweep them away a little more gently ; " interfering," as Moryson informs us, " to save their lives, *on condition of their instantly quitting the country !* " Now this seemed to the English (small wonder indeed) a very queer kind of " help." It was not what suited them at all ; and we

need not be suprised that soon Hugh's accusers in Dublin
and in London once more, and more vehemently than ever,
demanded his destruction.

It was now the statesmen and courtiers of England began to feel that craft may overleap itself.   In the moment
when first they seriously contemplated Hugh as a foe to the
queen, they felt like " the engineer hoist by his own petard.'
Here was their own pupil, trained under their own hands,
versed in their closest secrets, and let into their most subtle
arts ! Here was the steel they had polished and sharpened to
pierce the heart of Ireland, now turned against their own
breast ! No wonder there was dismay and consternation in
London and Dublin—it was so hard to devise any plan against
him that Hugh would not divine like one of themselves ! Failing any better resort, it was resolved to inveigle him into
Dublin by offering him a safe-conduct, and, this document
notwithstanding, to seize him at all hazards.   Accordingly
Hugh was duly notified of charges against his loyalty, and
a royal safe-conduct was given to him that he might "come
in and appear."   To the utter astonishment of the plotters,
he came with the greatest alacrity, and daringly confronted
them at the council-board in the Castle ! He would have been
seized in the room, but for the nobly honorable conduct of
the Earl of Ormond, whose indignant letter to the lord
treasurer Burleigh (in reply to the queen's order to seize
O'Neill) is recorded by Carte:—" My lord, I will never use
treachery to any man ; for it would both touch her highness's
honor and my own credit too much ; and whosoever gave the
queen advice thus to write, is fitter for such base service than
I am. Saving my duty to her majesty, I would I might have
revenge by my sword of any man that thus persuaded
the queen to write to me."   Ormond acquainted O'Neill with
the perfidy designed against him, and told him that if he did not
fly that night he was lost, as the false deputy was drawing a
cordon round Dublin. O'Neill made his escape and prepared
to meet the crisis which now he knew to be at hand. " News
soon reached him in the north," as Mr. Mitchel recounts, " that

England, consisting of veteran troops who had fought in Bretagne and Flanders under Sir John Norrys, the most experienced general in Elizabeth's service; and that garrisons were to be forced upon Ballyshannon and Belleek, commanding the passes into Tyrconnell, between Lough Erne and the sea. The strong fortress of Portmore also, on the southern bank of the Blackwater, was to be strengthened and well manned; thus forming, with Newry and Greencastle, a chain of forts across the island, and a basis for future operations against the north."

XLII.—O'NEILL IN ARMS FOR IRELAND. CLONTIBRET AND BEAL-AN-ATHA-BUIE.

HERE was no misunderstanding all this. "It was clear that, let King Philip send his promised aid, or send it not, open and vigorous resistance must be made to the further progress of foreign power, or Ulster would soon become an English province." Moreover, in all respects, save the aid from Spain, Hugh was well forward in organization and preparation. A great Northern Confederacy, the creation of his master-mind, now spanned the land from shore to shore, and waited only for him to take his rightful place as leader, and give the signal for such a war as had not tried the strength of England for two hundred years.

"At last," says Mitchel, "the time had come; and Dungannon with stern joy beheld unfurled the royal standard of O'Neill, displaying, as it floated proudly on the breeze, that terrible *Red Right Hand* upon its snow-white fold, waving defiance to the Saxon queen, dawning like a new Aurora upon the awakened children of Heremon.

"With a strong body of horse and foot, O'Neill suddenly appeared upon the Blackwater, stormed Portmore, and drove away its garrison, 'as carefully,' says an historian, 'as he would have driven poison from his heart;' then demolished

O'Reilly's country, everywhere driving the English and their adherents before him to the south (but without wanton bloodshed, slaying no man save in battle, for cruelty is no where charged against O'Neill); and, finally, with Mac Guire and Mac Mahon, he laid close siege to Monaghan, which was still held for the queen of England. O'Donnell, on his side, crossed the Saimer at the head of his fierce clan, burst into Connaught, and shutting up Bingham's troops in their strong places at Sligo, Ballymote, Tulsk, and Boyle, traversed the country with avenging fire and sword, putting to death every man *who could speak no Irish*, ravaging their lands, and sending the spoil to Tyrconnell. Then he crossed the Shannon, entered the Annally's, where O'Ferghal was living under English dominion, and devastated that country so furiously, that 'the whole firmament,' says the chronicle, 'was one black cloud of smoke.'"

This rapidity of action took the English at complete disadvantage. They accordingly (merely to gain time) feigned a great desire to " treat " with the two Hughs. Perhaps those noble gentlemen had been wronged. If so, the queen's tender heart yearned to have them reconciled ; and so forth. Hugh, owing to his court training, understood this kind of thing perfectly. It did not impose upon him for a moment ; yet he consented to give audience to the royal commissioners, whom he refused to see except at the head of his army, " nor would he enter any walled town as liege man of the queen of England." " So they met," we are told, " in the open plain, in the presence of both armies." The conditions of peace demanded by Hugh were :—

1. Complete cessation of attempts to disturb the Catholic Church in Ireland.

2. No more garrisons—no more sheriffs or English officials of any sort soever to be allowed into the Irish territories, which should be unrestrictedly under the jurisdiction of their lawfully elected native chiefs.

3. Payment by Marshal Bagnal to O'Neill of one thousand pounds of silver " as a marriage portion with the lady *whom he had raised to the dignity of an O'Neill's bride.*"

THE COMBAT BEFORE ARMAGH.

See pages 261, 262.

We may imagine how hard the royal commissioners must have found it to even hearken to these propositions, especially this last keen touch at Bagnal. Nevertheless, they were fain to declare them very reasonable indeed ; only they suggested —merely recommended for consideration—that as a sort of set-off, the confederates might lay down their arms, beg forgiveness, and " discover " their correspondence with foreign states. Phew ! There was a storm about their ears ! Beg " pardon " indeed ! " The rebels grew insolent, " says Moryson. The utmost that could be obtained from O'Neill was a truce of a few days' duration.

Early in June, Bagnal took the field with a strong force, and effecting a junction with Norreys, made good his march from Dundalk to Armagh. Not far from Monaghan is Clontibret—Cluain-Tuberaid, the " Lawn of the Spring." What befel there, I will relate in the words of Mr. Mitchel :—

" The castle of Monaghan, which had been taken by Con O'Neill, was now once more in the hands of the enemy, and once more was besieged by the Irish troops. Norreys, with his whole force, was in full march to relieve it ; and O'Neill, who had hitherto avoided pitched battles, and contented himself with harassing the enemy by continual skirmishes in their march through the woods and bogs, now resolved to meet this redoubtable general fairly in the open field. He chose his ground at Clontibret, about five miles from Monaghan, where a small stream runs northward through a valley enclosed by low hills. On the left bank of this stream the Irish, in battle array, awaited the approach of Norreys. We have no account of the numbers of each side, but when the English general came up, he thought himself strong enough to force a passage. Twice the English infantry tried to make good their way over the river, and twice were beaten back, their gallant leader each time charging at their head, and being the last to retire. The general and his brother, Sir Thomas, were both wounded in these conflicts, and the Irish counted the victory won, when a chosen body of English horse, led on by Segrave, a Meathian officer, of gigantic bone and height,

Tyrowen, commanded by their prince in person. Segrave singled out O'Neill, and the two leaders laid lance in rest for deadly combat, while the troops on each side lowered their weapons and held their breath, awaiting the shock in silence. The warrors met, and the lance of each was splintered on the other's corslet, but Segrave again dashed his horse against the chief, flung his giant frame against his enemy, and endeavored to unhorse him by the mere weight of his gauntletted hand. O'Neill grasped him in his arms, and the combatants rolled together in that fatal embrace to the ground :—

> ' Now gallant Saxon, hold thine own :
> No maiden's arms are round thee thrown.'

There was one moment's deadly wrestle and a death groan : the shortened sword of O'Neill was buried in the Englishmen's groin beneath his mail. Then from the Irish rank arose such a wild shout of triumph as those hills had never echoed before —the still thunder-cloud burst into a tempest—those equestrian statues become as winged demons, and with their battle cry *Lamh-dearg-aboo*, and their long lances poised in eastern fashion above their heads, down swept the chivalry of Tyrowen upon the astonished ranks of the Saxon. The banner of St. George wavered and went down before that furious charge. The English turned their bridle-reins and fled headlong over the stream, leaving the field covered with their dead, and, worse than all, leaving with the Irish that proud red-cross banner, the first of its disgraces in those Ulster wars. Norreys hastily retreated southwards, and the castle of Monaghan was yielded to the Irish."

This was opening the compaign in a manner truly worthy of a royal O'Neill. The flame thus lighted spread all over the northern land. Success shone on the Irish banners, and as the historian informs us, " at the close of the year 1595, the Irish power predominated in Ulster and Connacht."

The proceedings of the next two years—1596 and 1597— during which the struggle was varied by several efforts at negotiation, occupy too large a portion of history to be traced

steadily though slowly driven in upon the Pale from nearly all sides, and strenuous efforts were made to induce O'Neill to accept terms. He invariably professed the utmost readiness to do so; deplored the stern necessity that had driven him to claim his rights in the field, and debated conditions of peace; but, either mistrusting the designs of the English in treating with him, or because he had hopes far beyond anything they were likely to concede, he managed so that the negotiations somehow fell through at all times. On one occasion royal commissioners actually followed and chased him through the country with a royal "pardon" and treaty, which they were beseeching him to accept, but O'Neill continued to "miss" all appointments with them. More than once the English bitterly felt that their quondam pupil was feathering his keenest arrows against them with plumes plucked from their own wing! But it was not in what they called "diplomacy" alone Hugh showed them to their cost that he had not forgotten his lessons. He could enliven the tedium of a siege —and, indeed, terminate it—by a ruse worthy of a humorist as of a strategist. On the expiration of one of the truces, we are told, he attacked Norreys' encampment, with great fury, "and drove the English before him with heavy loss till they found shelter within the wall of Armagh." He sat down before the town and began a regular siege; "but the troops of Ulster were unused to a war of posts, and little skilled in reducing fortified places by mines, blockades, or artillery. They better loved a rushing charge in the open field, or the guerilla warfare of the woods and mountains, and soon tired of sitting idly before battlements of stone. O'Neill tried a stratagem. General Norreys had sent a quantity of provisions to relieve Armagh under a convoy of three companies of foot and a body of cavalry, and the Irish had surprised these troops by night, captured the stores, and made prisoners of all the convoy. O'Neill caused the English soldiers to be stripped of their uniform, and an equal number of his own men to be dressed in it, whom he ordered to appear by day break as if marching to relieve Armagh. Then, having stationed an am-

lying on the eastern side of the city, he sent another body of troops to meet the red-coated gallo-glasses, so that when day dawned the defenders of Armagh beheld what they imagined to be a strong body of their countrymen in full march to relieve them with supplies of provisions, then they saw O'Neill's troops rush to attack these, and a furious conflict seemed to proceed, but apparently the English were overmatched, many of them fell, and the Irish were pressing forward pouring in their shot and brandishing their battle axes with all the tumult of a deadly fight. The hungry garrison could not endure this sight. A strong rallying party issued from the city and rushed to support their friends; but when they came to the field of battle all the combatants on both sides turned their weapons against them alone.

" The English saw the snare that had been laid for them, and made for the walls again, but Con O'Neill and his party issued from the monastery and barred their retreat. They defended themselves gallantly, but were all cut to pieces, and the Irish entered Armagh in triumph. Stafford and the remnant of his garrison were allowed to retire to Dundalk, and O'Neill, who wanted no strong places, dismantled the fortifications and then abandoned the town."

Over several of the subsequent engagements in 1596 and 1597 I must pass rapidly, to reach the more important events in which the career of O'Neill culminated and closed. My young readers can trace for themselves on the page of Irish history the episodes of valor and patriotism that memorize " Tyrrell's pass" and " Portmore." The *ignis fatuus* of " aid from Spain" was still in O'Neill's eyes. He was waiting—but striking betimes, parleying with royal commissioners, and corresponding with King Philip, when he was not engaging Bagnal or Norreys: Red Hugh meanwhile echoing in Connacht every blow struck by O'Neill in Ulster. At length in the summer of 1598, he seems to have thrown aside all reliance upon foreign aid, and to have organized his countrymen for a still more resolute stand than any they yet had made against the national enemy.

Mac Hugh, then chief of the O'Byrnes, that he might fall upon the Pale, as they were about to make employment in the north for the troops of Ormond, and at the same time he detached fifteen hundred men and sent them to assist his ally, O'More, who was then besieging Porteloise, a fort of the English in Leix. Then he made a sudden stoop upon the castle of Portmore, which, says Moryson, 'was a great eye-sore to him lying upon the chiefe passage into his country,' hoping to carry it by assault.

"Ormond now perceived that a powerful effort must be made by the English to hold their ground in the north, or Ulster might at once be abandoned to the Irish. Strong reinforcements were sent from England, and O'Neill's spies soon brought him intelligence of large masses of troops moving northward, led by Marshal Sir Henry Bagnal, and composed of the choicest forces in the queen's service. Newry was their place of rendezvous, and early in August, Bagnal found himself at the head of the largest and best appointed army of veteran Englishmen that had ever fought in Ireland. He succeeded in relieving Armagh, and dislodging O'Neill from his encampment at Mullaghbane, where the chief himself narrowly escaped being taken, and then prepared to advance with his whole army to the Blackwater, and raise the siege of Portmore. Williams and his men were by this time nearly famished with hunger; they had eaten all their horses, and had come to feeding on the herbs and grass that grew upon the walls of the fortress. And every morning they gazed anxiously over the southern hills, and strained their eyes to see the waving of the red cross flag, or the glance of English spears in the rising sun.

"O'Neill hastily summond O'Donnell and MacWilliam to his aid, and determined to cross the marshal's path, and give him battle before he reached the Blackwater. His entire force on the day of battle, including the Scots and the troops of Connaught and Tyrconnell, consisted of four thousand five hundred foot and six hundred horse, and Bagnal's army amounted to an equal number of infantry and five hundred

gether with some field artillery, in which O'Neill was wholly
wanting.

"Hugh Roe O'Donnell had snuffed the coming battle from
afar, and on the 9th of August joined O'Neill with the clans
of Connaught and Tyrconnell. They drew up their main body
about a mile from Portmore, on the way to Armagh, where
the plain was narrowed to a pass, enclosed on one side by a
thick wood, and on the other by a bog. To arrive at that
plain from Armagh the enemy would have to penetrate through
wooded hills, divided by winding and marshy hollows, in
which flowed a sluggish and discolored stream from the bogs,
and hence the pass was called *Bcal-an-atha-buidhe*, 'the mouth
of the yellow ford.' Fearfasa O'Clery, a learned poet of
O'Donnell's, asked the name of that place, and when he heard
it, remembered (and proclaimed aloud to the army) that St.
Bercan had foretold a terrible battle to be fought at a yellow
ford, and a glorious victory to be won by the ancient Irish.

"Even so, Moran, son of Maoin! and for thee, wisest poet,
O'Clery, thou hast this day served thy country well, for to an
Irish army, auguries of good were more needful than a com-
missariat; and those bards' songs, like the Dorian flute of
Greece, breathed a passionate valor that no blare of English
trumpets could ever kindle.

"Bagnal's army rested that night in Armagh, and the Irish
bivouacked in the woods, each warrior covered by his shaggy
cloak, under the stars of a summer night, for to 'an Irish rebel,'
says Edmund Spenser, 'the wood is his house against all
weathers, and his mantle is his couch to sleep in.' But O'Neill,
we may well believe, slept not that night away; the morrow
was to put to proof what valor and discipline was in that
Irish army, which he had been so long organizing and training
to meet this very hour. Before him lay a splendid army of
tried English troops in full march for his ancient seat of Dungannon, and led on by his mortal enemy. And O'Neill would
not have had that host weakened by the desertion of a single
man, nor commanded—no, not for his white wand of chieftaincy—by any leader but this his dearest foe."

To Mr. Mitchel, whose vivid narrative I have so far been

quoting, we are indebted for the following stirring description
of O'Neill's greatest battle—ever memorable *Beal-an-atha
buie :—*

" The tenth morning of August rose bright and serene upon
the towers of Armagh and the silver waters of Avonmore.
Before day dawned the English army left the city in three divisions, and at sunrise they were winding through the hills
and woods behind the spot where now stands the little Church
of Grange.

" The sun was glancing on the corslets and spears of their
glittering cavalry, their banners waved proudly, and their
bugles rung clear in the morning air, when, suddenly, from
the thickets on both sides of their path, a deadly volley of
musketry swept through the foremost ranks. O'Neill had
stationed here five hundred light-armed troops to guard the
defiles, and in the shelter of thick grove of fir trees they had
silently waited for the enemy. Now they poured in their
shot, volley after volley, and killed great numbers of the English ; but the first division, led by Bagnal in person, after some
hard fighting, carried the pass, dislodged the marksmen from
their position, and drove them backwards into the plain.
The centre division under Cosby and Wingfield, and the rear-
guard led by Cuin and Billing, supported in flank by the cavalry under Brooke, Montacute, and Fleming, now pushed forward, speedily cleared the difficult country, and formed in
the open ground in front of the Irish lines. ' It was not quite
safe,' says an Irish chronicler (in admiration of Bagnal's disposition of his forces) ' to attack a nest of griffins and den of
lions in which were placed the soldiers of London.' Bagnal
at the head of his first division, and aided by a body of cavalry,
charged the Irish light-armed troops up to the very entrench-
ments, in front of which O'Neill's foresight had prepared some
pits, covered over with wattles and grass, and many of the
English cavalry rushing impetuously forward, rolled headlong,
both men and horses, into these trenches and perished. Still
the marshal's chosen troops, with loud cheers and shouts of
' St. George for merry England !' resolutely attacked the en-

cannon, and in one place succeeded, though with heavy loss, in forcing back their defenders. Then first the main body of O'Neill's troops was brought into action, and with bagpipes sounding a charge, they fell upon the English, shouting their fierce battle-cries, Lamh-dearg! and O'Donnell aboo! O'Neill himself, at the head of a body of horse, pricked forward to seek out Bagnal amidst the throng of battle, but they never met: the marshal, who had done his devoir that day like a good soldier, was shot through the brain by some unknown marksman. The division he had led was forced back by the furious onslaught of the Irish, and put to utter rout: and, what added to their confusion, a cart of gunpowder exploded amidst the English ranks and blew many of their men to atoms. And now the cavalry of Tyrconnell and Tyrowen dashed into the plain and bore down the remnant of Brook's and Flemming's horse; the columns of Wingfield and Cosby reeled before their rushing charge—while in front, to the war-cry of Bataillah-aboo! the swords and axes of the heavy armed gallowglasses were raging amongst the Saxon ranks. By this time the cannon were all taken; the cries of ' St. George ' had failed, or turned into death-shrieks; and once more, England's royal standard sank before the Red Hand of Tyrowen."

Twelve thousand gold pieces, thirty-four standards, and all the artillery of the vanquished army were taken. Nearly three thousand dead were left by the English on the field. The splendid army of the Pale was, in fact, annihilated.

Beal-an-atha-buie, or, as some of the English chroniclers call it, Blackwater, may be classed as one of the great battles of the Irish nation; perhaps the greatest fought in the course of the war against English invasion. Other victories as brilliant and complete may be found recorded in our annals; many defeats of English armies as utter and disastrous; but most of these were in a military point of view, not to be ranked for a moment with the " Yellow Ford." Very nearly all of them were defile surprises, conducted on the simplest principals of warfare common to struggles in mountainous country. But Beal-an-atha-buie was a deliberate engagement

armies which England and Ireland respectively were able to send forth, and was fought out on principles of military science in which both O'Neill and Bagnal were proficients. It was a fair stand-up fight between the picked troops and chosen generals of the two nations; and it must be told of the vanquished on that day, that, though defeated, they were not dishonored. The Irish annals and chants, one and all, do justice to the daring bravery and unflinching endurance displayed by Bagnal's army on the disastrous battle-field of Beal-an-atha-buie.

As might be supposed, a victory so considerable as this has been sung by a hundred bards. More than one notable poem in the native Gaelic has celebrated its glory; and quite a number of our modern bards have made it the theme of stirring lays. Of these latter, probably the best known is Drennan's ballad, from which I quote the opening and concluding verses:

> By O'Neill close beleaguer'd, the spirits might droop
> Of the Saxon three hundred shut up in their coop,
> Till Bagnal drew forth his Toledo, and swore
> On the sword of a soldier to succor Portmore.

> His veteran troops, in the foreign wars tried,
> Their features how bronz'd, and how haughty their stride,
> Step'd steadily on; it was thrilling to see
> That thunder-cloud brooding o'er Beal-an-atha-Buidh!

> The flash of their armor, inlaid with fine gold,
> Gleaming matchlocks and cannons that mutteringly roll'd,
> With the tramp and the clank of those stern cuirassiers,
> Dyed in blood of the Flemish and French cavaliers.

> •   •   •   •   •   •

> Land of Owen aboo! and the Irish rushed on:
> The foe fir'd but one volley—their gunners are gone.
> Before the bare bosoms the steel coats have fled,
> Or, despite casque or corslet, lie dying or dead.

> And brave Harry Bagnal, he fell while he fought,
> With many gay gallants; they slept as men ought,
> Their faces to Heaven; there were others, alack!

And the Irish got clothing, coin, colors, great store,
Arms, forage, and provender—plunder *go leor*.
They munch'd the white manchets, they champ'd the brown chine,
Fuliluah for that day, how the natives did dine !

The chieftain looked on, when O'Shanagan rose,
And cried : Hearken, O'Neill, I've a health to propose—
To our Sassenach hosts, and all quaffed in huge glee,
With *Cead mile failte go !* BEAL-AN-ATHA-BUIDH !

The same subject has been the inspiration of, perhaps, the most beautiful poem in Mr. Aubrey de Vere's *Lyrical Chronicle of Ireland :*—

THE WAR-SONG OF TYRCONNELL'S BARD AT THE BATTLE OF BLACKWATER.

Glory to God, and to the Powers that fight
          For Freedom and the Right !
We have them then, the invaders ! there they stand
          Once more on Oriel's land !
     They have pass'd the gorge stream cloven,
          And the mountain's purple bound ;
     Now the toils are round them woven,
          Now the nets are spread around !
Give them time : their steeds are blown ;
     Let them stand and round them stare,
     Breathing blasts of Irish air ;
Our eagles know their own !

Thou rising sun, fair fall
Thy greeting on Armagh's time-honored wall
And on the willows hoar
That fringe thy silver waters, Avonmore !
See ! on that hill of drifted sand
The far-famed marshal holds command,
Bagnal, their bravest :—to the right,
That recreant, neither chief nor knight,
"The Queen's O'Reilly," he that sold
His country, clan, and church for gold !
"Saint George for England ! "—recreant crew,
What are the saints ye spurn to you ?
They charge ; they pass yon grassy swell ;
They reach our pit-falls hidden well :
On !—warriors native to the sod !
Be on them, in the power of God !

          *   *   *   *   *

Seest thou yon stream, whose tawny waters glide
     Through weeds and yellow marsh lingeringly and slowly ?

THE STORY OF IRELAND.

There, ages past, Saint Bercan stood and cried,
"This spot shall quell one day th' invader's pride!"
   He saw in mystic trance
     The blood-stain flush yon rill!
    On!—hosts of God, advance!
     Your country's fate fulfil!

   *   *   *   *   *

Hark! the thunder of their meeting!
Hand meets hand, and rough the greeting!
Hark! the crash of shield and brand;
They mix, they mingle, band with band,
Like two horn-commingling stags,
Wrestling on the mountain crags,
Intertwined, intertangled,
Mangled forehead meeting mangled!
See! the wavering darkness through
I see the banner of Red Hugh;
Close beside is thine, O'Neill!
Now they stoop and now they reel,
Rise once more and onward sail,
Like two falcons on one gale!
O ye clansmen past me rushing,
Like mountain torrents seaward gushing,
Tell the chiefs that from this height
Their chief of bards beholds the fight;
That on theirs he pours his spirit;
Marks their deeds and chaunts their merit;
While the priesthood evermore,
Like him that ruled God's host of yore,
With arms outstretched that God implore!

   *   *   *   *

Glory be to God on high!
That shout rang up into the sky!
The plain lies bare; the smoke drifts by;
Again that cry: they fly! they fly!
O'er them standards thirty-four
Waved at morn! they wave no more.

Glory be to Him alone who holds the nations in His hand,
And to them the heavenly guardians of our Church and native land!
Sing, ye priests, your deep Te Deum: bards, make answer loud and long,
In your rapture flinging heavenward censers of triumphant song.
Isle for centuries blind in bondage, lift once more thine ancient boast,
From the cliffs of Innishowen southward on to Carbery's coast!
We have seen the right made perfect, seen the Hand that rules the spheres,

Glory fadeth, but this triumph is no barren mundane glory;
Rays of healing it shall scatter on the eyes that read our story:
Upon nations bound and torpid as they waken it shall shine,
As on Peter in his chains the angel shone, with light divine.
From th' unheeding, from th' unholy it may hide, like truth, its ray;
But when Truth and Justice conquer, on their crowns its beam shall play:
O'er the ken of troubled tyrants it shall trail a meteor's glare;
For the blameless it shall glitter as the star of morning fair;
Whensoever Erin triumphs, then its dawn it shall renew;
Then O'Neill shall be remember'd, and Tyrconnell's chief, Red Hugh!

The fame of this great victory filled the land. Not in Ireland alone did it create a sensation. The English historians
tell us that for months nothing was talked of at the court or
elsewhere throughout England, but O'Neill and the great
battle on the Blackwater, which had resulted so disastrously
for "her Highness." Moryson himself informs us that "the
generall voyce was of Tyrone amongst the English after
the defeat of Blackwater, as of Hannibal amongst the Romans
after the defeat at Cannæ." The event got noised abroad,
too, and in all the courts of Europe Hugh of Tyrone became
celebrated as a military commander and as a patriot leader.

XLIII.—HOW HUGH FORMED A GREAT NATIONAL CONFEDERACY AND BUILT UP A NATION ONCE MORE ON IRISH SOIL.

F Ulster was Ireland, Ireland now was free. But all that has been narrated so far, has affected only half the island. The south all this time lay in a heavy trance of helplessness, suffering and despair, that had supervened upon the desolating Desmond war. At best the south was very unlikely to second with equal zeal, energy, and success, such an effort as the north had made. Munster was almost exclusively possessed by Anglo-Irish lords, or Irish chiefs in the power of, and submissive to, the English. Ulster was the stronghold of the native cause ; and what was possible there might be, and in truth was, very far from feasible in the "colonized" southern province. Nevertheless, so irresistible was the inspiration of Hugh's victories in the north, that even the occupied, conquered, broken, divided, and desolated south began to take heart and look upward. Messengers were despatched to Hugh entreating him to send some duly authorized lieutenants to raise the standard of Church and Country in Munster, and take charge of the cause there. He complied by detaching Richard Tyrrell, of Fertullah, and Owen, son of Ruari O'Moore, at the head of a chosen band, to unfurl the national flag in the southern provinces. They were enthusiastically received. The Catholic Anglo-Norman lords and the native chiefs entered into the movement, and rose to arms on all sides. The newly planted "settlers," or "undertakers" as they were styled—(English adventurers amongst whom had been parcelled out the lands of several southern Catholic families, lawlessly seized on the ending of the Desmond rebellion)—fled pell mell, abandoning the stolen castles and ands to their rightful owners, and only too happy to escape with life.* The Lord President had to draw in every outpost,

---

* Amongst them was Spenser, a gentle poet and rapacious freebooter. His poesy

and abandon all Munster, except the garrison towns of Cork
and Kilmallock, within which, cooped up like prisoners, he
and his diminished troops were glad to find even momentary
shelter. By the beginning of 1599, "no English force was
able to keep the field throughout all Ireland." O'Neill's authority was paramount—was loyally recognized and obeyed
everywhere outside two or three garrison towns. He exercised the prerogatives of royalty; issued commissions, conferred offices, honors, and titles; removed or deposed lords
and chiefs actually or passively disloyal to the national authority, and appointed others in their stead. And all was done so
wisely, so impartially, so patriotically—with such scrupulous
and fixed regard for the one great object, and no other—
namely, the common cause of national independence and freedom—that even men chronically disposed to suspect family or
clan selfishness in every act, gave in their full confidence to
him as to a leader who had completely sunk the clan chief in
the national leader. In fine, since the days of Brian the
First, no native sovereign of equal capacity—singularly qualified as a soldier and as a statesman—had been known in Ireland. " He omitted no means of strengthening the league.
He renewed his intercourse with Spain; planted permanent
bodies of troops on the Foyle, Erne, and Blackwater; engaged
the services of some additional Scots from the Western Isles,
improved the discipline of his own troops, and on every side
made preparations to renew the conflict with his powerful
enemy. For he well knew that Elizabeth was not the monarch
to quit her deadly gripe of this fair island without a more terrible struggle than had yet been endured." *
That struggle was soon inaugurated. England at that time,
one of the strongest nations in Europe, and a match for the
best among them by land and sea, ruled over by one of the
ablest, the boldest, and the most crafty sovereigns that had
ever sat upon her throne, and served by statesmen, soldiers,

---

brutal, venal, and cowardly. He wooed the muses very blandly, living in a stolen
home, and philosophically counselled the extirpation of the Irish owners of the land,
for the greater security of himself and fellow adventurers.

* Mitchel.

philosophers, and writers, whose names are famous in history —was now about to put forth all her power in a combined naval and military armament against the almost reconstituted but as yet all too fragile Irish nation. Such an effort, under all the circumstances, could scarcely result otherwise than as it eventually did ; for there are, after all, odds against which no human effort can avail and for which no human valor can compensate. It was England's good fortune on this occasion, as on others previously and subsequently, that the Irish nation challenged her when she was at peace with all the world— when her hands were free and her resources undivided. Equally fortunate was she at all times, on the other hand, in the complete tranquillity of the Irish when desperate emergencies put her on her own defence, and left her no resources to spare for a campaign in Ireland, had she been challenged then. What we have to contemplate in the closing scenes of O'Neill's glorious career is the heroism of Thermopylæ, not the success of Salamis or Platæa.

Elizabeth's favorite, Essex, was despatched to Ireland with *twenty thousand* men at his back ; an army not only the largest England had put into the field for centuries, but in equip- ment, in drill, and in armament, the most complete ever assem- bled under her standard. Against this the Irish nowhere had ten thousand men concentrated in a regular army or movable corps. In equipment and in armament they were sadly deficient, while of sieging material they were altogether des- titute. Nevertheless, we are told " O'Neill and his confeder- ates were not dismayed by the arrival of this great army and its magnificent leader. " And had the question between the two nations depended solely upon such issues as armies settle, and superior skill and prowess control, neither O'Neill nor his confederates would have erred in the strong faith. the high hope, the exultant self-reliance that now animated them. The campaign of 1599—the disastrous failure of the courtly Essex and his magnificent army—must be told in a few lines. O'Neill completely out-generalled and over-awed or over-reached the haughty deputy. In more than one fatal engagement his

a constant stream of reinforcement from England, it had wasted away, and was no longer formidable in O'Neill's eyes. In vain the queen wrote letter after letter endeavoring to sting her quondam favorite into " something notable ;" that is a victory over O'Neill. Nothing could induce Essex to face the famous hero of Clontibret and the Yellow Ford, unless, indeed, in peaceful parley. At length having been taunted into a movement northward, he proceeded thither reluctantly and slowly. " On the high ground north of the Lagan, he found the host of O'Neill encamped, and received a courteous message from their leader, soliciting a personal interview. At an appointed hour the two commanders rode down to the opposite banks of the river, wholly unattended, the advanced guards of each looking curiously on from the uplands." * O'Neill, ever the flower of courtesy, spurred his horse into the stream up to the saddlegirths. " First they had a private conference, in which Lord Essex, won by the chivalrous bearing and kindly address of the chief, became, say the English historians, too confidential with an enemy of his sovereign, spoke without reserve of his daring hopes and most private thoughts of ambition, until O'Neill had sufficiently read his secret soul, fathomed his poor capacity, and understood the full meanness of his shallow treason. Then Cormac O'Neill and five other Irish leaders were summoned on the one side, on the other Lord Southampton and an equal number of English officers, and a solemn parley was opened in due form." † O'Neill offered terms : " first, complete liberty of conscience ; second, indemnity for his allies in all the four provinces ; third, the principal officers of state, the judges, and one-half the army to be henceforth Irish by birth." Essex considered these very far from extravagant demands from a man now virtually master in the island. He declared as much to O'Neill, and concluded a truce pending reply from London. Elizabeth saw in fury how completely O'Neill had dominated her favorite. She wrote him a frantic letter full of scornful taunt and upbraiding. Essex flung up all his duties in Ireland without leave, and hurried to London, to bring into requisition the personal influences he had undoubtedly possessed at one time with the queen. But he found her unapproachable. She stamped and swore at him, and ordered him to the tower, where the unfortunate earl paid, with his head upon the block, the forfeit for not having grappled successfully with the " Red Hand of Ulster."

The year 1600 was employed by O'Neill in a general circuit of the kingdom, for the more complete establishment of the national league and the better organization of the national resources. " He marched through the centre of the island at the head of his troops to the south," says his biographer, " a kind of royal progress, which he thought fit to call a pilgrimage to Holy Cross. He held princely state there, concerted measures with the southern lords, and distributed a manifesto announcing himself as the accredited Defender of the Faith." " In the beginning of March," says another authority, " the Catholic army halted at Inniscarra, upon the river Lee, about five miles west of Cork. Here O'Neill remained three weeks in camp consolidating the Catholic party in South Munster. During that time he was visited by the chiefs of the ancient Eugenian clans—O'Donohoe, O'Donovan, and O'Mahony. Thither also came two of the most remarkable men of the southern province: Florence McCarthy, lord of Carberry, and Donald O'Sullivan, lord of Bearhaven. McCarthy 'like Saul, higher by the head and shoulders than any of his house,' had brain in proportion to his brawn; O'Sullivan, as was afterwards shown, was possessed of military virtues of a high order. Florence was inaugurated with O'Neill's sanction as McCarthy More; and although the rival house of Muskerry fiercely resisted his claim to superiority at first, a wiser choice could not have been made had the times tended to confirm it.

" While at Inniscarra, O'Neill lost in single combat one of his most accomplished officers, the chief of Fermanagh. Maguire, accompanied only by a priest and two horsemen, was making observations nearer to the city than the camp, when Sir Warham St Leger, marshal of Munster, issued out of

Both were in advance of their attendants when they came unexpectedly face to face. Both were famous as horsemen and for the use of their weapons, and neither would retrace his steps. The Irish chief, poising his spear, dashed forward against his opponent, but received a pistol shot which proved mortal the same day. He, however, had strength enough left to drive his spear through the neck of St. Leger, and to effect his escape from the English cavalry. St. Leger was carried back to Cork where he expired. Maguire, on reaching the camp, had barely time left to make his last confession when he breathed his last. This untoward event, the necessity of preventing possible dissensions in Fermanagh, and still more the menacing movements of the new deputy, lately sworn in at Dublin, obliged O'Neill to return home earlier than he intended. Soon after reaching Dungannon he had the gratification of receiving a most gracious letter from Pope Clement the Eighth, together with a crown of phœnix feathers symbolical of the consideration with which he was regarded by the Sovereign Pontiff." *

XLIV.—HOW THE RECONSTRUCTED IRISH NATION WAS OVER-BORNE. HOW THE TWO HUGHS "FOUGHT BACK TO BACK" AGAINST THEIR OVERWHELMING FOES. HOW THE "SPANISH AID" RUINED THE IRISH CAUSE. THE DISASTROUS BATTLE OF KINSALE.

HERE now appear before us two remarkable men whose names are prominently identified with this memorable epoch in Irish history—Mountjoy, the new lord deputy; and Carew, the new lord president of Munster. In the hour in which these men were appointed to the conduct of affairs in Ireland, the Irish cause was lost. Immense resources were placed at their disposal, new levies and armaments were ordered; and again all the might of England by land and sea was to be put forth against Ireland. But Mount-joy and Carew alone were worth all the levies. They were men of indomitable energy, masters of subtlety, craft, and cunning, utterly unscrupulous as to the employment of means to an end; cold-blooded, callous, cruel, and brutal. Norreys and Bagnal were soldiers—able generals, illustrious in the field. Essex was a lordly courtier, vain and pomp-loving. Of these men— soldier and courtier—the Irish annals speak as of fair foes. But of Mountjoy and Carew a different memory is kept in Ireland. They did their work by the wile of the serpent, not by the skill of the soldier. Where the brave and manly Norreys tried the sword, they tried snares, treachery, and deceit, gold, flattery, promises, temptation, and seduction in every shape. To split up the confederation of chiefs was an end towards which they steadily labored by means the most subtle and crafty that human ingenuity could devise. Letters, for instance, were forged purporting to have been written secretly to the lord deputy by the Earl of Desmond, offering to betray one of his fellow confederates, O'Connor. These forgeries were "disclosed," as it were, to O'Connor, with an offer that he should "forestal" the earl, by seizing and giving up the latter to the government, for which, moreover, he was to have a thousand pounds in hand, besides other considerations promised. The plot succeeded. O'Connor betrayed the earl and handed him over a prisoner to the lord deputy, and of course going over himself as an ally also. This rent worked the dismemberment of the league in the south. Worse defections followed soon after; defections unaccountable, and, indeed, irretrievable. Art O'Neill and Nial Garv O'Donnell, under the operation of mysterious influences, went over to the English, and in all the subsequent events, were more active and effective than any other commanders on the queen's side! Nial Garv alone was worth a host. He was one of the ablest generals in the Irish camp. His treason fell upon the national leaders like a thunderbolt. This was the sort of "campaigning" on which Mountjoy relied most. Time and money were freely devoted to it, and not in vain. After the national confederation had been sufficiently split up and

weakened in this way—and when, north, and south, the de-
fecting chiefs were able of themselves to afford stiff employment for the national forces, the lord deputy took the field.

In the struggle that now ensued O'Neill and O'Donnell
presented one of those spectacles which, according to the language of the heathen classics, move gods and men to sympathy
and admiration! Hearts less brave might despair; but *they*,
like Leonidas and the immortal Three Hundred, would fight
out the battle of country while life remained. The English
now had in any one province a force superior to the entire
strength of the national army. The eventful campaign of
1601, we are told, was fought out in almost every part of the
kingdom. To hold the coast lines on the north—where Dowcra had landed (at Derry) four thousand foot and four hundred horse—was the task of O'Donnell; while to defend the
southern Ulster frontier was the peculiar charge of O'Neill.
" They thus," says the historian, " fought as it were back to
back against the opposite lines of attack." Through all the
spring and summer months that fight went on. From hill to
valley, from pass to plain, all over the island, it was one roll
of cannon and musketry, one ceaseless and universal engagement; the smoke of battle never lifted off the scene. The two
Hughs were all but ubiquitous; confronting and defeating an
attack to-day at one point; falling upon the foes next day at
another far distant from the scene of the last encounter! Between the two chiefs the most touching confidence and devoted affection subsisted. Let the roar of battle crash how it
might on the northern horizon, O'Neill relied that all was
well, for O'Donnell was at his post. No matter what myriads ·
of foes were massing in the south, it was enough for O'Donnell to know that O'Neill was there. " Back to back," indeed, as many a brave battle against desperate odds has been
fought, they maintained the unequal combat, giving blow for
blow, and so far holding their ground right nobly. By September, except in Munster, comparatively little had been
gained by the English beyond the successful planting of some
further garrisons; but the Irish were considerably exhausted,

came the exciting news that—at length !—a powerful auxiliary force from Spain had landed at Kinsale. The Anglo-Irish privy council were startled by the news while assembled in deliberation at Kilkenny. Instantly they ordered a concentration of all their available forces in the south, and resolved upon a winter campaign. They acted with a vigor and determination which plainly showed their conviction that on the quick crushing of the Spanish force hung the fate of their cause in Ireland. A powerful fleet was sent round the coast, and soon blockaded Kinsale ; while on the land side it was invested by a force of some fifteen thousand men.

This Spanish expedition, meant to aid, effected the ruin of the Irish cause. It consisted of little more than three thousand men, with a good supply of stores, arms, and ammunition. In all his letters to Spain, O'Neill is said to have strongly urged that if a force under five thousand men came, it should land in *Ulster*, where it would be morally and materially worth ten thousand landed elsewhere ; but that if Munster was to be the point of debarkation, anything less than eight or ten thousand men would be useless. The meaning of this is easily discerned. The south was the strong ground of the English, as the north was of the Irish side. A force landed in Munster should be able of itself to cope with the strong opposition which it was sure to encounter. These facts were not altogether lost sight of in Spain. The expedition as fitted out consisted of six thousand men ; but various mishaps and disappointments reduced it to half the number by the time it landed at Kinsale. Worse than all, the wrong man commanded it ; Don Juan D'Aquilla, a good soldier, but utterly unsuited for an enterprise like this. He was proud, sour-tempered, hasty, and irascible. He had heard nothing of the defections and disasters in the south. The seizure of Desmond and the ensnaring of Florence McCarthy—the latter the most influential and powerful of the southern nobles and chiefs—had paralyzed everything there ; and Don Juan, instead of finding himself in the midst of friends in arms, found himself surrounded by foes on land and sea. He gave way to his natural ill-temper in reproaches and complaints ; and in letters to O'Neill, bit-

terly demanded whether he and the other confederates meant
to hasten to his relief. For O'Neill and O'Donnell, with their
exhausted and weakened troops to abandon the north and undertake a winter march southward, was plain destruction.
At least it staked *everything* on the single issue of success or
defeat before Kinsale, and to prevent defeat and to insure
success there, much greater organization for coöperation and
concert, and much more careful preparation, were needed
than was possible now, hurried southward in this way by
D'Aquilla. Nevertheless, there was nothing else for it.
O'Neill clearly discerned that the crafty and politic Carew
had been insidiously working on the Spanish commander, to
disgust him with the enterprise, and induce him to sail homeward on liberal terms. And it was so. Don Juan, it is said,
agreed, or intimated that if, within a given time, an Irish army
did not appear to his relief, he would treat with Carew for
terms. It was, therefore, probable disaster for O'Neill to
proceed to the south, it was certain ruin for him to refuse ; so
with heavy hearts the northern chieftains set out on their
winter march for Munster, at the head of their thinned and
wasted troops. " O'Donnell, with his habitual ardor, was first
on the way. He was joined by Felim O'Doherty, MacSwi-
ney-na-Tuath, O'Boyle, O'Rorke, the brother of O'Connor
Sligo, the O'Connor Roe, MacDermott, O'Kelly, and others ;
mustering in all about two thousand five hundred men."
O'Neill, with MacDonnell of Antrim, MacGennis of Down,
MacMahon of Monaghan, and others of his suffragans, marched southward at the head of between three and four thousand
men. Holy-Cross was the point where both their forces appointed to effect their junction. O'Donnell was first at the
rendezvous. A desperate effort on the part of Carew to intercept and overwhelm him before O'Neill could come up,
was defeated only by a sudden night-march of *nearly forty
miles* by Red Hugh. O'Neill reached Belgooley, within sight
of Kinsale, on the 21st of December.
    In Munster, in the face of all odds—amidst the wreck of the
national confederacy, and in the presence of an overwhelming
army of occupation—a few chiefs there were, undismayed and

unfaltering, who rallied faithfully at the call of duty. Foremost amongst these was Donal O'Sullivan, Lord of Beare, a man in whose fidelity, intrepidity, and military ability, O'Neill appears to have reposed unbounded confidence. In all the south, the historian tells us, "only O'Sullivan Beare, O'Driscoll, and O'Connor Kerry declared openly for the national cause" in this momentous crisis. Some of the missing ships of the Spanish expedition reached Castlehaven in November, just as O'Donnell, who had made a detour westward, reached that place. Some of this Spanish contingent were detailed as garrisons for the forts of Dunboy, Baltimore, and Castlehaven, commanding three of the best havens in Munster. The rest joined O'Donnell's division, and which soon sat down before Kinsale.

When O'Neill came up, his master-mind at once scanned the whole position, and quickly discerned the true policy to be pursued. The English force was utterly failing in commissariat arrangements; and disease as well as hunger was committing rapid havoc in the besiegers' camp. O'Neill accordingly resolved to *besiege the besiegers;* to increase their difficulties in obtaining provision or provender, and to cut up their lines of communication. These tactics manifestly offered every advantage to the Irish and allied forces, and were certain to work the destruction of Carew's army. But the testy Don Juan could not brook this slow and cautious mode of procedure. "The Spaniards only felt their own inconveniences; they were cut off from escape by sea by a powerful English fleet; and," continues the historian, "Carew was already practising indirectly on their commander his 'wit and cunning' in the fabrication of rumors and the forging of letters. Don Juan wrote urgent appeals to the northern chiefs to attack the English lines without another day's delay; and a council of war in the Irish camp, on the third day after their arrival at Belgooley, decided that the attack should be made on the morrow." At this council, so strongly and vehemently was O'Neill opposed to the mad and foolish policy of risking an engagement, which, nevertheless, O'Donnell, ever impetuous, as violently supported, that for the first time the two friends were angrily at issue, and some writers even allege that on this occasion question was raised between them as to who should assume command-in-chief on the morrow. However this may have been, it is certain that once the vote of the council was taken, and the decision found to be against him, O'Neill loyally acquiesced in it, and prepared to do his duty.

"On the night of the 2d January (new style)—24th December old style, in use among the English—the Irish army left their camp in three divisions : the vanguard led by Tyrrell, the centre by O'Neill, and the rear by O'Donnell. The night was stormy and dark, with continuous peals and flashes of thunder and lightning. The guides lost their way, and the march, which even by the most circuitous route ought not to have exceeded four or five miles, was protracted through the whole night. At dawn of day, O'Neill, with whom were O'Sullivan and O'Campo, came in sight of the English lines, and to his infinite surprise found the men under arms, the cavalry in troops posted in advance of their quarters. O'Donnell's division was still to come up, and the veteran earl now found himself in the same dilemma into which Bagnal had fallen at the Yellow Ford. His embarrassment was perceived from the English camp ; the cavalry were at once ordered to advance. For an hour O'Neill maintained his ground alone ; at the end of that time he was forced to retire. Of O'Campo's 300 Spaniards, 40 survivors were with their gallant leader taken prisoners; O'Donnell at length arrived and drove back a wing of the English cavalry ; Tyrrell's horsemen also held their ground tenaciously. But the route of the centre proved irremediable. Fully 1,200 of the Irish were left dead on the field, and every prisoner taken was instantly executed. On the English side fell Sir Richard Graeme: Captains Danvers and Godolphin, with several others, were wounded ; their total loss they stated at two hundred, and the Anglo-Irish, of whom they seldom made count in their reports, must have lost in proportion. The earls of Thomond and Clanricarde were actively engaged with their followers, and their loss could hardly have been less than that of the English regulars.

council together at Innishannon, on the river Bandon, where it was agreed that O'Donnell should instantly take shipping for Spain to lay the true state of the contest before Philip the Third; that O'Sullivan should endeavor to hold his castle of Dunboy, as commanding a most important harbor ; that Rory O'Donnell, second brother of Hugh Roe, should act as chieftain of Tyrconnell, and that O'Neill should return into Ulster to make the best defence in his power. · The loss in men was not irreparable ; the loss in arms, colors, and reputation, was more painful to bear, and far more difficult to retrieve." *

XLV.—"THE LAST LORD OF BEARA." HOW DONAL OF DUN-BOY WAS ASSIGNED A PERILOUS PROMINENCE, AND NOBLY UNDERTOOK ITS DUTIES. HOW DON JUAN'S IMBECILITY OR TREASON RUINED THE IRISH CAUSE.

ONFESSEDLY for none of the defeated chiefs did the day's disaster at Kinsale involve such consequences as it presaged for the three southern leaders—O'Sulli-van, O'Driscoll, and O'Connor Kerry. The northern chieftains returning homeward, retired upon and within the strong lines of what we may call the vast entrenched camp of the native cause. But the three southerns—who alone of all their Munster compeers had dared to take the field against the English side in the recent crisis—were left isolated in a distant extremity of the island, the most remote from native support or coöperation, left at the mercy of Carew, now master of Munster, and leader of a powerful army flushed with victory. The northerns might have some chance, standing together and with a considerable district almost entirely in their hands, of holding out, or exacting good terms as they had done often before. But for the doomed southern chiefs, if aid from Spain came not soon, there was literally no prospect but the swift and immediate crash of Carew's vengeance ;

no hope save what the strong ramparts of Dunboy and the stout heart of its chieftain might encourage!

O'Neill, as I have already remarked, had a high opinion of O'Sullivan—of his devotedness to the national cause—of his prudence, skill, foresight, and courage.   And truly the character of the " last Lord of Beara " as writ upon the page of history—as depicted by contemporary writers, as revealed to us in his correspondence, and as displayed in his career and actions from the hour when, at the call of duty, with nothing to gain and all to peril, he committed himself to the national struggle—is one to command respect, sympathy, and admiration.   In extent of territorial sway and in " following " he was exceeded by many of the southern chiefs, but his personal character seems to have secured for him by common assent the position amongst them left vacant by the imprisonment of Florence Mac Carthy, *facile princeps* among the Irish of Munster, now fast held in London tower.   In manner, temperament, and disposition, O'Sullivan was singularly unlike most of the impulsive ardent Irish of his time.   He was of deep, quiet, calm demeanor; grave and thoughtful in his manner, yet, notably firm and inflexible in all that touched his personal honor, his duty towards his people,* or his loyalty to religion or country.   His family had flung themselves into the struggle of James Geraldine, and suffered the penalties that followed thereupon.   Early in Elizabeth's reign, Eoghan, or Eugene, styled by the English Sir Owen O'Sullivan, contrived to possess himself of the chieftaincy and territory of Beara, on the death of his brother Donal, father of the hero of Dunboy. Eugene accepted an English title. sat in Lord Deputy Perrot's parliament of 1585, in the records of which we find his name

---

* Nothing strikes the reader of Donal's correspondence with king Philip and the Spanish ministers, more forcibly than the constant solicitude, the deep feeling, and affectionate attachment he exhibits towards his " poor people," as he always calls them. Amidst the wreck of all his hopes, the loss of worldly wealth and possessions, home, country, friends, his chief concern is for his " poor people " abandoned to the persecution of the merciless English foe. In all his letters it is the same. No murmur, no repining for himself, but constant solicitude about Ireland, and constant sorrow for his poor people, left " like sheep without a shepherd when the storm shuts

duly registered, and took out a "patent" in his own name for the tribe land. His nephew, young Donal—Donal Mac Donal O'Sullivan, as he was called—vehemently disputed the validity of Sir Owen's title to the lands, and after a lengthy law-suit, a letter of partition was issued under the great seal in January, 1593, according to which Donal was to have the lordship, castles, and dependencies of Beara, while Sir Owen was to possess those eastward and northward of the peninsula. It is highly probable that by this decision the Pale authorities hoped to enthral Donal without losing Sir Owen, to make both branches of the family, as it were, compete in loyalty to the English power, and in any event, by putting enmity between them, cause them to split up and weaken their own influence. In this latter calculation they were not disappointed, as the sequel shows; but their speculations or expectations about Donal were all astray. He was indeed averse to hopeless and prospectless struggles against the power of England, and on attaining to the chieftaincy, directed his attention mainly to the internal regulation of his territory, and the bettering of the condition of his people in every respect, not by forays on neighboring clans, but by the peaceful influences of industry. But Donal, grave and placid of exterior, truly patriotic of heart, watched attentively the rise and progress of O'Neill's great movement in the north. For a time he believed it to be merely a quarrel between the queen's protege and his royal patroness, sure to be eventually adjusted ; and accordingly up to a recent period he displayed no sympathy with either side in the conflict. But when that conflict developed itself into a really national struggle, O'Sullivan never wavered for a moment in deciding what his attitude should be; and that attitude, once taken, was never abandoned, never varied, never compromised by act or word or wish, through all that followed of sacrifice and suffering and loss. O'Neill, who was a keen discerner of character, read O'Sullivan correctly when he estimated all the more highly his accession, because it was that of a man who acted not from hot impulse or selfish calculation, but from full deliberation and a pure sense of duty. In fine,

lord of Dunboy for such honorable but perilous prominence as to name him one of the three men to whom was committed, in the darkest crisis of their country, the future conduct of the national cause.*

We may imagine the memorable scene of the morn succeeding that night of sleepless consultation at Innishannon over "hapless Erinn's fate"—the parting of the chiefs! Wildly they embraced each other, and like clutch of iron was the farewell grasp of hand in hand, as each one turned away on the path of his allotted task! O'Neill marched northward, where we shall trace his movements subsequently. O'Donnell took shipping for Spain, and O'Sullivan at the head of his faithful clansmen marched westward for Bantry and Bearhaven. Had Don Juan D'Aquilla been a true and steadfast man—had he been at all worthy and fit to command or conduct such an enterprise—had he been at all capable of appreciating its peculiar exigencies and duties—the defeat at Kinsale, heavy and full of disaster as it was, might soon have been retrieved and the whole aspect to affairs reversed. Had he but held his ground (as not unreasonably he might have been expected to do, with three thousand men within the fortified and well stored town) until the arrival of the further reinforcements which he must have known his royal master was sending, or would quickly send, and thus coöperated in the scheme of operations planned by the Irish chiefs at Innishannon, nothing that had so far happened could be counted of such great moment as to warrant abandonment of the expedition. But D'Aquilla's conduct was miserably inexplicable. He could not act more despairingly if his last cartridge had been fired, if his last gunner had perished, if his "last horse had been eaten," or if assured that king Philip had utterly abandoned him. After a few sorties, easily repulsed, he offered to capitulate. Carew, who hereby saw that Don Juan was a fool, was, of course, only

---

* "These high Irishmen, namely, O'Neill and O'Donnell, ordered that the chief command and leadership of these (the Munster forces) should be given to O'Sullivan Beare, i. e., Donal, the son of Donal the son of Dermot ; for he was at this time the best commander among their allies in Munster for wisdom and valour."—*Annals of the Four Masters.*

too happy to grant him *any* terms that would ensure the departure of the Spanish aids. By conceding conditions highly flattering to D'Aquilla's personal vanity, the lord president induced that outwitted commander not only to draw off to Spain the entire force of the expedition, but to undertake to yield up to the English all the castles and fortresses of the Irish chiefs in which Spanish garrisons had been placed, and to order back to Spain any further troops that might arrive before his departure. This imbecility or treason ruined the Irish cause in the South, and ruining it there at such a juncture, ruined it everywhere. Such a capitulation was utter and swift destruction to the southern leaders. It "took the ground from under their feet." It reft them of bases of operations, and flung them as mere fugitives unsheltered and unprovisioned into the field, the forest, the morass or the mountain, to be hunted and harried, cut off in detail, and pitilessly put to the sword by Carew's numerous, powerful, and well-appointed field corps of scouring parties.

Don Juan's capitulation was signed 11th January, 1602 (N. S.). Seven days afterwards the lord deputy and the lord president drew off to Cork. " The day following the captains received directions to repair to sundry towns in Munster appointed for their garrisons ; and the same day Captain Roger Harvie and Captain George Flower were despatched with certain companies to go by sea to receive the castles of Castlehaven, Donnashed, and Donnelong at Baltimore, and Dunboy at Bearhaven." On the 12th February, the Spanish officer in command at Castlehaven gave up the castle to Harvie. On the 21st he proceeded to Baltimore, the two castles of which the Spanish officers therein gave up in like manner ; and in a few weeks all the coast district castles of the southwest, those of the Beara promontory alone excepted, were in the hands of the English. A month later (16th March) Don Juan sailed for Spain, most of his forces having been shipped thither previously.*

* On his return to Spain he was degraded from his rank for his too great intimacy with Carew, and confined a prisoner in his own house. He is said to have died of a

O'Sullivan heard with dismay and indignation of Don Juan's audacious undertaking to deliver up to his " cruel, cursed, misbelieving enemies," his castle of Dunboy, the key of his inheritance.* With speed, increased by this evil news, he pushed rapidly homeward, and in due time he appeared with the remnant of his little force † before the walls of the castle, demanding admittance. The Spaniards refused : they had heard of D'Aquilla's terms of capitulation, they regretted them but felt constrained to abide by them. Donal, however, knowing a portion of the outworks of the place which afforded some facilities for his purpose, availed himself of a dark and stormy night to effect an entrance, mining his way through the outer wall, and surprising and overpowering the Spaniards. He then addressed them feelingly on the conduct of D'Aquilla and the present posture of affairs, stating his resolution to hold the castle till King Philip would send fresh aid, and offering a choice to the Spaniards to remain with him or sail for home. Some of them decided to remain, and were amongst the most determined defenders of Dunboy in the subsequent siege. The rest, Donal sent to Spain, despatching at the same time envoys with letters to King Philip, urgently entreating speedy aid. Moreover, in charge of these messengers, he sent to the king, as guarantee of his good faith and perseverance, his oldest son, a boy of tender years.

Well knowing that soon he would have the foe upon him, Donal now set about preparing Dunboy for the tough and terrible trial before it. He had the outworks strengthened in every part ; and another castle of his, on Dursey Island (at the uttermost extremity of the peninsula, dividing Bantry

---

* "Among other places which were neither yielded nor taken toe the end that they should be delivered to the English, Don Juan tied himself to deliver my castell and haven, the only key of mine inheritance, whereupon the living of many thousand persons doth rest that live some twenty leagues upon the sea coast, into the hands of my cruell, cursed, misbelieving enemies."—Letter of Donal O'Sullivan Beare to the King of Spain.—*Pacata Hibernia.*

† O'Sullivan's contingent, we are told, " was amongst those who made the most determined fight on the disastrous day of Kinsale, and when the battle was lost it bravely protected some of the retreating troops of the northern chieftains, who but for

and Kenmare bays), garrisoned by a trusty band ; designing
this latter as a refuge for himself, his family and clansmen, in
the event of the worst befalling Dunboy.

———————

XLVI.—HOW THE QUEEN'S FORCES SET ABOUT "TRANQUIL-
LIZING" MUNSTER. HOW CAREW SENT EARL THOMOND ON A
MISSION INTO CARBERY, BEAR, AND BANTRY.

M E A N W H I L E the detachments detailed by Carew
were doing their savage and merciless work throughout Cork and Kerry. According to Carew's own
version, the occupation of these troops, day by day
was the seeking out and murdering in cold blood of all the
native inhabitants, men, women, and children ; and when
they were not murdering they were cow-stealing and corn
burning. How to *extirpate* the hapless people—how to blast
and desolate the land, rather than it should afford sustenance
to even a solitary fugitive of the doomed race—was the
constant effort of the English commanders. Carew was not
the first of his name to signalize himself in such work. It was
the process by which Munster had been " pacified"—*i. e.* desolated—barely thirty years before. It was that by which
Cromwell, forty years subsequently, pursued the same end.
It was a system, the infamy of which, amongst the nations of
the world, pagan or Christian, is wholly monopolized by England. The impartial reader, be his nationality English or
Irish, perusing the authentic documents stored in the State
Paper Office, is forced to admit that it was not *war* in even
its severest sense, but *murder* in its most hideous and heartless
atrocity, that was waged upon the Irish people in the process
of subjugating them. It was not that process of conquest the
wounds of which, though sharp and severe for the moment,
soon cicatrise with time. Such conquests other countries have
passed through, and time has either fused the conqueror and

them. Had Ireland, too, been conquered thus, like happy results might be looked for; but as the process was wofully
different, so has the product been; so must it ever be, till the
laws of nature are reversed and revolutionized, and grapes
grow on thorns and figs on thistles. It was not war—which
might be forgotten on both sides—but murder which to this
day is remembered on one side with a terrible memory.

A thoroughly English historian—Froude—writing in our
day on these events, has found the testimony of the State
Paper Office too powerful to resist; and with all his natural
and legitimate bias or sympathy in favor of his own country,
his candor as an historian more than once constitutes him an
accuser of the infamies to which I have been referring. " The
English nation," he says, " was shuddering over the atrocities
of the Duke of Alva. The children in the nurseries were being
inflamed to patriotic rage and madness by the tales of Spanish tyranny. Yet *Alva's* bloody sword never touched *the
young, the defenceless, or those whose sex even dogs can recognize
and respect.*" *

" Sir Peter Carew has been seen murdering women and
children, and *babies that had scarcely left the breast*, but Sir
Peter Carew was not called on to answer for his conduct, and
remained in favor with the deputy. Gilbert, who was left in
command at Kilmallock, was illustrating yet more signally
the same tendency."†

" Nor was Gilbert a bad man. As times went he passed
for a brave and chivalrous gentleman; not the least distinguished in that high band of adventurers who carried the English
flag into the western hemisphere, a founder of colonies, an
explorer of unknown seas, a man of science, and, above all,
a man of special piety. He regarded himself as dealing rather
with savage beasts than with human beings, and when he tracked them to their dens, he *strangled the cubs and rooted out the
entire broods.*"‡

" The Gilbert method of treatment," says Mr. Froude again,

---

* Froude's *History of England*, vol. x. page 508.

" has this disadvantage, that it must be carried out to the last extremity, or it ought not to be tried at all. The dead do not come back; and if the mothers and the babies are slaughtered with the men, the race gives no further trouble; but the work must be done thoroughly; partial and fitful cruelty lays up only a long debt of deserved and ever-deepening hate."

The work on this occasion happening not to be "done thoroughly," Mr. Froude immediately proceeds to explain :—

"In justice to the English soldiers, however, it must be said that it was no fault of theirs if any Irish child of that generation was allowed to live to manhood."*

The same historian frankly warns his readers against supposing that such work was exceptional on the part of the English forces. From the language of the official documents before him, he says "the inference is but too natural, that work of this kind was the road to preferment, and that this, or something like it, was the *ordinary* employment of the 'Saxon' garrisons in Ireland."†

Such, then, was the work in which Carew the Second and his garrisons occupied themselves on the fall of Kinsale. Sir Charles Wilmot at the head of fifteen hundred men was despatched to desolate Kerry; and on the 9th March, Carew formally issued a commission to the Earl of Thomond "to assemble his forces together, consisting of two thousand and five hundred foot in list, and fifty horse," for the purpose of wasting Carbery, Bear, and Bantry, and making a *reconnaissance* of Dunboy. ‡ Thomond accordingly " marched as far as the abbey of Bantrie, and there had notice that Donnell O'Sullivan Beare and his people, by the advice of two Span-

---

* Ibid., page 507.

† Ibid., page 512.

‡ " The service you are to performe is to doe all your endeavour to burne the rebels' Corne in Carbery, Bear, and Bantry, take their cowes, and to use all hostile prosecution upon the persons of the people, as in such cases of rebellion is accustomed.

When you are in Beare (if you may without any apparent perill), your lordship shall doe well to take a view of the Castle of Dunboy, whereby wee may be the better instructed how to proceed for the talking of it when time convenient shall be afforded."

iards, an Italian, and a fryer called Dominicke Collins, did still continue their workes about the castle of Dunboy." " Here-upon the earl left seven hundred men in list in the Whiddy (an island lying within the Bay of Bantrie) very convenient for the service, and himself with the rest of his forces returned to Corke, where having made relation of the particulars of his journey, it was found necessary that the president, with-out any protractions or delay, should draw *all the forces in the province* to a head against them." *

XLVII.—HOW THE LORD PRESIDENT GATHERED AN ARMY OF FOUR THOUSAND MEN TO CRUSH DOOMED DUNBOY, THE LAST HOPE OF THE NATIONAL CAUSE IN MUNSTER.

AREW set out from Cork on the 20th April, at the head of his army ; on the 30th they reached Dunamark, about a mile north of the town of Bantry, having on the way halted on the 23rd at Owneboy, near Kinsale ; 24th, at Timoleague ; 25th, at Roscarbery ; 26th, at Glenharahan, near Castlehaven ; 27th, at Baltimore, where they spent two days, Carew visiting Innisherkin ; 29th, " on the mountain, at a place called Recareneltaghe, neare unto Kilcoa, being a castel wherein the rebell Conoghor, eldest sonne to Sir Fin-nin O'Drischoll, knight, held a ward."

Carew spent a month in encampment at Dunamark, by the end of which time the fleet arrived at the same place, or in the bay close by, having come round the coast from Cork. Mean-time his message for a war muster against O'Sullivan had spread throughout Munster. On the other hand, such effort as was possible in their hapless plight, was made by the few patriot leaders in the province ; all perceiving that upon Dunboy now hung the fate of the Irish cause, and seeing clearly enough that if they could not keep off from O'Sullivan the tremendous force ordered against him, it must inevitably overwhelm him. Accordingly, spreading themselves east-ward around the base of the Beara promontory, and placing themselves on all the lines leading thereto, they desperately dis-puted the ground with the concentrating English contingents, beating them back or obstructing them as best they could. Above all, the endeavor was to keep Wilmot's Kerry contingent from coming up. Tyrrel was specially charged to watch Wil-mot—to hold him in check at Killarney, and at all hazard and at any cost to prevent his junction with Carew at Bantry. Tyr-rel posted his force so advantageously in the passes leading southward from Killarney, and held them so firmly, that for weeks Wilmot's most vehement efforts to force or flank them were vain. At length, by a feat which merits for him, as a mili-tary achievement, everlasting praise—a night march over Mangerton mountain—Wilmot evaded Tyrrel; pushed on through a mountain district scarcely passable at this day for horsemen, until he reached Inchigeela; thence he marched through Ceam-an-eigh Pass (unaccountably left unguarded), and so onward till he reached Bantry. By this junction Carew's force was raised to nearly four thousand men. While waiting for Wilmot, the daily occupation of the army, according to the lord president's account, was sheep-stealing and cow-steal-ing.* At Dunamark Carew was joined by the sons of Sir Owen Sullivan, uncle of Donal of Dunboy; and to the infor-

---

* " The first of May, Captaine Taffe's troop of Horse with certain light foote were sent from the Campe, who returned with *three hundred Cowes, many Sheepe, and a great number of Garrans* they got from the Rebels.

"The second Captaine John Barry brought into the Campe, five hundred Cowes, *three hundred Sheepe, three hundred Garrans, and had the killing of five Rebels;* and the same day we procured skirmish in the edge of the Fastnesse with the rebels, but no hurt of our part.

" The third, Owen Osulevan and his brothers, sonnes to Sir Owen Osulevan (who stands firme, and deserved well of her Majestie, being Competitours with Osulevan Beare) brought some *fiftie Cowes and some sheepe* from the enemy into the Campe.

" The Rebells receiving also notice, that the President was marched so neere to the Countrey of Beare, withdrew themselves out of Desmond (as before) into Glan-garve, whereby opportunitie was offered to the Governour of performing some good service. For Donnell Osulevan More, a malicious Rebell, remained with great store

mation and coöperation given his enemies by these perfidious cousins, Donal most largely owed the fate that subsequently befel him.

On the 14th of May a council of war was held in the English camp to determine their course to Bearhaven ; whereat it was decided to march by the southern shore of the bay, called Muinter-varia, to a point nearly opposite Bear Island ; from this point by means of the fleet, to transport the whole army across the bay to Bear Island ; and thence across to the mainland close by Dunboy ; this course being rendered necessary by the fact that Donal's forces defended the passes of Glengarriffe, through which alone Bearhaven could be reached by land from Bantry. On the 31st of May, accordingly, Carew marched from Dunamark to "Kilnamenghe on the sea side, in Mountervarry." The two next following days were occupied in transporting the army to Bear Island, upon which, eventually, the whole force was landed. A short march across the island brought them to its northern shore, in full view of Dunboy, barely a mile distant across the narrow entrance to Bearhaven harbor.

---

the fifth of May, hee secretly dispached a partie of men, which burnt and *spoyled all the Countrey*, and *returned with foure thousand Cowes, besides Sheepe and Garrans.*"

" A Sergeant of the Earle of Thomond's with a partie of his Company, drew to Down. Manus, whence hee brought a prey of *threescore and sixe Cowes, with a great many of Garrans.*"—*Pacata Hibernia.*

XLVIIL—THE LAST DAYS OF DUNBOY : A TALE OF HEROISM !.

WELL might consternation fill the breasts of the Beara clansmen on beholding the resources now displayed against them ; a well-appointed army of nearly four thousand men on the shore, and hostile war-ships encircling them by sea! Within the castle O'Sullivan had, according to the English accounts, exactly one hundred and forty-three men ; there being besides these not more than five or six hundred of his clansmen available at the moment for fighting purposes. But his was not a soul to be shaken by fears into abandonment of a cause which failing or gaining, was sacred and holy in his eyes—the cause of religion and country. So Donal, who knew that a word of submission would purchase for him not only

nor in still darker hours. He had "nailed his colors to the mast," and looked Fate calmly in the face.

It seems to have been a maxim with the lord president never to risk open fight until he had first tried to effect his purpose by secret treason. While staying at Bantry he had addressed a letter to the Spanish gunners in Dunboy, offering them all manner of inducements to betray O'Sullivan, to desert the castle, first taking care, as he says, " to cloy the ordnance or mayme their carriages, that when they shall have need of them they may prove useless ; for the which I will forthwith liberally recompense you answerable to the qualities of your merit." The infamous proposition was scouted by the men to whom it was addressed. Carew, unabashed, now resolved to try whether he could not corrupt the Constable of Dunboy, O'Sullivan's most trusted friend, a man whose memory is to this day held in worship by the people of Beara —Richard Mac Geoghegan, the impersonation of chivalrous fidelity, the very soul of truth, honor, and bravery ! Thomond was commissioned to invite the Constable of Dunboy to a parley. Mac Geoghegan acceded to the invitation, came across to Bear Island (5th June), and met the earl, in presence of, but apart from, their respective guards, on the shore: Of that memorable interview Carew has left us a brief but characteristic description. " All the eloquence and artifice which the Earle could use avayled nothing : for Mac Geoghegan was resolved to persevere in his wayes; and, in the great love which he pretended to beare unto the Earle (Thomond) he advised him not to hazard his life and landing upon the Mayne. . . . . . The Earle disdayning both his obstinacie and his vanie-glorious advice, broke off his speech, telling Mac Geoghegan that ere many days passed hee would repent that hee had not followed his (the Earl's) counsel."*

Carew had at first designed to cross over and land on the main at what seemed to be the only feasible point, a smooth strand at a spot now called Caematrangan. Within a few perches of this spot reaches one end of a small island ("Deenish") which stretches almost completely across the mouth of

* *Pacata Hibernia.*

the inner harbor of (modern) Castletown Beare. Carew landed a portion of his army on this small island; but O'Sullivan had erected a battery faced with gabions at Caematrangan, and had, moreover, his small force drawn up at hand to meet the invaders at the shore. Whereupon Carew, while making a feint as if about to attempt the passage there, directed the remainder of his force quickly to pass to the other (or eastern) extremity of Deenish, and effect a landing on the main at that point. This they were able to accomplish unopposed, for the distance thereto, from O'Sullivan's strand battery, owing to the sweep of the shore and a narrow arm of the sea intervening, was two or three miles, whereas directly across, by water or on Deenish island, was a reach of less than half a mile. Nevertheless, O'Sullivan, discerning, though all too late, the skilful use made by Carew of the natural advantages of the ground, hastened with all speed to confront the invaders, and unawed by the disparity of numbers against him—thousands against hundreds—boldly gave them battle. Carew himself seems to have been quite struck with the daring courage or "audacity" of this proceeding. After marvelling at such foolhardiness, as he thought it, he owns "they came on bravely," and maintained a very determined attack. It was only when additional regiments were hurried up, and utterly overwhelmed them by numbers, that Donal's little force had to abandon the unequal strife, leaving their dead and wounded upon the field.

That night, however, there reached Dunboy news well calculated to compensate for the gloom of perils so great and so near at hand. A Spanish ship had arrived at O'Sullivan's castle of Ardea (in Kenmare bay, on the northern shore of the Beara promontory) bringing to Donal letters and envoys from King Philip, and aid for the Munster chiefs in money, arms, and ammunition, committed to his care for distribution.

Moreover, there came by this ship the cheering intelligence that an expedition of some fifteen thousand men was being organized in Spain for Ireland when the vessel sailed! Here was glorious hope indeed! It was instantly decided that the chief himself should proceed with all promptitude to meet the envoys landed at Ardea,* and look to the important duties required of him by their messages ; meanwhile entrusting the defence of Dunboy to Mac Geoghegan and a chosen garrison. Next morning Donal, with all his available force, exclusive of a garrison of one hundred and forty-three picked men left in the castle, set out for Ardea. The farewell cheers that rang out from the ramparts behind him, gave token of brave resolve to do or die, and doubtless helped to lighten the chieftain's heart with whispers of hope. But alas! Donal had taken his last farewell of Dunboy. When next he gazed upon the once proud home of his fathers it was a smoking and blood-clotted ruin !—

> The halls where mirth and mistrelsy
> Than Beara's wind rose louder,
> Were flung in masses lonelily,
> And black with English powder !

For eleven days Mac Geoghegan fought Dunboy against Carew and his surrounding army of four thousand men! Eleven days, during which the thick white cloud of smoke never once lifted from battery and trench, and the deafening boom of cannon never once ceased to roll across the bay. By the 17th of June the castle had been knocked into a ruinous condition by an incessant bombardment from the well-appointed English batteries. The lord president devotes several pages of his journal to minute and copious descriptions of each day's labor in a siege which he declares to be unparalleled for obstinacy of defence ; and his narrative of the closing scenes of the struggle is told with painful particularity. Mr. Haverty condenses the tragic story very effectively as follows :—
" The garrison consisted of only one hundred and forty-three chosen fighting men, who had but a few small cannon, while

---

* These were the Most Rev. Dr. McEgan, Bishop of Ross, and Father Nealon. They brought, says Carew, " letters to sundry rebels, and twelve thousand pounds. The disposition of the money by appointment in Spaine was left principally to Donnall O'Sulevan Beare, Owen McEggan, James Archer, and some others." This same Bishop McEgan was subsequently killed near Bandon fighting gallantly, with his sword in one hand and his beads in the other. His remains were buried in the

the comparatively large army which assailed them were well supplied with artillery and all the means of attack. At length, on the 17th of June, when the castle had been nearly shattered to pieces, the garrison offered to surrender if allowed to depart with their arms ; but their messenger was immediately hanged and the order for the assault was given. Although the proportion of the assailants in point of numbers was overwhelming, the storming party were resisted with the most desperate bravery. From turret to turret, and in every part of the crumbling ruins, the struggle was successively maintained throughout the live-long day ; thirty of the gallant defenders attempted to escape by swimming, but soldiers had been posted in boats, who killed them in the water ; and at length the surviving portion of the garrison retreated into a cellar, into which the only access was by a narrow, winding flight of stone steps. Their leader, MacGeoghegan being mortally wounded, the command was given to Thomas Taylor, the son of an Englishman, and the intimate friend of Captain Tyrrell, to whose niece he was married. Nine barrels of gunpowder were stowed away in the cellar, and with these Taylor declared that he would blow up all that remained of the castle, burying himself and his companions with their enemies in the ruins, unless they received a promise of life. This was refused by the savage Carew, who, placing a guard upon the entrance to the cellar, as it was then after sunset, returned to the work of slaughter next morning. Cannons balls were discharged among the Irish in their last dark retreat, and Taylor was forced by his companions to surrender unconditionally ; but when some of the English officers descended into the cellar, they found the wounded Mac Geoghegan, with a lighted torch in his hand, staggering to throw it into the gunpowder. Captain Power thereupon seized him by the arms, and the others despatched him with their swords ; but the work of death was not yet completed. Fifty-eight of those who had surrendered were hanged that day in the English camp, and some others were hanged a few days after ; so that not one of the one hundred and forty-three

the remains of the castle were blown up by Carew with the gunpowder found therein."

Few episodes of Irish history have been more warmly eulogized than this heroic defence of Dunboy ; nor would it be easy to find in the history of any country one more largely calculated to excite sympathy and admiration. Dr. Robert Dwyer Joyce, in his published volume of *Ballads, Romances, and Songs,* contributes a truly graphic poem on the subject. Subjoined are the concluding stanzas :—

THE SACK OF DUNBUL.

*   ▸   ●   ●

Nearer yet they crowd and come,
With taunting and yelling and thundering drum,
   With taunting and yelling the hold they environ,
     And swear that its towers and defenders must fall,
While the cannon are set, and their death-hail of iron
   Crash wildly on bastion and turret and wall;
And the ramparts are torn from their base to their brow;
Ho! will they not yield to the murderers now ?
No ! its huge towers shall float over Cleena's bright sea,
Ere the Gael prove a craven in lonely Dunbui.

Like the fierce god of battle, Mac Geoghegan goes
From rampart to wall, in the face of his foes,
   Now his voice rises high o'er the cannon's fierce din,
Whilst the taunt of the Saxon is loud as before,
   But a yell thunders up from his warriors within,
And they dash through the gateway, down, down to the shore,
With their chief rushing on.   Like a storm in its wrath,
They sweep the cowed Saxon to death in their path ;
Ah ! dearly he'll purchase the fall of the free,
Of the lion-souled warriors of lonely Dunbui !

Leaving terror behind them, and death in their train,
Now they stand on their walls 'mid the dying and slain,
   And the night is around them—the battle is still—
That lone summer midnight, ah ! short is its reign ;
   For the morn springeth upward, and valley and hill
Fling back the fierce echoes of conflict again.
And see ! how the foe rushes up to the breach,
Towards the green waving banner he yet may not reach,
For look how the Gael flings him back to the sea,
From the blood-reeking ramparts of lonely Dunbui !

Night cometh again, and the white stars look down,
From the hold to the beach, where the batteries frown ;
  Night cometh again, but affrighted she flies,
Like a black Indian queen from the fierce panther's roar,
  And morning leaps up in the wide-spreading skies,
To his welcome of thunder and flame evermore ;
For the guns of the Saxon crush fearfully there,
Till the walls and the towers and ramparts are bare.
And the foe make their last mighty swoop on the free,
The brave-hearted warriors of lonely Dunbui !

Within the red breach see Mac Geoghegan stand,
With the blood of the foe on his arm and his brand,
  And he turns to his warriors and " fight we," says he,
" For country, for freedom, religion, and all :
  Better sink into death, and forever be free,
Than yield to the false Saxon's mercy and thrall !"
And they answer with brandish of sparth and of glaive :
" Let them come: we will give them a welcome and grave ;
Let them come : from their swords could we flinch, could we flee,
When we fight for our country, our God, and Dunbui ?"

They came, and the Gael met their merciless shock—
Flung them backward like spray from the lone Skellig rock;
  But they rally, as wolves springing up to the death
Of their brother of famine, the bear of the snow—
  He hurls them adown to the ice fields beneath,
Rushing back to his dark Norland cave from the foe ;—
So up to the breaches they savagely bound,
Thousands still thronging beneath and around,
Till the firm Gael is driven—till the brave Gael must flee
In, into the chambers of lonely Dunbui !

In chamber, in cellar, on stairway and tower,
Evermore they resisted the false Saxon's power ;
  Through the noon, through the eve, and the darkness of night
The clangor of battle rolls fearfully there,
  Till the morning leaps upward in glory and light.
Then, where are the true-hearted warriors of Beare ?
They have found them a refuge from torment and chain,
They have died with their chief, save the few who remain,
And that few—oh, fair Heaven ! on the high gallows tree,
They swing by the ruins of lonely Dunbui !

Long, long in the hearts of the brave and the free
Live the warriors who died in the lonely Dunbui—
  Down time's silent river their fair names shall go,

Can we find names so sweet for remembrance as they !
And we will hold their memories forever and aye,
A halo, a glory that ne'er shall decay,
We'll set them as stars o'er eternity's sea,
The names of the heroes who fell at Dunbui !

During the progress of the siege at Dunboy, Carew had
despatched a force to Dursey island, which, landing in the
night, succeeded in overpowering the small and indeed unwary garrison left there ; " so that," as a historian remarks, "no
roof now remained to the Lord of Bearhaven." Donal, collecting his people, one and all, men, women, and children, as
well as all the herds and removable property of the clan, now
retired eastward upon his great natural stronghold of Glengariffe. Here he defied and defeated every attempt to dislodge him.* For three months he awaited with increasing anxiety and suspense the daily-expected news from spain. Alas !
In the words of one of our historians, " the ill-news from Spain
in September, threw a gloom over those mountains deeper
than was ever cast by equinoctial storm." But here we must
pause for awhile to trace the movements of O'Donnell and
O'Neill after the parting at Innishannon.

---

* On one occasion a fierce and protracted battle ensued between him and the combined forces of Wilmot, Selsby, and Slingsby : "A bitter fight," says Carew, "maintained without intermission for sixe howers ; the Enemy not leaving their pursuit
until they came in sight of the campe ; for whose reliefe two regiments were drawne
forth to gieve countenance, and Downings was sent with one hundred and twenty
choisse men to the succour of Barry and Selby, who in the reare were so hotly charged
by the Rebels that they came to the Sword and Pike ; and the skirmish continued
till night parted them." Notwithstanding their immense superiority in numbers,
night was a welcome relief to the English ; for it not only saved them from a perilous
position, but enabled them to get off an immense spoil of cattle, which early in the
day they had taken from the Irish. Brilliant as was the victory for O'Sullivan in other
respects, the loss thus sustained must have been most severe—two thousand cows,
four thousand sheep, and one thousand horse, according to Carew : a store of sheep
and kine which, even in these days of "cattle shows" and " agricultural societies," it
would be difficult to collect in the same locality.

THE LAST STRUGGLE OF THE BRAVE MAC GEOGHEGAN.

See page 320

XLIX.—HOW THE FALL OF DUNBOY CAUSED KING PHILIP TO CHANGE ALL HIS PLANS, AND RECALL THE EXPEDITION FOR IRELAND ; AND HOW THE REVERSE BROKE THE BRAVE HEART OF RED HUGH. HOW THE " LION OF THE NORTH " STOOD AT BAY, AND MADE HIS FOES TREMBLE TO THE LAST.

HREE days after the defeat at Kinsale, O'Donnell—hav. ing deputed his brother Ruari to command the clan in his absence—accompanied by his confessor, his secretary, and some military *attachés* or *aides-de-camp*, sailed from Castlehaven for Corunna, where he arrived on the 14th of January. " He was received with high distinction by the Marquis of Caracena and other nobles, ' who evermore gave O'Donnell the right hand ; which within his government,' says Carew, ' he would not have done to the greatest duke in Spain.' He travelled through Gallicia, and at Santiago de Compostella was royally entertained by the archbishop and citizens ; but in bull-fighting on the stately Alameda he had small pleasure. With teeth set and heart on fire, the chieftain hurried on, traversed the mountains of Gallicia and Leon, and drew not bridle until he reached Zamora, where King Philip was then holding his court. With passionate zeal he pleaded his country's cause ; entreated that a greater fleet and a stronger army might be sent to Ireland without delay, unless his Catholic majesty desired to see his ancient Milesian kinsmen and allies utterly destroyed and trodden into earth by the tyrant Elizabeth ; and above all, whatever was to be done he prayed it might be done instantly, while O'Neil still held his army on foot and his banner flying ; while it was not yet too late to rescue poor Erin from the deadly fangs of those dogs of England. The king received him affectionately, treated him with high consideration, and actually gave orders for a powerful force to be drawn together at Corunna for another descent upon Ireland."*

" He returned to that port, from which he could every day look out across the western waves that lay between him and home, and where he could be kept constantly informed of what was passing in Ireland. Spring was over and gone, and summer too had passed away, but still the exigencies of Spanish policy delayed the promised expedition."* " That armament never sailed ; and poor O'Donnell never saw Ireland more ; for news arrived in Spain, a few months after, that Dun-baoi Castle, the last stronghold in Munster that held out for King Philip, was taken ; and Beare-haven, the last harbor in the south that was open to his ships, effectual'y guarded by the English. The Spanish preparations were countermanded, and Red Hugh was once more on his journey to the court, to renew his almost hopeless suit, and had arrived at Simancas, two leagues from Valladolid, when he suddenly fell sick ; his gallant heart was broken, and he died there on the 10th of September, 1602. He was buried by order of the king with royal honors, as befitted a prince of the Kinel-Conal ; and the chapter of the cathedral of St. Francis, in the stately city of Valladolid, holds the bones of as noble a chief and as stout a warrior as ever bore the wand of chieftaincy, or led a clan to battle." †

" Thus," says another writer, " closed the career of one of the brightest and noblest characters in any history. His youth, his early captivity, his princely generosity, his daring courage, his sincere piety, won the hearts of all who came in contact with him. He was the sword, as O'Neil was the brain, of the Ulster confederacy : the Ulysses and Achilles of the war, they fought side by side without jealousy or envy, for almost as long a period as their prototypes had spent in besieging Troy."

One cannot peruse unmoved the quaint and singular recital of O'Donnell's characteristic merits and virtues given by the Four Masters. Of him it can with scrupulous truth be said that—unlike not a few others, famed as soldiers, or rulers, or statesmen—his character, in *every* phase, was pure and noble ; and that his private life as well as his public career was worthy of admiration, without stain and without reproach.

Meanwhile O'Neill had set out homeward at the head of the shattered Ulster contingent; and now the lord deputy felt that the moment had come for a supreme effort to pour down upon and overwhelm him. The "Lion of the north" was struck, and, badly wounded, was retreating to his lair. This was surely the time for pressing him to the death—for surrounding, capturing, or slaying the once dreaded foe. So throughout Leinster, Connacht, and Ulster, the cry was spread for the English garrisons, and all natives who would mark themselves for favor and consideration, to rise simultaneously and burst in upon the territories of the confederate chiefs; while the deputy swiftly assembled troops to intercept, capture or destroy them on their homeward way from the south. The Irish cause was down—disastrously and hopelessly. Now, therefore, was the time for all who " bow the knee and worship the rising sun" to show their zeal on the winning side. Tyrconnell and Tyrowen, as well as the territories of O'Rorke and Maguire, were inundated by converging streams of regular troops and volunteer raiders; while O'Neill, like a " lion," indeed, who finds that the hunter is rifling his home, made the earth tremble in his path to the rescue! With the concentrated passion of desperation he tore through every obstacle, routed every opposing army, and marched—strode—to the succor of his people, as if a thunderbolt cleared the way. Soon his enemies were made to understand that the " Lion of the North" was still alive and unsubdued. But it was, insooth, a desperate cause that now taxed to its uttermost the genius of Hugh. The Lord deputy, Mountjoy, proceeded to the north to take command in person against him; while " Dowcra, marching out of Derry, pressed O'Neill from the north and northeast." Mountjoy advanced on Hugh's family seat, Dungannon; but O'Neill could ever better bear to see his ancestral home in ashes than to have it become the shelter of his foes. The Lord deputy " discovered it in the distance, as Norris had once before done, in flames, kindled by the hand of its straitened proprietor." With vigor and skill undiminished and

:measures of defensive operations. In fine, it was in this moment of apparent wreck and ruin and despair, that O'Neill's
character rose into positive grandeur and sublimity, and that
his glorious talents shone forth in their greatest splendor.
" Never," says one of our historians, " did the genius of Hugh
O'Neill shine out brighter than in these last defensive operations. In July, Mountjoy writes apologetically to the council, that ' notwithstanding her Majesty's great forces O'Neill
doth still live.' He bitterly complains of his consummate cau-
tion, his ' pestilent judgment to spread and to nourish his own
infection,' and of the reverence entertained for his person by
the native population. Early in August, Mountjoy had
arranged what he had hoped might prove the finishing stroke
in the struggle ; Dowcra from Derry, Chichester from Carrickfergus, Danvers from Armagh, and all who could be spared
from Mountjoy, Charlemont, and Mountnorris, were gathered
under his command, to the number of eight thousand men, for
a foray into the interior of Tyrone. Inisloghlin, on the borders of Down and Antrim, which contained a great quantity
of valuables belonging to O'Neill, was captured, Magherlow-
ney and Tulloghoge were next taken. At the latter place
stood the ancient stone chair on which the O'Neills were
inaugurated, time out of mind ; it was now broken into atoms
by Mountjoy's orders. But the most effective warfare was
made on the growing crops. The eight thousand men spread
themselves over the fertile fields, along the valleys of the Bann
and the Roe, destroying the standing grain with fire, where it
would burn, or with the *praca*, a peculiar kind of harrow, tearing it up by the roots. The horsemen trampled crops into the
earth which had generously nourished them ; the infantry shore
them down with their sabres ; and the sword, though in a very
different sense from that of Holy Scripture, was indeed, converted into a sickle. The harvest moon never shone upon
such fields in any Christian land. In September, Mountjoy
reported to Cecil, ' that between Tullaghoge and Toome there
lay unburied a thousand dead,' and that since his arrival on the
Blackwater—a period of a couple of months—there were three

of his clansmen drove the chief to surrender to Dowcra, and the news of Hugh Roe's death having reached Donegal, his brother repaired to Athlone, and made his submission to Mountjoy. Early in December, O'Neill, unable to maintain himself on the river Roe, retired with six hundred foot and sixty horse to Glencancean, near Lough Neagh, the most secure of his fastnesses. His brother Cormac, McMahon, and Art O'Neill, of Clandeboy, shared with him the wintry hardships of that asylum, while Tyrone, Clandeboy, and Monaghan, were given up to horrors surpassing any that had been known or dreamt of in former wars.

By this time O'Sullivan had bravely held his position in Glengarriffe for full six months against all the efforts of the Munster army. That picturesque glen, whose beauty is of worldwide fame, was for Donal a camp formed by nature, within which the old and helpless, the women and children of his clan, with their kine and a sheep, were safely placed, while the fighting force, which, with Tyrrell's contingent, did not exceed 800 men, guarded the few passes through which alone the alpine barriers of the glen could be penetrated. Here the little community, as we might call them, housed in tents of evergreen boughs, lived throughout the summer and autumn months, " waiting for the news from Spain." They fished the "fishful river" that winds through that elysian vale, and the myriad confluent streams that pour down from the "hundred lakes" of Caha. They hunted the deer that in those days, as in our own, roamed wild and free through the densely wooded craggy dells. Each morning the guards were told off for the mountain watches ; and each evening the bugles of the chief, returning from his daily inspection, or the joyous shouts of victory that proclaimed some new assault of the enemy repulsed, woke the echoes of the hills. And perhaps in the calm summer twilight, the laugh and the song went round ; the minstrels touched their harps, and the clansmen improvised their simple rustic sports, while the Chief and Lady Aileen moved through the groups with a gracious smile for all ! For they nothing doubted that soon would come the

then !—Beara would be swept of the hated foe, and their loved
Dunboy

          ————again would rise
        And mock the English rover!

Alas ! this happy dream was to fade in sorrow, and die out
in bitterest reality of despair ! News came indeed from Spain
at length; but it was news that sounded the knell of all their
hopes to O'Sullivan and his people ! O'Donnel was dead,
and on hearing of the fall of Dunboy the Spanish government
had countermanded the expedition assembled and on the
point of sailing for Ireland ! This was heart-crushing intelligence for Donal and his confederates. Nevertheless they
held out still. There remained one faint glimmer in the north;
and while there was a sword unsheathed any where in the
sacred cause of fatherland, they would not put up theirs.
They gave Carew's captains hot work throughout Desmond
for the remainder of the autumn, capturing several strong
positions, and driving in his outlying garrisons in Muskerry
and the Carberies. But soon even the northern ray went out,
and the skies all around were wrapt in cimmerian gloom.
There was room for hope no more!

What was now Donal's position? It is difficult adequately
to realize it ! Winter was upon him; the mountains were
deep in snow ; his resources were exhausted ; he was cooped
up in a remote glen, with a crowd of helpless people, the aged
and infirm, women and children, and with barely a few hundred fighting men to guard them. He was environed by foes
on all hands. The nearest point where an ally could be
reached was in Ulster, at the other extremity of Ireland—two
or three hundred miles away—and the country between him
and any such friendly ground was all in the hands of the English, and swarmed with their garrisons and scouring parties.

The resolution taken by O'Sullivan under these circumstances was one which has ever since excited amongst historical writers and military critics the liveliest sentiments of
astonishment and admiration. It was to pierce through his
surrounding foes, and fight his way northward inch by inch to

and wounded of his clan—in fine, all who might elect to claim his
protection and share his retreat rather than trust the perils of
remaining. It was this latter feature which preëminently
stamped the enterprise as almost without precedent. For
four hundred men, under such circumstances, to cut their
way from Glengariffe to Lietrim, even if divested of every
other charge or duty save the clearing of their own path,
would be sufficiently daring to form an episode of romance ;
and had Donald more regard for his own safety than for his
"poor people," this would have been the utmost attempted
by him. But he was resolved, let what might befal, not to
abandon even the humblest or the weakest amongst them.
While he had a sword to draw, he would defend them ; and
he would seek no safety or protection for himself that was not
shared by them. His own wife and, at least, the youngest of
his children, he left behind in charge of his devoted foster-
brother, Mac Swiney, who successfully concealed them until the chief's return, nearly eight months subsequently,
in an almost inaccessible spot at the foot of an immense
precipice in the Glengarriffe mountains, now known as the
Eagle's Nest. Many other families also elected to try the
chance of escape from Carew's scouring parties, and remained
behind, hidden in the fastnesses of that wild region.

L.—THE RETREAT TO LEITRIM; "THE MOST ROMANTIC AND GALLANT ACHIEVEMENT OF THE AGE."

N the last day of December, 1602, was commenced this memorable retreat, which every writer or commentator, whether of that period or of our own, civil or military, English or Irish, has concurred in characterizing as scarcely to be paralleled in history.* Tyrrell and other of the confederates had drawn off some time previously, when *sauve qui peut* evidently became the maxim with the despair-stricken band; so that O'Sullivan's force when setting out from Glengarriffe consisted exactly of four hundred fighting men, and about six hundred non-combatants, women, children, aged and infirm people, and servants.† Even in our own day, and in time of peace, with full facilities of transport and supply, the commissariat arrangements necessary to be made beforehand along the route of such a body—a thousand souls—would require some skill and organization. But O'Sullivan could on no day tell where or how his people were to find sustenance for the morrow. He had money enough,‡ it is true, to purchase supplies ; but no one durst sell them to him, or permit him to take them. Word was sent through the country by the lord president for all, *on peril of being treated as O'Sullivan's covert or open abettors,* to fall upon him, to cross his road, to bar his way, to watch him at the fords to come upon him by night ; and, above all, to drive off or destroy all cattle or other possible means of sustenance, so,

---

* " We read of nothing more like to the expedition of Cyrus and the Ten Thousand Greeks, than this retreat of O'Sullivan Beare."—*Abbé Mac Geoghegan.*

" One of the most extraordinary retreats recorded in history."—*Haverty.*

" A retreat almost unparalleled."—*M'Gee.*

" The most romantic and gallant achievement of the age."—*Davis.*

†*Historiæ Catholicæ Hiberniæ,* Haverty, M'Gee, Mac Geoghegan.

‡ Even on the last day of his terrible retreat, we find him able to pay a guide very

that of sheer necessity his party must perish on the way. Whose lands soever O'Sullivan would be found to have passed through unresisted, or whereupon he was allowed to find food of any kind, the government would consider forfeited. Such were the circumstances under which the Lord of Beara and his immortal Four Hundred set out on their mid-winter retreat on the 31st December, 1602.

That evening, Don Philip tells us, they reached and encamped at " a place on the borders of Muskerry, called by the natives Acharis." * Next day, 1st January, 1603, they reached "before noon," "Balebrunia" (Ballyvourny), famed as the retreat of St. Gubeneta, whose ruined church and penitential stations are still frequented by pious pilgrims. Here O'Sullivan and his entire force halted, that they might begin their journey by offering all their sufferings to God, and supplicating the powerful prayers of His saint. Donal and several members of his family made gifts to the altar, and the little army, having prayed for some time, resumed their weary march. The ordeal commenced for them soon. They were assailed and harassed all the way "by the sons of Thadeus Mac Carthy," several being wounded on both sides. They cleared their road, however, and that night encamped in "O'Kimbhi" (O'Keefe's country: Duhallow); "but," says Philip, "they had little rest at night after such a toilsome day, for they were constantly molested by the people of that place, and suffered most painfully from hunger. For they had been able to bring with them but one day's provisions and these they had consumed on the first day's march." Next morning they pushed forward towards the confines of Limerick, designing to reach that ancient refuge of the oppressed and vanquished, the historic Glen of Aherlow, where at least they

* I am not aware that any one hitherto has identified this spot ; but it is, nevertheless, plainly to be found. The place is the junction of some mountain roads. in a truly wild and solitary locality, about a mile north of the present village of Bealnageary, which is between Gougane Barra and Macroom. In a little grove the ruined church of *Agharis* (marked on the Ordnance maps) identifies the for us locality of "Acharis.' It is on the road to Ballyvourney by O'Sullivan's route, which was from Glengarriffe eastward by his castle of the Fawn's Rock ("Carrick-an-Asa"), where he left a ward;

hoped for rest in safety during a few days' halt, but their path now lay through the midst of their foes—right between the garrisons of Charleville and Buttevant, and they scarcely hoped to cross the river in their front without a heavy penalty. And truly enough, as the faint and weary cavalcade reached the bank, a strong force under the brother of Viscount Barry encountered them at Bellaghy Ford. The women and children were at once put to the rear, and the hunger-wasted company, nevertheless, all unflinching, came up to the conflict like horses. It was a bitter fight, but despair gave energy to that desperate fugitive band. They literally swept their foes before them, and would not have suffered a man to escape them had not hunger and terrible privation told upon them too severely to allow of a pursuit. Dr. Joyce chronicles this combat for us in one of his ballads :

> We stood so steady,
>   All under fire,
> We stood so steady,
> Our long spears ready
>   To vent our ire—
> To dash on the Saxon,
> Our mortal foe,
> And lay him low
>   In the bloody mire !
>
> 'T was by Blackwater,
>   When snows were white,
> 'T was by Blackwater,
> Our foes for the slaughter
>   Stood full in sight ;
> But we were ready
> With our long spears;
> And we had no fears
>   But we 'd win the fight.
>
> Their bullets came whistling
>   Upon our rank,
> Their bullets came whistling
> Their bay'nets were bristling
>   On th' other bank.
> Yet we stood steady,
> And each good blade
> Ere the morn did fade

"Hurra ! for Freedom !"
  Came from our van ;
" Hurra ! for Freedom !
Our swords—we'll feed 'em !
  As but we can—
With vengeance we'll feed 'em !"
Then down we crashed,
Through the wild ford dashed,
  And the fray began !

Horses to horses
  And man to man-
O'er dying horses
And blood and corses
  O'Sullivan,
Our general, thundered ;
And we were not slack
To slay at his back
  Till the flight began.

O ! how we scattered
  The foemen then—
Slaughtered and scattered
And chased and shattered,
  By shore and glen ;—
To the wall of Moyallo,
Few fled that day,—
Will they bar our way
  When we come again?

Our dead freres we buried,—
  They were but few,—
Our dead freres we buried
Where the dark waves hurried
  And flashed and flew :
O ! sweet be their slumber
Who thus have died
In the battle's tide,
  Innisfail, for you !

Pushing on for Aherlow—the unwounded of the soldiers carrying between them the wounded of the past three day's conflict—after a march of thirty miles they reached at length that " vast solitude," as Don Philip calls it. They were so worn-out by travel and hunger, toil and suffering, that the

perform their duty.* The prospect of recruiting strength by
a few days' repose here had to be abandoned, lest the foes
now gathering around their might bar all way to the Shannon.
So next morning, at dawn, having refreshed themselves with
the only food available, *herbs and water*,† they set out northward. On this day one of their severest battles had to be
fought—a conflict of eight hours' duration. O'Sullivan says
that, though the enemy exceeded greatly in numbers, they
were deficient in military skill, otherwise the men of Beara
must have been overpowered. From this forward the march
grew every day more painful. Nature itself could not continue to endure such suffering. The fugitives dropped on the
road from utter exhaustion, or strayed away in the wild
delirious search for food. In many instances the sentries at
night died at their posts from sheer privation. Arriving at
Dunnohill, the starving soldiery at once occupy the place.
The first who arrived ravenously devoured all the food; those
who came next, greedily ate everything in the way of corn,
etc. On by Ballynakill, Sleive Felim, and Lateragh; each
day a prolonged strife with foes on all sides. "It was not
only," says Don Philip, "that they had to fight against superior numbers; but every day O'Sullivan had fresh enemies,
while his soldiers were being worn out by cold, hunger, and
incessant fighting." Still they guarded faithfully the women
and children, and such of the aged as could walk without assistance; and maintained, though only by the utmost exertion,
that strict discipline and precaution to which O'Sullivan
largely owed his safety on this march. A vanguard of forty
men always went in front; next came the sick and wounded,
the women and children; next the baggage and the ammunition; and, last of all, protecting the rear, Donal himself
with the bulk of his little force. On the 6th January, they
reached the wood of Brosna (now Portland, in the Parish of
Lorha); and here Donal orders the little force to entrench
themselves. Their greatest peril is now at hand. The "lordly Shannon" wide and deep, is in their front; they have no

---

Historia Catholica Ibernia.   † Ibid.

boats; and the foe is crowding behind and around them. Donal's resort in this extremity was one worthy of his repu- tation as a skilful captain. Of the few horses now remaining in his cavalcade, he directed eleven to be killed. The skins he strained upon a firmly bound boat-frame which he had his soldiers to construct in the wood close by; the flesh was cooked as a luxury for the sick and wounded. In this boat, on the morning of the 8th January, he commenced to trans- port his little force across the Shannon, from Redwood. As he was in the act of so doing, there arrived on the southern bank, where the women and children, and only a portion of the rear-guard remained, the queen's sheriff of Tipperary and a strong force, who instantly "began to plunder the baggage, slaughter the camp followers, and throw the women and children into the river." * One of O'Sullivan's lieutenants, in charge of the small guard which, however, yet remained, fell upon them with such vehemence, that they retired, and the last of the fugitives crossed to the Connacht shore.

But there was still no rest for that hapless company. "The soldiers pressed by hunger divide themselves into two bands, and alternately sustain the attacks of the enemy, and collect provisions." Arriving at Aughrim-Hy-Maine a powerful and well ordered army under Sir Thomas Burke, Lord Clanri- carde's brother, and Colonel Henry Malby, lay across their route. Even Carew himself informs us that the English force vastly exceeded the gaunt and famished band of O'Sullivan; though he does not venture into particulars. In truth, Donal found himself compelled to face a pitched battle against a force of some eight hundred men with his wasted party, now re- duced to less than three hundred. Carew briefly tells the story, so bitter for him to tell. "Nevertheless, when they saw that either they must make their way by the sword or perish, they gave a brave charge upon our men, in which Captain Malby was slain; upon whose fall Sir Thomas and his troops fainting, with the loss of many men, studied their safety by flight."† The quaint record in the *Annals of the*

---

* *Historia Catholica.*

Four Masters is as follows:—" O'Sullivan, O'Connor-Kerry, and William Burke, with their small party, were obliged to remain at Aughrim-Hy-Many to engage fight, and sustain a battle-field,and test their true valor against the many hundreds oppressing and pursuing them. O'Sullivan, with rage, heroism, fury, and ferocity, rushed to the place where he saw the English, for it was against them that he cherished most animosity and hatred ; and made no delay until he reached the spot where he saw their chief ; so that he quickly and dexterously beheaded that noble Englishman, the son of Captain Malby. The forces there collected were then routed and a countless number of them slain."*   Besides Malby and Burke there were left on the field by the English "three standard bearers and several officers." It was a decisive victory for the prince of Beare ; but it only purchased for him a day's respite. That night, for the first time—terrible affliction—he had to march forward, unable to bring with him his sick or wounded ! Next day the English (who could not win the fight) came up and butchered these helpless ones in cold blood ! I summarize from the *Historiæ Catholicæ* the following narrative of the last days of this memorable retreat :—

" Next day at dawn he crossed Slieve Muire (Mount Mary) and came down to some villages where he hoped to procure provisions. But he found all the cattle and provisions carried away, and the people of the district arrayed against him, under the command of Mac David the lord of the place. He withdrew at dusk to some thick woods at Sleibh Iphlinn. But in the night he received information that the people intended to surround him and cut him off. Large fires were lighted to deceive his enemies, and he at once set off on a night march. The soldiers suffered exceedingly. They fell into deep snow drifts, whence they dragged each other out with great difficulty. " Next day they were overtaken by Mac David. But their deter-

---

and equanimity, a picture, hardly to be paralleled in the records of savagery :—" Next morning Sir Charles (Wilmot) coming to seeke the enemy in their campe, hee entered into their quarter without resistance. where he found *nothing but hurt and sick men. whose bains and lives by the soldiers were both determined.*"

mined attitude made their foes retire; and so they were allowed to betake themselves to another wood called Diamhbhrach, or the Solitude. Upon entering this refuge, the men, overpowered with fatigue, lay down and fell asleep. When O'Sullivan halted, finding only twelve companions with himself, he ordered fires to be lighted, in order that his scattered followers might know whither to turn upon waking.

" At dawn of next day numbers of the inhabitants flocked to O'Sullivan's bivouac, attracted by the unprecedented spectacle of so many fires in such a lonely solitude. They furnished him gratuitously with food, and subsequently informed Oliver Lombard, the governor of Connaught, that the fires had been kindled by the herdsmen. Many of the Catholics were found to suffer very much in their feet, by reason of the severity of the weather and the length of the march. O'Connor, especially, suffered grievously. To give as long a rest as possible, they remained all this day in the wood; but a night march was necessary for all. This was especially severe on O'Connor, as it was not possible that he could proceed on horseback. For, since the enemy occupied all the public routes and the paths practicable for a horse, they were obliged to creep along by out-of-the-way paths, and frequently to help each other in places where alone they could not move.

" A guide was wanted; but God provided one. A stranger presented himself, clad in a linen garment, with bare feet, having his head bound with a white cloth, and bearing a long pole shod with iron, and presenting an appearance well calculated to strike terror into the beholders. Having saluted O'Sullivan and the others, he thus addressed them: 'I know that you Catholics have been overwhelmed by various calamities, that you are fleeing from the tyranny of heretics, that at the hill of Aughrim you routed the queen's troops, and that you are now going to O'Ruarke, who is only fifteen miles off; but you want a guide. Therefore, a strong desire has come upon me of leading you thither.' After some hesitation O'Sullivan accepted his offer, and ordered him to receive two hundred gold pieces. These he took, 'not as a reward, but as a mark

ness of the night, their ignorance of the country, and their unavoidable suspicion of their guide multiplied their fears. The slippery condition of the rocks over which they had to climb, the snow piled up by the wind, their fatigue and weakness, the swelling of their feet, tormented the unfortunate walkers. But O'Connor suffered most of all. His feet and legs were inflamed, and rapidly broke into ulcers. He suffered excruciating pain ; but he bore it patiently for Jesus Christ. In the dead of the night they reached a hamlet, Knock Vicar (*Mons Vicarii*) where they refreshed themselves with fire and food. But when they were again about to proceed, O'Connor could not stand, much less walk. Then his fellow soldiers carried him in their arms in alternate batches of four, until they found a wretched horse, upon the back of which they placed him. At length, when they had passed Cor Sliebh, the sun having risen, their guide pointed out O'Ruarke's castle in the distance, and having assured them that all danger was now passed, he bade them farewell."

Not unlike the survivors of the Greek Ten Thousand, to whom they have been so often compared, who, when they first descried the sea, broke from their ranks and rushed forward wildly shouting " Thalatta ! Thalatta !" that group of mangled and bleeding fugitives—for now, alas ! they were no more—when they saw through the trees in the distance the towers of Leitrim Castle, sank upon the earth, and for the first time since they had quitted Beara, gave way to passionate weeping, overpowered by strange paroxysms of joy, grief, suffering, and exultation. At last—at last !—they were safe ! No more days of bloody combat, and nights of terror and unrest ! No more of hunger's maddening pangs ! No more of flight for life, with bleeding feet, over rugged roads, with murderous foes behind ! Relief is at hand ! They can sleep —they can rest. They are saved—they are saved ! Then, kneeling on the sward, from their bursting hearts they cried aloud to the God of their fathers, who through an ordeal so awful had brought them, few as they were, at last to a haven of refuge !

They pushed forward, and about eleven o'clock in the forenoon reached O'Rorke's castle. Here they were gazed upon as if they were objects of miraculous wonder. All that generous kindness and tender sympathy could devise, was quickly called to their aid. Their wounds and bruises were tended by a hundred eager hands. Their every want was anticipated. Alas! how few of them now remained to claim these kindly offices. Of the thousand souls who had set out from Glengarriffe, not one hundred entered the friendly portals of Brefny Hall. Only thirty-five came in with O'Sullivan that morning. Of these, but one was a woman—the aged mother of Don Philip, the historian; eighteen were attendants or camp-followers, and only sixteen were armed men! About fifty more came in next day, in twos and threes, or were found by searching parties sent out by O'Rorke. All the rest, except some three hundred in all, who nad strayed, perished on the way, by the sword, or by the terrible privations of the journey. This retreat was the last military achievement of Donal O'Sullivan. Some of the greatest commanders in history might be proud to claim an enterprise so heroic as their best title to the immortality of fame.

LI.—HOW THE GOVERNMENT AND HUGH MADE A TREATY OF
PEACE. HOW ENGLAND CAME UNDER THE SCOTTISH MON-
ARCHY ; AND HOW IRELAND HOPEFULLY HAILED THE GAELIC
SOVEREIGN.

THE succeeding year (1603) opened upon a state of gloom
and incertitude on all hands in Ireland. Like a strong
man overpowered, wounded, and cast down, after a
protracted and exhausting struggle, yet still unsub-
mitting and not totally reft of strength, the hapless Irish nation lay prostrate—fallen but unsubdued—unwilling to yield,
but too weak to rise. The English power, on the other hand,
was not without its sense of exhaustion also. It had passed
through an awful crisis; and had come out of the ordeal victorious, it is true, but greatly by happy chance, and at best only
by purchasing victory most dearly. O'Neill was still unconquered ; and though the vast majority of the lesser chiefs confederated with him in the recent struggle, had been compelled
to submit and sue for pardon, O'Donnell, O'Ruark, Maguire,
and O'Sullivan, remained to him ;* and, on the whole, he was
still master of elements capable of being organized into a formidable power, perhaps to renew the conflict at some future
favorable opportunity. Elizabeth and her ministers were too
wise and prudent to allow exultation over their success to
blind them to the fact that so much of it had been due to for-
tuitous circumstances, and that 'twere decidedly better, if
possible, to avoid having the combat tried over again. Mountjoy was instructed to "sound" the defeated, but unsubdued
and still dangerous Tyrone as to terms of peace and submission, lest, being hopeless of " pardon" (as they put it), he might

---

* " All that are out doe seeke for mercy excepting O'Rorke and O'Sullivan, who is

continue to stand out. Negotiations were accordingly opened with O'Neill. "Sir William Godolphin and Sir Garrett Moore were sent as commissioners to arrange with him the terms of peace,' the latter (ancestor of the present Marquis of Drogheda) being a warm personal friend of O'Neill's. "They found him," we are told, "in his retreat near Lough Neag, early in March, and obtained his promise to give the deputy an early meeting at Mellifont." "The negotiations," according to another writer, "were hurried on the deputy's part by private information which he had received of the queen's death; and fearing that O'Neill's views might be altered by that circumstance, he immediately desired the commissioners to close the agreement, and invite O'Neill under safe conduct to Drogheda to have it ratified without delay." On the 30th of March, 1603, Hugh met Mountjoy by appointment at Mellifont Abbey, where the terms of peace were duly ratified on each side, O'Neill having on his part gone through the necessary forms and declarations of submission. The singularly favorable conditions conceded to O'Neill show conclusively the estimate held by the English council of their victory over him, and of his still formidable influence. He was to have complete amnesty for the past; he was to be restored in blood, notwithstanding his attainder and outlawry; he was to be reinstated in his dignity of Earl of Tyrone; he and his people were to enjoy *full and free exercise of their religion ;* new "letters-patent" were to issue, regranting to him and other northern chiefs very nearly the whole of the lands occupied by their respective clans. On the other hand, Hugh was to renounce once and forever the title of "the O'Neill," should accept the English title of "Earl," and should allow English law to run through his territories.* Truly liberal terms,—generous, indeed, they might under all circumstances be called—if meant to be faithfully kept! It is hard to think O'Neill believed in the good faith of men whose subtle policy he knew so well. It may be that he doubted it thoroughly, but was powerless to accomplish more than to obtain such

---

* Mitchel.

terms, whatever their worth for the present, trusting to the future for the rest.

Yet it seemed as if, for the first time, a real and lasting peace was at hand. James the Sixth of Scotland, son of the beautiful and ill-fated Mary, Queen of Scots, succeeded Elizabeth on the English throne; and even before his express declaration of a conciliatory policy was put forth, there ran through Ireland, as if intuitively, a belief in his friendly dispositions. And, in truth, never before did such a happy opportunity offer for adjusting, at long last and forever, peacefully and amicably, the questions at issue between Ireland and England. In James the Irish—always so peculiarly swayed by considerations of race or kinship—beheld a Gaelic prince, a king of the sister kingdom, Scotland, to whom had reverted the kingdom and crown of England. Kings of England of the now extinct line had done them grievous wrong; but no king of friendly Scotland had broken the traditional kindly relations between Hibernia and Caledonia. Taking King James the Gael for a sovereign was not like bowing the neck to the yoke of the invading Normans or Tudors. As the son of his persecuted mother, he was peculiarly recommended to the friendly feelings of the Irish people. Mary of Scotland had much to entitle her to Irish sympathy. She was a princess of the royal line of Malcolm, tracing direct descent from the Milesian princes of Dalaradia. She was the representative of many a Scottish sovereign who had aided Ireland against the Normans. Moreover, she had just fallen a victim to the tigress Elizabeth of England, the same who had so deeply reddened with blood the soil of Ireland. She had suffered for the Catholic faith too; and if aught else were required to touch the Gaels of Ireland with compassion and sympathy, it was to be found in her youth and beauty, qualities which, when allied with innocence and misfortune, never fail to win the Irish heart. It was to the son of such a woman—the martyred Mary, Queen of Scots—that the English crown and kingdom had lapsed, and with these, such claim as England might be held to have upon the Irish kingdom. What wonder if amongst the Irish the idea prevailed that now at last they could heartily offer loyalty to the sovereign on the English throne, and feel that he was neither a stranger nor a subjugator ?

It was indeed a great opportunity, apparently—the first that had ever offered—for uniting the three kingdoms under one crown, without enforcing between any of them the humiliating relations of conqueror and conquered. There can be no doubt whatever, that, had James and his government appreciated the peculiar opportunity, and availed of it in a humane, wise, and generous spirit,

> "——an end was made, and nobly,
> Of the old centennial feud."

The Irish nation, there is every ground for concluding, would cheerfully and happily have come in to the arrangement ; and the simplest measure of justice from the government, a reasonable consideration for the national feelings, rights, and interests, might have realized that dream of a union between the kingdoms, which the compulsion of conquest could never—can never—accomplish. But that accurst greed of plunder—that unholy passion for Irish spoil—which from the first characterized the English adventurers in Ireland and which, unhappily, ever proved potential to mar any comparatively humane designs of the king, whenever, if ever, such designs were entertained, was now at hand to demand that Ireland should be given up to "settlers," by fair means or by foul, as a stranded ship might be abandoned to wreckers, or as a captured town might be given up to sack and pillage by the assaulting soldiery. There is, however, slight reason, if any, for thinking that the most unworthy and unnatural son of Mary Queen of Scots—the pedantic and pompous James—entertained any statesmanlike generosity or justice of design in reference to Ireland. The Irish expectations about him were doomed to be wofully disappointed. He became the mere creature of English policy; and the Anglo-Irish adventurers and "settlers," yelling for plunder, were able to force that policy in their own direction. They grumbled outright at the favorable terms of

been set on edge by the anticipation of the ricn spoils of the "confiscated" north, which they made sure would follow upon O'Neill's subjection. "It now seemed as if the entire object of that tremendous war had been, on the part of England, to force a coronet upon the unwilling brows of an Irish chieftain, and oblige him in his own despite to accept ' letters patent' and broad lands 'in fee.' Surely, if this were to be the ' conquest of Ulster,' if the rich valleys of the north, with all their woods and waters, mills and fishings, were to be given up to these O'Neills and O'Donnells, on whose heads a price had so lately been set for traitors; if, worse than all, their very religion was to be tolerated, and Ulster, with its verdant abbey-lands, and livings, and termon-lands, were still to set ' Refor-mation' at defiance ; surely, in this case, the crowd of esurient undertakers, lay and clerical, had ground of complaint. It was not for this they left their homes, and felled forests, and camped on the mountains, and plucked down the Red Hand from many a castlewall. Not for this they ' preached before the state in Christ Church,' and censured the backsliding of the times, and pointed out the mortal sin of a compromise with Jezabel !"

Notwithstanding that for a year or two subsequent to James's accession, the terms of the treaty of Mellifont were in most part observed by the government, O'Neill noted well the gathering storm of discontent, to which he saw but too clearly the government would succumb at an early opportu-nity. By degrees the skies began to lour, and unerring indi-cations foretold that a pretext was being sought for his immo-lation.

LII.—"THE FLIGHT OF THE EARLS." HOW THE PRINCES OF IRELAND WENT INTO EXILE, MENACED BY DESTRUCTION AT HOME.

IT was not long **wanting.** An anonymous **letter was** found, or was **pretended** to have been found, **at the** door of the council **chamber in** Dublin Castle, purporting **to dis-** close with great circum**stantiality** a conspiracy, of which **O'Neill** was the head, to seize the Castle, to murder the Lord Deputy and raise a general revolt.* The most artful means were re-

---

* There seems to have been a plot of some kind ; but it was one got up by the secretary of state, Cecil himself ; Lord Howth, his agent in this shocking business, inveigling O'Neill and O'Donnell into attendance at some of the meetings. " Artful Cecil," says Rev. Dr. Anderson, a Protestant divine, in his *Royal Genealogies*, a work printed in London in 1736, "employed one St. Lawrence to entrap the Earls of Tyrone and Tyrconnell, the Lord of Delvin, and other Irish chiefs, into a sham plot which had no evidence but his. But these chiefs being informed that witnesses were to be heard against them, foolishly fled from Dublin ; and so taking their guilt upon them, they were declared rebels, and six entire counties in Ulster were at once

sorted to by all whose interest it was to procure the ruin of
the northern chiefs, to get up a wild panic of real or effected
terror on this most opportune discovery! O'Neill well knew
the nature of the transaction, and the design behind it. The
vultures must have prey—his ruin had become a state-neces-
sity. In the month of May, he and the other northern chiefs
were cited to answer the capital charge thus preferred against
them.   This they were ready to do; but the government
plotters were not just yet ready to carry out their own schemes,
so the investigation was on some slight pretext postponed,
and O'Neill and O'Donnell were ordered to appear in London
on their defence at Michaelmas.   There is little doubt
that hereupon, or about this time, O'Neill formed and communicated to his northern kinsmen and fellow-victims, the
resolution of going into exile, and ,seeking on some friendly
shore that safety which it was plain he could hope for in Ireland no longer. They at once determined to share his fortunes,
and to take with them into exile their wives, children, relatives
and household attendants; in fine, to bid an eternal farewell
to the " fair hills of holy Ireland."   The sad sequel forms the
subject of that remarkable work—" The Flight of the Earls :
or the Fate and Fortunes of Tyrone and Tyrconnell," by the
Rev. C. P. Meehan, of Dublin; a work full of deep and sorrowful interest to every student of Irish history. I can but
briefly summarize here, as closely as possible, from various
authorities, that mournful chapter in our national annals.   " In
the beginning of September, 1607, nearly four months after
the pretended discovery of St. Lawrence's plot, O'Neil was
at Slane with the Lord Deputy, Sir Arthur Chichester; and
they conferred relative to a journey, which the former was
to make to London before Michaelmas, in compliance with a
summons from the king. While here a letter was delivered
to O'Neill from one John Bath, informing him that Maguire
had arrived in a French ship in Lough Swilly."   Sir John
Davis, the attorney-general of that day, says: " He, O'Neill,
pok leave of the lord deputy, in a more sad and passionate
manner than was usual with him. From thence he went to
Mellifont, and Sir Garrett Moore's house, where he wept

abundantly when he took his leave, giving a solemn farewell
to every child and every servant in the house, which made
them all marvel, because in general it was not his manner to
use such compliments." On his way northwards, we are told,
he remained two days at his own residence in Dungannon—it
was hard to quit the old rooftree for ever! Thence he proceeded hastily (travelling all night) to Rathmullen, on the
shore of Lough Swilly, where he found O'Donnell and several
of his friends waiting, and laying up stores in the French
ship. Amidst a scene of bitter anguish the illustrious party
soon embarked; numbering fifty persons in all, including attendants and domestics. With O'Neill, in that sorrowful company, we are told, went—his last countess, Catherina, daughter
of Maginnis; his three sons, Hugh, Baron of Dungannon, John,
and Brian; Art Oge, the son of his brother Cormac, and others
of his relatives; Ruari, or Roderic O'Donnell, Earl of Tyrconnell; Caffa or Cathbar, his brother, and his sister Nuala, who
was married to Niall Garve O'Donnell, but who abandoned
her husband when he became a traitor to his country; Hugh
O'Donnell, the Earl's son, and other members of his family;
Cuconnaught Maguire, and Owen Roe Mac Ward, chief bard
of Tyrconnell." " It is certain," say the Four Masters, "that
the sea has not borne, and the wind has not wafted in modern
times, a number of persons in one ship, more eminent, illustrious, or noble in point of genealogy, heroic deeds, valor,
feats of arms, and brave achievements, than they. Would
that God had but permitted them," continue the old annalists,
" to remain in their patrimonial inheritances until the children
should arrive at the age of manhood. Woe to the heart that
meditated—woe to the mind that conceived—woe to the
council that recommended the project of this expedition, without knowing whether they should to the end of their lives
be able to return to their ancient principalities and patrimonies."
" With gloomy looks and sad forebodings, the clansmen of
Tyrconnell gazed upon that fated ship, ' built in th' eclipse and
rigged with curses dark,' as she dropped down Lough Swilly,
and was hidden behind the cliffs of Fanad land. They never

They sailed direct to Normandy. On their arrival in France the English minister demanded their surrender as "rebels;" but Henry the Fourth would not give them up. Passing from France through the Netherlands, they were received with marked honors by the Archduke Albert. In all the courts of Europe, as they passed on their way to the eternal city, they were objects of attention, respect, and honor, from the various princes and potentates. But it was in that Rome to which from the earliest date their hearts fondly turned—"the common asylum of all Catholics," as it is called in the epitaph on young Hugh O'Neill's tomb—that the illustrious fugitives were received with truest, warmest, and tenderest welcome. Every mark of affection, every honorable distinction was conferred upon them by the venerable Pope, Pius the Fifth, who, in common with all the prelates and princes of Christendom, regarded them as confessors of the faith. In conjunction with the king of Spain, the Holy Father assigned to each of them a liberal annual pension for their support in a manner befitting their royal birth and princely state in their lost country. Through many a year, to them, or to other distinguished Irish exiles, the Papal treasury afforded a generous and princely bounty.

But those illustrious exiles drooped in the foreign climes, and soon, one by one, were laid in foreign graves. Ruari, Earl of Tyrconnell, died on the 28th of July, 1608. His brother Caffar, died on the 17th of the following September. Maguire died at Genoa on his way to Spain, on the 12th of the previous month—August, 1608. Young Hugh O'Neill, baron of Dungannon (son of O'Neill), died about a year afterwards, on the 23d September, 1609, in the twenty-fourth year of his age. Thus, in the short space of two years after the flight from Ireland, the aged prince of Ulster found himself almost the last of that illustrious company now left on earth.* Bow-

---

* Of all his sons, but two now survived, Conn and Henry. The latter was page to the Archduke Albert in the Low Countries, and like his father, was beset by English spies. When the old chieftain died at Rome, it was quickly perceived the removal of Henry would greatly free England from her nightmare apprehensions about

ed down with years and sorrows, his soul wrung with anguish as each day's tidings from distant Ireland brought news of unparalleled miseries and oppressions scourging his faithful people, he wandered from court to court, " eating his heart", for eight years. Who can imagine or describe with what earnest passion he pleaded with prelates and princes, and besought them to think upon the wrongs of Ireland ? " Ha !" (exclaims one of the writers from whom I have been summarizing), " if he had sped in that mission of vengeance—if he had persuaded Paul or Philip to give him some ten thousand Italians or Spaniards, how would it have fluttered those English in their dove-cots to behold his ships standing up Lough Foyle with the Bloody Hand displayed.* But not so was it written in the book. No potentate in Europe was willing to risk such a force as was needed." To deepen the gloom that shrouded the evening of his life, he lost his sight, became totally blind and, like another Belisarius, tottered mournfully to the grave ; the world on this side of which was now in every sense all dark to him, On the 20th July, 1616, the aged and heart-crushed prince passed from this earthly scene to realms

"——where souls are free;
Where tyrants taint not nature's bliss."

It was at Rome he died, and the Holy Father ordered him a public funeral ; directing arrangements to be forthwith made for celebrating his obsequies on a scale of grandeur such as is accorded only to royal princes and kings. The world, that bows in worship before the altar of Success, turns from the falling and the fallen ; but Rome, the friend of the weak and the un-

---

Brussels. The murder was enveloped in the profoundest mystery; but no one was at a loss to divine its cause and design. Henry had already, by his singular ability, and by certain movements duly reported by the spies, given but too much ground for concluding that if he lived he would yet be dangerous in Ireland.

* In all his movements on the continent he was surrounded by a crowd of English spies, whose letters and reports, now in the State Paper Office, give minute and singularly interesting information respecting his manners, habits, conversations, etc. One of them mentions that in the evenings, after dining, if the aged prince were " warm with wine," he had but one topic; his face would glow and striking the table,

fortunate, never measured its honors to nations or princes by the standard of their worldly fortunes. So the English, who would fain have stricken those illustrious fugitives of Ireland from fame and memory, as they had driven them from home and country, gnashed their teeth in rage, as they saw all Christendom assigning to the fallen Irish princes an exalted place amongst the martyr-heroes of Christian patriotism! On the hill of the Janiculum, in the Franciscan church of San Pietro di Montorio, they laid the Prince of Ulster in the grave which, a few years before, had been opened for his son, beside the last resting place of the Tyrconnell chiefs. Side by side they had fought through life ; side by side they now sleep in death. Above the grave where rest the ashes of those heroes many an Irish pilgrim has knelt, and prayed, and wept. In the calm evening, when the sunbeams slant upon the stones below, the Fathers of St. Francis often see some figure prostrate upon the tomb, which as often they find wetted by the tears of the mourner. Then they know that some exiled child of Ireland has sought and found the spot made sacred and holy for him and all his nation by ten thousand memories of mingled grief and glory.*

There is not perhaps in the elegaic poetry of any language any thing worthy of comparison with the " Lament for the Princes of Tyrone and Tyrconnell," composed by the aged and venerable bard of O'Donnell, Owen Roe Mac Ward. In this

---

* Some eighteen years ago a horrible desecration well nigh destroyed for ever all identification of the grave so dear to Irishmen. The Eternal City—the sanctuary of Christendom —was sacrilegiously violated by invaders as lawless and abhorrent as Alaric and his followers—the Carbonari of modern Europe, led by Mazzini and Garibaldi. The churches were profaned, the tombs were rifled, and *the church of San Pietro di Montorio was converted by Garibaldi into cavalry stables !* The trampling of the horses destroyed or effaced many of the tombstones, and the Irish in the city gave up all hope of safety for the one so sacred in their eyes. Happily, however, when Rome had been rescued by France on behalf of the Christian world, and when the filth and litter had been cleared away from the desecrated church, the tomb of the Irish princes was found to have escaped with very little permanent injury. Some there are, who perhaps, do not understand the sentiment—the principle —which claims Rome as belonging to Christendom—not to " Italy," or France, or Austria, or Naples. But in truth and fact, Rome represents not only " God's acre " of the world, but is the repository of priceless treasures, gifts, and relics, which belong in common to all

noble burst of sorrow, rich in plaintive eloquence and in all
the beauty of true poesy, the bard addresses himself to Lady
Nuala O'Donnell and her attendant mourners at the grave
of the princes. Happily, of this peerless poem we possess a
translation into English, of which it is not too much to say
that it is in every sense worthy of the original, to which it
adheres with great fidelity, while preserving all the spirit and
tenderness of the Gaelic idiom. I allude to Mangan's admirable translation, from which I take the following passages :—

O woman of the piercing wail !
  Who mournest o'er yon mound of clay
    With sigh and groan,
Would God thou wert among the Gael !
  Thou wouldst not then from day to day
    Weep thus alone.
'T were long before, around a grave
  In green Tyrconnell, one would find
    This loneliness ;
Near where Beann-Boirche's banners wave,
  Such grief as thine could ne'er have pined
    Companionless.

Beside the wave, in Donegal
  In Antrim's glen, or fair Dromore,
    Or Killilee,
Or where the sunny waters fall
  At Assaroe, near Erna's shore,
    This could not be.
On Derry's plains,—in rich Drumclieff,—
  Throughout Armagh the Great, renowned
    In olden years,
No day could pass, but woman's grief
  Would rain upon the burial-ground
    Fresh floods of tears !

O no ! —from Shannon, Boyne, and Suir,
  From high Dunluce's castle walls,
    From Lissadill,
Would flock alike both rich and poor.
  One wail would rise from Cruachan's halls
    To Tara's hill ;
And some would come from Barrow side,
  And many a maid would leave her home

And by melodious Banna's tide,
  And by the Mourne and Erne, to come
    And swell thy strains !

*   *   *   *   *   *

Two princes of the line of Conn
  Sleep in their cells of clay beside
    O'Donnell Roe ;
Three royal youths, alas ! are gone,
  Who lived for Erin's weal, but died
    For Erin's woe !
Ah ! could the men of Ireland reed
  The names these noteless burial stones
    Display to view ;
Their wounded hearts afresh would bleed,
  Their tears gush forth again, their groans
    Resound anew !

*   *   *   *   *   *

And who can marvel o'er thy grief,
  Or who can blame thy flowing tears,
    That knows their source?
O'Donnell, Dunnasava's chief,
  Cut off amid his vernal years,
    Lies here a corse,
Beside his brother Cathbar, whom
  Tirconnell of the Helmets mourns
    In deep despair—
For valor, truth, and comely bloom,
  For all that greatens and adorns,
    A peerless pair.

*   *   *   *   *   *

When high the shout of battle rose
  On fields where Freedom's torch still burned
    Through Erinn's gloom,
If one—if barely *one*—of those
  Were slain, all Ulster would have mourned
    The heroes doom !
If at Athboy, were hosts of brave
  Ulidian horsemen sank beneath
    The shock of spears,
Young Hugh O'Neill had found a grave,
  Long must the North have wept his death
    With heart-wrung tears !

What do I say? Ah, woe is me!
  Already we bewail in vain
    Their fatal fall!
And Erinn, once the Great and Free
  Now vainly mourns her breakless chain
    And iron thrall!
Then daughter of O'Donnell, dry
  Thine overflowing eyes, and turn
    Thy heart aside,
For Adam's race is born to die,
  And sternly the sepulchral urn
    Mocks human pride!

Look not, nor sigh, for earthly throne,
  Nor place thy trust in arm of clay;
    But on thy knees
Uplift thy soul to God alone,
  For all things go their destined way
    As He decrees.
Embrace the faithful crucifix,
  And seek the path of pain and prayer
    Thy Saviour trod;
Nor let thy spirit intermix
  With earthly hope and worldly care
    Its groans to God!

... And Thou, O mighty Lord! whose ways
  Are far above our feeble minds
    To understand;
Sustain us in those doleful days,
  And render light the chain that binds
    Our fallen land!
Look down upon our dreary state,
  And through the ages that may still
    Roll sadly on,
Watch Thou o'er hapless Erinn's fate,
  And shield at last from darker ill
    The blood of Conn!

There remains now but to trace the fortunes of O'Sullivan, the last of O'Neill's illustrious companions in arms. The special vengeance of England marked Donal for a fatal distinction among his fellow chiefs of the ruined confederacy. He was not included in the amnesty settled by the treaty of Mellifont. We may be sure it was a sore thought for O'Neill that he could not obtain for a friend so true and tried as O'Sul-

of the Northern chieftains. But the government was inexorable. The Northerns had yet some power left ; from the
Southern chief there now was naught to fear. So, we are
told, "there was no pardon for O'Sullivan." Donal accompanied O'Neill to London the year succeeding James's accession ; but he could obtain no relaxation of the policy decreed
against him. He returned to Ireland only to bid it an eternal farewell! Assembling all that now remained to him of
family and kindred, he sailed for Spain A. D. 1604. He was
received with all honor by king Philip, who forthwith created
him a grandee of Spain, knight of the military order of St.
Iago, and subsequently Earl of Bearhaven. The king, moreover, assigned to him a pension of "three hundred pieces
of gold monthly." The end of this illustrious exile was truly
tragic. His young son, Donal, had a quarrel with an ungrate-
ful Anglo-Irishman named Bath, to whom the old chief had
been a kind benefactor. Young Donal's cousin, Philip—the
author of the *Historiæ Catholicæ Iberniæ*—interfered with
mediative intentions, when Bath drew his sword, uttering
some grossly insulting observations against the O'Sullivans.
Philip and he at once attacked each other, but the former
soon overpowered Bath, and would have slain him but for the
interposition of friends ; for all this had occurred at a royal
monastery in the suberbs of Madrid within the precincts of
which it was a capital offence to engage in such a combat.
The parties were separated. Bath was drawn off, wounded
in the face, when he espied not far off the old chieftain, O'Sullivan Beare, returning from Mass, at which that morning, as
was his wont, he had received Holy Communion. He was
pacing slowly along, unaware of what had happened. His
head was bent upon his breast, he held in his hand his gloves
and his rosary beads, and appeared to be engaged in mental
prayer. Bath, filled with fury, rushed suddenly behind the
aged lord of Beare, and ran him through the body. O'Sullivan fell to earth ; they raised him up—he was dead. Thus
mournfully perished, in the fifty-seventh year of his age, Donal the "Last Lord of Beare," as he is most frequently styled,
a man whose personal virtues and public worth won for him

THE IRISH PRINCES RECEIVED BY THE SOVEREIGN PONTIFF.

See page 330.

His nephew Philip became an officer in the Spanish navy, and is known to literary fame as the author of the standard work of history which bears his name, as well as of several publications of lesser note. Young Donal, son of the murdered chieftain, entered the army and fell at Belgrade, fighting against the Turks. The father of Philip the historian (Dermod, brother of Donal, Prince of Beare,) died at Corunna, at the advanced age of a hundred years, and was followed to the grave soon after by his long-wedded wife.

> "Two pillars of a ruined aisle—two old trees of the land ;
> Two voyagers on a sea of grief ; long sufferers hand in hand."

———∞———

LIII.—A MEMORABLE EPOCH. HOW MILESIAN IRELAND FINALLY DISAPPEARED FROM HISTORY ; AND HOW A NEW IRELAND— IRELAND IN EXILE—APPEARED FOR THE FIRST TIME. HOW "PLANTATIONS" OF FOREIGNERS WERE DESIGNED FOR THE "COLONIZATION" OF IRELAND, AND THE EXTIRPATION OF THE NATIVE RACE.

HAVE narrated at very considerable length the events of that period of Irish history with which the name of Hugh O'Neill is identified. I have done so because that era was one of most peculiar importance to Ireland ; and it is greatly necessary for Irishmen to fully understand and appreciate the momentous meaning of its results. The war of 1599–1602 was *the last struggle of the ancient native rule* to sustain itself against the conquerors and the jurisdiction of their civil and religious code. Thenceforth— at least for two hundred years subsequently— the wars in Ireland which eventuated in completing the spoliation, ruin, and extinction of the native nobility, were *wars in behalf of the English sovereign as the rightful sovereign of Ireland also.* Never more in Irish history do we find the authority of the

er more do we find the ancient laws and judicature undisturb-
edly prevailing in any portion of the land. With the flight of
the northern chieftains all claims of ancient native dynasties
to sovereignty of power, rights, or privileges disappeared,
never once to re-appear; and the ancient laws and constitution
of Ireland, the venerable code that had come down inviolate
through the space of fifteen hundred years, vanished totally
and for ever! Taking leave, therefore, of the chapter of history to which I have devoted so much space, we bid farewell
to Milesian Ireland—Ireland claiming to be ruled by its own
native princes, and henceforth have to deal with Ireland as a
kingdom subject to the Scoto-English sovereign.

The date at which we have arrived is one most remarkable
in our history in other respects also. If it witnessed the disappearance of Milesian Ireland, it witnessed the first appearance in history of that other Ireland, which from that day to
the present has been in so great a degree the hope and the
glory of the parent nation—a rainbow set in the tearful sky of
its captivity—*Ireland in exile !* In the beginning of the seventeenth century "the Irish abroad" are first heard of as a distinct
political element. The new power thus born into the world
was fated to perform a great and marvellous part in the designs
of Providence. It has endured through the shock of centuries
—has outlived the rise and fall of dynasties and states—has
grown into gigantic size and shape ; and in the influence it ex-
ercises at this moment on the course and policy of England,
affords, perhaps, the most remarkable illustration recorded
outside Holy Writ, of the inevitability of retributive justice.
To expel the people of Ireland from their own country, to
thrust them out as outcast wanderers and exiles all over the
world—to seize their homes and possess their heritage, will be
found to have been for centuries the policy, the aim, and untiring endeavor of the English government. The scheme
which we are about to see King James prosecuting (Munster
witnessed its inauguration in the previous reign) has ever since
haunted the English mind ; namely, the expulsion of the native
Irish race, and the "planting" or "colonizing" of their coun-

parallel for such a design, pursued so relentlessly through such a great space of time. But God did not more signally preserve His chosen people of the Old Law than he has preserved the Irish nation in captivity and in exile. They have not melt-ed away, as the calculations of their evicters anticipated. They have not becomed fused or transformed by time or change. They have not perished where ordinary probabilities threatened to the human race impossibility of existence. Prosperity and adversity in their new homes have alike failed to kill in their hearts the sentiment of nationality, the holy love of Ireland, the resolution of fulfilling their destiny as the Heraclidæ of modern history. They preserve to-day, all over the world, their individuality as markedly as the children of Israel did theirs in Babylon or in Egypt.

The flight of the earls threw all the hungry adventurers into ecstasies! Now, at least, there would be plunder. The vultures flapped their wings and wetted their beaks. Prey in abundance was about to be flung them by the royal hand. To help still further the schemes of confiscation now being matured in Dublin Castle, Sir Cahir O'Doherty—who had been a queen's man most dutifully so far—was skilfully pushed into a revolt which afforded the necessity pretext for adding the entire peninsula of Innishowen to the area of " plantation." Ulster was now parcelled out into lots, and divided among court favorites and clamoring " undertakers ;" the owners and occupiers, the native inhabitants, being as little regarded as the wild grouse of the hill ! The guilds, or trade companies of London, got a vast share of plunder ; something like one hundred and ten thousand acres of the richest lands of the O'Neills and O'Donnells—lands which the said London companies hold to this day. To encourage and maintain these " plantations," various privileges were conferred upon or offered to the " colonists ;" the conditions required of them on the other hand being simply to exclude or kill off the owners, to hunt down the native population as they would any other wild game ; and above all, to banish and keep out "Popery." In fine, they and their " heirs, executers,

to consider themselves a standing army of occupation in the English Protestant interest.

For two hundred years of history we shall find that " colonized " province, and the " colonists " generally, endowed, nursed, petted, protected, privileged—the especial care of the English government—whilst the helpless native population were, during the same period, proscribed, " dead in law," forbidden to trade, forbidden to educate, forbidden to own property ; for each which prohibition, and many besides to a like intent, acts of parliament with day and date, word and letter, may be cited.

So great was the excitement created amongst the needy and greedy of all classes in England by the profuse dispensations of splendid estates, rich, fertile, and almost at their own doors, that the millions of acres in Ulster were soon all gone ; and still there were crowds of hungry adventurers yelling for "more, more." James soon found a way for providing " more." He constituted a roving commission of inquiry into " defective titles," as he was pleased to phrase it—a peripatetic inquisition on the hunt for spoil. The commissioners soon reported 385,000 acres in Leinster as " discovered," inasmuch as the " titles"‘were not such as ought (in their judgment) to stand in the way of his majesty's designs. The working of this commission need scarcely be described. Even the historian, Leland, who would have been its apologist if he could, tells us there were not wanting " proofs of the most iniquitous practices, of hardened cruelty, of vile perjury, and scandalous subornation, employed to despoil the unfortunate proprietor of his inheritance." Old and obsolete claims, we are told, some of them dating as far back as Henry the Second, were revived, and advantage was taken of the most trivial flaws and minute informalities. In the midst of his plundering and colonizing James died, 27th March, 1625, and was succeeded by his son, Charles. Bitterly as the Irish Catholics had been undeceived as to James's friendly dispositions, they gave themselves up more warmly than ever to the belief that the young prince now just come to the throne

here we have to trace a chapter of cruelest deceit, fraud, and betrayal of a too confiding people. The king and his favorite ministers secretly encouraged these expectations. Charles needed money sorely, and his Irish representative, Lord. Faulkland, told the Catholic lords that if they would present to his majesty, as a voluntary subsidy, a good round sum of money, he would grant them certain protections or immunities, called " royal graces " in the records of the time. "The more important were those which provided 'that recusants should be allowed to practise in the courts of law, and to sue out the livery of their lands on taking an oath of civil allegiance in lieu of the oath of supremacy ; that the undertakers in the several plantations should have time allowed them to fulfil the condition of their tenures; that the claims of the crown should be limited to the last sixty years ; and that the inhabitants of Connaught should be permitted to make a new enrolment of their estates.' The contract was duly ratified by a royal proclamation, in which the concessions were accompanied by a promise that a parliament should be held to confirm them. The first instalment of the money was paid, and the Irish agents returned home, but only to learn that an order had been issued against ' the Popish regular clergy,' and that the royal promise was to be evaded in the most shameful manner. When the Catholics pressed for the fulfilment of the compact, the essential formalities for calling an Irish parliament were found to have been omitted by the officials, and thus the matter fell to the ground for the present."*

In other words, the Irish Catholics were royally swindled. The miserable Charles pocketed the morey, and then pleaded that certain of the "graces" were very " unreasonable." He found that already the mere suspicion of an inclination on his part to arrest the progress of persecution and plunder, was arousing and inflaming against him the fanatical Calvinistic section of English Protestantism, while his high-handed assertions of royal prerogative were daily bringing him into more dangerous conflict with his English parliament. To complete the complications surrounding him, the attempts to force

Episcopalian Protestantism on the Calvinistic Scots led to open revolt. A Scottish rebel army * took the field, demanding that the attempt to extend Episcopacy into Scotland should be given up, and that Calvinistic Presbyterianism should be acknowledged as the established religion of that kingdom. Charles marshalled an army to march against them. The parliament would not vote him supplies—indeed the now dominant party in parliament sympathized with and encouraged the rebels ; but Charles, raising money as best he could, proceeded northward. Nevertheless, he appears to have recoiled from the idea of spilling the blood of his countrymen for a consideration of spiritual supremacy. He came to an arrangement with the rebel " Covenanters" granting to them the liberty of conscience—nay, religious supremacy— which they demanded, and even *paying* their army for a portion of the time it was under service in the rebellion.

All this could not fail to attract the deepest attention of the Irish Catholic nobility and gentry, who found themselves in far worse plight than that which had moved the Calvinistic Scots to successful rebellion. Much less indeed than had been conceded to the rebel Covenanters would satisfy them. They did not demand that the Catholic religion should be set up as the established creed in Ireland ; they merely asked that the sword of persecution should not be bared against it : and for themselves they sought nothing beyond protection as good citizens in person and property, and simple equality of civil rights. Wentworth, Charles's representative in Ireland, had been pursuing against them a course of the most scandalous and heartless robbery, pushing on the operations of the commission of inquiry into defective titles. " He commenced the work of plunder with Roscommon, and as a preliminary step, directed the sheriff to select such jurors as might be made amenable, 'in case they should prevaricate ;' or in other words, they might be ruined by *enormous fines, if they refused to find a verdict for the king.* The jurors were

---

* Often called "Covenanters," from their demands or articles of confederation in the rebellion being called their " solemn league and covenant."

told that the object of the commission was to find 'a clear and undoubted title in the crown to the province of Connaught,' and to make them 'a civil and rich people' by means of a plantation; for which purpose his majesty should, of course, have the lands in his own hands to distribute to fit and proper persons. Under threats which could not be misunderstood, the jury found for the king, whereupon Wentworth commended the foreman, Sir Lucas Dillon, to his majesty, that he might be remembered upon the dividing of the lands,' and also obtained a competent reward for the judges.

"Similar means had a like success in Mayo and Sligo; but when it came to the turn of the more wealthy and populous county of Galway, the jury refused to sanction the nefarious robbery by their verdict. Wentworth was furious at this rebuff, and the unhappy jurors were punished without mercy for their 'contumacy.' They were compelled to appear in the castle chamber, where each of them was fined four thousand pounds, and their estates were seized and they themselves imprisoned until these fines should be paid, while the sheriff was fined four thousand pounds, and being unable to pay that sum died in prison. Wentworth proposed to seize the lands, not only of the jurors, but of all the gentry who neglected 'to lay hold on his majesty's grace;' he called for an increase of the army 'until the intended plantation should be settled,' and recommended that the counsel who argued the cases against the king before the commissioners should be silenced until they took the oath of supremacy, which was accordingly done. 'The gentlemen of Connaught,' says Carte (*Life of Ormond*, vol. i.), 'labored under a particular hardship on this occasion; for their not having enrolled their patents and surrenders of the 13th Jacobi (which was what alone rendered their titles defective) was not their fault, but the neglect of a clerk entrusted by them. For they had paid near three thousand pounds to the officers in Dublin for the enrolment of these surrenders and patents, which was never made.'" *

Meanwhile, as I have already described, the Scots whose

"grievances" were in nowise to be compared with these, had obtained full redress by an armed demonstration. It was not to be expected in the nature of things, that events, so suggestive would be thrown away on the spoiliated Catholic nobles and gentry of Ireland. Accordingly, we find them about this period conferring, confederating, or conspiring, on the basis of an Irish and Catholic " solemn league and covenant "—of much more modest pretentions, however, than the Scottish Calvinistic original. Their movement too was still more notably distinguished from that demonstration by the most emphatic and explicit loyalty to the king, whom indeed they still credited with just and tolerant dispositions, if freed from the restraint of the persecuting Puritan faction. They saw too that the king and the parliament were at utter issue, and judged that by a bold *coup* they might secure for themselves royal recognition and support, and turn the scale against their bitter foes and the king's.

Moreover, by this time the " other Irish nation"—" the Irish abroad," had grown to be a power. Already the exiles on the continent possessed ready to hand a considerable military force, and a goodly store of money, arms, and ammunition· For they had " not forgotten Jerusalem," and wherever they served or fought, they never gave up that hope of " a good day yet in Ireland." The English state-paper office holds several of the letters or reports of the spies retained by the government at this time to watch their movements ; and singularly enough, these documents describe to us a state of things not unlike that existing at this day, towards the close of the nineteenth century !—the Irish in exile, organized in the design of returning and liberating their native land, *assessing themselves out of their scanty pay for contributions to the general fund !** The Irish abroad had, moreover, what greatly en-

---

* Mr. Haverty, the historian, quotes one of these "reports" which, as he says, was first brought to light in the *Nation* newspaper of 5th February, 1859, having been copied from the original in the state paper office. It is a list or return of the names of the " dangerous " Irish abroad supplied by one of the English spies. " The list begins with Don Richardo Burke, 'a man much experienced in martial affairs,' and ' a good inginiere.' He served many years under the Spaniards in Naples and the

hanced their military influence—*prestige*. Already, they had become honorably known as "bravest of the brave" on the battlefields of Spain, France, and the Netherlands.

Communications were at once opened between the exiles and the confederates at home, the chief agent or promoter of the movement being a private gentleman, Mr. Roger O'More, or O'Moore, a member of the ancient family of that name,

---

West Indies, and was the governor of Leghorn for the Duke of Florence. Next, 'Phellomy O'Neill, nephew unto old Tyrone, liveth in great respect (in Milan), and is a captain of a troop of horse.' Then come James Rowthe or Rothe, an alfaros or standard-bearer in the Spanish army, aud his brother Captain John Rothe, 'a pensioner in Naples, who carried Tyrone out of Ireland.' One Captain Solomon Mac Da, a Geraldine, resided at Florence, and Sir Thomas Talbot, a knight of Malta, and 'a resolute and well beloved man,' lived at Naples, in which latter city 'there were some other Irish captains and officers.' The list then proceeds. 'In Spain Captain Phellomy Cavanagh, son-in-law to Donell Spaniagh serveth under the king by sea; Captain Somlevayne (O'Sullivan), a man of noted courage. These live commonly at Lisbonne, and are sea-captains. Besides others of the Irish, Captain Driscoll, the younger, sonne to old Captain Driscoll ; both men reckoned valorous. In the court of Spaine liveth the sonne of Richard Burke, which was nephew untoe William, who died at Valladolid . . . he is in high favor with the king, and (as it is reported) is to be made a marquis; Captain Toby Bourke, a pensioner in the court of Spain, another nephew of the said William, deceased ; Captain John Bourke M'Shane, who served long time in Flanders, and now liveth on his pension assigned on the Groyne. Captain Daniell, a pensioner at Antwerp. In the Low Countries, under the Archduke, John O'Neill, sonne of the arch-traitor Tyrone, colonel of the Irish regiment. Young O'Donnell, sonne of the late traitorous Earl of Tirconnell. Owen O'Neill (Owen Roe), sergeant-major (equivalent to the present lieutenant -colonel) of the Irish regiment. Captain Art O'Neill, Captain Cormac O'Neill, Captain Donel O'Donel, Captain Thady O'Sullivane, Captain Preston, Captain Fitz Gerrott; old Captain Fitz Gerrott continues sergeant-major, now a pensioner ; Captain Edmond O'Mor, Captain Bryan O'Kelly, Captain Stanihurst, Captain Corton, Captain Daniell, Captain Walshe. There are diverse other captaines and officers of the Irish under the Archduchess (Isabella), some of whose companies are cast, and they made pensioners. Of these serving under the Archduchess, there are about one hundred able to command companies, and twenty fit to be colonels. Many of them are descended of gentlemen's families and some of noblemen. These Irish soldiers and pensioners doe stay their resolutions until they see whether England makes peace or war with Spaine. If peace, they have practised already with other soveraine princes, from whom they have received hopes of assistance ; if war doe ensue, they are confident of greater ayde. They have been long providing of arms for any attempt against Ireland, and had in readiness five or six thousand arms laid up in Antwerp for that purpose, bought oute of the deduction of their monthly pay, as will be proved, and it is thought they have

chiefs of Leix. With him there soon became associated Lord
Maguire, an Irish nobleman who retained a small fragment of
the ancient patrimony of his family in Fermanagh ; his brother
Roger Maguire, Sir Felim O'Neill of Kinnard, Sir Con
Magennis, Colonel Hugh Oge Mac Mahon, Very Rev. Heber
Mac Mahon, Vicar-General of Clogher, and a number of others.

About May Nial O'Neill arrived in Ireland from the titular
Earl of Tyrone (John, son of Hugh O'Neill), in Spain, to inform his friends that he had obtained from Cardinal Richelieu
a promise of arms, ammunition, and money for Ireland when
required, and desiring them to hold themselves in readiness.
The confederates sent back the messenger with information
as to their proceedings, and to announce that they would be
prepared to rise a few days before or after All-Hallow-tide, according as opportunity answered. But scarcely was the messenger despatched when news was received that the Earl
of Tyrone was killed, and another messenger was sent with all
speed into the Low Countries to (his cousin) Colonel Owen
(Roe) O'Neill, who was the next entitled to be their leader.
" In the course of September their plans were matured ; and,
after some changes as to the day, the 23rd of October was
finally fixed upon for the rising."*

The plan agreed upon by the confederates included four
main features. I. A rising after the harvest was gathered in,
and a campaign during the winter months. II. A simultaneous attack on one and the same day or night on all the fortresses within reach of their friends. III. To surprise the
Castle of Dublin, which was said to contain arms for 12,000
men. All the details of this project were carried successfully
into effect, except the seizure of Dublin Castle—the most difficult, as it would have been the most decisive blow to strike."†
The government, which at this time had a cloud of spies on
the Continent watching the exiles, seems to have been in utter
ignorance of this vast conspiracy at home, wrapping nearly
the entire of three provinces, and which perfected all its arrangements throughout several months of preparation, to the

knowledge of thousands of the population, without one traitorous Irishman being found, up to the night for the simultaneous movement, to disclose the fact of its existence.

On the night appointed, without failure or miscarriage at any
point, save *one*, out of all at which simultaneousness of action
was designed, the confederate rising was accomplished. *In
one night* the people had swept out of sight, if not from existence, almost every vestige of English rule throughout three
provinces. The forts of Charlemont and Mountjoy, and the
town of Dungannon, were seized on the night of the 22d, by
Phelim O'Neill or his lieutenants. On the next day Sir Connor Magennis took the town of Newry ; the M'Mahons possessed themselves of Carrickmacross and Castleblayney ; the
O'Hanlons, Tandragee ; while Philip O'Rielly and Roger
Maguire raised Cavan and Fermanagh. A proclamation of
the northern leaders appeared the same day, dated from Dungannon, setting forth their "true intent and meaning" to be,
"*not hostility to his majesty the king*, nor to any of his subjects,
neither English or Scotch ; but only for the defence and liberty
of ourselves and the Irish natives of this kingdom." "A more
elaborate manifesto appeared shortly afterwards from the pen
of O'Moore, in which the oppressions of the Catholics for
conscience sake were detailed, the king's intended graces,
acknowledged, and their frustration by the malice of the
Puritan party exhibited ; it also endeavored to show that a
common danger threatened the Protestants of the Episcopal
Church with Roman Catholics, and asserted in the strongest
terms the devotion of the Catholics to the crown. In the
same politic and tolerant spirit, Sir Connor Magennis wrote
from Newry on the 25th to the officers commanding at Down.
' We are,' he wrote, ' for our lives and liberties. *We desire no
blood to be shed ; but if you mean to shed our blood, be sure we
shall be as ready as you for that purpose.*' This threat of retaliation, so customary in all wars, was made on the third day of
the rising, and refers wholly to future contingencies ; the
monstrous fictions which were afterwards circulated of a wholesale massacre committed on the 23d, were not as yet invented,

Ireland in the last week of October, or during the first days of November, so much as allude to those tales of blood and horror afterwards so industriously circulated and so greedily swallowed."*

The one point at which miscarriage occurred was, unfortunately for the conspirators, the chief one in their scheme—Dublin; and here the escape of the government was narrow and close indeed. On the night fixed for the rising, 23d October, one of the Irish leaders, Colonel Hugh MacMahon, confided the design to one Owen Connolly, whom he thought to be worthy of trust, but who, however, happened to be a follower of Sir John Clotworthy, one of the most rabid of the Puritanical party. Connolly, who, by the way, was drunk at the time, instantly hurried to the private residence of one of the lords justices, and excitedly proclaimed to him that that night the castle was to be seized, as part of a vast simultaneous movement all over the country. Sir W. Parsons, the lord justice, judging the story to be merely the raving of a half-drunken man, was on the point of turning Connolly out of doors, when, fortunately for him, he thought it better to test the matter. He hurriedly consulted his colleague, Sir John Borlase ; they decided to double the guards, shut the city gates, and search the houses wherein, according to Connolly's story, the leaders of the conspiracy were at that moment awaiting the hour of action. Colonel Mac Mahon was seized at his lodgings, near the King's Inns ; Lord Maguire was captured next morning in a house in Cooke Street ; but O'Moore, Plunkett, and Byrne, succeeded in making good their escape out of the city. Mac Mahon, on being put to question before the lords justices in the Castle, boldly avowed his part in the national movement , nay, proudly gloried in it, telling his questioners, that let them do what they might, their best or their worst, with him, " the rising was now beyond all human power to arrest." While the lords justices looked astounded, haggard, and aghast, Mac Mahon, his face radiant with exultation, his form appearing to dilate with proud defiance of the bloody fate he knew to be inevitable for himself, told them to bear him as soon as they pleased to the block, but that already Ireland had burst her chains! Next day, they found to their dismay that this was no empty vaunt. Before forty-eight hours the whole structure of British " colonization " in the North was a wreck. The " plantation " system vanished like " the baseless fabric of a vision ; " and while the ship was bearing away to England the gallant Mac Mahon and his hapless colleague, Lord Maguire—that an impotent vengeance might glut itself with their blood upon the scaffold—from all the towers and steeples in the north joy bells were ringing merry peals, and bonfires blazed, proclaiming that the spoliators had been swept away, and that the rightful owners enjoyed their own again! The people, with the characteristic exuberance of their nature, gave themselves up to the most demonstrative joy and exultation. No words can better enable us to realize the popular feeling at this moment than Mr. Gavan Duffy's celebrated poem, " The Muster of the North :"

Joy ! joy ! the day is come at last, the day of hope and pride,
And, see ! our crackling bonfires light old Bann's rejoicing tide !
And gladsome bell and bugle-horn, from Newry's captured tow'rs,
Hark ! how they tell the Saxon swine, this land is ours— *is* OURS !

Glory to God ! my eyes have seen the ransomed fields of Down,
My ears have drunk the joyful news, "Stout Phelim hath his own."
Oh ! may they see and hear no more, oh ! may they rot to clay,
When they forget to triumph in the conquest of to-day.

Now, now, we'll teach the shameless Scot to purge his thievish maw ;
Now, now, the courts may fall to pray, for Justice is the Law;
Now shall the undertaker square for once his loose accounts,
We'll strike, brave boys, a fair result from all his false amounts.

Come, trample down their robber rule, and smite its venal spawn,
Their foreign laws, their foreign church, their ermine and their lawn,
With all the specious fry of fraud that robbed us of our own,
And plant our ancient laws again beneath our lineal throne.

　　　　*　　　*　　　*　　　*　　　*　　　*　　　*

Down from the sacred hills whereon a saint commun'd with God,
Up from the vale where Bagnal's blood manured the recking sod,
Out from the stately woods of Trangh, M'Kenna's plundered home,

Then, brethren, on !—O'Neill's dear shade would frown to see you pause—
Our banished Hugh, our martyred Hugh, is watching o'er your cause—
His generous error lost the land—he deemed the Norman true,
O ! forward, friends ! it must not lose the land again in you !

———

LIV.—HOW THE LORDS JUSTICES GOT UP THE NEEDFUL BLOODY
FURY IN ENGLAND BY A " DREADFUL MASSACRE " STORY.
HOW THE CONFEDERATION OF KILKENNY CAME ABOUT.

HE Puritanical party, which ever since Wentworth's
execution had the government of Ireland in their
hands, began to consider that this desperate condition
of their affairs rendered some extraordinary resort
necessary, if the island was not to slip totally and for ever
from their grasp. The situation was evidently one full of
peculiar difficulty and embarrassment for them. The national
confederacy, which by this time had most of the kingdom in
its hands, declared utmost loyalty to the king, and in truth, as
time subsequently showed, meant him more honest and loyal
service than those who now surrounded him as ministers and
officials.

Hence it was more than likely to be extremely difficult to
arouse against the Irish movement that strong and general
effusion of public feeling in England which would result in
vigorous action against it. For obviously enough (so reasoned the Puritanical executive in Dublin Castle) that section of
the English nation which supports the king will be inclined
to side with this Irish movement ; they will call it far more
justifiable and far more loyal than that of the rebel Scotch
covenanters ; they will counsel negotiation with its leaders,
perhaps the concession of their demands ; in any event they
will reprehend and prevent any extreme measures against
them. In which case, of course, the result must be fatal to
the pious project of robbing the native Irish, and " planting "

MAC MAHON BEFORE THE LORDS JUSTICES.

See page 394.

In this extremity it was discerned that there was barely one way of averting all these dangers and disasters—just one way of preventing any favorable opinion of the Irish movement taking root in England—one sure way for arousing against it such a cry as must render it impossible for even the king himself to resist or refrain from joining in the demand for its suppression at all hazards. This happy idea was to start the story of an "awful, bloody, and altogether tremendous massacre of Protestants."

To be sure they knew there had been no massacre—quite the contrary ; but this made little matter. With proper vehemence of assertion, and sufficient construction of circumstantial stories to that effect, no difficulty was apprehended on this score. But the real embarrassment lay in the fact that it was *rather late* to start the thing. Several days or weeks had elapsed, and several accounts of the rising had been transmitted without any mention of such a proceeding as a "wholesale massacre," which ordinarily should have been the first thing proclaimed with all horror. The Lords Justices and their advisers, who were all most pious men, long and with grave trouble of mind considered this stumbling block ; for it was truly distressing that such a promising project should be thwarted. Eventually they decided to chance the story any way, and trust to extra zeal in the use of horror narratives, to get up such a bloody fury in England as would render close scrutiny of the facts out of the question.*

* Several of our recent historians have gone to great pains, citing original documents, state papers, and letters of Protestant witnesses, to expose the baseness and wickedness of this massacre story ; but at this time of day one might as well occupy himself in gravely demonstrating the villany of Titus Oate's "informations." The great Popish Massacre story has had its day, but it is now dead and gone. The fact that there were excesses committed by the insurgents in a few cases—instantly denounced and punished as violations of the emphatic orders of their leaders promulgated to the contrary—has nothing to say to this question of *massacre*. Let it always be said that even *one* case of lawless violence or life-taking —even *one* excess of the laws of honorable warfare – is a thing to abominate and deplore ; as the Irish confederate leaders denounced and deplored the cases of excesses reported to them by some of Sir Phelim O'Neill's armed band. Not only did the Irish leaders vehemently inculcate moderation, but the Protestant chroniclers of the time abundantly testify that

So—albeit long after date—suddenly a terrific outcry arose about the awful " massacre" in Ireland ; the great wholesale and simultaneous massacre of Protestants. Horrors were piled on horrors, as each succeeding mail brought from the government officials in Dublin " further particulars" of the dreadful massacre which had, they declared, taken place all over Ulster on the night of the rising. Several of the minis- ters in London were in the secret of this massacre story ; but there is no doubt it was sincerely credited by the bulk of the English people at the time ; and, as might be expected, a sort of frenzy seized the populace. A cry arose against the bloody Irish Popish rebels. Everywhere the shout was to " stamp them out." The wisdom and sagacity of the venerable Lords Justices—the pre-eminent merits of their device—were triumphantly attested !

For a time there was a danger that the whole scheme might be spoiled—shaken in public credulity—by the in- judicious zeal of some of the furnishers of "further par-

---

tice. Leland, the Protestant historian, declares that the Catholic priests "labored zealously to moderate the excesses of war," and frequently protected the English where danger threatened, *by concealing them in their places of worship and even under their altars !* The Protestant Bishop Burnet, in his life of Dr. Bedel, who was titular Protestant Bishop of Dromore at the time, tells us that Dr. Bedel, with the tumul- tuous sea of the "rising" foaming around him on all sides in Cavan, enjoyed, both himself and all who sought the shelter of his house, "to a miracle perfect quiet," though he had neither guard nor defence, save the respect and forbearance of the "insurgents." One fact alone, recorded by the Protestant historians themselves, affords eloquent testimony on this point. This Bishop Bedel died while the "rising" was in full rush around him. He was very ardent as a Protestant ; but he refused to join in, and, indeed, reprobated the scandalous robberies and persecutions pursued against the Catholic Irish. The natives —the insurgents—the Catholic nobles and peasants—*en masse,* attended his funeral, and one of Sir Phelim O'Neill's regiments, with reversed arms, followed the bier. When the grave was closed (says the Protestant historian whom I am quoting, they fired a farewell volley over it, the leaders crying out: *" Requiescat in pace, ultimus Anglorum !"* (" Rest in peace, last of the English.") For they had often said that as he was the best man of the English religion, he ought to be the last ! Such was the conduct of the Irish insurgents. In no country, unfortu- nately, are popular risings unaccompanied by excesses; never in any country, probably, did a people rising against diabolical oppression, sweep away their plunderers with *so few* excesses as did the Irish in 1641. But all this, in any event, has nought to say to such a proceeding as a massacre. *That was* an afterthought of the lords jus-

ticulars," by whom the thing was a little over-done. Some thought twenty thousand would suffice for the number of massacred Protestants; others would go for a hundred thousand; while the more bold and energetic still stood out for putting it at two or three hundred thousand, though there were not that number of Protestants in all Ireland at the time. As a consequence, there were some most awkward contradictions and inconsistencies; but so great was the fury aroused in England, that happily these little dangers passed away smoothly, and King Charles himself joined in the shout against the horrid Popish rebellion! The English soldiers in Ireland were exhorted to slay* and spare not; additional regiments were quickly sent over—the men maddened by the massacre stories—to join in the work of "revenge." And, just as might be expected, then indeed massacre in earnest appeared upon the scene. The Irish had in the very first hour of their movement—in the very flush of victory— humanely and generously proclaimed that they would seek righteous ends by righteous means; that they would fight their cause, if fight they must, by fair and honorable warfare. They had, with exceptions so rare as truly to "prove the rule," exhibited marvellous forbearance and magnanimity. But now the English Puritan soldiery, infuriated to the fiercest pitch, were set upon them, and atrocities that sicken the heart to contemplate made the land reek from shore to shore. The covenanters of Scotland also, who had just previously secured by rebellion all they demanded for themselves, were filled with a holy desire to bear a part in the pious work of stamping out the Irish Popish rebellion. King Charles, who was at the time in Edinburgh endeavoring to conciliate the Scottish parliament, was quite ready to gratify them; and accordingly a force of some two thousand Scots were despatched across the channel, landing at Antrim, where they were reinforced by a recruitment from the remnant of the "colonies" planted by James the First. It was this force which inaugurated what may be called "massacres." Before their arrival the Puritan commanders in the south had, it is true, left no atrocity untried; but the Scots went at the work wholesale. They drove all the native population of one vast district—(or rather all the aged and infirm, the women and children; for the adult males were away serving in the confederate armies)—into a promontory, almost an island, on the coast, called Island Magee. Here, when the helpless crowd were hemmed in, the Scots fell upon them sword in hand, and drove them over the cliffs into the sea, or butchered them to the last, irrespective of age or sex. "From this day forward until the accession of Owen Roe O'Neill to the command, the northern war assumed a ferocity of character foreign to the nature of O'Moore, O'Kelly, and Magennis. Horrors and barbarities on each side made humanity shudder. The confederate leaders had proposed, hoped for, and on their parts had done everything to insure the conducting of the war according to the usages of fair and honorable warfare. The government, on the other hand, so far from reciprocating this spirit, in all their proclamations breathed savage and merciless fury against the Irish; and every exhortation of their commanders (in strange contrast with the humane and honorable manifestoes of the confederates) called upon the soldiery to glut their swords and spare neither young nor old, child or woman.

The conduct of the government armies soon widened the area of revolt. So far the native Irish alone, or almost exclusively, had participated in it, the Anglo-Irish Catholic Lords and Pale gentry holding aloof. But these latter could not fail to see that the Puritan faction, which now constituted the local government, were resolved not to spare Catholics whether of Celtic or Anglo-Irish race, and were moreover bent on strengthening their own hands to league with the English parliamentarians against the king. Loyalty to the king, and considerations for their own safety, alike counselled them to take some decisive step. Everything rendered hesitation more perilous. Although they had in no way encouraged, or, so far, sympathized with, the northern rising, their possessions were ravaged by the Puritan armies. Fingal, Santry, and Swords—districts in profound peace—were the scenes of bloody excesses on the part of the government soldiery. The Anglo-Irish Catholic nobility and gentry of these districts in vain remonstrated. They drew up a memorial to the throne, and forwarded it by one of their number, Sir John Read. He was instantly seized, imprisoned, and put to the rack in Dublin Castle ; " one of the questions which he was pressed to answer being whether the king and queen were privy to the Irish rebellion." In fine the English or Anglo-Iish Catholic families of the Pale for the first time in history began to feel that with the native Irish, between whom and them hitherto so wide a gulf had yawned, their side must be taken. After some negotiation between them and the Irish leaders, " on the invitation of Lord Gormanstown a meeting of Catholic noblemen and gentry was held on the hill of Crofty, in Meath. Among those who attended were the Earl of Fingal, Lords Gormanstown, Slane, Louth, Dunsany, Trimleston, and Netterville ; Sir Patrick Barnwell, Sir Christopher Bellew, Patrick Barnwell of Kilbrew, Nicholas Darcy of Platten, James Bath, Gerald Aylmer, Cusack of Gormanstown, Malone of Lismullen, Segrave of Kileglan, etc. After being there a few hours a party of armed men on horse-back, with a guard of musketeers, were seen to approach. The former were the insurgent leaders, Roger O'More, Philip O'Reilly, Mac Mahon, Captains Byrne and Fox, etc. The lords and gentry rode towards them, and Lord Gormanstown as spokesman demanded, ' for what reason they came armed into the Pale ?' O'More answered ' that the ground of their coming thither and taking up arms, was for the freedom and liberty of their consciences, the maintenance of his majesty's prerogative, in which they understood he was abridged, and the making the subjects of this kingdom as free as those of England.' "* " The leaders then embraced amid the acclamations of their followers, and the general conditions of their union having been unanimously agreed upon, a warrant was drawn out authorizing the Sheriff of Meath to summon the gentry of the country to a final meeting at the Hill of Tara on the 24th December."†

From this meeting sprang the Irish Confederation of 1642, formally and solemnly inaugurated three months subsequently at Kilkenny.

———co———

.

LV.—SOMETHING ABOUT THE CONFLICTING ELEMENTS OF THE CIVIL WAR IN 1642-9. HOW THE CONFEDERATE CATHOLICS MADE GOOD THEIR POSITION, AND ESTABLISHED A NATIONAL GOVERNMENT IN IRELAND.

EW chapters of Irish history are more important, none have been more momentous in their results, than that which chronicles the career of the confederation of 1642. But it is of all, the most intricate and involved, and the most difficult to summarize with fitting brevity and clearness for young readers. In that struggle there were not two but at least *four* or *five* distinct parties, with distinct, separate, and to a greater or lesser degree conflicting, interests and views; partially and momentarily combining, shifting positions, and changing alliances; so that the conflict as it proceeded was, in its character and component parts, truly "chameleonic." As for the unfortunate king, if he was greatly to be blamed, he was also greatly to be pitied. He was not a man of passion, malice, or injustice. He was mild, kindly, and justly disposed; but weak, vacillating, and self-willed; and, under the pressure of necessity and danger, his weakness degenerated into miserable duplicity at times. In the storm gathering against him in England, his enemies found great advantage in accusing him of "Popish leanings," and insinuating that he was secretly authorizing and encouraging the Irish Popish rebels—the same who had just massacred all the Protestants that were and were not in the newly planted province of Ulster. To rid himself of this suspicion, Charles went into the extreme of anxiety to crush those hated Irish Papists. He denounced them in proclamations, and applied to parliament for leave to cross over and head an army against them himself. The parliament replied, by maliciously insinuating a belief that his real object was to get to the head of the Irish Popish rebellion, which (they would have it) he only hypocritically affected to denounce.

The newly-settled Anglo-Irish Protestants became from the outset of this struggle bitter Puritans; the old families of the Pale mostly remaining royalists. The former sided with the parliamentarians and against the king, because they mistrusted his declarations of intolerance against the Catholics, and secretly feared he would allow them to live and hold possession of lands in Ireland; in which case there would be no plunder, no " plantations." The Covenanting Scots—the classes from whom in James's reign the Ulster colonists had largely been drawn, had just the same cause of quarrel against the Irish, whom the English parliamentarians hated with a fierceness for which there could be no parallel. This latter party combined religious fanaticism with revolutionary passion, and to one and the other the Irish were intolerably obnoxious; to the one, because they were Papists, idolaters, followers of Antichrist, whom to slay was work good and holy; to the other, because they had sided with the " tyrant" Charles.

The Catholic prelates and clergy could not be expected to look on idly while a fierce struggle in defence of the Catholic religion, and in sustainment of the sovereign against rebellious foes, was raging in the land. In such a war they could not be neutral. A provincial synod was held at Kells, 22d March, 1642, whereat, after full examination and deliberation, the cause of the confederates—" God and the King," freedom of worship and loyalty to the sovereign—was declared just and holy. The assembled prelates issued an address vehemently denouncing excesses or severities of any kind, and finally took steps to convoke a national synod at Kilkenny on the 10th of May following.

On that day accordingly (10th of May, 1643), the national synod met in the city of St. Canice. " The occasion was most solemn, and the proceedings were characterized by calm dignity and an enlightened tone. An oath of association, which all Catholics throughout the land were enjoined to take, was framed ; and those who were bound together by this solemn tie were called the 'Confederate Catholics of Ireland.' A manifesto explanatory of their motives, and containing rules to guide the confederation, and an admirable plan of provisional government, was issued. It was ordained that a general assembly, comprising all the lords spiritual and temporal, and the gentry of their party, should be held ; and that the assembly should select members from its body, to represent the different provinces and principal cities, and to be called the Supreme Council, which should sit from day to day, dispense justice, appoint to offices, and carry on, as it were, the executive government of the country. Severe penalties were pronounced against all who made the war an excuse for the commission of crime ; and after three days' sittings this important conference brought its labors to a close."*

" The national synod did not break up till about the end of May, and long before that period the proclamation issued by the prelates and lay-lords, calling on the people to take the oath of association, had the happiest results. Agents from the synod crossed over into France, Spain and Italy, to solicit support and sympathy from the Catholic princes. Father Luke Wadding was indefatigably employed collecting moneys and inciting the Irish officers serving in the continental armies to return and give their services to their own land. Lord Mountgarret was appointed president of the council, and the October following was fixed for a general assembly of the whole kingdom."†

On the 23d October following the general assembly thus convoked, assembled in Kilkenny, " eleven bishops and fourteen lay-lords represented the Irish peerage ; two hundred and twenty-six commoners, the large majority of the constituencies. The celebrated lawyer Patrick Darcy, a member of the commons house, was chosen as chancellor, and everything was conducted with the gravity and deliberation befitting so venerable an asssembly and so great an occasion." A Supreme Council of six members for each province was elect-

---

* Haverty.   † Rev. C. P. Meehan's *Confd. Kilkenny.*

ed. The archbishops of Armagh, Dublin, and Tuam, the bishops of Down and of Clonfert, Lord Gormanstown, Lord Mountgarret, Lord Roche, and Lord Mayo, with fifteen of the most eminent commoners, composed this council.

Such was the national government and legislature under which Ireland fought a formidable struggle for three years· It was loyally obeyed and served throughout the land ; in fact it was the only sovereign ruling power recognized at all out-side of two or three walled cities for the greater part of that

OWEN ROE O'NEILL.
From a portrait in Flanders, painted from life.

time. It undertook all the functions properly appertaining to its high office ; coined money at a national mint ; appointed judges who went circuit and held assizes ; sent ambassadors or agents abroad, and commissioned officers to the national armies—amongst the latter being Owen Roe O'Neill, who had landed at Doe Castle in Donegal in July of that year, and now formally assumed command of the army of Ulster.

While that governing body held together, unrent by trea-son or division, the Irish nation was able to hold its crowding

.

LVI.—HOW KING CHARLES OPENED NEGOTIATIONS WITH THE
CONFEDERATE COUNCIL. HOW THE ANGLO-IRISH 'PARTY
WOULD "HAVE PEACE AT ANY PRICE," AND THE "NATIVE
IRISH" PARTY STOOD OUT FOR PEACE WITH HONOR. HOW
POPE INNOCENT THE TENTH SENT AN ENVOY—"NOT EMPTY-
HANDED"—TO AID THE IRISH CAUSE.

"THE very power of the confederates," says one of our
historians, "now became the root of their misfortunes.
It led the king to desire to come to terms with them, not
from any intention to do them justice, but with the hope
of deriving assistance from them in his difficulties: and it exposed them to all those assaults of diplomatic craft, and that
policy of fomenting internal division, which ultimately proved their ruin.

The mere idea of the king desiring to treat with them, un-
settled the whole body of the Anglo-Irish lords and nobles.
They would have peace with the king on almost any terms
—they would trust everything to him. The old Irish, the
native or national party, on the other hand, were for holding
firmly by the power that had caused the king to value and
respect them; yielding in nowise unless the demands specifi-
cally laid down in the articles of confederation were efficient-
ly secured. On this fatal issue the supreme council and the
confederation were surely split from the first hour. Two
parties were on the instant created—two bitter factions they
became—the "peace party" or "Ormondists;" and the "national party," subsequently designated the "Nuncionist,"
from the circumstance of the papal nuncio being its firmest
supporter, if not its leader.

The first negotiations were conducted on the royal side by
a plenipotentiary whom the Anglo-Irish lords not only regarded as a friend of the king, but knew to be as much oppos-

of Ormond, a man of profound ability, of winning manners, and deeply skilled in diplomacy. To induce the confederates to lay down their arms, to abandon their vantage ground in Ireland, and send their troops across to Scotland or England to fight for Charles, was his great aim. In return he would offer little more than "trust to the king, when he shall have put his enemies down." In the very first negotiation the compromise party prevailed. On the 15th September, 1643, a cessation of arms was signed in Ormond's tent at Sigginstown, near Naas. In this the confederates were completely outwitted. *They* kept the truce; but they found Ormond either unable or unwilling to compel to obedience of its provisions the Puritan government generals, foremost amongst whom in savagery were Munroe in the north, leader of the covenanting Scotch army, and Murrough O'Brien, Lord Inchiquin (son-in-law of Sentleger, lord president of Munster), in the south. Meanwhile Ormond, as we are told, "amused the confederates with negotiations for a *permanent* peace and settlement from spring till midsummer;" time working all against the confederates, inasmuch as internal division was widening every day. It turned out that the marquis, whose prejudices against the Catholics were stronger than his loyalty to the waning fortunes of the king, was deceiving both parties; for while he was skilfully procrastinating and baffling any decisive action, Charles was really importuning him to hasten the peace, and come to terms with the Irish, whose aid was every day becoming more necessary. At this stage, the king privately sent over Lord Glamorgan to conclude a secret treaty with the confederates. Lords Mountgarret and Muskerry met the royal commissioner on the part of the confederation, and the terms of a treaty fully acceptable were duly agreed upon. I. The Catholics of Ireland were to enjoy the free and public exercise of their religion. II. They were to hold and have secured for their use all the Catholic churches not then in actual possession of the Protestants. III. They were to be exempt from the jurisdiction of the Protestant clergy. IV. The confederates (as the

ship in their own faith) were to send 10,000 men fully armed
to the relief of Chester and the general succor of the king.
Lastly, on the king's part it was stipulated that this treaty
should be kept secret while his troubles with English malcontents were pending. The pretence was that Ormond (by this
time lord lieutenant) knew nothing of this secret negotiation,
but he and Glamorgan and the king understood each other
well. On his way to Kilkenney the royal agent called upon
and had a long sitting with Ormond ; and from Kilkenney,
Glamorgan and the confederate plenipotentiaries went to
Dublin, where, during several private interviews, the lord
lieutenant argued over all the points of the treaty with them. He
evidently thought the 10,000 men might be had of the confederates for less concessions. Meanwhile Charles's fortunes were
in the balance. Ormond was well-disposed to serve the king,
but not at the risk of danger to himself. After having fully
reasoned over all the points of the treaty for several days with
Glamorgan and the confederate lords, suddenly, one afternoon, Ormond arrested Glamorgan with every show of excitement and panic, and flung him into prison on a charge of
high treason, in having improperly treated in the king's name
with the confederates ! A tremendous sensation was created
in Dublin by the event ; Ormond feigning that only by accident that day had Glamorgan's conduct been discovered !
The meaning of all this was, that on the person of the archbishop of Tuam, who had been killed a few days previously,
bravely fighting against some of the marauding murderers in
the west, there was found a copy of the treaty, which thus
became public. Ormond saw that as the affair was prematurely disclosed, he must needs affect surprise and indignation
at, and disavow it. Of course Glamorgan was softly whispered to lie still, if he would save the king, and offer no con-
tradiction of the viceregal falsehoods. With which Glamorgan duly complied. The duped confederates were to bear
all the odium and discomfiture !

It was during the Glamorgan negotiation—towards its
close—that there arrived in Kilkenny a man whose name is

engraved in Irish memory—John Baptist Rinuccini, archbishop of Fermo, in the marches of Ancona, chosen by the
new pope, Innocent the Tenth, as nuncio to the confederated
Catholics of Ireland. As the pope, from the first hour when
the Irish were driven into a war in defence of religion, never
sent an envoy empty-handed, Rinuccini brought with him,
purchased by moneys contributed by the Holy Father, besides 36,000 dollars forwarded by Father Luke Wadding,
" 2,000 muskets, 2,000 cartouche belts, 4,000 swords, 2,000
pike-heads, 400 brace of pistols, 20,000 pounds of powder,
with match, shot, and other stores." He landed from his
frigate, the *San Pietro*, at Ardtully, in Kenmare Bay. He
then proceeded by way of Kilgarven to Macroom, whither
the supreme council sent some troops of calvary to meet him
as a guard of honor. Thence by way of Kilmallock and Limerick, as rapidly as his feeble health admitted—(he had to be
borne on a litter or palanquin)—he proceeded to Kilkenny,
now practically the capital of the kingdom—the seat of the
national government—where there awaited him a reception
such as a monarch might envy. It was Catholic Ireland's
salutation to the "royal pope."

That memorable scene is described for us as follows by a
writer to whom we owe the only succinct account which we
possess in the English language of the great events of the period now before us : " At a short distance from the gate, he
descended from the litter, and having put on the cope and pon-
tifical hat, the insignia of his office, he mounted a horse caparisoned for the occasion. The secular and regular clergy had
assembled in the church of St. Patrick, close by the gate, and
when it was announced that the nuncio was in readiness, they
advanced into the city in processional array, preceded by the
standard-bearers of their respective orders. Under the old
arch, called St. Patrick's gate, he was met by the vicar-general
of the diocese of Ossory, and the magistrates of the city and
county, who joined in the procession. The streets were lined
by regiments of infantry, and the bells of the Black Abbey
and the church of St. Francis pealed a gladsome chime. The

on which the splendid old fane, sacred to St. Canice, is erected. At the grand entrance he was received by the venerable bishop of Ossory, whose feebleness prevented his walking in procession. After mutual salutations, the bishop handed him the aspersorium and incense, and then both entered the cathedral, which, even in the palmiest days of Catholicity, had never held within its precincts a more solemn or gorgeous assemblage. The nuncio ascended the steps of the grand altar, intonated the *Te Deum*, which was caught up by a thousand voices, till crypt and chancel resounded with the psalmody, and when it ceased he pronounced a blessing on the immense multitude which crowded the aisles and nave. . . . These ceremonies concluded, he retired for a while to the residence prepared for him in the city, and shortly afterwards was waited on by General Preston and Lord Muskerry. He then proceeded on foot to visit Lord Mountgarret, the president of the assembly. The reception took place in the castle. At the foot of the grand staircase he was met by Thomas Fleming, archbishop of Dublin, and Walsh, archbishop of Cashel. At the end of the great gallery, Lord Mountgarret was seated, waiting his arrival, and when the nuncio approached, he got up from his chair, without moving a single inch in advance. The seat designed for Rinuccini was of damask and gold, with a little more ornament than that occupied by the president. . . . The nuncio immediately addressed the president in Latin, and declared that the object of his mission was to sustain the king, then so perilously circumstanced; but above all, to rescue from pains and penalties the people of Ireland, and to assist them in securing the free and public exercise of the Catholic religion, and the restoration of the churches and church property of which fraud and violence had so long deprived their rightful inheritors."*

From the very first the nuncio discerned the pernicious workings of the " compromise " idea in paralyzing the power of the confederacy; and perceiving all its bitter mischief, he seems to have had little patience with it. He saw that the old

English of the Pale were more than anxious for a compromise, and to this end would allow the astute Ormond to fool them to the last, to the utter ruin of the confederate cause. They were, however, the majority, and eventually on the 28th of March, 1646, concluded with Ormond a treaty of peace which was a modification of Glamorgan's original propositions.

On the character and merits of this treaty turns one of the most injurious and mournful controversies that ever agitated Ireland. " A base peace" the populace called it when made public: but it might have been a wise one for all that. In the denunciations put forward against it by all who followed the nuncio's views, full justice has not been done this memorable pact. It contained one patent and fatal defect—it failed to make such express and adequate stipulations for the security of the Catholic religion as the oath of Confederation demanded. Failing this, it was substantially a good treaty under all the circumstances. It secured (as far as a treaty with a double-dealing and now virtually discrowned king might be held to secure anything) all, or nearly all, that the Irish Catholics expected then, or have since demanded. There can be no doubt that the majority of the supreme council honestly judged it the best peace attainable, nay wondrously advantageous, all things considered ; and judging so, it is not to be marvelled at that they bitterly complained of and inveighed against the nuncio and the party following him, as mad and culpable " extremists," who would lose all by unreasonably grasping at too much. But the nuncio and the "native" party argued, that if the confederates were but true to themselves, they would not need to be false to their oaths—that they had it in their power by vigorous and patriotic effort to win equality and freedom, not merely tolerance. Above all, Rinuccini pointed out that dealing with men like Charles the king and Ormond the viceroy, circumstanced as the royalist cause then was, the confederates were utterly without security. They were selling their whole power and position for the " promise to pay" of a bankrupt.

LVII.—HOW THE NUNCIO FREED AND ARMED THE HAND OF
OWEN ROE, AND BADE HIM STRIKE AT LEAST ONE WORTHY
BLOW FOR GOD AND IRELAND. HOW GLORIOUSLY OWEN
STRUCK THAT BLOW AT BEINBURB.

T was even so. Two months
afterwards, May, 1649,
Charles, all powerless,
fled form the dangers en-
vironing him in England, and took
refuge with the Scottish parliament. Meanwhile the Scottish
covenanting marauders in Ulster
had been wasting the land un-
checked since the fatal " truce "
and "peace negotiation" had tied up the hands of the confederates. The nuncio had early discerned the supreme abilities of
Owen Roe O'Neill (the favorite general of the national party
or "old Irish faction " in the council), and now he resolved to
strike a blow which might show the country what was possible

to O'Neill the greater part of the supplies which he had brought with him from abroad, and told the Ulster commander that on him it now lay to open the eyes alike of Puritan rebels, English royalists, and half-hearted confederates.

O'Neil was not slow to respond to this summons. For three long years, like a chained eagle, he had pined in weary idleness, ignoble " truces" fettering him. At last he was free; and now he resolved to show weak friend and arrogant foe how he who had defended Arras, could strike for God and liberty at home.

With the first days of June he was on the march from his late " truce " station on the borders of Leinster, at the head of five thousand foot and four hundred horse, to attack Monroe. " The Scottish general received timely notice of this movement, and setting out with six thousand infantry and eight hundred horse, encamped about ten miles from Armagh. His army was thus considerably superior to that of O'Neill in point of numbers, as it must also have been in equipments ; yet he sent word to his brother, Colonel George Monroe, to hasten from Coleraine to reinforce him with his cavalry. He appointed Glasslough, in the south of Monaghan, as their rendezvous; but the march of the Irish was quicker than he expected, and he learned on the 4th of June that O'Neill had not only reached that point, but had crossed the Blackwater into Tyrone, and encamped at Benburb. O'Neill drew up his army between two small hills, protected in the rear by a wood, with the river Blackwater on his right and a bog on his left, and occupied some brushwood in front with musketeers, so that his position was admirably selected. He was well informed of Monroe's plans, and despatched two regiments to prevent the junction of Colonel George Monroe's forces with those of his brother. Finding that the Irish were in possession of the ford at Benburb, Monroe crossed the river at Kinard, a considerable distance in O'Neill's rear, and then by a circuitous march approached him in front from the east and south. The manner in which the 5th of June was passed in the Irish camp was singularly solemn. ' The whole army.' says Rinuccini, ' having confessed, and the gen-

eral, with the other officers, having received the holy communion with the greatest piety, made a profession of faith,
and the chaplain deputed by the nuncio for the spiritual care
of the army, after a brief exhortation, gave them his blessing. On the other hand the Scots were inflamed with fierce
animosity against their foe, and an ardent desire for battle.*' "

"As they advanced," says another writer, "they were met
by Colonel Richard O'Ferral, who occupied a narrow defile
through which it was necessary for the Scotch troops to
pass in order to face the Irish. The fire of Monroe's guns,
however, compelled O'Neill's officer to retire." Lieutenant-
Colonel Cunningham having thus cleared the pass for the
Scotch horse, who were commanded by the Lord Viscount
of Ardes, in the absence of Colonel Monroe, "the whole army
advanced to dislodge Owen Roe; but a shower of bullets
from the 'scrogs and bushes,' which covered O'Neill's infantry, checked him; and then the Scotch cannon opened its
fire with little effect; as, owing to the admirable position of
the Catholic troops, only one man was struck by the shot.
In vain did Monroe's cavalry charge; with the river on their
right and 'a marish bog' on the left, it was hopeless to think
of stirring the confederates. For four hours did the Fabius
of his country amuse the enemy with skirmishing. During
all that time the wind rolling the smoke of Monroe's musketry and cannon in the face of the Irish ranks, concealed the
adverse ranks from their sight, and the sun had shone all day
in their eyes, blinding them with its dazzling glare; but ·that
sun was now descending, and producing the same effect on the
Scotch, when Monroe perceived the entire of the Irish army
making ready for a general assault with horse and foot.

"It was the decisive moment. The Irish general, throwing
himself into the midst of his men, and pointing out to them that
retreat must be fatal to the enemy, ordered them to pursue
vigorously, assuring them of victory. 'I myself,' said he,
'with the aid of heaven, will lead the way let those who
fail to follow me remember that they abandon their general.'

---

* Haverty.

This address was received with one unanimous shout by the army. The colonels threw themselves from their horses, to cut themselves off from every chance of retreat, and charged with incredible impetuosity.

"Monroe had given orders to a squadron of horse to break through the columns of the Irish foot as they advanced; but that squadron became panic-striken, and retreated disorderly through their own foot, pursued by O'Neill's cavalry. Nevertheless, Monroe's infantry stood firm and received the Irish, body to body, with push of pike, till at last the cavalry reserve, being routed in a second charge, fell pell mell amongst his infantry, which, being now broken and disordered, had no way to retreat but over the river which lay in their front."

"The Scots now fled to the river," says another historian; "but O'Neill held possession of the ford, and the flying masses were driven into the deep water where such numbers perished that tradition says, one might have crossed over dryshod on the bodies. Monroe himself fled so precipitately that his hat, sword, and cloak, were among the spoils, and he halted not till he reached Lisburn. Lord Montgomery was taken prisoner, with twenty-one officers and about one hundred and fifty soldiers; and over three thousand of the Scots were left on the field besides those killed in the pursuit, which was resumed next morning. All the Scotch artillery, tents, and provisions, with a vast quantity of arms, and ammunition, and thirty-two colors, fell into the hands of the Irish, who, on their side, had only seventy men killed, and two hundred wounded."

Father Hartigan, one of the army chaplains, was sent to bear the glad news of this victory to the nuncio at Limerick, taking with him the trophies captured from the enemy. He arrived on Saturday, 13th of June, and his tidings flung the queen city of the Shannon into ecstacies of jubilation. "On the following day (Sunday) at four o'clock, p. m., all the troops in garrison at Limerick assembled before the church of St. Francis, where the nuncio had deposited thirty-two standards taken by the Irish general from the Scotch. These trophies

* Rev. P. Meehan's *Confederation of Kilkenny.*

were then borne in solemn procession by the chiefs of the nobility, followed by the nuncio, the archbishop of Cashel, and the bishops of Limerick, Clonfert, and Ardfert. After these came the supreme council, the mayor and the magistrates, with the entire population of the city. The procession moved on till it reached St. Mary's cathedral, where the *Te Deum* was chanted, and on the next day a mass of thanksgiving was offered to the Lord, ' who fought among the valiant ones, and overthrew the nations that were resembled against them to destroy the sanctuary.' "

Mr. Aubrey de Vere, who is never truer poet, never more nobly inspired, than when the victory of an O'Neill is to be sung, gives us the following splendid chant of Beinburb :

At midnight I gazed on the moonless skies ;
There glisten'd 'mid other star blazonries,
A sword all stars ; then heaven, I knew,
Hath holy work for a sword to do.
Be true, ye clansmen of Nial ! Be true !

At morning I look'd as the sun uprose
On the fair hills of Antrim, late white with snows;
Was it morning only that dyed them red ?
Martyr'd hosts methought had bled
On their sanguine ridges for years not few !
Ye clansmen of Conn, this day be true !

There is felt once more on the earth
    The step of a kingly man :
Like a dead man hidden he lay from his birth
    Exile from his country and clan.

This day his standard he flingeth forth ;
    He tramples the bond and ban :
Let them look in his face that usurp'd his hearth
    Let them vanquish him, they who can !

Own Roe, our own O'Neill !
    He treads once more our land !
The sword in his hand is of Spanish steel !
    But the hand is an Irish hand !

Montgomery, Conway ! base-born crew !
This day ye shall learn an old lesson anew !

Thou art red with sunset this hour, Blackwater ;
But twice ere now thou wert red with slaughter !
Another O'Neill by the ford they met ;
And " the bloody loaming" men name it ye !

 Owen Roe, our own O'Neill—
  He treads once more our land
 The sword in his hand is of Spanish steel,
  But the hand is an Irish hand !

The storm of battle rings out ! On ! on !
Shine well in their faces thou setting sun!
The smoke grows crimson: from left to right
Swift flashes the spleenful and racing light ;
The horses stretched forward with belly to ground
On ! on ! like a lake which has burst its boun
Through the clangor of brands rolls the laughter of cannon !
Wind-borne it shall reach thine old walls, Dungannon.
Our widow'd cathedrals an ancient strain
To-morrow triumphant shall chant again.
On ! on ! This night on thy banks, Lough Neagh,
Men born in bondage shall couch them free.
On ! warriors, launched by a warrior's hand !
Four years ye were leash'd in a brazen band ;
He counted your bones, and he meted your might,
This hour he dashes you into the fight !
Strong Sun of the battle ! — great chief, whose eye
Wherever it gazes makes victory —
This hour thou shalt see them do or die !

 Owen Roe, our own O'Neill —
  He treads once more our land !
 The sword in his hand is of Spanish steel,
  But the hand is an Irish hand !

Through the dust and the mist of the golden west,
 New hosts draw nigh : —is it friend or foe ?
They come ! They are ours ! Like a cloud their vanguard lours !
 No help from thy brother this day, Monro !
They form : there stand they one moment, still—
 Now, now they charge under banner and sign :
They breast, unbroken, the slope of the hill :
 It breaks before them, the invader's line !
Their horse and their foot are crushed together
 Like harbor-locked ships in the winter weather,
Each dashed upon each, the churn'd wave strewing
With wreck upon wreck, and ruin on ruin.
The spine of their battle gave way with a yell :
Down drop their standards ! that cry was their knell !

Some on the bank, and some in the river,
Struggling they lie that shall rally never.

'T was God fought for us ! with hands of might
From on high He kneaded and shaped the fight.
To Him be the praise ; what He wills must be :
With Him is the future : for blind are we.
Let Ormond at will make terms or refuse them ;
Let Charles the confederates win or lose them ;
Uplift the old faith, and annul the old strife
Or cheat us, and forfeit his kingdom and life ;
Come hereafter what must or may,
Ulster, thy cause is avenged to-day !
What fraud took from us and force, the sword
That strikes in daylight makes ours restored.

Owen Roe, our own O'Neill—
He treads once more our land !
The sword in his hand is of Spanish steel,
But the hand is an Irish hand !

LVIII.—HOW THE KING DISAVOWED THE TREATY, AND THE IRISH REPUDIATED IT. HOW THE COUNCIL BY A WORSE BLUNDER CLASPED HANDS WITH A SACRILEGIOUS MURDER- ER, AND INCURRED EXCOMMUNICATION. HOW AT LENGTH THE ROYALISTS AND CONFEDERATES CONCLUDED AN HONOR- ABLE PEACE.

ELATED by this great victory, that party in the confed- eration of which O'Neill was the military favorite, and the nuncio the head, now became outspoken and vehement in their denunciations of the temporizers. And opportunely for them came the news from England that the miserable Charles, on finding that his commission to Glamorgan had been discovered, repudiated and denied the whole transaction, notwithstanding the formal commission duly signed and sealed by him, exhibited to the confederate council by his envoy! Ormond, nevertheless, as strongly exhorted the "peace party" to hold firm, and to consider for, the hard position of the king, which compelled him to pre- varicate! But the popular spirit was aroused, and Rinuccini, finding the tide with him, acted with a high hand against the "Ormondists," treating them as malcontents, even arresting and imprisoning them as half-traitors, whereas, howsoever wrong their judgment and halting their action, they were the (majority of the) lawfully elected government of the confeder- ation.

New elections were ordered throughout the country for a new general assembly, which accordingly met at Kilkenny, 10th January, 1647. This body by an overwhelming major- ity condemned the peace as invalid *ab initio*, inasmuch as it notably fell short of the oath of federation ; but the conduct of the commissioners and majority of the council was gener- ously, and indeed justly, declared to have been animated by

but superficially healed ; discord and suspicion caused the confederate generals, according as they belonged to the conflicting parties—the " Pale English " or the " native Irish "—to fear each other as much as the Puritan enemy. Meanwhile an Irish Attila was drenching Munster in blood—Morrough O'Brien, Lord Inchiquin, called to this day in popular traditions " Morrough of the Burnings," from the fact that the firmament over his line of march was usually blackened by the smoke of his burnings and devastations.* One monster massacre on his part filled all the land with horror. He besieged and stormed Cashel. The women and children took refuge in the grand cathedral on the rock, the ruins of which still excite the tourist's admiration. " Inchiquin poured in volleys of musket balls through the doors and windows, unmoved by the piercing shrieks of the crowded victims within, and then sent in his troopers to finish with pike and sabre the work which the bullets had left incomplete. The floor was encumbered with piles of mangled bodies, and *twenty priests* who had sought shelter *under the altars* were dragged forth and slaughtered with a fury which the mere extinction of life could not half appease."† Ere the horror excited by this hideous butchery had died away, the country heard with consternation that the Supreme Council of the Confederation had concluded a treaty with Inchiquin, as a first step towards securing his alliance. In vain the nuncio and the bishops protested against alliance or union with the man whose hands were still wet and red with the blood of anointed priests, massacred at the altar. The majority of the council evidently judged—sincerely, it may be credited—that under all the circumstances in was a substantial good to make terms with, and possibly

---

* This dreadful man was one of the first and bitterest fruits of the "Court of Wards," scheme, which in the previous reign was appointed for the purpose of seizing the infant children of the Catholic nobility, and bringing them up in hatred and horror of the faith of their fathers. O'Brien had been thus seized when a child, and thus brought up by the " Court of Wards"—to what purpose has just been illustrated. It would hardly be fair to the English to say such a scheme had no parallel; for history records that *the Turks* used to seize the children of the subject Christians, and train them up to be the bloodiest in fury against their own race and creed!

draw over to the royal cause, a foe so powerful. The bishops did not look on the question thus; nor did the lay (native) Irish leaders. The former recoiled in horror from communion with a sacrilegious murderer; the latter, to like aversion joined an absolute suspicion of his treachery, and time justified their suspicions. The truce nevertheless was signed at Dungarvan on the 20th of May, 1648. Fully conscious that the nuncio and the national party would resist such an unholy pact, the contracting parties bound themselves to unite their forces against whomsoever would assail it. Accordingly Preston, the favorite general of the "Ormondist" Confederates, joined his troops to those of Inchiquin to crush O'Neill, whom with good cause they feared the most. Five days after the "league with sacrilege and murder" was signed, the nuncio published a sentence of excommunication against its abettors, and an interdict against all cities and towns receiving it. Having posted this proclamation on the gates of the cathedral, he made his escape from the city, and repaired to the camp of O'Neill, at Maryboro.' Four months of wild confused conflict—all the old actors, with barely a few exceptions, having changed sides or allies—were ended in September, by the arrival of Ormond at Cork—(he had fled to France after an unaccountable if not traitorous surrendor of Dublin to the Puritans)—expressing willingness to negotiate anew with the confederation on the part of the king and his friends, on the basis of Glamorgan's *first* treaty. Four months subsequently —on the 17th January, 1649—this treaty, fully acceptable to all parties, was finally ratified and published amidst great re-joicings ; and the seven years' war was brought to an end !

Ormond and his royal master had wasted four years in vain,

news of the king's death in London shocked the land. Charles, as already mentioned, had flung himself upon the loyalty of the Scottish parliament, in which the Lowland covenanting element predominated. His rebellious subjects on the southern side of the border, thirsting for his blood, offered to buy him from the Scots. After a short time spent in hagging over the bargain, those canny saints sold the unfortunate Charles for a money price of four hundred thousand pounds —an infamy for which the world has not a parallel. The blood-money was duly paid, and the English bore their king to London, where they murdered him publicly at Whitehall on the 30th January, 1649.

A few weeks after this event the uncompromising and true-hearted, but impetuous and imperious nuncio, Rinuccini, bade adieu to the hapless land into whose cause he had entered heart and soul, but whose distractions prostrated his warm hopes. He sailed from Galway for home, in his ship the *San Pietro*, on the 23d February, 1649.

And now, while the at-length united confederates and royalists are proclaiming the young Prince of Wales as king throughout Ireland, lo! the huge black shadow of a giant destroyer near at hand is flung across the scene!

LIX.—HOW CROMWELL LED THE PURITAN REBELS INTO
IRELAND. HOW IRELAND BY A LESSON TOO TERRIBLE TO
BE FORGOTTEN WAS TAUGHT THE DANGER OF TOO MUCH
LOYALTY TO AN ENGLISH SOVEREIGN.

T is the figure of the great Regicide that looms up at this
period, like a huge colossus of power and wrath. The
English nation caused Oliver Cromwell's body to be
disinterred and hung in chains, and buried at the gallows foot. Even in our own day that nation, I believe, refuses
to him a place amidst the statues of its famous public men, set
up in the legislative palace at Westminster. If England honored none of her heroes who were not *good* as well as *great*,
this would be more intelligible and less inconsistent. She
gave birth to few greater men, whose greatness is judged apart
from virtue ; and, if she honors as her greatest philosopher and
moralist the corrupt and venal lord chancellor Bacon, degraded for selling his decisions to the highest bribe, it is the
merest squeamishness to ostracise the " Great Protector," because one king was among his murdered victims.

England has had for half a thousand years few sovereign
rulers to compare in intellect with this " bankrupt brewer of
Huntingdon." She owes much of her latter day European
prestige to his undoubted national spirit ; for, though a despot,
a bigot, and a canting hypocrite, he was a thorough nationalist
as an Englishman. And she owes not a little of her constitutional liberty to the democratic principles with which the
republican party, on whose shoulders he mounted to power,
leavened the nation.

In 1649, the Puritan revolution had consumed all opposition
in England ; but Ireland presented an inviting field for what
the Protector and his soldiery called " the work of the Lord.'·
There their passions would be *fully* aroused ; and there their

vengeance would have full scope. To pull down the throne, and cut off Charles' head, was, after all (according to their ideas), overthrowing only a political tyranny and an episcopal dominance amongst their own fellow countrymen and fellow Protestants. But in Ireland there was an idolatrous people to be put to the sword, and their fertile country to be possessed. Glory halleluja! The bare prospect of a campaign *there* threw all the Puritan regiments in ecstasies. It was the summons of the Lord to His chosen people to cross the Jordan and enter the promised land!

In this spirit Cromwell came to Ireland, landing at Dublin on the 14th August, 1649. He remained nine months. Never, perhaps, in the same space of time, had one man more of horror and desolation to show for himself. It is not for any of the ordinary severities of war that Cromwell's name is infamous in Ireland. War is no child's play and those who take to it must not wail if its fair penalties fall upon them ever so hard and heavy. If Cromwell, therefore, was merely a vigorous and "thorough" soldier, it would be unjust to cast special odium upon him. To call him "savage" because the slain of his enemies in battle might have been enormous in amount, would be simply contemptible. But it is for a far different reason Cromwell is execrated in Ireland. It is for such butcheries of the unarmed and defenceless non-combatants—the ruthless slaughter of inoffensive women and children —as Drogheda and Wexford witnessed, that he is justly regarded as a bloody and brutal tyrant. Bitterly, bitterly, did the Irish people pay for their loyalty to the English sovereign; an error they had just barely learned to commit, although scourged for centuries by England compelling them thereto! I spare myself the recital of the horrors of that time. Yet it is meet to record the fact that not even before the terrors of such a man did the Irish exhibit a craven or cowardly spirit. Unhappily for their worldly fortunes, if not for their fame, they were high-spirited and unfearing, where pusillanimity would certainly have been safety, and might have been only prudence. Owen Roe O'Neil was struck down by death early in the struggle, and by the common testimony of friend and foe, in him the Irish lost the only military leader capable of coping with Cromwell.* Nevertheless, with that courage which unflinchingly looks ruin in the face, and chooses death before dishonor, the Irish fought the issue out. At length, after a fearful and bloody struggle of nearly three years' duration, " on the 12th May, 1652, the Leinster army of the Irish surrendered on terms signed at Kilkenny, which were adopted successively by the other principal armies between that time and the September following, when the Ulster forces surrendered."

LX.—THE AGONY OF A NATION.

HAT ensued upon the Cromwellian conquest of Ireland has been told recently in a book written under most singular circumstances—a compilation from state records and official documents—a book which the reader may take in his hand and challenge the wide world for another such true story.

About one-and-twenty years ago an Irish professional gentleman, a member of the bar, a Protestant, educated in England, belonging to one of those noble Anglo-Norman families who early indentified themselves in sympathy with Ireland as the country of their adoption, " received a commission from England to make some pedigree researches in Tipperary." He was well qualified for a task which enlisted at once the abilities of a jurist and the attainments of an archæologist. By inclination and habit far removed from the stormy atmosphere of politics, his life had been largely devoted to the

---

* He died 6th November, 1649, at Cloughoughter Castle, county Caven, on his way southward to effect a junction with Ormond for a campaign against Cromwell. . He was buried in the cemetery of the Franciscan convent in the town of Caven. A popular tradition, absurdly erroneous, to the effect that he died by poison—" having danced in poisoned slippers"—has been adopted by Davis in his " Lament for the death of Owen Roe." The story, however, is quite apocryphal.

tranquil pursuits of study at home or in other lands. His literary and philosophic tastes, his legal schooling, and above
all his professional experience, which in various occupations
had brought him largely into contact with the practical realities of life in Ireland, all tended to give him an interest in the
subject thus committed to his investigations.   His client little
thought, however—for a long time he little dreamt himself—
that to the accident of such a commission would be traceable
the existence subsequently of one of the most remarkable
books ever printed in the English language—" The Cromwellian Settlement of Ireland," by Mr. John P. Prendergast.

It would be hopeless to attempt to abbreviate or summarize
the startling romance, the mournful tragedy of history—" the
records of a nation's woes"—which Mr. Prendergast, as he tells
us, discovered in the dust-covered cell of that gloomy tower
in Dublin Castle yard, apparently the same that once was the
dungeon of Hugh Roe O'Donnell.*   I therefore relinquish all

---

* " I now thought of searching the Record Commissioners' Reports, and found there
were several volumes of the very date required, 1650 –1659, in the custody of the
clerk of the privy council, preserved in the heavily embattled tower which forms the
most striking feature of the Castle of Dublin.   They were only accessible at that
day through the order of the lord lieutenant or chief secretary for Ireland.   I obtained, at length, in the month of September, 1849, an order.   It may be easily imagined
with what interest I followed the porter up the dark winding stone staircase of this
gloomy tower, once the prison of the castle, and was ushered into a small central
space that seemed dark, even after the dark stairs we had just left.   As the eye became accustomed to the spot, it appeared that the doors of five cells made in the
prodigious thickness of the tower walls, opened on the central space.   From one of
them Hugh Roe O'Donel is said to have escaped, by getting down the privy of his
cell to the Poddle River that runs around the base of the tower.   The place was covered with the dust of twenty years; but opening a couple of volumes of the statutes—one
as a clean spot to place my coat upon, and the other to sit on—I took my seat in the
cell exactly opposite to the one just mentioned, as it looked to the south over the
castle garden, and had better light.   In this tower I found a series of Order Books
of the Commissioners of the Parliament of the Commonwealth of England for the affairs of Ireland, together with domestic correspondence and Books of Establishments
from 1650 to 1659.   They were marked on the back by the letter A over a number,
as will be observed in the various references in the notes to the present sketch.
Here I found the records of a nation's woes.   I felt that I had at last reached the haven I had been so long seeking.   There I sat, extracting, for many weeks, until I began to know the voices of many of the corporals that came with the guard to relieve
the sentry in the castle yard below, and every drum and bugle call of the regiment

idea of following in detail the transactions which immediately followed upon the capitulation of the Irish armies : " when," says Mr. Prendergast, " there took place a scene not witnessed in Europe since the conquest of Spain by the Vandals." " Indeed," he continues, " it is injustice to the Vandals to equal them with the English of 1652 ; for the Vandals came as strangers and conquerors in an age of force and barbarism ; nor did they banish the people, though they seized and divided their lands by lot ; but the English of 1652 were of the same nation as half of the chief families in Ireland, and had at that time had the island under their sway for five hundred years.

" The captains and men of war of the Irish, amounting to forty thousand men and upwards, they banished into Spain, where they took service under that king ; others of them with a crowd of orphan girls were transported to serve the English planters in the West Indies ; and the remnant of the nation not banished or transported were to be transplanted into Connaught, while the conquering army divided the ancient inheritances of the Irish amongst them by lot."

James essayed the plantation of Ulster, as Henry and Elizabeth had the colonization of Munster. The republican parliament went much farther, " improving" to the full their dreadful " opportunity." They decided to colonize *three* provinces—Leinster, Munster, and Ulster—converting the fourth (Connaught) into a vast encircled prison, into which such of the doomed natives as were not either transported as white slaves to Barbadoes, kept for servitude by the new settlers, or allowed to expatriate themselves as a privilege, might be driven on pain of immediate death ; the calculation being, that in the desolate tracts assigned as their unsheltered prison they must inevitably perish ere long.

The American poet, Longfellow, has, in the poem of

quartered in the Ship Street barracks. At length, between the labor of copying and excitement at the astonishing drama performing, as it were, before my eyes, my heart by some strange movements warned me it was necessary to retire for a time.

"Evangeline," immortalized the story of Acadia. How many a heart has melted into pity, how many an eye has filled with tears, perusing his metrical relation of the "transplanting" and dispersion of that *one* little community "on the shore of the basin of Minas!" But alas! how few recall or realize the fact—if, indeed, aware of it at all—that not *one* but *hundreds* of such dispersions, infinitely more tragical and more romantic, were witnessed in Ireland in the year 1654, when in every hamlet throughout three provinces "the sentence of expulsion was sped from door to door!" Longfellow describes to us how the English captain read aloud to the dismayed and grief-stricken villagers of Grand Pre the decree for their dispersion. Unconsciously, the poet merely described the form directed by an act of the English parliament to be adopted all over Ireland, when "*by beat of drumme and sound of trumpett,*" on some markett day, within tenn days after the same shall come unto them within their respective precincts," "the governor and commissioners of revenue, or any two or more of them within every precinct," were ordered to publish and proclaim "this present declaration;" to wit, that "all the ancient estates and farms of the people of Ireland were to belong to the adventurers and the army of England, and that the parliament had assigned Connaught (America was not then accessible) for the habitation of the Irish nation, *whither they must transplant with their wives and daughters and children before the 1st May following* (1654), *under penalty of death, if found on this side of the Shannon after that day.*

"Connaught was selected for the habitation of all the Irish nation," we are reminded, "by reason of its being surrounded by the sea and the Shannon all but ten miles, and the whole easily made into line by a few forts.* To further secure the imprisonment of the nation, and to cut them off from relief by the sea, a belt four miles wide, commencing one mile west of Sligo, and so winding along the sea coast and the Shannon,

---

* "9th March, 1654-5.—Order Passes over the Shannon between Jamestown and Sligo to be closed, so as to make one entire line between Connaught and the adja-

was reserved by the act (27th September, 1653) from being set
out to the Irish, and was to be given to the soldiery to plant."
The Irish were not to attempt to pass " the four mile line," as
it was called, or to enter a walled town (or to come within
five miles of certain specified towns) *"on pain of death."**

Need we marvel that all over the land the loud wail of grief
and despair resounded for days together? It was one universal scene of distracted leave-taking, and then along every road
that led towards Connaught, each a *via dolorosa*, the sorrowing
cavalcades streamed, weary, fainting, and foot-sore, weeping
aloud !

Towards the seaports moved other processions ; alas ! of not
less mournful character—the Irish regiments marching to em-
bark for exile ; or the gangs in charge to be transported and
sold into slavery in the pestilential settlements of the West
Indies ! Of young boys and girls alone Sir William Petty
confesses six thousand were thus transported ; " but the total
number of Irish sent to perish in the tobacco islands, as they
were called, were estimated in some Irish accounts at one
hundred thousand." Force was necessary to collect them ;
but vain was all resistance. Bands of soldiery went about
tearing from the arms of their shrieking parents, young children of ten or twelve years, then chaining them in gangs, they
marched them to the nearest port ! " Henry Cromwell (Oliver's son,) who was most active in the kidnapping of Irish
' white slaves,' writing from Ireland to Secretary Thurloe, says:
' I think it might be of like advantage to your affairs there, and
ours here, if you should think to send one thousand five hundred or two thousand young boys of twelve or fourteen years
of age to the place aforementioned (West Indies). Who knows
but it may be the means to make them Englishmen—I mean,
rather, Christians. Thurloe answers : ' The committee of the

---

* "How strict was the imprisonment of the transplanted in Connaught may be judged when it required a special order for Lord Trimbleston, Sir Richard Barnwell, Mr.
Patrick Netterville, and others, then dwelling in the suburbs of Athlone on the Connaught side, to pass and repass the bridge into the part of the town on the Leinster
side on their business ; and only on given security not to pass without special leave

council have voted one thousand *girls* and as many youths to be *taken up* for that purpose.' "

The *piety* of the amiable kidnapper will be noted. But it was always so with his class ; whether confiscating or transplanting, whether robbing the Irish, or selling them into slavery, it was always for their spiritual or temporal good —to sanctify or to civilize them. Accordingly we read that at this period " the parliamentary commissioners in Dublin published a proclamation by which and other edicts any Catholic priest found in Ireland after twenty days, was guilty of high treason, and liable to be hanged, drawn, and quartered ; any person harboring such clergymen was liable to the penalty of death, and loss of goods and chattels ; and any person knowing the place of concealment of a priest and not disclosing it to the authorities, might be publicly whipped, and further punished with amputation of ears.

" Any person absent from the parish church on a Sunday was liable to a fine of thirty pence ; magistrates might take away the children of Catholics and send them to England for education, and might tender the oath of abjuration to all persons at the age of twenty-one years, who, on refusal, were liable to imprisonment during pleasure, and the forfeiture of two-thirds of their real and personal estates.

" The same price of five pounds was set on the head of a priest and on that of a wolf, and the production of either head was a sufficient claim for the reward. The military being distributed in small parties over the country, and their vigilance kept alive by sectarian rancor and the promise of reward, it must have been difficult for a priest to escape detection, but many of them, nevertheless, braved the danger for their poor scattered flocks ; and, residing in caverns in the mountains, or in lonely hovels in the bogs, they issued forth at night to carry the consolations of religion to the huts of their oppressed and suffering countrymen."*

" Ludlow," continues the same author, "relates in his Memoirs (vol. i,, page 422 de Vevay, 1691) how, when marching from Dundalk to Castleblaney, probably near the close of 1652, he discovered a few of the Irish in a cave, and how his party spent two days in endeavoring to smother them by smoke. It appears that the poor fugitives preserved themselves from suffocation during this operation, by holding their faces close to the surface of some running water in the cavern, and that one of this party was armed with a pistol, with which he shot the foremost of the troopers who where entering the mouth of the cave after the first day's smoking. Ludlow caused the trial to be repeated, and the crevices through which the smoke escaped having been closed, ' another smoke was made.' The next time the soldiers entered with helmets and breast-plates, but they found the only armed man dead, inside the entrance, where he was suffocated at his post ; while the other fugitives still preserved life at the little brook. Fifteen were put to the sword within the cave, and four dragged out alive ; but Ludlow does not mention whether he hanged these then or not; but one at least of the original number was a Catholic priest, for the soldiers found a crucifix, chalice, and priest's robes in the cavern.

Of our kindred, old or young, sold into slavery in the " tobacco islands," we hear no more in history, and shall hear no more until the last great accounting day. Of those little ones—just old enough to feel all the pangs of such a ruthless and eternal severance from loving mother, from fond father, from brothers and playmates, from all of happiness on earth—no record tells the fate. We only know that a few years subsequently there survived of them in the islands barely the remembrance that they came in shiploads and perished soon—too young to stand the climate or endure the toil! But at home—in the rifled nest of the parent's heart—what a memory of them was kept! There the image of each little victim was enshrined ; and father and mother, bowed with years and suffering, went down to the grave " still thinking, ever thinking " of the absent, the cherished one, whom they were never to see on earth again, now writhing beneath a planter's lash, or filling a nameless grave in Jamaican soil ! Yes, that army of innocents vanish

slaughters of Herod, has kept a reckoning of the crime that in that hour so notably likened Ireland to Rachel weeping for her children.

But there was another army—other of the expatriated—of whom we are not to lose sight, the "Irish Swordmen," so called in the European writings of the time ; the Irish regiments who elected to go into exile, preferring to

> .   .   .   .   .   . " roam
> Where freedom and their God might lead,"

rather than be bondsman under a bigot-yoke at home. "Foreign nations were apprised by the Kilkenny Articles that the Irish were to be allowed to engage in the service of any state in amity with the Commonwealth. The valor of the Irish soldier was well known abroad. From the time of the Munster plantation by Queen Elizabeth, numerous exiles had taken service in the Spanish army. There were Irish regiments serving in the Low Countries. The prince of Orange declared they were 'born soldiers;' and Henry the Fourth of France publicly called Hugh O'Neill 'the third soldier of the age,' and he said there was no nation made better troops than the Irish when drilled. Agents from the King of Spain, the King of Poland, and the Prince de Condé, were now contending for the services of Irish troops. Don Ricardo White, in May, 1652, shipped seven thousand in batches from Waterford, Kinsale, Galway, Limerick, and Bantry, for the King of Spain. Colonel Christopher Mayo got liberty in September, 1652, to beat his drums to raise three thousand for the same king. Lord Muskerry took five thousand to the King of Poland. In July, 1654, three thousand five hundred, commanded by Colonel Edmund Droyer, went to serve the Prince de Condé. Sir Walter Dungan and others got liberty to beat their drums in different garrisons, to a rallying of their men that laid down arms with them in order to a rendezvous, and to depart for Spain. They got permission to march their men together to the different ports, their pipers perhaps playing 'Ha til, Ha til, Ha til, mi tulidh'—' We return, we return no more!* .

---

* " The tune with which the departing Highlanders usually bid farewell to their.

SEIZING THE IRISH CHILDREN FOR SLAVE GANGS IN BARRADOES.

See page 389.

Between 1661 and 1664, thirty-four thousand (of whom few ever saw their loved native land again) were transported into foreign parts."*

While the roads to Connaught were as I have described witnessing a stream of hapless fugitives—prisoners rather, plodding wearily to their dungeon and grave—a singular scene was going on in London. At an office or bureau. appointed for the purpose by government, a *lottery* was held, whereat the farms, houses, and estates from which the owners had thus been driven, were being "drawn" by or on behalf of the soldiers and officers of the army, and the " adventurers " —*i. e.* petty shopkeepers in London, and others who had lent money for the war on the Irish. The mode of conducting the lottery or drawing was regulated by public ordinance. Not unfrequently a vulgar and illiterate trooper "drew" the mansion and estate of an Irish nobleman, who was glad to accept permission to inhabit, for a few weeks merely, the stable or the cowshed† with his lady and children, pending their setting out for Connaught ! This same lottery was the " settlement " (varíed a little by further confiscations to the same end forty years subsequently) by which the now existing landed proprietary was "planted" upon Ireland. Between a proprietary thus planted and the bulk of the population, as well as the tenantry under them, it is not to be marvelled that feelings the reverse of cordial prevailed. From the first they scowled at each other. The plundered and trampled people despised and hated the "Cromwellian brood," as they were called, never regarding them as more than vulgar and violent usurpers of other men's estates. The Cromwellians, on the other hand, feared and hated the serf-peasantry, whose secret sentiments and desires of hostility they well knew. Nothing but the fusing spirit of nationality obliterates such feelings as these ; but no such spirit was allowed to fuse the Cromwellian " landlords " and the Irish tenantry. The former were taught

---

* Prendergast's *Crom. Settlement.*

† See the case of the then proprietor of the magnificent place now called **Woodlands**

to consider themselves as a foreign garrison, endowed to watch and keep down, and levy a land-tribute off the native tillers of the soil; moreover "the salt of the land," the " elect of the Lord," the ruling class, alone entitled to be ranked as saints or citizens. So they looked to and leaned all on England, without whom they thought they must be massacred. "Aliens in race, in language, and in religion," they had not one tie in common with the subject population ; and so both classes unhappily grew up to be what they remain very much in our own day—more of taskmasters and bondsmen than landlords and tenants.

———

LXI.—HOW KING CHARLES THE SECOND CAME BACK ON A COMPROMISE. HOW A NEW MASSACRE STORY WAS SET TO WORK. THE MARTYRDOM OF PRIMATE PLUNKETT.

POSSESSED of supreme power, Cromwell by a bold stroke of usurpation, now changed the republic to what he called a " protectorate," with himself as " Protector ;" in other words, a kingdom with Oliver as king, *vice* Charles, decapitated. This *coup d' état* completely disgusted the sincere republicans of the Pym and Ludlow school ; and on the death of the iron-willed Protector, 3d September, 1658, the whole structure set up by the revolution on the ruins of the monarchy in England tottered and fell.

Communication had been opened with the second Charles, a worthless, empty-headed creature, and it was made clear to him, that if he would only undertake not to disturb too much the "vested interests " created during the revolution—that is, if he would undertake to let the "settlement of property" (as they were pleased to call their stealing of other men's estates) alone—his return to the throne might be made easy. Charles was delighted. This proposal only asked of him to sacrifice his friends, now no longer powerful, since they had lost all in his behalf. He acquiesced, and the monarchy was restored.

had been so fearfully scourged for the sin of loyalty to his father now joyfully expected that right would be done, and that they would enjoy their own once more. They were soon undeceived. Such of the "lottery " speculators, or army officers and soldiers as were actually in possession of the estates of royalist owners, were not to be disturbed. Such estates only as had not actually been "taken up"were to be restored to the owners. There was one class, however, whom all the others readily agreed might be robbed without any danger— nay, whom it was loudly declared to be a crime to desist from robbing to the last—namely, the Catholics—especially the *"Irish* Papists." The reason why, was not clear. Everybody, on the contrary, saw that they had suffered most of all for their devoted loyalty to the murdered king. After a while a low murmur of compassion—muttering even of justice for them— began to be heard about the court. This danger created great alarm. The monstrous idea of justice to the Catholics was surely not to be endured ; but what was to be done ? " Happy thought"—imitate the skilful ruse of the Irish Puritans in starting the massacre story of 1641. But where was the scene of massacre to be laid this time, and when must they say it had taken place ? This was found to be an irresistible stopper on a new massacre story in the past, but then the great boundless future was open to them : could they not say it was *yet to take place ?* A blessed inspiration the saintly people called this. Yes : they could get up an anti-Catholic frenzy with a massacre-story about the future, as well as one relating to the past !

Accordingly, in 1678 the diabolical fabrication known as the " Great Popish Plot" made its appearance. The great Protestant historian, Charles James Fox, declared that the

But the plot-story did its appointed work splendidly and completely, and all the sentimental horror of a thousand Macaulays could nought avail, once that work was done. A proper fury had been got up against the Catholics, arresting the idea of compassionating them, giving full impetus to merciless persecution of Popish priests, and, above all (crowning merit!) effectually silencing all suggestions about restoring to Irish Catholic royalists their estates and possessions. Shaftesbury, one of the chief promoters of the plot-story, was indeed dragged to the tower as an abominable and perjured miscreant, but not until the scaffold had drunk deep of Catholic blood, and Tyburn had been the scene of that mournful tragedy—that foul and heartless murder—of which Oliver Plunkett, the sainted martyr-primate of Ireland, was the victim.

This venerable man was at Rome when the Pope selected him for the primacy. A bloody persecution was at the moment raging in Ireland; and Dr. Plunkett felt that the appointment was a summons to martyrdom. Nevertheless he hastened to Ireland, and assumed the duties of his position. Such was his gentleness and purity of character, his profound learning, the piety, and indeed sanctity, of his life, that even the Protestant officials and gentry round about came to entertain for him the highest respect and personal regard. Prudent and circumspect, he rigidly abstained from interference in the troubled politics of the period, and devoted himself exclusively to rigorous reforms of such irregularities and abuses as had crept into parochial or diocesan affairs during

---

* Few episodes in Irish history are more tragic and touching than that with which the name of the Martyr-Primate is associated, and there have been few more valuable contributions to Irish Catholic or historical literature in our generation than the "Memoir" of this illustrious prelate by the Rev. Dr. Moran. In it the learned reverend author has utilized the rich stores of original manuscripts relating to the period—many of them letters in the Martyr-Primate's handwriting—preserved in Rome, and has made his book not only a "memoir" of the murdered archbishop, but an authentic history of a period momentous in its importance and interest for Irishmen. A much briefer work is the *Life and Death of Oliver Plunkett* by the Rev. George Crolly, a little book which tells a sad story in language full of simple pathos

the past century of civil war and social chaos. For the support of the "intended massacre" story it was clearly necessary to extend the scene of the plot to Ireland (so much more Popish than England), and casting about for some one to put down as chief conspirator, the constructors of the story thought the head of the Popish prelates ought to be the man, *ex officio.* The London government accordingly wrote to the Irish lord lieutenant to announce that the "Popish plot" existed in Ireland also. He complied. Next he was to resume energetically the statutory persecutions of the Papists. This he also obeyed. Next he was directed to arrest the Popish primate for complicity in the plot. Here he halted. From the correspondence it would appear that he wrote back to the effect that this was rather too strong, inasmuch as even amongst the ultra-Protestants, the idea of Dr. Plunkett being concerned in any such business would be scouted. Besides, he pointed out there was *no evidence.* He was told that this made no matter, to obey his orders, and arrest the Primate. He complied reluctantly. An agent of the Oates and Shaftesbury gang in London, Hetherington by name, was now sent over to Dublin to get up evidence, and soon proclamations were circulated through all the jails, offering pardon to any criminal—murderer, robber, tory, or traitor—who could (would) give the necessary evidence against the Primate; and accordingly crown witnesses by the dozen competed in willingness to swear anything that was required. The Primate was brought to trial at Drogheda, but the grand jury, though ultra-Protestant to a man, threw out the bill ; the perjury of the crown witnesses was too gross, the innocence of the meek and venerable man before them too apparent. When the news reached London, great was the indignation there. The lord lieutenant was at once directed to send the Primate thither, where no such squeamishness of jurors would mar the ends of justice. The hapless prelate was shipped to London and brought to trial there. Macaulay himself has described for us from original authorities the manner in which those "trials" were conducted. Here is his description of

" A wretch named Carstairs, who had earned a living in
Scotland by going disguised to conventicles, and then inform
ing against the preachers, led the way ; Bedloe, a noted
swindler, followed ; and soon from all the brothels, gambling-
houses, and sponging-houses of London, false witnesses poured
forth to swear away the lives of Roman Catholics. . . .
Oates, that he might not be eclipsed by his imitators, soon
added a large supplement to his original narrative. The vulgar believed, and the highest magistrates *pretended* to believe,
even such fictions as these. The chief judges of the kingdom
were corrupt, cruel, and timid. . . . . The juries partook of the feelings then common throughout the nation, and
were encouraged by the bench to indulge those feelings without restraint. The multitude applauded Oates and his confederates, hooted and pelted the witnesses who appeared on
behalf of the accused, and shouted with joy when the verdict
of guilty was pronounced."

Before such a tribunal, on the 8th of June, 1681, the aged
and venerable Primate was arraigned, and of course convicted. The scene in court was ineffably brutal. In accordance
with the law in that time, the accused was allowed no counsel
whereas the crown was represented by the Attorney-General
and Sergeant Maynard ; the judges being fully as ferocious
as the official prosecutors. Every attempt made by the venerable victim at the bar to defend himself, only elicited a roar
of anger or a malignant taunt from one side or the other.
The scene has not inappropriately been likened, rather to the
torturing of a victim at the stake by savage Indians, dancing
and shouting wildly round him, than the trial of a prisoner
in a court of law. At length the verdict was delivered ; to
which, when he heard it, the archbishop simply answered :
" *Deo gratias !*" Then he was sentenced to be drawn on a
hurdle to Tyburn, there and then to be hanged, cut down
while alive, his body quartered, and the entrails burned in
fire. He heard this infamous decree with serene composure.

"But looking upward full of grace,
God's glory smote him on the face."

felt greatly shocked by this conviction. The thing was *too* glaring. The Protestant archbishop of Dublin (who seems to have been a humane and honorable man) expressed aloud his horror, and fearlessly declared the Catholic primate as innocent of the crimes alleged as an unborn child. But no one durst take on himself at the moment to stem the tide of English popular fury. The Earl of Essex, indeed, hurried to the king and vehemently besought him to save the Irish primate by a royal pardon. Charles, terribly excited, declared that he, as well as every one of them, knew the primate to be innocent, "but," cried he with passionate earnestness, "*ye* could have saved him; *I* cannot—you know well I *dare* not."

Then, like Pontius Pilate, he desired "the blood of this innocent man" to be on their heads, not his. The law should take its course.

" The law" did " take its course." The sainted Plunkett was dragged on a hurdle to Tyburn amidst the yells of the London populace. There he was hanged, beheaded, quartered and disembowelled, "according to law," July 1st, 1681.

Soon after, as I have already intimated, the popular delirium cooled down and everybody began to see that rivers of innocent Catholic blood had been made to flow without cause, crime, or offence. But what of that ? A most salutary check had been administered to the apprehended design of restoring to Catholic royalists the lands they had lost through their devotion to the late king. The " Popish Plot" story of 1678, like the great massacre story of 1641, had accomplished its allotted work.

LXII.—HOW KING JAMES THE SECOND, BY ARBITRARILY AS-
SERTING LIBERTY OF CONSCIENCE, UTTERLY VIOLATED
THE WILL OF THE ENGLISH NATION. HOW THE ENGLISH
AGREED, CONFEDERATED, COMBINED, AND CONSPIRED TO
DEPOSE THE KING, AND BEAT UP FOR " FOREIGN EMIS-
SARIES" TO COME AND BEGIN THE REBELLION FOR THEM.

N the 6th February, 1685, Charles the Second closed
a life the chronicles of which may be searched in vain,
for a notable act of goodness, wisdom, valor, or virtue. On his death-bed he openly professed the faith
which for years past, if not at all times, he had secretly believed in, but dared not publicly avow—Catholicity. The
man, however, on whom now devolved the triple crown of
England, Scotland, and Ireland—Charles' brother, James,
Duke of York—was one who had neither dissembled nor concealed his religious convictions. He was a sincere Catholic,
and had endured much of trouble and persecution in consequence of his profession of that faith. He was married to the
young and beautiful princess, Mary of Modena, an ardent
Catholic like himself,* and the ultra-Protestant party witnessed his accession to the throne with undisguised chagrin
and sullen discontent.

All writers have agreed in attributing to James the Second
a disregard of the plainest dictates of prudence, if not of the
plainest limits of legality, in the measures he adopted for the
accomplishment of a purpose unquestionably equitable, laud-
able, and beneficent—namely, the abolition of proscription
and persecution for conscience sake, and the establishment of

---

* She was his second wife, and had been married to him at the age of fifteen. By
his first wife, Ann, daughter of Chancellor Hyde, he had too daughters, who were
brought up Protestants by their mother. They were married, one, Mary, to Prince

religious freedom and equality. It may be said, and with perfect truth, that though this was so, though James was rash and headlong, it mattered little after all, for the end he aimed at was so utterly opposed to the will of the English people, so inconsistent with " vested interests" throughout all three kingdoms, that it was out of all possibility he could have succeeded, whether he were politic and cautious, or straightforward. arbitrary, and rash. For the English nation was too strongly bent on thorough persecution, to be barred in its cause, or diverted into tolerance or humanity by any power of king or queen; and already the English people had made it plain that no man should be ruler over them who would not be of their mind on this subject. But James's conduct rendered his overthrow simply inevitable. Before he was well seated on the throne, he had precipitated conflicts with the judges, the bishops, and parliament; the point of contention, to be sure, being mainly his resolution of granting freedom of conscience to all creeds. It was in Ireland, however, that this startling programme evoked the wildest sensation of alarm on the one hand, and rejoicing on the other; and it was there that, inevitably, owing to the vast preponderance of the Catholic population, relative equality appeared to the Protestant eye as absolute Catholic dominance. Two Catholic judges and one Protestant may have been even short of the Catholic proportion; yet the Protestant colony would not look at the question in this way at all, and they called it intolerable Popish ascendancy. James had selected for the carrying out of his views in Ireland a man whose faults greatly resembled his own, Richard Talbot, subsequently Earl and Duke of Tyrconnell. He was devotedly attached to the king; a courtier, not a statesman; rash, vain, self-willed; a faithful and loyal friend, but a famous man to lose a kingdom with.

If the Irish Catholics had indulged in hopes on the accession successively of James's grandfather, father, and brother, what must have been their feelings now? Here, assuredly, there was no room for mistake or doubt. A king resolved to befriend them was on the throne! The land burst forth into

cavern and fastness, came hunted prelate and priest, the surplice and the stole, the chalice and the patten ; and once more, in the open day and in the public churches, the ancient rites were seen. The people, awakened as if from a long trance of sorrow, heaved with a new life, and with faces all beaming and radiant went about in crowds chanting songs of joy and gratitude. One after one, the barriers of exclusion were laid low, and the bulk of the population admitted to equal rights with the colonist-Protestants. In fine, all men were declared equal in the eye of the law, irrespective of creed or race ; an utter reversion of the previous system, which constituted the " colony" the jailors of the fettered nation.

Ireland and England accordingly seethed with Protestant disaffection, but there was an idea that the king would die without legitimate male issue,* and so the general resolution seemed to be that in a few years all would be right, and these abominable ideas of religious tolerance swept away once more. To the consternation and dismay of the anti-tolerance party, however, a son was born to James in June, 1688. There was no standing this. It was the signal for revolt.

On this occasion no native insurrection initiated the revolution. In this crisis of their history—this moment in which was moulded and laid down the basis of the English constitution as it exists to our own time—the English nation asserted by precept and practice the truly singular doctrine, that even for the purpose of overthrowing a legitimate native sovereign, conspiring malcontents act well and wisely in depending upon "foreign emissaries" to come and begin the work—and complete it too! So they invited the Dutch, and the Danes, and the Swedes, and the French calvinists—and indeed, for that matter, foreign emissaries from every country or any country who would aid them—to come and help them in their rebellion against their king. To the Stadtholder of Holland, William Prince of Orange, they offered the throne, having ascertained that he would accept it without any

---

* Four children born to him by his second wife, all died young, and some year

qualms, on the ground that the king to be beheaded or driven away was at once his own uncle and father-in-law.

This remarkable man has been greatly misunderstood, owing to the fact of his name being made the shibboleth of a faction whose sanguinary fanaticism he despised and repudiated. William Henry, Prince of Orange was now in his thirty-seventh year. An impartial and discriminating Catholic historian justly discribes him to us as "fearless of danger, patient, silent, imperious to his enemies, rather a soldier than a statesman, indifferent in religion, and personally adverse to persecution for conscience sake," his great and almost his only public passion being the humiliation of France through the instrumentality of a European coalition. In the great struggle against French preponderance on the continent then being waged by the league of Augsburg, William was on the same side with the rulers of Austria, Germany, and Spain, and even with the Pope ; James, on the other hand, being altogether atttached to France. In his designs on the English throne, however, the Dutch prince practised the grossest deceit on his confederates of the league, protesting to them that he was coming to England solely to compose in a friendly way a domestic quarrel, one of the results of which would be to detach James from the side of France and add England to the league. By means of this duplicity he was able to bring to the aid of his English schemes, men, money, and material contributed tor league purposes by his continental colleagues.

On the 5th of November, 1688, William landed at Torbay in Devonshire. He brought with him a Dutch fleet of twenty-two men of war, twenty-five frigates, twenty-five fire-ships, and about four hundred transports ; conveying in all about fifteen thousand men. If the royal army could have been relied upon, James might easily have disposed of these "invaders" or "liberators ;" but the army went over wholesale to the "foreign emissaries." Thus finding himself surrounded by treason, and having the fate of his hapless father in remembrance, James took refuge in France, where he arrived on 25th December, 1688 ; the Queen and infant Prince

conveyed thither some short time previously, the revolutionary party affected to think the escape of the king an abdication,
the theory being, that by not waiting to be beheaded he had
forfeited the throne.

England and Scotland unmistakably declared for the revolution. Ireland as unquestionably—indeed enthusiastically—
declared for the king ; any other course would be impossible
to a people amongst whom ingratitude has been held infamous,
and against whom want of chivalry or generosity has never
been alleged. In proportion as the Catholic population expressed their sympathy with the king, the "colony" Protestants and Cromwellianite garrisons manifested their adhesion
to the rebel cause, and began to flock from all sides into
the strong places of Ulster, bringing with them their arms
and ammunition. Tyrconnel, who had vainly endeavored
to call in the government arms in their hands (as militia,)
now commissioned several of the Catholic nobility and gentry
to raise regiments of more certain loyalty for the king's service. Of recruits there was no lack, but of the use of arms or
knowledge of drill or discipline, these recruits knew absolutely
nothing ; and of arms, of equipments, or of war material—especially of cannon—Tyrconnel found himself almost entirely destitute. The malcontents, on the other hand, constituted that class
which for at least forty years past had enjoyed by law the sole
right to possess arms, and who had from childhood, of necessity, been trained to use them. The royalist force which
the viceroy sent to occupy Derry (a Catholic regiment newly
raised by Lord Antrim), incredible as it may appear, had for
the greater part no better arms than clubs and skians. It is
not greatly to be wondered at that the Protestant citizens—
amongst whom, as well as throughout all the Protestant districts in Ireland, anonymous letters had been circulated, giving
out an "intended Popish massacre " * of all the Protestants on
the 9th December—feared to admit such a gathering within
their walls. "The impression made by the report of the intended massacre, and the contempt naturally entertained for

toes armed in so rude a fashion," were as a matter of fact the chief incentives to the "closing of the gates of Derry," which event we may set down as the formal inauguration of the rebellion in Ireland.

LXIII.—HOW WILLIAM AND JAMES MET FACE TO FACE AT THE BOYNE. A PLAIN SKETCH OF THE BATTLE FIELD AND THE TACTICS OF THE DAY.

EIGHTEEN months afterwards, two armies stood face to face on the banks of the Boyne. King James and Prince William for the first time were to contest in person the issues between them.

The interval had not been without its events. In England the revolution encountered no opposition, and William was free to bring against Ireland and Scotland the full strength of his British levies, as well as of his foreign auxiliaries. Ireland, Tyrconnell was quite sanguine of holding for King James, even though at the worst England should be lost ; and to arouse to the full the enthusiasm of the devoted Gaels, nay possibly to bring back to their allegiance the rebellious Ulster Protestants, he urged the king to come to Ireland and assume in person the direction of affairs. King Louis of France concurred in those views, and a squadron was prepared at Brest to carry the fugitive back to his dominions. "Accompanied by his natural sons, the Duke of Berwick and the Grand Prior Fitzjames, by Lieutenant-Generals de Rosen and de Maumont, Majors-General de Persignan and de Lery (or Geraldine), about a hundred officers of all ranks, and one thousand two hundred veterans, James sailed from Brest with a fleet of thirty-three vessels, and landed at Kinsale on the 12th day of March (old style). His reception by the southern population was enthusiastic in the extreme. From Kinsale to Cork, from Cork to Dublin, his progress was accompanied by Gaelic songs and dances, by Latin orations, loyal addresses, and all the demonstrations with which a popular favorite can

be welcomed. Nothing was remembered by that easily pacified people but his great misfortunes, and his steady fidelity
to his and their religion. The royal entry into Dublin was the
crowning pageant of this delusive restoration. With the tact
and taste for such demonstrations hereditary in the citizens,
the trades and arts were marshalled before him. Two venerable harpers played on their national instruments near the
gate by which he entered ; a number of religious in their robes,
with a huge cross at their head, chanted as they went ; forty
young girls dressed in white, danced the ancient *Rinka*, scat-
tering flowers as they danced. The Earl of Tyrconnell, lately
raised to a dukedom, the judges, the mayor and corporation,
completed the procession which marched over newly sanded
streets beneath arches of evergreens, and windows hung with
' tapestry and cloth of Arras.' But, of all the incidents of that
striking ceremonial, nothing more powerfully impressed the
popular imagination than the green flag floating from the
main tower of the castle bearing the significant inscription :
' *now or never—now and for ever.*' "

So far well ; but when he came to look into the important
matter of material for war, a woful state of things confronted
James. As we have already seen, for forty years past, in
pursuance of acts of parliament rigorously enforced, no Catholic or native Irishman had been allowed to learn a trade,
to inhabit walled towns, or to possess arms. As a consequence, when the Protestants, whom alone for nearly half a
century the law allowed to learn to make, repair, or use firearms, fled to the north, there was in all the island scarcely a
gunsmith or armorer on whom the king could rely. Such
Protestant artizans as remained, "when obliged to set about
repairing guns or forging spears, threw every possible obstacle
in the way, or executed the duty in such a manner as to leave
the weapon next to useless in the hour of action ; while night
and day the fires blazed and the anvils rang in the preparation of the best arms for the Williamites." The want of cannon was most keenly felt on the king's side. At the time of
the so-called siege of Derry (progressing when James
arrived), "there was not a single battering cannon fit for use

in Ireland; and there were only twelve field pieces." As a consequence, there was, as there could have been, no real *siege* of Derry. The place was *blockaded* more or less loosely for some months—closely towards the end. The inhabitants bore the privations of the blockade with great endurance and heroism, though certainly not greater than that exhibited by the besieged in severer blockades elsewhere during the war.* It were pitiful and unworthy to deny to the brave rebels of Derry all that such heroic perseverance as theirs deserves. Such qualities as they displayed—such sufferings cheerfully borne for a cause they judged just and holy—deserve honor and acclaim wherever found. But, after all, as I have pointed out, it was a blockade, not a siege, they endured; and their courage was put to no such test as that which tried the citizens of Limerick two or three years subsequently.

"Meanwhile a splendidly appointed Williamite army had been collected at Chester. It was commanded by the veteran Duke Schomberg, and amounted to ten thousand men. They landed at Bangor, county Down, 13th August, 1689, and on the 17th took possession of Belfast." Little was accomplished on either side up to the summer following, when the news that William himself had resolved to take the field in Ireland, flung the Ulster rebels into a state of enthusiastic rejoicing, and filled the royalists with concern. All felt now that the crisis was at hand. On the 14th June William landed at Carrickfergus, surrounded by a throng of veteran generals of continental fame, princes and peers, English and foreign. "At Belfast, his first headquarters, he ascertained the forces at his disposal to be upwards of forty thousand men, 'a strange medley of all nations'—Scandinavians, Swiss, Dutch, Prussians,

---

* Notably, for instance, Fort Charlemont, held for the king by the gallant O'Regan with eight hundred men; besieged by Schomberg at the head of more than as many thousands, with a splendid artillery train. The garrison, we are told, were reduced by hunger, to the last extremity, and at length offered to surrender if allowed to march out with all the honors of war. Schomberg complied, and then, says a chronicler, "eight hundred men, with a large number of women and children, came forth, eagerly gnawing pieces of dry hides with the hair on; a small portion of filthy meal and a few pounds of tainted beef being the only provisions remaining in the fort."

Huguenot-French, English, Scotch, Scotch-Irish, and Anglo-Irish." "On the 16th of June, James, informed of William's arrival, marched northward at the head of twenty thousand men, French and Irish, to meet him. On the 22d James was at Dundalk, and William at Newry. As the latter advanced, the Jacobites retired and finally chose their ground at the Boyne, resolved to hazard a battle (even against such odds) for the preservation of Dublin and the safety of the province of Leinster. *

No military opinion has ever been uttered of that reso-lution, save that it never should have been taken. The won-der is not that William forced the Boyne ; all the marvel and the madness was that such an army as James's (especially, when commanded by such a man) ever attempted to defend it. Not merely had William nearly 50,000 men against James's 23,000 ; but whereas the former force, all save a few thousand of the Ulster levies (and these, skilful and experienced sharp-shooters), were veteran troops, horse and foot, splendidly equipped, and supported by the finest park of artillery per-haps ever seen in Ireland ; the latter army, with the exception of a few thousand French, were nearly all raw recruits hasti-ly collected within a few months past from a population un-acquainted with the use of firearms, and who had, of course, never been under fire in the field, and now had of artillery but six field pieces to support them. But even if this disparity had never existed, the contrast between the commanders would in itself have made all the difference possible. William was an experienced military tactician, brave, cool, prescient, firm and resolute. James, as Duke of York, had distinguished himself bravely and honorably on land and sea, so that the charges of absolute cowardice often urged against him can scarcely be just. But his whole conduct of affairs in this Irish campaign was simply miserable. Weak, vacillating. capricious, selfish, it is no wonder that one of the French officers, stung to mad-ness by his inexplicable pusillanimity and disgraceful bung-ling, should have exclaimed aloud to him : " Sire, if you had a hundred kingdoms you would lose them all." A like sentiment found utterance in the memorable words of an Irish officer when brought a prisoner after the battle into the presence of the Williamite council of war : *Exchange commanders with us*, gentlemen, and even with all the other odds against us, *we'll fight the battle over again.*

But now the die was cast. The resolve on James's part most falteringly taken,* was fixed at last. Uncle and nephew, sovereign and invader, were to put their quarrel to the issue of a battle on the morrow.

---

* Even when the whole of such arrangements and dispositions for battle as he (after innumerable vacillations had ordered, had been made, James, at the last moment, on the very eve of battle, once again capriciously changed his mind, said he would fall back to Dublin, and actually sent off thither on the moment the baggage, together with six of the twelve cannon which constituted his entire artillery, and some portion of his troops ! Then, again, after these had gone off beyond recall, he as capriciously changed his mind once more, and resolved to await battle then and there at the Boyne !

LXIV.—" BEFORE THE BATTLE."

ARLY on the **morning of** the 30th June, 1690, Wil- liam's army **approached** the Boyne in **three divi-** sions. "Such was his **impatience** to behold the enemy **he was to** fight, and the ground **they had** taken up, that by the **time the ad-** vance guard was **within view of** the Jacobite camp, **he was in front** of them, having ridden forward from the head of his own division. Then it was that he beheld a sight which, yet un- stirred by soldier shout or cannon shot, unstained by blood or death, might well gladden the heart of him who gazed, and warm with its glorious beauties even a colder nature than his! He stood upon a height, and beheld beneath him and beyond him, with the clearness of a map and the gorgeous beauty of a dream, a view as beautiful as the eye can scan.

harvest were blended with green fields and greener trees, and a sweet river flowing calmly on in winding beauty through a valley whose banks rose gently from its waters, until in lofty hills they touch the opposite horizon, bending and undulating into forms of beauty." * " To the south-east the steeples and castle of Drogheda, from which floated the flags of James and Louis, appeared in the mid-distance ; whilst seaward might be seen the splendid fleet which attended the motions of the Williamite army. But of more interest to the phlegmatic but experienced commander, whose eagle eye now wandered over the enchanting panorama, were the lines of white tents, the waving banners, and moving bodies of troops which, to the south-west, between the river and Donore Hill indicated the position of James's camp." †

Having viewed the ground carefully, William selected the Oldbridge fords for the principal attack, and fixed upon sites for batteries to command the opposite or Jacobite bank. He then rode a short way up the river, and alighted to take some refreshment. On his return he was fired upon by some field pieces at the other side of the river, the first shot striking to the earth one of the group beside the prince. A second shot followed ; the ball struck the river bank, glanced upwards, and wounded William slightly. He sank upon his horse's neck, and a shout of exultation burst from the Irish camp, where it was believed he was killed. He was not much hurt, however, and rode amongst his own lines to assure his troops of his safety ; and shouts of triumph and defiance from the Williamite ranks soon apprised the Irish of their error.

That night—that anxious night !—was devoted by William to the most careful planning and arrangement for the morrow's strife. But ere we notice these plans or approach that struggle, it may be well to describe for young readers with all possible simplicity the battlefield of the Boyne, and the nature of the military operations of which it was the scene.

The Boyne enters the Irish sea a mile or more to the east of

---

* *Williamite and Jacobite Wars in Ireland*, by Dr. Cane.

† The *Hart* for March, 1870: The " Battle of the Boyne " by M. J. M'Cann

Drogheda, but for a mile or two above or to the west of that
town, the sea-tides reach and rise and fall in the river. Two
miles and a half up the river from Drogheda, on the southern
bank, is the little village of Oldbridge. About five miles in a
direct line due west of Oldbridge (but considerably more by
the curve of the river, which between these points bends deeply southward), stands the town of Slane on the northern
bank. The ground rises rather rapidly from the river at Oldbridge, sloping backwards, or southwards, about a mile, to
the hill of Donore, on the crest of which stand a little ruined
church (it was a ruin even in 1690) and a grave-yard ; three
miles and a half further southward than Donore, on the road
to Dublin from Oldbridge, stands Duleek.

James's camp was pitched on the northern slopes of Donore,
looking down upon the river at Oldbridge. James himself
slept and had his headquarters in the little ruined church already mentioned.

Directly opposite to Oldbridge, on the northern side of the
river, the ground, as on the south side, rises rather abruptly,
sloping backward, forming a hill called Tullyallen. This hill
is intersected by a ravine north and south, leading down to
the river, its mouth on the northern brink being directly opposite to Oldbridge. The ravine is now called King William's
Glen. On and behind Tullyallen Hill, William's camp was
pitched, looking southwards, towards, but not altogether in
sight of James's, on the other side of the river.

At this time of the year, July, the Boyne was fordable at several places up the river towards Slane. The easiest fords, however, were at Oldbridge, where, when the sea-tide was at
lowest ebb, the water was not three feet deep.

To force these fords, or some of them, was William's task.
To defend them, was James's endeavor.

The main difficulty in crossing a ford in the face of an opposing army, is that the enemy almost invariably has batteries
to play on the fords with shot and shell, and troops ready at
hand to charge the crossing party the instant they attempt to
" form " on reaching the bank, if they succeed in reaching it.

vice, and if assailants have batteries to "cover" the passage of their fording parties by a strong cannonade, *i. e.* to prevent (by shot and shell fired over their heads at the bank they rush for) the formation there of any troops to charge them on reaching the shore, the ford is, as a general rule, sure to be forced.

James had not a single cannon or howitzer at the fords. From fifty splendid field pieces and mortars William rained shot and shell on the Jacobite bank.

William's plan of attack was to outflank James's left by sending a strong force up the river towards Slane, where they were to cross and attack the Jacobite flank and rear; while he, with the full strength of his main army (the centre under Schomberg senior, the extreme left under himself), would, under cover of a furious cannonade, force all the fords at and below Oldbridge.

It was only at the last moment that James was brought to perceive the deadly danger of being flanked from Slane, and he then detailed merely a force of five hundred dragoons under the gallant Sir Neal O'Neill to defend the extreme left there. His attention until the mid-hour of battle next day, was mainly given to the (Oldbridge) fords in his front, and his sole reliance for their defence was on some poor breast-works and farm-buildings to shelter musketry-men; trusting for the rest to hand-to-hand encounters when the enemy should have come across! In fact, he had no other reliance, since he was without artillery to defend the fords.

All else being settled, ere the anxious council-holders on each side sought their couches, the pass-word for the morning and the distinguishing badges were announced. The Jacobite soldiers wore white cockades. William chose *green* for *his* colors. Every man on his side was ordered to wear a green bough or sprig in his hat, and the word was to be "Westminster."

LXV.—THE BATTLE OF THE BOYNE.

UESDAY the 1st July, 1690, dawned cloudlessly on
those embattled hosts, and as the early sunlight
streamed out from over the eastern hills, the stillness of
that summer morning was broken by the Williamite
drums and bugles sounding the *generale.* In accordance with
the plan of battle arranged the previous night, the first move on
William's side was the march of ten thousand men (the Scotch
foot-guards under Lieutenant-General Douglas, and the Danish horse under Meinhart Schomberg), with five pieces of artillery, for the bridge of Slane, where, and at the fords between it and Ross-na-ree, (two miles nearer to Oldbridge), they
were to cross the river, and turn the left flank of James's army.
The infantry portion of this force crossing at Slane, while the
horse were getting over at Ross-na-ree, came upon Sir Neal
O'Neill and his five hundred dragoons on the extreme left of
the Jacobite position. For fully an hour did the gallant
O'Neill hold this force in check, he himself falling mortally
wounded in the thick of the fight. But soon, the Danish horse
crossing at Ross-na-ree, the full force of ten thousand men
united and advanced upon the Jacobite flank, endeavoring to
get between the royalist army and Duleek. Just at this moment, however, there arrived a force of French and Swiss infantry, and some Irish horse and foot, with six pieces of cannon under Lauzun, sent up hurriedly from Oldbridge by James,
who now began to think all the fight would be on his left.
Lauzun so skilfully posted his checking force on the slope of
a hill with a marsh in front, that Douglas and Schomberg,
notwithstanding their enormous numerical superiority, halted
and did not venture on an attack until they had sent for and
obtained an additional supply of troops. Then only did their

Duleek, completely overlapping or flanking the Jacobite left wing.

Meanwhile, about ten o'clock in the forenoon, Schomberg the elder (in charge of the Williamite centre), finding that his son and Douglas had made good their way across on the extreme right, and had the Jacobites well engaged there, gave the word for the passage of Oldbridge fords. Tyrconnel's regiment of foot guards, with other Irish foot (only a few of them being armed with muskets), occupied the ruined breastwork fences and farm buildings on the opposite side; having some cavalry drawn up behind the low hills close by to support them. But the Williamites had a way for emptying these breastworks and clearing the bank for their fording parties. Fifty pieces of cannon that had during the morning almost completely battered down the temporary defences on the southern bank, now opened simultaneously, shaking the hills with their thunders, and sweeping the whole of the Irish position with their iron storm; while the bombs from William's mortar batteries searched every part of the field. Under cover of this tremendous fire, to which the Irish had not even a single field-piece to reply, * the van of the splendidly-appointed Williamite infantry issued from King William's Glen, and plunged into the stream. "Count Solme's Dutch Blue Guards, two thousand strong, reputed the best infantry regiment in the world, led the way at the principal ford opposite Oldbridge, followed by the Brandenburghers. Close on their left were the Londonderries and Enniskillen foot; below whom entered a long column of French Huguenots, under the veteran Calimotte. A little below the Huguenots were the main body of the English, under Sir John Hanmer and Count Nassau; and still lower down, the Danes, under Colonel Cutts. In all about ten thousand of the flower of the infantry of Europe, struggling through a quarter of a mile of the river, and almost hidden beneath flashing arms and green boughs." †

---

* The six retained by James had been forwarded to Lauzun on the extreme left.

† *Battle of the Boyne*, by M. J. M'Cann. No one desiring to trace closely, and fully understand the events of this memorable battle, should omit to read (Sir Wil-

As they neared the southern bank, the roar of cannon ceased —a breathless pause of suspense ensued. Then a wild cheer rung from the Irish lines ; and such of the troops as had guns opened fire. An utterly ineffective volley it was ; so ill-directed, that the Williamite accounts say it did not kill a man ; and then the veterans of a hundred continental battle-fields knew they had only raw Irish peasant levies on the bank before them. There being no artillery (as already frequently noted) to play on the fording parties while crossing, and there being so little water in the river, the passage of the fords was easily effected.

The Dutch Guards were the first to the bank, where they instantly formed. Here they were charged by the Irish foot ; but before the withering fire of the cool and skilful foreign veterans, these raw levies were cut up instantly, and driven flying behind the fences. The truth became plain after two or three endeavors to bring them to the charge, that they were not fit for such work. Now, however, was the time for Hamilton, at the head of the only well-disciplined Irish force on the field—the horse—to show what his men could do. The hedges, which had not been levelled for the purpose, did not prevent their charge. The ground literally trembled beneath the onset of this splendid force. Irresistible as an avalanche, they struck the third battalion of Dutch Blues while yet in the stream, and hurled them back. The Brandenburghers turned and fled. The Huguenots, who were not so quick in escape, were broken through, and their commander Calimotte cut down.

Schomberg had remained on the northern bank with a chosen body of foot as a reserve. He saw with excitement the sudden crash of the Irish horse and its effects ; and was prepared to push forward the reserve, when word reached him that his old friend Calimotte had fallen ! Without waiting for helmet or cuirass he dashed forward, his white hair float-

---

liam) Wilde's beautiful and valuable work the *Boyne und Blackwater.* I follow as closely as possible the briefer accounts of the battle by Mr. M'Cann in the *Harp,* and by Dr. Cane in his *Williamite Wars,* with occasional corrections from *Macariæ Excidium,* from Sir William Wilde's work, and other authorities.

ing in the wind. In the river he met and strove to rally the flying Huguenots. " Come on, come on, messieurs ; behold your persecutors," cried the old warrior, alluding to the French infantry on the other side. They were the last words he ever spoke. Tyrconnel's Irish horse-guards, returning from one of their charges, again broke clear through and through the Huguenots, cleaving Schomberg's head with two fearful sabre wounds, and lodging a bullet in his neck. When the wave of battle had passed, the lifeless body of the old general lay amongst the human debris that marked its track. He had quickly followed, not only across the Boyne but to another world, his brave companion in arms whose fall he had sought to avenge.

All this time William, at the head of some five thousand of the flower of his cavalry, lay behind the slopes of Tullyallen, close by the lowest ford on the extreme left of his army, wait- ing anxiously for news of Schomberg's passage at Oldbridge. But now learning that his centre had been repulsed, he dis- engaged his wounded arm from its sling, and calling aloud to his troops to follow him, plunged boldly into the stream. The water was deepest at this ford, for it was nearest to the sea, and the tide, which was out at the hour fixed for crossing in the morning, was now beginning to rise. William and his five thousand cavalry reached the south bank with difficulty. Marshalling his force on the shore with marvellous celerity, he did not wait to be charged, but rushed furiously forward upon the Irish right flank. The Irish command at this point was held by the young Duke of Berwick with some squadrons of Irish horse, some French infantry, and Irish pikemen. The Irish were just starting to charge the Williamites at the back, when the latter, as already noted, dashed forward to anticipate such a movement by a charge upon them, so that both bodies of horse were simultaneously under way, filled with all the vehemence and fury which could be imparted by consciousness of the issues depending on the collision now at hand. As they neared each other the excitement became choking, and above the thunder of the horses' feet on the sward could be heard

shouts of every troop officer "Close—close up ; for God's sake,
closer! closer!" On they came, careering like the whirlwind
—and then!—What a crash! Like a thunder-bolt the Irish
horse broke clear through the Williamites. Those who watched from the hill above, say that when both those furious billows
met, there was barely a second of time (a year of agonized
suspense it seemed at the moment to some of the lookers on)
during which the wild surges rendered it uncertain which one
was to bear down the other. But in one instant the gazers
beheld the white plumed form of young Berwick at the head
of the Irish cavalry far into the middle of the Williamite mass ;
and soon, with a shout—a roar that rose over all the din of battle—a frantic peal of exultation and vengeance—the Irish absolutely swept the Dutch and Enniskillen cavalry down the
slopes upon the river, leaving in their track only a broken
crowd of unhorsed or ridden-down foes, whom the Irish pikemen finished.

But now the heavy firing from Oldbridge announced that
the Williamite centre was crossing once more, and soon it
became clear that even though the Irish repulsed man for man,
there still were enough of their foes to make a lodgment on
the bank too powerful to be resisted. Bodies of his troops
streaming down to him from the centre, gladly proclaimed to
William that they were across again there. Rallying his left
wing with these aids he advanced once more. He now had
infantry to check the ever-dreaded charges of the Irish horse,
and so pressing steadily onward, he drove the Irish back along
the lane leading from the river to Sheephouse, a small hamlet
half way between Donore and the Boyne. Here the Irish
were evidently prepared to make a stand. William, who
throughout this battle exhibited a bravery—a cool, courageous recklessness of personal peril, which no general ever
surpassed, now led in person a charge by all his left wing
forces. But he found himself flanked by the Irish foot posted
in the hedges and cabins, and confronted by the invincible
cavalry. He turned a moment from the head of the Ennis-
killens and rode to the rear to hurry up the Dutch. The Ennis-

they thought the king's movement was to be followed by them, so they turned, and William coming up with the Dutch, met them flying pell mell. He now handed over the Dutch to Ginckle, and took himself the unsteady Ulstermen in charge. He appealed entreatingly to them to rally and stand by him, and not to ruin all by their weakness at such a critical moment. By this time the Huguenot horse also came up, and the whole combining, William a third time advanced. The Williamite accounts describe to us the conflict that now ensued at this point as one of the most desperate cavalry combats of the whole war. According to the same authorities, the Dutch recoiled, and Ginckle had to throw himself in their rear to prevent a disordered flight.* William, dauntless and daring, was in the thickest of the fight, cheering, exhorting, leading his men. The gallant Berwick and Sheldon, on the other hand, now assisted by some additional Irish hurried up from the centre, pressed their foes with resistless energy. Brave and highly disciplined those foes were undoubtedly ; nevertheless, once more down the lane went the Williamite horse and foot, with the Irish cavalry in full pursuit.

This time, "like Rupert at the battle of Edge Hill," the Irish " pursued too far." While all that has been described so far was occurring on the Jacobite right, at the centre (Oldbridge), overwhelming masses of William's cavalry and infantry had, notwithstanding the best efforts of the French and Irish foot, forced all the fords and mastered everything at that point. In detached masses they were now penetrating all the approaches to Donore, in the direction of Sheephouse, driving the Jacobites before them. While the Irish cavalry on the right, as above described, were in pursuit of the Williamites, the lane leading to Sheephouse was left unoccupied. This being observed by two regiments of Williamite dragoons, they quickly dismounted and lined the hedges of the lane, at the same time sending word to Ginckle to take advantage of what they were about to do. The Irish cavalry after their charge, now returned slowly through the lane to

resume their position.   Suddenly and to their utter consternation they found themselves assailed by a close and
deadly fusillade from the ambuscade around them, so close,
so deadly, the guns almost touched each horseman ; and
there was no room for evolution in the narrow place.   While
they were thus disordered, whole masses of troops were flung
upon them ; Ginckle in their rear, their lately routed but now
rallied foes on the right, and all combining, pressed the over-
borne but not outbraved heroes up the lane upon Donore.

Here the Irish turned doggedly for a resolute stand ; and
William saw that though forced indeed from the river, they
considered themselves far from being beaten yet.   After a few
ineffectual charges, he suspended the attack, in order to reform his ranks for a grand assault in full force.

It was at this moment—while his devoted little army, still
all undaunted, were nerving themselves for the crisis of their
fate—that James, yielding readily to the advice of Tyrconnel
and Lauzun (which quite accorded with his own anxiety),
fled precipitately for Dublin; taking with him as a guard for
his person the indignant and exasperated Sarsfield and his
splendid cavalry regiment, at that moment so sorely needed
on the field!

Some Irish writers, embittered against James for this
flight, go so far as to contend that had he remained and
handled his troops skilfully, it was still within possibility to
turn the fortunes of the day, and drive William beyond the
river.   The point is untenable.   The Jacobite left, right, and
centre had been driven in, and the Williamite forces were all
now in full conjunction in front.   It was possible to hold
William in check; to dispute with him each mile of ground
to Dublin ; but Napoleon himself could not (*with only six field
pieces*) have beaten William at the Boyne.

It is certain, however, that the Irish troops themselves
were not of this mind ; for when they heard that Donore was
to be relinquished, and that they must fall back on Duleek,
they murmured and groaned aloud, and passionately declared it was snatching from them a certain victory ! * Never-

theless, to fall back was now essential to their safety; for already bodies of Williamite troops were streaming away on the Jacobite left towards Duleek, designing to get in the Irish rear. To meet this movement, the Irish left was swung round accordingly, and pushed on also, mile for mile, with the flanking Williamites; until eventually the struggle in front was virtually abandoned by both parties, and the competition was all as to the manœuvres and counter-manœuvres on the Duleek road; the Irish falling back, yet facing the enemy, and making their retreat the retiring movement of an overpowered army, by no means the flight of one routed. At Duleek they turned to bay, taking up a strong position on the south of the little stream which passes the town. The Williamites came on, and having looked at the ground and the disposition of the Jacobite forces, deemed it well to offer battle no further, but to rest content, as well they might, with the substantial victory of having forced the Boyne and vanquished the Stuart king.

LXVI.—HOW JAMES ABANDONED THE STRUGGLE; BUT THE IRISH WOULD NOT GIVE UP.

ITH all the odds at which this battle was fought, and important as were its ultimate consequences, the immediate gain for William was simply that he had crossed the Boyne. He had not a captured gun, and scarcely a standard,* to show for his victory. The vanquished had, as we have seen, effected a retreat in almost perfect order, bringing off the few guns they possessed at the beginning of the fight. In fine, of the usual tokens of a victory—namely, captured guns, standards, baggage, or prisoners—William's own chroniclers confess he had nought to show; while, according to the same accounts, his loss in killed and wounded nearly equalled that of the royalists.

This was almost entirely owing to the Irish and French cavalry regiments. They saved the army. They did more—their conduct on that day surrounded the lost cause with a halo of glory which defeat could not dim.

Could there have been any such " exchange of commanders " as the captured Irish officer challenged—had the Irish a general of real ability, of heart and courage, zeal and determination, to command them,—all that had so far been lost or gained at the Boyne would have proved of little account indeed. But James seemed imbecile. He fled early in the day, reached Dublin before evening ; recommended that no further struggle should be attempted in Ireland; and advised his adherents to make the best terms they could for themselves. He had seen a newly raised and only half-armed Irish foot regiment, it seems, torn by shot and shell,

---

* Story, the Williamite chaplain, says: "Only one or two," and complains of

break and fly in utter confusion when charged by cavalry, and the miserable man could talk of nothing but of their bad conduct that had lost him the crown! While he, most fleet at flying, was thus childishly scolding in Dublin Castle, the devoted Irish were even yet keeping William's fifty thousand men at bay, retreating slowly and in good order from Donore!

At five o'clock next morning he quitted Dublin; and, leaving two troops of horse "to defend the bridge at Bray as long as they could, should the enemy come up," he fled through Wicklow to the south of Ireland. At Kinsale he hurriedly embarked on board the French squadron, and sailed for Brest, where he arrived on the 20th July; being himself the first messenger with the news of his defeat.

The Irish army on reaching Dublin found they were without king or captain-general. They had been abandoned and advised to make favor with the conquerer. This, however, was not their mind. James mistook his men. *He* might fly and resign if he would; but the cause—the country —*La Patrie*—remained. So the Irish resolved not to surrender. They had fought for James at the Boyne; they would now fight for Ireland on the Shannon.

"To Limerick! To Limerick!" became the cry. The superior wisdom of the plan of campaign advised by Sarsfield from the beginning—defence of the line of the Shannon—was now triumphantly vindicated. Freely surrendering as indefensible, Dublin, Kilkenny, Waterford, and Dungannon, to Limerick the Irish now turned from all directions. The chronicles of the time state that the soldiers came to that rallying point from the most distant places, "in companies, in scores, in groups; nay, in twos and threes," without any order or command to that effect. On the contrary, James had directed them all to surrender, and every consideration of personal safety counselled them to disband and seek their homes. But no! They had an idea that on the Shannon Sarsfield would yet make a gallant stand beneath the green flag; and so thither their steps were bent!

place was at this time held by an old hero, whose name deserved to be linked with that of Sarsfield—Colonel Richard Grace, a confederate Catholic royalist of 1641, now laden with years, but as bold of heart and brave of spirit as when first he drew a sword for Ireland. To reduce Athlone, William detached from his main army at Dublin, Lieutenant-General Douglas with twelve thousand men, a train of twelve cannon, and two mortars. The town stood then, as it stands now, partly on the Leinster, and partly on the Connacht side of the Shannon river, or rather of the short and narrow neck of water, which at that point links two of the "loughs" or wide expanses of the river, that like a great chain of lakes runs north and south for fifty miles between Limerick and Lough Allen. That portion of Athlone on the west, or Connacht side of the river was called the "Irish town;" that on the east or Leinster side, the "English town." The castle and chief fortifications lay on the west side. The governor deemed the English town untenable against Douglas's artillery, so he demolished that entire suburb, broke down the bridge, and put all defences on the western side of the river into the best condition possible to withstand assault.

On the 17th of July, 1690, Douglas arrived before Athlone, and sent an insolent message to the governor demanding immediate surrender. Veteran Grace drew a pistol from his belt, and firing over the head of the affrighted envoy, answered to the effect that "that was his answer" *this* time, but something severer would be his reply to any such message repeated. Next day Douglas with great earnestness planted his batteries, and for two days following played on the old castle walls with might and main. But he received in return such compliments of the same kind from Colonel Grace as to make him more than dubious as to the result of his bombardment. After a week had been thus spent, news full of alarm for Douglas reached him. Sarsfield—name of terror already—was said to be coming up from Limerick to catch him at Athlone! If old Grace would only surrender now; just to let him, Douglas, get away in time, it would be a blessed

the 24th the old hero on the Connacht side *hung out the red flag.** Douglas, maddened at this, opened on the instant a furious cannonade, but received just as furious a salute from Governor Grace, accompanied moreover by the most unkind shouts of derision and defiance from the western shore. Douglas now gave up : there was nothing for it but to run ! Sarsfield might be upon him if he longer delayed. So he and his ten thousand fled from Athlone, revenging themselves for their discomfiture there by ravaging the inhabitants of all the country through which they passed. Old Governor Grace made a triumphal circuit of Athlone walls, amidst the enthusiastic ovations of the garrison and townspeople. Athlone was saved—this time. Once again, however, it was to endure a siege as memorable, and to make a defence still more glorious, though not, like this one, crowned with victory !

---

* Which betokens resistance *a l' outrance ;* refusal of capitulation or quarter.

LXVII.—HOW WILLIAM SAT DOWN BEFORE LIMERICK AND BE-
GAN THE SIEGE. SARSFIELD'S MIDNIGHT RIDE—THE FATE
OF WILLIAM'S SIEGE TRAIN.

PON Limerick now all interest centred. On the 7th of
August William reached Cahirconlish, about seven
miles south-east of the city, where he encamped, his
force amounting to about twenty-eight thousand men.
On the evening of the 8th, Douglas with the ten thousand
runaway besiegers of Athlone, joined him, raising his force to
thirty-eight thousand. At this time there were, on the other
hand, in the city barely ten thousand infantry ; about four
thousand cavalry being encamped on the Clare side. When
the courtier commanders, Tyrconnel and Lauzun, had estimated William's forces, and viewed the defences of the city,
they absolutely scoffed at the idea of defending it, and directed its surrender. Sarsfield and the Irish royalists, however,
boldly declared they would not submit to this, and said they
would themselves defend the city. In this they were
thoroughly and heartily seconded and supported by the gallant Berwick. Lauzun again inspected the walls, gates, bastions, etc., and as his final opinion declared that the place
" could be taken *with roasted apples.*" Hereupon Tyrconnel,
Lauzun, and all the French and Swiss departed for Galway,
taking with them everything they could control of stores,
arms, and ammunition !

This looked like desertion and betrayal indeed. The taking
away of the stores and ammunition, after Sarsfield and Berwick, and even *the citizens themselves*, had declared they
would defend the city, was the most scandalous part of the
proceeding. Nevertheless, undismayed, Sarsfield, assisted by
a French officer of engineers, De Boisseleau, who, dissenting

boldly set about preparing Limerick for siege. Happily for the national honor of Ireland, the miserable court party thus cruelly deserted Limerick. That base abandonment left all the glory of its defence to the brave heroes who remained.

De Boisseleau was named governor of the city, and Sarsfield commander of the horse. It was decided that the latter force should be posted on the Clare side of the Shannon, opposite the city (with which communication was kept up by the bridges), its chief duty being at all hazards to prevent the Williamites from crossing to that shore at any of the fords above the city. De Boisseleau meanwhile was to conduct the engineering operations of the defence.

It was true enough that Lauzun, when he scoffed at those defences, saw very poor chance for the city, as far as ramparts of stone and mortar were concerned. "The city," we are told, "had neither outworks, glacis, fosses, half-moons, or horn works. An old wall flanked with a few tottering towers, but without either ditch or parapet, was its only defence."* However, De Boisseleau soon set to work to improve upon these, mounting batteries, and digging covered ways or counterscarps ; the citizens, gentle and simple, and even the women and children, working from sunrise to sunset at the construction or strengthening of defences.

Early on the 9th of August, 1690, William drew from his encampment at Cahirconlish, and, confident of an easy victory, sat down before Limerick. That day he occupied himself in selecting favorable sites for batteries to command the city, and in truth, owing to the formation of the ground, the city was at nearly every point nakedly exposed to his guns. He next sent in a summons to surrender, but De Boisseleau courteously replied that " he hoped he should merit his opinion more by a vigorous defence than a shameful surrender of a fortress which he had been entrusted with."†

The siege now began. William's bombardment, however, proceeded slowly ; and the Limerick gunners, on the other

---

* *First Siege of Limerick :* M. J. M'Cann

hand, were much more active and vigorous than he had expected. On Monday, the 11th, their fire compelled him to shift his field train entirely out of range; and on the next day, as if intent on following up such practice, their balls fell so thickly about his own tent, killing several persons, that he had to shift his own quarters also. But in a day or two he meant to be in a position to pay back these attentions with heavy interest, and to reduce those old walls despite all resistance. In fine, there was coming up to him from Waterford a magnificent battering train, together with immense stores of ammunition, and, what was nearly as effective for him as the seige train, a number of pontoon-boats of tin or sheet copper, which would soon enable him to pass the Shannon where he pleased. So he took very coolly the resistance so far offered from the city. For in a day more Limerick would be absolutely at his mercy!

So thought William; and so seemed the inevitable fact. But there was a bold heart and an active brain at work at that very moment planning a deed destined to immortalize its author to all time, and to baffle William's now all-but-accomplished designs on Limerick!

On Sunday, the 10th, the battering train and its convoy had reached Cashel. On Monday, the 11th, they reached a place called Ballyncety, within nine or ten miles of the Williamite camp. The country through which they had passed was all in the hands of their own garrisons or patrols; yet they had so important and precious a charge that they had watched it jealously so far; but now there were virtually at the camp—only a few miles in its rear: and so the convoy, when night fell, drew the siege train and the vast line of ammunition wagons, the pontoon boats and store-loads, into a field close to an old ruined castle, and, duly posting night sentries, gave themselves to repose.

That day, an Anglicized Irishman, one Manus O'Brien, a Protestant landlord in the neighborhood of Limerick, came into the Williamite camp with a piece of news. Sarsfield at the head of five hundred picked men, had ridden off the night before on some mysterious enterprise in the direction of Killaloe ; and the informer, from Sarsfield's character judged rightly that something important was afoot, and earnestly assured the Williamites that nothing was too desperate for that commander to accomplish.

The Williamite officers made little of this. They thought the fellow was only anxious to make much of a trifle, by way of securing favor for himself. Besides, they knew of nothing in the direction of Killaloe that could affect them. William, at length, was informed of the story. He, too, failed to discern what Sarsfield could be at ; but his mind anxiously reverting to his grand battering train—albeit it was now barely a few miles off—he, to make safety doubly sure, ordered Sir John Lanier to proceed at once with five hundred horse to meet the convoy. By some curious chance, Sir John—perhaps deeming his night ride quite needless—did not greatly hurry to set forth. At two o'clock, Tuesday morning, instead of at nine o'clock on Monday evening, he rode leisurely off. His delay of five hours made all the difference in the world, as we shall see.

It was indeed true that Sarsfield, on Sunday night, had secretly quitted his camp on the Clare side, at the head of a chosen body of his best horsemen ; and, true enough, also, that it was upon an enterprise worthy of his reputation he had set forth. In fine, he had heard of the approach of the siege train, and had planned nothing less than its surprise, capture, and destruction !

On Sunday night he rode to Killaloe, distant twelve miles above Limerick on the river. The bridge here was guarded by a party of the enemy ; but favored by the darkness, he proceeded further up the river until he came to a ford near Ballyvally, where he crossed the Shannon, and passed into Tipperary county. The country around him now was all in the enemy's hands ; but he had one with him as a guide on this eventful occasion, whose familiarity with the locality enabled Sarsfield to evade all the Williamite patrols, and but for whose services it may be doubted if his ride this night had not been his last. This was Hogan, the rapparee

By paths and passes known only to riders "native to the sod," he turned into the deep gorges of Silver Mines, and ere day had dawned was bivouacked in a wild ravine of the Keeper Mountains. Here he lay *perdu* all day on Monday. When night fell there was anxious tightening of horsegirths and girding of swords with Sarsfield's five hundred. They knew the siege train was at Cashel on the previous day, and must by this time have reached near to the Williamite lines. The midnight ride before them was long, devious, difficult, and perillous ; the task at the end of it was crucial and momentous indeed. Led by their trusty guide, they set out southward, still keeping in by-ways and mountain roads. Meanwhile, as already mentioned, the siege train and convoy had that evening reached Ballyneety, where the guns were parked and convoy bivouacked. It was three o'clock in the morning when Sarsfield, reaching within a mile or two of the spot, learnt from a peasant that the prize was now not far off ahead of him. And here we encounter a fact which gives the touch of true romance to the whole story ! It happened, by one of those coincidences that often startle us with their singularity, that the pass-word with the Williamite convoy on that night was " *Sarsfield !* " That Sarsfield obtained the pass-word before he reached the halted convoy, is also unquestionable, though how he came by his information is variously stated. The painstaking historian of Limerick states that from a wo- man, wife of a sergeant in the Williamite convoy, unfeelingly left behind on the road by her own party in the evening, but most humanely and kindly treated by Sarsfield's men, the word was obtained. * Riding softly to within a short distance of the place indicated, he halted and sent out a few trusted scouts to scan the whole position narrowly. They returned reporting that besides the sentries there were only a few score troopers drowsing beside the watch fires, on guard ; the rest of the convoy being sleeping in all the immunity of fancied safety. Sarsfield now gave his final–orders—silence or death, till they were in upon the sentries ; then, forward

like a lightning flash upon the guards. One of the Williamite
sentries fancied he heard the beat of horsehoofs approaching
him; he never dreamt of foes; he thought it must be one of
their own patrols. And truly enough, through the gloom he
saw the figure of an officer evidently at the head of a body of
cavalry, whether phantom or reality he could not tell. The
sentry challenged, and, still imagining he had friends, demanded the " word." Suddenly, as if from the spirit land, and
with a wild, weird shout that startled all the sleepers, the
" phantom troop " shot .past like a thunderbolt; the leader
crying as he drew his sword, " *Sarsfield* is the word, *and Sarsfield is the man !*" The guards dashed forward, the bugles
screamed the alarm, the sleepers rushed to arms, but theirs
was scarcely an effort. The broadswords of Sarsfield's five
hundred were in their midst; and to the affrighted gaze of the
panic-stricken victims, that five hundred seemed thousands !
Short, desperate, and bloody was that scene; so short, so
sudden, so fearful, that it seemed like the work of incantation.
In a few minutes the whole of the convoy were cut down or
dispersed; and William's splendid siege train was in Sarsfield's
hands! But his task was as yet only half accomplished.
Morning was approaching; William's camp was barely eight
or ten miles distant, and thither some of the escaped had
hurriedly fled. There was scant time for the important work
yet to be done. The siege guns and mortars were filled with
powder, and each muzzle buried in the earth; upon and
around the guns were piled the pontoon boats, the contents of
the ammunition wagons, and all the stores of various kinds,
of which there was a vast quantity. A train of powder was
laid to this huge pyre, and Sarsfield, removing all the wounded
Williamites to a safe distance, * drew off his men, halting
them while the train was being fired. There was a flash that
lighted all the heavens and showed with dazzling brightness
the country for miles around. Then the ground rocked and
heaved beneath the gazer's feet, as, with a deafening roar
that seemed to rend the firmament, the vast mass burst into

---

* Even the Williamite chroniclers make mention of Sarsfield's kindness to the

the sky ; and as suddenly all was gloom again ! The sentinels on Limerick walls heard that awful peal. It rolled like a thunder storm away by the heights of Cratloe, and wakened sleepers amidst the hills of Clare. William heard it too ; and he at least needed no interpreter of that fearful sound. He knew in that moment his splendid siege train had perished, destroyed by a feat that only one man could have so planned and executed ; an achievement destined to surround with unfading glory the name of Patrick Sarsfield !

Sir John Lanier's party, coming up in no wise rapidly, saw the flash that, as they said, gave broad daylight for a second, and felt the ground shake beneath them as if by an earthquake, and then their leader found he was just in time to be too late. Rushing on he sighted Sarsfield's rear-guard ; but there were memories of the Irish cavalry at the Boyne in no way encouraging him to force an encounter. From the Williamite camp two other powerful bodies of horse were sent out instantly on the explosion being heard, to surround Sarsfield and cut him off from the Shannon. But all was vain, and on Tuesday evening he and his Five Hundred rode into camp amidst a scene such as Limerick had not witnessed for centuries. The whole force turned out ; the citizens came with laurel boughs to line the way, and as he marched in amidst a conqueror's ovation, the gunners on the bold bastions across the river gave a royal salute to him whom they all now hailed as the saviour of the city !

LXVIII.—HOW WILLIAM PROCURED A NEW SIEGE TRAIN AND
BREACHED THE WALL. HOW THE WOMEN OF LIMERICK WON
THEIR FAME IN IRISH HISTORY. HOW THE BREACH WAS
STORMED AND THE MINE SPRUNG. HOW WILLIAM FLED
FROM "UNCONQUERED LIMERICK."

IN the Williamite camp the event caused proportionate
dismay, depression, and discouragement. But William was not a man easily thwarted or disconcerted.
A week later he had another siege train of thirty-six
guns and four mortars brought up from Waterford,
pouring red hot shot into the devoted city. A perfect storm
of bombs, "fire-balls," "carcasses," and other diabolical con-
trivances, rained upon every part of the town, firing it in
several places. Sarsfield and De Boisseleau now ordered that
all the women and children should withdraw into the Clare
suburb. The women *en masse* rebelled against the order!
They vehemently declared that no terrors should cause them
to quit their husbands and brothers in this dreadful hour,
fighting for God and country. They had already bravely
aided in erecting the defences ; they were now resolved to
aid in the struggle behind them, ready to die in the breach or
on the walls beside their kindred, ere the hated foe should
enter Limerick.

And the women of Limerick were true to that resolve!
Then might be seen, say the chroniclers, day after day, women, old and young, full of enthusiasm and determination,
laboring in the breaches, mines, and counterscarps, digging
the earth, filling the gabions, piling the shot, and drawing up
ammunition, while around them showered balls, bombs, and
grenades.

By this time the surface of the whole of the surrounding
suburbs on the southern side was cut up into a vast maze of

26th their trenches were within *a few feet* of the palisades, and a breach had been made in the walls at St. John's Gate. William moreover pursued mining to a great extent. But if he mined, Sarsfield countermined, and it turned out that the Irish mines were far beyond anything the siegers could have credited. In fact the scientific skill, the ingenuity and fertility of engineering resorts, appliances, and devices, exhibited by the defenders of Limerick have seldom been surpassed. The miraculous magic of devoted zeal and earnest activity transformed the old city wall into a line of defences such as Todleben himself in our own day might gaze upon with admiration. * Food, however, was lamentably scarce, but in truth none of the besieged gave thought to any privation ; their whole souls were centred in one great object—defence of the walls, defeat of the foe.

On Wednesday, the 27th August, the breach having been still further increased by a furious bombardment, William gave orders for the assault. Ten thousand men were ordered to support the storming party ; and at half-past three in the afternoon, at a given signal, five hundred grenadiers leaped from the trenches, fired their pieces, flung their grenades, and in a few moments had mounted the breach. The Irish were not unprepared, although at that moment the attack was not expected. Unknown to the besiegers, Boisseleau had caused an intrenchment to be made inside the breach. Behind this intrenchment he had planted a few pieces of cannon, and from these a cross fire now opened with murderous effect on the assailants, after they had filled the space between the breach and the entrenchment. For a moment they halted—staggered by this fatal surprise ; but they next pushed forward with the courage and fury of lions. A bloody hand-to-hand struggle ensued. Spear and dagger, sword and butted musket could alone be used, and they were brought into deadly requisition. The instant William found his storming party

---

* Among numerous other happy resorts and ingenious adaptations of the means at hand to the purpose of defence, we read that, wool stores being numerous in the city, the wool was packed into strong sacks and cases, a lining of which was hung out over

had fastened well upon the breach, the supports in thousands were flung forward. On the Irish side, too, aids were hurried up; but eventually, with a tremendous rush, the assaulting party burst through their opponents, and in a moment more poured into the town.

That feat which usually gives victory to an assault, was, however, in this instance, only the sure occasion of repulse and utter defeat for William's regiments. The news that the foe had penetrated into the town, so far from causing dismay to inhabitants or garrison, seemed to act like the summons of a magician on the countless hosts of enchantment. Down through street, and lane, and alley poured the citizens, women and men; the butcher with his axe, the shipwright with his adze; each man with such weapon as he had been able most readily to grasp; the women, "like liberated furies," flinging stones, bricks, glass bottles, delft-ware, and other missiles, with fury on the foe. Some of the Irish cavalry on the Clare side, hearing the news, dashed across the bridges, "the pavements blazing beneath the horses' hoofs as they galloped to Ball's Bridge, where dismounting and flinging their horses loose, they charged into Broad Street, and sword in hand joined their countrymen in the *mélée*." Even the phlegmatic William, under whose eye the assault was made, became excited as he gazed on the struggle from "Cromwell's Fort," ever and anon ordering forward additional troops to the sustainment of his assaulting column. For *three hours* this bloody hand-to-hand fight in the streets and the breach went on. The women, says Story (the Williamite chaplain), rush boldly into the breach, and stood nearer to our men than to their own, hurling stones and broken bottles right into the faces of

besieged as they hurled from the walls, as they thought, the
last remnant of the Dutch battalions.   But William had yet a
grip upon those walls.   In the wild confusion of the three hours'
struggle, the Brandenburghers, when being pressed back upon
the breach, got in at the rear of one of the Irish batteries, into,
and over which, we are told, they now swarmed in a dense black
mass.   In a moment, however, the whole struggle was suddenly and decisively terminated by the crowning feat of the
defence.   At the very instant when the Brandenburghers—
little knowing that the ground beneath them was every rood
a *mine*—were exulting over what they thought at least an instalment of success, the earth heaved and yawned under their
feet and with a roar like thunder, mingled with a thousand
despairing death-shrieks, battery and Brandenburghers went
flying into the air !   For a moment there was a pause ; each
side alike seeming to feel the awfulness of the fate that had
so suddenly annihilated the devoted regiment.   Then, indeed,
a shout wild and high went up from the walls, wafted from
end to end of the city, and caught up on the Thomond shore,
and a final salvo from the unconquered battlements, by way
of parting salute to the flying foe, proclaimed that patriotism
and heroism had won the victory.

Far more honorable at all times than conquering prowess
in battle—far more worthy of admiration and fame—is humanity to the fallen and the wounded, generosity to the vanquished.
Let the youth of Ireland, therefore, know, when with bound-
ing heart they read or relate so far this glorious story of Limerick, that there remains to be added the brightest ray to the
halo of its fame.   At the moment when the last overwhelming
rush of the garrison and inhabitants swept the assailants from
the breach, in the impetuosity of the onset the pursuing Irish
penetrated at one point into the Williamite camp and in the
mélée the Williamite hospital took fire.   What follows deserves to be recorded in letters of gold.   The Irish instantaneously turned from all pursuit and conflict—some of them
rushed into the flames to bear away to safety from the burning building its wounded occupants, while others of them

the flames! It was only when all danger from the conflagration was over, that they gave thought to their own safety, and fought their way back to the town!

William, resolving to renew the assault next day, could not persuade his men to advance, though he offered to lead them in person! "Whereupon," says the Protestant historian who relates the fact, "in all rage he left the camp, and never stopped till he came to Waterford, where he took shipping for England, his army in the meantime retiring by night from Limerick." *

LXIX.—HOW THE FRENCH SAILED OFF, AND THE DESERTED IRISH ARMY STARVED IN RAGS, BUT WOULD NOT GIVE UP THE RIGHT. ARRIVAL OF "ST. RUTH, THE VAIN AND BRAVE."

HILE William's cowed and beaten army were flying from Limerick, and the queen city of the Shannon was holding high carnival of rejoicing, a French fleet was anchoring in Galway to take off Lauzun and the French auxiliaries! James had represented in France that all was lost—that the struggle was over—that the Irish would not fight; so King Louis sent a fleet imperatively to bring away his men. Accordingly, Lauzun and his division embarked and sailed from Galway. Tyrconnell, however, proceeded to France at the same time, to represent to James his error as to the condition of affairs in Ireland, and to obtain from King Louis a new expedition in aid of the struggle.

An army in the field is a costly engine. Who was to supply the Irish with a "military chest?" How were the forces to be paid, supported, clothed? And, above all, how were military stores, ammunition, arms, and the myriad of other necessaries for the very existence of an army, to be had? The struggle was not merely against so many thousand Williamites—Dutch.

Danish, or English—on Irish soil: but against so many as a
wing of the English nation, or mercenaries in its pay with
the constituted government, the wealth, the taxes, the levies,
the arsenals and the foundries of powerful England behind
them. We need hardly wonder that while, every day, transports arrived from England with arms, ammunition, and military stores, new uniform; tents, baggage, and transport appliances, for the Williamite army, the hapless Irish garrisons
were literally in rags, unpaid, unsupplied, short of food, and
wretchedly off for ammunition. Matters were somewhat
mended by the arrival of Tyrconnell at Limerick, in February
of the following year (1691) with a small supply of money and
some shiploads of provisions, but no men. He brought, however, news, which to the half-famished and ragged garrisons
were more welcome than piles of uniform clothing, or chests
of gold—the cheering intelligence that King Louis was preparing for Ireland military assistance on a scale beyond anything France had yet afforded!

On the 8th of May following, a French fleet arrived in the
Shannon, bringing some provisions, clothing, arms, and ammunition for the Irish troops, but no money and no troops.
In this fleet, however, came Lieutenant-General St. Ruth, a
French officer of great bravery, ability, energy, and experience,
sent to take the chief command of the Irish army. This appointment, it may be remarked, in effect reduced to a fifth
subordinate position Sarsfield, the man to whom was mainly
owing the existence of any army at all in Ireland at this juncture, and on whom during the past winter had practically devolved all the responsibilities of the chief military and civil
authority.

" Every fortunate accident," says one of our historians, " had
combined to elevate that gallant cavalry officer into the position of national leadership. He was the son of a member of
the Irish commons proscribed for his patriotism and religion
in 1641 ; his mother being Anna O'Moore, daughter of the
organizer of the Catholic Confederation. He was a Catholic
in religion ; spoke Gaelic as fluently as English ; was brave, im-

During Tyrconnel's absence every sincere lover of his country came to him with intelligence and looked to him for direction."

The viceroy had brought him from France the rank and title of Earl of Lucan ; "a title drawn from that pleasant hamlet in the valley of the Liffey, where he had learned to lisp the catechism of a patriot at the knee of Anna O'Moore." But it was not for titles or personal honors Sarsfield fought. More dear to him was the cause he had at heart ; and though unquestionably the denial to him of a higher position of command in this campaign led to the bitterest feeling in the army —with the worst of results ultimately—in his own breast there rested no thought but how to forward that cause, no ambition but to serve it, whether as commoner or earl, as subaltern or as chief.

LXX.—HOW GINCKLE BESIEGED ATHLONE. HOW THE IRISH "KEPT THE BRIDGE," AND HOW THE BRAVE CUSTUME AND HIS GLORIOUS COMPANIONS " DIED FOR IRELAND." HOW ATHLONE, THUS SAVED, WAS LOST IN AN HOUR!

THE Williamite army rendezvoused at Mullingar towards the end of May, under Generals De Ginckle, Talmash, and Mackay. ' On the 7th June, they moved westward for Athlone, "the ranks one blaze of scarlet, and the artillery such as had never before been seen in Ireland." * They were detained ten days besieging an Irish out-post, Ballymore castle, heroically defended by Lieutenant-Colonel Ulick Burke and a force of twelve hundred men against Ginckle's army of thirteen thousand, and that artillery described for us by Macaulay. On the 18th Ginckle was joined by the Duke of Wirtemburg, the Prince of Hesse, and the Count of Nassau, with seven thousand foreign mercenaries.

On the 19th their full force appeared before Athlone and summoned the town to surrender.

On the previous occasion, when beseiged by Douglas, the governor (Colonel Grace) relinquished as untenable the Leinster (or " English") side of the town, and made his stand successfully from the Connacht (or " Irish") side.   The governor on this occasion—Colonel Fitzgerald—resolved to defend both the " English " and " Irish" sides, St. Ruth having strongly counselled him so to do, and promised to reach him soon with the bulk of the Irish army from Limerick.   Colonel Fitzgerald had not more than three hundred and fifty men as a garrison ; nevertheless, knowing that all depended on holding out till St. Ruth could come up, he did not wait for Ginckle to appear in sight, but sallied out with his small force, and disputed with the Williamite army the approaches to the town, thus successfully retarding them for five or six hours. But Ginckle had merely to plant his artillery, and the only walls Athlone possessed—on *that* side at least—were breached and crumbled like pastry.   Towards evening, on the 17th June, the whole of the bastion at the "Dublin Gate," near the river on the north side, being levelled, the (English) town was assaulted.   The storming party, as told off, were four thousand men, headed by three hundred grenadiers, under Mackay, and with profuse supports besides.   To meet these, Fitzgerald had barely the survivors of his three hundred and fifty men, now exhausted after forty-eight hours' constant fighting.   In the breach, when the assault was delivered, *two hundred* of that gallant band fell to rise no more.   The remainder, fiercely fighting, fell back inch by inch towards the bridge, pressed by their four thousand foes.   From the Williamite shouts now arose on all sides of, " *the bridge—the bridge ;* " and a furious rush was made to get over the bridge along with, if not before, the retreating Irish.   In this event, of course, all was lost ; but the brave Fitzgerald and his handful of heroes knew the fact well.   Turning to bay at the bridge-end, they opposed themselves like an impenetrable wall to the mass of the enemy ; while above the din of battle and the shouts of the combatants

ed no explanation—*the Irish were breaking down the arches be-hind,* while yet they fought in front! "*They are destroying the bridge,*" he shouted wildly: "On! on! save the bridge—the bridge!" Flinging themselves in hundreds on the few score men now resisting them, the stormers sought to clear the way by freely giving man for man, life for life, nay four for one; but it would not do. There Fitzgerald and his companions stood like adamant; the space at the bridge-end was small; one man could keep five at bay; and a few paces behind, wielding pick, and spade, and crowbar, like furies, were the engineers of the Irish garrison. Soon a low rumbling noise was heard, follow-ed by a crash; and a shout of triumph broke from the Irish side; a yell of rage from the assailants; a portion, but a por-tion only, of two arches had fallen into the stream; the bridge was still passable! Again a wild eager shout from Mackay: "On! on! Now! now! the bridge!" But still there stood the decimated defenders, with clutched guns and clenched teeth, resolved to die but not to yield. Suddenly a cry from the Irish rear: "Back, back, men, *for your lives!*" The brave band turned from the front, and saw the half-broken arches behind them tottering. Most of them rushed with lightning speed over the falling mass; but the last company—it had wheeled round even at that moment to face and keep back the enemy—were too late! As they rushed for the passage, the mass of masonry heaved over with a roar into the boiling surges, leaving the devoted band on the brink in the midst of their foes! There was a moment's pause, and almost a wail burst from the Irish on the Connacht side; but just as the enemy rushed with vengeance upon the doomed group, they were seen to draw back a pace or two from the edge of the chasm, fling away their arms, then dash forward and plunge into the stream. Like a clap of thunder broke a volley from a thousand guns of the Leinster shore, tearing the water into foam. There was a minute of suspense on each side, and then a cheer rang out—of defiance, exultation, victory—as the brave fellows were seen to reach the other bank, pulled to land by a hun-

heard next day that the English town had fallen. " He instantly set out at the head of fifteen hundred horse and foot,
leaving the main army to follow as quickly as possible. On
his arrival, he encamped about two miles west of the town,
and appointed Lieutenant-General D'Usson governor instead
of the gallant Fitzgerald, as being best skilled in defending
fortified places." *   Now came the opportunity for that
splendid artillery, "the like of which," Macaulay has told us,
" had never been seen in Ireland." For seven long days of
midsummer they poured against the Irish town such a storm
of iron from seven batteries of heavy siege guns and mortars,
that by the 27th the place was literally a mass of ruins,
amongst which, we are told, "two men could not walk a-
breast." On that day "a hundred wagons arrived in the
Williamite camp from Dublin, laden with a further supply of
ammunition for the siege guns." That evening the enemy
by grenades set on fire the fascines of the Irish breastwork at
the bridge, and that night, under cover of a tremendous bombardment, they succeeded in flinging some beams over the
broken arches, and partially planking them. Next morning—
it was Sunday, the 28th June—the Irish saw with consternation that barely a few planks more laid on would complete
the bridge. Their own few cannon were now nearly all
buried in the ruined masonry, and the enemy beyond had
battery on battery trained on the narrow spot—it was *death*
to show in the line of the all but finished causeway !

Out stepped from the ranks of Maxwell's regiment, a sergeant of dragoons, Custume by name. " Are there ten men
here who will die with me for Ireland?" A hundred eager
voices shouted, Aye : " Then," said he, " we will save Athlone;
the bridge must go down."

Grasping axes and crow-bars, the devoted band rushed
from behind the breastwork, and dashed forward upon the
newly laid beams. A peal of artillery—a fusillade of musketry—from the other side, and the space was swept with
grape-shot and bullets. When the smoke cleared away, the

bodies of the brave Custume and his ten heroes lay on the bridge, riddled with balls. They had torn away some of the beams, but *every man of the eleven had perished !*

Out from the ranks of the same regiment dashed as many more volunteers. " There are eleven men more who will die for Ireland." Again across the bridge rushed the heroes. Again the spot is swept by a murderous fusillade. The smoke lifts from the scene ; nine of the second band lie dead upon the bridge—two survive, but the work is done ! The last beam is gone ; Athlone once more is saved !

I am not repeating a romance of fiction, but narrating a true story, recorded by lookers on, and corroborated in all its substance by writers on the Williamite and on the Jacobite side. When, therefore, young Irishmen read in Roman history of Horatius Cocles and his comrades, who

> " kept the bridge
> In the brave days of old,"

let them remember that the authentic annals of Ireland record a scene of heroism not dissimilar in many of its features, not less glorious in aught ! And when they read also of the fabled Roman patriot who plunged into the abyss at the forum, to save the city, let them remember that such devotion, not in fable, but in fact, has been still more memorably exhibited by Irishmen ; and let them honor beyond the apocryphal Curtius, the brave Custume and his glorious companions, who died for Ireland at Athlone.

The town was saved once more--yet awhile.. " Ginckle, thus a second time defeated in striving to cross the Shannon, resolved to renew his approaches over the bridge by the more cautious method of a covered walk, or ' close gallery,' and to support the new mode of attack by several others in different directions." * The whole of that day he cannonaded the Irish town with great violence, "as I believe never town was," writes a spectator. Nevertheless, the Irish, burrowing and trenching amidst the chaotic mass of ruins and piles of

rubbish once called the town of Athlone, continued to form
new defences as fast as the old were levelled, and Ginckle
was at his wit's end what to rely upon if his "close gallery"
should fail. A council of war in the Williamite camp decided
that on the morning of the 29th, the passage of the river
should be a third time attempted, and in greater force than
ever. A bridge of boats was to be thrown across the river
some distance below the old stone structure, and it occurred to
some one to suggest that as the summer had been exceedingly dry, and as the water in the river appeared to be unpre-
cedentedly low, it might be worth while to try sounding for
a ford.

This hap-hazard thought—this apparently fugitive sugges-
tion—won Athlone.

"Three Danish soldiers, under sentence of death for some
crime, were offered their pardon if they would undertake to
try the river. The men readily consented, and, putting on
armor, entered at three several places. The English in the
trenches were ordered to fire seemingly *at* them, but in reali-
ity over their heads, whence the Irish naturally concluded
them to be *deserters*, and did not fire till they saw them returning, when the English by their great and small shot,
obliged the Irish to be covered. It was discovered that the
deepest part of the river did not reach their breasts." Thereupon it was decided to assail the town next morning suddenly and by surprise at three points ; one party to go over the
bridge by the "close gallery ;" a second to cross by the pon-
toons or boat bridge; the third, by one of the fords. Once
more Mackay was to lead the assault, which was fixed for
ten o'clock next morning ; again, as at the Boyne, each
Williamite soldier was to mount a green bough or sprig in
his hat ; and this time the word was to be "Kilkenny."

That night a deserter swam the river below the town, and
revealed to St. Ruth that an assault was to be made by a
boat-bridge and "close gallery" early next morning; and lo!
when day dawned, the Williamites could descry the *main
army* of the Irish defiling into the town, and detachments

HOW THEY KEPT THE BRIDGE AT ATHLONE.

See page 463, 464.

have been "a surprise." To make matters worse, the boats were not ready till ten o'clock, instead of at six. Nevertheless the assault was proceeded with, and the storm of grenades began to fly. It had been decided to begin the conflict at or on the bridge, close to the broken arches, where (on their own side) the English had a breastwork, up to which the "close gallery" had been advanced, and upon the attack at this point the other operations were to depend. After an hour's hot work the Irish set on fire the fascines of the English breastwork. There being a strong breeze blowing, in a few minutes the flames spread rapidly; the breastwork had to be abandoned; the "close gallery" was almost destroyed; and the storming columns were called off. The Williamite assault upon Athlone a third time had proved a total failure.

Great was the exultation on the Irish side of the river at the triumphant defeat and utter abandonment of this, the final attempt, as they regarded it, on the part of the foe. After waiting till near five o'clock to behold the last of the Williamites called to the rear, and every other sign of defeat exhibited on their side, St. Ruth drew off the victorious Irish army to the camp three miles distant, and, over-confidently, if not vain-gloriously, declaring the siege as good as raised, invited the resident gentry of the neighborhood and the officers of the army to a grand ball at his quarters that evening.

Meanwhile Ginckle, a prey to the most torturing reflections, wavered between a hundred conflicting resolutions or momentary impulses. At last he decided to raise the siege, but wishing for the decision of a council to shield him somewhat from the outcry he apprehended in Dublin and in London, a meeting was held to consider the point. After a hot and bitter disputation, a resolution, at first laughed at by the majority, was adopted—namely, to try *that very evening*, nay *that very hour*, a sudden dash across the river *by the fords*, as (it was rightly conjectured) the Irish would now be off their guard. As a last refuge from disgrace, Ginckle resolved to try this chance.

side, sent word to the General (St. Ruth) that he thought there were signs of a movement on the opposite bank, and suggesting that additional guards be sent in, as only a few companies had remained in the town. St. Ruth replied by a sharp and testy remark, reflecting on the courage of the officer, to the effect that he was frightened by fancy. By the time this brusk reply had reached him the officer saw enough to convince him infallibly that an assault was about to be made and he again sent with all speed to the camp entreating the general to credit the fact. St. Ruth replied by saying that if the officer in charge was afraid of such attacks, he might turn over the command to another. Sarsfield was present at this last reply, and he at once judged the whole situation correctly. He implored St. Ruth not to treat so lightly a report so grave from an officer of undoubted bravery. The Frenchman—courageous, energetic, and highly-gifted as he unquestionably was—unfortunately was short-tempered, imperious, and vain. He and Sarsfield exchanged hot and angry words ; St. Ruth resenting Sarsfield's interference, and intimating that the latter henceforth should " know his place." While yet this fatal altercation was proceeding, an *aid-de-camp* galloped up all breathless from the town—*the English were across the river and into the defences of Athlone!* Even now St. Ruth's overweening self-confidence would not yield. " Then let us drive them back again," was his answer, at the same time directing troops to hurry forward for that purpose. But it was too late. The lodgment had been made in force. The English were now in the defences. The walls of the town on the camp side had been left standing, and only a siege could now dispossess the new occupants. Athlone was lost ! *

---

* Amongst the slain on the Irish side in this siege was the glorious old veteran, Colonel Richard Grace, who was governor the preceding year. His great age—he was now nearly ninety years of age—caused him to be relieved of such a laborious position in this siege, but nothing could induce him to seek, either in retirement or in less exposed and dangerous duty, that quiet which all his compeers felt to be the o'd man's right. He would insist on remaining in the thickest of the fighting, and he died " with his harness on his back." He was one of the most glorious characters to

LXXI.—" THE CULLODEN OF IRELAND." HOW AUGHRIM WAS FOUGHT AND LOST. A STORY OF THE BATTLE-FIELD ; " THE DOG OF AUGHRIM," OR, FIDELITY IN DEATH !

ST. RUTH fell back to Ballinasloe, on Ginckle's road to Galway, which city was now held by the Irish, and was in truth one of their most important possessions. The Frenchman was a prey to conscious guilty feeling. He knew that Sarsfield held him accountable for the loss of Athlone, and his pride was painfully mortified. How often do dire events from trivial causes spring ! This estrangement between St. Ruth and Sarsfield was fated to effect the destinies of Ireland, for to it may be traced the loss of the battle of Aughrim, as we shall see.

taken up, but St. Ruth moved off to Aughrim about three miles distant on the road to Galway. The new position was not less strong than that which had just been quitted. In truth its selection, and the uses to which St. Ruth turned each and all of its natural advantages, showed him to be a man of consummate ability.

Close to the little village of Aughrim—destined to give name to the last great battle between Catholic and Protestant royalty on the soil of Ireland—is the Hill of Kilcommedan. The hill slopes gradually and smoothly upward to a height of about three hundred feet from its base, running lengthways for about two miles from north to south. On its east side or slope, looking towards the way by which Ginckle must approach on his march westward to Galway, the Irish army was encamped, having on its right flank the pass or causeway of Urrachree, and its left flank resting on the village of Augh- rim. A large morass lay at the foot of Kilcommedan (on the east, sweeping round the northern end of the hill) which might be crossed in summer by footmen, but was impracti- cable for cavalry. Through its centre, from south to north, ran a little stream, which with winter rains flooded all the sur- rounding marsh. Two narrow causeways, " passes," or roads ran across the morass to the hill; one at Urrachree, the other at the town of Aughrim; the latter one being defended or commanded by an old ruin, Aughrim Castle at the hill base. * Along the slopes of the hill, parallel with its base, ran two or three lines of whitethorn hedge-rows, growing out of thick earth fences, affording admirable position and protection for musketeers. It may be questioned if the genius of a Welling- ton could have devised or directed aught that St. Ruth had not done to turn every feature of the ground and every inch of this position to advantage. Yet by one sin of omission he placed all the fortunes of the day on the hazard of his

* The most intelligible, if not the only intelligible, descriptions of this battle-field are those of Mr. M. J. M'Cann, in the *Harp* for June, 1859; and in a work recently issued in America, *Battle-fields of Ireland*, unquestionably the most attractive and

own life ; he communicated his plan of battle to *no one.* Sars-field was the man next entitled and fitted to command, in the event of anything befalling the general; yet he in particular was kept from any knowledge of the tactics or strategy upon which the battle was to turn. Indeed he was posted at a point critical and important enough in some senses, yet away from, and out of sight of the part of the field where the main struggle was to take place ; and St. Ruth rather hurtfully gave him imperative instructions not to stir from the position thus assigned him, without a written order from himself. " At Aughrim," says an intelligent Protestant literary periodical, " three apparent accidents gave the victory to Ginckle. The musketeers defending the pass at the old castle found them-selves supplied with cannon balls instead of bullets ; the flank movement of a regiment was mistaken for a retreat; and St. Ruth lost his life by a cannon shot." * The last mentioned, which was really the accident that wrested undoubted victory from the Irish grasp, would have had no such disastrous re-sult had St. Ruth confided his plan of battle to his lieutenant-general, and taken him heartily and thoroughly into joint command on the field.

I know of no account of this battle, which, within the same space exhibits so much completeness, clearness, and simplicity of narration, as Mr. Haverty's, which accordingly I here bor-row with very little abridgement :—

" The advanced guards of the Williamites came in sight of the Irish on the 11th of July, and the following morning, which was Sunday, 12th of July, 1691, while the Irish army was as-sisting at mass, the whole force of the enemy drew up in line of battle on the high ground to the east beyond the morass. As nearly as the strength of the two armies can be estimated, that of the Irish was about fifteen thousand horse and foot, and that of the Williamites from twenty to twenty-five thou-sand, the latter having besides a numerous artillery, while the Irish had but nine field pieces.

---

* *Dublin University Magazine,* for February, 1867.—" Some Episodes of the Irish

" Ginckle, knowing his own great superiority in artillery, hoped by the aid of that arm alone to dislodge the Irish centre force from their advantageous ground; and as quickly as his guns could be brought into position, he opened fire upon the enemy. He also directed some cavalry movements on his left at the pass of Urraghree, but with strict orders that the Irish should not be followed beyond the ' pass,' lest any fighting there should force on a general engagement, for which he had not then made up his mind. His orders on this point, however, were not punctually obeyed ; the consequence being some hot skirmishing, which brought larger bodies into action, until about three o'clock, when the Williamites retired from the pass.

" Ginckle now held a council of war and the prevalent opinion seemed to be that the attack should be deferred until an early hour next morning, but the final decision of the council was for an immediate battle. At five o'clock accordingly, the attack was renewed at Urraghree, and for an hour and a half there was considerable fighting in that quarter; several attempts to force the pass having been made in the interval, and the Irish cavalry continuing to maintain their ground gallantly, although against double their numbers.

" At length, at half-past six, Ginckle, having previously caused the morass in front of the Irish centre to be sounded, ordered his infantry to advance on the point where the line of the fences at the Irish side projected most into the marsh, and where the morass was, consequently, narrowest. This, it appears, was in the Irish right centre, or in the direction of Urraghree. The four regiments of colonels Erle, Herbert, Creighton, and Brewer, were the first to wade through the mud and water, and to advance against the nearest of the hedges, where they were received with a smart fire by the Irish, who then retired behind their next line of hedges, to which the assailants in their turn approached. The Williamite infantry were thus gradually drawn from one line of fences to another, up the slope from the morass, to a greater distance than was contemplated in the plan of attack, according to which they were to hold their ground near the morass until they could be sup-

ported by reinforcements of infantry in the rear, and by cavalry on the flanks. The Irish retired by such short distances,
that the Williamites pursued what they considered to be an
advantage, until they found themselves face to face with the
main line of the Irish, who now charged them in front; while
by passages cut specially for such a purpose through the line
of hedges by St. Ruth, the Irish cavalry rushed down with
irresistible force and attacked them in the flanks. The effect was instantaneous. In vain did Colonel Erle endeavor
to encourage his men by crying out that 'there was no way
to come off but to be brave.' They were thrown into total
disorder, and fled towards the morass, the Irish cavalry cutting them down in the rear, and the infantry pouring in a
deadly fire, until they were driven beyond the quagmire, which
separated the two armies. Colonels Erle and Herbert were
taken prisoners ; but the former, after being taken and retaken,
and receiving some wounds, was finally rescued.

" Whilst this was going forward towards the Irish right,
several other Williamite regiments crossed the bog nearer to
Aughrim, and were in like manner repulsed ; but not having
ventured among the Irish hedges, their loss was not so considerable, although they were pursued so far in their retreat,
that the Irish, says Story, 'got almost in a line with some of
our great guns,' or, in other words, had advanced into the
English battle-ground. It was no wonder that at this moment
St. Ruth should have exclaimed with national enthusiasm,
' The day is ours, *mes enfants !* '

"The manœuvres of the Dutch general on the other side
evinced consummate ability, and the peril of his present
position obliged him to make desperate efforts to retrieve it.
His army being much more numerous than that of the Irish,
he could afford to extend his left wing considerably beyond
their right, and this causing a fear that he intended to flank
them at that side, St. Ruth ordered the second line of his left
to march to the right, the officer who received the instructions taking with him also a battalion from the centre, which
left a weak point not unobserved by the enemy. St. Ruth

to the great extent of bog, and the extreme narrowness of the causeway near Aughrim Castle. The Williamite commander perceived this confidence, and resolved to take advantage of it. Hence his movement at the opposite extremity of his line, which was a mere feint, the troops which he sent to his left not firing a shot during the day, while some of the best regiments of the Irish were drawn away to watch them. The point of weakening the Irish left having been thus gained, the object of doing so soon became apparent. A movement of the Williamite cavalry to the causeway at Aughrim was observed. Some horsemen were seen crossing the narrow part of the causeway with great difficulty, being scarcely able to ride two abreast. St. Ruth still believed that pass impregnable, as indeed it would have been, but for the mischances which we have yet to mention, and he is reported to have exclaimed, when he saw the enemy's cavalry scrambling over it, 'They are brave fellows, 'tis a pity they should be so exposed.' They were not, however, so exposed to destruction as he then imagined. Artillery had come to their aid, and as the men crossed, they began to form in squadrons on the firm ground near the old castle. What were the garrison of the castle doing at this time? and what the reserve of cavalry beyond the castle to the extreme left? As to the former, an unlucky circumstance rendered their efforts nugatory. It was found on examining the ammunition with which they had been supplied, that while the men were armed with French firelocks, the balls that had been served to them were cast for English muskets, of which the calibre was larger, and that they were consequently useless. In this emergency the men cut the small globular buttons from their jackets, and used them for bullets, but their fire was ineffective, however briskly it was sustained, and few of the enemy's horse crossing the causeway were hit. This was but one of the mischances connected with the unhappy left of St. Ruth's position. We have seen how an Irish officer, when ordered with reserves to the right wing, removed a battalion from the left centre. This error *

---

* Many Irish authorities assert it was no "error," but downright treason. The officer who perpetrated it being the traitor, Luttrel, subsequently discovered to have

was immediately followed by the crossing of the morass at that weakened point by three Williamite regiments, who employed hurdles to facilitate their passage, and who, meeting with a comparatively feeble resistance at the front line of fences, succeeded in making a lodgment in a corn-field on the Irish side."

It was, however—as the historian just quoted remarks in continuation—still very easy to remedy the effects of these errors or mishaps thus momentarily threatening to render questionable the victory already substantially won by the Irish ; and St. Ruth, for the purpose of so doing—and, in fact, delivering the *coup de grace* to the beaten foe—left his position of observation in front of the camp on the crest of the hill and, placing himself in joyous pride at the head of a cavalry brigade, hastened down the slope to charge the confused bodies of Williamite horse gaining a foot-hold below. Those who saw him at this moment say that his face was aglow with enthusiasm and triumph. He had, as he thought, at last vindicated his name and fame ; he had shown what St. Ruth could do. And, indeed, never for an instant had he doubted the result of this battle, or anticipated for it any other issue than a victory. He had attired himself, we are told, in his most gorgeous uniform, wearing all his decorations and costly ornaments, and constantly told those around him that he was to-day about to win a battle that would wrest Ireland from William's grasp. About half-way down the hill he halted a moment to give some directions to the artillerymen at one of the field batteries. Then, drawing his sword, and giving the word to advance for a charge, he exclaimed to his officers : " They are beaten, gentlemen ; let us drive them back to the gates of Dublin." With a cheer, rising above the roar of the artillery—which, from the other side, was playing furiously on this decisive Irish advance—the squadron made reply : when suddenly, louder still, at its close, there rose a cry—a shriek— from some one near the general. All eyes were turned upon the spot, and for an instant many failed to discern the cause of such a startling utterance. There sat the glittering uni-

second glance to detect the horrible catastrophe that had
befallen. There sat the body of St. Ruth indeed, but it was
his *lifeless corpse*—a headless trunk. A cannon shot from the
Williamite batteries had struck the head from his body, as if
the Tyburn axe and block had done their fearful work. St.
Ruth, the vain, the brave, was no more!

The staff crowded around the fallen commander in sad dismay. The brigade itself, ignorant at first of the true nature
of what happened, but conscious that some serious disaster
had occurred, halted in confusion. Indecision and confusion
in the face of the enemy, and under fire of his batteries, has
ever but one result. The brigade broke, and rode to the
right. No one knew on whom the command devolved. Sarsfield was next in rank ; but every one knew him to be posted
at a distant part of the field, and it was unhappily notorious
that he had not been made acquainted with any of the lost
general's plan. This indecision and confusion was not long
spreading from the cavalry brigade which St. Ruth had been
leading, to other bodies of the troops. The Williamites plainly
perceived that something fatal had happened on the Irish
side, which, if taken advantage of promptly, might give them
victory in the very moment of defeat. They halted, rallied,
and returned. A general attack in full force on all points was
ordered. "Still the Irish centre and right wing maintained
their ground obstinately, and the fight was renewed with as
much vigor as ever. The Irish infantry were so hotly engaged,
that they were not aware either of the death of St. Ruth, or
of the flight of the cavalry, until they themselves were almost
surrounded. A panic and confused flight were the result.
The cavalry of the right wing, who were the first in action
that day, were the last to quit their ground. Sarsfield, with
the reserve horse of the centre, had to retire with the rest
without striking one blow, 'although,' says the Williamite
captain Parker, ' he had the greatest and best part of the
cavalry with him.' St. Ruth fell about sunset ; and about
nine, after three hours' hard fighting, the last of the Irish
army had left the field. The cavalry retreated along the high
road to Loughrae, and the infantry, who mostly flung away

their arms, fled to a large red bog on their left, where great numbers of them were massacred unarmed and in cold blood : but a thick misty rain coming on, and the night setting in, the pursuit was soon relinquished."

The peasantry to this day point out a small gorge on the hill side, still called " Gleann-na-Fola," * where two of the Irish regiments, deeming flight vain, or scorning to fly, halted, and throughout the night waited their doom in sullen determination. There they were found in the morning, and *were slaughtered to a man.* The slogan of the conqueror was : " No quarter." †

Above five hundred prisoners, with thirty-two pairs of colors, eleven standards, and a large quantity of small arms, fell into the hands of the victors. The English loss in killed and wounded was about three thousand ; the Irish lost over four thousand, chiefly in the flight, as the Williamites gave no quarter, and the wounded, if they were not, in comparative mercy, shot as they lay on the field, were allowed to perish unfriended where they fell.

To the music of one of the most plaintive of our Irish melodies—"The Lamentation of Aughrim"—Moore (a second time touched by this sad theme) has wedded the well-known verses here quoted :

---

* The Glen of Slaughter.—The Bloody Glen.

† Moore, who seems to have been powerfully affected by the whole story of Aughrim —" the Culloden of Ireland "—is said to have found in this mournful tragedy the subject of his exquisite song, " After the Battle : "—

> Night closed around the conqueror's way,
>   And lightning showed the distant hill,
> Where those who lost that dreadful day
>   Stood few and faint—but fearless still.
> The soldier's hope—the patriot's zeal, :
>   For ever dimmed, for ever crossed !
> Oh ! who can say what heroes feel
>   When all but life and honor's lost !
>
> The last sad hour of freedom's dream
>   And valor's task moved slowly by ;
> And mute they watched till morning's beam
>   Should rise and give them light to die !
> There's yet a world where souls are free,

Forget not the field where they perished—
The truest, the last of the brave;
All gone—and the bright hopes we cherished
Gone with them, and quenched in the grave.

Oh ! could we from death but recover
Those hearts as they bounded before,
In the face of high Heaven to fight over
The combat for freedom once more ;

Could the chain for a moment be riven
Which Tyranny flung round us then—
No !—'tis not in Man, nor in Heaven,
To let Tyranny bind it again !

But 'tis past ; and though blazoned in story
The name of our victor may be;
Accurst is the march of that glory
Which threads o'er the hearts of the free !

Far dearer the grave or the prison
Illumed by one patriot name,
Than the trophies of all who have risen
On Liberty's ruins to fame !

We cannot take leave of the field of Aughrim and pass un-
noticed an episode connected with that scene which may well
claim a place in history ; a true story, which, if it rested on
any other authority than that of the hostile and unsympathiz-
ing Williamite chaplain, might be deemed either the creation
of poetic fancy or the warmly tinged picture of exaggerated fact.

The bodies of the fallen Irish, as already mentioned, were
for the most part left unburied on the ground, " a prey to the
birds of the air and the beasts of the field." " There is," says
the Williamite chronicler, "a true and remarkable story of a
greyhound, * belonging to an Irish officer. The gentleman
was killed and stripped in the battle,† whose body the dog re-

---

* It was a wolf-hound, or a wolf-dog.

† Meaning to say, killed in the battle and stripped after it by the Williamite camp-
followers, with whom stripping and robbing the slain was a common practice. They
did not spare even the corpse of their own lieutenant-colonel, the Right Rev. Dr.
Walker, Protestant Bishop of Derry, which they stripped naked at the Boyne.

mained by night and day; and though he fed upon *other* corpses with the rest of the dogs, yet he would not allow them or anything else to touch that of his master. When all the corpses were consumed, the other dogs departed; but this one used to go in the night to the adjacent villages for food, and presently return to the place where his master's bones only were then left. And thus he continued (from July when the battle was fought) till January following, when one of Colonel Foulkes's soldiers, being quartered nigh at hand, and going that way by chance, the dog *fearing he came to disturb his master's bones* flew upon the soldier, who, being surprised at the suddenness of the thing, unslung his piece then upon his back and shot the poor dog." * "He expired," adds Mr. O'Callaghan, "with the same fidelity to the remains of his unfortunate master, as that master had shown devotion to the cause of his unhappy country. In the history of nations there are few spectacles more entitled to the admiration of the noble mind and the sympathy of the generous and feeling heart, than the fate of the gallant men and the faithful dog of Aughrim." †

---

* Story's *Cont. Imp. Hist.*, p. 147.
† *Green Book*, p. 459.

LXXII.—HOW GLORIOUS LIMERICK ONCE MORE BRAVED THE
ORDEAL. HOW AT LENGTH A TREATY AND CAPITULATION
WAS AGREED UPON. HOW SARSFIELD AND THE IRISH ARMY
SAILED INTO EXILE.

GALWAY surrendered on favorable terms ten days after
the battle. Sligo also, the last western garrison, succumbed soon after, and its governor, the brave Sir
Teige O'Regan, the hero of Charlemont, marched his
six hundred survivors southward to Limerick."

"Thus once more all eyes and hearts in the British Islands
were turned towards the well-known city of the lower Shannon." *

On the 25th of August, Ginckle, reinforced by all the troops
he could gather in with safety, invested the place on three
sides. It appears he had powers, and indeed urgent directions, from William long previously, to let no hesitation in
granting favorable terms keep him from ending the war, if
it could be ended by such means, and it is said he apprehended
serious censure for not having proclaimed such disposition
before he assaulted Athlone. He now resolved to use without
stint the powers given to him, in the anxious hope of thereby
averting the necessity of trying to succeed where William
himself had failed—beneath the unconquered walls of Limerick.

Accordingly, a proclamation was issued by Ginckle, offering
a full and free pardon of all "treasons" (so-called—meaning
thereby loyalty to the king, and resistance of the foreign
emissaries), with restoration for all to their estates "forfeited"
by such "treason," and employment in his majesty's service
for all who would accept it, if the Irish army would abandon
the war.

It is not to be wondered at that this proclamation developed on the instant a " peace party " within the Irish lines. Not even the most sanguine could now hope to snatch the crown from William's head, and replace it on that of the fugitive James. For what object, therefore, if not simply to secure honorable terms, should they prolong the struggle? And did not this proclamation afford a fair and reasonable basis for negotiation? The Anglo-Irish Catholic nobles and gentry, *whose estates were thus offered to be secured to them*, may well be pardoned, if they exhibited weakness at this stage. To battle further was, in their judgment, to peril all for a shadow.

Nevertheless, the national party, led by Sarsfield, prevailed, and Ginckle's summons to surrender was courteously but firmly refused. Once more glorious Limerick was to brave the fiery ordeal. Sixty guns, none of less than twelve pounds calibre, opened their deadly fire against it. An English fleet ascended the river, hurling its missiles right and left. Bombardment by land and water showered destruction upon the city—in vain! Ginckle now gave up all hope of reducing the place by assault, and resolved to turn the siege into a *blockade*. Starvation must, in time, effect what fire and sword had so often and so vainly tried to accomplish. The treason of an Anglo-Irish officer long suspected, Luttrell, betrayed to Ginckle the pass over the Shannon above the city ; and one morning the Irish, to their horror, beheld the foe upon the Clare side of the river. Ginckle again offered to grant almost any terms, if the city would but capitulate ; for even still he judged it rather a forlorn chance to await its capture. The announcement of this offer placed further resistance out of the question.

and bitter grief. They ran to the ramparts, from which they so often had hurled the foe, and broke their swords in pieces. " Muskets that had scattered fire and death amidst the British grenadiers, were broken in a frenzy of desperation, and the tough shafts of pikes that had resisted William's choicest cavalry, crashed across the knees of maddened rapparees." The citizens, too, ran to the walls, with the arms they had treasured proudly as mementoes of the last year's glorious struggle, and shivered them into fragments, exclaiming with husky voices : " We need them no longer. *Ireland is no more !*"

On the 26th September the negotiations were opened, hostages were exchanged, and Sarsfield and Major-General Wauchop dined with Ginckle in the English camp. The terms of capitulation were settled soon after; but the Irish, happily —resolved to leave no pretext for subsequent repudiation of Ginckle's treaty, even though he showed them his formal powers—demanded that *the lords justices* should come down from Dublin to ratify the articles. This was done ; and on the 3rd of October, 1691, the several contracting parties met in full state at a spot on the Clare side of the river, to sign and exchange the treaty. That memorable spot is marked by a large stone, which remains to this day, proudly guarded and preserved by the people of that city, for whom it is a monument more glorious than the Titan arch for Rome. The visitor who seeks it on the Shannon side, needs but to name the object of his search, when a hundred eager volunteers, their faces all radiant with pride, will point him out that memorial of Irish honor and heroism, that silent witness of English troth—*punica fides*—the " Treaty Stone of Limerick."

The treaty consisted of military articles, or clauses, twenty-nine in number ; and civil articles, thirteen. Set out in all the formal and precise language of the original document, those forty-two articles would occupy a great space. They were substantially as follows: The military articles provided that all persons willing to expatriate themselves, as well officers and soldiers, as rapparees and volunteers, should have free liberty to do so, to any place beyond seas, except Eng-

companies, or parties; that, if plundered by the way, William's government should make good their loss; that fifty ships, of two hundred tons each, should be provided for their transportation, besides two men-of-war for the principal officers; that the garrison of Limerick might march out with all their arms, guns, and baggage, colors flying, drums beating, and matches lighting! The garrison of Limerick, moreover, were to be at liberty to take away any six brass guns they might choose, with two mortars, and half the ammunition in the place. It was also agreed that those who so wished might enter the service of William, retaining their rank and pay.

"The civil articles were thirteen in number. Article I. guaranteed to members of that denomination remaining in the kingdom, such privileges in the exercise of their religion as are consistent with the law of Ireland, or as they enjoyed in the reign of King Charles the Second'; this article further provided that, 'their majesties, as soon as their affairs will permit them to summon a parliament in this kingdom, will endeavor the said Roman Catholics such further security in that particular as may preserve them from any disturbance.'" Article II guaranteed pardon and protection to all who had served king James, on taking the oath of allegiance prescribed in Article IX., as follows :—

"I, A. B., do solemnly promise and swear that I will be faithful and bear true allegiance to their majesties, King William and Queen Mary: so help me God."

Articles III., IV., V., and VI., extended the provisions of Articles I. and II. to merchants and other classes of men. Article VII. permits "every nobleman and gentleman compromised in the said articles" to carry side arms, and keep "a gun in their houses." Article VIII. gives the right of removing goods and chattels without search. Article IX. is as follows :—

"The oath to be administered to such Roman Catholics as submit to their majesties' government shall be the oath aforesaid, and no other."

Article X. guarantees that "no person or persons who shall hereafter break these articles, or any of them, shall thereby make or cause any other person or persons to forfeit or lose the benefit of them." Articles XI and XII. relate to the ratification of the articles "within eight months or sooner." Article XIII. refers to the debts of "Colonel John Brown, commissary of the Irish army, to several Protestants," and arranges for their satisfaction.

On the morning of the 5th of October, 1691, a singular scene was witnessed on the northern shore of the Shannon, beyond the city walls. On that day the Irish regiments were to make their choice between exile for life, or service in the armies of their conqueror. At each end of a gently rising ground beyond the suburbs, were planted on one side the royal standard of France, and on the other that of England. It was agreed that the regiments, as they marched out— "with all the honors of war, drums beating, colors flying, and matches lighting"—should, on reaching this spot, wheel to the left or to the right beneath that flag under which they elected to serve. At the head of the Irish marched the foot guards—the finest regiment in the service—fourteen hundred strong. All eyes were fixed on this splendid body of men. On they came, amidst breathless silence and acute suspense ; for well both the English and Irish generals knew that the choice of the first regiment would powerfully influence all the rest. The guards marched up to the critical spot and— in a body wheeled to the colors of France ; barely *seven* men turning to the English side Ginckle, we are told, was greatly agitated as he witnessed the proceeding. The next regiment, however (Lord Iveagh's) marched as unanimously to the Williamite banner, as did also portions of two others. But the bulk of the Irish army defiled under the *Fleur de lis* of king Louis ; only one thousand and forty-six, out of nearly fourteen thousand men, preferring the service of England !

A few days afterwards a French fleet sailed up the Shannon with an aiding army, and bringing money, arms, ammunition, stores, food, and clothing ! Ginckle, affrighted, imagined the Irish would now disclaim the articles, and renew the war. But it was not *the Irish* who were to break the Treaty of Limerick. Sarsfield, when told that a powerful fleet was sailing up the river, seemed stunned by the news! He was silent for a moment, and then, in mournful accents, replied: " *Too late.* The treaty is signed; our honor is pledged—the honor of Ireland. *Though a hundred thousand Frenchmen offered to aid us now, we must keep our plighted troth !* "

He forbade the expedition to land, with a scrupulous sense of honor contending that *the spirit* if not *the letter* of the capitulation extended to any such arrival! The French ships, accordingly, were used only to transport to France the Irish army that had volunteered for foreign service. Soldiers and civilians, nobles, gentry, and clergy, there sailed in all nineteen thousand and twenty-five persons. Most of the officers, like their illustrious leader, Sarsfield, * gave up fortune, family, home, and friends, refusing the most tempting offers from William, whose anxiety to enrol them in his own service was earnestly and perseveringly pressed upon them to the last. Hard was their choice ; great was the sacrifice. Full of anguish was that parting, whose sorrowful spirit has been so faithfully expressed by Mr. Aubrey de Vere, in the following simple and touching verses—the soliloquy of a brigade soldier sailing away from Limerick :—

> I snatched a stone from the bloodied brook,
> And hurled it at my household door !
> No farewell of my love I took :
> I shall see my friend no more.
>
> I dashed across the church-yard bound:
> I knelt not by my parents' grave :
> There rang from my heart a clarion's sound,
> That summoned me o'er the wave.
>
> No land to me can native be
> That strangers trample, and tyrants stain :
> When the valleys I loved are cleansed and free,
> They are mine, they are mine again !
>
> Till then, in sunshine or sunless weather,
> By Seine and Loire, and the broad Garonne
> My war-horse and I roam on together
> Wherever God will. On ! on !

---

* His patrimonial estates near Lucan, county Dublin, were, even at that day, worth

These were not wholly lost to Ireland, though not a man of them ever saw Ireland more. They served her abroad when they could no longer strike for her at home. They made her sad yet glorious story familiar in the courts of Christendom. They made her valor felt and respected on the battle-fields of Europe. And as they had not quitted her soil until they exacted terms from the conqueror, which if observed, might have been for her a charter of protection, so did they in their exile take a terrible vengeance upon that conqueror for his foul and treacherous violation of that treaty.

No! These men were not, in all, lost to Ireland. Their deeds are the proudest in her story. History may parallel, but it can adduce nothing to surpass the chivalrous devotion of the men who comprised this second great armed migration of Irish valor, faith, and patriotism.

LXXIII.—HOW THE TREATY OF LIMERICK WAS BROKEN AND TRAMPLED UNDER FOOT BY THE " PROTESTANT INTEREST," YELLING FOR MORE PLUNDER AND MORE PERSECUTION.

THERE is no more bitter memory in the Irish breast than that which tells how the Treaty of Limerick was violated ; and there is not probably on record a breach of public faith more nakedly and confessedly infamous than was that violation.

None of this damning blot touches William—now king *de facto* of two islands. *He* did *his* part ; and the truthful historian is bound on good evidence to assume for him that he saw with indignation and disgust the shameless and dastardly breach of that treaty by the dominant and all-powerful Protestant faction. We have seen how the lords justices came down from Dublin and approved and signed the treaty at Limerick.* The king bound public faith to it still more firmly, formally, and solemnly, by the issue of royal letters patent confirmatory of all its articles, issued from Westminster, 24th February, 1692, in the name of himself and queen Mary.

We shall now see how this treaty was *kept* toward the Irish Catholics.

The " Protestant interest" of Ireland, as they called themselves, no sooner found the last of the Irish regiments shipped

---

* Here it may be well to note an occurrence which some writers regard as a deliberate and foul attempt to overreach and trick Sarsfield in the treaty, but which might, after all, have been accident. The day after the treaty was signed in "fair copy," it was discovered that *one line*—containing however one of the most important stipulations in the entire treaty—had been omitted in the "fair copy" by the Williamites, though duly set out in the "first draft" signed by both parties. The instant it was discovered, Sarsfield called on Ginckle to answer for it. The latter, and all the Williamite "contracting parties," declared the omission purely accidental—inserted the line in its right place, and, by a supplemental agreement, solemnly covenanted that this identical line should have a special confirmation from the king and parlia-

from the Shannon, than they openly announced that the
treaty would not, and ought not to be kept! It was the old
story. Whenever the English sovereign or government desired to pause in the work of persecution and plunder, if not
to treat the native Irish in a spirit of conciliation or justice, the
"colony," the "plantation," the garrison, the "Protestant interest," screamed in frantic resistance. It was so in the reign of
James the First ; it was so in the reign of Charles the First ;
it was so in the reign of Charles the Second ; it was so in the
reign of James the Second ; it was so in the reign of William
and Mary. Any attempt of king or government to mete to
the native Catholic population of Ireland any measure of
treatment save what the robber and murderer metes out to his
helpless victim was denounced—absolutely complained of—
as a daring wrong and grievance against what was, and is
still called the " Protestant interest," or "*our* glorious rights
and liberties." *   Indeed, no sooner had the lords justices
returned from Limerick, than the Protestant pulpits commenced to resound with denunciations of those who would ob-
serve the treaty ; and Dopping, titular Protestant bishop of
Meath, as Protestant historians record, preached before the
lords justices themselves a notable sermon on "*the crime* of
keeping faith with Papists."

The " Protestant interest " party saw with indignation that
the king meant to keep faith with the capitulated Catholics ;
nay, possibly to consolidate the country by a comparatively
conciliatory, just, and generous policy ; which was, they con-
tended, *monstrous*. It quickly occurred to them, however,
that as they were sure to be a strong majority in the parliament, they could take into their own hands the work of " re-
construction," when they might freely wreak their will on the
vanquished, and laugh to scorn all treaty faith.

There was some danger of obstruction from the powerful

Catholic minority entitled to sit in both houses of parliament; but, for this danger the dominant faction found a specific. By an unconstitutional straining of the theory that each house was judge of the qualification of its members, they framed test oaths to exclude the minority. In utter violation of the treaty of Limerick—a clause in which, as we have seen, covenanted that no oath should be required of a Catholic other than the oath of allegiance therein set out—the parliamentary majority framed a test oath explicitly denying and denouncing the doctrines of transubstantiation, invocation of saints, and the sacrifice of the Mass, as "damnable and indolatrous." Of course the Catholic peers and commoners retired rather than take these tests, and the way was now all clear for the bloody work of persecution.

In the so-called "Catholic parliament"—the parliament which assembled in Dublin in 1690, and which was opened by king James in person—the Catholics greatly preponderated (in just such proportion as the population was Catholic or Protestant); yet no attempt was made by *that* majority to trample down or exclude the minority. Nay, the Protestant prelates all took their seats in the peers chamber, and debated and divided as stoutly as ever throughout the session, while *not a Catholic prelate* sat in that "Catholic parliament" at all. It was the Catholics' day of power, and they used it generously, magnanimously, nobly. Sustainment of the king, suppression of rebellion, were the all-pervading sentiments. *Tolerance of all creeds—freedom of conscience* for Protestant and for Catholic—were the watchwords in that "Catholic parliament."

And now, how was all this requited? Alas! We have just seen how! Well might the Catholic in that hour, exclaim in the language used for him by Mr. De Vere in his poem :—

> We, too, had our day—it was brief: it is ended—
> When a king dwelt among us, no strange king but ours ;
> When the shout of a people delivered ascended,
> And shook the broad banner that hung on his tow'rs.
> We saw it like trees in a summer breeze shiver
> We read the gold legend that blazoned it o'er :

> How fared it that season, our lords and our masters,
>   In that spring of our freedom, how fared it with you !
> Did we trample your faith ?   Did we mock your disasters ?
>   We restored but his own to the leal and the true.
> Ye had fallen ! 'Twas a season of tempest and troubles,
>   But against you we drew not the knife ye had drawn ;
> In the war-field we meet : but your prelates and nobles
>   Stood up mid the senate in ermine and lawn!

It was even so, indeed. But *now*. What a contrast. Strangers to every sentiment of magnanimity, justice or compassion, the victorious majority went at the work of proscription wholesale. The king, through lord justice Sydney, offered some resistance ; but,.by refusing to vote him adequate
supplies, they soon taught William that he had better not in-
terfere with their designs. After four years' hesitancy, he
yielded in unconcealed disgust. Forthwith ample supplies
were voted to his majesty, and the parliament proceeded to
practise freely the doctrine of "no faith to be kept with Papists."

Of course they began with confiscations. Plunder was ever
the beginning and the end of their faith and practice.
Soon 1,060,792 acres were declared "escheated to the crown."
Then they looked into the *existing* powers of persecution, to
see how far they were capable of extension. These were
found to be atrocious enough ; nevertheless, the new parliament added the following fresh enactments :—"1. An act to deprive Catholics of the means of educating their children at home
and abroad, and to render them incapable of being guardians of
their own or any other person's children : 2. An act to disarm
the Catholics ; and 3. Another, to banish all the Catholic priests
and prelates. Having thus violated the treaty, they gravely
brought in a bill ' to confirm the Articles of Limerick.' ' The
very title of the bill,' says Dr. Crooke Taylor, 'contains evidence of its injustice. It is styled, " A bill for the confirmation
of Articles (not *the* articles) made at the surrender of Limerick."
And the preamble shows that the little word ' *the* ' was not accidentally omitted. It runs thus :—" That the said articles, or
*so much of them as may consist with the safety and welfare of your
majesty's subjects in these kingdoms*, may be confirmed," etc. The

parts that appeared to these legislators inconsistent with 'the safety and welfare of his majesty's subjects' was the first article, which provided for the security of the Catholics from all disturbances on account of their religion ; those parts of the second article which confirmed the Catholic gentry of Limerick, Clare, Cork, Kerry, and Mayo, in the possession of their estates, and allowed all Catholics to exercise their trades and professions without obstruction ; the fourth article, which extended the benefit of the peace to certain Irish officers then abroad ; the seventh article, which allowed the Catholic gentry to ride armed ; the.ninth article, which provides that the oath of allegiance shall be the only oath required from Catholics, and one or two others of minor importance. All of these are omitted in the bill for ' The confirmation of articles made at the surrender of Limerick,'

" The Commons passed the bill without much difficulty. The House of Lords, however, contained some few of the ancient nobility and some prelates who refused to acknowledge the dogma, ' that no faith should be kept with Papists,' as an article of their creed. The bill was strenuously resisted, and when it was at length carried, a strong protest against it was signed by lords Londonderry, Tyrone, and Duncannon, the Barons of Ossory, Limerick, Killaloe, Kerry, Howth, Kingston, and Strabane, and, to their eternal honor be it said, the Protestant bishops of Kildare, Elphin, Derry, Clonfert, and Killala ! " *

Thus was that solemn pact, which was in truth the treaty of the Irish nation with the newly set-up English *regime*, torn and trampled under foot by a tyrannic bigotry.

---

* M'Gee.

LXXIV.—" THE PENAL TIMES." HOW "PROTESTANT ASCEN-
DANCY" BY A BLOODY PENAL CODE ENDEAVORED TO
BRUTIFY THE MIND, DESTROY THE INTELLECT, AND DE-
FORM THE PHYSICAL AND MORAL FEATURES OF THE SUB-
JECT CATHOLICS.

T was now there fell upon Ireland that night of deepest
horror—that agony the most awful, the most prolonged,
of any recorded on the blotted page of human suffering.

It would be little creditable to an Irish Catholic to own himself capable of narrating this chapter of Irish history with
calmness and without all-conquering emotion. For my part
I content myself with citing the descriptions of it supplied
by Protestant and English writers.

" The eighteenth century," says one of these, writing on the
penal laws in Ireland, " was the era of persecution, in which
the law did the work of the sword more effectually and more
safely. Then was established a code framed with almost
*diabolical ingenuity to extinguish natural affection—to foster per-
fidy and hypocrisy—to petrify conscience—to perpetuate brutal ignorance—to facilitate the work of tyranny*—by rendering the
vices of slavery inherent and natural in the Irish character,
and to make Protestantism almost irredeemably odious as the
monstrous incarnation of all moral perversions.

" Too well," he continues, " did it accomplish its deadly
work of debasement on the intellects, morals, and physical
condition of a people sinking in degeneracy from age to age,
till all manly spirit, all virtuous sense of personal independence
and responsibility, was nearly extinct, and the very features
—vacant, timid, cunning, and unreflective—betrayed the

In the presence of the terrible facts he is called upon to chronicle, the generous nature of the Protestant historian whom I am quoting, warms into indignation. Unable to endure the reflection, that they who thus labored to deform and brutify the Irish people are for ever reproaching them before the world for bearing traces of the infamous effort, he bursts forth into the following noble vindication of the calumniated victims of oppression :

" Having no rights or franchises—no legal protection of life or property—disqualified to handle a gun, even as a common soldier or a gamekeeper—forbidden to acquire the elements of knowledge at home or abroad—forbidden even to render to God what conscience dictated as His due—what could the Irish be but abject serfs? What nation in their circumstances could have been otherwise? Is it not amazing that any social virtue could have survived such an ordeal ?— that any seeds of good, any roots of national greatness, could have outlived such a long tempestuous winter ?"

" These laws," he continues, " were aimed not only at the religion of the Catholic, but still more at his liberty and his property. He could enjoy no freehold property, nor was he allowed to have a lease for a longer term than thirty-one years ; but as even as this term was long enough to encourage an industrious man to reclaim waste lands and improve his worldly circumstances, it was enacted that if a Papist should have a farm producing a profit greater than one-third of the rent, his right to such should immediately cease, and pass over to the first Protestant who should discover the rate of profit ! "

This was the age that gave to Irish topography the " Corrig-an-Affrion," found so thickly marked on every barony map in Ireland. " The Mass Rock ! " What memories cling around each hallowed moss-clad stone or rocky ledge on the mountain side, or in the deep recess of some desolate glen, whereon, for years and years, the Holy Sacrifice was offered up in stealth and secrecy, the death-penalty hanging over

priest and worshipper! Not unfrequently Mass was interrupted by the approach of the bandogs of the law; for, quickened by the rewards to be earned, there sprang up in those
days the infamous trade of priest-hunting, "five pounds"
being equally the government price for the head of a priest
as for the head of a wolf. The utmost care was necessary
in divulging intelligence of the night on which Mass would
next be celebrated; and when the congregation had furtively
stolen to the spot, sentries were posted all around before the
Mass began. Yet in instances not a few, the worshippers
were taken by surprise, and the blood of the murdered priest
wetted the altar stone.

Well might our Protestant national poet, Davis, exclaim,
contemplating this deep night-time of suffering and sorrow:

> Oh! weep those days—the penal days,
>   When Ireland hopelessly complained:
> Oh! weep those days—the penal days
>   When godless persecution reigned.
>
> .   •   •
>
> They bribed the flock, they bribed the son,
>   To sell the priests and rob the sire;
> Their dogs were taught alike to run
>   Upon the scent of wolf and friar.
>   Among the poor,
>   Or on the moor,
> Were hid the pious and the true-
>   While traitor, knave
>   And recreant slave
> Had riches, rank, and retinue,
>   And, exiled in those penal days,
>   Our banners over Europe blaze.

A hundred years of such a code in active operation, ought,
according to all human calculations, to have succeeded in accomplishing its malefic purpose. But again, all human calculations, all natural consequences and probabilities, were set
aside, and God, as if by a miracle, preserved the faith, the
virtue, the vitality, and power of the Irish race. He decreed
that they should win a victory more glorious than a hundred

MASS ON THE MOUNTAIN, IN THE PENAL TIMES.

See page 475.

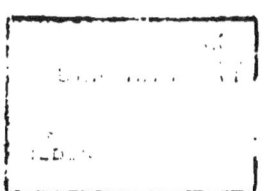

results—in their triumph over the penal code. After three half centuries of seeming death, Irish Catholicity has rolled away the stone from its guarded sepulchre, and walked forth full of life! It could be no human faith that, after such a crucifixion and burial, could thus raise glorious and immortal! This triumph, the greatest, has been Ireland's; and God, in His own good time, will assuredly give her the fulness of victory.

———— ◦◦ ————

LXXV.—THE IRISH ARMY IN EXILE. HOW SARSFIELD FELL ON LANDEN PLAIN. HOW THE REGIMENTS OF BURKE AND O'MAHONY SAVED CREMONA, FIGHTING IN " MUSKETS AND SHIRTS." THE GLORIOUS VICTORY OF FONTENOY! HOW THE IRISH EXILES, FAITHFUL TO THE END, SHARED THE LAST GALLANT EFFORT OF PRINCE CHARLES EDWARD

THE glory of Ireland was all abroad in those years. Spurned from the portals of the constitution established by the conqueror, the Irish slave followed with eager gaze the meteor track of " the Brigade." Namur, Steenkirk, Staffardo, Cremona, Ramillies, Fontenoy—each, in its turn, sent a thrill through the heart of Ireland. The trampled captive furtively lifted his head from the earth, and looked eastward, and his face was lighted up as by the beam of the morning sun.

For a hundred years, that magnificent body, the Irish Brigade—(continuously recruited from home, though death was the penalty by English law)—made the Irish name synonymous with heroism and fidelity throughout Europe. Sarsfield was amongst the first to meet a soldier's death. But he fell in the arms of victory, and died, as the old annalists would say, with his mind and his heart turned to Ireland. In the bloody battle of Landen, fought 29th July, 1693, he fell mortally wounded, while leading a victorious charge of

he lay on the field his corslet was removed in order that the
wound might be examined. He himself, in a pang of pain,
put his hand to his breast as if to staunch the wound. When
he took away his hand, it was full of blood. Gazing at it for
a moment sorrowfully, he faintly gasped out : "*Oh ! that this
were for Ireland !*" He never spoke again !

His place was soon filled from the ranks of the exiled Irish
nobles--those illustrious men whose names are emblazoned
on the glory roll of France—and the Brigade went forward in its path of victory. At Cremona, 1702, an Irish regiment, most of the men fighting *in their shirts*—(the place had
been surprised in the dead of night by treachery)—saved the
town under most singular circumstances. Duke Villeroy,
commanding the French army, including two Irish regiments
under O'Mahony and Burke, held Cremona ; his adversary,
Prince Eugene, commanding the Germans, being encamped
around Mantua. Treason was at work, however, to betray
Cremona. One night a partisan of the Germans within the
walls, traitorously opened one of the gates to the Austrian
troops. Before the disaster was discovered, the French general, most of the officers, the military chests, etc., were taken,
and the German horse and foot were in possession of the town,
excepting one place only--the Po Gate, which was guarded
by the two Irish regiments. In fact, Prince Eugene had already taken up his head-quarters in the town hall, and
Cremona was virtually in his hands. The Irish were called
on to surrender the Po Gate. They answered with a volley.
The Austrian general, on learning they were Irish troops,
desired to save brave men from utter sacrifice--for he had
Irish in his own service, and held the men of Ireland in high
estimation. He sent to expostulate with them, and show
them the madness of sacrificing their lives where they could
have no probability of relief, and to assure them that if they
would enter into the imperial service, they should be directly
and honorably promoted. " The first part of this proposal,"
says the authority I have been following, "they heard with
impatience ; the second, with disdain. ' Tell the prince,' said
they, ' that we have hitherto preserved the honor of our

country, and that we hope this day to convince him we are worthy of his esteem. *While one of us exists, the German eagle shall not be displayed upon these walls.'*" The attack upon them was forthwith commenced by a large body of foot, supported by five thousand cuirassiers. As I have already noted, the Irish, having been aroused from their sleep, had barely time to clutch their arms and rush forth undressed. Davis, in his ballad of Cremona, informs us, indeed (very probably more for " rhyme " than with " reason ") that

——the major is drest;

adding, however, the undoubted fact—

But *muskets and shirts* are the clothes of the rest.

A blooay scene of street fighting now ensued, and before the morning sun had risen high, the naked Irish had recovered nearly half the city!

"In on them," said Friedberg—"and Dillon is broke,
Like forest flowers crushed by the fall of the oak."
Through the naked battalions the cuirassiers go, —
But the man, not the dress, makes the soldier, I trow.
Upon them with grapple, with bay'net, and ball,
Like wolves, upon gaze-hounds the Irishmen fall—
Black Friedberg is slain by O'Mahony's steel,
And back from the bullets the cuirassiers reel.

Oh! hear you their shout in your quarters, Eugene?   .
In vain on Prince Vaudemont for succor you lean!
The bridge has been broken, and mark! how pell-mell
Come riderless horses and volley and yell !
He's a veteran soldier—he clenches his hands,
He springs on his horse, disengages his bands—
He rallies, he urges, till, hopeless of aid,
He is chased through the gates by the *Irish Brigade*."

It was even so. " Before evening," we are told, " the enemy were completely expelled the town, *and the general and military chests recovered!*" Well might the poet undertake to describe as here quoted the effects of the news in Austria, England, France, and Ireland—

' News, news in Vienna!—King Leopold's sad.
News, news in St. James's !—King William is mad.

News, news in old Ireland !—high rises her pride,
And loud sounds her wail for her children who died ;
And deep is her prayer—" God send I may see
MacDonnell and Mahoney fighting for me ! "   .

Far more memorable, however, far more important, was
the ever-glorious day of Fontenoy—a name which to this day
thrills the Irish heart with pride. Of this great battle—fought
11th May, 1745—in which the Irish Brigade turned the fortunes of the day, and saved the honor of France, I take the
subjoined account, prefixed to Davis's well-known poem,
which I also quote :—

"A French army of seventy-nine thousand men, commanded by Marshal Saxe, and encouraged by the presence of both
the King and the Dauphin, laid siege to Tournay, early in
May, 1745. The Duke of Cumberland advanced at the head
of fifty-five thousand men, chiefly English and Dutch, to
relieve the town. At the Duke's approach, Saxe and the
King advanced a few miles from Tournay with forty-five
thousand men, leaving eighteen thousand to continue the
siege, and six thousand to guard the Scheldt. Saxe posted
his army along a range of slopes thus: his centre was on the
village of Fontenoy, his left stretched off through the wood
of Barri, his right reached to the town of St. Antoine, close
to the Scheldt. He fortified his right and centre by the
villages of Fontenoy and St. Antoine, and redoubts near
them. His extreme left was also strengthened by a redoubt
in the wood of Barri; but his left centre, between that wood
and the village of Fontenoy, was not guarded by anything
save slight lines. Cumberland had the Dutch, under
Waldeck, on his left, and twice they attempted to carry St.
Antoine, but were repelled with heavy loss. The same fate
attended the English in the centre, who thrice forced their
way to Fontenoy, but returned fewer and sadder men. In-
goldsby was then ordered to attack the wood of Barri with
Cumberland's right. He did so, and broke into the wood,
when the artillery of the redoubt suddenly opened on him,
which, assisted by a constant fire from the French tirailleurs

"The Duke now resolved to make one great and final effort. He selected his best regiments, veteran English corps, and formed them into a single column of six thousand men. At its head were six cannon, and as many more on the flanks, which did good service. Lord John Hay commanded this great mass. Everything being now ready, the column advanced slowly and evenly as if on the parade ground. It mounted the slope of Saxe's position, and pressed on between the wood of Barri and the village of Fontenoy. In doing so, it was exposed to a cruel fire of artillery and sharpshooters, but it stood the storm, and *got behind Fontenoy!*

"The moment the object of the column was seen, the French troops were hurried in upon them. The cavalry charged ; but the English hardly paused to offer the raised bayonet, and then poured in a fatal fire. On they went, till within a short distance, and then threw in their balls with great precision, the officers actually laying their canes along the muskets to make the men fire low. Mass after mass of infantry was broken, and on went the column, reduced but still apparently invincible ! Duc Richelieu had four cannon hurried to the front, and he literally battered the head of the column, while the household cavalry surrounded them, and in repeated charges, wore down their strength. But these French were fearful sufferers. The day seemed virtually lost, and King Louis was about to leave the field. In this juncture, Saxe ordered up *his last reserve—the Irish Brigade.* It consisted that day of the regiments of Clare, Lally, Dillon, Berwick, Roth, and Buckley, with Fitzjames's horse. O'Brien, Lord Clare, was in command. Aided by the French regiments of Normandy and Vaisseany, they were ordered to charge upon the flank of the English with fixed bayonets without firing. Upon the approach of this splendid body of men, the English were halted on the slope of a hill and up that slope the Brigade rushed rapidly and in fine order ; the stimulating cry of 'Cuimhnigidh ar Liumneac, agus ar fheile na Sacsanach,' '*Remember Limerick and British faith.*' being re-echoed from man to man. The fortune of

with a long day's fighting, cut up by cannon, charge, and
musketry, and dispirited by the appearance of the Brigade.
Still they gave their fire well and fatally ; but they were
literally stunned by the shout, and shattered by the Irish
charge. They broke before the Irish bayonets, and tumbled
down the far side of the hill disorganized, hopeless and falling
by hundreds. The victory was bloody and complete. Louis
is said to have ridden down to the Irish bivouac, and personally thanked them ; and George the second, on hearing
it, uttered that memorable imprecation on the penal code,
'Cursed be the laws which deprive me of such subjects.'
The one English volley and the short struggle on the crest
of the hill cost the Irish dear. One-fourth of the officers, including Colonel Dillon, were killed, and one-third of the
men. The capture of Ghent, Bruges, Ostend, and Oudenard,
followed the victory of Fontenoy."

Thrice, at the huts of Fontenoy, the English column failed,
And thrice the lines of St. Antonie the Dutch in vain assailed ;
For town and slope were filled with foot and flanking battery,
And well they swept the English ranks and Dutch auxiliary.
As vainly, through De Barri's Wood the British soldier burst,
The French artillery drove them back, diminished and dispersed.
The bloody Duke of Cumberland beheld with anxious eye,
And ordered up his last reserve, his latest chance to try.
On Fontenoy, on Fontenoy, how fast his generals ride !
And mustering come his chosen troops, like clouds at eventide.

Six thousand English veterans in stately column tread ;
Their cannon blaze in front and flank ; Lord Hay is at their head ;
Steady they step adown the slope—steady they climb the hill,
Steady they load—steady they fire, moving right onward still.
Betwixt the wood and Fontenoy, as through a furnace blast,
Through rampart, trench, and pallisade, and bullets showering fast ;
And on the open plain above they rose and kept their course,
With ready fire and grim resolve, that mocked at hostile force.
Past Fontenoy, past Fontenoy, while thinner grow their ranks—
They break as broke the Zuyder Zee through Holland's ocean banks.

More idly than the summer flies, French tirailleurs rush round ;
As stubble to the lava tide, French squadrons strew the ground ;
Bombshell and grape, and round shot tore, still on they marched and fired—
Fast from each volley grenadier and voltigeur retired.
"Push on my household cavalry," King Louis madly cried.

On through the camp the column trod—King Louis turns his rein:
" *Not yet*, my liege," Saxe interposed, " *the Irish* troops remain;"
And Fontenoy, famed Fontenoy had been a Waterloo,
Were not these exiles ready then, fresh, vehement, and true.

"Lord Clare," he says, " you have your wish: there are your Saxon foes!"
The Marshal almost smiles to see, so furiously he goes!
How fierce the smiles these exiles wear, who're wont to look so gay;
The treasured wrongs of fifty years are in their hearts to-day.
The treaty broken ere the ink wherewith 'twas writ could dry,
Their plundered homes, their ruined shrines, their women's parting cry,
Their priesthood hunted down like wolves, their country overthrown!
Each looks as if revenge for all were staked on him alone.
On Fontenoy, on Fontenoy, nor ever yet elsewhere,
Pushed on to fight a nobler band than those proud exiles were.

O'Brien's voice is hoarse with joy, as halting he commands,
" Fix bay'nets—charge."—Like mountain storm rush on these fiery bands!
Thin is the English column now, and faint their volleys grow,
Yet must'ring all the strength they have, they made a gallant show.
They dress their ranks upon the hill to face that battle wind;
Their bayonets the breakers' foam; like rocks the men behind!
One volley crashes from their line, when through the surging smoke,
With empty guns clutched in their hands, the headlong Irish broke,
On Fontenoy, on Fontenoy, hark to that fierce huzza!
" Revenge! remember Limerick! dash down the Sassenagh!

Like lions leaping at a fold when mad with hunger's pang,
Right up against the English line the Irish exiles sprang.
Bright was their steel, 'tis bloody now, their guns are filled with gore;
Through shattered ranks, and severed piles, and trampled flags they tore;
The English strove with desperate strength, paused, rallied, staggered, fled—
The green hill-side is matted close with dying and with dead.
Across the plain and far away passed on that hideous wrack,
While cavalier and fantassin dash in upon their track.
On Fontenoy, on Fontenoy, like eagles in the sun,
With bloody plumes the Irish stand—the field is fought and won!

In the year of Fontenoy, 1745, Prince Charles Edward made his bold and romantic attempt to recover the lost crown of the Stuarts. His expedition, we are told, " was undertaken and conducted by Irish aid, quite as much as by French or Scottish." His chief of command was Colonel O'Sullivan; the most of the funds were supplied by the two Waters—father and son—Irish bankers at Paris, " who advanced one hundred

Walsh, a merchant at Nantes, putting "a privateer of eighteen guns into the venture." Indeed, one of Charles' English adherents, Lord Elcho, who kept a journal of the campaign, notes complainingly the Irish influence under which the prince acted. On the 19th July, he landed near Moidart, in the north of Scotland. "Clanronald, Cameron of Lochiel, the Laird of M'Leod, and a few others having arrived, the royal standard was unfurled on the 19th August at Glenfinan, where that evening, twelve thousand men—the entire army, so far—were formed into camp under the orders of O'Sullivan. From that day until the day of Culloden, O'Sullivan seems to have manœuvred the prince's forces. At Perth, at Edinburgh, at Manchester, at Culloden, he took command in the field or in the garrison; and even after the sad result, he adhered to his sovereign's son with an honorable fidelity which defied despair." *

In Ireland no corresponding movement took place. Yet this is the period which has given to native Irish minstrelsy, as it now survives, its abiding characteristic of deep, fervent, unchangeable, abiding devotion to the Stuart cause. The Gaelic harp never gave forth richer melody, Gaelic poetry never found nobler inspiration, than in its service. In those matchless songs, which, under the general designation of "Jacobite Relics," are, and ever will be, so potential to touch the Irish heart with sadness or enthusiam, under a thousand forms of allegory the coming of Prince Charles, the restoration of the ancient faith, and the deliverance of Ireland by the "rightful prince," are prophesied and apostrophied. Now it is "Dark Rosaleen;" now it is "Kathaleen-na-Houlahan;" now it is the "Blackbird," the "Drimin Don Deelish," the "Silk of the Kine," or "Ma Chrevin Evin Algan Og." From this rich store of Gaelic poetry of the eighteenth century I quote one specimen a poem written about the period of Charles Edward's landing at Moidart, by William Heffernan "Dall" ("the Blind") of Shronehill, county Tipperary, and addressed to the Prince of Ossory, Michael Mac Giolla Kerin, known as Mehal Dhu, or Dark Michael. The translation into English is by Mangan :—

Lift up the drooping head,
    Meehal Dhu Mac-Giolla-Kierin;
Her blood yet boundeth red
    Through the myriad veins of Erin;
No! no! she is not dead—
    Meehal Dhu Mac-Giolla-Kierin!
    Lo! she redeems
The lost years of bygone ages—
    New glory beams
Henceforth on her history's pages!
Her long penitential Night of Sorrow
Yields at length before the reddening morrow!

You heard the thunder-shout,
    Meehal Dhu Mac-Giolla-Kierin
Saw the lightning streaming out
    O'er the purple hills of Erin!
And bide you still in doubt,
    Meehal Dhu Mac-Giolla-Kierin?
    Oh! doubt no more!
Through Ulidia's voiceful valleys,
    On Shannon's shore,
Freedom's burning spirit rallies,
Earth and heaven unite in sign and omen
Bodeful of the downfall of our foemen.
    *   *   *   *   *

Charles leaves the Grampian hills,
    Meehal Dhu Mac-Giolla-Kierin,
Charles whose appeal yet thrills
    Like a clarion blast through Erin.
Charles, he whose image fills
    Thy soul too, Mac-Giolla-Kierin!
    Ten thousand strong
His clans move in brilliant order,
    Sure that ere long
He will march them o'er the border,
While the dark-haired daughters of the Highlands
Crown with wreaths the monarch of these islands.

But it was only in the passionate poesy of the native minstrels that any echo of the shouts from Moidart resounded midst the hills of Erin. During all this time the hapless Irish

fallen them.   For a moment victory gleamed on the Stuart banner, and the young prince marched southward to claim his own in London.   Still Ireland made no sign.   Hope had fled.   The prostrate and exhausted nation slept heavily in its blood-clotted chain !

————0————

LXXVI.—HOW IRELAND BEGAN TO AWAKEN FROM THE SLEEP OF SLAVERY.   THE DAWN OF LEGISLATIVE INDEPENDENCE.

RELAND lay long in that heavy trance.   The signal for her awakening came across the western ocean.   " A voice from America," says Flood, " shouted 'Liberty ;'   and every hill and valley of this rejoicing island answered, ' Liberty !' "

For two centuries the claim of the English parliament to control, direct, and bind the Irish legislature, had been the subject of bitter dispute.   The claim was first formally asserted and imposed in the reign of Henry the Seventh, when a servile " parliament," gathered at Drogheda, in November, 1495, by lord deputy Poynings, amongst other acts of self-degradation, at the bidding of the English official, enacted that henceforth no law could be originated in the Irish legislature, or proceeded with, until the heads of it had first been sent to England, submitted to the king and council there, and returned with their approbation under seal.   This was the celebrated " Poynings' Act," or " Poynings' Law," which readers of Grattan's *Life and Times* will find mentioned so frequently. It was imposed as a most secure chain—a ponderous curb— at a crisis when resistance was out of the question.   It was, in moments of like weakness or distraction, submitted to ; but ever and anon in flashes of spirit, the Irish parliaments repudiated the claim as illegal, unconstitutional, and unjust.   On the 16th February, 1640, the Irish House of Commons submitted a set of queries to the judges, the nature of which may be inferred from the question—" Whether the subjects of this kingdom be a free people, and to be governed only by the common *law of England* and *statutes passed in this kingdom ?* " When the answers 'received were deemed insufficient, the House turned the questions into the form of resolutions, and proceeded to vote on them, one by one, affirming in every point the rights, the liberties, and the privileges of their constituents. The Confederation of Kilkenny still more explicitly and boldly enunciated and asserted the doctrine that Ireland was a distinct, free, sovereign, and independent nation, subject only to the triple-crown of the three kingdoms. The Cromwellian rebellion tore down this, as it trampled upon so many other of the rights and liberties of all three kingdoms. The " restoration " came ; but in the reign of the second Charles, the Dublin parliament was too busy in scrambling for retention of plunder and resistance of restitution, to utter an aspiration for liberty ; it bowed the neck to " Poynings' law." To the so-called "Catholic Parliament " of Ireland in James the Second's reign belongs the proud honor of making the next notable declaration of independence ; amongst the first acts of this legislature being one declaring the complete and perfect freedom of the Irish Parliament. " Though they were ' Papists,' " says Grattan, " these men were not slaves ; they wrung a constitution from King James before they accompanied him to the field." Once more, however, came successful rebellion to overthrow the sovereign and the parliament, and again the doctrine of national independence disappeared. The Irish legislature in the first years of the new *regime* sunk into the abject condition of a mere committee of the English parliament.

Soon, however, the spirit of resistance began to appear. For a quarter of a century the Protestant party had been so busy at the work of persecution-- so deeply occupied in forging chains for their Catholic fellow-countrymen—that they never took thought of the political thraldom being imposed upon themselves by the English parliament. "The Irish Protestant," says Mr. Wyse, " had succeeded in excluding the Catholics from power, and for a moment held triumphant and

locum tenens for a more powerful conqueror, a jackal for the lion, an Irish steward for an English master. The exclusive system was turned against him ; he made' the executive exclusively *Protestant ;* the Whigs of George the First made it almost entirely *English.* His victory proved the way for another far easier and far more important. Popery fell, but Ireland fell with it."* In 1719, the question came to a direct issue. In a lawsuit between Hester Sherlock, appellant, and Maurice Annesley, respondent, relating to some property in the County Kildare, the Irish Court of Exchequer decided in favor of the respondent. On an appeal to the *Irish* House of Peers, this judgment was reversed. The respondent, Annesley, now appealed to the *English* House of Peers in England, which body annulled the decision of the Irish Peers, and confirmed that of the Exchequer Court. The Sheriff of Kildare, however, recognizing the decision of the Irish Peers, and declining to recognize the jurisdiction of the English tribunal, refused to obey an order calling on him to put Annesley into possession of the estate. The Irish Court of Exchequer thereupon inflicted a fine upon the sheriff. The Irish peers removed the fine, and voted that the sheriff " had behaved with integrity and courage." This bold course evoked the following galling enactment by the English House:

" Whereas, ... the lords of Ireland have of late, against law, assumed to themselves a power and jurisdiction to examine and amend the judgments and decrees of the courts of justice in Ireland ; therefore, etc., it is declared and enacted, etc. . . . . that the King's Majesty, by and with the advice and consent of the lords spiritual and temporal and commons *of Great Britain* in parliament assembled, had, hath, and of right ought to have, full power and authority to make laws and statutes of sufficient force and validity to bind the people of the kingdom of Ireland. And it is further enacted and declared, that the House of Lords of Ireland have not, nor of right ought to have, any jurisdiction to judge of, affirm, or reverse any judgment, etc., made in any court in the said kingdom."

His. Cath. Association. page 27.

Here was " Poynings' law " reënacted with savage explicitness; a heavy bit set between the jaws of the restive Irish legislature.

This rough and insulting assertion of subjugation stung the Protestants to the quick. They submitted ; but soon there began to break forth from amongst them men who commenced to utter the words Country and Patriotism. These " rash " and " extreme," *doctrinaires* were long almost singular in their views. Wise men considered them insane when they " raved " of recovering the freedom of parliament. " Repeal Poynings' law !—*restore the heptarchy !* " cried one philosopher. " Liberate the parliament !—a splendid phantom ! " cried another. Nevertheless, the so-called doctrinaires grew in popularity. Their leader was the Very Rev. Jonathan Swift, Protestant dean of St. Patrick's. His precursor was William Molyneux, member for the Dublin University, who, in 1691, published the first great argumentative vindication of Irish legislative independence—*The Case of Ireland Stated.* Immediately on its appearance, the English parliament took alarm, and ordered the book to be " burned by the hands of the common hangman." Swift took up the doctrines and arguments of Molyneux, and made them all-prevalent amongst the masses of the people. But the " upper classes " thought them " visionary " and " impracticable ; " nay, seditious and disloyal. Later on—in the middle of the century—Dr. Charles Lucas, a Dublin apothecary, became the leader of the anti-English party. Of course, he was set down as disaffected. A resolution of the servile Irish House of Commons declared him " an enemy to his country : " and he had to fly from Ireland for a time. His popularity however increased and the popula-

and the chancellor were roughly handled ; a privy councillor was thrown into the river ; the attorney-general was wounded and obliged to take refuge in the College ; Lord Inchiquin was abused till he said his name was O'Brien, when the rage of the people was turned into acclamations. The speaker, Mr. Ponsonby, and the chief secretary, Mr. Rigby, had to appear in the porch of the House of Commons, solemnly to assure the citizens that no union was dreamed of, and if it was proposed that they would be the first to oppose it." *

The union scheme had to be abandoned ; and Lucas soon after returned from exile, to wield increased power. The " seditious agitator," the solemnly declared " enemy of his country," was triumphantly returned to parliament by the citizens of Dublin, having as fellow-laborers, returned at the same time, Hussey Burgh and Henry Flood. Lucas did not live many years to enjoy his well-earned honors. In 1770 he was followed to the grave by every demonstration of national regret. " At his funeral the pall was borne by the Marquis of Kildare, Lord Charlemont, Mr. Flood, Mr. Hussey Burgh, Sir Lucius O'Brien, and Mr. Ponsonby." And the citizens of Dublin, to perpetuate the memory of the once banished " disloyalist," set up his marble statue in their civic forum, where it stands to this day. †

While the country was thus seething with discontent, chafing under the "Poyning" yoke, there rolled across the Atlantic the echoes of Bunker's Hill ; Protestant dominancy paused in its work of persecution, and bowed in homage to the divine spirit of Liberty !

---

* M'Gee.

† Lucas was, politically, a thorough nationalist, but, religiously, a bigot. The Irish nation he conceived to be the Irish Protestants. The idea of admitting the Catholics – the mass of the population—within the Constitution, found in him a rabid opponent. Yet the Catholics of Ireland, to their eternal honor, have ever condoned his rabid bigotry against themselves, remembering his labors for the principle of nationality.

LXXVII.—HOW THE IRISH VOLUNTEERS ACHIEVED THE LEGIS-LATIVE INDEPENDENCE OF IRELAND ; OR, HOW THE MORAL FORCE OF A CITIZEN ARMY EFFECTED A PEACEFUL, LEGAL, AND CONSTITUTIONAL REVOLUTION.

T HE first effort of the " patriot party," as for some years past they had been called, was to limit the duration of parliaments (at this time elected for the life of the king), so that the constituents might oftener have an opportunity—even by such cumbrous and wretchedly in-effective means as the existing electoral system provided—of judging the conduct of their members. In 1760, Lucas and his fellow-nationalists succeeded in carrying resolutions for " heads of a bill," limiting the parliaments to seven years. In accordance with " Poynings' law," the "heads" were trans-mitted to London for sanction, but were never heard of more. In 1763, they were again carried in the Irish house, again sent to London, again cancelled there. Irish popular feeling now began to be excited. Again, a third time, the "Septennial Bill " was carried through the Irish parliament, again sent to London, and again ignominiously vetoed there. But now the infatuation of England had overleaped itself. A spirit was aroused in Ireland before which the government quailed. A *fourth* time, amidst ominous demonstrations of popular de-termination, the thrice rejected "heads of a bill " were sent across. This time they were returned approved ; but the *seven* years were altered to *eight* years, a paltry and miserable assertion of mastery, even while yielding under fear. But the impartial student will note that by some malign fatality it happens that even up to the present hour every concession granted by England to Irish demands was invariably refused till passion was inflamed, and has been conceded only on compulsion. The concession that, had it been made cheerful-ly and graciously at first, might have elicited good will and

be withheld, and been granted only when some home or foreign difficulty rendered Irish discontent full of danger.

Concessions thus made are taken without thanks, and only give strength and determination to further demands. The patriot party followed up their first decisive victory by campaigns upon the pension list, the dependence of the judges, the voting of supply, etc. ; the result being continuous, violent and bitter conflict between the parliament and the viceroy; popular feeling rising and intensifying, gaining strength and force every hour.

Meanwhile America, on issues almost identical, had taken the field, and, aided by France, was holding England in deadly struggle. Towards the close of the year 1779, while Ireland as well as England was denuded of troops, the government sent warning that some French or American privateers might be expected on the Irish coast, but confessing that no regular troops could be spared for local defence. The people of Belfast were the first to make a significant answer to this warning, by enrolling volunteer corps. The movement spread rapidly throughout the island, and in a short time the government with dismay beheld the patriot party in parliament surrounded by a volunteer army filled with patriotic ardor and enthusiasm. Every additional battalion of volunteers enrolled added to the moral power wielded by those leaders, whose utterance grew in boldness amidst the flashing swords and bayonets of a citizen army one hundred thousand strong. The nation by this time had become unanimous in its resolution to be free ; a corrupt or timid group of courtiers or placemen alone making a sullen and half-hearted fight against the now all-powerful nationalists. Under the healing influence of this sentiment of patriotism, the gaping wounds of a century began to close. The Catholic slave, though still outside the pale of the constitution, forgot his griefs and his wrongs for the moment, and gave all his energies in aid of the national movement. He bought the musket which law denied to himself the right to bear, and placing it in the hand of his Protest-

Free trade became now the great object of endeavor. The trade of Ireland at this time had been almost extinguished by repressive enactments passed by the English parliament in London, or by its shadow in Dublin in by-gone years. Immediately on the accession of William the Third, the English lords and commons addressed the king, praying his majesty to declare to his Irish subjects that " the growth and increase of the woollen manufacture hath long been, and will ever be looked upon with great jealousy," and threatening very plainly that they might otherwise have to enact " *very strict laws totally to abolish the same.*"* William answered them, promising to do "all that in him lay " to "discourage the woollen manufacture there." 'Twere long to trace and to recapitulate the multifarious laws passed to crush manufacture and commerce of *all* kinds in Ireland in accordance with the above-cited address and royal promise. Englishmen in our day are constantly reproaching Ireland with absence of manufactures and commerce, and inviting this country to "wake up " and compete with England in the markets of the world. This may be malignant sarcasm, or it may be the ignorance of defective information. When one country has been by law forbidden to engage in manufactures or commerce, until the other has protected and nursed her own into vigor and maturity, and has secured possession of the world's markets, the invitation to the long restricted and now crippled country to "compete " on the basis of free trade, is as much of a mockery, as to call for a race between a trained athlete and a half-crippled captive, who has, moreover, been forcibly and foully detained till the other has neared the winning post.

To liberate Irish trade from such restraints was now the resolve of the patriot party in the Irish parliament. On the 12th October, 1779, they carried an address to the viceroy, declaring that " by free trade alone " could the nation be saved from impending ruin. Again England ungraciously and sourly complied, and once more clogged her compliance with embittering addenda! These concessions, which the secretary

of state was assuring the Irish parliament were freely bestowed
by English generosity, were no sooner made public in England
than Mr. Pitt had to send circular letters to the manufacturing
towns, assuring them " that nothing effectual had been granted
in Ireland. "

But the Irish leaders were now about to crown their liberating efforts by a work which would henceforth place the
destinies of Irish trade beyond the power of English jealousy,
and beneath the protecting aegis of a free and independent
native legislature. On the 19th April, 1780, Grattan moved
that resolution which is the sum and substance in its simple
completeness of the Irish national constitutional doctrine :—
"*that no power on earth, save that of the king, lords, and commons of Ireland, has a right to make laws to bind this kingdom.*"
The motion was unsuccessful ; but this was the commencement of the great struggle; and over the vital issue now raised—complete   legislative   independence—the   government
fought with an unscrupulous energy.   Throughout two years
the contest was pursued with unintermitting severity, when
suddenly Europe was electrified by the intelligence that the
British armies had capitulated to the " rebel colonists," and
the " star-spangled banner " appeared on the western horizon,
proclaiming the birth of a new power destined to be the terror of tyrants, the hope of the oppressed, all over the world.

It was England's day of humiliation and dismay. By clutch-
ing at the right of oppression in her hour of fancied strength,
she had lost America.   It was not clear that through the same
course she was not about to drive Ireland also from the demand for legislative independence into the choice of complete
separation.

The Ulster volunteers now decided to hold a national convention of delegates from every citizen regiment in the province.   On the day fixed —Friday, 15th February, 1782—and
at the appointed place of meeting—the Protestant church of
Dungannon, county Tyrone, the convention assembled ; and
there, amidst a scene the most glorious witnessed in Ireland
for years, the delegates of the citizen army solemnly swore

"unconstitutional, illegal, and a grievance," "the claim of any body of men, other than the king, lords, and commons *of Ireland*, to make laws to bind this kingdom." The Dungannon resolutions were enthusiastically ratified and reasserted by the several volunteer corps, the municipal corporations, and public meetings, all over the island ; and soon, outside the circle of corrupt and servile castle placemen, no voice durst be raised against the demand for liberty.

A conciliatory, that is, a temporizing ministry now came into power in London, and in their choice of lord lieutenant for Ireland—the duke of Portland—they found a very suitable man, apparently, for their designs or experiments. But the duke ." on his arrival found the nation in a state in which neither procrastination nor evasion was any longer practicable." He reported to England the danger of resistance and the advisability of temporizing, that is, of yielding as little as possible, but yielding *all* if necessary. Accordingly, a message was delivered by the king to the British parliament, setting forth " that mistrusts and jealousies had arisen in Ireland, and that it was highly necessary to take the same into immediate consideration in order to a *final* adjustment." Meanwhile the viceroy in Dublin was plausibly endeavoring to wheedle Grattan and the other patriot leaders into procrastination, or, failing this, to tone down, to " moderate," the terms of the popular demand. Happily Grattan was sternly firm. He would not consent to even a *day's* postponement of the question, and refused to alter a jot of the national ultimatum. An eye-witness has described for us the great scene of the 16th of April, 1782 :

" Whoever has individually experienced the sensation of ardent expectation, trembling suspense, burning impatience, and determined resolution, and can suppose all those sensations possessing an entire nation, may form some, but yet an inadequate idea of the feelings of the Irish people on the 16th of April, 1782, which was the day peremptorily fixed by Mr. Grattan for moving that delaration of rights, which was the proximate cause of Ireland's short-lived prosperity, and the

were the minds of the public wound up on the eve of that
momentous day, that the volunteers flew to their arms without having an enemy to encounter, and, almost breathless with
impatience, inquired eagerly after the probability of events,
which the close of the same day must certainly determine.

" Early on the 16th of April, 1782, the great street before
the house of parliament was thronged by a multitude of people, of every class and description, though many hours must
elapse before the house would meet, or business be proceeded
with. The parliament had been summoned to attend this
momentous question by an unusual and special call of the house,
and by four o'clock a full meeting took place. The body of
the House of Commons was crowded with its members, a
great proportion of the peerage attended as auditors, and the
capacious gallery which surrounded the interior magnificent
dome of the house contained above four hundred ladies of the
highest distinction, who partook of the same national fire
which had enlightened their parents, their husbands, and their
relatives, and by the sympathetic influence of their presence
and zeal they communicated an instinctive chivalrous impulse
to eloquence and patriotism.

"A calm but deep solicitude was apparent on almost every
countenance when Mr. Grattan entered, accompanied by Mr.
Brownlow and several others, the determined and important
advocates for the declaration of Irish independence. Mr.
Grattan's preceding exertions and anxiety had manifestly
injured his health; his tottering frame seemed barely sufficient
to sustain his laboring mind, replete with the unprecedented
importance and responsibility of the measure he was about to
bring forward." *

"For a short time," continues Sir Jonah Barrington, "a
profound silence ensued." It was expected that Grattan would
rise; but, to the mortification and confusion of the government
leaders, he kept his seat, putting on them the responsibility
of opening the proceedings and of fixing their attitude before
being allowed to "feel their way," as they greatly desired to

do. The secretary of state, resigning himself to the worst, thought it better to declare for concession. He announced that " his majesty, being concerned to find that discontents and jealousies were prevailing amongst his loyal subjects in Ireland upon matters of great weight and importance, recommended to the house to take the same into their most serious consideration, in order to effect such a *final* adjustment as might give satisfaction to both kingdoms." The secretary, however, added, that he was not officially authorized to say more than to deliver the message.

After an interval of embarrassing silence and curiosity, Mr. George Ponsonby rose, and moved a weak and procrastinating reply, "thanking the king for his goodness and condescension." But it would not do. The national determination was not to be trifled with. At length, after a solemn pause, Grattan, slowly rising from his seat, commenced " the most luminous, brilliant, and effective oration ever delivered in the Irish parliament ; " a speech which, " rising in its progress, applied equally to the sense, the pride, and the spirit of the nation." " Amidst an universal cry of approbation," he concluded by moving as an amendment to Mr. Ponsonby's inconsequential motion, the ever-memorable DECLARATION OF IRISH INDEPENDENCE :

" That the kingdom of Ireland is a distinct kingdom, with a parliament of her own, the sole legislature thereof ; that there is no body of men competent to make laws to bind the nation, but the kings, lords, and commons of Ireland, nor any parliament which hath any authority or power of any sort whatever in this country, save only the parliament of Ireland ; to assure his majesty, that we humbly conceive that in this right the very essence of our liberty exists, a right which we, on the part of all the people of Ireland, do claim as their birthright, and which we cannot yield but with our lives."

Grattan's amendment was seconded by Mr. Brownlow, member for Armagh county, in point of wealth and reputation one of the first country gentlemen in Ireland. "The whole house," says Barrington, "in a moment caught the patriotic flame. All further debate ceased ; the speaker put the question on Mr. Grattan's amendment ; an *unanimous* shout

the question. The applause redoubled. A moment of tumul-
tuous exultation followed : and after centuries of oppression,
Ireland at length declared herself an independent nation.

Word of the event no sooner reached the impatient crowd
outside the building, than a cry of joy and triumph burst forth
all over the city. "The news soon spread through the nation,
and the rejoicings of the people were beyond all description;
every city, town, and village in Ireland blazed with the emblems of exultation, and resounded with the shouts of triumph."

"Never was a new nation more nobly heralded into existence! Never was an old nation more reverently and tenderly
lifted up and restored! The houses adjourned to give England
time to consider Ireland's ultimatum. Within a month it was
accepted by the new British administration." The "visionary "
and "impracticable " idea had become an accomplished fact.
The "splendid phantom " had become a glorious reality.
The heptarchy had not been restored ; yet Ireland had won
complete legislative independence !

LXXVIII.—WHAT NATIONAL INDEPENDENCE ACCOMPLISHED FOR IRELAND. HOW ENGLAND ONCE MORE BROKE FAITH WITH IRELAND, AND REPAID GENEROUS TRUST WITH BASE BETRAYAL.

IF mankind needed at so late a period of the world's age as the close of the eighteenth century, any experiment to prove the substantial benefits of national freedom, the progress of Ireland during this brief but bright and glorious era of independence would suffice to establish the fact for ever. Happily, when referring to the events of that time, we treat of no remote period of history. Living men remember it. Irishmen of this generation have listened at their parent's knee to reminiscences and relations, facts and particulars, that mark it as the day of Ireland's true, real, and visible prosperity. Statistics—invulnerable—irrefragable —full of eloquence—momentous in their meaning—attest the same truth. Manufacture, trade, and commerce developed to a greater extent in *ten* years of native rule than they had done in the previous *hundred* under English mastery, and in a much greater proportion than they had developed in the *sixty-seven* years of subsequent " union " legislation.

Ireland's freedom and prosperity did not mean England's injury, nor England's pause in the like onward march. The history of the period we are now treating of disposes of more than one fallacy used by the advocates of Irish national extinction. It proves that Ireland's right does not involve England's wrong. Never before were the two countries more free from jealousy, rivalry, or hostility. Never before was discontent banished from Ireland—as never since has disaffection been absent.

Lust of dominion—sheer covetousness of mastery—has in all ages been the source and origin of the most wanton inva-

Englishmen themselves does any writer now hesitate to characterize as nefarious, treacherous? and abominable, the scheme by which England invaded and overthrew in 1800 the happily established freedom of Ireland. *

Scarcely had the rusty chain of "Poynings' Act" been wrenched off, than the English minister began to consider how a stronger one might be forged and bound on the liber‑ ated Irish nation! The king's voice characterized the happy and amicable settlement just concluded as "*final.*" The Brit‑ ish minister and the British parliament in the most solemn manner declared the same ; and surely nothing but morbid suspiciousness could discover fair ground for crediting that England would play Ireland false upon that promise—that she would seize the earliest opportunity of not merely break‑ ing that "final adjustment," and shackling the Irish parliament anew, but of destroying it utterly and forever! Yet there were men amongst the Irish patriots who did not hesitate to express such suspicions at the moment, and foremost amongst these was Flood. He pressed for further and more specific and formal renunciation. Grattan, on the other hand, vio‑ lently resisted this, as an ungenerous effort to put England "on her knees"—to humiliate her—to plainly treat her as a sus‑ pected blackleg. On this issue the two patriot leaders vio‑ lently, acrimoniously, and irreconcilably quarreled ; Flood and his following contending that England would surely be‑ tray Ireland on the "final adjustment," and Grattan, with the bulk of the national party, vehemently refusing to put such ungenerous insult and indignity on England as to suppose her capable of such conduct.

Alas ! *At that very moment*—as the now published corres‑

---

* English readers as yet uninformed on the subject, and disposed to receive with hesitation the statements of Irish writers as to the infamous means resorted to by the English government to overthrow the Irish constitution in 1800, may be referred to the Castlereagh Papers and the Cornwallis Correspondence‑‑the private letters of the chief agents in the scheme. Mr. Massey, chairman of committies in the English House of Commons, published, a few years ago, a volume which exposes and charac‑ terizes that nefarious transaction in language which might by deemed too strong if

pondence of the English statesmen engaged in the transaction discloses—the British ministers were discussing, devising, and directing preparations for accomplishing, by the most iniquitous means, that crime against Ireland of which Grattan considered it ungenerous and wicked to express even a suspicion !

It was with good reason the national party, soon after the accomplishment of legislative independence, directed their energies to the question of parliamentary reform. The legislative body, which in a moment of great public excitement and enthusiasm, had been made for a moment to reflect correctly the national will, was after all returned by an antique electoral system, which was a gross farce on representation. Boroughs and seats were at the time openly and literally *owned* by particular persons or families, the voting "constituency" sometimes being not more than a dozen in number. As a matter of fact, less than a hundred persons *owned* seats or boroughs capable of making a majority in the commons.

The patriot party naturally and wisely judged that with such a parliament the retention of freedom would be precarious, and the representation of the national will uncertain ; so the question of parliamentary reform came to be agitated with a vehemence second only to that of parliamentary independence in the then recent campaign. By this time, however, the British minister had equally detected, that while with such a parliament he might accomplish his treacherous designs, with a parliament really amenable to the people, he never could. Concealing the real motive and the remote object, the government, through its myriad devious channels of influence, as well as openly and avowedly, resisted the demand for reform. Apart from the government, the "vested interests" of the existing system were able to make a protracted fight. Ere long both these sections were leagued together, and they hopelessly outnumbered the popular party.

The government now began to feel itself strong, and it accordingly commenced the work of deliberately destroying the parliament of Ireland. Those whom it could influence.

in market overt. Those who were true to honor and duty, it insolently threatened, insulted, and assailed. The popular demands were treated with defiance and contumely by the minister and his co-conspirators. Soon a malign opportunity presented itself for putting Ireland utterly, hopelessly, help-lessly into their hands—the sheep committed to the grasp of the wolf for security and protection!

------cᴓ------

LXXIX.—HOW THE ENGLISH MINISTER SAW HIS ADVANTAGE IN PROVOKING IRELAND INTO AN ARMED STRUGGLE; AND HOW HEARTLESSLY HE LABORED TO THAT END.

HILE these events were transpiring in Ireland the French revolution had burst forth, shaking the whole fabric of European society, rending old systems with the terrible force of a newly-appeared explosive pow-er. Everywhere its effects were felt. Everywhere men were struck with wonder. Everywhere the subtle intoxi-cation of the revolutionary doctrines, symbolized by the terrible *drapeau rouge*, fired the blood of political enthusi-asts. Some hailed the birth of the French republic as the avatar of freedom; * others saw in it the incarnation of an-

---

* The sentiments evoked in the breasts of most Irish patriots by the first outburst and subsequent proceedings of the French revolution— enthusiasms, joy, and hope, followed by grief, horror, and despair—have been truthfully expressed by Moore in the following matchless verses : —

> 'Tis gone and for ever—the light we saw breaking
> Like heaven's first dawn o'er the sleep of the dead ;
> When man from the slumber of ages awaking,
> Looked upward and blessed the pure ray ere it fled.
> 'Tis gone—and the gleam it has left of its burning
> But deepens the long night of bondage and mourning
> That dark o'er the kingdoms of earth is returning,
> But darkest of all, hapless Erin, o'er thee.
>
> How high was thy hope when those glories were darting
> Around thee through all the gross clouds of the world
> When Truth, from her fetters indignantly starting,

archy and infidelity ; and organized war upon social order and upon the Christian religion. It instantly arrayed all Europe in two fiercely hostile camps. Each side spoke and acted with a passionate energy. Old parties and schools of political thought were broken up ; old friendships and alliances were sundered forever, on the question whether the French revolution was an emanation from hell or an inspiration from heaven.

Ireland so peculiarly circumstanced, could not fail to be powerfully moved by the great drama unfolded before the world in Paris. Side by side with the march of events there, from 1789 to 1795, was the revelation of England's treason against the "final adjustment" of Irish national rights, and the exasperating demeanor, language, and action of the government in its now avowed determination to conquor right by might.

Towards the close of 1791, Theobald Wolfe Tone—a young Protestant barrister of great ability, who had devoted himself to the service of the Catholics in their efforts for emancipation—visiting Belfast (then the centre and citadel of democratic and liberal, if not indeed of republican opinions),* met there some of the popular leaders. They had marked the treacherous conduct of the government, and they saw no hope for averting the ruin designed for Ireland, save in a union of *all* Irishmen, irrespective of creed or class, in an open, legal, and constitutional organization for the accomplishment of *parliamentary reform* and *Catholic emancipation*. Such an or-

---

Oh I never shall earth see a moment so splendid ;
Then—then—had one Hymn of Deliverance blended
The tongues of all nations, how sweet had ascended
 The first note of liberty, Erin, from thee !

But shame on those tyrants who envied the blessing,
 And shame on the light race unworthy its good,
Who at Death's reeking altar, like furies caressing
 The young hope of Freedom, baptized it in blood,
Then vanished for ever that fair sunny vision
Which, spite of the slavish, the cold heart's derision,
Shall long be remembered—pure, bright, and elysian
 As first it arose, my lost Erin on thee !

* In July of that year (1791), the French revolution was celebrated with military

ganization they forthwith established. Tone, on his return
to Dublin, pushed its operations there, and it soon embraced
every man of note on the people's side in politics. The association thus established was called the Society of United
Irishmen. For some time it pursued its labors zealously, and,
as its first principles exacted, openly, legally, and constitu-
tionally, towards the attainment of its most legitimate objects.
But the government was winning against the United Irish
leaders by strides—pandering to the grossest passions and
vices of the oligarchical party, now sedulously inflamed
against all popular opinions by the mad-dog cry of " French
principles." One by one the popular leaders tired in the hopeless struggle—were overpowered by despair of resisting the
gross and naked tyranny of the government, which was absolutely and designedly pushing them out of constitutional action. Some of them retired from public life. Others of them
yielded to the conviction that outside the constitution, if not
within it, the struggle might be fought, and the United Irishmen gradually became an oath-bound secret society.

From the first hour when an armed struggle came to be
contemplated by the United Irish leaders, they very naturally
fixed their hopes on France: and envoys passed and repassed
between them and the French Directory. The government
had early knowledge of the fact. It was to them news the
most welcome. Indeed they so clearly saw their advantage
—their certain success—in arraying on their side all who
feared a Jacobin revolution, and in identifying in the minds
of the property classes anti-Englishism with revolution and
infidelity, that their greatest anxiety was to make sure that
the United Irishmen would go far enough and deep enough
into the scheme. And the government left nothing undone
to secure that result.

Meanwhile, the society in its new character extended itself
with marvellous success. Its organization was ingenious, and
of course its leaders believed it to be "spy-proof." Nearly
half a million of earnest and determined men were enrolled,
and a considerable portion of them were armed either with

likely that the government conspirators might find they had over-shot their own purpose, and had allowed the organization to develop too far. Up to 1796 they never took into calculation as a serious probability that France would really cast her powerful aid into the scale with Ireland. In the instant when England, startled beyond conception, was awakened to her error on this point by the appearance in Bantry Bay, in December, 1796, of a formidable expedition under Hoche *— a sense of danger and alarm possessed her, and it was decided to burst up the insurrectionary design—to *force* it into conflict at once ;—the peril now being that the armed and organized Irish might " bide their time."

To drive the Irish into the field—to goad them into action in the hour of England's choice, not their own—was the problem. Its accomplishment was arrived at by proceedings over which the historical writer or student shudders in horror. Early in 1796, an Insurrection Act was passed, making the administration of an oath identical with or similar to that of the United Irishmen punishable with *death !* An army of fifty thousand men, subsequently increased to eighty thousand, was let loose upon the country on the atrocious system of " free quarters." Irresponsible power was conferred on the military officers and local magistracy. The yeomanry, mainly composed of Orangemen, were quartered on the most Catholic districts, while the Irish militia regiments suspected of any sympathy with the population were shipped off to England in exchange for foreign troops. " The military tribunals did not wait for the idle formalities of the civil courts. Soldiers and civilians, yeomen and townsmen, against whom the informer pointed his finger, were taken out and summarily executed. Ghastly forms hung upon the thickest gibbets, not only in the market places of the country towns and before the public prisons, but on all the bridges of the metropolis. The horrid torture of picketing, and the

---

* This expedition had been obtained from the French Directory by the energy and perseverance of Wolfe Tone, who had been obliged to fly from Ireland. It was dis-

blood-stained lash, were constantly resorted to, to extort accusations or confessions." * Lord Holland gives us a like picture of "burning cottages, tortured backs, and frequent executions." " The fact is incontrovertible," he says, "that the people of Ireland were driven to resistance (which, possibly, they meditated before) by the free quarters and excesses of the soldiery, which were such as are not permitted in civilized warfare even in an enemy's country. Dr. Dickson, Lord Bishop of Down, assured me that he had *seen* families returning peaceably from Mass, assailed without provocation by drunken troops and yeomanry, and their wives and daughters exposed to every species of indignity, brutality, and outrage, from which neither his (the Bishop's) remonstrances, nor those of other Protestant gentlemen, could rescue them." †

No wonder the gallant and humane Sir John Moore—appalled at the infamies of that lustful and brutal soldiery, and unable to repress his sympathy with the helpless Irish peasantry—should have exclaimed, " *If I were an Irishman I would be a rebel !*"

---

* M'Gee.
† Lord Holland, *Memoirs of the Whig Party.*

LXXX.—HOW THE BRITISH MINISTER FORCED ON THE RISING. —THE FATE OF THE BRAVE LORD EDWARD.—HOW THE BROTHERS SHEARES DIED HAND-IN-HAND.—THE RISING OF 'NINETY-EIGHT.

HILE the government, by such frightful agencies, was trying to *force* an insurrection, the United Irish leaders were straining every energy to keep the people in restraint until such time as they could strike and not strike in vain. But in this dreadful game the government was sure to win eventually. By a decisive blow at the Society, on the 12th March, 1798, it compelled the United Irishmen to take the field forthwith or perish. This was the seizure, on that day, in one swoop, of the Supreme Council or Directory, with all its returns, lists, and muster-rolls, while sitting in deliberation, at the house of Mr. Oliver Bond (one of the council) in Bridge Street, Dublin.

This terrible stroke was almost irreparable. One man, however, escaped by the accident of not having attended, as he intended, that day's council meeting ; and him of all others the government desired to capture. This was Lord Edward Fitzgerald, son of the Duke of Leinster, commander-in-chief of the United Irish military organization.

Of all the men who have given their lives in the fatal struggle against the English yoke, not one is more endeared

Edward the *beau ideal* of a popular leader. " He was, " says
a writer whose labors to assure the fame and vindicate in
history the gallant band of whom the youthful Geraldine was
amongst the foremost, should never be forgotten by Irishmen—"as playful and humble as a child, as mild and timid as
a lady, and, when necessary, as brave as a lion." *

Such was the man on whose head a price of one thousand
pounds was now set by the government. On the arrest of
the directory at Bond's, three men of position and ability
stepped forward into the vacant council-seats ; the brothers
John and Henry Sheares, and Doctor Lawless; and upon
these and Lord Edward now devolved the responsibility of
controlling the organization. Lord Edward insisted on an
immediate rising. He saw that by the aid of spies and in-
formers the government was in possession of their inmost secrets, and that very day would be ruining their organization.
To wait further for aid from France would be utter destruction to all their plans. Accordingly, it was decided that on
the 23d May next following, the standard of insurrection
should be unfurled, and Ireland appeal to the *ultima ratio* of
oppressed nations.

The government heard this, through their spies, with a
sense of relief and of diabolical satisfaction. Efforts to secure
Lord Edward were now pursued with desperate activity ;
yet he remained in Dublin eluding his enemies for eight weeks
after the arrests at Bond's, guarded, convoyed, sheltered by
the people with a devotion for which history has scarcely a
parallel. The 23d of May was approaching fast, and still
Lord Edward was at large. The Castle conspirators began
to fear that after all their machinations they might find themselves face to face with an Irish Washington. Within a few
days, however, of the ominous 23d, treason gave them the
victory, and placed the noble Geraldine within their grasp.

On the night of the 18th May, he was brought to the house
of a Mr. Nicholas Murphy, a feather merchant of 153 Thomas
Street. He had been secreted in this same house before, but

had been removed, as it was deemed essential to change his place of concealment very frequently. After spending some short time at each of several other places in the interval, he was, on the night already mentioned, a second time brought to Mr. Murphy's house. On the evening of the next day, Lord Edward, after dining with his host, retired to his chamber, intending to lie down for a while, being suffering from a cold. Mr. Murphy followed him up stairs to speak to him about something, when the noise of feet softly but quickly springing up the stair caught his ear, and instantly the door was thrown open and a police magistrate named Swan, accompanied by a soldier, rushed into the room. Lord Edward was lying on the bed with his coat and vest off. He sprang from the bed snatching from under the pillow a dagger. Swan thrust his right hand into an inside breast pocket where his pistols were ; but Lord Edward divining the object, struck at that spot, and sent his dagger through Swan's hand, penetrating his body. Swan shouted that he was "murdered ;" nevertheless, with his wounded hand he managed to draw his pistol and fire at Lord Edward. The shot missed ; but at this moment another of the police party, named Ryan, (a yeomanry captain) rushed in, armed with a drawn cane-sword, and Major Sirr with half a dozen soldiers, hurried up stairs. Ryan flung himself on Lord Edward, and tried to hold him down on the bed, but he could not, and the pair, locked in deadly combat, rolled upon the floor. Lord Edward received some deadly thrusts from Ryan's sword, but he succeeded in freeing his right hand, and as quick as he could draw his arm, plunged the dagger again and again into Ryan's body. The yeomanry captain, though wounded mortally all over, was still struggling with Lord Edward on the floor when Sirr and the soldiers arrived. Sirr, pistol in hand, feared to grapple with the enraged Geraldine; but, watching his opportunity, took deliberate aim at him and fired. The ball struck Lord Edward in the right shoulder ; the dagger fell from his grasp, and Sirr and the soldiers flung themselves upon him in a body. Still it required their utmost efforts to hold him down, some of them stabbing and hacking at him with shortened swords and clubbed pistols, while others held him fast. At length, weakened from wounds and loss of blood, he fainted. They took a sheet off the bed and rolled the almost inanimate body in it, and dragged their victim down the narrow stair. The floor of the room, all over blood, an eye-witness says, resembled a slaughter house, and even the walls were dashed with gore.

Meantime a crowd had assembled in the street, attracted by the presence of the soldiers around the house. The instant it became known that it was Lord Edward that had been captured, the people flung themselves on the military, and after a desperate struggle had overpowered them but for the arrival of a large body of cavalry, who eventually succeeded in bringing off Lord Edward to the castle.

Here his wounds were dressed. On being told by the doctor that they were not likely to prove fatal, he exclaimed: " I am sorry to hear it." He was removed to Newgate, none of his friends being allowed access to him until the 3d of June, when they were told *that he was dying!* His aunt, Lady Louisa Connolly, and his brother, Lord Henry Fitzgerald, were then permitted to see him. They found him delirious. As he lay on his fever pallet in the dark and narrow cell of that accursed bastile, his ears were dinned with horrid noises that his brutal jailors took care to tell him were caused by the workmen erecting barriers around the gallows fixed for a forthcoming execution.   .

Next day 4th June, 1798, he expired. As he died unconvicted, his body was given up to his friends, but only on condition that no funeral would be attempted. In the dead of night they conveyed the last remains of the noble Lord Edward from Newgate to the Kildare vault beneath St. Werburgh's Protestant Church, Dublin, where they now repose.

A few days after Lord Edward's capture—on Monday, 21st May—the brothers Sheares were arrested, one at his residence in lower Baggot Street, the other at a friend's house in French Street, having been betrayed by a government agent named Armstrong, who had wormed himself into their friendship and confidence for the purpose of effecting their ruin. On the evening previous to their capture he was a guest in the

CAPTURE OF LORD EDWARD.

See pages 511, 512.

bosom of their family, sitting at their fireside, fondling on his knee the infant child of one of the victims, whose blood was to drip from the scaffold in Green Street, a few weeks later, through his unequalled infamy.

On the 12th July, John and Henry Sheares were brought to trial, and the fiend Armstrong appeared on the witness table and swore away their lives. Two days afterwards the martyr-brothers were executed, side by side. Indeed they fell through the drop *hand clasped in hand*, having, as they stood blindfolded on the trap, in the brief moment before the bolt was drawn, by an instinct of holy affection strong in death each one reached out as best he could his pinioned hand, and grasped that of his brother!

The capture of Lord Edward, so quickly followed by the arrest of the brothers Sheares, was a deathblow to the insurrection, as far as concerned any preconcerted movement. On the night of the appointed day an abortive rising took place in the neighborhood of the metropolis. On the same day Kildare, Lord Edward's county, took the field, and against hopeless disadvantages made a gallant stand. Meath also kept its troth, as did Down and Antrim in the north keep theirs, but only to a like bloody sacrifice, and in a few days it seemed that all was over. But a county almost free from complicity in the organization, a county in which no one on either side had apprehended the revolt, was now about to show the world what Irish peasants, driven to desperation defending their homes and altars, could dare and do. Wexford, heroic and glorious Wexford, was now about to show that even *one* county of Ireland's *thirty-two* could engage more than half the available army of England!

Wexford rose, not in obedience to any call from the united Irish organization, but purely and solely from the instinct of self-preservation. Although there was probably no district in Ireland so free from participation in the designs of that association (there were scarcely two hundred enrolled United Irishmen amongst its entire population), all the horrors of free-quarters and martial law had been let loose on the county. Atrocities that sicken the heart in their contemplation, filled

with terror the homes of that peaceful and inoffensive people.
The midnight skies were reddened with the flames of burning cottages, and the glens resounded with shrieks of agony,
vengeance, and despair. Homes desolated, female virtue made
the victim of crimes that cannot be named, the gibbet and
the triangle erected in every hamlet, and finally, the temples
of God desecrated and given to the torch, left manhood in
Wexford no choice but that which to its eternal honor it
made.

Well and bravely Wexford fought that fight. It was the
wild rush to arms of a tortured peasantry, unprepared, un-
organized, unarmed. Yet no Irishman has need to " hang his
head for shame " when men speak of gallant Wexford in ninety-
eight. Battle for battle, the men of that county beat the
best armies of the king, until their relative forces became out of
all proportion. Neither Tell in Switzerland nor Hofer in the
Tyrol earned immortality more gloriously than that noble
band of " the sister-counties," Wexford and Wicklow—
Beauchamp Bagenal Harvey ; Colclough of Tintern Abbey ;
Fitzgerald of Newpark ; Miles Byrne, and Edmund Kyan, in
the one ; and the patriot brothers Byrne of Ballymanus, with
Holt, Hackett, and " brave Michael Dwyer," in the other.
And, as he who studies the history of this country will note,
in all its struggles for seven hundred years, the priests of Ireland, ever fearless to brave the anger of the maddened people,
restraining them while the conflict might be avoided, were ever
readiest to die,

> Whether on the scaffold high,
> Or in the battle's van—

side by side with the people, when driven to the last resort.
Fathers John and Michael Murphy, Father Roche, and Father
Clinch, are names that should ever be remembered by Irishmen
when tempters whisper that the voice of the Catholic pastor,
raised in warning or restraint, is the utterance of one who
cannot feel for, who would not *die* for, the flock he desires to
save.

appeared in Killala Bay the first instalment of that aid from France for which the United Irish leaders had desired to wait! If they could have resisted the government endeavors to precipitate the rising for barely three or four months longer, it is impossible to say how the movement might have resulted. On the 22d August, the French general Humbert, landed at Killala with barely one thousand men. Miserable as was this force, a few months earlier it would have counted for twenty thousand; but now, ten thousand, much less ten hundred, would not avail. They came too late, or the rising was too soon. Nevertheless, with this handful of men, joined by a few thousand hardy Mayo peasantry, Humbert literally chased the government troops before him across the island; and it was not until the viceroy himself, Lord Cornwallis, hurrying from Dublin, concentrated around the Franco-Irish army of *three thousand* men a force of nearly *thirty thousand*, enveloping them on all sides—and of course, hopelessly overpowering them—that the victorious march of the daring Frenchmen was arrested by the complete defeat and capitulation of Ballinamuck, on the morning of the 8th September, 1798.

It was the last battle of the insurrection. Within a fortnight subsequently two further and smaller expeditions from France reached the northern coast; one accompanied by Napper Tandy (an exiled United Irish leader), and another under Admiral Bompart with Wolfe Tone on board. The latter one was attacked by a powerful English fleet and captured. Tone, the heroic and indefatigable, was sent in irons to Dublin, where he was tried by court-martial and sentenced to be hung. He pleaded hard for a soldier's death; but his judges were inexorable. It turned out, however, that his trial and conviction were utterly illegal, as martial law had ceased, and the ordinary tribunals were sitting at the time. At the instance of the illustrious Irish advocate, orator, and patriot, Curran, an order was obtained against the military authorities to deliver Tone over to the civil court. The order was at first resisted, but ultimately the official of the court was informed that the prisoner " had committed suicide." He

ed by himself, to avert the indignity he so earnestly deprecat-
ed ; but not improbably, as popular conviction has it, the work
of a murderous hand ; for fouler deeds were done in the government dungeons in " those dark and evil days."

The insurrection of '98 was the first *rebellion* on the part of
the Irish people for hundreds of years. The revolt of the
Puritan colonists in 1641, and that of their descendants, the
Protestant rebels of 1690, were not *Irish* movements in any
sense of the phrase. It was only after 1605 that the English
government could, by any code of moral obligations whatever,
be held entitled to the obedience of the Irish people, whose
struggles previous to that date were lawful efforts in defence of
their native and legitimate rulers against the English invaders.
And never, subsequently to 1605, up to the period at which
we have now arrived—1798—did the Irish people revolt or
rebel against the new sovereignty. On the contrary, in 1641,
they fought for the king, and lost heavily by their loyalty.
In 1690 once more they fought for the king, and again they
paid a terrible penalty for their fidelity to the sovereign. In
plain truth, the Irish are, of all people, the most disposed
to respect constituted authority where it is entitled to respect,
and the most ready to repay even the shortest measure of
justice on the part of the sovereign, by generous, faithful,
enduring, and self-sacrificing loyalty. They are a law-abiding
people—or rather a justice-loving people ; for their contempt
for law becomes extreme when it is made the antithesis of
justice. Nothing but terrible provocation could have driven
such a people into rebellion.

Rebellion against just and lawful government is a great
crime. Rebellion against constituted government of any
character is a terrible responsibility. There are circumstances
under which resistance is a duty, and where, it may be said,
the crime would be rather in slavish or cowardly acquiescence ;
but awful is the accountability of him who undertakes to judge
that the measure of justification is full, that the moral duty of
resistance is established by the circumstances, and that, nor
merely in figure of speech, but in solemn reality, no other
resort remains.

But, however all this may be, the public code of which it is a part, rightly recognizes a great distinction in favor of a people who are driven into the field to defend their homes and altars against brutal military violence. Such were the heroic men of Wexford; and of the United Irishmen it is to be remembered that if they pursued an object unquestionably good and virtuous in itself, outside, not within, the constitution, it was not by their own choice. They were no apostles of anarchy, no lovers of revolution, no "rebels for a theory." They were not men who decried or opposed the more peaceful action of moral force agencies. They would have preferred them, had a choice fairly been left them. There was undoubtedly a French Jacobinical spirit tingeing the views of many of the Dublin and Ulster leaders towards the close, but under all the circumstances this was inevitable. With scarcely an exception, they were men of exemplary moral characters, high social position, of unsullied integrity, of brilliant intellect, of pure and lofty patriotism. They were men who honestly desired and endeavored, while it was permitted to them so to do, by lawful and constitutional means, to save and serve their country, but who, by an infamous conspiracy of the government, were deliberately forced upon resistance as a patriot's duty, and who at the last sealed with their blood their devotion to Ireland.

"More than twenty years have passed away," says Lord Holland; "many of my political opinions are softened, my predilections for some men weakened, my prejudices against others removed; but my approbation of Lord Edward Fitzgerald's actions remains unaltered and unshaken. His country was bleeding under one of the hardest tyrannies that our times have witnessed. He who thinks that a man can be even excused in such circumstances by any other consideration than that of despair from opposing by force a pretended government, seems to me to sanction a principle which would insure impunity to the greatest of all human delinquents, or at least to those who produce the greatest misery among mankind." *

_____

* Lord Holland's *Memoirs of the Whig Party.*

LXXXI.—HOW THE GOVERNMENT CONSPIRACY NOW ACHIEVED
ITS PURPOSE.—HOW THE PARLIAMENT OF IRELAND WAS
EXTINGUISHED.

ORRORS," says Sir Jonah Barrington, " were everywhere recommenced, executions were multiplied. The
government had now achieved the very climax of
public terror on which they had so much counted for
inducing Ireland to throw herself into the arms of the
'protecting' country.   Mr. Pitt conceived that the moment
had arrived to try the effect of his previous measures, to
promote a legislative union, and annihilate the parliament of
Ireland."

"On the 22d January, 1799, the Irish legislature met
under circumstances of great interest and excitement.   The
city of Dublin, always keenly alive to its metropolitan interests, sent its eager thousands by every avenue towards
College Green.   The viceroy went down to the houses with
a more than ordinary guard, and being seated on the throne
in the House of Lords, the Commons were summoned to the
bar.   The viceregal speech congratulated both houses on
the suppression of the late rebellion, on the defeat of Bompart's squadron, and the recent French victories of Lord
Nelson ; then came, amid profound expectation, this concluding sentence :—

" ' The unremitting industry,' said the viceroy, ' with which our enemies persevere
in their avowed design of endeavoring to effect a separation of this kingdom from
Great Britain must have engaged your attention, and his Majesty commands me to
express his anxious hope that this consideration, joined to the sentiment of mutual
affection and common interest, may dispose the parliaments in both kingdoms to
provide the most effectual means of maintaining and improving a connection
essential to their common security, and of consolidating, as far as possible, into one
firm and lasting fabric, the strength, the power, and the resources of the British
empire.'

" On the paragraph of the address reëchoing this sentiment
(which was carried by a large majority in *the lords*). a debate

ensued in the commons which lasted till one o'clock of the following day, about twenty consecutive hours. The galleries and lobbies were crowded all night by the first people of the city, of both sexes, and when the division was being taken the most intense anxiety was manifested within doors and without."*

" One hundred and eleven members had declared against the Union, and when the doors were opened, one hundred and five were discovered to be the total number of the minister's adherents. The gratification of the anti-Unionists was unbounded ; and as they walked deliberately in, one by one, to be counted, the eager spectators, ladies as well as gentlemen, leaning over the galleries ignorant of the result, were panting with expectation. Lady Castlereagh, then one of the finest women of the court, appeared in the sergeant's box, palpitating for her husband's fate. The desponding appearance and fallen crests of the ministerial benches and the exulting air of the opposition members as they entered, were intelligible. The murmurs of suppressed anxiety would have excited an interest even in the most unconnected stranger, who had known the objects and importance of the contest. How much more, therefore, must every Irish breast which panted in the galleries, have experienced that thrilling enthusiasm which accompanies the achievement of patriotic actions, when the minister's defeat was announced from the chair! A due sense of respect and decorum restrained the galleries within proper bounds ; but a low cry of satisfaction from the female audience could not be prevented, and no sooner was the event made known out of doors, than the crowds that had waited during the entire night with increasing impatience for the vote which was to decide on the independence of their country, sent forth loud and reiterated shouts of exultation, which, resounding through the corridors, and penetrating to the body of the house, added to the triumph of the conquerors, and to the misery of the adherents of the conquered minister."†

The minister was utterly and unexpectedly worsted in his

first attack; but he was not shaken from his purpose. He could scarcely have credited that, notwithstanding his previous laborious machinations of terror and seduction, there could still be found so much of virtue, courage, and independence in the parliament. However, this bitter defeat merely caused him to fall back for the purpose of approaching by mine the citadel he had failed to carry by assault. The majority against him was narrow. The gaining of twenty or thirty members would make a difference of twice that number on a division. "All the weapons of seduction were in his hands," says Sir Jonah Barrington, "and to acquire a majority, he had only to overcome the wavering and the feeble." "Thirty-two new county judgeships," says another writer, "were created; a great number of additional inspectorships were also placed at the minister's disposal; thirteen members had peerages for themselves or for their wives, with remainder to their children, and nineteen others were presented to various lucrative offices."

Both parties—Unionists and anti-Unionists, traitors and patriots—felt that during the parliamentary recess the issue would really be decided; for by the time the next session opened the minister would have secured his majority if such an end was possible. The interval, accordingly, was one of painfully exciting struggle, each party straining every energy. The government had a persuasive story for every sectional interest in the country. It secretly assured the Catholic bishops, nay, solemnly pledged itself, that if the Union were carried, one of the first acts of the imperial parliament should be Catholic emancipation. " An *Irish* parliament will never grant it, can never afford to grant it," said the Castle tempter. " The fears of the Protestant minority in this country will make them too much afraid of you. *We* alone can afford to rise above this miserable dread of your numbers." To the Protestants, on the other hand, the minister held out arguments just as insidious, as treacherous, and as fraudulent. "Behold the never-ceasing efforts of these Catholics! Do what you will, some day they must overwhelm you, being

security or the Irish Protestant Church establishment, unless in a union with us. In Ireland, as a kingdom, you are in a miserable minority, sure to be some day overwhelmed and destroyed. United to Great Britain, you will be an indivisible part of one vast Protestant majority, and can afford to defy the Papists."

Again, to the landed gentry, the terrors of "French principles," constant plots and rebellions, were artfully held forth. "No safety for society, no security for property, except in a union with Great Britain." Even the populace, the peasantry, were attempted to be overreached also, by inflaming them against the landlords as base yeomanry tyrants, whose fears of the people would ever make them merciless oppressors!

And it is curious to note that in that day—1799 and 1800— the identical great things that in our own time are still *about* to happen, and always have been *about* to happen, (but are *never happening*) since 1800, were loudly proclaimed as the inevitable first fruits of a union. "*English capital*" was to flow into Ireland by the million, "owing," as the ministerialists sagaciously put it, "to the stability of Irish institutions when guaranteed by the union." Like infallible arguments were ready to show that commerce must instantaneously expand beyond calculation, and manufactures spring up as if by magic, all over the island. Peace, tranquillity, prosperity, contentment, and loyalty, must, it was likewise sagely argued, flow from the measure; for the Irish would see the uselessness of rebelling against an united empire, and would be so happy that disaffection must become utterly unknown. Nay, whosoever consults the journals of that period, will find even the "government dock-yard at Cork," and other stock jobs of promised "concession," figuring then just as they figure now. *

But the endeavor to influence public opinion proved futile, and the minister found he must make up his mind to go

---

* The vote of Mr. Robert Fitzgerald, of Corkabeg, was secured by "Lord Cornwallis assuring him that in the event of the union a royal dock-yard would be built at Cork, which would double the value of his estates."—Barrington's *Rise and Fall*

through with a naked, unsparing, unscrupulous, and unblushing corruption of individuals.   Many of the Catholic bishops were overreached by the solemn pledge of emancipation; but the overwhelming majority of the clergy, and the laity almost unanimously, scouted the idea of expediting their emancipation by an eternal betrayal of their country.   The Orangemen, on the other hand, were equally patriotic.   All the 'Protestant bishops but two were gained over by the minister; yet the Protestant organizations everywhere passed resolutions, strong almost to sedition, against the union. Most important of all was the patriotic conduct of the Irish Bar. They held a meeting to discuss the proposition of a "union," and notwithstanding the open threats of government vengeance, and public offers of " reward " or bribe there were found but only two members of the bar to support the ministerial proposition, while one hundred and sixty-six voted it a treason against the country.

The next session, the last of the Irish parliament, assembled on the 15th January, 1800.   The minister had counted every man, and by means the most iniquitous secured the requisite majority.   Twenty-seven new peers had been added to the House of Lords, making the union project all safe there. In the Commons some thirty or forty seats had been changed by bargain with the owners of the boroughs.   It was doubtful that any *bona fide* constituency in Ireland—even one— could be got to sanction the union scheme; so the minister had to carry on his operations with what were called " patronage boroughs," or " pocket-boroughs."

The patriot party felt convinced that they were outnumbered, but they resolved to fight the battle vehemently while a chance remained.   At the worst, if overborne in such a cause, they could expose the real nature of the transaction, and cause its illegality, infamy, and fraud, to be confessed; so that posterity might know and feel the right and the duty of appealing against, and recovering against, the crime of that hour. They persuaded Grattan to reënter parliament * to aid them

* Three years before, he and many others of the patriot party had quitted parlia-

in this last defence of his and their country's liberties. He was at the moment lying on a bed of sickness, yet he assented, and it was decided to have him returned for Wicklow town, that borough being the property of a friend. The writ was duly applied for, but the government withheld its issue up to the last moment allowed by law, designing to prevent Grattan's return in time for the debate on the address to the throne, the first trial of strength. Nevertheless, by a feat almost unprecedented in parliamentary annals, that object was attained. " It was not until the day of the meeting of parliament that the writ was delivered to the returning officer. By extraordinary exertions, and perhaps by following the example of government in overstraining the law, the election was held immediately on the arrival of the writ; a sufficient number of votes were collected to return Mr. Grattan before midnight. By one o'clock the return was on its road to Dublin; it arrived by five; a party of Mr. Grattan's friends repaired to the house of the proper officer, and making him get out of bed, compelled him to present the writ in parliament before seven in the morning, when the house was in warm debate on the Union. A whisper ran through every party that Mr. Grattan was elected and would immediately take his seat. The ministerialists smiled with incredulous derision, and the opposition thought the news too good to be true.

"Mr. Egan was speaking strongly against the measure when Mr. George Ponsonby and Mr. Arthur Moore walked out, and immediately returned, leading, or rather helping Mr. Grattan, in a state of feebleness and debility. The effect was electric. Mr. Grattan's illness and deep chagrin had reduced a form never symmetrical, and a visage at all times thin, nearly to the appearance of a spectre. As he feebly tottered into the house, every member simultaneously rose from his seat. He moved slowly to the table; his languid countenance seemed to revive as he took those oaths that restored him to his preëminent station; the smile of inward satisfaction obviously illuminated his features, and reanimation and energy seemed to kindle by the labor of his mind. The house was

almost breathless, as if by instinct attempted to rise, but was
unable to stand ; he paused, and with difficulty requested permission of the house to deliver his sentiments without moving
from his seat.   This was acceded to by acclamation, and he
who had left his bed of sickness to accord as he thought his
last words in the parliament of his country, kindled gradually
till his language glowed with an energy and feeling which he
had seldom surpassed.   After nearly two hours of the most
powerful eloquence, he concluded with an undiminished vigor
miraculous to those who were unacquainted with his intellect."
     The debate lasted for sixteen consecutive hours.   It com-
menced at seven o'clock on the evening of the 15th, continued
throughout the entire night, and did not terminate until eleven
o'clock of the forenoon on the 16th, when the division was
taken.   Then the minister's triumph was made clear.   The
patriots reckoned one hundred and fifteen votes ; the government one hundred and fifty-eight.   There were twenty-seven
absent from various causes, nearly every man an anti-Unionist ;
but even these, if present, could not have turned the scale.
The discussion clearly showed that Ireland's doom was
sealed.
     There now commenced that struggle in the Irish senate
house in College Green, over which the Irish reader becomes
irresistibly excited.   The minister felt that the plunge was
taken, and now there must be no qualms, no scruples, as to
the means of success.   Strong in his purchased majority, he
grew insolent, and the patriot minority found themselves subjected to every conceivable mode of assault and menace.   The
houses of parliament were invariably surrounded with soldiery.
The debates were protracted throughout the entire night,
and far into the forenoon of the next day.   In all this, the calculation was, that in a wearying and exhausting struggle of
this kind, men who were on the weak and losing side, and
who had no personal interest to advance, must surely give
way before the perseverance of men on the strong and winning side, who had each a large money price from the minister.
But that gallant band, with Grattan, Ponsonby, Parsons, and

that seemed to experience no exhaustion. In order to be at hand in the house, and to sit out the eighteen and twenty hour debates, the ministerialists formed a "dining club," and ate, drank, dined, slept, and breakfasted, like a military guard, in one of the committee rooms. The patriot party followed the same course; and through various other manœuvres met the enemy move for move.

But the most daring and singular step of all was now taken by the government party—*the formation of a duelling club.* The premier (Lord Castlereagh) invited to a dinner party, at his own residence, a picked band of twenty of the most noted duellists amongst the ministerial followers; and then and there it was decided to form a club, the members of which should be bound to "call out" any anti-Unionist expressing himself "immoderately" against the conduct of the government! In plain words, Grattan and his colleagues were to be shot down' in designedly provoked duels!

Even this did not appal the patriot minority. With spirit undaunted they resolved to meet force by force. Grattan proposed that they should not give the ministerial "shooting club" any time for choosing its men, but that they themselves should forestal the government by a bold assumption of the offensive. He was himself the first to lead the way in the daring course he counselled. On the 17th February, the House went into committee on the articles of union, which, after a desperate struggle, as usual, were carried through by a major-ity of *twenty* votes; one hundred and sixty to one hundred and forty. It was on this occasion Corry, the Chancellor of the Exchequer, made, for the third or fourth time that session, a virulent attack on the enfeebled and almost prostrate Grat-tan. But soon Corry found that though physically prostrated, the glorious intellect of Grattan was as proud and strong as ever, and that the heart of a lion beat in the patriot leader's breast. Grattan answered the chancellor by "that famous philippic, unequalled in our language for its well-suppressed passion and finely condensed denunciation." A challenge pass-ed on the instant, and Grattan, having the choice of time, in-as daylight would admit. Accordingly, leaving the house in full debate, about day dawn the principals and their seconds drove to the Phœnix Park. Before half-an-hour Grattan had shot his man, terminating, in one decisive encounter, the Castlereagh campaign of "fighting down the opposition." The ministerial "duelling club" was heard of no more.

"Throughout the months of February and March, with an occasional adjournment, the constitutional battle was fought on every point permitted by the forms of the house." On the 25th March the committee finally reported the Union resolutions, which were passed in the house by forty-seven of a majority. After six weeks of an interval, to allow the British parliament to make like progress, the Union Bill was (25th May, 1800) introduced into the Irish Commons, and on the 7th of June the Irish parliament met for the last time. " The closing scene," as Mr. M'Gee truly remarks, " has been often described, but never so graphically as by the diamond pen of Sir Jonah Barrington." That description I quote unabridged:

" The Commons House of Parliament on the last evening afforded the most melancholy example of an independent people, betrayed, divided, sold, and as a State annihilated. British clerks and officers were smuggled into her parliament to vote away the constitution of a country to which they were strangers, and in which they had neither interest nor connection. They were employed to cancel the royal charter of the Irish nation, guaranteed by the British government, sanctioned by the British legislature, and unequivocally confirmed by the words, the signature, and the great seal of their monarch !

" The situation of the Speaker on that night was of the most distressing nature. A sincere and ardent enemy of the measure, he headed its opponents, he resisted it with all the power of his mind, the resources of his experience, his influence, and his eloquence.

" It was, however, through his voice that it was to be proclaimed and consummated. His only alternative (resignation) would have been unavailing, and could have added nothing to his character. His expressive countenance bespoke the

glance, and his embarrassment was obvious in every word he uttered.

"The galleries were full, but the change was lamentable; they were no longer crowded with those who had been accustomed to witness the eloquence and to animate the debates of that devoted assembly. A monotonous and melancholy murmur ran through the benches, scarcely a word was exchanged amongst the members, nobody seemed at ease, no cheerfulness was apparent, and the ordinary business for a short time proceeded in the usual manner.

"At length the expected moment arrived, the order of the day for the third reading of the bill for a 'Legislative Union between Great Britain and Ireland,' was moved by Lord Castlereagh. Unvaried, tame, cold-blooded, the words seemed frozen as they issued from his lips, and as if a simple citizen of the world, he seemed to have no sensation on the subject. At that moment he had no country, no god but his ambition. He made his motion, and resumed his seat with the utmost composure and indifference.

"Confused murmurs again ran through the house; it was visibly affected; every character in a moment seemed involuntarily rushing to its index; some pale, some flushed, some agitated; there were few countenances to which the heart did not despatch some messenger. Several members withdrew before the question could be repeated, and an awful momentary silence succeeded their departure. The Speaker rose slowly from that chair which had been the proud source of his honors and his high character; for a moment he resumed his seat, but the strength of his mind sustained him in his duty, though his struggle was apparent. With that dignity which never failed to signalize his official actions, he held up the bill for a moment in silence: he looked steadily around him on the last agony of the expiring parliament. He at length repeated in an emphatic tone, ' As many as are of opinion that this bill do pass, say aye.' The affirmative was languid but indisputable: another momentary pause ensued, again his lips seemed to decline their office; at length with an eye averted

voice,' *The ayes have it*.' The fatal sentence was now pronounced; for an instant he stood statue-like, then indignantly, and with disgust, flung the bill upon the table, and sunk into his chair with an exhausted spirit. An independent country was thus degraded into a province : Ireland as a nation was extinguished."*

The subjoined verses, written on the night of that sorrowful scene—by some attributed to the pen of Moore, by others to that of Furlong—immediately made their appearance; a Dirge and a Prophecy we may assuredly call them :—

O Ireland! my country, the hour
Of thy pride and thy splendor is past;
And the chain that was spurned in thy moment of power,
Hangs heavy around thee at last.
There are marks in the fate of each clime :—
There are turns in the fortunes of men;
But the changes of realms, and the chances of time,
Can never restore thee again.

Thou art chain'd to the wheel of thy foe
By links which the world shall not sever.
With thy tyrant, thro' storm and thro' calm shalt thou go,
And thy sentence is—bondage for ever.
Thou art doom'd for the thankless to toil,
Thou art left for the proud to disdain,
And the blood of thy sons and the wealth of thy soil
Shall be wasted, and wasted in vain.

Thy riches with taunts shall be taken,
Thy valor with coldness repaid ;
And of millions who see thee thus sunk and forsaken
Not one shall stand forth in thine aid.
In the nations thy place is left void,
Thou art lost in the list of the free,
Even realms by the plague or the earthquake destroy'd
May revive : but no hope is for thee.

---

* In their private correspondence at the time, the ministers were very candid as to the villany of their conduct. The letters of Lord Castlereagh and Lord Cornwallis, abound with the most startling revelations and admissions. The former (Lord Castlereagh) writing to Secretary Cook, 21st June, 1800 (expostulating against an intention of the government to break some of the bargains of corruption, as too excessive, now that the deed was accomplished), says: " It will be no secret what has been promised, *and by what means the Union had been carried*. Disappointment will encourage, not prevent disclosures : and the only effect of such a proceeding on their (the ministers,) part will be to add the weight of their testimony to that of the anti-Unionists in proclaiming *the profligacy of the means by which the measure was accom-*

LXXXII.—IRELAND AFTER THE UNION. THE STORY OF ROBERT
EMMET.

HE peasants of Podolia, when no Russian myrmidon is
nigh, chant aloud the national hymn of their captivity
—" *Poland is not dead yet.*" Whoever reads the story
of this *western* Poland—this " Poland of the seas "—
will be powerfully struck with the one all-prominent fact of
Ireland's indestructible vitality. Under circumstances where
any other people would have succumbed for ever, where any
other nation would have resigned itself to subjugation and
accepted death, the Irish nation scorns to yield, and refuses
to die.

It survived the four centuries of war from the second to the
eighth Henry of England. It survived the exterminations of
Elizabeth, by which Froude has been so profoundly appalled.
It survived the butcheries of Cromwell, and the merciless
persecutions of the Penal times. It survived the bloody
policy of Ninety-eight. Confiscations, such as are to be
found in the history of no other country in Europe, again and
again tore up society by the roots in Ireland, trampling the
noble and the gentle into poverty and obscurity. The mind
was sought to be quenched, the intellect extinguished, the
manners debased and brutified. "The perverted ingenuity
of man" could go no further in the untiring endeavor to kill
out all aspirations of freedom, all instinct of nationality in the
Irish breast. Yet this indestructible nation has arisen under
the blows of her murderous persecutors, triumphant and immortal. She has survived even England's latest and most
deadly blow, designed to be the final stroke—the Union.

Almost on the threshold of the new century, the conspiracy
of Robert Emmet startled the land like the sudden explosion
of a mine. In the place assigned in Irish memory to the youth-

trated the all-absorbing, all-indulging love of a people for
those who purely give up life on the altar of Country. Many
considerations might seem to invoke on Emmet the censure
of stern judgment for the apparently criminal hopelessness of
his scheme. Napoleon once said that "nothing consolidates
a new dynasty like an unsuccessful insurrection ;" and unquestionably Emmet's *emeute* gave all possible consolidation
to the "Union" *regime*. It brought down on Ireland the
terrible penalty of a *five years'* suspension of the Habeas Corpus
Act, and a contemporaneous continuance of the bloody " Insurrection Act," aggravating tenfold all the miseries of the
country. Nevertheless, the Irish nation has canonized his
memory—has fondly placed his name on the roll of its patriot
martyrs. His extreme youth, his pure and gentle nature, his
lofty and noble aims, his beautiful and touching speech in the
dock, and his tragic death upon the scaffold, have been all-
efficacious with his countrymen to shield his memory from
breath of blame.

Robert Emmet was the youngest brother of Thomas Addis
Emmet, one of the most distinguished and illustrious of the
United Irish leaders. He formed the daring design of surprising the castle of Dublin, and, by the seizure of the capital,
the inauguration of a rebellion throughout the provinces. Indeed it was, as Mr. M'Gee remarks, the plan of Roger O'More
and Lord Maguire in 1641. In this project he was joined by
several of the leaders in the recent insurrection, amongst them
being Thomas Russell, one of the bravest and noblest characters that ever appeared on the page of history, and Michael
Dwyer, of Wicklow, who still, as for the past five years, held
his ground in the defiles of Glenmalure and Imall, defying
and defeating all attempts to capture him. But, beside the
men whose names were openly revealed in connection with
the plot, and these comprised some of the best and worthiest
in the land, it is beyond question that there were others not
discovered, filling high positions in Ireland, in England and in
France, who approved, counselled, and assisted in Emmet's

in Dublin alone, not a man betrayed the secret to the last; and Emmet went on with his preparations of arms and ammunition in two or three depôts in the city. Even when one of these exploded accidentally, the government failed to divine what was afoot, though their suspicions were excited. On the night of the 23d of July, 1803, Emmet sallied forth from one of the depôts at the head of less than a hundred men. But the whole scheme of arrangements—although it certainly was one of the most ingenious and perfect ever devised by the skill of man—like most of other conspiracies of the kind, crumbled in all its parts at the moment of action. " There was failure everywhere;" and to further insure defeat, a few hours before the moment fixed for the march upon the Castle, intelligence reached the government *from Kildare*, that some outbreak was to take place that night, as bodies of the disaffected peasantry from the county had been observed making towards the city. The authorities were accordingly on the *qui vive* to some extent when Emmet reached the street. His expected musters had not appeared; his own band dwindled to a score; and to him the most poignant affliction of all, an act of lawless bloodshed, the murder of Lord Justice Kilwarden, one of the most humane and honorable judges, stained the short-lived *emeute.* Incensed beyond expression by this act, and perceiving the ruin of his attempt, Emmet gave peremptory orders for its instantaneous abandonment. He himself hurried off towards Wicklow in time to countermand the rising there and in Wexford and Kildare. It is beyond question that his prompt and strenuous exertions, his aversion to the useless sacrifice of life, alone prevented a protracted struggle in those counties.

His friends now urged him to escape, and several means of escape were offered to him. He, however, insisted on postponing his departure for a few days. He refused to disclose his reason for this perilous delay; but it was eventually discovered. Between himself and the young daughter of the illustrious Curran there existed the most tender and devoted attachment, and he was resolved not to quit Ireland without

While awaiting an opportunity for an interview with Miss Curran, he was arrested on the 25th August, 1803, at a house on the east side of Harold's Cross Road, a few perches beyond the canal bridge. On the 19th of the following month he was tried at Green Street ; upon which occasion, after conviction, he delivered that speech which has probably more than ought else tended to immortalize his name. Next morning, 20th September, 1803, he was led out to die. There is a story that Sarah Curran was admitted to a farewell interview with her hapless lover on the night preceding his execution, but it rests on slender authority, and is opposed to probabilities. But it is true that as he was being led to execution, a last farewell was exchanged between them. A carriage, containing Miss Curran and a friend, was drawn up on the roadside, near Kilmainham, and, evidently by preconcert, as the vehicle containing Emmet passed by on the way to the place of execution the unhappy pair exchanged their last greeting on earth.*

In Thomas Street, at the head of Bridgefoot Street, and directly opposite the Protestant church of St. Catherine, the fatal beam and platform were erected. It is said that Emmet had been led to expect a rescue at the last, either by Russell (who was in town for that purpose), or by Michael Dwyer and his mountain band. He mounted the scaffold with firmness, and gazed about him long and wistfully, as if he expected to read the signal of hope from some familiar face in the crowd. He protracted all the arrangements as much as possible, and even when at length the fatal noose was placed upon his neck, he begged a little pause. The executioner again and again asked him was he ready, and each time was answered : "Not yet, not yet." Again the same question, and, says one who was present, while the words "Not yet" were still being uttered by Emmet, the bolt was drawn, and he was launched into eternity. The head was severed from his body, and "according to law," held up to the public gaze by the executioner as the "head of a traitor." An hour afterwards,

as an eyewitness tells us, the dogs of the street were lapping
from the ground the blood of the pure and gentle Robert
Emmet.

Moore was the fellow-student and companion of Emmet,
and, like all who knew him, ever spoke in fervent admiration
of the youthful patriot-martyr as the impersonation of all that
was virtuous, generous, and exalted! More than once did
the minstrel dedicate his strain to the memory of that friend
whom he never ceased to mourn. The following verses are
familiar to most Irish readers:

> Oh! breathe not his name; let it sleep in the shade
> Where cold and unhonored his relics are laid.
> Sad, silent, and dark be the tear that is shed,
> Like the night-dew that falls on the grass o'er his head.

> But the night-dew that falls, though in secret it weeps,
> Still freshens with verdure the grave where he sleeps;
> So the tear that is shed, while in secret it rolls,
> Shall long keep its memory green in our souls!

Soon afterwards the gallant and noble-hearted Russell was
executed at Downpatrick, and for months subsequently the
executioner was busy at his bloody work in Dublin. Michael
Dwyer, however, the guerilla of the Wicklow hills, held his
ground in the fastnesses of Luggielaw, Glendalough, and
Glenmalure. In vain regiment after regiment was sent
against him. Dwyer and his trusty band defeated every effort of their foes. The military detachments one by one
were wearied and worn out by the privations of campaigning
in that wild region of dense forest and trackless mountain.
The guerilla chief was apparently ubiquitous, always invisible
when wanted by his pursuers, but terribly visible when not
expected by them. In the end some of the soldiers * became
nearly as friendly to him as the peasantry, frequently sending
him word of any movement intended against him. More than
a year passed by, and the powerful British government, that

---

* They were Highland regiments. Through the insurrections of 1798 and 1803,
the Highland regiments behaved with the greatest humanity and, where possible,
kindness towards the Irish peasantry.

could suppress the insurrection at large in a few months found itself, so far quite unable to subdue the indomitable Outlaw of Glenmalure. At length it was decided to "open .up" the district which formed his stronghold, by a series of military roads and a chain of mountain forts, barricks, and outposts. The scheme was carried out, and the tourist who now seeks the beauties of Glencree, Luggielaw, and Glendalough, will travel by the "military roads," and pass the mountain forts or barricks, which the government of England found it necessary to construct before it could wrest from Michael Dwyer the dominion of those romantic scenes.

The well authenticated stories of Dwyer's hairbreadth escapes by flood and field would fill a goodly volume. One of them reveals an instance of devoted heroism—of self-immolation—which deserves to be recorded in letters of gold.

One day the Outlaw Chief had been so closely pursued that his little band had to scatter, the more easily to escape, or to distract the pursuers, who on this occasion, were out in tremendous force scouring hill and plain. Some hours after nightfall, Dwyer, accompanied by only four of his party (and fully believing that he had successfully eluded his foes), entered a peasant's cottage in the wild and picturesque solitude of Imall. He was, of course, joyously welcomed; and he and his tired companions soon tasted such humble hospitality as the poor mountaineer's hut could afford. Then they gave themselves to repose.

But the Outlaw Patriot had *not* shaken the foe from his track that evening. He had been traced to the mountain hut with sleuth-hound patience and certainty ; and now, while he slept in fancied security, the little sheeling was being stealthily surrounded by soldiery!

Some stir on the outside, some chance rattle of a musket, or clank of a sabre, awakened one of the sleepers within. A glance through a door-chink soon revealed all; and Dwyer, at the first whisper springing to his feet, found that after nearly five years of proud defiance and successful struggle, he was at length in the toils! Presently the officer in command out-

answered, demanding his business. The officer said he knew that Michael Dwyer the Outlaw was inside. " Yes," said Dwyer, "I am the man." " Then," rejoined the officer, "as I desire to avoid useless bloodshed, surrender. This house is surrounded ; we must take you, alive or dead." " If you are averse to ·unnecessary bloodshed," said Dwyer, " first let the poor man whose house this is, and his innocent wife and children, pass through. I came into this house unbidden, unexpectedly. They are guiltless. Let them go free, and then I shall consider your proposition as regards myself."

The officer assented. The poor cottager, his wife, and children were passed through.

" Now, then," cried the officer, " surrender in the name of the king."

" Never !" shouted Dwyer ; " we defy you in the name of Ireland."

The hills echoed to the deafening peals that followed on this response. For *nearly an hour* Dwyer and his four companions defended the sheeling, keeping their foes at bay. But by this time one of them lay mortally wounded. Soon a shout of savage joy from the soldiery outside was followed by a lurid glare all around. They had set the cabin on fire over the heads of the doomed outlaws !

Then spoke up Dwyer's wounded companion, Alexander MacAlister : " My death is near ; my hour is come. Even if the way was clear, there is no hope for me. Promise to do as I direct, and I will save you all." Then the poor fellow desired them to prop him up, gun in hand, immediately inside the door. " Now," continued he, " they are expecting you to rush out, and they have their rifles levelled at the door. Fling it open. Seeing me, they will all fire at me. Do you then quickly dash out through the smoke, before they can load again ! "

They did as the dying hero bade them. They flung the door aside. There was an instantaneous volley, and the brave MacAlister fell pierced by fifty bullets. Quick as lightning, Dwyer and his three comrades dashed through the smoke.

diers; and once outside in the darkness, on those trackless hills he was lost to all pursuit!

Nor was he ever captured. Long afterwards, every effort to that end having been tried for years in vain, he was offered honorable conditions of surrender. He accepted them; but, when was a treaty kept towards the Irish brave? Its specific terms were basely violated by the government, and he was banished to Australia.

The mountaineers of Wicklow to this day keep up the traditions of Michael Dwyer—of his heroism, his patriotism—of his daring feats, his marvellous escapes. But it is of the devoted MacAlister that they treasure the most tender memory; and around their firesides in the winter evenings, the cottagers of Glenmalure, in rustic ballad or simple story, recount with tearful eyes and beating hearts how he died to save his chief in the sheeling of Imall.

The following ballad, by Mr. T. D. Sullivan, follows literally the story of the hero-martyr MacAlister:

> " At length, brave Michael Dwyer, you and your trusty men
> Are hunted o'er the mountains and tracked into the glen.
> Sleep not, but watch and listen; keep ready blade and ball;
> The soldiers know you're hiding to-night in wild Imaal."

> The soldiers searched the valley, and towards the dawn of day
> Discovered where the outlaws, the dauntless rebels lay.
> Around the little cottage they formed into a ring,
> And called out, " Michael Dwyer! surrender to the king!"

> Thus answered Michael Dwyer: " Into this house we came,
> Unasked by those who own it—they cannot be to blame.
> Then let these peaceful people unquestioned pass you through,
> And when they're placed in safety, I'll tell you what we'll do."

> 'Twas done, " And now, " said Dwyer, " your work you may begin;
> You are a hundred outside—we're only four within.
> We've heard your haughty summons, and this is our reply:
> We're true United Irishmen, we'll fight until we die."

> Then burst the war's red lightning, then poured the leaden rain,
> The hills around reëchoed the thunder peals again.
> The soldiers falling round him, brave Dwyer sees with pride—

Yet there are three remaining good battle still to do;
Their hands are strong and steady, their aim is quick and true
But hark that furious shouting the savage soldiers raise!
The house is fired around them! the roof is in a blaze!

And brighter every moment the lurid flame arose,
And louder swelled the laughter and cheering of their foes.
Then spake the brave M'Alister, the weak and wounded man :
"You can escape, my comrades, and this shall be your plan:

"Place in my hands a musket, then lie upon the floor :
I'll stand before the soldiers, and open wide the door :
They'll pour into my bosom the fire of their array :
Then whilst their guns are empty, dash through them and away."

He stood before his foemen revealed amidst the flame,
From out their levelled pieces the wished-for volley came;
Up sprang the three survivors for whom the hero died,
But only Michael Dwyer broke through the ranks outside.

He baffled his pursuers, who followed like the wind;
He swam the river Slaney, and left them far behind,
But many an English soldier he promised soon should fall,
For these, his gallant comrades, who died in wild Imaal.

The surrender of Michael Dwyer was the last event of the insurrection of 1798—1803. But, for several years subsequently, the Habeas Corpus Act continued suspended and an insurrection act was in full force. Never up to the hour of Napoleon's abdication at Fontainbleau, did the spectre of a French invasion of Ireland cease to haunt the mind of England.

LXXXIII.—HOW THE IRISH CATHOLICS, UNDER THE LEADER-
SHIP OF O'CONNELL, WON CATHOLIC EMANCIPATION.

MMET'S insurrection riveted the Union chain on Ireland. It was for a time the death-blow of public life
in the country. When political action reappeared, a
startling change, a complete revolution, had been
wrought. An entirely new order of things appeared in politics—an entirely new phase of national life and effort; new
forces in new positions and with new tactics. Everything
seemed changed.

Hitherto political Ireland meant the Protestant minority of
the population alone. Within this section there were nationalists and anti-nationalists, whigs and tories, emancipationists
and anti-emancipationists. They talked of, and at, and about
the Catholics (the overwhelming mass of the population)
very much as parties in America, previous to 1860, debated
the theoretical views and doctrines relating to negro emancipation. Some went so far as to maintain that a Catholic was
" a man and a brother." Others declared this a revolutionary
proposition, subversive of the crown and government. The
parties discussed the matter as a speculative subject. But now
the Catholic millions themselves appeared on the scene, to
plead and agitate their own cause, and alongside the huge
reality of their power, the exclusively Protestant political
fabric sunk into insignificance, and as such disappeared forever. In *theory*—legal theory—no doubt the Protestant minority were for a long time subsequently " The State," but men
ignored the theory and dealt with the fact. From 1810 to 1829,
the politics of Ireland were bound up in the one question—
emancipation or no emancipation. The Catholics had many true
and staunch friends amongst the Protestant patriots. Grattan,

ten by enfranchised Catholic Irishmen. But by all British parties and party leaders alike they found themselves in turn deceived, abandoned, betrayed. Denounced by the king, assailed by the tories, betrayed by the whigs; one moment favored by a premier, a cabinet, or a section of a cabinet; the next forbidden to hope, and commanded to desist from further effort on the peril of fresh chains and scourges—the enslaved millions at length took the work of their redemption out of the hands of English party chiefs and cliques, and resolved to make it a question of national emergency, not of party expediency.

The great victory of Catholic Emancipation was won outside of the Parliament, but within the lines of constitutional action. It was mainly the work of one man, whose place in the hearts of his countrymen was rarely, if ever before, reached, and probably will be rarely reached again by king or commoner. The people called him "Liberator." Others styled him truly the "Father of his Country"—the "Uncrowned Monarch of Ireland." All the nations of Christendom, as the simplest yet truest homage to his fame, recognize him in the world's history as "O'Connell."

It may well be doubted if any other man or any other tactics could have succeeded, where the majestic genius, the indomitable energy, and the *protean strategy* of O'Connell were so notably victorious. Irishmen of this generation can scarcely form an adequate conception of the herculean task that confronted the young barrister of 1812. The condition of Ireland was unlike that of any other country in the world in any age. The Catholic nobility and old gentry had read history so mournfully that the soul had quietly departed from

out to the government that, for their parts, they reprobated any thing that might displease the king or embarrass the ministry.

Nor was it the Catholic nobility and gentry alone whose un-exampled pusillanimity long thwarted and retarded O'Connell. The Catholic bishops for a long time received him and the "advanced" school of emancipationists with unconcealed dis-like and alarm. They had seen the terrors and rigors of the penal times ; and "leave to live," even by mere connivance, seemed to them a great boon. The "extreme"ideas of this young O'Connell and his party could only result in mischief. Could he not go on in the old slow and prudent way ? What could he gain by "extreme" and "impracticable" demands ?

In nothing did O'Connell's supreme tact and prudence man-ifest itself more notably than in his dealings with the Catholic bishops who were opposed to and unfriendly to him. He never attempted to excite popular indignation against them as "Castle politicians ;" he never allowed a word disrespect-ful towards them to be uttered ; he never attempted to degrade them in public estimation, even on the specious plea that it was "only in the capacity of politicians" he assailed them. Many and painful were the provocations he received ; yet he never was betrayed from his impregnable position of mingled firmness and prudence. It was hard to find the powers of an oppressive government—fines and penalties, proclamations and prosecutions—smiting him at every step, and withal be-hold not only the Catholic aristocracy, but the chief members of the hierarchy also arrayed against him, negatively sustain-ing and encouraging the tyranny of the government. But he bore it all ; for he well knew that, calamitous as was the con-duct of those prelates, it proceeded from no corrupt or selfish consideration, but arose from weakness of judgment, when dealing with such critical, legal and political questions. He bore their negative if not positive opposition long and patient-ly, and in the end had the triumph of seeing many converts from amongst his early opponents zealous in action by his side, and of feeling that no word or act of his had weakened the respect, veneration, and affection due from a Catholic peo-ple to their pastors and prelates.

From the outset he was loyally sustained by the Catholic mercantile classes, by the body of the clergy, and by the masses of the population in town and country. Owing to the attitude of the bishops, the secular or parochial clergy for a time deemed it prudent to hold aloof from any very prominent participation in the movement, though their sentiments were never doubted. But the regular clergy—the religious orders—flung themselves ardently into the people's cause. When every other place of meeting, owing to one cause or another, was closed against the young Catholic leaders, the Carmelite Church in Clarendon Street became their rallying point and place of assembly in Dublin, freely given for the purpose by the community.

O'Connell laid down as the basis of his political action in Ireland this proposition, " *Ireland cannot fight England.*" From this he evolved others. " If Ireland try to fight England, she will be worsted. She has tried too often. She must not try it any more." That acumen, that prescience, in which he excelled all men of his generation, taught him that a change was coming over the world, and that superior might—brute force—would not always be able to resist the power of opinion, could not always afford to be made odious and rendered morally weak. Above all, he knew that there remained, at the worst, to an oppressed people unable to match their oppressors in a military struggle, the grand policy of *Passive Resistance*, by which the weak can drag down the haughty and the strong.

Moulding all his movements on these principles, O'Connell resolved to show his countrymen that they could win their rights by action strictly within the constitution. And, very naturally, therefore, he regarded the man who would even ever so slightly tempt them outside of it, as their direst enemy. He happily combined in himself all the qualifications for guiding them through that system of guerilla warfare in politics, which alone could enable them to defeat the government, without violating the law ; quick to meet each dexterous evolution of the foe by some equally ingenious artifice ; evading

one guise, only to start up in another. No man but himself
could have carried the people, as he did safely and victoriously
through such a campaign, with the scanty political resources
then possessed by Irish Catholics. It was scarcely hyperbole
to call him the Moses of the modern Israel.

His was no smooth and straight road. Young Irishmen
can scarcely realize the discouragements and difficulties, the
repeated failings—*seeming* failures—the reverses, that often
flung him backward, apparently defeated. But with him
there was no such word as fail. The people trusted him and
followed him with the docile and trustful obedience of troops
obeying the commands of a chosen general. For them—for
the service of Ireland—he gave up his professional prospects.
He labored for them, he thought for them, he lived but for
them ; and he was ready to die for them. A trained shot— a
chosen bravo—D'Esterre—was set on by the Orange corporation of Dublin to shoot him down in a duel. O'Connell met
his adversary at eighteen paces, and laid him mortally wounded on the field. By degrees even those who for long years
had held aloof from the Catholic leader began to bow in homage to the sovereignty conferred by the popular will and English ministries, one by one, found themselves powerless to
grapple with the influence he wielded. If, indeed, they could
but goad or entrap him into a breach of the law ; if they
could only persuade the banded Irish millions to obligingly
meet England in the arena of her choice—namely, the field of
war—then the ministerial anxieties would be over. They
could soon make an end of the Catholic cause there. But,
most provokingly, O'Connell was able to baffle this idea—
was able to keep the most high-spirited, impetuous, and war
loving people in the world *deaf*, as it were, to all such chal-
lenges ; callous, as it were, to all such provocations. They
would, most vexatiously, persist in choosing their own ground,
their own tactics, their own time and mode of action, and would
not allow England to force hers upon them at all. Such a
policy broke the heart and maddened the brain of English oppression. In vain the king stormed and the Duke of York
swore. In vain the old " saws " of " utopian dreams " and

"splendid phantoms " were flung at the emancipationists. Men sagely pointed out that emancipation was " inconsistent with the coronation oath," was " incompatible with the British constitution ;" that it involved " the severence of the countries," the dismemberment of the empire," and "that England would spend her last shilling, and her last man, rather than grant it." Others, equally profound, declared that in a week after emancipation, " Irish Catholics and Protestants would be cutting each other's throats ; " that there would be a massacre of Protestants all over the island, and that it was England's duty, in the interests of good order, civilization, and humanity, not to afford an opportunity for such anarchy.

There is a most ancient and fish-like smell about these precious arguments. They are indeed very old and much decayed ; yet my young readers will find them always used whenever an Irish demand for freedom cannot be encountered *on the merits.*

But none of them could impose upon or frighten O'Connell. He went on, rousing the whole people into one mass of fierce earnestness and enthusiasm, until the island glowed and heaved like a volcano. Peel and Wellington threatened war. Coercion acts followed each other in quick succession. Suddenly there appeared a sight as horrific to English oppression as the hand upon the wall to Belshazzar—*Irish regiments cheering for O'Connell !* Then, indeed, the hand that held the chain shook with the palsy of mortal fear. Peel and Wellington—those same ministers whose special " platform " was resistance *à l' outrance* to Catholic emancipation—came down to the House of Commons and told the assembled parliament that Catholic emancipation *must* be granted. The " Man of the People " had conquered.

LXXXIV.—HOW THE IRISH PEOPLE NEXT SOUGHT TO ACHIEVE THE RESTORATION OF THEIR LEGISLATIVE INDEPENDENCE. HOW ENGLAND ANSWERED THEM WITH A CHALLENGE TO THE SWORD.

EMANCIPATION was won; yet there was a question nearer and dearer even than emancipation to O'Connell's heart; the question of national independence—the repeal of the iniquitous Union. It might be thought that as an emancipated Catholic he would be drawn towards the legislature that had freed him, rather than to that which had forged the shackles thus struck off. But O'Connell had the spirit and the manhood of a patriot. While yet he wore those penal chains, he publicly declared that he would willingly forfeit all chance of emancipation from the British parliament for the certainty of repeal. His first public speech had been made against the Union; and even so early as 1812, he contemplated relinquishing the agitation for emancipation, and devoting all his energies to a movement for repeal, but was dissuaded from that purpose by his colleagues.

Now, however, his hands were free, and scarcely had he been a year in parliamentary harness, when he unfurled the standard of repeal. His new organization was instantaneously suppressed by proclamation—the act of the Irish secretary, Sir Henry Hardinge. The proclamation was illegal, yet O'Connell bowed to it. He denounced it, however, as "an atrocious Polignac proclamation," and plainly intimated his conviction that Hardinge designed to force the country into a fight. Not that O'Connell "abjured the sword and stigmatized the sword" in the abstract; but, as he himself expressed it, the time had not come. "Why," said he, "I would rather be a dog, and bay the moon, than the Irishman who would tamely submit to so infamous a proclamation. I have

people, and give our enemies a triumph. But I will oppose it, and that, too, not in the way that the paltry Castle scribe would wish—by force. No. Ireland is not in a state for repelling force by force. Too short a period has elapsed since the cause of contention between Protestants and Catholics was removed—too little time has been given for healing the wounds of factious contention, to allow Ireland to use physical force in the attainment of her rights or her punishment of wrong.

Hardly had his first repeal society been suppressed by the " Polignac proclamation," than he established a second, styled " The Irish Volunteers for the Repeal of the Union." Another government proclamation as quickly appeared suppressing this body also. O'Connell, ever fertile of resort, now organized what he called "Repeal breakfasts." " If the government," said he, " think fit to proclaim down breakfasts, then we will resort to a political lunch. If the luncheon be equally dangerous to the peace of the great duke (the viceroy), we shall have political dinners. If the dinners be proclaimed down, we must, like certain sanctified dames, resort to ' tea and tracts.' " The breakfasts *were* "proclaimed," but, in defiance of the proclamation, went on as usual. Whereupon O'Connell was arrested and held to bail to await his trial. He was not daunted. " Were I fated to-morrow," said he, " to ascend the scaffold or go down to the grave, I should bequeath to my children *eternal hatred of the Union.*"

The prosecution was subsequently abandoned, and soon afterwards it became plain that O'Connell had been persuaded by the English reform leaders that *the* question for Ireland was what they called " the great cause of reform,"—and that from a reformed parliament Ireland would obtain full justice. Accordingly he flung himself heartily into the ranks of the English reformers. Reform was carried ; and almost the first act of the reformed parliament was to pass a Coercion Bill for Ireland more atrocious than any of its numerous

"Union with English liberals"—union with "the great liberal party"—was now made to appear to him the best hope of Ireland. To yoke this giant to the whig chariot, the whig leaders were willing to pay a high price. Place, pension, emolument to any extent, O'Connell might have had from them at will. The most lucrative and exalted posts—positions in which he and all his family might have lived and died in ease and affluence—were at his acceptance. But O'Connell was neither corrupt nor selfish, though in his alliance with the whigs he exhibited a lack of his usual firmness and perspicuity. He would accept nothing for himself, but he demanded the nomination in great part of the Irish executive, and a veto on the selection of a viceroy. The terms were granted, and it is unquestioned and unquestionable that the Irish executive thus chosen—the administration of Lord Mulgrave—was the only one Ireland had known for nigh two hundred years—the first, and the only one in the present century—that possessed the confidence and commanded the respect, attachment, and sympathy of the Irish people.

"*Men*, not *measures*," however, was the sum total of advantage O'Connell found derivable from his alliance with the great liberal party. Excellent appointments were made, and numerous Catholics were, to the horror of the Orange faction, placed in administrative positions throughout the country. But this modicum of good (which had, moreover, as we shall see, its counterbalancing evil) did not, in O'Connell's estimation, compensate for the inability or indisposition of the administration to pass adequate remedial *measures* for the country. He had given the Union system a fair trial under its most favorable circumstances, and the experiment only taught him that in Home Rule alone could Ireland hope for just or protective government.

Impelled by this conviction, on the 15th April, 1840, he established the Loyal National Repeal Association, a body destined to play an important part in Irish politics.

The new association was a very weak and unpromising project for some time. Men were not, at first, convinced that

tended so much to ruin the association, was now, even in its incipient stages, beginning to be felt. The appointment by government of popular leaders to places of emolument—an apparent boon—a flattering concession, as it seemed, to the spirit of emancipation—opened up to the administration an entirely new field of action in their designs against any embarrassing popular movement. O'Connell himself was a tower of personal and public integrity, but amongst his subordinates were men who by no means possessed his adamantine virtue. It was only when the Melbourne (whig) ministry fell, and the Peel (tory) ministry came into power, that (government places for Catholic agitators being no longer in the market) the full force of his old following rallied to O'Connell's side in his repeal campaign. It would have been well for Ireland, if most of them had never taken such a step. Some of them were at best intrinsically rude, and, almost worthless, instruments, whom O'Connell in past days had been obliged in sheer necessity to use. Others of them, of a better stamp, had had their day of usefulness and virtue, but now it was gone. Decay, physical and moral, had set in. A new generation was just stepping into manhood, with severer ideas of personal and public morality, with purer tastes and loftier ambitions, with more intense and fiery ardor. Yet there were also amongst the abherents of the great tribune, some who brought to the repeal cause a fidelity not to be surpassed, integrity beyond price, ability of the highest order; and a matured experience, in which, of course, the new growth of men were entirely deficient.

In three years the movement for national autonomy swelled into a magnitude that startled the world. Never did a nation so strikingly manifest its will. About three million of associates paid yearly towards the repeal association funds. As many more were allied to the cause by sympathy. Meetings to petition against the Union were at several places attended by six hundred thousand persons: by eight hundred thousand at two places ; and by nearly a million at one—Tara hill. All these gigantic demonstrations, about forty in num-

infringement of the peace. Order, sobriety, respect for the laws, were the watchwords of the millions. England was stripped of the slightest chance of deceiving the world as to the nature of her relations with Ireland. The people of Israel, with one voice, besought Pharaoh to let them go free; but the heart of Pharaoh was hard as stone.

O'Connell was not prepared for the obduracy of tyrannic strength which he encountered. So completely was he impressed with the conviction that the ministry *must* yield to the array of an almost unanimous people, that in 1843 he committed himself to a specific promise and solemn undertaking that within "six months" repeal would be an accomplished fact.

This fatal promise—the gigantic error of his life—suggested to the minister the sure means to effect the overthrow of O'Connell and his movement. To break the spell of his magic influence over the people—to destroy their hitherto unshaken confidence in him—to publicly discredit his most solemn and formal covenant with them—(that if they would but keep the peace and obey his instructions, he would as surely as the sun shone on them, obtain repeal within six months)—it was now necessary merely to hold out for six or twelve months longer, and by some bold stroke, even at the risk of a civil war, to fall upon O'Connell and his colleagues with all the rigors of the law, and publicly degrade them.

This daring and dangerous scheme Peel carried out. First he garrisoned the country with an overwhelming force, and then, so far from yielding repeal, trampled on the constitution, challenged the people to war, prepared for a massacre at Clontarf—averted only by the utmost exertions of the popular leaders—and, finally, he had O'Connell and his colleagues publicly arraigned, tried, and convicted as conspirators, and dragged to jail as criminals.

O'Connell's promise was defeated. His spell was broken from that hour. All the worse for England.

All the worse for England, as crime is always, even where it wins present advantage, all the worse for those who avail of it. For, what had England done? Here was a man, the corner stones of whose policy, the first principles of whose public teaching, were—loyalty, firm and fervent, to the throne ; respect, strict and scrupulous, for the laws ; confidence in the prevalence of reasoning force ; reliance, complete and exclusive, upon the efficacy of peaceful, legal, and constitutional action.

Yet this was the man whom England prosecuted as a *conspirator !* These were the teachings she punished with fine and imprisonment!

The Irish people, through O'Connell, had said to England : " Let us reason this question. Let there be an end to resort to force." England answered by a flourish of the mailed hand. She would have no reasoning on the subject. She pointed to her armies and fleets, her arsenals and dock-yards, her shotted gun and whetted sabre.

In that hour a silent revolution was wrought in the popular mind of Ireland. Up to that moment a peaceable, an amicable, a friendly settlement of the question between the two countries, was easy enough. But now!

The law lords in the British house of peers, by three votes· to two, decided that the conviction of O'Connell and his colleagues was wrongful. Every one knew that. There was what the minister judged to be a "state necessity" for showing that the government could and would publicly defy and degrade O'Connell by conviction and imprisonment, innocent or guilty; and as this had been triumphantly accomplished, Peer cared not a jot that the full term of punishment was thus cut short. O'Connell left his prison cell a broken man. Overwhelming demonstrations of unchanged affection and personal attachment poured in upon him from his countrymen. Their faith in his devotion to Ireland was increased a hundred fold, but their faith in the efficacy of his policy, or the surety of his promises, was gone.

He himself saw and felt it, and marking the effect the government course had wrought upon the new generation of Irishmen, he was troubled in soul. England had dared them to grapple with her power. He trembled at the thought of what

crop of Irish manhood had become recognizable as a distinct political element—a distinct school of thought and action. At the head of this party blazed a galaxy of genius—Poets, Orators, Scholars, Writers, and Organizers. It was the party of Youth with its generous impulses, its roseate hopes, its classic models, its glorious daring, its pure devotion. The old man feared the issue between this hot blood and the cold stern tyranny that had shown its disregard for law and conscience. Age was now heavily upon him, and, moreover, there were those around him full of jealousy against the young leaders of the Irish Gironde—full of envy of their brilliant genius, their public fame, their popular influence. The gloomiest forebodings arose to the old man's mind, or were sedulously conjured up before it by those who surrounded him.

Soon a darker shade came to deepen the gloom that was settling on the horizon of his future. Famine—terrible and merciless—fell upon the land. Or rather, one crop, out of the many grown on Irish soil—that one on which the masses of the people fed—perished ; and it became plain the government would let the people perish too. In 1846 the long spell of conservative rule came to a close, and the whigs came into office. Place was once more to be had by facile Catholic agitators, and now the Castle backstairs was literally thronged with the old hacks of Irish agitation, filled with a fine glowing indignation against those " purists " of the new school who denied that it was a good thing to have friends in office. Here was a new source of division between the old and new elements in Irish popular politics. O'Connell himself was as far as ever from bending to the acceptance of personal favor from the government; but some of his near relatives and long-time colleagues or subordinates in agitation were one by one being " placed " by the Viceroy, amidst fierce invectives from the " Young Ireland " party as they were called.

All these troubles seemed to be shaking from its foundations the mind of the old Tribune, who every day sunk more and more into the hands of his personal adherents. He became

young party. He framed a test declaration for members of the association, repudiating, disclaiming, denouncing, and abhorring the use of physical force *under any possible circumstances or in any age or country.* This monstrous absurdity showed that the once glorious intellect of O'Connell was gone. In his constant brooding over the dangers of an insurrection in which the people would be slaughtered like sheep, he struck upon this resort, apparently unable to see that it was opposed to all his own past teaching and practice—nay, opposed to all law, human and divine, that it would conserve and enthrone the most iniquitous tyrannies, and render man the abject slave of power.

The young party offered to take this test as far as related to the *present* or the *future of Ireland ;* but they refused to stigmatize the patriot brave of all history, who had bled and died for liberty. This would not suffice, and the painful fact became clear enough that the monstrous test resolutions were meant to drive them from the association. On the 27th of July, 1846, the Young Ireland leaders, refusing a test which was a treason against truth, justice, and liberty, quitted Conciliation Hall, and Irish Ireland was rent into bitterly hostile parties.

Not long afterwards the insidious disease, the approach of which was proclaimed clearly enough in O'Connell's recent proceedings—softening of the brain—laid the old chieftain low. He had felt the approach of dissolution, and set out on a pilgrimage that had been his lifelong dream—a visit to Rome. And assuredly a splendid welcome awaited him there ; the first Catholic Layman in Europe, the Emancipator of seven millions of Catholics, the most illustrious Christian patriot of his age. But heaven decreed otherwise. A brighter welcome in a better land awaited the toil-worn soldier of faith and fatherland. At Marseilles, on his way to Rome, it became clear that a crisis was at hand ; yet he would fain push onward for the Eternal city. In Genoa the Superb he breathed his last ; bequeathing, with his dying breath, his body to Ireland, his heart to Rome, his soul to God. All Christendom was plunged into mourning. The world poured its homage of respect over his bier. Ireland, the land for which he had lived and labored, gave him a funeral nobly befitting his title of Uncrowned Monarch. But more honoring than funeral pageant, more worthy of his memory, was the abiding grief that fell upon the people who had loved him with such a deep devotion.

LXXXV.—HOW THE HORRORS OF THE FAMINE HAD THEIR EF-
FECT ON IRISH POLITICS. HOW THE FRENCH REVOLUTION
SET EUROPE IN A FLAME. HOW IRELAND MADE A VAIN AT-
TEMPT AT INSURRECTION.

AMIDST the horrors of "Black Forty-seven," the reason of strong men gave way in Ireland. The people lay dead in hundreds on the highways and in the fields. There was food in abundance in the country; * but the government said it should not be touched, unless in accordance with the teachings of Adam Smith and the "laws of political economy."

The mechanism of an absentee government utterly broke down, even in carrying out its own tardy and inefficient measures. The charity of the English people towards the end, generously endeavored to compensate for the inefficiency or the heartlessness of the government. But it could not be done. The people perished in thousands. Ireland was one huge charnel pit.

It is not wonderful that amid scenes like these some passionate natures burst into rash resolves. Better, they cried, the people died bravely with arms in their hands, ridding themselves of such an imbecile *regime ;* better Ireland were reduced to a cinder, than endure the horrible physical and moral ruin being wrought before men's eyes. The daring apostle of these doctrines was John Mitchel. Men called him mad.

* The corn *exported* from Ireland that year would alone, it is computed, have sufficed to feed a larger population.

Well might it have been so. Few natures like his could have calmly looked on at a people perishing—rotting away—under the hands of blundering and incompetent, if not callous and heartless foreign rulers. But he protested he was "not mad, most noble Festus." An unforeseen circumstance came to the aid of the phrensied leader. In February, 1848, the people rose in the streets of Paris, and in three days' struggle pulled down one of the strongest military governments in Europe. All the continent burst into a flame. North, south, east and west, the people rose, thrones tottered, and rulers fell. Once again the blood of Ireland was turned to fire. What nation of them all, it was asked, had such maddening wrongs as Ireland? While all around her were rising in appeals to the god of battles, was she alone to crouch and whine like a beggar? Was England stronger than other governments that now daily crumbled at the first shock of conflict?

Even a people less impulsive and hot-blooded than the Irish would have been powerless to withstand these incitements. The Young Ireland leaders had almost unanimously condemned Mitchel's policy when first it had been preached ; but this new state of things was too much for them. They were swept off their feet by the fierce billows of popular excitement. To resist the cry for war was deemed "cowardly." Ere long even the calmest of the Young Ireland chiefs yielded to the epidemic, and became persuaded that the time at length had come when Ireland might safely and righteously appeal for justice to God and her own strong right arm.

Alas ! all this was the fire of fever in the blood, not the strength of health, in that wasted, famine-stricken nation !

Nevertheless, the government was filled with alarm. It fell upon the popular leaders with savage fury. Mitchel was the first victim. He had openly defied government to the issue. He had openly said and preached that English government was murdering the people, and ought to be swept away at once and for ever. So prevalent was this conviction—at all events its first proposition*—in Ireland at the time, that

---

* So distressingly obvious was the callousness of the government to the horrors of

the government felt that according to the rules of fair constitutional procedure, Mitchel would be sustained in a court of
justice. That is to say, a "jury of his countrymen" *fairly* empanelled, would, considering all the circumstances, declare
him a patriot, not a criminal. So the government was fain to
collect twelve of its own creatures, or partizans, and send
them into a jury box to convict him in imitation of a "trial."
Standing in the dock where Emmet stood half a century before,
he gloried in the sacrifice he was about to consummate for
Ireland, and like another Scævola, told his judges that three
hundred comrades were ready to dare the same fate. The
court rang with shouts from the crowding auditors, that each
one and all were ready to follow him—that not three hundred,
but three hundred thousand, were his companions in the
"crime" of which he stood convicted. Before the echoes had
quite died away in Green Street, John Mitchel, loaded with
irons, was hurried on board a government transport ship,
and carried off into captivity.

He had not promised all in vain. Into his vacant place
there now stepped one of the most remarkable men—one of
the purest and most devoted patriots—Ireland ever produced.
Gentle and guileless as a child, modest and retiring, disliking
turmoil, and naturally averse to violence, his was, withal,
true courage, and rarest, noblest daring. This was "John
Martin, of Loughorne," a Presbyterian gentleman of Ulster,
who now, quitting the congenial tranquillity and easy independence of his northern home, took his place, all calmly,
but lion-hearted, in the gap of danger. He loved peace, but
he loved truth, honor, and manhood, and he hated tyranny,
and was ready to give his life for Ireland. He now as boldly
as Mitchel proclaimed that the English usurpation was
murderous in its result, and hateful to all just men. Martin
was seized also, and like Mitchel, was denied real trial by
jury. He was brought before twelve government partizans

than the corn market should be "disturbed" by the action of the State—that coro-
ners' juries in several places, empanelled in the cases of famine victims, found as
their verdict, on oath, "Wilful murder against Lord John Russel" (the premier)
and his fellow cabinet ministers.

selected for the purpose, convicted, sentenced, and hurried off in chains.

Seizures and convictions now multiplied rapidly. The people would have risen in insurrection immediately on Mitchel's conviction, but for the exhortations of other leaders, who pointed out the ruin of such a course at a moment when the food question alone would defeat them. In harvest, it was resolved on all sides to take the field, and the interval was to be devoted to energetic preparation.

But the government was not going to permit this choice of time nor this interval of preparation. In the last week of June a bill to suspend the Habeas Corpus act was suddenly hurried through parliament, and the Young Ireland leaders, scattered through the country in the work of organization, taken utterly by surprise, and without opportunity or time for communication or concert, were absolutely flung into the field.

The result was what might be expected: no other result was possible, as human affairs are ordinarily determined. An abortive rising took place in Tipperary, and once more some of the purest, the bravest, and the best of Irishmen were fugitives or captives for "the old crime of their race"—high treason against England.

The leader in this movement was William Smith O'Brien, brother of the present Earl of Inchiquin, and a lineal descendant of the victor of Clontarf. Like some other of the ancient families of Ireland of royal lineage, O'Briens had, generations before his time, become completely indentified with the Anglo-Irish nobility in political and religious faith. He was, therefore, by birth an aristocrat, and was by early education a "conservative" in politics. But he had a thoroughly Irish heart withal, and its promptings, seconded by the force of reason, brought him in 1844 into the ranks of the national movement. This act—the result of pure self-sacrificing conviction and sense of duty—sundered all the ties of his past life, and placed him in utter antagonism with his nearest and dearest relatives and friends. He was a man

humanity ; a lofty integrity, a proud dignity, a perfect *inability*, so to speak, to fall into an ignoble or unworthy thought or action.   Unfriendly critics called him haughty, and said he was proud of his family ; and there was a proportion of truth in the charge.   But it was not a failing to blush for, after all, and might well be held excusable in a scion of the royal house of Thomond, filled with the glorious spirit of his ancestors.

Such was the man—noble by birth, fortune, education, and social and public position—who, towards the close of 1848, lay in an Irish dungeon awaiting the fate of the Irish patriot who loves his country " not wisely but too well."

In those days the Irish peasantry—the wreck of that splendid population, which a few years before were matchless in the world—were enduring all the pangs of famine, or the humiliations of "out-door" pauper life.   Amidst this starving peasantry scores of political fugitives were now scattered, pursued by all the rigors of the government, and with a price set on each head.   Not a man—*not one*—of the proscribed patriots who thus sought asylum amidst the people was betrayed.   The starving peasant housed them, sheltered them, shared with them his own scanty meal, guarded them while they slept, and guided them safely on their way. He knew that hundreds of pounds were on their heads but he shrank as from perdition from the thought of selling for blood-money men whose crime was that they had dared and lost all for poor Ireland.*

Dillon, Doheny, and O'Gorman, made good their escape to America.   O'Brien, Meagher, and MacManus, were sent

---

* This devotedness, this singular fidelity, was strikingly illustrated in the conduct of some Tipperary peasants brought forward compulsorily by the crown as witnesses on the trial of Smith O'Brien for high treason.   They were marched in between files of bayonets.   The crown were aware that they could supply the evidence required and they were now called upon to give it.   One and all they refused to give evidence. One and all they made answer to the warnings of the court that such refusal would be punished by lengthened imprisonment :—" *Take us out and shoot us if you like, but a word we wont swear against the noble gentleman in the dock.*" The threatened

to follow Mitchel, Martin, and O'Doherty into the convict chain-gangs of Van Diemen's Land. One man alone came scathless, as by miracle, out of the lions' den of British law: Gavan Duffy, the brain of the Young Ireland party. *Three times* he was brought to the torture of trial, each time defying his foes as proudly as if victory had crowned the venture of his colleagues. Despite packing of juries, the crown again and again failed to obtain a verdict against him, and at length had to let him go free. "Free"—but broken and ruined in health and fortune, yet not in hope.

Thus fell that party whose genius won the admiration of the world, the purity of whose motives, the chivalry of whose actions, even their direst foes confessed. They were wrecked in a hurricane of popular enthusiasm, to which they fatally spread sail. It is easy for us now to discern and declare the huge error into which they were impelled—the error of meditating an insurrection—the error of judging that a famishing peasantry, unarmed and undisciplined, could fight and conquer England at peace with all the world. But it is always easy to be wise after the fact. At the time—in the midst of that delirium of excitement, of passionate resolve and sanguine hope—it was not easy for generous natures to choose and determine otherwise than as they did. The verdict of public opinion—the judgment of their own country—the judgment of the world—has done them justice. It has proclaimed their unwise course, the error of noble, generous, and self-sacrificing men.

LXXXVI.—HOW THE IRISH EXODUS CAME ABOUT, AND THE
ENGLISH PRESS GLOATED OVER THE ANTICIPATED EX-
TIRPATION OF THE IRISH RACE.

IGHTEEN hundred and forty-nine found Ireland in a
plight as wretched as had been hers for centuries. A
year before, intoxicated with hope, delirious with enthusiasm—now, she endured the sickening miseries of a
fearful reaction. She had vowed daring deeds—deeds beyond
her strength—and now, sick at heart, she looked like one who
wished for death's relief from a lot of misery and despair.
Political action was utterly given up. No political organization of any kind survived Mr. Birch and Lord Clarendon.
There was not even a whisper to disturb the repose of the
"Jailer-General :"—

> Even he, the tyrant Arab, slept;
> Calm while a nation round him wept. *

The parliament, for the benefit of the English people, had
recently abolished the duty on imported foreign corn. Previously Ireland had grown corn extensively for the English
market ; but now, obliged to compete with corn-growing
countries where the land was not weighted with such oppressive rents as had been laid on and exacted in Ireland under
the old system, the Irish farmer found himself ruined by " tillage" or grain-raising. Coincidently came an increased demand
for cattle to supply the English meat-market. *Corn* might be
safely and cheaply brought to England from even the most
distant climes, but *cattle* could not. Ireland was close at hand,
destined by nature, said one British statesman, to grow meat
for " our great hives of human industry;" " clearly intended by
Providence," said another, " to be the fruitful mother of flocks

A SCENE FROM THE IRISH EXODUS.

See pages 563, 564.

and herds." That is to say, if high rents cannot be paid in Ireland by growing corn, in consequence of "free trade," they can by raising cattle.

But turning a country from *grain*-raising to *cattle*-raising meant the annihilation of the agricultural population. For bullock-ranges and sheep-runs needed the consolidation of farms and the sweeping away of the human occupants. Two or three herdsmen or shepherds would alone be required throughout miles of such "ranges" and "runs," where, under the tillage system thousands of peasant families found employment and lived in peaceful contentment.

Thus, *cleared-farms* came to be desirable with the landlords. For, as a consequence of "free-trade," either the old rents must be abandoned, or the agricultural population be swept away *en masse*.

Then was witnessed a monstrous proceeding. In 1846 and 1847—the famine years—while the people lay perishing, the land lay wasted. Wherever seed was put in the ground, the hunger-maddened victims rooted it out and ate it raw. No crops were raised, and of course no rents were paid. In any other land on earth the first duty of the state would be to remit, or compound with the land owners for any claims advanced for the rents of those famine years. But alas! in cruelties of oppression endured, Ireland is like no other country in the world. With the permission, concurrence, and sustainment of the government, the landlords now commenced to demand what they called the arrears of rent for the past three years! And then—the object for which this monstrous demand was made—failing payment, "notices to quit" by the thousand carried the sentence of expulsion through the homesteads of the doomed people! The ring of the crowbar, the crash of the falling roof-tree, the shriek of the evicted, flung on the road-side to die, resounded all over the island. Thousands of families, panic-stricken, did not wait for receipt of the dread mandate at their own door. With breaking hearts they quenched the hearth, and bade eternal farewell to the scenes of home, flying in crowds to the Land of Liberty in

that startled Christendom ; but the English press burst into a pæan of joy and triumph : for now at last the Irish question would be settled. Now at last England would be at ease. Now at last this turbulent, disaffected, untameable race would be cleared out. " In a short time," said the *Times*, " *a Catholic Celt will be as rare in Ireland as a Red Indian on the shores of Manhattan*."

Their own countrymen who remained—their kindred—their own flesh and blood—their pastors and prelates—could not witness unmoved this spectacle, unexampled in history, the flight *en masse* of a population from their own beautiful land, not as adventurous emigrants, but as heart-crushed victims of expulsion. Some voices, accordingly, were raised to deplore this calamity—to appeal to England, to warn her that evil would come of it in the future. But as England did not see this—did not see it *then*—she turned heartlessly from the appeal, and laughed scornfully at the warning. There were philosopher statesmen ready at hand to argue that the flying thousands were " *surplus population*." This was the cold-blooded official way of expressing it. The English press, however, went more directly to the mark. They called the sorrowful cavalcade wending their way to the emigrant ship, a race of assassins, creatures of superstition, lazy, ignorant, and brutified. Far in the progress of this exodus—even long after some of its baleful effects began to be felt—the London *Saturday Review* answered in the following language to a very natural expression of sympathy and grief wrung from an Irish prelate witnessing the destruction of his people :—

" The Lion of St. Jarlath's surveys with an envious eye the Irish exodus, and *sighs over the departing demons of assassination and murder. So complete is the rush of departing marauders, whose lives were profitably occupied in shooting Protestants from behind a hedge, that silence reigns over the vast solitude of Ireland*." *

Pages might be filled with extracts of a like nature from the press of England ; many still more coarse and brutal.

There may, probably, be some Englishmen who *now* wish such language had not been used ; that such blistering libels had not been rained on a departing people, to nourish in their hearts the terrible vow of vengeance with which they landed on American shores. But *then*—in that hour, when it seemed *safe* to be brutal and merciless—the grief-stricken, thrust-out people

"Found not a generous friend, a pitying foe."

And so they went into banishment in thousands and tens of thousands, with hands uplifted to the just God who saw all this ; and they cried aloud, *Quousque Domine ? Quousque ?*

An effort was made in Ireland to invoke legislative remedy for the state of things which was thus depopulating the country. A parliamentary party was formed to obtain some measure of protection for the agricultural population. For even where *no* arrears—for "famine years," or any other years—were due, even where the rent was paid to the day, the landlords stepped in, according to law, swept off the tenant, and confiscated his property. To terminate this shocking system, to secure from such robbery the property of the tenant, while strictly protecting that of the landlord, it was resolved to press for an Act of Parliament.

At vast sacrifices the suffering people, braving the anger of their landlords, returned to the legislature a number of representatives pledged to their cause. But the English minister, as if bent on teaching Irishmen to despair of redress by constitutional agencies, resisted those most just and equitable demands, and deliberately set himself to corrupt and break up that party. To humiliate and exasperate the people more and more, to mock them and insult them, the faithless men who had betrayed them were set over them as judges and rulers. And when, by means as nefarious as those that had carried the union, this last attempt of the Irish people to devote themselves to peaceful and constitutional action was baffled, defeated, trampled down, when the "Tenant League" had been broken up, and its leaders scattered—when Gavan Duffy had

broken-hearted into the grave, and Moore, the intrepid leader, the unequalled orator, had been relegated to private life, a shout of victory again went up from the press of England, as if a Trafalgar had been won.

————∞————

LXXXVII.—HOW SOME IRISHMEN TOOK "THE POLITICS OF DESPAIR." HOW ENGLAND'S REVOLUTIONARY TEACHINGS "CAME HOME TO ROOST." HOW GENERAL JOHN O'NEILL GAVE COLONEL BOOKER A TOUCH OF FONTENOY AT RIDGE-WAY.

ALL may deplore, but none can wonder, that under circumstances such as those, a considerable section of the Irish people should have lent a ready ear to "the politics of despair."

> In vain the hero's heart had bled,
> The sage's voice had warned in vain.

In the face of all the lessons of history they would conspire anew, and dream once more of grappling with England on the battlefield !

They were in the mood to hearken to any proposal, no matter how wild ; to dare any risk, no matter how great ; to follow any man, no matter whom he might be, promising to lead them to vengeance. Such a proposal presented itself in the shape of a conspiracy, an oath-bound secret society, designated the "Fenian Brotherhood," which made its appearance about this time. The project was strenuously apprehended by every one of the "Forty-eight" leaders with scarcely an exception, and by the Catholic clergy universally ; in other words, by every patriotic influence in Ireland not reft of reason by despair. The first leaders of the conspiracy were not men well recom-

which they assailed all who endeavored to dissuade the people from their plot, they showed that they had not only copied the forms, but imbibed the spirit of the continental secret societies. But the maddened people were ready to follow and worship *any leader* whose project gave voice to the terrible passions surging in their breasts. They were ready to believe in him in the face of all warning, and at his bidding to distrust and denounce friends and guides whom, ordinarily, they would have followed to the death.

In simple truth the fatuous conduct of England had so prepared the soil and sown the seed, that the conspirator had but to step in and reap the crop. In 1843 she had answered to the people that their case *would not be listened to*. To the peaceful and amicable desire of Ireland to reason the questions at issue, England answered in the well-remembered words of the *Times : " Repeal must not be argued with."*—" *If the Union were gall it must be maintained."* In other words, England, unable to rely on the weight of any other argument, flung the sword into the scale, and cried out: **Væ Victis !** "

In the same year she showed the Irish people that loyalty to the throne, respect for the laws, and reliance exclusively on moral force, did not avail to save them from violence. When *O'Connell* was dragged to jail as a "conspirator"—a man notoriously the most loyal, peaceable, and law-respecting in the land—the people unhappily seemed to conclude that they might as well be *real* conspirators, for any distinction England would draw between Irishmen pleading the just cause of their country.

But there was yet a further reach of infatuation, and apparently England was resolved to leave no incitement unused in driving the Irish upon the policy of violence—of hate and hostility implacable.

At the very time when the agents of the secret society were preaching to the Irish people the doctrines of revolution, *the English press resounded with like teachings.* The Sovereign and her ministers proclaimed them; parliament re echoed them : England with unanimous voice shouted them aloud.

or *fancying themselves*, oppressed, to conspire and revolt against their rulers—even native and legitimate rulers—was day by day thundered forth by the English journals. Yet more than this. The most blistering taunts were flung against peoples who, fancying themselves oppressed, hope to be righted by any means save by conspiracy, revolt, war, bloodshed, eternal resistance and hostility. " Let all such peoples know," wrote the *Times*, that " *liberty is a thing to be fought out with knives and swords and hatchets.*"

To be sure these general propositions were formulated for the express use of the *Italians* at the time. So utterly had England's anxiety to overthrow the papacy blinded her, that she never once recollected that those incitements were being hearkened to by a hot-blooded and passionate people like the Irish. At the worst, however, she judged the Irish to be too completely cowed to dream of applying them to their own case. At the very moment when William Smith O'Brien was freely sacrificing or perilling his popularity in the endeavor to keep his countrymen from the revolutionary secret society, the *Times*—blind, stone-blind, to the state of the facts—blinded by intense national prejudice—assailed him truculently, as an antiquated traitor who could not get *one man—not even one man*—in all Ireland to share his "crazy dream" of national autonomy.

Alas! So much for England's ability to understand the Irish people! So much for her ignorance of a country which she insists on ruling !

Up to 1864 the Fenian enterprise—the absurd idea of challenging England (or rather accepting *her* challenge) to a war-duel—strenuously resisted by the Catholic clergy and other patriotic influences, made comparatively little headway in Ireland. In America, almost from the outset it secured large support. For England had filled the western continent with an Irish population burning for vengeance upon the power that had hunted them from their own land. On the termination of the great civil war of 1861—1864, a vast army of Irish soldiers, trained, disciplined, and experienced—of valor proven on many a well-fought field, and each man willing to cross the globe a hundred times for "a blow at England"—were disengaged from service.

Suddenly the Irish revolutionary enterprise assumed in America a magnitude that startled and overwhelmed its originators. It was no longer the desperate following of an autocratic chief-conspirator, blindly bowing to his nod. It grew into the dimensions of a great national confederation with an army and a treasury at its disposal. The expansion in America was not without a corresponding effect in Ireland; but it was after all nothing proportionate. There was up to the last a fatuous amount of delusion maintained by the " Head Centre " on this side of the Atlantic, James Stephens, a man of marvellous subtlety and wondrous powers of plausible imposition; crafty, cunning, and quite unscrupulous as to the employment of means to an end. However, the army ready to hand in America, if not utilized at once, would soon be melted away and gone, like the snows of past winters. So in the middle of 1865 it was resolved to take the field in the approaching autumn.

It is hard to contemplate this decision or declaration, without deeming it either insincere or wicked on the part of the leader or leaders, who at the moment knew the *real* condition of affairs in Ireland. That the enrolled members, howsoever few, would respond when called upon, was certain at any time; for the Irish are not cowards; the men who joined this desperate enterprise were sure to prove themselves courageous, if not either prudent or wise. But the pretence of the revolutionary chief, that there was a force able to afford the merest chance of success, was too utterly false not to be plainly criminal.

Toward the close of 1865, came almost contemporaneously the government swoop on the Irish revolutionary executive, and the deposition—after solemn judicial trial, as prescribed by the laws of the society—of O'Mahoney, the American " Head Centre," for crimes and offences alleged to be worse than mere imbecility, and the election in his stead of Colonel William R. Roberts, an Irish-American merchant of high

generously aided Irish patriotic, charitable, or religious purposes. The deposed official, however, did not submit to the application of the society rules. He set up a rival association, a course in which he was supported by the Irish Head Centre ; and a painful scene of factious and acrimonious contention between the two parties thus antagonized, caused the English government to hope—nay, for a moment, fully to believe—that the disappearance of both must soon follow.

This hope quickly vanished when, on reliable intelligence, it was announced that the Irish-Americans, under the Roberts' presidency, were substituting for the unreal or insincere project of an expedition to Ireland, as the first move, the plainly practicable scheme of an invasion of British North America in the first instance. The *Times* at once declared that now indeed England had need to buckle on her armor, for that the adoption of this new project showed the men in America to be in earnest, and to have sound military judgment in their councils. An invasion of Ireland by the Irish in the United States all might laugh at, but an invasion of Canada from the same quarter was quite another matter ; the southern frontier of British North America being one impossible to defend in its entirety, unless by an army of one hundred thousand men. Clearly a vulnerable point of the British empire had been discovered.

This was a grievous hardship on the people of Canada. They had done no wrong to Ireland or to the Irish people. In Canada Irishmen had found friendly asylum, liberty, and protection. It seemed, therefore, a cruel resolve to visit on Canada the terrible penalty of war for the offences of the parent country. To this the reply from the confederate Irish in the States was, that they would wage no war on the Canadian people; that it was only against British power their hostility would be exercised ; and that Canada had no right to expect enjoyment of all the advantages, without experiencing, on the other hand, the disadvantages of British connection.

It seemed very clear that England stood a serious chance of

remained. If the American government would but defend the frontier on its own side, and cut the invading parties from their base of supplies, the enterprise must naturally and inevitably fail. It seemed impossible, however, that the American government could be prevailed upon thus to become a British preventive police. During the civil war the Washington executive, and, indeed, the universal sentiment and action of the American people, had plainly and expressly encouraged the Fenian organization ; and even so recently as the spring as 1866, the American government had sold to the agents of Colonel Roberts thousands of pounds' worth of arms and munitions of war, with the clear, though unofficial, knowledge that they were intended for the projected Canadian enterprise. Nevertheless, as we shall see, the American executive had no qualms about adopting an outrageously inconsistent course.

By the month of May, 1866, Roberts had established a line of depots along the Canadian frontier, and in great part filled them with the arms and material of war sold to him by the Washington government. Towards the close of the month the various " circles " throughout the Union received the command to start their contingents for the frontier. Never, probably, in Irish history was a call to the field more enthusiastically obeyed. From every State in the Union there was a simultaneous movement northwards of bodies of Irishmen : the most intense excitement pervading the Irish population from Maine to Texas. At this moment, however, the Washington government flung off the mask. A vehement and bitterly-worded proclamation called for the instantaneous abandonment of the Irish projects. A powerful military force was marched to the northern frontier; United States gunboats were posted on the lakes and on the St. Lawrence river ; all the arms and war material of the Irish were sought out, seized, and confiscated, and all the arriving contingents, on mere suspicion of their destination, were arrested.

This course of proceeding fell like a thunderbolt on the Irish ! It seemed impossible to credit its reality ! Despite all those obstacles, however—a British army on one shore, an

American, guarding the waters between—one small battalion
of the Irish under Colonel John O'Neill succeeded in crossing
to the Canadian side on the night of the 31st May, 1866. They
landed on British ground close to Fort Erie, which place they
at once occupied, hauling down the royal ensign of England,
and hoisting over Fort Erie in its stead, amidst a scene of
boundless enthusiasm and joy, the Irish standard of green and
gold.

The news that the Irish were across the St. Lawrence—that
once more, for the first time for half a century, the green flag
waved in the broad sunlight over the serried lines of men in
arms for "the good old cause"—sent the Irish millions in the
States into wild excitement. In twenty-four hours fifty thousand volunteers offered for service, ready to march at an hour's
notice. But the Washington government stopped all action
on the part of the Irish organization. Colonel Roberts, his
military chief officer, and other officials, were arrested, and it
soon became plain the unexpected intervention of the American executive had utterly destroyed, for the time, the Canadian project, and saved to Great Britain her North American
colonies.

Meanwhile O'Neill and his small force were in the enemy's
country—in the midst of their foes. From all parts of Canada
troops were hurried forward by rail to crush at once by overwhelming force the now isolated Irish battalion. On the morning of the 1st of June, 1866, Colonel Booker, at the head of the
combined British force of regular infantry of the line and some
volunteer regiments, marched against the invaders. At a
place called Limestone Ridge, close by the village of Ridgeway, the advanced guard of the British found O'Neill drawn
up in position ready for battle. The action forthwith commenced. The Irish skirmishers appeared to fall back slowly
before their assailants, a circumstance which caused the Canadian volunteer regiments to conclude hastily that the day was
going very easily in their favor. Suddenly, however, the Irish
skirmishers halted, and the British, to their dismay, found
themselves face to face with the main force of the Irish. post-

part of O'Neill. Booker ordered an assault in full force on the Irish position, which was, however, disastrously repulsed. While the British commander was hesitating as to whether he should renew the battle, or await reinforcements reported to be coming up from Hamilton, his deliberations were cut short by a shout from the Irish lines, and a cry of alarm from his own—the Irish were advancing to a charge. They came on with a wild rush and a ringing cheer, bursting through the British ranks. There was a short but desperate struggle, when some one of the Canadian officers, observing an Irish aid-de-camp galloping through a wood close by, thought it was a body of Irish horse, and raised the cry of "cavalry! cavalry!" Some of the regular regiments made a vain effort to form a square —a fatal blunder, there being no cavalry at hand; others, however, broke into confusion, and took to flight, the general, Booker, it is alleged, being the fleetest of the fugitives. The British rout soon became complete, the day was hopelessly lost, and the victorious Irish, with the captured British stand-ards in their hands, stood on Ridgeway heights as proudly as their compeers at Fontenoy—"The field was fought and won."

LXXXVIII.—THE UNFINISHED CHAPTER OF EIGHTEEN HUN-
DRED AND SIXTY-SEVEN. HOW IRELAND, "OFT DOOMED TO
DEATH," HAS SHOWN THAT SHE IS "FATED NOT TO DIE."

UDGED by the forces engaged, Ridgeway was an
inconsiderable engagement. Yet the effect produced
by the news in Canada, in the States, in England, and
of course, most of all in Ireland, could scarcely have
been surpassed by the announcement of a second Fontenoy.
Irish troops had met the levies of England in pitched battle
and defeated them. English colors, trophies of victory, were
in the hands of an Irish general. The green flag had come
triumphant through the storm of battle. At home and
abroad the Irish saw only these facts, and these appeared to
be all-sufficient for national pride.

O'Neill, on the morrow of his victory, learned with poignant feelings that his supports and supplies had been all cut
off by the American gun-boats. In his front the enemy were
concentrating in thousands. Behind him rolled the St. Lawrence, cruised by United States war steamers. He was
ready to fight the British, but he could not match the combined powers of Britain and America. He saw the enterprise
was defeated hopelessly, for this time, by the action of the
Washington executive, and, feeling that he had truly "done
enough for valor," he surrendered to the United States naval
commander.

This brief episode at Ridgeway was for the confederated
Irish the one gleam to lighten the page of their history for
1866. That page was otherwise darkened and blotted by a record of humiliating and disgraceful exposures in connection
with the Irish Head Centre. In autumn of that year he proceeded to America, and finding his authority repudiated and

be difficult to characterize too strongly. By way of attracting a following to his own standard, and obtaining a flush of money, he publicly announced that in the winter months close at hand, and before the new year dawned, he would (sealing his undertaking with an awful invocation of the Most High) be in Ireland, leading the long promised insurrection. Had this been a mere " intention " which might be " disappointed," it was still manifestly criminal thus to announce it to the British government, unless indeed, his resources in hand were so enormous as to render England's preparations a matter of indifference. But it was not as an " intention" he announced it, and swore to it. He threatened with the most serious personal consequences any and every man soever, who might dare to express a doubt that the event would come off as he swore. The few months remaining of the year flew by; his intimate adherents spread the rumor that he had sailed for the scene of action, and in Ireland the news occasioned almost a panic. One day, towards the close of December, however, all New York rang with the exposure that Stephens had never quitted for Ireland, but was hiding from his own enraged followers in Brooklyn. The scenes that ensued were such as may well be omitted from these pages. In that bitter hour thousands of honest, impulsive, and self-sacrificing Irishmen endured the anguish of discovering that they had been deceived as never had men been before; that an idol worshipped with frenzied devotion was, after all, a thing of clay.

There was great rejoicing by the government party in Ireland over this exposure of Stephens' failure. Now, at least, it was hoped, nay, confidently assumed, there would be an end of the revolutionary enterprise!

And now, assuredly there would have been an end of it had Irish disaffection been a growth of yesterday ; or had the unhappy war between England and the Irish race been merely a passing contention, a momentary flash of excitement. But it was not so; and these very exposures, and scandals, and recriminations seemed only fated to try in the fiery ordeal the strength, depth, and intensity of that disaffection.

In Ireland, where Stephens had been most implicitly be-

lieved in, the news of this collapse—which reached early in
1887—filled the circles with keen humiliation. The more
dispassionate wisely rejoiced that he had not attempted to
keep a promise, the making of which was in itself a crime ;
but the desire to wipe out the reproach supposed to be cast
on the whole enrolment by his public defection became so
overpowering, that a rising was arranged to come off simultaneously all over Ireland on the 5th March, 1867.

Of all the insensate attempts at revolution recorded in history, this one assuredly was preëminent. The most extravagant of the ancient Fenian tales supplies nothing more absurd.
The inmates of a lunatic asylum could scarcely have produced
a more impossible scheme. The one redeeming feature in
the whole proceeding was the conduct of the hapless men
who engaged in it. Firstly, their courage in responding to
such a summons at all, unarmed and unaided as they were.
Secondly, their intense religious feeling. On the days immediately preceding the 5th March, the Catholic churches were
crowded by the youth of the country, making spiritual preparations for what they believed would be a struggle in
which many would fall and few survive. Thirdly, their noble
humanity to the prisoners whom they captured, their scrupulous regard for private property, and their earnest anxiety to
carry on their struggle without infraction in aught of the laws
and rules of honorable warfare.

In the vicinity of Dublin, and in Tipperary, Cork, and
Limerick counties, attacks were made on the police stations,
several of which were captured by or surrendered to the insurgents. But a circumstance as singular as any recorded
in history, intervened to suppress the movement more effectually than the armies and fleets of England ten times told
could do. On the next night following the rising—the 6th
March—there commenced a snowstorm which will long be
remembered in Ireland, as it was probably without precedent
in our annals. For twelve days and nights without intermission, a tempest of snow and sleet raged over the land, piling
snow to the depth of yards on all the mountains, streets, and
highways. The plan of the insurrection evidently had for its

chief feature desultory warfare in the mountain districts, but this intervention of the elements utterly frustrated the project, and saved Ireland from the horrors of a protracted struggle.

The last episode of the "rising" was one, the immediate and remote effects of which on public feeling were of astonishing magnitude,—the capture and death of Peter O'Neill Crowley in Kilclooney Wood, near Mitchelstown. Crowley was a man highly esteemed, widely popular, and greatly loved in the neighborhood ; a man of respectable position, and of good education, and of character so pure and life so blameless, that the peasantry revered him almost as a saint. Towards the close of March, the government authorities had information that some of the leaders in the late rising were concealed in Kilclooney Wood, and it was surrounded with military, "beating" the copse for the human game. Suddenly they came on Crowley and two comrades, and a bitter fusillade proclaimed the discovery. The fugitives defended themselves bravely, but eventually Crowley was shot down, and brought a corpse into the neighboring town. Around his neck (inside his shirt) hung a small silver crucifix and a medal of the Immaculate Conception. A bullet had struck the latter, and dinged it into a cup shape. Another had struck the crucifix. It turned out that the fugitives, during their concealment in the wood, under Crowley's direction, never omitted compliance with the customary Lenten devotions. Every night they knelt around the embers of their watch-fire, and recited aloud the Rosary, and at the moment of their surprise by the soldiery they were at their morning prayers. All these circumstances—Crowley's high character, his edifying life, his tragic fate—profoundly impressed the public mind. While the government was felicitating itself on the "final" suppression of its protean foe, Irish disaffection, and the English press was commencing anew the old vaunting story about how Ireland's "crazy dream" of nationality had been dispelled for ever, a startling change, a silent revolution, was being wrought in the feelings, the sentiments, the resolutions of the Irish nation. First came compassion and sympathy ; then anger and indignation, soon changing into resentment

and hostility. The people heard their abstention from the
impossible project of "Fenianism" construed into an approbation and sustainment of the existing rule—an acceptance of
provincialism. They heard the hapless victims of the late
rising reviled as "ruffians," "murderers," "robbers," "marauders," animated by a desire for plunder. They knew the
horrible falseness, the baseness and cruelty of all this, coming
as it did too from the press of a nation ready enough to
hound on revolutionary cut-throats abroad, while venting
such brutality upon Irishmen like Peter O'Neill Crowley.
Ireland could not stand this. No people with a spark of manhood
or of honor left, could be silent or neutral here. In the end proposed to themselves by those slain or captured Irishmen—the
desire to lift their country up from her fallen state, to staunch
her wounds, to right her wrongs—their countrymen *all* were
at one with them ; and the purity, the *virtue* of their motives,
were warmly recognized by men who had been foremost in
reprehending the hapless course by which they had immo-
lated themselves. For whatever disorders had arisen from
this conspiracy, for whatever there was to reprehend in it,
the judgment of the Irish people held English policy and
English acts and teachings to account. For, who made
those men conspirators ? Who taught them to look to violence ? Who challenged them to a trial of force ? When
they who had done these things now turned round on the
victims of a noble and generous impulse, and calumniated
them, assuredly their fellow-countrymen could not stand by
unmoved. And the conduct of "the men in the dock" brought
all Ireland to their side. Never in any age, or in any country,
did men bear themselves in such strait more nobly than those
men of '67. They were not men to blush for. Captured at
hazard by the government from amongst thousands, yet did
they one and all demean themselves with a dignity a fortitude,
a heroism worthy of

> The holiest cause that tongue or sword
> Of mortal ever lost or gained.

others were soldiers, many were artizans. Not a man of them all quailed in the dock. Not one of them spoke a word or did an act which could bring a blush to the cheek of a Christian patriot. Some of them—like Peter O'Neill Crowley—had lived stainless lives, and met their fate with the spirit of the first Christian martyrs. Their last words were of God and Ireland. Their every thought and utterance seemed an inspiration of virtue, of patriotism, or of religion. As man after man of them was brought to his doom, and met it with bravery, the heart of Ireland swelled and throbbed with a force unknown for long years.

Meanwhile an almost permanent court-martial was sitting in Dublin for the trial of soldiers charged, some with sedition, others simply with the utterance of patriotic sentiments ; and scenes which might be deemed incredible in years' to come, had they not public witnesses and public record in the press, were filling to the brim the cup of public horror and indignation. The shrieks of Irish soldiers given over to the knout, resounded almost daily. Blood-clots from the lash sprinkled the barrick yards all over. Many of the Irishmen thus sentenced walked to the triangle, stripped themselves for the torture, bore it without a groan, and, when all was finished —while their comrades were turning away sickened and fainting—*cheered anew for "poor Ireland,"* or repeated the "seditious" aspiration for which they had just suffered !

Amidst such scenes, under such circumstances, a momentous transformation took place in Ireland. In the fires of such affliction the whole nation became fused. All minor political distinctions seemed to crumble or fade away, all passed contentions seemed forgotten, and only two great parties seemed to exist in the island, those who loved the *regime* of the blood-clotted lash, the penal chain, and the gibbet, and those who hated it. Out of the ashes of " Fenianism," out of the shattered *débris* of that insane and hopeless enterprise, arose a gigantic power ; and eighteen hundred and sixty-seven beheld Irish nationality more of a visible and potential reality than it had been for centuries.

Here abruptly pauses the " Story of Ireland ;" not ended, because " *Ireland is not dead yet.*" Like that faith to which she
has clung through ages of persecution, it may be said of her
that, though "oft doomed to death," she is "fated not to
die."

Victory must be with her.   Already it is with her.   Other
nations have bowed to the yoke of conquest, and been wiped
out from history.   Other peoples have given up the faith
of their fathers at the bidding of the sword.   Other races
have sold the glories of their past and the hopes of their future
for a mess of pottage ; as if there was nothing nobler in man's
destiny than to feed, and sleep, and die.   But Ireland, after
centuries of suffering and sacrifice such as have tried no
other nation in the world, has successfully, proudly, gloriously, defended and retained her life, her faith, her nationality.
Well may her children, proclaiming aloud that "there is a
God in Israel," look forward to a serene and happy future,
beyond the tearful clouds of this troubled present.   Assuredly
a people who have survived so much, resisted so much, retained so much, are destined to receive the rich reward of
such devotion, such constancy, such heroism.

VALEDICTORY.

DEAR YOUNG FELLOW-COUNTRYMEN,

The Story of our Country, which I have endeavored to narrate for your instruction and entertainment, terminates here—for the present. Time as it rolls onward will always be adding to its chapters. Let us hope it may be adding to its glories.

The lesson which the " Story of Ireland" teaches is, Hope, Faith, Confidence in God. Tracing the struggles of the Irish people, one finds himself overpowered by the conviction that an all-wise Providence has sustained and preserved them as a nation for a great purpose, for a glorious destiny.

My task is done; and now I bid farewell to my young friends who have followed my story-telling so far. I trust I have not failed in the purpose, and shall not be disappointed in the hopes, which impelled me to this labor of love.

God Save Ireland!

STORY OF IRELAND;

FROM 1867

TO

THE PRESENT TIME.

BEING

A CONTINUATION

OF THE

STORY OF A. M. SULLIVAN, M. P.

BY

JAMES LUBY.

" Never 'till the latest day,
Shall the memory pass away
Of the gallant lives, thus given for our land;
But on the cause must go,
Through joy or weal or woe
'Till we make our isle, a nation free and grand."
T. D. SULLIVAN.

NEW YORK:
P. J. KENEDY,
Excelsior Catholic Publishing House,
5 BARCLAY STREET.

CONTINUATION.

CHAPTER LXXXIX.

A YEAR OF EXCITEMENT AND ALARM. SEQUEL OF THE LAM-
ENTABLE RISING OF 1867. THE JACKNELL EXPEDITION.
THE MANCHESTER RESCUE. " GOD SAVE IRELAND."

HE "unfinished chapter of 1867" still remains unfinished. The forces that were active in that troublous year are still working in Ireland and America;
the agitations of to-day are the natural and lineal
offspring of the national endeavors of that time. In this,
Fenianism differs from the preceding movements of the century. Each of these reached a climax, and died a sudden
death, leaving the nation sorrowing and prostrated. Sorrow
enough indeed has followed in the track of Fenianism, but
since the days when Stephens and his lieutenants awoke the
country from the lethargy that followed 1849, despair has
never visited the people, nor has sloth been a reproach to
their leaders.

Since Fenianism was published to the world as a fact
through the seizure of the "Irish People" newspaper in the
end of 1865, one national movement has but given place to
another, and the foreign government has been subjected to a
constant succession of alarms.

The Amnesty movement proved the adherence of the
nation to the revolutionary leaders. It was a great popular
endorsement of revolutionary principles. The Home Rule
agitation brought into active hostility,—at least in a certain
sense—to the government, a large and influential class which

had long held aloof from national politics. It renewed the
fight against England at a time when the position of armed resistance was no longer tenable. The Land League served three
good purposes. It worried and weakened the British government and caused division among the leaders thereof; it brought
into the fight the tenant farmers who had not as a class been
very active in any agitation since O'Connell's day; but above
all, it showed the nation that when united and unswerving, it
might become an irresistible power for its own redemption.

I remember, years ago, just before the disestablishment of
the Irish Church, hearing a young man, who was not as wise
as he was patriotic, express regret because that great concession was about to be granted. " The more their wrongs
are redressed, the less discontented the masses will be, and the
less earnestly they will seek their freedom;"—such was his
argument. This of course involves a very mean opinion of
the people's standard of patriotism; it implies a surrender
on their part of the national principle, the right to national
existence and independence; but even putting that out of the
question, the speech was a foolish one, as I think. I regard
every concession won from England as a battle gained in the
war against her. The better the condition of the people becomes, the better they will be able to maintain future struggles;
the more victories they win,—no matter how they win them,
—the greater their self-confidence, and the greater the impetus with which they will make their next attack.

Mr. Sullivan has given some account of the revolutionary
attempt with which 1867 opened. I do not purpose going
over the same ground, though my memory flies back to the
bitter winter night when a constant stream of men passed
along the road that ran at the back of the house where I lived
on the outskirts of Dublin, and I remember being told—I was
only eleven years old—to say a prayer for the poor fellows
who were going out to fight.

It was the night of March 4th, and the men were hasten-
ing to Tallaght. The affair was a failure in all save the tem-

their soldierly respect for private rights, they covered themselves with honor. There are two things to regret about the whole business,—one that it ever took place; the other, that since it did, there was not a better fight. One advantage indeed was gained ; it was once again made manifest that there are at all times thousands of Irishmen ready to take up arms for the overthrow of English rule in their native land, however desperate the venture.

But this unhappy attempt was only the first of the series of alarms that the government had to· undergo during 1867. Next in order, came the famous Jacknell expedition. On the 12th of April, under the impression that their native country was in arms, a gallant little band of Irishmen set sail from New York harbor on board the brigantine, Jacknell. The vessel was cleared for a port in Cuba. According to her papers, she was laden with pianos, sewing machines, and wine in casks, and in fact the barrels, and oddly shaped cases that filled her hold seemed adapted to such a cargo. The vessel left Sandy Hook steering to the southward, but when the shades of evening fell upon the ocean, her course was changed, and she sped away for the shores of Ireland, on an errand of adventure that might not have misbecome the early and romantic voyagers upon the Spanish Main.

To invade the British Empire fifty strong,—with a brigantine for a navy, and sewing machines for an armament!

But no, these gallant madmen had some method in their undertaking. On the bright bracing morning of April 29th— it was Easter Sunday,—the Jacknell sank into the past, and the Sunburst floated in the breeze as the ensign of the Erin's Hope. The barrels were broached on this occasion, and powder and ball were distributed among the crew. From the piano cases, rifles and bayonets were taken—they contained 5000 stand—and it was announced amidst cheers and general handshaking that, instead of sewing-machines, three field pieces were stored in the hold.

The voyage was long, and only on May 20th, did a "mysterious brigantine" appear in Sligo Bay. The coast guards

and then the royal gunboats steamed out from neighboring
harbors to investigate. Meanwhile an agent had gone off to
the vessel from the revolutionary party. Colonel Richard
O'Sullivan Burke was the man. His mission was a sad one.
The illusions of the little invading party were broken by his
coming. There was no fight—no hope.

Still, the vessel hovered around the Irish shore, escaping almost miraculously the cruisers of the enemy. But very early
in June, it became evident that nothing could be done. The
vessel must return to America. But how? The provisions
were exhausted in the two months' cruise ; there was no hope
of a fresh supply. Then thirty men decided to take all risks
to save the rest. Two fishing smacks were seized off Helvick
Head in the County Waterford near Dungarvan ; the thirty
landed and were arrested. A traitor, Daniel J. Buckley, was
in their midst, and a prison was their resting place at the close
of their adventure. Most of them were held but a few
months under the suspended *habeas corpus* act ; only two were
brought to trial and sentenced to penal servitude. They
were Colonel John Warren, who was sentenced to fifteen
years, and Captain Augustine E. Costello, who got twelve.

These trials had an important consequence. Colonel Warren was a native of Clonakilty, County Cork, Costello
was born in Galway, but both were naturalized American
citizens. This fact was ignored, and they were denied the
right of trial by a half-alien jury,—a right guaranteed to foreigners by English law. The United States government took
the matter up in time, and insisted on the release of the two
prisoners. In 1870, Parliament passed the " Warren and Costello Act," by which the right of a British subject to abandon
his allegiance, and become naturalized under another government, was for the first time acknowledged.

Those who remained in the Brigantine brought her back
in safety to America, suffering much on the voyage from
shortness of provisions. The cargo was safely landed, and
years after, John O'Mahoney showed me some of the mould-
ering weapons in the office of the expiring Fenian Brother-

This expedition, like nearly all the incidents of Fenianism, teaches an important practical lesson. It proves that the best equipped fleet, and the most vigilant coastguards cannot prevent the landing of munitions of war in aid of a struggling people. Had there been men in the field in Ireland, I have no doubt that all the Jacknell's stores might have been placed in their hands, the English fleet notwithstanding; and if men of the right metal engaged in the work, I think five out of six ships, leaving America with a similar object, might accomplish it successfully. Of course, the crew of the sixth might become meat for the. Lion's jaws—and scant mercy they would get—but such risks are inseparable from all revolution.

The Hyde road, leading out of Manchester, is a broad thoroughfare, thickly built up near the city with shops—as they call them there—of the smaller class,—barbers' shops, public houses, greengroceries, and little haberdasheries and linen-drapers' places. About a mile out, these begin to thin away in numbers, and near the point where the road is crossed by a railroad bridge, long lines of low brick fence, with here and there a straggling house, fill up either side of the road.

Here occurred the celebrated Manchester Rescue, the third in point of time of the striking events of 1867. About 3.30 o'clock in the afternoon of September 18th, the ordinary prison van came driving along this road on its way to the county jail at Salford. The residents along the road, who had daily watched the journey of this vehicle for years, were awakened to unwonted interest in it this day, for besides the customary driver, four policemen occupied the box, the guard behind was doubled, and following the van came a cab with three more officers.

"There go the Fenians," ran from mouth to mouth. It was true. In the van were Colonel Thomas J. Kelly, and Captain John Deasey—the former, the head of the revolutionary body in England and Ireland, the latter one of his most trusted lieutenants. They had been arrested as vagrants a few days

They were now going back to the jail on remand, and they were handcuffed and locked into separate compartments in the van. There were in the vehicle besides, three loose women and a boy, and Police Sergeant Brett, who was in charge of the party, and who had had the keys passed in to him through a ventilator after the door had been locked from without.

But as the van approaches the railroad bridge, a man is seen standing in the middle of the road. Presently he draws a pistol, and shouts to the driver of the van to stop. The driver plies his whip. How can one man expect to stop the wheels of the law, with a powerful pair of horses to keep them going, and ten uniformed guardians of the peace to watch over their progress? But now from over the low brick walls on either side come leaping, other men of strong and active figure, and terribly determined aspect. They have pistols too, which papably shoot, for one of the powerful horses of the law—poor brute— falls bleeding. Lest they too, bleed, these ten gallant guardians, five from the box, two from the rear, and three from the accompanying cab, take flight.

Now the gallant rescuers for a minute hold the field unhampered.

" Give up the keys," cries one to Sergeant Brett.

" Never," replies the officer.

A fatal blunder had been made. No means were at hand to force open the prison van. I have heard that levers and wedges had been provided, but were forgotten at the rendezvous by the rescuers when they set out on their desperate undertaking. I have also been told, however, that a foolhardy confidence had been entertained that the keys would be at once surrendered, and hence no provision was made for the other contingency. I am inclined to believe the former story, but it really matters little which was true. The lack of proper tools was fatal.

The cowardly police who fled, soon gathered a great throng to their aid. At first the sight of the rescuers' pistols kept the crowd at a distance, but as numbers poured in, the English spirit began to wax brave, and paving stones and other missiles began to fall thick about the little band.

Still the parley went on, and Brett swore he would never
surrender.

" There is no more time to lose," said some one, " blow off
the lock with your pistol." Then a man—he is now living in
America I believe, but for obvious reasons his name must remain concealed,—did apply his weapon to the keyhole, and
fired.

Unhappy Sergeant Brett. The ball which was meant to
break the lock, lodged in his obstinate head. The women in
the van screamed, and one of them took the keys from the
prostrate officer, and passed them out. The door was opened,
and Brett rolled dying on the road. A young man, named
Allen, stepped past him, and, opening the door of Kelly's cell,
exclaimed, " I told you, Kelly, I'd die before I parted with you."

Let me hurry over the sequel,—the chase through the fields,
the brutal treatment of those who were overtaken,—there is
nothing so barbarous on earth as a low British mob—the ar-
raignment of the prisoners in irons, the packed jury, the perjured witnesses, the prejudiced judges, the murderous verdict.

Brett died, and by construction of law, every member of
the rescuing party was responsible for killing him—responsible with his life. Five men were arraigned together on the
capital charge of murder—Edward O'Meagher Condon
(known as Shore,) Thomas Maguire, William Philip Allen,
Michael O'Brien, (known as Gould,) and Michael Larkin.
All were convicted in one verdict, and on the same testimony.

But it soon became evident that McGuire, a marine in the
royal service, was absolutely innocent—had not been at the
scene, and had no knowledge of, or complicity in the affair, was
in fact a " loyal" subject. He was pardoned. But if the verdict was wrong in one case, why not in all ? When the one
mistake was admitted by the government, every one concluded that at least the lives of the other four convicts would
be spared. Not so ; it is announced that they will certainly
be executed.

Weeks shorten to days, and hope gives way to despair.
But at the eleventh hour, it is proclaimed that another of the
condemned is to be respited, and of all others, the one se-

lected is Condon—Condon who boldly avowed his devotion to his country in the dock ; who all but admitted his participancy in the rescue ; · who proclaimed to the world that he was not afraid to die 'in a good cause ; who first uttered that brief prayer that has since become the watchword of nationality —who cried out in an English court, in the face of a bench of English judges, " God save Ireland."

The reason of Condon's respite is not hard to find. He was an American citizen. England was quite ready to hang, but utterly unprepared to answer for her murderous course, to a possibl evindicator of her victim's rights. So Condon's sentence was commuted.

But now at length the world felt that none would hang. A line might have been drawn at Maguire, but, as the English ministry well knew, Condon was the man most deeply concerned in the affair, the "guiltiest " save him who fired the fatal shot. Could it be possible then that the government would hang the remaining three?

Yes. The dreadful preparations were advanced ; bayonets and batteries were massed in terrible array about the scaffold. The blood-thirsty Tory ministers encased their souls in adamant ; the vile British mob howled words of derision and insult through the windows of the condemned men's cells.

At last, one cold bleak morning – November 23d, 1867—the final scene took place. Let us draw a veil over it.

Within a few days of the tragedy, a ballad appeared in print in Dublin, which caught at once the popular mind. The author was Mr. T. D. Sullivan, and his verses have now become the national song of Ireland. I give them here, in full, in the hope that every young Irishman may commit their words to memory, and take their lesson to his heart The song is called

GOD SAVE IRELAND.

High upon the gallows tree,
Swung the noble-hearted three,
By the vengeful tyrant stricken in their bloom ;
But they met him face to face,
With the spirit of their race,
And they went with souls undaunted to their doom.

"God save Ireland!" said the heroes;
"God save Ireland!" said they all:
"Whether on the scaffold high
"Or the battle-field we die,
Oh, what matter, when for Erin dear we fall!"

Girt around with cruel foes,
Still their courage proudly rose,
For they thought of hearts that loved them, far and near.
Of the millions true and brave
O'er the ocean's swelling wave,
And the friends in holy Ireland ever dear.
"God save Ireland!" said they proudly;
"God save Ireland!" said they all:
"Whether on the scaffold high
"Or the battle-field we die,
"Oh, what matter, when for Erin dear we fall!"

Climbed they up the rugged stair,
Rung their voices out in prayer,
Then with England's fatal cord around them cast,
Close beneath the gallows tree,
Kissed like brothers lovingly,
True to home and faith and freedom to the last.
"God save Ireland!" prayed they loudly;
"God save Ireland!" prayed they all:
"Whether on the scaffold high
"Or the battle-field we die,
"Oh, what matter, when for Erin dear we fall!"

Never till the latest day
Shall the memory pass away
Of the gallant lives thus given for our land;
But on the cause must go,
Through joy, or weal, or woe,
Till we make our isle a nation free and grand
"God save Ireland!" say we proudly;
"God save Ireland!" say we all:
"Whether on the scaffold high
"Or the battle-field we die,
"Oh, what matter, when for Erin dear we fall!"

Not in vain did these martyrs die. The fall of the drop beneath their feet sent a thrill through the heart of Ireland that will not wholly subside so long as the nation exists. I can compare the profound feeling of the time to nothing I have seen, save the great mourning of the American people

for their lately murdered president. The whole Irish race
sorrowed.

The weeks immediately following the execution saw a
long series of funeral demonstrations in Ireland, in England,
in America, and at the Antipodes. Tens of thousands participated. I myself had a very small part in the great funeral
procession in Dublin on December 8th. From thirty-five to
sixty thousand people—according to various estimates—
marched for miles that Sunday through such rain and slush
as I have seldom seen, wearing emblems of green upon their
breasts, veiled with crape. Two hundred thousand men,
women and children, patient of cold, and wet, and wearisome
delay, lined the streets through which the procession moved,
standing for hours in mournful silence, only offering prayers
for the martyrs' rest, when three empty hearses passed along.

As the cortege passed the spot where Robert Emmet gave
up his life,—it is in Thomas Street, just by St. Catherine's
Church, I know it well; a round stone in the pavement is said
to mark the spot where the gallows stood,—every man uncovered his head in reverence. This procession was headed
by John Martin, A. M. Sullivan, and Dr. J. C. Waters, walking arm in arm. At the gate of Glasnevin Cemetery where
the line of march terminated, John Martin made a touching
and patriotic address. For their part in the affair, these three
gentlemen and others were prosecuted, but the jury which
tried them disagreed.

These immediate results of the Manchester execution were
as nothing to its subsequent effects. Could the government
have forecast the future, would the death penalty have ever
been exacted? Not a single anniversary of the tragedy has
passed without commemoration by the Irish people at home
and abroad, in Ireland and in America. The martyred three
have passed into the heart of hearts of the nation, and it is indeed true that never till the latest day shall their memory cease
to fire their countrymen to deeds of bravery and sacrifice.

The mission of these men was to suffer and to die ; their
reward is a remembrance that will not perish.

CHAPTER XC.

REVIVAL OF PARLIAMENTARY AGITATION IN IRELAND. THE DEMAND FOR AMNESTY A PRACTICAL ENDORSEMENT OF FENIANISM. DISESTABLISHMENT. O'DONOVAN ROSSA, M. P.

ONE other startling event occurred in 1867—the Clerkenwell explosion, but I will postpone the discussion of it to another place, and, skipping a few months, I will take up that period which is marked by the revival of parliamentary agitation.

The end of 1867 and all the former half of 1868 were taken up with prosecutions. Assizes and commissions, regular and special, for months kept swelling the army of political convicts. From all parts of Ireland, and many parts of England the recruits were gathered. Presently there came a lull; but hardly had the last sentence been pronounced, hardly was the last felon dressed in his convict garb, when a new voice spoke out from the country, a small weak voice at first, but one which swelled in volume until it clamored in the ears of England's ministers with tones of thunder.

Think of it! England had trampled down the Irish people's aspirations, had degraded—so far as she was able—their leaders, and now she found the nation rising up defiantly in the hour of supposed defeat, reiterating the old principle, and paying homage to the old leaders under the guidance of new ones.

The movement first took definite shape about November, 1868, but, in fact, in newspaper articles, in general conversation, and even in some public speeches, the demand for amnesty had been foreshadowed. Anyway, in November, 1868, we find the Central Amnesty Committee in regular weekly

persons in the chair at various times, most notable among
them Isaac Butt, the eloquent and statesmanlike defender of
the Fenians before the British tribunals, and of the nation
in the British forum—a man whose character and career
might, in Carlylean phrase, be described as at once meteoric
and fuliginous.   I am inclined to the opinion that Isaac Butt
cannot in any proper sense be classed among the leaders of the
Irish people.   I hardly think he ever really led the movements
that he headed.   But his splendid gifts of imagination, intellect,
and speech, and his admirable acquirements. made him a most
available man to thrust forward in great affairs, while men of
less showy parts and less real genius too, but of more skill in
the manipulation of parties, lurked in the background and
pulled the wires.

But at least, Butt was the first man at this time to proclaim
the demands of the Irish people from a public platform in the
presence of a great assemblage.   He was the first too, who
saw with statesmanlike eye, and publicly proclaimed, the true
meaning of these demands.

The first of a long series of great amnesty demonstrations
took place at the Rotunda, Dublin.   It was on the evening of
January 24th, 1869, and the Lord Mayor presided.   Letters from
half a dozen Roman Catholic Bishops, and many other clerics
both Catholic and Protestant were read, all asking " mercy "
from the crown.   Mr. Butt moved the first resolution.   It
was this :—

> Resolved, that it is the persuasion of this meeting that the grant of a general am-
> nesty to all persons convicted of political offences would be most grateful to the feel-
> ings of the people of the Irish Nation.

The hall was crowded, and those who have seen an Irish
political meeting can well imagine the roar of endorsement
with which this proposition was received.   Butt's right manly and patriotic speech which followed, gave the keynote of
the whole campaign.   He spoke of the swelling popular tide
in favor of amnesty as a great popular ratification of the principles of the prisoners, as a mighty protest against the ignorant,
unsympathetic, oppressive government of England.

The ball set rolling at this meeting did not soon stop, and as it rolled it gained in weight and impetus. In February, 1869, the first concession was made. According to a Dublin newspaper, published at the time, there were then in prison eighty-one civilians charged with treason-felony, besides many military convicts, and persons charged with murder or other deeds of violence. Of the treason-felony men, forty-two had been shipped to Western Australia, the rest were scattered among various convict settlements in England, where they were treated with the utmost rigor of the ordinary penal rule. About the end of February it was announced that forty-nine prisoners,—thirty-four in Australia, and fifteen in England, were to receive free pardons. When the names were made known, it was found that Charles James Kickham—now dead, unhappily,—was the only man of first-rate importance in the number, though James O'Connor, and James F. X. O'Brien might be classed as formidable. The rest were men who had occupied subordinate positions in Mr. Stephens' organization ; but, for some unexplained reason, several men equally obscure and unimportant were still held in prison.

This half-hearted amnesty may serve me as a bridge to reach another very important series of events which was coming to a climax while the amnesty agitation was only dawning. The disestablishment of the Protestant church in Ireland, the first of the great measures of reform which Mr. Gladstone has bestowed upon the country, was now on the eve of accomplishment. It cannot be said that this particular concession was urgently sought by the great body of the people, nor did it bring them any considerable relief from their burdens. It was a concession to the "respectable element," to the bishops and better class Catholics. No doubt it terminated a crying injustice, no doubt it effaced the last marks of conquest which had served to keep Catholics divided from their fellow-countrymen of the dominant religion. Still, to the masses the satisfaction was only sentimental ; the reform was, of all that might have been introduced, the one which did them least good.

According to Mr. Sullivan's account of the matter,* the singling out of this church grievance was the result of what, in America, we call a "deal," made in the autumn of 1864, between the Roman Catholic bishops and that portion of the English liberal party, of which John Bright is the type man. Denominational education had before been the object of the bishops, but there was no hope of an agreement on this head with the Whigs. Therefore with a facility which should prove instructive to all Irish politicians of whatever stripe, they abandoned their old position from which no advancement could be made, for that new one which promised a speedy victory, fully expecting to return,—as indeed they did, —to their old ground with redoubled strength. The first steps in the new movement were not auspicious. The "National" Association was a failure, and shorty after it was founded,—June, 1866,—the Russell-Gladstone ministry fell, and Lord Derby and Mr. Disraeli assumed the reins of government. Under this ministry, all the most troublous events of Fenianism passed. This was the ministry of coercion laws and penal tortures. This was the administration that hanged the Manchester rescuers, and that kept Lord Strathnairn, the butcher of the Sepoys, on hand in Ireland to deal with a possible revolt. The rule of the Tories lasted nominally until December 2d, 1868. While the full excitement of Fenianism prevailed, Mr. Disraeli had been able to hold his own. But now the ferment was subsiding, and the fact remained, made by that formidable movement too plain to be ignored, that Ireland was discontented to the core, and with good reason. Some sop should be thrown at once to the people, but Mr. Disraeli had no remedy ready. Then the old negotiations between the bishops and the Liberals bore fruit. Mr. Gladstone and his followers attacked at once the Irish Church and the Tories. They defeated the Tories in the House of Commons in May, 1868, soon a series of resolutions, proposed by Mr. Gladstone himself, declarative of the propriety of disestablishing the Church. Mr. Disraeli dissolved parliament and in the general election the Liberals swept their adversaries out of the field. But in the course of this election Mr. Gladstone's utterances had been such that when he became prime minister on the reassembly of parliament, no choice remained for him but to grant some measure of amnesty. What he did has been already told. His half-hearted clemency, instead of awakening popular gratitude, raised a tempest of indignation in the country.

This is the peculiar fatuity of English statesmen in dealing with Ireland. They give so grudgingly, so scantily that they never win a cordial response from the people. Mr. Gladstone made two mistakes at this time. His amnesty failed to please the people at large, and his Church Act failed to relieve their sufferings.

Mr. Gladstone perfected his disestablishment scheme with the greatest possible rapidity. The actual reforms were three; every office in Ireland, except the Lord Lieutenancy, was thrown open to Roman Catholics; all special oaths to be taken by Catholics on assuming public office were abolished; and all pecuniary support on the part of the Government was withdrawn from the Protestant Church,—the vested rights of individuals only, being respected.

So far as regards the Protestant Church, the results of this change were most favorable. The hour of political downfall, proved the hour of spiritual revival. A suitable organization was perfected, and as an independent body, the Church is today strong, influential, and useful in an eminent degree. The Catholic peasant derived no profit whatever. Reduction of taxation brought no reduction of rents. The money that the landlord had formerly paid to the government for the support of the established religion, he now put into his own pocket, leaving his poor tenants to enjoy the sentimental advantages of Mr. Gladstone's great concession.

The actual disestablishment bill was passed May 31st, 1869, and on July 26th, it received the royal assent. It had no effect whatever in checking the Amnesty agitation. When the summer came, a series of great open air meetings was begun. One

England, or at least the Irish in England, joined in the agitation. I was present myself at two of the open air meetings, one of them early in the summer at Bray ; the other, the monster demonstration at Cabra. Both of these scenes come vividly before my mind : I am sure none that saw has ever forgotten them.

The meeting at Bray took place upon a balmy day. It was Sunday, the sun was bright, and in the early morning the vale through which the river Bray runs brawling down to the sea, and the village nestling in its bosom, made a scene full of freshness and peace. But as the day wore on, and the noontide came, great crowds from the metropolis, and from the neighboring country began to fill the quiet roads. Green emblems were on many a breast, and patriotic words were in every mouth. In due time, Mr. Butt and the other speakers came driving through the crowd to the place of meeting, a field of some half-dozen acres, which was in a minute black with people. But now from afar, martial strains float over the vale, and long lines of men come marching from various outlying districts. Meeting within sight of the constabulary barricks, where Her Majesty's hirelings watch the proceedings from their picturesque battlements, the different contingents unite in a procession, and with banners waving overhead, and with bursts of patriotic music, they wind along the sloping roads until they reach the place of meeting and are swallowed up in the general mass. It was indeed a scene not easily forgotten when, amid the freshness and beauty of their own native land, ten thousand Irishmen gathered together to proclaim their devotion to her cause, and their confidence in her destiny.

Still another glorious scene, though of a somewhat different kind, was that of the Cabra meeting. There was nothing in the natural surroundings to lend a charm. The meeting took place in a great sloping meadow on the right hand side,— going out of town,—of the Cabra road. A wide gap in the fence gave admittance to the crowds : the platform was set up at the side of the field farthest from the road.

The programme for the day had included a procession of

the trades and other civil bodies, but this was prohibited by proclamation from the castle. Nevertheless, most of the organizations went severally over the projected line of march, filling the streets with the afflatus of their determined patriotism. I remember that the heart of the city was wondrously quiet, for the whole population had flocked out to Cabra, and the sounds that reached the ear of the chance wayfarer from time to time, of martial music and marching men, were awe-inspiring in the midst of the general solitude.

The meeting was in the afternoon, and I have seldom seen such multitudes as were gathered in the northern portion of the city, about the Mater Misericordiæ Hospital, and out along the Phibsborough Road. The field where the speaking took place was one vast sea of people. Around the outskirts were displayed the banners of the trades, mounted high on wagonettes and drags, drawn by teams of four and six horses. What enthusiasm pervaded the throng! What cheers rent the air! What noble sentiments were uttered!

I have read these last in later years, for I was not then of an age to appreciate oratory,—I think Butt was the only man who had awakened my attention—and so I will pass the speeches by. In truth, I never got within earshot of the platform. But as I left the field, I remembered catching a glimpse of a fine pale face, surmounting a dark close-fitting habit, and I remember the people held in a wonderful stillness by a voice that came to me then over the heads of the crowd with a sad cadence, like an echo from afar, and that comes back to me now with an added tinge of melancholy, as if from the speaker's grave. It was George Henry Moore, a man of pure and lofty motives, of unselfish patriotism, of high intellectual pow-

When the meeting was over, the trades and other bodies marched from the field in processional array. The evening was glorious with the rays of the setting sun. Headed with bands, with their banners flapping heavily overhead, and bearing bannerets and pennants of green and gold, they came marching down the road. Orange mingled with the green, in badges and rosettes ; a new spirit of unity, of strength, of purpose, pervaded the ranks. The blare of the trumpets mingled with the vociferations of the thousands lining the way. It seems as if the march that evening might be taken as a type of the Nation's progress, in the course of which old jealousies must be swept away, and the efforts of all her sons be blended into one power to work out her salvation.

Only one other instance of those days of the Amnesty movement will I stop to mention here—one that caused infinite amusement, and yet carried no small weight at the time, but which, as I think, has produced rather lamentable results in later days. This was the election of O'Donovan Rossa to Parliament by the County Tipperary, in November, 1869. As a manifestation of the sort of man the people of Ireland wish to represent them,—or rather, I should say, as a signalization of the principles they wished their representatives to hold, the election of Rossa to the House of Commons was an event of unsurpassed importance. It was one of the strongest endorsements of Fenianism that the period afforded.

The vacancy in Tipperary was caused by the death of one of the sitting members. Mr. Denis Caulfield Heron, a lawyer, was the regular Whig candidate. The fight was between him and Rossa. The latter had been chosen for the contest as the extremest—to use an un-English word,—of the prisoners. His swaggering defiance of the judges, and indeed of the whole machinery of the law at his trial, had tickled the fancy of the people. The ill-usage which he brought on himself in prison by his useless, ill-timed, and undignified resistance to rule, won for him the popular sympathy. Rumors— erroneous of course—were rife that he had been flogged in prison, and it was known that he had spent days in the dark cells. These things made him an available candidate for a struggle where everything depended upon catching the popular fancy. The Catholic clergy were opposed to him, but the bulk of those who voted were opposed to England above all things. Rossa defeated his opponent by 1054 votes to 898.

It is needless to say that Rossa was never allowed to take his seat in Parliament; but the protest against Westminster legislation conveyed in his triumphant return over all difficulties at the polls was just as strong as though he had been allowed to refuse the oath of allegiance at the speaker's table, clad in his convict gray.

To dispose of the subject of the Fenian prisoners briefly, it only remains to be said here, that the British government long resisted the demand for amnesty; but at last, in December, 1870, Mr. Gladstone announced the intention of the government to extend " pardons " to all the remaining non-military treason-felony convicts, on condition that they should leave the United Kingdom and remain abroad until the expiration of their several sentences. Thirty-seven men were set at liberty on these conditions, most of whom sooner or later proceeded to America. Of the imprisoned soldiers, six were rescued from the convict settlement at Swan River near Freemantle in Western Australia, on Easter·Monday, 1876, through the gallantry and ability of John J. Breslin,—who had also aided in the escape of James Stephens from Richmond Bridewell, in Dublin —backed by the financial resources of an American Association of Nationalists. Many others were from time to time released on tickets-of-leave or otherwise, and the last man remaining in prison on any charge growing out of the Fenian movement was James Clancy, an ex-soldier of the Royal Engineers, who was arrested for treason-felony, and sentenced to penal servitude for life for firing at the policeman who captured him. Clancy was released in October, 1878, and a short time after came to America.

CHAPTER XCI.

HOW IRISHMEN OF OPPOSITE OPINIONS COMBINED AT LAST
IN THEIR COUNTRY'S CAUSE. STRENGTH AT THE HUSTINGS
AND WEAKNESS IN THE COMMONS. JOHN MITCHEL.

IN this chapter I am to begin the story of the Home
Rule movement. I believe the narrative will illustrate the important truth that in politics as in all other
affairs of life, clearness of aim, and untiring aggression
are indispensable to success. We shall find the Home Rule
movement weak, languishing, and fruitless, so long as its policy
is one of conciliation and patient waiting. But as soon as a
man of bold determined character, and vigorous activity as-
sumes the leadership, the party develops into a great power ; as
soon as a single, well-defined, and paramount object becomes
the focus of its endeavors, these progress to great results.

The period on which we are now entering, opened with a
national disaster. George Henry Moore died at his residence,
Moore Hall, in the County Mayo, on the 19th of April, 1870.
This was just one month before the founding of the Home
Rule organization. There can be no doubt as to the part that
this man would have taken in the new agitation, and it is impossible to exaggerate the greatness of his loss at this time.
What indecision, what delays, what feeble measures, what
hampering of all the energetic tendencies of the nation he
might have prevented ! His death threw the undivided leadership into the hands of Isaac Butt, and Butt proved wholly
unequal to the trust.

I cannot refrain from saying a few words about the death
of Moore. It fell like a pall upon the nation. But a day or
two before, his name had been in every mouth as a word of
hope, and when he died the people were dismayed. A great
throng gathered to follow him to the grave. From every

side, the most notable men of the popular party hastened to the house of mourning. Not a few conservative gentlemen too, who admired the deceased for his personal qualities, came to pay a last tribute of respect. Not in the presence of these, however, was the highest honor done to the dead man's memory ; but in the gathering of the poor and the lowly,—of the oppressed people who revered and loved him, and who had begun to hope for brighter days under his leadership. The peasantry and townfolk of fifty miles around flocked to the house that chill April morning, and I am told that hundreds of men of humble means went from Dublin to the funeral.

As the body was borne from the house, the women on a sudden raised the *kaoine*, or Celtic funeral wail. The sensation created in the crowd was terrible. For a moment the mourners stood appalled. Men in the surrounding crowd broke into tears. Another memorable scene was enacted by the grave. A fussy parish priest, it appears, had insisted on his right to deliver the funeral sermon, and after some remonstrance, the point had been yielded. He performed his part with grandiloquent mediocrity. But there was among the mourners that day another priest, Father Patrick Lavelle—noted alike for his ability and patriotism, and for his pugnacity more than for either,—who had been the friend of the deceased, who understood him, and could speak of him as no other man could. When the coffin had been lowered, and the earth smoothed over it, Father Lavelle, at the instance of many of those present, came forward to address the crowd.

For two or three minutes, he stood with bent head, gazing at the new-made grave. Then he threw up his arms, and raising his face to the sky, burst into a passion of weeping, while his auditors, thrilled to the heart, broke out into loud sobs and cries of lamentation.

The Home Rule movement had its origin at a meeting or conference held at the Bilton Hotel, Dublin, on the evening of May 19th, 1870. The assemblage was a strange one for Ireland, and it showed the far-reaching effects that Fenianism

that it wrought, had such a gathering become possible. In the days of Protestant ascendancy, it could never have come to pass that Orangemen and Catholics, conservatives and revolutionists should meet in harmony, as they did that night, to consult and combine for the general advancement of their country's cause; nor could many of those who were present that night, have been brought to see that Ireland had any cause at all, demanding effort on their part, had it not been for the great leavening that the country had just undergone. Fenianism failed to bring much enlightenment to England as to the wrongs, the needs, the resolves of the Irish people. To this day, England as a nation, is blind as regards Ireland. But at least, the great conspiracy caused the eyes of many thousand Irishmen to open.

Profit may be found in the study simply of the names of those who attended the meeting, and I am sorry I have not space to give the list in full. I select a few men from it, however, and the statement of their religious and political opinions will enable the reader to judge how great a change had been wrought by disestablishment. First in prominence was Isaac Butt, in his youth a conservative and the opponent of O'Connell, but now classed as a " Protestant nationalist." In contrast with him, may be put James V. Mackay, J. P., an Orangeman. The Lord Mayor of Dublin and two ex-Lord Mayors were present. The incumbent and one of his predecessors were Protestant conservatives; the other ex-Lord Mayor was a Catholic liberal. The Rev. Joseph E. Galbraith, a Fellow of Trinity College, was a Protestant conservative, and so were Sir William Wilde, Major Knox, (proprietor of the "Irish Times,") Archdeacon Gould, Captain Edward R. King-Harman, the Hon. Lawrence Harman King-Harman, and George F. Shaw, Fellow of Trinity College. William Shaw, M. P. was a Protestant liberal; John Martin was a Presbyterian nationalist; John Nolan (Secretary of the Amnesty Association) was a Catholic nationalist; James O'Connor, and James J. O'Kelly were in opinion,—if not in fact—Fenians,—both were Catholics; A. M. Sullivan classes himself the same head; Alfred Webb was a Quaker and a nationalist.

In a word, every stripe of Irish party politics was represented, as well as the three leading religions of the country. The deliberations were harmonious, and they ended by the adoption of a resolution, proposed by Butt, and couched in these terms :—

Resolved, that it is the opinion of this meeting that the true remedy for the evils of Ireland is the establishment of an Irish parliament with full control over our domestic affairs.

This was adopted, Mr. Sullivan tells us* without a dissentient voice. He adds, " Every one, greatly astonished, burst into a cheer; the first heard that evening, so grave and earnest and almost solemn had been the tone of the deliberations."

An auspicious beginning, indeed, for a patriotic movement! The succeeding months too were full of promise. The people took up the cry of Home Rule enthusiastically enough. Thousands were attracted by the idea who had never before been on the popular side in politics. The formal organization was called the Home Government Association of Ireland, but it never, as an organization, occupied a place of first-rate importance. Such strength as the movement ever had, lay in the spontaneous mustering of the people to the leaders' support whenever an opportunity for action arose.

The plan of operations being one of peaceful and parliamentary agitation, the effort to form a Home Rule party in the House of Commons was begun as soon as ever a fair opportunity arose. Several gentlemen who represented Irish constituencies when the Association was formed, had given in their adhesion to it at once, and so had become the nucleus of a parliamentary party, but the first man actually chosen to the House as a professed Home Ruler was John Martin, the Forty-eight nationalist, who had in 1869 been defeated in a memorable contest for Longford. In 1871, a vacancy occurred in Meath. It was at once determined that Martin should

* "New Ireland," Chapter XXVIII.

contest the seat. The Hon. Mr. Plunkett, a Roman Catholic, and brother of Lord Fingall, was his apponent. He was the regular candidate of the Liberal party, and had the nominal support of the Roman Catholic clergy. He laughed at the Home Ruler's pretensions, and indeed, few persons really expected to see Martin returned. The situation, however, was critical, and the popular leaders bent their energies to the struggle. They had staked their all upon a single cast. Defeat, in truth, meant ruin. But the people of Meath proved worthy of the confidence that had been placed in them ; the priests proved practically neutral : and the administration party, combating against forces which they did not comprehend, and which they far underestimated, were seriously handicapped. The result justified the enterprise of the Home Rule leaders. The close of the fight found Martin head of the polls by a vote of 1149 to 684.

The moral effect of this event was very great. The victors made no delay in following up their advantage. The next vacant seat in Parliament was for Galway, and the election came in February, 1871. Mr. Mitchel-Henry, the son of an Irishman settled in Lancashire, and himself a surgeon of high repute but retired from practice, became the Home Rule candidate. He owned a handsome place in the county, and his family had of old been one of some influence there. From the first, his election was a foregone conclusion, so much so that no candidate appeared to oppose him. He was returned without contest. The next noteworthy incident occurred in June. Mr. P. J. Smyth, a Young Irelander, a speaker of excellent capacity, and a man of unquestionable patriotism, but intractable in character, and Utopian in ideas, was elected member for Westmeath also without contest. In September, Mr. Butt was similarly elected from Limerick. Finally, in January, 1872, after a contest of desperate rancor, in which both sides fairly exhausted their resources, Mr. Rowland Ponsonby Blennerhassett, a mere boy, fresh from Oxford, but occupying by birth an influential position, and professing the Home Rule doctrine, was triumphantly chosen to represent Kerry, defeating the forces of landlordism and foreign ascen-

With this event ends the first period of the Home Rule agitation, the period of evolution. The party was now firmly established in the country, had shown its power, was confessed by enemies as well as friends to constitute a new and formidable element in Irish politics. I have dwelt on the history of this first period in order to illustrate the precise position of the movement among the masses of the people. The vision of a parliament of their own was one of joy and promise to them. From this time forward, the advocacy of Home Rule has been indispensable in any one desiring to represent an Irish constituency. But it was always the idea that the nation rallied to support, and not the party. The people were never very generally aroused to share in the agitation. Whenever the occasion offered to strike a blow at England, by defeating the representative of a regular English party, then they shook off their lethargy, and boldly vindicated their rights and their aspirations. But the general run of demonstrations in support of the Home Rule policy fell far short in numbers, in enthusiasm, and in moral force, of those which had supported O'Connell's demands, or endorsed the principles of Fenianism during the great Amnesty year.

In the autumn of 1873, a great project was formed to give new vigor to the somewhat languishing movement. In October, a call for a great National Conference was circulated through the country, and in a short time the names of twenty-five thousand men of influence and standing were affixed to it. On Tuesday, November 18, 1873, the Conference met in the Round Room of the Rotunda, Dublin. It was numerously attended, and by men of a high order of intelligence. Every shade of party feeling, and all the leading religious sects were represented. Mr. William Shaw, M. P., presided; the proceedings lasted for three days, and, throughout, were dignified, patriotic, and harmonious. There was no mistaking the general current of feeling in the assembly; there was no mistaking the general endorsement of the Home Rule principle; but there was equally plainly a lack of a master

stimulus of a popular awakening ; nothing was done to give solidity, strength, or definiteness to the movement ; and no plans were formulated which were calculated to have any appreciable effect in modifying the policy of England.

Still, the immediate effect of the conference for good was very considerable. A general election followed shortly after. Parliament was dissolved by Mr. Gladstone in January, 1874. The event came as a surprise not to Ireland only, but to the entire Empire. The newly founded Home Rule League,—it was organized by the conference—was ill prepared for such an emergency. Home Rule candidates were lacking for the various counties and boroughs that were eager to elect them ; organization, money, experience, everything was deficient that might be considered necessary to success. But there was no deficiency of spirit among the people. The Ballot Act of 1872 had broken down the power of landlords, and employers. Every man could vote according to his conscience without fearing the vengeance of a disappointed master. This was the first opportunity the people had had to avail themselves of their new found liberty. They did so without stint. Sixty-two Home Rulers sought the suffrages of the voters in various parts of the country ; sixty of them were returned triumphantly. Let it be remembered that Ireland had but a hundred and three representatives to elect. Of these, though taken by surprise, she elected at her very first opportunity a clear majority, solemnly pledged to combat the forced and unnatural union with England, to assert the people's right, as a distinct nationality, to rule themselves and care for themselves.

While these events were occurring in Ireland, a very lively contest was in progress in America, which, though it was waged over the musty relics of a bygone century, yet had a considerable practical influence upon the current time. How close was the bond between the Irish people in America and at home ; how warmly the former cherished their traditions of hate for England ; and how formidable an aux-

British government had well learned during the Fenian excitement. The United States—though indeed the Federal administration had been shamefully inactive in defending its citizens,—had then been the only barrier between England and her vengeance. Now in more tranquil days, to provide for future contingencies, a British emissary came to the United States, for the purpose of poisoning the American mind against Ireland and her national efforts. James Anthony Froude was the man who undertook this honorable task. The nature of his calumnies is well known. They may be seen in detail in his libellous " English in Ireland." His character as a historian has been exposed by English as well as Irish scholars. I desire in this place only to say a word as to the actual consequences of his mission. On the American people, he made no impression. They received him hospitably and listened to him politely ; they dined him, wined him, complimented him —and disbelieved him. But among the Irish people in America, he roused up a host of defenders of their race. A storm of indignation was levelled against him and his employers, and a great revival of interest in Irish history, with consequent accession of bitter feeling over old grievances, was the immediate outcome of his mission.

Two men stood out from all the rest of Froude's refuters, both from their previous reputation, and the effect of their replies to him. These two were John Mitchel, the felon of Forty-eight, and Father Thomas Burke the Dominican orator. Of the former, I have to speak again ; and I need only allude here to the remarkable scholarship and trenchant satire which marked his answers to Froude. They were published in a New York weekly newspaper, and I believe have since been collected and republished. Father Burke made use of his admirable oratorical gifts to reply to the slanderer of his country and his faith. His popularity, then at its zenith, the attractive form of his answers, and the wide circulation given them through the press of the country, combined to make him the means of carrying the truth to thousands who would otherwise have taken small interest in the controversy. A man was he of

of fancy, and of strong feeling. His sway over masses of people was remarkable. His voice was always heard on the side of patriotism and justice, and through his eloquence, I believe, as many hearts have been saved to Ireland as souls to Heaven. Lately he has passed away from the scene of his labors, but he has left behind the sorrowing affection that a sincere, unselfish spirit, and a warm sympathetic heart must always beget.

John Mitchel revisited Ireland in 1874. This seems a simple matter, yet it was the beginning of one of the most romantic episodes of later Irish history.

Mitchel was an outlaw in great Britain—and escaped convict, and an unrepentant rebel. His liberty was not worth an hour's purchase once he set foot on Irish soil. Yet broken with age, and enfeebled by sickness as he was, he had resolved that he would not die until he once more breathed the air of his native Ulster, until he fought one more fight in the cause to which he had given up his life.

" It is quite true the government may cause my arrest," said he to a newspaper man in New York the day before he sailed ; " but on the whole, I hardly think they will. If they think fit to do so, I shall be quite content to have them bring on themselves the odium that must result from such a proceeding."

A little while before, he had written thus to Mr. A. M, Sullivan :—

When certain friends bethought themselves of putting me in nomination for Cork city, at the last election, and asked me the question *per cable*, " Will you come over if elected ? " Only one answer was possible.   I would have gone at once, by the very next steamer calling at Queenstown.

He had been put in nomination for Tipperary as well as Cork city, but had been given no previous notice whatever. His famous dictum, that no good thing could come from the British Parliament, was well known to the people.   They doubted whether he would consider an election to that body an insult, or a compliment.   Under the circumstances, it is not strange that he was defeated.

But now it was certain that he was willing to be a candidate. Had he changed his opinions ?   Was he in his old age, coming to regard "moral force" as the solution of Ireland's cause? No, to the latest breath, he was the same determined enemy of all things British, the same fierce advocate of the extremest measures. But he had hit on a novel scheme of warfare of his own.

If he were elected, one of two alternatives should arise. His election might be accepted by the House of Commons, or it might be rejected on the ground of his position as a ticket-of-leave man, who had broken his parole—of course, he had done this in no dishonorable sense, but only according to British fiction. If the government would permit him, then, he proposed to go to London, and, at the bar of the commons, make solemn protest against English domination of his native country. He would recount the bloodshed, the rapine, the fraud, the sacrilege by which it had been brought about. He would, in the British Halls of Legislature, lay bare the corruption of the Act of Union. He would describe in tones that all the world should hear, the true condition of his country, down-trodden and impoverished; of her people given over to ignorance and starvation. He would attack even the "golden link of the crown," and show that for Ireland to be truly prosperous and happy, she must take her place as a free sovereign power among the nations of the earth.

But as he says himself, Parliament could, and would find some means of disqualifying him. It would declare the seat for Tipperary vacant again. Of this possibility he says in the letter quoted above:

That would suit me very well, because I would offer myself again—would be elected again, for the electors are the sole judges of the eligibility. And if Parliament disfranchised Tipperary altogether, then I would go across the county boundary into Clare, or into Kilkenny, get elected there, and so procure the happy disfranchisement of county after county.

Speaking of the fears of the Home Rulers that this candidature might injure their cause, he utters an important principle which applies with equal truth to every so-called constitutional movement, from the Emancipation agitation to the

I think also that your party is under a mistake in supposing that I, if returned for
an Irish constituency, would be likely to introduce confusion or weakness into the
Home Rule ranks. On the contrary, I might act in the opposite direction, and do
you service, for the greatest strength and support you would have in England would
be the knowledge of the fact that behind you there is an extreme party—an extreme
Left, so you would be the Left Centre.

He sailed from New York on July 14, and landed at Queenstown on the 25th. A characteristic anecdote is told of his arrival in the harbor. It appears that when he sailed from it as
a convict, five and twenty years before, a drizzling rain obscured the retreating hills from his longing gaze. As the steamer on which he returned steered into the " Cove," a similar
rain hung like a veil over the shores.

"Good God," said Mitchel, " isn't that shower over yet ? "

His landing at Queenstown was unexpected, and his presence was unknown until he arrived at Cork. There, ten
thousand people marched in procession to his hotel to welcome him. He made a little speech on that occasion which
was very affecting. He told them he always loved Cork—
what part of Ireland did he not love?—but that after that
meeting with her sons, he would love and honor her more
than ever.

A day or two after, he hastened to Newry, his native town.
There he rested very quietly for several months. His health
grew wonderfully better; but as there seemed no prospects
of a Parliamentary vacancy, he returned to New York in
October.

In February, 1875, the member who had before defeated
him in Tipperary, resigned, and Mitchel was put in the field
as a candidate. He sailed forthwith from America to make
a personal canvass of the county, but the day before he
landed,—February 16th,—he was declared elected without opposition. He at once went quietly to Dromolane near Newry, to the house of his fathers.

But Parliament quashed the election. John Martin, Mr.
Sullivan, and a few others made a gallant stand in the debate
which preceded this action. Even some English members
denounced the haste of the proceedings as indecent. It was in

vain. On February 20th, upon the motion of Mr. Disraeli, the House of Commons by a vote of 250 to 100—approximately—declared that the man of the people's choice was ineligible to represent them.

Then Mitchel kept his word. He went to Tipperary, and so far as his strength—now ebbing fast away—would allow, he personally sought the suffrages of the constituency. A certain Mr. Moore, a Tory and a seeker after cheap honors, took the field against him. The polling was on March 11th, and the result was that Mitchel had 3114 votes; Moore, 746.

Mitchel again repaired to Dromolane " to rest," while Parliament deliberated. But his battles were now over; he had stood before his fellow men for the last time in vindication of the principles of liberty and patriotism to which he had devoted himself. His small remaining vitality burned away faster and faster day by day, in the heat of the conflict in which he was engaged. His spirit passed away on the morning of March 20th, about day-break, and the same roof under which he was born, sheltered his death-bed.

Thus died John Mitchel,—not in a way to be sorrowed for, I am sure, but after a manner, rather, to awaken exultation, —sustained and comforted by the trust and affection of his people, resting in the land he loved so well, facing the foe he had combated all his life, yet for the moment pausing from the strife. Death touched him gently at the end, and the peace of his closing scene was in affecting contrast with the wear and struggle of his life. He has taken as the motto of his History of Ireland, written in his later years, these lines of the poet :—

"The Star of the West shall yet rise in its glory,
And the land that was darkest, be brightest in story;—
I too may be gone ; but my name shall be spoken
When Erin awakes, and her fetters are broken."

I have never read these lines, in this place, without a peculiar emotion. It seems to me as if this man, as the shadows began to gather about him, was granted one vision of the future.

He saw more surely than is often granted, tne destined end of the fight in which he had engaged. His mind's eye rested on the picture of an Ireland flourishing and free, and he saw that in the hearts of the people his life would not be without its recompense. Like Moses, he gazed from afar upon the Promised Land, and then he blessed God and died.

CHAPTER XCII.

OBSTRUCTION. MEN AND METHODS THAT WORRIED THE HOUSE
OF COMMONS. A NEW AND HAPPY DEPARTURE. FAMINE.
LAND FOR THE LANDLESS PEOPLE. PARNELL, DEVOY,
DAVITT.

HE general history of the years from 1873 to 1877,
presents little that is pleasant to dwell upon.
Vacillation in the Home Rule policy, division among
its chiefs, weakness in its leader, defeat in all its
efforts, gradually expiring confidence in the country—such
are the characteristics of the time. The design of the party
had been to agitate in Parliament for minor reforms; its
hope, to gradually accustom England to doing justice to
Ireland. One great annual debate on constitutional separation was to be secured, the result was to be left to time and
Providence. I know no better way of showing how this
plan succeeded, than to borrow from Mr. Sullivan's "New
Ireland," a record of the efforts made in behalf of the subject
nation during the period indicated, and the manner in which
they were disposed of by the representatives of the ruling people:—

Amendment to the Address on Home Rule; March 20th, 1874; Irish vote,—ayes
48, noes 26; defeated by 288 British votes.
Amendment to the Address on Home Rule, July 2d, 1874; Irish vote,—ayes 53,
noes 37; defeated by 421 British votes.
Amendment to the Address on Home Rule, June 30th, 1876; Irish vote,—ayes 52,
noes 33; defeated by 258 British votes.
Amendment to the Address on Home Rule, April 24th, 1877, shows similar results.
April 17th, 1874, Irish Municipal Franchise Bill; Irish vote,—ayes 43, noes 14;
thrown out by 111 British votes.
June 18th, 1874; Municipal Privileges Bill; Irish vote,—ayes 22, noes 9; rejected
by 66 British votes.
April 28th, 1874; Purchase of Irish Railways Bill; Irish vote,—ayes 45, noes 6;
defeated by 236 British votes.

March 23d, 1875; Irish Municipal Corporations Bill; Irish vote,—ayes 43, noes 18; thrown out by 127 British votes.

March 1st, 1875; Irish Municipal Franchise Bill; Irish vote,—ayes 41, noes 16; flung out by 160 British votes.

March 22d, 1876; Irish Fisheries Bill; Irish vote,—ayes 54, noes 6; rejected by 209 British votes.

March 28th, 1876; Irish Borough Franchise Bill; Irish vote,—ayes 57, noes 17; flung out by 162 British votes.

May 3d, 1876; Irish Registration of Voters Bill; Irish vote,—ayes 41, noes 23; rejected by 212 British votes.

July 8th, 1875; Irish Lunatic Asylum Bill; Irish vote,—ayes 28, noes 7; rejected by 111 British votes.

June 2d, 1875; Irish Land Bill; Irish vote,—ayes 44, noes 22; rejected by 279 British votes.

June 11th, 1875; Motion for Enquiry into the Working of the 1870 Land Act; Irish vote,—ayes 30, noes 11; rejected by 97 British votes.

June 30th, 1875; Grand Jury Reform Bill; Irish vote,—ayes 32, noes 22; thrown out by 160 British votes.

June 29th, 1876; Irish Land Bill; Irish vote,—ayes 48, noes 33; rejected by 257 British votes.

April 24th, 1877; Irish Land Bill; Irish vote,—ayes 48, noes 24; flung out by 320 British votes.

The great weakness of the Home Rule party was the lack of a clear and united purpose, and a definite scheme whereby to accomplish it. The fundamental resolutions of the Home Government Association simply contained a declaration in favor of a separate legislature to manage the domestic affairs of Ireland, while the affairs of the Empire at large were to be entrusted to an Imperial Parliament. The adherents of the party were understood to concur in the effort to bring about such an arrangement, yet no one was "committed to any political opinion, save the desirability of seeking for Ireland the amount of self-government indicated."

Now, the "amount of self-government indicated," on the most liberal construction, was not enough to enkindle the popular imagination, or excite great national enthusiasm; and it very soon became evident that nobody quite knew what the amount was. One distinguished leader of opinion was confessedly seeking repeal, pure and simple, while another was willing to give up to a purely English parliament, all international and Imperial concerns, on condition that Ireland should be allowed to do all her petty internal legislation for herself.

If any one should have known just what the Home Rule party wanted, surely that man must have been Butt. Butt, however, had no enlightenment to give the people. He wavered now in this direction, now in that, according as this or that doctrine was uppermost before the public. He never made any serious effort to define the object he sought, and still less attempted to formulate a definite system by which the difficulties incidental to Home Rule in any degree, should necessarily be accompanied. Only one point Butt seemed really determined upon,—he would not give offence to England or her statesmen. He would agitate for minor reforms, he would calmly argue the case of Ireland, he would deferentially request attention to her grievances ; but he would patiently await the time when a sense of justice would cause her masters to afford her some relief. The English government, meanwhile, treated almost contemptuously a party which had neither definite objects nor feasible schemes, and the people lost confidence in leaders who were united only in name, divided on every tangible issue.

Such was the situation in 1877, when, from the most unexpected source, a new energy, potent both in Parliament and with the people, came into being.

Charles Stewart Parnell was a young gentleman of the County Wicklow. His family had long been famous in Ireland for high mental powers, and incorruptible political virtue. The poet Parnell, to whom Alexander Pope has dedicated a poem, takes no mean rank in letters ; nor did he lack regard for the country of his birth, in his day just emerging from almost the darkest period of her history. Again we find a Parnell, worthily styled by his fellow-countrymen *par excellence* " The Incorruptible," ranking among the purest public servants of his day, and among the bitterest opponents of the Act of Union. A grandson of this gentleman married the daughter of another terrible enemy of England—Miss Delia Stewart, the daughter of that Commodore Stewart who was the father of the triumphant American navy of 1812, who himself sailed and fought through several glorious cruises the

lives in American history ? b American hearts under the
grim but expressive title of " Old Ironsides."

The son of this marriage, the descendant of " Old Ironsides"
and " The Incorruptible," is to-day the chosen chief of the
Irish people, the leader under whom they have accomplished
no small results, the guide whom they hope to follow to still
greater things.   Charles Stewart Parnell was born in June,
1846, at Avondale, the family seat in Wicklow.   He was
brought up in England, and he graduated at Cambridge
University.   Originally, his acquaintance with Irish affairs was
very slight.   His sympathies, Mr. Sullivan tells us, were first
attracted to the popular cause by the Manchester executions.
However that may be, he seems quite early in life to have formed strong patriotic opinions and aspirations.   He was chosen to
Parliament as a Home Ruler by the County Meath, in 1875,
when John Martin, the purest, simplest, and most devoted of
men, so closely followed his old comrade Mitchel to the
.grave.

In the spring of 1877, Parnell became the founder of the
now celebrated " Obstruction " policy.   He seems to have
drifted into it by accident, to have persisted in it from deliberation.   The course of action is simply to retard the operations of the House of Commons by every parliamentary
device.   Exhaustive speeches are indulged in on every side
issue ; motions to adjourn, motions that the speaker " leave the
chair," personal explanations, and all the other tricks and
devices known to parliamentarians are unsparingly resorted
to, to check the progress of obnoxious measures.   At first,
Parnell was only one of a group of members who fought
against the practice of bringing important measures up for
action at advanced hours of the night.   The first great obstruction combat took place on the English Prisons Bill, on
March 26th, 1877.   A number of salutary amendments were
moved during the evening by Mr. Parnell and others.   They
were all rigorously voted down.   At last, in the early hours of
the morning, Mr. Biggar moved an adjournment of the House.
Even then his proposal was supported by some English members.   His motion was defeated by 138 noes to 10 ayes.

Then Parnell plunged into the fight, and for two long hours he maintained a guerrilla warfare such as Parliament had never known before. This was the entering wedge. Parnell quickly conceived the idea of forcing Ireland's grievances upon the attention of the House by showing that her representatives came to Westminster not to plead, but to fight.

From the beginning, he had the unfailing support of three other members—Joseph Biggar, who sat for Cavan; Frank Hugh O'Donnell, representing Dungarvan; and John O'Connor Power, member for Mayo. These men, Parnell, Biggar, O'Donnell, and Power, were the four first known as "Obstructionists," and during the greater part of two sessions they carried on their fight almost by their own unaided resources. They were a remarkable little band. Parnell, a tall, fair, handsome young man, with a refined manner, a clear voice, and a slightly English accent, spoke calmly, logically, incisively. His bearing was cold, and reserved. Perseverance, courage, and energy, were three of his most marked traits. He always kept his presence of mind and his temper. He studiously avoided even the appearance of discourtesy· He would delay the house for hours upon some trivial point; he would rise time and again to speak at length regarding some side issue,—he would move an adjournment ten times in a couple of hours; but he would always take the floor with a smile, and would preface his remarks with a few words of seeming conciliation and deprecation. O'Donnell, a writer for the press, possessed an unusual knowledge of foreign and colonial affairs, both of which were subjects of special concern at this time. He made his information the means of goading Cabinet ministers well nigh to desperation. His scornful smile as he rose to speak, was an exasperation which the House never failed to resent; but he seemed to revel in the anger of his fellow legislators. Biggar has of late been before the public under the guise of a gay and fickle Lothario. He has been the defendant in a suit for breach of promise, This is all the more odd as he is personally deformed, and is gifted, it is said, with a voice which reminds the hearer of

upon the ears of the unhappy ministry of Mr. Disraeli,—who, by the way, had come into office after Mr. Gladstone's ill-advised dissolution coup of 1874. None of the Obstructionists has ever been more hateful to English members than Biggar. His North-of-Ireland accent, his savage sarcasm, and his shrewd business talent alike rendered him obnoxious to his adversaries. Of John O'Connor Power, there is little to be said. He is a man of great ability of an every day kind. He started in life in a comparatively humble station, and with "Advanced National" opinions. As he emerged from his humility, he abandoned his revolutionary notions. His career in Parliament was rendered successful by his skill as a debater.

Night after night while the Prisons Bill was going through the house, the contest was renewed, and indescribable scenes took place. English members hooted and groaned, while the Irishmen talked against time. This must be said for the Obstructionists:—they always kept on the side of liberality, justice, and advanced thought. Every one of the amendments they proposed to the Prisons Bill was in the line of improvement, and on almost every point, they had the co-operation of certain liberal-minded English members. They received frequent assistance, too, from Irish Home Rule members who did not wholly give in adhesion to their methods. Major Purcell O'Gorman was their most reliable ally. Mr. Callan after his election to Parliament gave them constant support. The O'Gorman Mahon, Mr. A. M. Sullivan, Major Nolan, the "Whip" of the Home Rulers, and others from time to time voted with them. Butt, it is true, came down to the House one night, and roundly abused the whole obstruction scheme and all its advocates. I think it was the most discreditable act of his life, even if he disapproved the scheme. But his denunciation had no effect whatever, and the Obstructionists gathered strength and popularity day by day. Butt died soon after, having lived just long enough to reap the harvest of his own weakness. He witnessed the failure of his conciliatory plans, and he saw the tide of opinion in the Home Rule party and in the country at large,

Mr. William Shaw, M. P., of Cork, was chosen leader of the Home Rule party upon the death of Mr. Butt. His leadership, however, was only nominal. Even while the majority of the Home Rule members yet ranged themselves under his banner, all the progressive force of the party was concentrated with the Obstructionists, and on them and on their doings, public attention thenceforward remained fixed. After the Prisons Bill, the Parnellites turned their attention to the Mutiny Bill,—the law annually adopted by Parliament, it may be necessary to explain to American readers, for the government and discipline of the army. They assailed with unsparing vigor the inhuman provisions of this measure, which had been passed without material change, year after year from beyond the memory of this generation. They laid its barbarity open to the eyes of the world. Then the British members assailed them more freely than ever. The Irishmen's speeches were drowned in tempests of coughs, jeers, hootings, and threats. Scenes more suited to a cockpit than a senate chamber were enacted. A retaliatory policy of applying the rules of the House to the discomfiture of Obstructionists was also begun. Efforts were made to bring the refractory members under the censure of their fellows as factionists and incendiaries. Members—that is Irish ones—were called to order for words they never uttered ; such words as they did use were tortured and perverted from their true meaning into breaches of parliamentary decorum. In time, suspensions for periods more or less prolonged succeeded to rebukes by the speaker ; but all had no effect. In the face of overwhelming odds, despite discouragement, obloquy and persecution, the gallant little band kept up its fight until victory at last perched upon its banner. The struggle was particularly bitter over the South Africa Bill,—whereby the annexation of the Transvaal was perfected. On this, as on all the other questions they touched, the Irish were in the right ; but, it is needless to say, the government carried the bill despite their opposition. With it the session of 1878 practically closed. In 1878 and 1879, Obstruction developed into a regular sys-

line of improving English legislation. In the years mentioned, the Factories and Workshops Act, and the Army Discipline Act, were passed. On both Parnell and his followers left their mark, and always in the direction of liberality to the oppressed classes, and relief to those who were most liable to tyrannous ill-usage.

Was Obstruction justifiable? some one may ask. Can there be any doubt, I reply, since it was always used against bad, and for good measures? But even in the abstract it was quite justifiable. When the "Liberal" party entered on a canvass of the country before the general election of 1880, its spokesmen pronounced an obstructive policy the right of small minorities, as their only means of securing attention. Magazine articles and speeches to this effect were frequent, and this is the truth of the matter. But of course power was accompanied by oblivion when it came to the Whigs, and the ministry of Mr. Gladstone has done more to limit the privileges of Parliament than all the Tory governments since the Commonwealth, together.

On October 25th, 1878, a cable despatch was sent to Dublin to be submitted to Mr. Parnell, after it had received the approval of the leaders of the Advanced National party in Ireland. It was signed by Dr. William Carroll, of Philadelphia; John J. Breslin, F. F. Millen, and John Devoy of New York; and Patrick Mahon of Rochester, all of whom were prominent in the Irish revolutionary ranks in America. The essential portion of the despatch read thus:—

The Nationalists here will support you (Mr. Parnell) on the following conditions:—

First. Abandonment of the federal demand, and substitution of a general declaration in favor of self-government.

Second. Vigorous agitation of the Land Question on a basis of peasant proprietary, while accepting concessions tending to abolish arbitrary eviction.

Third. Exclusion of all sectarian issues from the platform.

Fourth. Irish members to vote together on all Imperial and Home questions, adopt an aggressive policy, and energetically resist coercive legislation.

Fifth. Advocacy of all struggling nationalities in the British Empire and elsewhere.

These proposals constitute the celebrated "New Departure"

abuse; which has been more wilfully misunderstood, and more practically carried out; which has brought more trouble and misconstruction upon the projector, and more benefit to the nation than any other political combination in the latter days of Irish history. The policy of utter abstinence from constitutional agitation grew out of John Mitchel's principle that no good thing could come from the English Parliament. The practical application of the principle was entirely the product of James Stephens' leadership. It was one of his mistakes,—one of his worst mistakes. The nation had been accustomed to look up to such men as Grattan and O'Connell as patriots—in no limited sense of the word either—and I know no reason why that estimate of them should be altered, and none why such a man as Parnell should be held in any less esteem. In truth, I think Stephens' bitter opposition to all the open movements of his time was hurtful alike to his own organization and the country's prospects.

Therefore I consider the "New Departure" as the dawn of a brighter period in Irish politics,—a period of toleration and coördinate effort among the several sections of the National party. If the "New Departure" in the remotest degree compromised the great national claim to sovereign independence, no one would condemn it more strongly than I; but it simply meant that while every effort was being made towards that great goal, every minor advantage possible should be wrested from the enemy for the benefit of the people.

There is no man living who more steadfastly longs for the complete separation of Ireland from England than the projector of the "New Departure" scheme; there is hardly any one known to me who has suffered more or sacrificed more for his convictions. The man is John Devoy, formerly one of the Fenian convicts, later one of the Fenian exiles, and always a devoted Irishman,—a man from whom a distressed fellow-countryman has never gone away empty handed; a man who has sacrificed professional prospects, private comfort, everything which is generally prized, for the cause to which he has given up his life; a man whose warm heart, honesty of purpose, and devoted earnestness have—to my personal knowledge—won respect for himself and the principles he advocates, in quarters where Irish nationalism is ordinarily regarded with dislike or contempt.

The terms proposed in the cablegram from New York, were not formally accepted by Mr. Parnell and his adherents. The circumstances of the hour rendered such acceptance impossible. But since that period, the aggressive Parliamentary party has had the support of the vast majority of Advanced Nationalists both in Ireland and America,—not perhaps as a body, but with all the force of numbers, intelligence, and determination. Mitchel's saying, in his letter to Mr. Sullivan, has been realized in an unlooked for way. The parliamentary party is now, and has been since the " New Departure," in the position of a " Left Centre," backed and supported by an " Extreme Left," and much of its success has resulted from the appreciation which the English government has of that fact.

On Sunday, April 28th, 1879, an open-air meeting was held at Irishtown, County Mayo, which has passed into history as the first public step in the founding of the Land League. It was not a very large meeting nor were the speakers—Mr. O'Connor Power, M. P., perhaps excepted—men of any very great note or influence. They were Mr. James Daly of Castlebar, who presided ; Mr. Power ; Mr. John Ferguson of Glasgow ; Mr. Thomas Brennan, and Mr. J. J. Louden. But what the meeting lacked in other respects was made up in the novelty and boldness of the doctrines expounded. These did not fail to attract the notice of the press and the public, and in England, and from the ruling classes generally, a howl of "righteous" indignation went up to the skies. Communism, socialism, treason, were the favorite terms used by the English press, then and for many months later, to describe these doctrines, which in reality were neither more nor less than the assertion that the peasant had some rights in the soil he cultivated, and in the products of his own labor.

Those who have read the preceding portion of this book will understand the situation of the Irish tenant farmers.—will know something of the horrors of 1847, when the people starved to death in thousands by the roadsides. Two great changes had happened since that period ;—one in Ireland, the other in the world at large. The Irish people had been visited with the blessings of education and enlightenment ; they had learned much as to their rights, and something of their power. All Christendom had, even in a quarter of a century or less, been filled with a broader spirit of mercy and justice. Those who said that the scenes of 1847 could never be repeated in Ireland were right, for the danger brought the remedy.

Save in enlightenment, the condition of the Irish farmer was little different in 1879 from what it was in 1847. As the lands had improved, rents had been raised,—sometimes the increase of rent had far exceeded, in proportion, the increase of value. Leases had gradually been becoming things of the past, and the wretched tenants-at-will suffered all that the tyranny and greed of foreign masters could inflict. Of course, from time to time, " Whiteboy " outrages had taken place in various parts of the country, and England, on such occasions, had waxed virtuous and wroth. But for years nothing had been done to remove the cause of the trouble.

At last one terrible episode, the slaughter at Ballycohey, had turned the spirit of concession which Fenianism had evoked in England, into an agrarian direction, and one of those half-hearted measures of reform for which Englishmen are famous, had been enacted. The tragedy had occurred on Friday, August 14th, 1868. Mr. William Scully, a landlord already infamous for his behavior towards his tenantry, had started out with a great posse of police for a wholesale service of ejectment notices in Ballycohey, which is a townland of Tipperary a few miles from Limerick Junction. The people having fortified one of the farm houses, had poured a hot fire from it upon Scully and his myrmidons. He, though his dastard breast was covered with a coat of chain mail, had received six bullet wounds,—unhappily he survived them ;—his bailiff and a constable had been killed, and several men had been wounded. Those who fired from the house were never

favorable to Mr. Scully or to landlordism generally. The ultimate consequence had been the Land Act of 1870, by which Mr. Gladstone tried to secure to the tenants some compensation for arbitrary eviction. The landlords, however, had almost from the first, found means to evade this law, and in 1879, it had become almost a dead letter. At that time, I believe, the material condition of the Irish peasant classes was almost as bad as it had ever been before.

It is remarkable that the man who conceived and created the Land League was not present at the first meeting at Irishtown. The mere accident of missing a train prevented him from being there. But he had conducted all the previous negotiations, he had caused the meeting to be called, he had selected the place—his father had once been a tenant farmer near by, and had been evicted in 1848,—and he had drafted the resolutions which were adopted, obtaining for them in advance, the approval of Patrick Egan, Brennan and others.

This man was Michael Davitt, a phenomenal character ; one born to great ends and struggling to their achievement through clouds of darkness and difficulty. When he was a boy, his family lived in great poverty in Lancashire, England. He was sent very early to work in a mill, and he lost his arm in the machinery. This accident gave him yet a little time for study. In early manhood, he was an ardent Fenian, and once again accident intervened to cause his arrest and conviction in 1870, at a time when Fenianism had ceased to be a matter of alarm. He was sentenced to fifteen years penal servitude ; he served eight. The early woes of his family gave his mind its bent. The condition of the agricultural classes filled his thoughts while he was in prison. On his release he came to America, and at once began an effort to create land agitation. " Land for the landless people," became the burden of all his speech, and the aim of all his work. He got a certain degree of encouragement in America, from those who advocated the " New Departure." When he returned to Ireland, he gradually won support there.

The circumstances of the time favored him. A catastrophe

of 1877 had proved a failure. It fell several millions of pounds sterling below the average value. The farmers had to borrow money to sow for the next year. Who can exaggerate the crisis when the autumn of 1878 again brought disaster? The crops a second time fell millions of pounds below the general standard. Then rents began to be deficient, and evictions frequent. The wretched people made feeble efforts to reduce the expenses of living,—already near the border of starvation. What a winter was that which brought 1878 to a close, and opened 1879! In hunger and cold, and in still more agonizing suspense, the people waited for the spring and summer; waited to learn whether homes and food for their wives and little ones, or the poorhouse, the emigrant ship and the roadside were to be their portion. In this dark hour, Davitt took his first step. At his instance, the call for the Irishtown meeting was circulated among the farmers of Mayo.

This meeting was succeeded by many others, and the movement rapidly grew strong in the remote poverty-stricken districts of the west. Meanwhile, as the summer wore on, it became evident that the crops would for the third time be deficient. Then famine—absolute famine stared the country and its rulers in the face. Parnell and his followers—in fact the Irish members generally,—were alive to the situation. They urged the House of Commons to take some steps to meet the emergency,—at least to appoint a committee of enquiry. The Rt. Hon. James Lowther, Chief Secretary for Ireland, disposed of the whole subject in a sentence. He was glad, he said, to think that though depression undoubtedly existed in Ireland, it was not so serious as that which prevailed in other parts of the "United" Kingdom.

After this preciously oracular dictum, Mr. Parnell went to Ireland, and entered into the land movement with all his soul. At a meeting at Westport on June 8th, he told the people to " keep a firm grip on their holdings." This principle became the fundamental one of the whole fight. The farmer resisted eviction by every means short of violence,—occasionally even

League took place at a convention of tenant farmers held in Dublin. The scheme of organization provided that the objects of the League were to obtain a reduction of rack rents, and to bring about the establishment of a peasant proprietary. The plan of campaign embraced the following methods :—1. The promotion of organization among the tenant farmers. 2. The legal defence of those threatened with eviction for non-payment of unjust rents. 3. To facilitate the working of the " Bright Clauses " of the Land Act of 1878, which in some degree provided for the purchase of farms by the actual cultivators. 4. Agitation for such further reform of the land laws as would make it possible for tenants to become owners of their holdings by the payment of fair sums annually for a certain term of years. Mr. Parnell was chosen president of the League, Thomas Brennan, secretary, and Patrick Egan, a Dublin baker, treasurer.

As the distress grew deeper in the country, the League grew stronger. The Catholic clergy presently came over to it, and their immense influence insured its success. They combined with the leaders to prevent deeds of violence, and their aid was all-important in carrying on the work of relieving distress, one of the most prominent features of the League programme.

In December, Mr. Parnell made his memorable visit to the United States. It would be superfluous at this time, and writing in New York, to enter into any details as to his reception or his doings. I regard the visit, as on the whole, a triumph for him and for his party. He made, it must be admitted, more than one most regretable mistake ; the American press was anything but favorably disposed towards him either at the beginning or the end of his stay ; but the people of Irish race rallied around him with an enthusiasm seldom equalled, and all the great work that has been done in this country ever since, has been the result, direct or indirect, of his mission. The immediate result was the raising of enormous sums for the redemption of the famine-stricken people from starvation. At the period of his visit, two relief committees, besides that of the League, were at work in Ireland—one headed by the Duchess of Marlborough, wife of the Lord Lieutenant, the

of distressed Ireland with bounteous liberality. The United States government gave the use of a war vessel, in which supplies were forwarded,—best among them, a store of seed potatoes to take the place of the diseased roots which were propagating the germs of famine year after year. The "New York Herald" headed a subscription list of its own with the splendid offering of $100,000. Its fund reached half a million of dollars, which was distributed by its own agents in Ireland. The Land League fund received from America three-quarters of a million that year alone, and ever since, large sums have been forwarded to Ireland from time to time, chiefly through the medium of the "Irish World" newspaper, and of the Rev. Father Walsh, of Waterbury, Conn., the national treasurer of the American branch of the Land League, throughout the existence of that body.

The results of all this magnificent alms-giving were not unworthy of the spirit that prompted it. So far as I have ever heard, no man or woman perished of sheer hunger in Ireland. To paint the privation and suffering of the winter of 1879-80 would be a task that I cannot undertake here. The imagination of the reader can hardly color the picture in too sombre tones. Sickness, want, and sorrow of every kind oppressed the land. The depression of that time will yet be felt for years to come. But at least, I believe, the final horror was spared, and no man died of famine.

While Parnell was yet in America, those notable allies, the Afghans, the Zulus, and the Obstructionists became too much for Mr. Disraeli and his Tory followers. The statesman of dazzling ideas threw himself upon the country, and the country rejected him. A general election was held in April, 1880, and the Conservatives suffered crushing defeat. Mr. Gladstone became prime-minister in May, with a majority of about a hundred votes in the House of Commons. The Home Rule party made a net gain of ten votes. This was the time when Mr. Healey, Mr. T. P. O'Connor, and others of Mr. Parnell's best-known followers, were elected to Parliament for the first time. In 1880, only a partial measure of relief, the Disturb-

All through the autumn and winter, though the harvest was a fair one, the distress continued, and the agitation was maintained at its height. This was the era of the celebrated " Boycotting " system, called after its first victim, an Englishman named Boycott, who had leased the farm of an evicted tenant. The system consisted simply in the entire withdrawal of the people from social or business relations with the obnoxious person,—generally a bailiff or constable, or someone who, like Boycott, had settled upon the land of an evicted tenant. No person would speak to one who fell under the ban, no person would buy from him, sell to him, or work for him.

At this time crimes of violence were at their lowest point among the peasantry. The English press, it is true, teemed with agrarian outrages ; but under scrutiny, nine out of ten of these were reduced to mere frivolities, or vanished into fiction altogether. In October, 1880, Messrs. Parnell, Dillon, Egan, Brennan, Boyton, and others, were arraigned in the Court of Queen's Bench, in Dublin, for publicly inciting tenants to refuse to pay rent. The jury that tried them disagreed, standing ten votes for acquittal to two for conviction.

When Parliament met in 1881, Mr. Gladstone's followers, smarting under this defeat, forced him to open the session by proposing a coercion bill. In doing so, he promised that as soon as it had become law, a scheme of land reform should be proposed. He held this promise out as a bribe to the Home Rulers, to allow the speedy passage of the measure of oppression. But the Irish members made no base surrender of their principles. They recognized that their first duty was to resist all aggression on the people's rights. Then were renewed the obstruction scenes of the days of the Mutiny Act. Parnell and his followers fought with all their might. The struggle was prolonged for a month. Every resource was exhausted. But of course, the government prevailed. Besides the coercion law for Ireland, one for the House of Commons was enacted. Worried beyond endurance by the tactics of the Parnellites, a short-sighted " Liberal " majority legalized a set of rules to muzzle free debate. Thus does Eng-

does she in anticipation destroy, for all purposes of conciliation, every reform that stern necessity forces her to grant.

Mr. Gladstone's Land Bill was introduced on April 7th,
1881, and became law on August 22d, after the Lords had
done their worst to kill it, and, failing in that, to deprive it
of all value. The chief feature of the bill, as it was finally
carried, was the establishment of a system of land courts with
power to adjudicate as to the fair rents of all property not
held by lease. Something further was done besides towards
facilitating the purchase of holdings by the tenants, the government engaging to lend certain fractions of the purchase
money under certain circumstances.

The bill had several fatal defects,—worst among them, the
lack of any relief for the tenants from the dreadful arrears of
rent that had been accumulating, and of means for preventing
evictions, until the land courts could consider at least some of
the cases that were brought before them in tens of thousands.
Still, take it all in all, the bill was a wonderful concession
from a British Parliament, a wonderful victory for the Irish
people. Its passage marks the climax of the Land League
movement, and also, so far as now appears, of the career of
Davitt, and no unworthy climax was it for either. It marks
a great step in the progress of Ireland ; it teaches a great lesson,—that with union, discretion, and determination, the
people wield irresistible power.

But while doing justice to the energy and genius of Davitt,
and the splendid leadership of Parnell, it would, in my opinion, be unjust to withhold a word of gratitude from the statesman
who has for many years felt deep sympathy for Ireland, and
who has done more to alleviate her sufferings, than any other
of his race. It seems to me that those Irishmen who are in the
habit of heaping abuse on Mr. Gladstone, forget that he is an
Englishman, and that, after all, his first duty is to his own
country. It is true he has the failing of dealing sometimes in
half-measures ; but I think the time will come when the motives that have actuated him throughout the turmoil of the
Land League agitation, will be vindicated, and the people

CHAPTER XCIII.

Decline of the Land League. "No Rent." Dynamite and the Dagger. The Phœnix Park Tragedy
and its Sequel. Hope again. The Chapter still
Unfinished.

N this chapter I shall be under the disadvantage of
dealing with contemporaneous matters,—matters
which are still the subjects of violent passions and excited opinions, not to say prejudices. Concerning
things which are past and settled, even though they be
separated from the present by only half a decade, we can
have some toleration for views opposed to our own. It is human nature, however, to receive impatiently whatever conflicts with our ideas upon subjects of immediate interest.

Now, like every one else, I have very strong opinions touching the " No Rent " manifesto, the " Invincible " conspiracy,
and the " Dynamite " system of politics. I believe the " No
Rent " manifesto was an error, and, alike on grounds of conscience and expediency, I hold in aversion all schemes of
assassination, or for the wholesale destruction of property.

It appears that a large portion of my fellow-countrymen
and probable readers differ from me radically, some on one,
some on all of these subjects. This is a matter of great regret
to me, and I feel I should be doing less than my duty if I
failed to make at least one appeal to the honor, to the sense
of right, and to the practical judgment of my readers ; if I
should fail to warn them against acts and methods which, to
take no higher view, must strengthen rather than weaken the
position of England. But when I come to narrate the events
of the last three years, I shall refrain from all criticism.
I shall present the facts plainly as they occurred, and, content
with putting my own conscientious opinions on record,

I shall leave it to my readers to form their own inferences, and to the fulness of time to vindicate the eternal principles of right.

The Land Act of 1881 really marks the climax of the Land League movement. For nearly two years more, the agitation was kept at an excited pitch in Ireland, and several victories—notably the passage of the law for the adjustment of the arrears of rent—were won. This was done in the face of determined governmental opposition. As soon as the Land Bill became law, a fierce crusade against the Land League was begun ; yet, only for the Land League, the new measure would have failed to afford relief to the people, would, in fact, have only come into general application by very slow degrees. As it was, Mr. Parnell, while demanding further concessions from Parliament, determined that the people should have all the benefits of those already secured. Money was therefore furnished by the League to the peasantry to bring their grievances before the newly established land courts. Lawyers were found to plead their causes, support was afforded them while their cases were pending, appeals were made from unjust decisions—in short, everything was done to render Mr. Gladstone's law a real measure of relief, and not a mere piece of documentary benevolence, as the landlords would have wished.

In the midst of these endeavors the League leaders were rudely interrupted. Their organization was declared illegal, and its suppression was determined upon. Then began an era of persecution. Meetings were broken up by the police, local leaders were arrested by scores, editors of nationalist newspapers were prosecuted. At length even the parliamentary chiefs of the party were assailed. Parnell, Dillon, J. J. O'Kelly and a number of others were seized and cast into prison as persons dangerous to the public peace. Michael Davitt was arrested in Dublin and consigned to Milbank convict-prison as a ticket-of-leave man who had broken his parole. Patrick Egan was obliged to flee to Paris,—not for the sake

League beyond the danger of seizure by the Government, and to keep a channel open by which the peasantry, still living on the verge of famine, might receive the generous sums raised in America for their salvation.

In this country, the Land League had, at the time now re‑ ferred to, far greater numbers, strength, and enthusiasm than any other Irish-American body has ever attained to, except, perhaps, the Fenian Brotherhood. Without depriving any one of due credit, I think I may say this strength was the result of a great uprising of popular spirit rather than of the teach‑ ings of any man or group of men. The immediate sufferings of the Irish peasantry were of a kind that a majority of their fellow-countrymen in the United States had practical expe‑ rience of. Famine, or eviction, had driven themselves or their fathers to seek a refuge beyond the seas, and their souls were full of bitter wrath when they were reminded of the system that was depopulating their mother country. Almost spontaneously they organized in all the cities and villages of the Union, and for months they continued to pour out their offerings to aid the League at home in its double work of fighting the oppressor and relieving the down-trodden people.

In this work there was one man who, more than any other, was the chosen and devoted servant of the people. This was the Rev. Lawrence Walsh, a priest and a man of sincere pa‑ triotism. During his most active connection with Irish affairs he was pastor of the Immaculate Conception parish in Wa‑ terbury, Connecticut. It would be out of place for me to touch upon his ecclesiastical career in this place; suffice it to say it was notable for active piety ;—but the part which he play‑ ed in the history of the Land League, in view of his recent and lamentable death, calls for at least a brief outline. When the danger of a famine became imminent in Ireland, he collected three thousand dollars among his parishioners in Waterbury, and sent it direct by cable to the bishops and priests in those districts in Ireland, where the greatest distress prevailed. When Parnell visited America, and the urgent need for gen‑ eral relief became a certainty, he embarked heart and soul

Treasurer of the League of the United States by a convention held at Trenor Hall, New York, in 1880. In 1881 he was re-elected by the convention held at Buffalo ; and again in 1882 he was the unanimous choice of the delegates at Washington. He was a central figure in the great conventions of all the Irish societies held at Chicago in the close of 1881, and at Philadelphia in 1883. He would undoubtedly have been chosen General Treasurer of the newly organized National League, if his health had permitted him to be a candidate. But the shadow of death was already upon him, and though the devotion of his spirit to his country never abated, the most active work of his last days was consecrated to the service of that Church of which he was no unworthy minister.

In the midst of the persecution that the government directed against the Land League, the women of Ireland displayed an energy and devotion worthy of their race. Some of them endured even imprisonment for the national cause. The Ladies' Land League became the active agency for keeping up the agitation, and for relieving the distress among the peasantry. These women were the persons who really gave Mr. Gladstone's Land Bill vitality, by enabling the peasantry to bring their grievances before the Land Courts. Thousands of tenants were evicted at the same time on account of the hopeless arrears of rent for 1879 and 1880, and only the work of the Ladies' Land League kept such unfortunates, with their wives and children, from perishing of cold and want upon the open roadsides. It is probable that but for the work of these ladies, and the great generosity of the Irish in America, thousands would have starved to death in the midst of comparative plenty.

During the greater part of this time, Mr. Parnell and his lieutenants were kept in prison, under the provisions of a Coercion Act which gave the British rulers arbitrary power over the liberty of every Irishman. When this act was before the House of Commons, it was, of course, opposed by the Irish nationalist members, and the ministry secured

against "village ruffians," who were said to be inciting their
simple neighbors to wild acts of violence. But when the act
was passed, the government forthwith adopted a policy in
direct violation of its pledges. Under the false pretence
that the country was a prey to disorder growing out of the
Land League movement, the leaders of that movement were
seized and hurried off to prison. The immediate effect of
this proceeding was a great increase in agrarian crime. Actual deeds of violence against landowners took the place
of the fabrications which the castle authorities had been accustomed to invent week after week for the purpose of manufacturing public opinion against the Irish peasantry.

This increase of crime was naturally to be expected. Mr.
Parnell, Davitt, and the other League leaders, had been the
strongest advocates of peace in the country. Peace was the
first principle of their policy, and their influence was the
only force in the country capable of securing passive endurance among the goaded people. Mr. Parnell repeatedly
represented these facts to the government and the British
public; but without result. He and his trusted lieutenants
were, with gross injustice, kept under close ward, while the
state of things, throughout the country, became daily worse
and worse.

Under this exasperation, Mr. Parnell promulgated the celebrated "No Rent" manifesto. It was intended purely as a
measure of retaliation. Its instructions to the people were
that they should pay no rent until the "suspects," as the imprisoned popular leaders were called by the government,
should be liberated. Mr. Healy, M. P., and Mr. Frank
Hugh O'Donnell, both leaders of the Land League, and both
journalists of high repute, are authorities for the statement
that this manifesto was obeyed to a very limited extent among
the people. In fact, the circumstances of the time made absolute obedience to it impossible. The literal carrying out of
the manifesto would have amounted to revolution, and the
people were in far too enfeebled a condition to attempt, not
to say accomplish, any revolutionary proceeding.

though enforced by "Buckshot" Forster with unsparing
rigor, had daily less and less effect in checking it. At last
Mr. Gladstone resolved on a change of policy. The imprisoned "suspects," leaders and all alike, were set at liberty ;
Mr. Foster, in whose heart there was no mercy for an agrarian
reformer or a down-trodden peasant, was superseded in office ;
tranquillity for the moment prevailed, and a period of recip-
rocal toleration seemed to be beginning. The tranquillity
was short-lived. It was broken by the ever-to-be-deplored
tragedy of the Phœnix Park, on May 6th, 1882.

It was Saturday evening, and Lord Frederick Cavendish,
the new Chief Secretary for Ireland—who had just come
over in Mr. Forster's place to institute the *régime* of conciliation—and Mr. Thomas H. Burke, the Under Secretary,
were walking together from the Castle to their lodges—as
the official residences are called—in the park. Near the
Phœnix Monument, they were met by a band of men armed
with knives, who forthwith attacked them. The struggle
was of the briefest. The two officials were unarmed, and
unguarded. They were taken utterly by suprise, and in a
minute's space both lay upon the dusty road, weltering in
their blood and breathing their last.

The attack had been aimed against Burke, who was regarded by the people—and with good reason—as responsible
for much of the Castle tyranny. Cavendish was an accidental victim. His death was the result of a chance meeting between him and Burke a few minutes before the attack, which
had been planned against the latter, was made. There had
not been the slightest intention of killing Cavendish. The
murderers did not even know who their second victim was,
until they found out from the newspapers. This fact, obvious
though it was,—that Burke alone had been aimed at,—was
utterly lost sight of amid the horror of the hour. The world
forgot, too, that the government which had driven the people
to desperation was ultimately responsible for the crime.

Some credit is due to Mr. Gladstone, that this awful tragedy,
and the tremendous burst of public feeling against Ireland

not prevent him from enacting the Arrears Bill, the necessary supplement to the Land Act. It is also highly honorable to Mr. Parnell that, despite unequalled discouragement, he brave-ly fought the measure which Gladstone, under overwhelming pressure of popular opinion, introduced into Parliament for the suppression of political offences in Ireland. Parnell's re-sistance was, of course, unavailing, and a terrible system was legalized which gave the government powers equal to those of Russian despotism. The passage of this measure was made the first work of Parliament after the funerals of Burke and Cavendish had taken place. It gave the government the power to try even capital cases before a bench of judges in-stead of by jury ; inquisitorial methods in the treatment of unwilling witnesses were authorized ; and the freedom of the press, and the right of public meeting, were made dependent on the pleasure of the Castle officials.

The Arrears Act became law shortly after the Crimes Act. The House of Lords retarded its passage by attempts to "amend " away all the benefits that it was intended to confer upon the people. As has been usual in later times, the prej-udices of that antiquated assembly had to give way before the pressure of justice and public opinion. It finally passed the bill on August 11th, 1882, and, shortly after, the measure received the Royal signature, and came into effect.

The act was designed to neutralize in part the results of the dreadful years of partial famine. When the Land Act was passed, thousands of the peasantry were in arrears with their rent for three years. The landlords were insisting that the whole amount should be paid in full, and the people, being utterly unable to meet the demand, were being ejected by wholesale daily, while still more sweeping evictions were imminent. The Land Act made no provision for this phase of the prevailing distress. It had no retrospective action, and, as long as he was behind with his rent, the tenant could gain no help from the land courts. The new measure, which was laid out principally in accordance with suggestions of Mr. Parnell, effected a reasonable compromise. It was ar-ranged that the landlords should forego one-third of the amounts due to them ; that the tenants should pay one-third of the amounts for which they were liable ; and that the government should pay to the landlords the remaining third out of the public treasury.

The Phœnix Park murderers jumped on cars, and driving away from the scene of the tragedy, contrived to evade detection for some time. The power bestowed upon the administration by the new Coercion, or Crimes Act, however, enabled it, in time, to solve the mystery of their identity. It was found that a widespread conspiracy to assassinate prominent English and Anglo-Irish officials existed under the name of the " Irish Invincibles." The head of this body, a man, it is said, named Tynan, who has been known to the world by the mystic title of " No. 1," escaped to America. A large number of persons connected with the killing of Burke and Cavendish were, however, arrested.

Their trials took place in Dublin, and lasted from February 3 to May 2, 1883. One of the most deeply involved of all the prisoners—in fact, the designer and leader of the Phœnix Park affair, a man who had also planned the murder of various other persons—the infamous James Carey—became informer when he found his own miserable life in danger. On his evidence, five of his companions were convicted and hanged. Their names and the dates of their executions were as follows :—Joseph Brady, May 14, 1883 ; Daniel Curley, May 18 ; Michael Fagan, May 28 ; Thomas Caffrey, June 2 ; and Timothy Kelly, June 9. Several other men were sentenced to periods of penal servitude of greater or less duration for complicity in the murders.

However great was the guilt of these men, the acceptance by the government of the evidence of their leader to secure their punishment, caused a shock to the moral sense of the entire world. Happily, the wretch did not long survive his monstrous treachery.

As soon as his usefulness was at an end, the government shipped Carey and his unfortunate wife and children to Port

to his final destination, on board the steamer *Melrose*, his thin disguise was penetrated by Patrick O'Donnell, an Irish-American of national proclivities, who was proceeding to the same point. During the voyage, on Sunday, July 29, 1883, O'Donnell shot Carey, firing at him twice and killing him.

No other person saw these shots fired. When O'Donnell was tried for the killing of Carey, his lawyers endeavored to show that they were fired in self-defence, as the result of a quarrel between the men. O'Donnell even made statements to that effect several times before his conviction. He said Carey had a pistol and drew it on him. He had come, he said, from a section of this country where a man never hesitated to shoot the instant he saw a revolver in an adversary's hand. He fired because he believed it was necessary to do so for his own safety. After his conviction, however, O'Donnell placed in the hands of his counsel an avowal that he had killed Carey deliberately, as a punishment for the miscreant's treason.

The shooting having taken place upon the high seas, O'Donnell was taken to London to be tried by an English judge and an English jury. The case occupied several days. The defence was carried on by the aid of funds subscribed in Ireland and America, $55,098.78 being raised in the United States by the *Irish World*, as shown in an audit recently published in the columns of that paper. The counsel were Mr. Charles Russell, Q. C., and Mr. A. M. Sullivan, assisted by Mr. Roger A. Pryor, of the New York bar. Their pleading was able, but unavailing. After considerable deliberation, the jury convicted O'Donnell of "wilful murder," and he was sentenced to be hanged. A feeble attempt at interference in his behalf by the American government, and efforts made by his counsel to obtain the "clemency of the crown," were barren of result. Victor Hugo, the great French patriot and poet, addressed a personal appeal to Queen Victoria in the condemned man's behalf. Her Majesty referred the matter to her ministers, who advised "that the law should take its course."

don, at eight o'clock on the morning of December 17, 1883. He died courageously. As the slayer of an informer, and especially of so vile a traitor as Carey, he had in his death the sympathy not only of the Irish people, but of the world in general. Even those who did not think his action wholly justifiable, were far from considering that it required expiation upon the gallows. On January 24, 1884, a great funeral procession in his memory took place at Derrybeg, his birthplace, in the County Donegal. A requiem Mass was celebrated, and an empty coffin was deposited in the grave of his family.

The first appearance of the explosive element in Irish politics was in the effort to rescue Richard O'S. Burke from Clerkenwell Prison in 1867. The wall of the jail yard, in which it was supposed Burke was exercising, was blown down with gunpowder. Those concerned in the scheme made the dreadful mistake of using a whole barrel of the explosive. The shock laid the entire neighborhood in ruins, and twelve people were killed, one hundred and twenty maimed or hurt. The young man, Barrett, who was hanged for this affair, was not, I believe, a principal in it. Anyway, the moral guilt of the authors of the tragedy was not great. There was no intention whatever to destroy human life, or even to injure property. The whole affair was a blunder. Had Burke been where his friends supposed he was, he would inevitably have been blown to atoms. No persons were more terribly shocked by the disastrous results than those who planned the explosion.

The dynamite school of revolutionists, properly so-called, was founded by O'Donovan Rossa, who started the "Skirmishing Fund," well known by name to all Irish-Americans, in 1875, with the avowed object of assailing England with dynamite in her ships and strongholds, in her palaces and her centres of wealth. A little later, March, 1877, certain other prominent Irishmen insisted on a change in the trusteeship. The fund has since that time been called the

It is managed by a board of trustees, who are a strictly secret body. What may or may not have been done with the money, or any portion of it, no one can say outside the board ; but I am assured by members of that board, and I believe that no part has been used for any of the recent demonstrations in England.

Shortly after the change of trustees, Rossa ceased to have any share in the management of the fund. Since that time, he has repeatedly appealed to the public, through newspapers of which he has been editor, for money for dynamite projects, and more or less has from time to time been contributed. Meanwhile a certain activity on the part of the dynamite element has been unmistakably evident in England. The attempt to blow up the London Mansion House in 1881, was only the first of a series of alarms to which England has been subjected. At various times since, dynamite cartridges have been discovered at various points; and while it is probable that English socialists were responsible for some of these, it is quite as likely that they were introduced into the country by Irish Revolutionists. No person can pretend to doubt that the attempt to blow up the offices of the Local Government board, early in 1883, was the work of the same men who had established a magazine of dynamite in Manchester, and whose agents were arrested in London, Glasgow, Manchester, and other points. Most of those who were arrested are now undergoing penal servitude.

Whether Rossa is the real head of the conspiracy which had thus been at work in England, whether he was the instigator of the unfortunate men who are now suffering a hopeless imprisonment, whether he furnished the money and material for the attempts that marked the course of 1883, or for the still more recent explosion in the Victoria Railway Station, London, I am sure I cannot pretend to say. He has never directly admitted any part in the matter, but while dealing only in hints and generalities, he has given good ground for the conclusion that he is the prime mover in the dynamite campaign.

upon the political field of Ireland is the continued activity of the Parnellite party, which, like the phœnix from its ashes, has arisen strong and vigorous from the ruins of the Land League.

Let me say here again, as I said in opening these supplementary chapters, that the characteristic of the present period of Irish history is the determination with which the struggle against England has been kept alive. One national movement has subsided only to make room for another. Since I first placed this remark upon paper, a fresh exemplification of the fact has been afforded. Seeing that the Land League could no longer be made a means of success, Parnell and his fellow leaders declared its dissolution, and at a National Conference, held in the Ancient Concert Rooms, Dublin, on October 7th, 1882, founded the National League, with broader principles and higher aims than had yet actuated their agitation. The programme outlined at this conference was subsequently rendered more definite by a convention which sat at the Rotunda. At this convention a constitution was adopted, setting forth that the League was organized to attain for the Irish people the following objects :—

1st. National Self-Government.
2d. Land Law Reform.
3d. Local Self-Government.
4th. Extension of the Parliamentary and Municipal Franchises.
5th. The development and encouragement of the Labor and Industrial Interests of Ireland.

America has given an enthusiastic sanction to the new movement. The Philadelphia convention held in June, 1883, proclaimed the dissolution of the Land League of the United States, and the establishment of the National League. In a general convention, delegates from almost all the Irish associations in the country participated. The result was an organization which went further towards harmonizing various elements than any other that Irishmen had ever formed in this country.

finished chapter.   What a day may bring to Ireland is uncertain.   I hope for great things from the League, for great
things from the new spirit of energy, union, and self-reliance
that has grown up among the people.   But whatever the near
future may bring, I am certain that no one who has studied
the history of this century, and especially of the later dec-
ades, can doubt what the ultimate result will be.   I have
a firm trust that,—whether in this generation or the next, I
know not, but certainly at some not very far off day,—the
chains rusty with the blood of centuries will be cast aside, and
Ireland will once again take her place, free and independent,
among the nations of the earth.

ROBERT EMMET.

DYING SPEECH OF THE GREAT PATRIOT OF '98—WORDS
THAT WILL EVER THRILL THE HEARTS OF FREEMEN.

"Not in Power, Not in Profit, but in the Glory of the Achievement,"
His Only Ambition.

What have I to say why sentence of death should not be
pronounced on me, according to law? I have nothing to
say which can alter your predetermination, nor that it becomes me to say with any view to the mitigation of that
sentence which you are here to pronounce, and by which I
must abide. But I have that to say which interests me
more than life, and which you have labored, as was necessarily your office in the present circumstances of this oppressed country, to destroy. I have much to say why my
reputation should be rescued from the load of false accusa-
tion and calumny which has been heaped upon it. I do not
imagine that, seated where you are, your minds can be so
free from impurity as to receive the least impression from
what I am about to utter. I have no hope that I can anchor
my character in the breast of a court constituted and tram-
melled as this is. I only wish, and it is the utmost I expect,
that your lordships may suffer it to float down your memories untainted by the foul breath of prejudice, until it
finds some more hospitable harbor to shelter it from the
rude storm by which it is at present buffeted. Were I only
to suffer death, after being adjudged guilty by your tribunal,
I should bow in silence, and meet the fate that awaits me
without a murmur; but the sentence of the law which de-
livers my body to the executioner will, through the ministry of the law, labor in its own vindication to consign my

whether in the sentence of the court, or in the catastrophe, posterity must determine. A man in my situation, my lords, has not only to encounter the difficulties of fortune and the force of power over minds which it has corrupted or subjugated, but the difficulties of established prejudice. The man dies, but his memory lives. That mine may not perish, that it may live in the respect of my countrymen, I seize upon this opportunity to vindicate myself from some of the charges alleged against me. When my spirit shall be wafted to a more friendly port—when my shade shall have joined the bands of those martyred heroes who have shed their blood on the scaffold and in the field in defence of their country and of virtue, this is my hope—I wish that my memory and name may animate those who survive me while I look down with complacency on the destruction of that perfidious government which upholds its domination by blasphemy of the Most High ; which displays its power over man, as over the beasts of the forest ; which sets man upon his brother, and lifts his hand, in the name of God, against the throat of his fellow who believes or doubts a little more or a little less than the government standard—a government which is steeled to barbarity by the cries of the orphans and the tears of the widows which it has made.

LORD NORBURY—"The weak and wicked enthusiasts who feel as you feel are un-equal to the accomplishment of their wild designs."

I appeal to the immaculate God—I swear by the Throne of Heaven before which I must shortly appear—by the blood of the murdered patriots who have gone before me—that my conduct has been, through all this peril, and through all my purposes, governed only by the convictions which I have uttered, and by no other view than that of the emancipation of my country from the superinhuman oppression under which she has so long and too patiently travailed ; and I confidently and assuredly hope that, wild and chimerical as it may appear, there is still union and strength in Ireland to accomplish this noblest enterprise. Of this I speak with the confidence of intimate knowledge and with the consolation that appertains to that confidence. Think not, my lords, that I say this for the petty gratification of giving you a transitory uneasiness. A man who never yet raised his voice to utter a lie will not hazard his character with posterity by asserting a falsehood on a subject so important to his country and on an occasion like this. Yes, my lords, a man who does not wish to have his epitaph written until his country is liberated will not leave a weapon in the power of envy nor a pretence to impeach the probity which he means to preserve, even in the grave to which tyranny consigns him.

LORD NORBURY—"You proceed to unwarrantable lengths in order to exasperate or delude the unwary, and circulate opinions of the most dangerous tendency for purposes of mischief."

Again I say that what I have spoken was not intended for your lordship, whose situation I commiserate rather than envy; my expressions were for my countrymen. If there is a true Irishman present, let my last words cheer him in the hour of his affliction—

LORD NORBURY—"What you have hitherto said confirms and justifies the verdict of the jury."

I have always understood it to be the duty of a judge, when a prisoner has been convicted, to pronounce the sentence of the law. I have understood that judges sometimes think it their duty to hear with patience, and to speak with humanity; to exhort the victim of the laws, and to offer, with tender benignity, their opinions of the motives by which he was actuated in the crime of which he was adjudged guilty. That a judge has thought it his duty so to have done, I have no doubt; but where is that boasted freedom of your institutions—where is the vaunted impartiality, clemency, and mildness of your courts of justice, if an unfortunate prisoner, whom your policy, and not justice, is about to deliver into the hands of the executioner, is not suffered to explain his motives sincerely and truly, and to vindicate the principles by which he was actuated? My lords, it may be a part of the system of angry justice to bow a man's mind by humiliation to the purposed ignominy of the scaffold; but worse to me than the purposed shame of the scaffold's terror would be the shame of such foul and unfounded imputations as have been laid against me in this court. You, my lord,

are a judge; I am the supposed culprit. I am a man; you
are a man also.   By a revolution of power we might change
places, though we never could change characters. If I
stand at the bar of this court and dare not vindicate my
character, what a farce is your justice? If I stand at this bar
and dare not vindicate my character, how dare you calumni-
ate it? Does the sentence of death, which your unhallowed
policy inflicts upon my body, also condemn my tongue to
silence and my reputation to reproach? Your executioner
may abridge the period of my existence, but while I exist I
shall not forbear to vindicate my character and motives from
your aspersions; as a man to whom fame is dearer than life
I will make the last use of that life in doing justice to that
reputation which is to live after me, and which is the only
legacy I can leave to those I honor and love, and for whom
I am proud to perish. As men, my lord, we must appear on
the great day at one common tribunal, and it will then remain
for the Searcher of all hearts to show a collective universe
who was engaged in the most virtuous actions or actuated by the purest motives—my country's oppressor, or—
    LORD NORBURY—"Stop, sir! Listen to the sentence of the law."

My lord, shall a dying man be denied the legal privilege
of exculpating himself in the eyes of the community from an
undeserved reproach thrown upon him during his trial, by
charging him with ambition, and attempting to cast away,
for a paltry consideration, the liberties of his country?
Why did your lordship insult me? Or rather, why insult
justice in demanding of me why sentence of death should
not be pronounced? I know, my lord, that form prescribes
that you should ask the question. The form also presumes
the right of answering. This, no doubt, may be dispensed
with, and so might the whole ceremony of the trial, since
the sentence was already pronounced at the Castle before
your jury were impaneled. Your lordships are but the
priests of the oracle. I submit to the sacrifice, but I insist on the whole of the forms.
    LORD NORBURY—"You may proceed, sir."

emissary of France! And for what end? It is alleged that I wished to sell the independence of my countrymen ; and for what end? Was this the object of my ambition? And is this the mode by which a tribunal of justice reconciles contradictions? No; I am no emissary. My ambition was to hold a place among the deliverers of my country—not in power, not in profit, but in the glory of the achievement. Sell my country's independence to France! And for what? A change of masters? No : but for my ambition. Oh, my country! was it personal ambition that influenced me, had it been the soul of my actions, could it not, by my education and fortune, by the rank of my family, have placed myself amongst the proudest of your oppressors? My country was my idol. To it I sacrificed every selfish, every endearing sentiment; and for it I now offer myself, O God! No, my lords; I acted as an Irishman, determined on delivering my country from the yoke of a foreign and unrelenting tyranny, and from the more galling yoke of a domestic faction, its joint partner and perpetrator in the patricide, whose reward is the ignominy of existing with an exterior of splendor and a consciousness of depravity. It was the wish of my heart to extricate my country from this doubly-riveted despotism—I wished to place her independence beyond the reach of any power on earth. I wished to exalt her to that proud station in the world which Providence had destined her to fill. Connection with France was, indeed, intended, but only so far as mutual interest would sanction or require. Were the French to assume any authority inconsistent with the purest independence it would be the signal for their destruction. We sought their aid—and we sought it as we had assurance we could obtain it—as auxiliaries in war and allies in peace. Were the French to come as invaders or enemies, uninvited by the wishes of the people, I should oppose them to the utmost of my strength. Yes! my countrymen, I should advise you to meet them on the beach with a sword in one hand and a torch in the other. I would meet them with all the destructive fury of war, and I would animate my

had contaminated the soil of my country. If they succeeded in landing, and if forced to retire before superior
discipline, I would dispute every inch of ground, raze
every house, burn every blade of grass ; the last spot on
which the hope of freedom should desert me, there would I
hold, and the lost entrenchment of liberty should be my grave.
What I could not do myself in my fall, I should leave as a
last charge to my countrymen to accomplish ; because I
should feel conscious that life, any more than death, is dishonorable when a foreign nation holds my country in subjection. But it was not as an enemy that the succors of
France were to land. I looked, indeed, for the assistance of
France ; I wished to prove to France and to the world that
Irishmen deserve to be assisted—that they were indignant at
slavery, and ready to assert the independence and liberty of
their country ; I wished to procure for my country the guarantee which Washington procured for America—to procure
aid which, by its example, would be as important as its valor ;
disciplined, gallant, pregnant with science and experience ;
that of allies who would perceive the good and polish the
rough points of our character. They would come to us as
strangers, and leave us as friends, after sharing in our trials
and elevating our destiny. These were my objects ; not to
receive new taskmasters, but to expel old tyrants. And it
was for these ends I sought aid from France ; because
France, even as an enemy, could not be more implicable
than the enemy already in the bosom of my country.

*   *   *   *   *   *   *   *   *   *

LORD NORBURY—"I exhort you not to depart this life with such sentiments of
rooted hostility to your country as those which you have expressed."

Let no man dare, when I am dead, to charge me with dishonor ; let no man attaint my memory by believing that I
could have engaged in any cause but that of my country's
liberty and independence ; or that I could have become the
pliant minion of power in the oppression and misery of my
countrymen. The proclamation of the Provisional Government speaks my views, no inference can be tortured from it

humiliation or treachery from abroad. I would not have submitted to a foreign oppressor for the same reason that I would resist the domestic tyrant. In the dignity of freedom I would have fought upon the threshold of my country, and its enemy should only enter by passing over my lifeless corpse. And am I, who lived but for my country, who have subjected myself to the dangers of the jealous and watchful oppressor, and now the bondage of the grave, only to give my countrymen their rights and my country her independence,—am I to be loaded with calumny and not suffered to resent it? No; God forbid!

Here Lord Norbury told Mr. Emmet that his sentiments and language disgraced his family and his education, but more particularly his father, Dr. Emmet, who was a man, if alive, that would not countenance such opinions. To which Mr. Emmet replied:—

If the spirits of the illustrious dead participate in the concerns and cares of those who were dear to them in this transitory life, O! ever dear and venerated shade of my departed father, look down with scrutiny upon the conduct of your suffering son, and see if I have, even for a moment, deviated from those principles of morality and patriotism which it was your care to instil into my youthful mind, and for which I am now about to offer up my life. My lords, you seem impatient for the sacrifice. The blood for which you thirst is not congealed by the artificial terrors which surround your victim [the soldiery filled and surrounded the Sessions House]—it circulates warmly and unruffled through the channels which God created for noble purposes, but which you are now bent to destroy, for purposes so grievous that they cry to Heaven. Be yet patient! I have but a few more words to say. I am going to my cold and silent grave; my lamp of life is nearly extinguished; my race is run; the grave is open to receive me, and I sink into its bosom. I have but one request to ask at my departure from this world; it is—THE CHARITY OF ITS SILENCE. Let no man write my epitaph; for as no man who knows my motives dare now vindicate them, let them and me rest in obscurity and peace, and my name remain uninscribed until other times and other men can do justice to my character. When my country takes her place among the nations of the earth, then, and not till then, let my epitaph be written. I have done.

CONTENTS.

CONTINUATION.